THE
RARE

TRILOGY OMNIBUS

DIANE ANTHONY

AUTHORS 4 AUTHORS PUBLISHING
Marysville, WA, USA

Published by Authors 4 Authors Publishing
1214 6th St
Marysville, WA 98270
www.authors4authorspublishing.com

Library of Congress Control Number: 2022948042

E-book ISBN: 978-1-64477-161-7
Paperback ISBN: 978-1-64477-162-4
Hard cover ISBN: 978-1-64477-167-9
Audiobook ISBN: 978-1-64477-163-1

Edited by Rebecca Mikkelson
Copyedited by Brandi Spencer and Renee Frey

Cover design ©2022 Practically Perfect Covers. All rights reserved.
Interior design by Brandi Spencer

Authors 4 Authors Publishing branding is set in Bavire. Title and headings are set in Pirulen. Author name and chapter numbers are set in Perfect Thoughts. Correspondence text is set in Segoe Print. All other text is set in Garamond.

THE RARE

TRILOGY OMNIBUS

DIANE ANTHONY

Authors 4 Authors Content Rating

This title has been rated 14+, suitable for teens, and contains:

- moderate language
- intense violence
- brief kissing
- brief implied sexual violence
- negative mild tobacco, illicit, and fantasy drug use
- discussions of suicide, self-harm, mental illness, and sexual abuse
- governmental conspiracy

Please, keep the following in mind when using our rating system:

1. A content rating is not a measure of quality.

Great stories can be found for every audience. One book with many content warnings and another with none at all may be of equal depth and sophistication. Our ratings can work both ways: to avoid content or to find it.

2. Ratings are merely a tool.

For our young adult (YA) and children's titles, age ratings are generalized suggestions. For parents, our descriptive ratings can help you make informed decisions, but at the end of the day, only you know what kinds of content are appropriate for your individual child. This is why we provide details in addition to the general age rating.

For more information on our rating system, please, visit our Content Guide at: www.authors4authorspublishing.com/books/ratings

DEDICATION

To Sage and my Three Kings.

WORKS BY
DIANE ANTHONY

Supernova

The Rare Trilogy

The Rare
The Remnant
The Return

TABLE OF CONTENTS

THE RARE

THE REMNANT

TABLE OF CONTENTS

THE
RARE

DIANE ANTHONY

1

A continuous, rhythmic beeping pulls me out of my dreamless slumber.

Crap! I'm not dead.

This is the third time I've tried but failed to free myself from this dismal existence. I keep my eyes closed, hoping not to bring unwanted attention to my awakening. I don't need the looks of disappointment, the words of false concern, or the endless questions about why I would do such a thing.

I wince in pain as I try to swallow. My throat is raw and swollen. They must have pumped my stomach again. The first time I tried to end my life was with a whole bottle of my Zoloft prescription. I thought the irony of killing myself with a bottle of antidepressants was amusing. This time, it was a container of aspirin washed down with a bottle of Benadryl. It seemed like a better way to go than my last attempt. Let me tell you, drowning is not as poetic of a way to go as you might think. The burning in my lungs, the pain and dizziness in my head from lack of oxygen, and the subsequent retching and coughing of water after being pulled from my moment of death were so unpleasant it made me vow to never try it again.

I crack my eyelids open just enough to peer through my eyelashes. I want to see if I can spot my mother. I can make out a blurry form in the corner. I open my eyes just a bit more. I'm not wearing my glasses, but I can tell by the way her head is leaning off to the side that she is asleep in the rocking chair.

Good.

I have an itch on my nose that has been driving me mad since I woke up. I try to lift my hand as slowly and silently as I can, so as not to wake her, but something pulls on my wrist, and my hand stops only inches off the bed.

What the...?

I try to lift my other hand, but it, too, is strapped down. My heart races, causing the beeping of my heart monitor to quicken. I start hyperventilating as a panic attack sets in. All I can think about is freeing myself from this newest prison.

I start to thrash around as everything fades to black. It's as though I'm looking through a narrow tunnel, seeing nothing but the painting hanging on the wall across the room. My hyperventilating turns into a full-blown asthma attack. So much for being inconspicuous. My mom is awake now and rushes over to the call button to get a nurse in here.

"What's going on? Why am I strapped down?" I squeak between shallow breaths.

"Calm down. You need to just calm down," my mom says.

I squeeze my eyes shut, tears leaking down my cheeks, and I try to hold still. My chest is heaving as I struggle to take an adequate breath. I know the drill. I have had so many asthma attacks in my life it seems as though I spend more time using my inhaler than I do breathing on my own. My muscles tremble from the adrenaline that is coursing through my body.

Why couldn't I have just died this time? I hate my life!

My mom grabs my inhaler from her purse and holds it up to my mouth.

"Ready? One, two, three, breathe," she says as she squeezes the medicine down my throat. I try hard to hold my breath for the ten seconds before exhaling, but my lungs burn from a desire to cough.

Hold it…hold it…

I let my breath out with a chest-wrenching cough. My already sore throat feels like it's about to rip out of my neck.

"What's going on in here?" asks a plump nurse as she makes her way to my bed, followed closely by a man dressed in white.

"She's having a panic attack, which triggered an asthma attack," my mom answers.

"Give her another dose of her inhaler while I go get something for the panic attack," the nurse says, turning around and waddling back out of the room. The man stands at the foot of my bed, watching me closely.

Every muscle in my body is shaking now. I'm still not breathing well enough, and my face starts tingling from the insufficient amount of air.

"Here you go. One, two, three, breathe," Mom says again.

I breathe in the medicine, and I'm able to hold my breath this time. My mom puts my glasses on me so I can see again.

"Where am I?" I eye the man who hasn't moved an inch since coming in. My heart is still racing. I wish I could run away right now.

"You're in the psychiatric ward of St. Mary's hospital, Olivia."

I shudder at the thought. I'm in the looney bin? Great. I pull at my restraints again, hoping they will break so I can fight my way out of here.

The nurse makes her way back into the room holding a syringe.

"Orderly, I need you to expose her backside."

I start yelling incomprehensibly. Every word I utter dies in my injured throat.

"Hold still, please," the nurse says, annoyingly calm but firm. "I'm giving you a dose of diazepam. It will help you calm down. It'll take a little bit to kick in, though. I suggest you try to relax until then."

There's a pinch in my butt where she injects the medicine, and then the orderly lets me go. I stop pulling at my restraints, but my heart is still pounding, and my head is fuzzy.

"How…" I try to clear my throat so I can spit out my question. "How much longer do I have to be tied down?"

"Until we feel that you will not try to run away or injure yourself again," the nurse answers. "You will be staying here in the hospital wing until you're healed. Once you no longer need medical attention, we'll move you to a different room in the psychiatric ward, but until then, you need to stay in this bed and rest. I'll be back to check on you in a little while to make sure the medicine has taken effect."

"Maybe if you remove the restraints, I'll be able to calm down better," I plead. "I promise I won't run away," I say as innocently as possible. I have every intention of getting out of here once no one is looking. A psychiatric ward? I don't think so!

"Nice try. The medicine should kick in soon, and then we'll have a chat," the nurse says, turning to walk out of the room. The orderly follows.

I huff in frustration. I lay my head back down on the pillow and focus on a crack in the opposite wall. I try to do my breathing exercises to settle myself down.

"You did this to yourself you know," my mom says accusingly.

"No, I didn't. I planned on dying, not being thrown in a mental hospital and strapped to a bed."

"Olivia! Why do you want to die so badly?"

"My life is hell, Mom! You of all people should know this! I'm in and out of hospitals constantly; I have such severe asthma that I need to have at least two inhalers with me at all times, in case one of them should run out during the day and leave me unable to breathe; I'm practically blind without these coke bottle glasses; I have no friends—"

"You have David," my mom interrupts.

"Yes. I have David. Another human who happens to be in the same boat as me." I roll my eyes. "If you recall, we met in a hospital."

"Well, you can't expect to make friends if you don't try."

"Mom, everyone at school thinks I'm a weakling and an idiot. I'm failing most of my classes because I'm not smart enough. I get picked last in gym all the time, which I guess I don't blame them. I would pick me last too."

"You're struggling in school because your hospital visits set you back. You'll catch on eventually if you would stop trying to do this..." she says, gesturing at me.

I roll my eyes. There is no talking to this woman. She will never understand the hell I have to live with. I'm not sure I have ever seen my mother sick in all my life. I, on the other hand, spend more time in and out of hospitals with illnesses than should be humanly possible. I just want it to end.

"Once you get home, I think you should invite Susan over again. You seemed to have a nice time together the last time she was over," my mom offers.

"Yeah, maybe," I agree, trying to dodge the topic.

Susan is my next-door neighbor in the apartment complex we live in. What Mom doesn't know is that I made a deal with Susan that day. If she pretended to be having a good time whenever my mother was around, I would give her my week's allowance. She was a surprisingly great actress. When my mom would walk in the room, Susan would put on a big smile and laugh extra loud, as though I said something profoundly hilarious. Once my mother would leave, we would go back to stony silence, and Susan would sit, texting anyone and everyone she could. Susan isn't one of the popular girls in my class, but she has enough friends to keep her texting fingers busy and her big blue eyes glued to the phone screen. I'm not sure why she isn't popular. Must be by choice or something. She has beautiful long black hair, a pretty face complete with long lashes and pouty lips, and a toned athletic frame. A great deal different from my short blonde hair, plain face, and sickly, thin body. I can't seem to put on any weight between hospital visits. Most of the illnesses leave me with no appetite.

Now that I've calmed down, my muscles start to release tension. My breathing slows, and the tingling stops. My mom has returned to the rocking chair and keeps glancing at me. I know she's trying hard to hold her tongue and not lecture me some more like the last time I was in the hospital after trying to commit suicide. She went on and on about how foolish I was and how I have my whole life ahead of me and whether I know how expensive these hospital stays are. I finally screamed at her to just get out, and she left me for a couple of days before returning to apologize. And that's our relationship in a nutshell ever since I can remember: fighting, accusations, arguing, and then apologies and tolerance until the next fight. I don't think my mom was ready to be a mom when she got pregnant with me, and with my Dad gone, she's had to do it all alone. She tries to be a good mom sometimes, but I'm pretty sure she resents my existence.

I take a deep breath in and close my eyes. My muscles are relaxed enough now that I slowly start to fade into the state of waking dreams, that is, until the city's air raid sirens start blaring. I get sucked out of my dream and reflexively try to sit up, but the restraints tug at my wrists, and I flop back into the pillow.

My mom is at the door, peeking her head out.

"Nurse? Nurse!" she calls out, trying to get somebody's attention.

The hospital emergency system starts going off to match the sirens. The cacophony makes me want to cover my ears, but of course, I can't.

"Excuse me! What's going on?" I hear my mom yelling out the door now.

"This is not a drill. All patients and personnel are required to stay inside until further notice. This facility is in a lockdown. I repeat this is not a drill. All patients and personnel..." repeats an unnervingly calm voice over the P.A. system.

I look over at the door to see my mom reach out and grab a nurse's arm as she hustles by.

"What's going on? Are we being attacked?"

"No, ma'am. It's raining," the nurse answers as she pulls her arm out of my mother's grip and quickly walks away.

2

I instinctively glance out the window, but I can't see anything in this unceasing fog. I sure hope they gave enough warning this time. The last time it rained, eleven people died because they didn't get out of the rain fast enough. Scientists call it "poison rain," but everyone I talk to calls it "death rain." It's different from acid rain, which destroys buildings. This just destroys humans.

Scientists tried to come up with umbrellas that can handle the rain, but they are rudimentary, at best. I have seen higher quality rain protection gear, but it's only for the rich. Not many people can afford it.

My mom is always paranoid that the sirens mean there is another attack happening like the one that got our country in the mess it's in now. But it is always just the rain.

The sirens continue to blare for a couple more minutes, but they shut it off once the lockdown is complete. I lay my head back onto the pillow and start to fall back to sleep.

Everything is green. The sunlight dances through the trees as the wind gently sends them swaying. The breeze is cool on my face, cutting through the intense heat of the day. I take a deep breath of the sweet smelling air and find that my lungs fill without protest from my asthma. I take a good look around. Everything is so green!

I'm in the woods. At least, I assume it's the woods. I have only ever seen them on TV or in pictures in books. What am I doing here? I need to get back home before some wild beast gets me! I glance around, hoping to find a trail that will take me back to the city. I stumble over branches and undergrowth that seem to grab at my feet. I pass between two giant boulders draped with soft green moss, and I stop short. There is a black figure up ahead in the shadows about forty feet away. I can't seem to make out what it is. I slowly start to back up, hoping to hide behind one of the boulders until it leaves. Is it looking in this direction? I make my movements slow and calculated. It seems to be hunched over something. I'm almost back to the boulder when my foot steps down on a branch with a resounding crack.

The dark figure spins around to face me. Just as it does, the wind picks up, and a beam of sunlight lands on its dark mottled fur. Its eyes are pools of inky black. Its long snout is crimson and wet. It bares its teeth, revealing needle-sharp fangs, dripping with blood. It looks as though it had once been a wolf, but its stature is larger and disfigured. It lets out an unearthly growl and starts bounding toward me. There is no way I'm going to get away from this thing! I turn around to run, but a pair of hands grab me and pulls me behind a boulder. I hear a twang sound, and then a loud whine comes from the direction of the beast. I look up and see a man standing on the boulder, nocking another arrow. He lets it loose, and I hear a loud thud accompanied by the breaking of branches and then silence. He must have killed it.

The man jumps down from the boulder to make sure the beast is dead. I turn around to get a look at the person who pulled me out of harm's way. He looks to be in his early twenties, although it's hard to tell with his face covered in a thick beard. His brown hair is long and tied back with a strip of cloth. His clothes look worn and dirty. His eyes are a crystal clear blue that seems to hold my gaze and won't let go. The hunter comes back around the boulder and breaks this guy's scrutiny of me. He turns from me and gives his friend a slap on the back.

The man who killed the beast looks remarkably like the young guy who pulled me behind the boulder, only older, maybe in his late forties. His brown hair is cut short in odd angles, as though he did it with a knife. A thick brown beard with streaks of gray grows on his face, and he has green eyes. His clothes are also in a state of disrepair but are covered by a garment made of animal fur. Black fur. A lot like the beast he just killed.

"Thank you for saving me. I don't even know how I got here." I look back and forth between the two men.

"You're welcome, Olivia," the older man says.

"Olivia!" my mom shouts.

I awake with a start. My legs are twisted up in the sheets, and I'm drenched with sweat.

"Are you okay? You were thrashing around in your bed, moaning. I've been trying to wake you up for a couple of minutes now."

"Um...yeah. I'm fine...I think," I mumble, trying to make sense of what's going on. That dream. It seemed so real. Who were those people?

My mom helps me straighten out the sheets and gets me comfortable again. I try to fix my hair, but then remember that I'm still tied down to the bed. She hesitantly strokes some strands of hair out of my face. She bends down and picks my glasses up off the floor and puts them back on me.

"How're you feeling?"

"How do I look?" I snap back. My mom looks down at the floor, dejected. Oh jeez. Now I hurt her feelings.

"I'm sorry, Mom. I shouldn't have snapped at you. I feel like crap, and it's making me moody."

There's a quiet knock at the door, followed by a head with greasy black hair.

"David? What're you doing here?" I croak out.

"I was having a follow-up appointment to make sure the pneumonia was cleared up this time. I heard you were here and thought I would come visit," he says, finishing off with a deep chest cough.

"You sound like garbage," I say.

"You look like garbage," he replies, putting his hand up to his ear and fiddling with his hearing aid.

"Stop it, you two. David, is your mother here with you? I would like to talk to her," my mom says.

"Yes, Mrs. Sloane. She's waiting for me in the hallway."

My mom heads out to the hallway, quietly closing the door behind her.

"What'd you do this time?" David asks.

"Tried to kill myself with aspirin and Benadryl."

"Looks like you failed," David says with a hint of a smirk playing at his lips.

"No crap," I roll my eyes.

"So, when do you get out?" He pushes my legs over so he can sit on my bed.

"No idea. Looks like they're sending me to the psychiatric ward after I'm healed."

"Yikes. I almost got locked up once in the padded room for throwing a chair at the window."

"Why'd you throw a chair at the window? Trying to prove that you belonged there or something?" I ask, watching him pick at a huge zit on his chin. I turn my head away before I throw up.

"I was playing truth or dare with Bartholomew. He dared me to do it."

"You idiot. Bartholomew isn't real. I think they should put you in the loony bin permanently."

"Yeah, whatever. I told you before, Bartholomew shows up right before I'm about to get sick. It's like he's my guardian angel or something..."

"Right. A guardian angel who dares you to throw a chair at a window in the psychiatric ward."

"He said he was sorry. He got carried away."

David stops looking at me and stares up at the ceiling.

"What? Do you see him?" I roll my eyes.

He doesn't reply and continues staring. He's having a seizure again. I sigh, waiting for it to end.

After a few seconds, David looks back at me. "What were we talking about?"

"You just had another seizure."

"Damn it. This medicine isn't working either," David says with tears welling up in his muddy brown eyes.

"I'm sorry. I'm sure they'll figure something out," I offer gently.

"Maybe I should be like you and just try to end this sad excuse of a life. I could just run out into the rain and let my flesh melt off my bones." He stops to think about it and then shudders, shaking his head. "Who am I kidding? I could never do it."

"Me neither. Once you're dead, it wouldn't matter, but what a crappy way to go."

"Maybe we should run away into the woods."

"Ugh. Not this again. What is your obsession with running off into the wilderness? Do you want to be eaten?"

"No...yes...I don't know. I have this strange feeling that there's something else out there."

"I had a dream about the woods. I have no idea how I got there, but I was trying to get back to the city, and there was a beast that tried to kill me. I was saved by these two guys who, I swear, seemed really familiar."

"Maybe it's a sign."

"No, David. Look at me! Does it look like I'm in any condition to go traipsing out into the woods? And what about you and your epilepsy? You wouldn't last two minutes out there."

"Fine," David huffs, looking away.

We fall into an awkward silence. I hate it when he starts going on and on about the woods. I have no idea what he thinks is out there that's so important. We aren't even allowed to leave city limits unless it's on a train. The woods are a dangerous place full of numerous ways to die. I've heard stories. If you manage to not get eaten by any animals, the plants themselves will kill you. I just read an article a year or so ago about a group of botanists who went to the woods to document the plant life. Some of the foliage looked different, and they wanted to take samples. Their bodies were found just outside of the fence. The doctors still weren't sure what plants could cause this. Little barbs were found inside of the scientists' skin, and their internal organs had been decomposed to mush.

"So, are you headed back to school tomorrow?" I ask, trying to break the silence.

"Yeah, they gave me the all clear. I can gather some of your homework and try to bring it to you if you want."

I rattle my restraints in response.

"I suppose you won't be able to get much done with your hands tied down."

"There's no way I'm ever going to catch up on my school work. I will probably have to do junior year again."

"I'm sure it won't be that bad. I can tutor you once you get out of the loony bin," David offers with a wide smile that exposes his crooked yellow teeth. I glance away again.

"Yeah, maybe."

We hear my mom come back into the room.

"David, the rain has stopped, and it's time for you to head home," my mom says.

"See you later, Liv."

"See ya," I mumble as David steps out the door.

My mom walks over to me, holding a bottle of vitamins, and shakes a large red pill out into her hand. I have to take two extra drinks to get the vitamin to finally slide down my throat. I cringe at the pain as well as the taste. I wish we had some of our bottled water here. I hate the way the tap water tastes. The government has a filtration system put in so everyone can have drinking water and not get poisoned by the rain, but I don't like it, so my mom buys bottled water for us to drink.

The next couple of days I spend quietly lying in bed, staring off into nowhere, earning the fat nurse's trust so she will take my restraints off. Once she finally does, she makes me promise that I won't try to run away.

I wait for my mom to fall asleep that night and slip my way out of the hospital bed. I peek my head out of the door, and there's no one in the hall. I make it about three rooms away before I hear someone coming and try to scramble into the closest room, but I'm caught and strapped back into my bed by none other than Nurse Tubby. I finally realize that there is no way I am going to sneak my way out of here.

I try to apologize to the nurse, but she's skeptical of me now. We don't get along well. I'm pretty sure she has ordered unnecessary tests to be done just so she can take extra vials of my blood. She's not too gentle with that needle either. I guess I might deserve it, though. I lied about running away. Just to get back at her, I wet my bed on purpose once, after a particularly nasty blood draw. I'm confident she missed my vein intentionally. She made me stand cuffed to the bed in my wet hospital gown while she changed the sheets, cursing under her breath and giving me death glares. My mom chewed me out and seemed so worked up that I decided to lay off Nurse Chunk. It's probably better that way anyway since I'm not getting out of this hospital anytime soon.

My mom has to go to work every day, but she comes back and stays with me at the hospital at night. I usually allow myself to cry while she's gone. It's easier to hold it in and let it all out when I don't have an audience. Our relationship is tense as it is, and I don't want to stress her out more with my depression. My mom and David are the only people in the world who actually seem to like me.

A couple more days pass, and I can finally eat and take my vitamin without pain now. The last time Nurse Fatso was in here, she asked me to rate my pain between one and ten. I hate it when they ask me that. I mean, I get it; they want an indication of how bad your pain is, but pain can be so different for so many people. I just have a swollen throat and asthma attacks. How can I compare that to someone who has their legs chopped off or a broken bone protruding out of their skin? I feel I can't say over a five without looking like a complete doofus.

I hear a tapping on the door.

"Well, girly," says Nurse Pudge, "looks like you're all healed up. It's time to move to your new quarters."

"Will I be getting my own room?" I ask hopefully. I don't want to be stuck with some psycho.

After the nurse finally stops laughing so hard that her rotund belly shakes violently under her scrubs, she answers, "This ain't no five-star hotel, deary. Don't worry. I picked out someone perfect to be your roommate."

That evil look in her eyes makes my stomach drop. I'm in trouble!

3

I shuffle behind the nurse, following her down the bleached white hallway, passing room after room before I make it to my new living space. I hear a few screams coming from behind some of the doors. I hope my roommate isn't a screamer.

Luckily the room is empty when I arrive, so I can get settled in before they show up. I wonder what kind of nut job the nurse put me with.

"I've been told you have a half hour before mandatory group time. They run a tight ship around here. Be on time or else," the nurse warns as she turns around to head back to the hospital wing. Once she closes the door behind her, I flip her the bird. I shouldn't have done that. They probably have cameras in the rooms to monitor the patients. My eyes drift around the room, looking for cameras. I can't spot one, but I should be a little more careful, just in case.

My room is plain. There are two twin beds with gray metal frames on opposite sides of the room. I sit down on one and find that the beds are adorned with scratchy white sheets and a threadbare light blue blanket. There are two waist-high dressers for our clothes next to the beds and a window in between the dressers. The floors and ceiling are stark white, which is quite the contrast to the walls: a faded yellow color that makes me think the last resident was a chain smoker. I walk over to the barred window to get a look at the view from this room. We are four stories up, which makes it challenging to see anything on the ground through the fog. I can make out the outlines of a few people, hurrying off to do important things with their freedom. How nice that must be.

"Get away from the window!" A high-pitched voice squeals at me.

I turn around and see a short girl standing in the doorway, staring at me wide-eyed. She looks to be about twelve years old, her black hair pulled back into a ponytail.

"Why? What's wrong with the window?" I look back and forth between the window and the girl.

"They'll see you!"

"Who?" I step slowly away from the window and back over to my bed.

"The monsters. They're always watching. Waiting. We're never alone. Just stay away from the window. I don't want to lose another roommate." She keeps her back to the wall as she sidesteps her way to her bed.

I am officially freaked out.

"What happened to your roommate?" I ask, not really wanting to hear her answer.

She responds with an ear-piercing scream. I cover my ears so she doesn't bust my eardrums. Moments later, a nurse comes bounding into our room with a syringe.

The girl starts swatting at the nurse, trying to knock the syringe out of her hand, but the girl is no match for the large, muscular nurse. Once the medicine has been injected, the girl lies still on her bed, panting.

"What happened?" the nurse asks.

"I don't know. She told me to stay away from the window and mentioned something about her roommate. I asked her what happened, and she started screaming..."

"Do us both a favor, and never ask about her roommate again. Got it?"

"Yeah...sure." I agree. Holy crap! What have I gotten myself into?

The nurse leaves the room, closing the door with a resounding thump. I sit on my bed, glancing at the girl now and again. After about five awkward minutes of silence, she sits up, letting her legs dangle over the edge of the bed. She holds her head down in her hands as though she has an intense headache. Suddenly, she looks up and locks eyes with me. The pale blue color of her eyes is kind of creeping me out. They are so pale they almost look white.

"My name's Cindy," she says innocently.

"I'm Olivia."

She smiles wide, the corner of her lips curling up, making her look like a female Joker.

"I think we are going to be best friends, Olivia. I got this place figured out. I can give you tips."

"Um. Okay. Tips for what, exactly?"

"Scoring extra drugs like I just demonstrated, which nurses let you get away with certain stuff, how to say just the right things to the other patients to get them to have an episode to end group time...you know. Stuff like that."

What a brat!

"How long have you been here?" I ask.

"Pretty much my whole life." Cindy kicks her feet back and forth with her toes brushing the floor. "Why're you here?"

"I tried to kill myself."

"How fun! I've done that too." She shows me the insides of her arms. Thick scars run down her wrists.

"How old are you? You seem too young to want to die."

"Oh, you're too kind! I'm older than I look. I'm twenty-five."

"Twenty-five? No offense, but I thought you were, like, twelve when you first came in."

"Twelve?" She says, laughing hysterically. "I'll admit, I'm a little short for my age, but damn. You really thought I looked twelve? You sure you don't need to have your eyes checked?"

I've had enough of this chick already.

"I'm kinda tired. I think I'll lie down for a little bit before group time."

"Yeah, sure thing." Cindy scooches her back to the wall.

I lie down facing toward her. I'm not sure I trust her enough to turn my back to her. As soon as I close my eyes, I hear her clicking her tongue like a clock. I sigh loudly, hoping it will make her stop. She does, but then she starts humming "The Itsy-Bitsy Spider" slowly and ominously. I open my eyes to glare at her and find that she is doing the motions to go along with the song.

"Cindy, do you mind being a little quieter so I can sleep."

"Oh. Sorry." She brings a finger to her lips.

Silence. I'm starting to relax when I hear the squeak of her bed. What is she doing now? I open my eyes just a bit, but I don't see her. I hear the click of the bathroom door. She's just using the bathroom. I take a deep calming breath, filling my lungs as full as I can, and let it out slowly. These beds are pretty comfy. I might actually get some sleep. After I let all the air out of my lungs, I start to take my next breath, and my nose is filled with the stench of rancid milk and candy. I open my eyes and find Cindy's face inches away from mine. I scramble to sit up.

"You're pretty when you sleep."

"Don't do that! You need to stay on your side of the room! I get panic attacks really easily." I feel my chest tightening. I probably shouldn't have told her that.

"You do? Well, I'll just have to keep that in mind." She bounces her way back to her bed.

I take a dose of my inhaler and glare at Cindy.

"Group time, girls," a nurse says, standing in the doorway.

I stand up and follow the nurse, hoping they have separate groups. I don't want to be around Cindy anymore.

"Where should I go?" I ask the nurse.

"Your group time will be held in the room next to the cafeteria down that way," she says, pointing down the hallway behind us. She turns back around to continue informing the rest of the patients about group time.

I make it to the room I'm supposed to be in and see a circle of people already there. Cindy is nowhere in sight. What a relief.

My group time is boring. The nurse tries to coax people out of their shells. Nobody seems to want to share much, though. People say their name and how they're feeling. A lot of "fines" and "tireds." We had one exciting part when a patient started punching the catatonic guy in the leg because he thought he saw a spider. I don't know why I thought it was funny, but I had to hide my chuckle behind a coughing fit.

After group time is lunch time. Sitting next to the cafeteria made me hungry. Once I have my tray of food, though, I am sorely disappointed. I'm not sure I can identify most of it. Gray mush, green slimy stuff, a stale dinner roll, and a pile of canned fruit I think must be pears. Yum, yum.

I see Cindy walk through the door, so I scan for a place to sit where she won't be able to sit by me. I find a spot between two people from my group, spider guy and an old lady named Gretchen who rocks back and forth continuously. We all eat in silence. I can handle this.

I finally make it back to my room after hours of grueling group sessions and "free time," which just means I can watch the TV that is playing old black and white movies, I can make a craft, or I can stare out the window. Meds were handed out right after supper. I looked in my little cup to see if I could identify what they're trying to give. Luckily, it was only my daily vitamin. I don't know what I would have done if they tried to give me some random medication. Now it's lights out in an hour. I sit down on my bed, exhausted for some reason, and notice that Cindy isn't back yet. I wonder what kind of trouble she's getting into.

I stare out the window for a little while, watching the hazy daylight fade away to darkness. I decide that my best bet is to just comply, and maybe I'll be released sooner. I whip around when I hear a startled intake of breath.

"Who're you?" Cindy asks, eyes filled with fear.

"Olivia, your roommate," I say, confused.

"Oh. Nice to meet you. I'm Joselyn." She offers her hand for a handshake.

"Joselyn? You told me your name was Cindy."

"No! No, no, no, no!" Joselyn screams, pounding her fists against her head. "Not again! Cindy's trying to kill me!"

4

"Nurse!" I yell. "We need a nurse in here!"

She continues punching her head with her fists, screaming, "Get away from me! I hate you!"

"Hey, this isn't just a show, is it?" I ask, remembering her last plot to get more drugs. I suddenly feel guilty for even asking. If she is faking it, she is an astounding actress.

The same nurse as before comes into our room, carrying a syringe. She injects the medicine and then holds the girl's hands in a tight grip so she stops punching at her head. The look of terror slowly fades off Cindy's face. The nurse lets her go and takes a few steps back, watching as she falls over on the bed and appears to be sleeping.

"You okay?" The nurse asks. It isn't until I look at her that I realize she was talking to me.

"Um...yeah. What's wrong with her?" I take a dose of my inhaler. "She just told me her name is Joselyn. Is she a pathological liar or something?"

"No. She has dissociative identity disorder. So far, you have met two of her personalities, Cindy and Joselyn."

"You mean, there are more?" I ask incredulously.

"Unfortunately, yes. We've found a medicine that seems to help, but it only works if she actually takes it. I think she cheeks the medicine and spits it out later, but we haven't figured out how she does it."

"Why would she do that if the medicine works?"

"She complains about feeling stupid while on the medicine. I tend to think that Cindy is a much stronger personality than we care to believe. She doesn't like the idea of being erased, and so she tends to take over more often."

"Cindy told me she fakes episodes so she can get more drugs."

"We'll look into it. I need to get back to the nurse's station. You need anything else?"

"A new room?" I plead.

"No can do. Nighty-night!"

I let out a big huff and sit down on my bed. I hate you Nurse Chubs! Why did they have to stick me with her?

"I heard you talking about me."

I look over at Joselyn and see her slowly opening her eyes, and although they are still the creepy pale blue color, they seem to have a childlike innocence to them. She seems more scared than anything.

"Yeah. Sorry."

"I hate Cindy. She's ruining my life," Joselyn says, starting to cry.

I stand up and make my way over to the foot of her bed. I slowly sit, cautiously waiting for her to start freaking out again. She just lies there sobbing instead.

"She said the medicine helps. Maybe you should take it."

"I can't," Joselyn says between sobs. "I feel dumb when I'm on them. I can't finish a sentence or even a thought."

"If you hate Cindy so much, isn't it worth feeling a little dumb if it means getting rid of her?" I offer.

"Yeah, maybe," she says, calming down a bit. "I hate that these are my options! I either live with a bunch of personalities where I don't know who I'm going to wake up as and have no memory of what happened while I was someone else, or I can take medicine that makes me feel like an idiot. I lose no matter what."

"It sounds like it sucks." I pat her leg again. "I'm sorry you have to deal with this."

"It could be worse, I guess. I have a guy in my group who believes he's a squirrel. He's hilarious to watch eat. He nibbles his food and sometimes shoves things in his cheeks until they puff out like this." She blows her cheeks up.

We both laugh for a moment. This Joselyn kid isn't so bad.

"Cindy told me she's twenty-five. How old are you really?"

"I'm twelve."

I knew it!

"So, how long have you been here?" I ask.

"As long as I can remember. My dad died when I was real little, and that's when Cindy showed up. So, my mom sent me here and never came back to see me." Fresh tears roll down her cheeks. "Cindy tried to kill herself—I mean, us, and that's when other personalities came. I just don't know what to do," Joselyn says, sobbing.

I sit by her for a little while, patting her leg while she cries. After a few minutes, I realize she's quiet. She fell asleep. I make my way back over to my bed just before the lights shut out. I hope I can get out of here soon.

5

In the morning, I awake with a start when something brushes against my cheek. It would appear Cindy has come back to visit. She's sitting on the edge of my bed, staring at me with those creepy pale eyes boring into my soul.

"Who's David?" She asks with a smirk.

"He's a friend." I rub the sleep out of my eyes. "Why?"

"You were calling out his name while you slept. 'David...David...no, don't go there!' Where was he trying to go? Your panties?" She finishes with a wicked laugh.

"No! You're sick!" I say, disgusted.

"Correct you are, Dr. Olivia." Cindy titters, standing back up and twirling in circles to her bed.

I sit up, knowing that I will not be getting any more sleep with psycho girl over there. After sitting for a couple of minutes, watching her twirl her ponytail and hum "Pop Goes the Weasel," I decide to play at her level and stir up the bees' nest a bit.

"So, why did the nurse tell me not to ask about your roommate? What happened?"

"Cassandra was my first roommate. She was an annoying wench who kept trying to help Joselyn make me go away permanently, so I took it upon myself to make her life a living hell. I pulled pranks on her every chance I could get. I made her wet the bed with the fingers-in-warm-water trick; tied individual strands of her long hair to the bedpost bars while she slept so when she got up, it would rip them out; I left bugs in her bed that I would find around the joint. I even made myself throw up on her favorite shoes once, pretending I was sick," Cindy says, eyes glistening as she reminisces about her evil ploys. "Anyway, she couldn't prove I was behind any of it, and nobody would believe her when she blamed me. That didn't sit so well with her bipolar disorder. Nope, nope, nope! She got more and more depressed until finally, she stole a knife from the kitchen one day and killed herself over by that window," Cindy finishes with a slight giggle as she mimics stabbing herself in the heart.

I stare at her, horrified.

"Oh, don't worry, Olivia! I would never do those things to you. I want us to be best friends! Don't you?" Cindy's eyes bulge slightly as she smiles.

I try to smile, but my muscles just spasm a few times. I swallow hard and find that my mouth has gone completely dry. I need to try to stay on her good side. I just nod my head a little. That seems to appease her, and she goes back to twirling her hair and humming to herself.

The rest of the day was uneventful after that. We have to have blood drawn every morning. They say it's so they can analyze it to know how much medication to give. I think they just like sticking us with needles. We had to go through another hospital lockdown because it's raining again today, but nobody seemed to notice; it happens so frequently. I try extra hard at group time to participate and appear happier so I can get myself home sooner.

I return to my room that evening and lie down, waiting for Cindy to return, hoping it will be Joselyn instead. Before I know it, the lights are turned out, and she hasn't come back. I'm afraid to go to sleep, wondering what horrors Cindy has in store for me, but exhaustion wins out.

I wake up in the morning and find that her bed is still empty. I wonder where they are—I mean, where she is.

I ask a nurse, and I'm told that Cindy got herself thrown into solitary confinement after being caught whispering in the ear of a patient with severe paranoia. Once they calmed the patient down, she informed them that Cindy threatened to smother her with a pillow while she was asleep. Looks like I will get the room to myself for a while.

■■■■■

"Well, Olivia. I think you've made some real progress here," says Dr. Regan Hughes, the head of the department. It's been three days since Cindy was taken to solitary confinement. Three days that I have busted my butt to participate in any way that I could. I was rewarded with good behavior yesterday after I helped calm the spider guy down when he saw a spider on the windowsill. They let me choose what to watch on the TV during free time. There wasn't a whole lot to choose from, but a movie from this century was a far cry better than the boring crap they usually played.

Dr. Hughes continually pushes his large round glasses back up his oily nose as he studies my file. I stare at his bald head reflecting the lamplight, wondering if he polishes it in the morning before he comes to work. He looks up at me, and I quickly meet his eye line. His dark brown eyes stare at me expectantly, waiting for a response.

"Oh, uh, I have made progress. I feel a lot better. I know now that it was silly of me to try to kill myself. I have so much to live for," I say, laying it on thick.

"Yes, well, I think with a few more sessions you should be able to go home."

"A few more? Can't I just go home now? I promise I'm better," I plead.

"Slow down, Olivia. We need to make sure you are completely rehabilitated."

"I am. I won't ever try to kill myself again. I promise! Please, just let me go home to my mom."

He looks at me with his bushy eyebrows furrowed, scrutinizing me. How can he possibly have that much hair above his eyes when his entire head is as bald as a cue ball?

"No. There's something else going on here. I don't think it's because you miss your mom." He glances back at my file. "There are no notes about you saying you miss your mom in any of the sessions. So, tell me: why do you want to leave so badly?"

"Fine. My roommate Cindy is being released from confinement, and I would rather not be here when she gets back," I say sheepishly. "I really do feel better, though."

"Ah...Cindy. Yes, she is a hard one to handle." Dr. Hughes sighs, clicking his pen a few times, thinking. "All right, I'll make a deal with you. Go to today's sessions, and we'll talk tomorrow."

"Really?"

"Yes, well, as I said, you have made some real progress. I believe you will be ready to return home tomorrow."

I would rather have gone home today, but I'll take what I can get.

Dr. Hughes dismisses me to head to my session. I can't seem to wipe the smile off my face, knowing I'll be going home tomorrow. That is until I walk into my session and see Cindy sitting there. She's staring down at the floor. I don't think she notices me sit down.

"Hello," she says in a deadpan tone. I look over at her, and she is glaring at me through her long black hair, which is usually pulled up in a high ponytail. Her long bangs drape over her face, obscuring one of her eyes.

"Hi, Cindy," I say cautiously.

"I'm not Cindy," she says with the same emotionless tone.

"Sorry, Joselyn?"

"Nope. The name's Landon."

"Landon? Isn't that a guy's name?"

"Yeah?" She gives me a weird look like I'm an idiot.

I decide to just stop talking. A dude? One of Joselyn's personalities is a dude? Weird.

"Who're you?" Landon asks.

"I'm Olivia. Your roommate," I say slowly. That's right. *Landon* wouldn't know that.

She nods her head and goes back to brooding. I feel horrible for Joselyn. I can't figure out why she would want to deal with all these personalities instead of taking her medicine and making them go away.

During the session, they only get one-word responses from Landon. He—I mean she— Oh, this is so confusing! He just stares at the floor, only looking up at me once in a while. I'm not sure if I'm imagining it, but the malice I usually see in Cindy's eyes has been replaced with a look of pain in Landon's.

Once it's lunchtime, I seek Landon out to sit with. Perhaps if I tell him there's a way to make the pain and suffering go away, he'll try taking the medicine Joselyn needs to get better.

"Hey, Landon. Do you mind if I sit with you?"

"Go for it." He stabs his fork at what looks like a pile of mashed potatoes. I take the seat across from him.

"If you don't mind me asking, what are you in here for?" I ask, curious as to what his response might be.

He brushes his bangs out of his eyes to look at me quizzically. I give a little smile to let him know I'm not being a jerk.

"I've been told that I'm just a personality inside of a girl named Joselyn. Pretty effed up, if you ask me," he says, continuing to smoosh around his food.

"Yeah. That's gotta be hard."

When he doesn't respond, I try to continue as gently as I can.

"Look, Landon, I can tell this is not an easy position to be in. The little girl that you are stuck inside could really use your help. She has another personality that is bad news—"

"Cindy. I know about her." He looks up at me abruptly. "I've been told all of this before. What do you want me to do about it?"

"If you could take the medicine that will make Joselyn better, you wouldn't have to be in pain anymore. You know... knowing you're not..." I stop and clear my throat, not sure if I should continue. I see that he is looking at me, almost as though he's wondering if I have the guts to finish my sentence. I take a deep breath and try to say it quick, like ripping a band-aid off. "Knowing you're not a real person. She's a sweet kid who's got a tough life."

"So, you want me to take medicine to make myself go away?"

"Well...yeah. I guess that's what I'm asking. I'm sorry, Landon. I'm just trying to help Joselyn out. You seem to be unhappy. I thought maybe you would like to have a way to escape the pain of knowing you're just a personality inside of a twelve-year-old girl's body. You would be sacrificing yourself to save someone," I finish.

He sighs and lets his head hang, his hair almost falling into his food.

"You're right. I don't belong here. I never have," he agrees. "I'll take the medicine, but I can't control what Cindy does. Nobody can."

We eat the rest of our lunch in silence and continue on with our day. Once medication time comes, I look around the room to see if I can spot Landon. He's standing a couple of places behind me in line. I take my vitamin and stand off to the side to encourage him. Once it's his turn, he grabs the little cup and dumps it in his mouth, washing it down with the water. I give him a big smile and two thumbs up. He gives me a strange look and shakes his head vigorously as though trying to shake a bug away. He looks at the little cup in his hand, and his eyes go wide. "Damn it!" he yells and runs off to the bathroom. I follow quickly behind and stand outside of the door, listening to what's going on. Suddenly, I hear vomiting.

I start banging on the door. "Don't do that!" I yell. "Nurse!"

"What are you yelling about?" a nurse scolds in hushed tones. "You're going to get the other patients worked up."

"I convinced Landon to take the medicine that will help Joselyn out, but he started acting weird, and now he's in there throwing up!"

"Ah, yes. This has happened before. That seems to be the trigger for Cindy. Why don't you head back to your room? I'll take care of this."

I go back to the room and change into my pajamas. Only moments after I lie down, Cindy comes barging into the room.

"You're trying to get rid of me, aren't you?" Cindy glares at me.

"I was just trying to help Joselyn out. She seems like a good kid," I say defensively.

"You're trying to recruit that weak-minded moron, Landon, to get rid of me? You're gonna have to try harder than that." Cindy flops down on the bed.

"Why do you want to stick around so badly when you know you don't belong? You're a twenty-five-year-old personality trapped inside a twelve-year-old. Doesn't that seem wrong to you?"

"No. The alternative is that I don't exist at all. Stay out of it, Olivia, or I swear, I'll kill you," she threatens.

I huff and lie my head back down on the pillow. I'm afraid to go to sleep. I lie awake for hours that night, continually checking to see if Cindy is going to do something to me.

I finally fall asleep sometime around two o'clock. After a few hours, I wake up to find Cindy sitting on her bed, back against the wall, staring at me again.

"Heard you're going home today," she says.

"Hopefully."

"We'll see about that. I may have told Dr. Hughes that you talked about killing yourself again last night."

"You *what?*"

"Consider it a little payback for trying to get rid of me."

6

I race down to Dr. Hughes' office. I knock on the door, shifting my weight back and forth, waiting for a response. Come on, come on, come on! I put my ear against the door. Nothing. I squat down to look through the keyhole. I can almost see his desk...

"What are you doing, Olivia?"

I jump so hard, I smack my head against the doorknob. Rubbing the sore spot, I stand up and see that Dr. Hughes is back with a steaming cup of coffee.

"Cindy just told me that she told you that I told her that I was thinking about killing myself." I shake my head at my inability to form proper sentences when I'm upset. I take a deep breath. "I just wanted to come down here to let you know that Cindy lied. I never talked about killing myself. You have to believe me!"

"Of course, I do. Come into my office," he says, opening the door.

I follow him in and have a seat. It is only then that I realize I'm still in my pajamas. I wonder if he notices me blushing.

"I was told that you tried to help Joselyn out by means of Landon. I'm really impressed by the way you want to help people, Olivia. Keep that up. I believe helping others out can really help lift your own spirits when you're feeling down."

I nod my head in agreement. "So, does this mean...I can go home?" I ask quietly, afraid he is going to say no.

"Yes. I've already called your mother. She's on her way."

"Oh, thank you, thank you, thank you!" I clap my hands. He gives me a big smile.

"You can head back to your room and gather your things together. Don't take this the wrong way, but I hope I never see you again," Dr. Hughes says with a wink.

I smile and skip back to my room. Cindy isn't there when I return. Good! I pack my things up and wait for my mom. Suddenly, the sirens start going off. I race to the window and see rain sliding down the pane of glass. No! It's raining again.

I make my way to breakfast, hoping the rain stops soon so I can go home. I sit down at a table to eat with spider guy and Charlotte, a girl who believes she has magical powers. I've only ever seen her around here once or twice. She's quiet and keeps to herself most of the time. I'm hoping to have a peaceful breakfast.

"Stop taking it, Olivia," Charlotte says through a mouthful of food.

"What? Stop taking what?"

"It takes your powers away so you can't use the magic within."

"What magic? Charlotte, we have no magic. There is no such thing as magic."

"You're wrong!" Charlotte yells, standing up and storming off to another table. I sigh, hoping I didn't just ruin my chance to get out of here. What in the world was she talking about?

I lean over to take a bite of food when I feel hair being ripped out of the back of my head. I turn around and see Cindy holding a few strands of my hair.

"Oops. Sorry. It was an accident." Cindy drops my hair on the floor. She just turns around and walks away. I hate her. I can't wait to get out of here. I really want to stand up and punch her right in her stupid face, but my desire to get home keeps me in my seat.

Finally, after two hours of sitting around staring at the window, waiting for the rain to stop, I see my mother walk through the door. Out of relief, I run over and give her a big hug.

"I'm so glad to see you. Let's get out of here, Mom."

She awkwardly hugs me in return. We don't usually show big signs of affection; in fact, this might be one of the first genuine hugs I've given her in years.

I hear shouts of "goodbye" and "hope to never see you again." I stop by my room and grab my stuff. As I'm finally walking down the sidewalk outside, I feel like I'm being watched. I turn around to look up at the fourth floor and can just barely make out Cindy standing at the window, watching me walk away. I give her a little wave, and she gives me the middle finger. I will definitely not miss you, Cindy.

Once I'm home, I walk into my apartment and take a deep calming breath. The welcoming scent of familiarity hits my nose. The hospital always smelled like bleach and other assorted chemicals. Our apartment smells like the lilac potpourri my mom always has lying around and the woody smell of the cedar chest my mom keeps extra blankets in.

"Welcome home, Olivia. I'm going to make you your favorite supper tonight..."

"Tacos?" I ask excitedly. "I miss tacos so much. That hospital food was terrible!"

My mom smiles, and I head off to my room to get unpacked. As I'm pulling out the few changes of clothes I had, the phone rings, and my mother shouts, "Got it!" I finish setting my hairbrush on my dresser and head to the kitchen to get a snack. I hear my mom talking on the phone in the living room in almost a whisper. I stand against the wall next to the doorway and listen, curious to know why she would be whispering.

"Hey, this isn't my fault. She was in your care... She didn't mention anything to me about her... Yes, I know it is important that we stay on task... I will keep giving it to her and report to you should anything change... Yes, thank you, Doctor. Mmm-hmm. Yup, goodbye."

I race to the dining room table with my snack and wait for my mom to come in.

"Who called?" I ask in what I hope is a nonchalant tone.

"Oh...um...just your doctor checking in to see how everything is going."

"That seems a little soon. We just got home."

"Yes, well, they want to be thorough. Anyway, there's your homework." She points to the end of the table that is stacked with about a foot of paper and textbooks. "Why don't you get started on it and get some done before supper?"

Mom is acting weird. I wonder what she's up to.

I sit down and grab the first folder of homework. I'll be lucky if I can ever get this done.

By the time my mom announces that the tacos are done, my hand is cramped, and I have a killer headache.

The tacos are so delicious that I scarf down three before I realize I should slow down, or they might be making a reappearance. We eat in silence. My mom keeps looking at me as though she's about to say something, but she stays quiet. I don't mind the silence. There was always someone chattering at the hospital. It's nice to have some peace.

After I've finally had my fill of tacos, I help my mom clean up the table and get back to my homework. As I'm staring at my trigonometry worksheet, trying to make heads and tails of it, my mom calls from the other room, "Olivia, David is on the phone." I am so grateful for the break, I run to my room to take the call.

"Hey!"

"Hi, Olivia. Glad to hear you're back home. Are you coming to school tomorrow?"

"Yeah, I think I'll give it a try. I'm taking a crack at my homework, but I think I might have to take you up on your offer to tutor me. I can't figure out what I'm supposed to be doing on my trigonometry."

"Not sure I will be much help to you with trigonometry, but I can give it a try."

"So, what have I missed at school? I mean, besides classes. Give me the dirty details."

"Let's see, Victoria broke up with Eddie and is now dating Preston."

"Tramp," I interject, rolling my eyes. "How long did that relationship last? Two weeks this time?"

"Yeah, well, she caught him making out with Rose at some party."

"Rose? Why Rose? She's not even part of 'The Group.'"

"Hey, don't pick on Rose. She's a nice girl."

"Oh yeah, sorry. I forgot you had a *thing* for her."

"Well, maybe if you would finally go out with me..."

"We're getting off topic here," I say, trying to dodge yet another advance from David. He has wanted to date me since the seventh grade.

"Fine. Um, let's see. I guess I haven't really been paying that much attention to the drama at school. I've been more worried about you and my battle with pneumonia."

"Olivia! You need to get off the phone and get some homework done!" my mom yells from the other room.

"I gotta go, David. I'll see you tomorrow at school."

I change into my pajamas and drag myself back to the table to get more work done. So much for my mother's sympathy.

7.

My alarm wakes me from my fitful sleep. I was dreaming about the woods again. Why I keep dreaming about somewhere I've never been, I have no idea. This time it wasn't as realistic. Just a nightmare. I was running through the woods with Cindy chasing me.

She kept yelling in a sing-songy voice, "Olivia, I'm coming to get you. Come out, come out, wherever you are! I want to be your best friend!"

I ran as fast as my legs would let me.

I do *not* miss Cindy.

I try to look at the time, but the clock is just blurry light, thanks to my poor eyesight. I grab my glasses and begrudgingly leave my warm bed. After taking a dose of my control inhaler, I get myself dressed in my school uniform: a tan A-line skirt that hangs just below my knees, a white blouse that's way too big on me because they didn't have anything smaller than a large, a tan and black striped tie, and black dress shoes. Some girls try to fancy up their outfits with brightly colored socks, which I don't think they're supposed to do, but they get away with it. I just wear the standard issue white dress socks. I don't want to stand out. It's not my thing.

Just as I sit down to eat my bowl of cereal, my mom starts lecturing me while she gets herself ready for work.

"Now remember, Olivia, you don't have to tell anyone where you were or why you were in the hospital. It's none of their business." She drops my vitamin on the table as she walks past me to head to her room.

"Mmm-hmm."

"And pay close attention in class. You might be able to catch up on what you've missed. You're going to have to work hard to keep up!" she shouts from her room.

"Yup," I grunt, staring down into my bowl of cereal as I shovel another bite into my mouth.

"Remember to ask Susan if she would like to come over sometime. I think it would be good for you to spend time with friends," she says, walking to the bathroom while trying to get her earring into her ear.

I roll my eyes in response. She's not really paying attention to me anyway. After a couple of minutes of silence, she's back at it.

"Don't forget to grab your extra inhaler on your way out. And make sure you eat all the lunch I packed for you. You need to be getting enough nutrition."

"Mom! I'll be fine!" I snap.

She stops and looks at me. "You're right. I'm being overbearing."

She goes back to getting ready for work, and I stuff my homework back into my bag. I'm feeling pretty nervous. I hope David will be there.

My mom drops me off and gives me one last look of concern, but she keeps her mouth shut. I wave goodbye and walk through the hazy fog to head into school. So far, nobody has even given me a second glance. Good. I open my locker, and a piece of paper falls to the ground by my feet. I pick it up and see bubbly handwriting with a heart dotting the i.

"Try harder next time."

I know who wrote this. That stupid tramp, Victoria. I glance around the hallway to see if I can spot her. There she is standing with her minions down the hall, giggling with each other. I'm not sure if they saw me read it or not, and I don't care. I crumple the note up and throw it on the bottom of my locker.

My chest is tight at the moment, but I don't want to take my inhaler in front of anyone. I slip into the bathroom and find a stall to hide in. I can't help but think about how much nicer it would have been if I had just died with my last suicide attempt. I don't need this bullcrap.

As I'm finishing up, I hear a group of girls come into the bathroom, laughing about something. I stand as still as possible, hoping they don't know I'm here.

"Did you see her? She looks even uglier than before, all pale and skeletal," Victoria says.

"I didn't even think that was possible." Her best friend Marcy giggles.

"She could have done us all a favor and just finished the job. Sometimes I'm worried I'm going to lose my lunch when I look at that butch hair and flat chest." Victoria pretends to gag. The group of girls starts laughing and even though their words hurt, I can't help but picture them as a bunch of slack-jawed hyenas. I stifle a giggle.

The bell rings, and the preppy girls shuffle their way out. I wait until I hear the door close and make my way to the sink. I look at myself in the mirror and sigh. I have dark circles under my eyes, and my hair is slightly bed-headish. I guess I didn't put too much effort into my looks this morning. I wet my hands and try to flatten it out before heading off to class.

I head back to my locker to grab my books for first period. As I shut my locker and turn around, Victoria slams into me, knocking my books out of my arms.

"Watch where you're going, freak!" Victoria sneers.

I glare at her and start picking my papers up off the floor. A hand suddenly appears holding some papers out for me. I look up and see that David is helping me.

"Thanks, David," I say, relieved to see him.

"Don't let them get to you, Olivia. They're just jealous."

I start laughing so hard, I think I might need my inhaler again. "What are you talking about? What could they possibly be jealous of?"

"Me! They want me bad and can't have all this," David smirks, gesturing to his gangly body. "I'm your best friend, and they're jealous."

I punch him in the arm, and we walk to class, laughing. David always seems to know how to make me laugh.

By the time it's lunch hour, I am exhausted, physically and mentally. There is no way I'm ever going to catch up on school. I came close to having a panic attack when Mr. Schuller, the chemistry teacher, paired Victoria and me together at the lab table. I tried my hardest to keep a civil tongue when she almost dripped the sulfuric acid on my arm. Luckily, Mr. Schuller was coming around to our table, and Victoria had to abandon her efforts to burn my arm. She repeatedly reminded me that she hated me under her breath, though. Nothing I'm not used to.

When I see David sitting alone in the corner of the cafeteria, I quicken my pace to join him. I sit down beside him and stare at my food. A tear rolls down my cheek.

"Hey. What's the matter, Olivia?" David asks, concerned. "Wait—hold on second—let me turn up my hearing."

He likes to turn his hearing aid down when he's in the cafeteria to block out some of the excess noise. I wish I could do the same.

"I can't do this, David. I can't... I can't do any of it," I say, allowing myself to have a moment of grief.

"What can't you do?"

"I am never going to catch up in school; I feel so physically drained that I could collapse right now, and I'm not sure I would be able to get back up, and if Victoria tells me that she hates me one more time...I think I might rip her stupid hair out of her stupid head!"

David is quiet for a moment, staring down at his tray of food.

"What?" I ask, suddenly worried that he's having another seizure.

"Let's leave," David mumbles.

"You mean, leave school? I'm not sure that's going to help."

"No," David says, suddenly looking into my eyes intensely. "I mean run away. Stop rolling your eyes for a second and listen to me. Our lives suck enough as it is. We don't need the constant bullying from these losers at school. I say we pack up our stuff and see what's out there!"

"Out where, David? There is nothing outside of the fences but death! That's why there are fences. To keep all the bad stuff out."

"Or is it to keep us all in here? How do we know what's out there? We only know what they tell us. I would rather die going on an adventure and seeking truths than die inside a hospital never having lived. I want you to come with me," David pleads. He then whispers, "You just tried to kill yourself, Olivia. If you are fine with dying, then why not die trying to find answers. It's been bothering me. What if there is more out there? What if we are being lied to?"

I just stare down at my food and don't respond to him because I honestly don't know what to say.

He huffs, "Think about it," and then leaves me alone in the cafeteria.

I spend the rest of the day barely holding on. Maybe a full day of school wasn't the best idea. Once I finally get home, I collapse on the couch, unable to move. My body aches everywhere. Before I know it, my mom is calling me to eat supper. I push myself off the couch onto the floor and struggle to stand up, my muscles protesting from the effort. I shuffle my way slowly to the table and flop down, glad to be off my feet again.

"How was your first day back?" She scoops a heaping pile of mashed potatoes onto my plate.

"Sucked," I mumble.

My mom lets out a huge sigh. "You'll get there. Just keep trying." Clearly, she thinks I'm talking about the school work. I have no energy to tell her otherwise. Besides, she'll just rattle on and on about how I need to make an effort to get to know people if I really want to have friends.

She finishes dishing up my plate and encourages me to "eat up." I have no appetite. I just shove the food around my plate with my fork and take bites only when my mom says something about me needing to eat.

After supper, I plod off to my room to do some homework. I open my history book and land on a page that has pictures of The Vietnam War. I stop on the page and stare. Not at the people but at the jungle behind them. There is something about the trees and all the green that intrigues me. We don't have trees here in the part of the city where I live. The only park we have has a sad group of trees that don't get enough light from the sun in this unending fog. Their sickly yellow-green leaves are the only indication that the trees are still alive.

Suddenly, something clicks in my head. I remember seeing the pictures they took of the woods when those two scientists died while trying to take samples from outside of the city. The leaves were all green. How? Every plant in the city is a pale chartreuse color. Farmers struggle to grow enough food to feed everyone because the fog never lets enough sunlight in. How are the woods outside the city so green? Plus, how come we were even able to see the trees in the picture. Shouldn't there have been a backdrop of fog? Maybe David is on to something. Maybe there is something more out there that we're missing.

8

I wake up to the sounds of my mother pounding on the door, yelling that I'm going to be late if I don't get up *now*. I put my glasses on and see that it's 7:25. I must have dismissed my alarm by accident. I sit up, but my entire body aches, and I fall back down on the bed. I can't do it. Call it laziness if you must, but I have no desire to try to go to school today.

"I can't, Mom," I half yell back.

She opens the door and stares at me with her hands on her hips.

"And what's the matter now?" She asks skeptically.

"I can't sit up. My whole body hurts."

"Well, I'm sorry to hear that. You need to get your butt to school."

"Why can't I just stay home and rest, Mom? I feel like crap."

"Honestly, I think you're just trying to use your recent hospital visit as an excuse to stay home from school. Need I remind you that you were the one who did this to yourself?"

"Nope. No need to remind me. Thank you." I roll my eyes.

"Good. Now get out of bed and hurry up. We have very little time to get you to school, and I'm going to be late for a very important meeting!"

My mom works for the United World Coalition for Peace, which is the government that was set into place after the war was over. She won't tell me what she does exactly, but that her job is "very important." I bet she's just a secretary or something.

"I'm not going!" I pout, covering my head up with my blankets. Not sure what I hope to accomplish by acting childish.

"Oh yes, you are!" my mom says, on the verge of yelling. She storms over to my bed and rips my blankets off.

"Ugh! What is wrong with you? Why are you being so mean?"

She heaves a big sigh and pinches the bridge of her nose. "I'm sorry, Olivia. I'm just so stressed out over this meeting. I didn't get much sleep, and now we're running late. Please get ready for school. I don't think you should miss any more of your classes," she pleads.

I huff and sit up on the edge of the bed.

"Thank you. Now, I'll go get something for you to eat on the way to school. You've got five minutes," she says, hurrying out to the kitchen.

I reluctantly get myself ready. I don't say much on the ride. I just eat my granola bar and take my vitamin and my painkillers. Technically I'm not supposed to have any painkillers because of my recent stunt, but I snuck some anyway. There is no way I'm going to make it through this morning without them. I chance a look at my mom to see if she noticed me pop the pills, but she didn't. The way she keeps chewing at her fingernails, and her eyes keep darting to the clock every few seconds, tells me she's pretty tense about today. I'm not sure she would even notice if I opened the car door and fell out right now.

"So, what's your meeting about?" I finally ask once we're about a half mile from school.

She starts at my voice breaking the silence. "I can't tell you that," she says, half-laughing.

"Why not? It's not like I have a lot of friends to tell."

"Doesn't matter. I'm not allowed to speak about what we're doing with anyone," she says resolutely.

"Whatever," I mumble. I'm about to fall back into stony silence, but a question keeps needling me. "Mom, last night, I was flipping through my history book and saw a picture of a jungle, and then I remembered the picture of the scientists who died while trying to get a sample from the woods..."

"Yeah?"

"The trees were so green. How come the trees in that picture were so green when all the trees and plants in the city are yellow and sickly? You work for President Turk. Is there something going on that they're not telling us?"

Her eyes narrow, and her cheeks flush a bit, but then she smiles at me with a smile that doesn't quite reach her eyes. "Of course not! I'm sure that photograph was just doctored up on someone's computer to make it seem more colorful."

"I suppose..."

"And why would President Turk be trying to hide anything?" she says, her eyes getting all misty when she says the president's name. "The government is here to help people. If it weren't for the vitamins they hand out, everyone would be suffering from a severe lack of vitamin D."

"Okay, Mom..." I say as we pull into the school parking lot.

"Not to mention how they're protecting us from getting attacked by not only animals but humans too. The war your grandparents had to go through was terrible! The world was out of control, and the war wiped half of the human race off the face of Earth! The damage those nuclear bombs did..." She pauses, tears welling up in her eyes. "I, for one, am glad we have President Turk and the Coalition working around the clock to keep the rest of us safe so something like that doesn't happen again."

"Sorry I asked..." I mumble, opening the car door to head into school. I turn around and see my mom wiping a tear off her cheek as she drives away. She's so touchy about this subject.

"Hey, Liv!" David yells.

I turn around and see him quickly limping his way toward me.

"What happened to you?" I ask once he's caught up.

"Ah, nothing. I twisted my ankle getting off the bus. It was the humiliation from everyone laughing that hurt more, though."

"Aw. Does your ego need a hug?" I joke. He gives me a playful shove as we walk into the school.

"Hey, you wanna come over to my house to study tonight?" he asks.

"Study? Study for what?" I push my backpack into my locker.

"For our history test," he says.

"We have a test? I don't remember him mentioning a test. I've only been back for a day. I'm nowhere near being up to speed on what I've missed. Mr. Carlyle has to give me more time to catch up with everyone."

"I don't know, Liv. He's pretty tough."

"I'll ask him about it. If he's going to be an ass, then sure, I'll come over to study."

The bell rings, and we head off to our first-period class. The morning drags on as usual, and Victoria has plenty of insults to hurl at me during science class. I just keep my head down and try hard to control my tongue.

By lunchtime, my painkillers have worn off, and I'm just about ready to keel over. I find a table in the corner and plop down with my super-nutritious vending-machine lunch of potato chips, a Milky Way, and a Mountain Dew. I didn't have enough time to pack myself a lunch, so Mom gave me a couple bucks to get hot lunch. After taking a good look at the wilty salads, mystery meat, and shriveled baked potatoes that are being served for lunch, I decided this might be a safer route. At least, I know I won't get food poisoning. Soon David joins me.

"Jeez, Liv! You look like you just climbed Mt. Everest or something. You feeling okay?"

"Not really, but I'll survive. By the way, it was a no-go with Mr. Carlyle. Apparently, he doesn't really care that I've missed school and have four other classes to catch up on. What a jerk. So, I guess I'll come over to study after supper. I'm sure my mom won't mind giving me a ride to your place."

A huge smile spreads across his face. "Great! I'll get some snacks for us and plenty of Mountain Dew to keep you awake."

"Good plan." I rest my head on the table, wishing I was still in my warm bed sleeping.

At the end of the day, I stand by the parking lot, waiting for my mom to come and get me. I pace back and forth as I watch car after car pull out, leaving only a few stragglers behind. No sign of my mom. After twenty minutes of standing there looking stupid, I turn to head back inside to the office to see if I can give her a call at work. It's so embarrassing to have to use the phone in the office when everyone in the whole school has a cell phone, except me. My mom doesn't believe I should own a cell phone until I'm an adult. Cheapskate. I stop dead in my tracks when I hear a quick honk of a horn and turn around to see my mom pull in.

"It's about time!" I slam the door.

"Sorry. The meeting went late, and I couldn't leave to call the school."

"I was standing there for almost half an hour! I was hoping to take a nap when I got home."

"I said I was sorry, Olivia," she says testily.

I roll my eyes and rest my head against the back of the seat, keeping my eyes closed in hopes that she won't talk to me.

Once home, I storm up to our second-floor apartment and flop down on the couch.

"Don't you have homework to do?" she says, putting her keys in the basket by the door and sorting through the day's mail. She hands me a letter, and I just grab it without looking at it, fold it, and shove it in my pants pocket.

"Yeah. But I have a nap to take too." I turn on my side to face toward the back of the couch.

"Olivia, you need to get to work on your homework. You will not be flunking out of junior year."

"And what difference does it make if I do junior year over again or not?" I yawn.

"It makes a pretty big difference because you're moving out once you turn eighteen! I can only protect you for so long."

"Protect me? What are you talking about?" I turn to face her. She has her hand clapped over her mouth.

"Nothing. Now go to your room, and get going on your homework..."

"No. What are you talking about 'protecting me'? From what? If it's from getting sick or from having a terrible life, you're really doing a bang-up job, Mom."

I can tell I hit a nerve as I watch her face turn a dark shade of maroon and her eyes narrow until they are almost closed. I'm on my feet, shaking from either exhaustion or anger, I can't tell.

"I am trying my hardest, Olivia! I have done nothing but provide for you. I cook; I clean; I work hard to try to pay the medical bills you've racked up."

"I'm sorry I'm such a problem!" I yell. "I wish Dad were still alive!"

"Don't you *dare* bring up your father!" She points her finger at me.

"Why? You never talk about him."

"I can't! It hurts too much!" Tears leak down her cheeks, leaving tracks of black eyeliner.

"I want to know what happened to Dad! I deserve that much! I have spent my entire life without a father, and my mother won't tell me anything about him!"

She glares at me with an intensity that makes me back up a few steps and sit down on the armrest of the couch.

"Fine. You wanna know?" She asks me with a quiet, dangerous tone. "He joined the military and was sent overseas to fight in a war we shouldn't even be a part of. I was young, pregnant with you, and terrified. I pleaded with him to stay with me, but he signed up anyway. And he never returned. No body. Nothing. They say a bomb fell where he was stationed, and they found nothing left of him to return to me."

I stare down at the floor, tears starting to form in my eyes.

"What? You got nothing more to say? Nothing to throw in my face to make me feel even worse? I have been nothing but patient with you through all your suicidal attempts, psychiatric stays, bad attitudes, and rudeness. But if you keep treating me like this...like your enemy...you can just get the hell out of here. I have put up with enough for today. Now, go to your room."

Huh. I've never seen my mom get so pissed at me before. I oblige and head to my room, giving the door a good slam in defiance. That must have been one hell of a meeting to put her in such a mood.

9

I lie on my bed, with my feet up on my wall, trying to make up my mind about what I'm going to do. She wants me gone? Fine. I decide that I'm going to go over to David's house, but I want to wait until my mom won't see me leave. Something is poking my thigh, and then I remember that I had shoved a letter in my pocket. I sit up and look for whom it's from. There is no return address.

> Dear Olivia,
> I miss you being here. I can't stand what Cindy is doing to me. I just woke up in solitary confinement again. It's so cold and dark in there. Please, help me!
> Joselyn

I stare at the words "help me" until my eyes blur. Poor Joselyn. I wish there were something I could do. I grab a piece of paper and write back.

> Joselyn,
> I'm so sorry. Stay strong! You need to keep taking your medicine. Cindy can be controlled if you just take it. I hope to someday see you outside of the hospital, Cindy-free. Until then, keep fighting!
> Olivia

I search online to find the address for the hospital. After I finish the letter, I stay in my room for about half an hour and finally get the nerve to crack my door open and peek out to see where my mom is. The door of her bedroom is open slightly, and I can hear her snoring. So much for supper. Oh well. This is my chance.

I pull my door open just enough to squeeze through it, hoping the door doesn't creak and wake her up. I slide my sneakers on and make my way as quietly out the front door as possible. I see the keys in the basket beside the door but decide that I'll just walk. I don't want to give her a reason to call the cops on me, saying I stole her car or something. I drop the letter I wrote to Joselyn into the mailbox on my way out.

The fog gives me a feeling of being enclosed that I don't like. I quicken my pace, hoping I can make it the five blocks to David's house. By the time I get there, my legs are like jelly, and I stop outside of his door to take a dose of my inhaler. I ring the doorbell and see David's ruddy face look through the curtain of the side window before opening the door.

"Hey! You made it."

"Barely." I lean against the doorframe, breathing heavily.

"What'd you do? Walk here?" he asks, closing the door behind me.

"I had to. I had a big fight with my mom. She doesn't know I'm here."

He leads me through the kitchen.

"Hi, Olivia. How're you?" David's mother asks me from the stove. She's a portly woman with long brown hair and a kind face. She looks up from the stove and gives me a friendly smile.

"I'm doing okay, Mrs. Beckett."

"Did you eat? We're having spaghetti and meatballs. There's enough if you want some."

"Um...sure. Thank you."

"Mom, we're going to go to my room and start studying. Let us know when supper's done." David takes my arm and pulls me to his room.

"Remember to keep the door open, David." Mr. Beckett calls after us from the living room, reminding him of their house rules. Like I would ever do anything with him that would require the door to be closed.

I walk into his surprisingly clean room and have a seat on his bed. He closes the door until there is a sliver of light shining through, just enough to be able to say he's following the rules.

"Wow. Your room looks so clean."

"I knew you were coming over, so I tidied up a bit," he says, sitting in a chair across from me. "So, what did you and your mom fight about this time?"

"She was being a total witch and wouldn't let me lie down to take a nap, so I told her I wish Dad were still alive, and she snapped. I finally got her to tell me what happened to him, though..."

"Oh yeah? Do tell."

"He signed up with the military and was shipped overseas. I guess a bomb dropped on his location, and there was nothing left of him to deliver home."

"They didn't find his body?" David asks with a faraway look in his eyes.

"That's what she said. Anyway, she told me she was tired of my attitude and said I should leave if I wasn't going to stop being this way. I went to my room, waited for her to cool off, and after a while, I found she was sleeping, so I snuck over here."

"Great! Now she's going to come looking for you and get mad at me."

"Nah, I think she's going to sleep until morning. She didn't get a lot of sleep last night because of the 'big, important meeting' she had today."

David looks up at me abruptly. "A big important meeting? Did she say what it was about?"

David is always intrigued by what my mom could be doing at the government building. He's working his way into being a full-fledged conspiracy theorist. Like a lot of people, he neither likes nor trusts President Reginald Turk. David believes Turk is a sleazy, smooth-talking viper of a man who has no business being our president. He was appointed by the UN, instead of being voted in like things were done in the United States before the war.

"No. She said it was classified and wouldn't tell me anything. The meeting ran late, and she picked me up half an hour after school let out. Then she was all cranky and short-tempered. She did say something that seemed odd, though."

"What?" David's eyes glisten.

"She told me that I needed to finish school because I have to move out when I'm eighteen because she can only protect me for so long."

"What? What does that mean?"

"I know, right! I asked her, but she started telling me to go do my homework."

"Hmm...interesting." David strokes his chin in a conspiratorial way.

"You're not going to go all tinfoil-hat on me now, are you?"

"Well, there's obviously something your mom is hiding."

I start to huff at him but then remember the conversation I had with her on my way to school.

"Actually...you know what? It was kind of weird when I asked her if the Coalition was hiding something about the woods and why they are so green when everything in the city is half dead, she started getting all defensive. 'Why would the Coalition try to hide anything from us? The government is here to protect us from uncertain doom' and crap like that."

"Of course, someone working for the government is going to defend what they're doing. They've probably been told by *President Turk*," David says with as much disdain as he can muster into saying the president's name, "to not speak to anyone about their lying and manipulation. There probably isn't anything actually wrong with the woods. Like I said before: what if they are just trying to keep us in the city like sheep in a pen."

"For what purpose?"

"Control. Power. Fear is a good motivator for compliance. If they have everyone inside of the city, they can keep tabs on what everybody is doing. And everyone will continue living like good little robots."

"Is that a bad thing? Sounds to me like they just want to make sure everyone is safe."

"I don't know, Liv. As long as you aren't hurting other people or their property, who cares what you do? Why does the president care so much about people leaving the city? If I want to leave the city, knowing the risks involved, I should be able to, but they have the entrance so heavily guarded you can't just leave."

"David! It's time for supper!" Mrs. Beckett calls from the kitchen.

"Did you just say something?" David looks around.

"No, turn up your hearing aid," I say with a playful eye roll. "Food's ready."

"To be continued." David fiddles with his ear.

As I sit at the table, eating the delicious supper—*I wish my mother cooked this well*—I keep replaying what David said. He's right. The president has no right to lock us up in the city. The fence is there to keep animals out, and the guards are there to keep enemies out, but what about us? What if we want to take the risk to leave? Is keeping us contained like prisoners really a good way to protect us?

"Liv...*Liv*!" David shouts, snapping his fingers in front of my face.

"What? I'm sorry. I was lost in thought."

"My mom asked if you would like a ride home after we're done studying."

"Oh, sure. That would be great." I give her a small smile.

We help clean up the dishes and then head back to David's room.

"What was up with you at supper?" David asks, closing his door most of the way again. "It's like you went all zombie on me."

"Sorry. I was thinking hard about what you were saying."

"Really?" David smiles wide. "So, are you finally going to agree to run away with me?"

"Shhh!" I hush, glancing at the door. "Just hold on. Say we did decide to go see what's out there. How are we even going to get out?"

"I've thought a lot about this." David scoots his chair closer to me so we can keep our voices down.

"Don't tell me you want to try to sneak through the bad part of town," I say nervously.

After the war, there was only a part of the city that was still standing and livable. To the east of us is the rundown part of the city, where criminals and homeless people live. The Coalition put up a fence around that part of town too to keep wild animals out, but they don't station guards there anymore. After a few guards were killed by druggies, they stopped caring what happened to the people in that area and left them to fend for themselves.

"No, of course not. We wait until it's dark, pick a section of the fence between guard towers, and use my dad's bolt cutters to cut a hole in the fence. It doesn't have to be big—I mean, look at us," he continues, gesturing to his scrawny body. I nod my head in agreement. "The fog will help conceal us as we make a break for it."

"But our parents will know we're missing, the hole will be discovered, and they'll come find us. We're not exactly top physical specimens able to outrun anyone."

"That's why we leave in the middle of the night, and by the time they realize we're missing, we'll be hours ahead of them out in the woods," David says, excitement lighting up his face.

"I still don't know, David. A part of me wants to know what's out there, but I'm scared. How are we going to protect ourselves if there are monsters in the woods?"

"With this." David leans down and grabs a shoebox from under his bed. He glances at the door before opening the box, making sure his parents aren't standing out there, peeking at us through the crack. He grabs a sock from inside it and slides whatever is in the sock out. A small black handgun rests on his palm.

"Where did you get that?" I say a little too loudly.

"Shh!" David warns, glancing at the door again. He quickly shoves the gun back into the sock and puts it all back.

"David, where did you get that? All the guns were supposed to have been turned in after the war. Only military are allowed to use them."

"I know. My grandpa gave this to me before he died. He told me he kept it because 'if you don't have the freedom to defend yourself, then you might as well be dead.' It was small enough that he hid it under a loose floorboard when soldiers came through to search people's houses for guns. My parents don't know I have it. Grandpa told me to keep it a secret."

"Do you know how to use it?" I ask, unsure of this whole idea.

"Well...no. Not really. I mean, I understand the concept. You point and shoot. But I can't exactly go outside and practice with it."

I take a deep breath. This talking about running away has me on edge.

"What about if it rains? The umbrellas we have are pretty much worthless."

"We won't go if it's raining, and once we are out of the city and in the woods, the trees should be able to block a lot of it. We'll take a couple of extra umbrellas with us and make a little shelter for ourselves if it does rain. We might be able to find a cave or something to hide in too."

"All right, say we do get out, and there aren't any threats... Then what?"

"I don't know. We explore. We discover. We'll pack food and clothes and matches, things we need for survival, and we go find answers. Why are Turk and the Coalition keeping us in here? What else is out there? Are we being lied to?"

I stare at the floor in thought. A sense of excitement is welling up in my chest. Maybe this kind of adventure is what I need. Maybe I need to get away from my mother and the bullies at school for a while.

"Okay, David. I'll go with you," I say, keeping my eyes on the floor. *What am I getting myself into?*

David jumps up out of his seat and fist-pumps the air.

"But I need time to get ready. How about we go next week sometime? Give me an opportunity to pack and maybe get some extra inhalers stockpiled. I'll just tell mom that I've been having a harder time with my asthma and that I need refills."

"Good idea. That'll give me time to sneak some more food," David says. "I can't believe we're doing this! I have been dreaming about this for a long time now."

I'm glad he's excited about it. I'm just hoping we don't die a horrible, painful death.

10

"You're a nice girl, Olivia," Mrs. Beckett says as we pull onto my road.

"Thank you, Mrs. Beckett," I reply, knowing where this is headed.

"David thinks very highly of you. He's a good boy. Maybe you should give him a chance and go on a date with him."

I really wish David had decided to ride with us. This is so freaking awkward.

"I know. I'm just not really interested in dating anyone right now, what with all of my sicknesses and being so behind in school."

"I understand. Just...give it some thought, okay?" she says, pulling up to my apartment.

I nod my head and thank her for the ride as I get out of the car. I think she's worried that David will never find someone to love him with all his physical needs. She's hoping that since I suffer from a long list of problems too, that maybe we would be able to take care of each other and be understanding to each other. But who's going to take care of both of us should we get sick at the same time?

I head up to the apartment, hoping that my mom is still asleep. I need some time to think about this plan I made with David. Just as my hand is on the knob, the door swings open.

"*Where have you been?*"

Crap. She's awake.

"I went over to David's to study for the history test I have tomorrow," I answer, trying to sidestep to get past her. She blocks my way.

"I wake up, and there's no note or anything! You're supposed to tell me where you're going. How would I know where to start looking for you if you hadn't come back?"

"I'm fine! I didn't realize you cared so much. You certainly didn't seem to give a crap about me a few hours ago...you know, when you told me to stop acting bratty or leave?" I duck under her arm and head to my room.

She grabs my wrist and spins me around to face her. She takes a moment to check her anger, and finally, her face softens. "I'm sorry about that, Olivia. I know I'm not the greatest mom in the world. I say things I don't mean sometimes."

Looks like we're back to the apologetic/tolerant part of our relationship again. I was actually okay with her being angry with me. I could leave without feeling guilty.

I sigh. "It's okay, Mom. I'm sorry for being so cranky lately."

"We both have. I'll try harder if you promise to do the same."

"Sure," I agree, hoping she'll let me go to my room.

She holds my wrist a little longer, staring at my face. I look at the floor, slightly uncomfortable with this moment of...affection? She's got my wrist held pretty tightly, almost threateningly.

"I never told you this, but you have your father's eyes," she says quietly. My eyes are an emerald green, while hers are a dark brown.

"That's because you never talk about him," I say, trying to keep my tone light.

"Yes, well, you got me thinking about him again. It was easier to just not think about him, and the pain would numb. But I guess that's not really fair to you." She lets go of my wrist.

"That's okay. We don't have to talk about him right now," I offer. "I was hoping to go over my notes once more for the history test before going to bed."

She nods her head. "That's a good idea."

I head to my room and close my door gently. I really do need to go over my notes since David and I didn't do any studying whatsoever because we were too busy working on our plans. I sit on my bed with my back against the wall and stare at the notes without seeing them.

Are we really going to do this? What if we get caught? What is my mom going to say when she finds out I ran away? She'll probably put me back in the looney bin, making sure I share a room with Cindy. Oh god!

After about an hour of getting nowhere on my studying, I get up and pace around the room. I stop by my door when I hear my mother's muffled voice coming from her bedroom. I crack the door open slightly to let her voice in clearer. She must have called someone, because I didn't hear the phone ring.

"I can't do it. You know how I feel..." She pauses, listening to the other end of the line. "No. We will not go forward with the original plan. She's back home, and she's fine... You don't know that! Look, we will continue doing things this way until I say we're done! Yes...okay...talk to you soon."

Who was she talking to? I don't have a lot of time to think about it, though, because my mom is headed toward my room. I quickly run and hop onto my bed, adjusting myself up against the wall just in time for her to open my door. I wonder if she will notice my heavy breathing.

"Hey. I just wanted to check to see how you're doing. Need any snacks or anything?"

"Nope. I'm fine."

"Okay. Well, I'm going to go take a shower and then head to bed," she says, stifling a yawn. "It's been one hell of a day."

I nod my head as she closes my door. I slip off my bed and listen at the door for the shower to turn on. Once I hear the water running, I slide out of my room and tiptoe my way into her room, looking for her cell phone. I want to know who she was talking to about me.

I find it on the bedside table and start searching immediately. My mom doesn't take long showers, so I need to make this quick. Huh. It says that she hasn't made or received any calls for days. I pick up our cordless landline, and there aren't any calls on there either. Who was she talking to? My curiosity is eating away at me. I hear the bathroom door open, and I make a mad dash to leave, but she meets me in the doorway of her bedroom.

"What are you doing in here?" She jumps a little when she sees me.

"Oh, um, I was just looking to see if you had any extra inhalers in here..." I say lamely. "I've been going through mine like crazy, and I just wanted to check for spares."

"No, I don't keep any in here," she says, eyeing me up skeptically, as she adjusts the towel tighter around her chest.

"Okay, well, would you mind picking up a couple extra ones for me?"

"Sure." She steps past me, leaving the scent of her shampoo lingering in her wake.

"Close the door behind you, please. Goodnight."

I close the door and hurry back to my room. That was too close. My mother likes her secrets, and I don't want to find out what she would do if she found me snooping around on her phone.

11

By the time it's the weekend, I'm ready to do nothing but lie around and eat ludicrous amounts of junk food. My mom seems to have cooled off a bit from our last fight and lets me binge watch my favorite movies. She spends most of her time working on her laptop at the kitchen table. I can hear the keys clacking away while I get up to put *The Lord of the Rings* in the DVD player. She occasionally reminds me that I need to do some homework this weekend—pretty much whenever she walks past me to go to the bathroom. I reassure her by grunting, "Maybe after this movie."

I talk to David a few times to finalize our plans. We're going to leave Wednesday night because my mom has a meeting on Thursday morning, and she always tries to get extra sleep the night before meetings.

Before I know it, it's Sunday night, and I got absolutely nothing accomplished this weekend. My mom finally finishes whatever it is she has been working on and is now hassling me to do my homework.

"It's not a big deal! I worked on some of it last night before I went to bed," I lie. "I'll go work on some more of it now."

"You'd better," she says, yawing big. "I'm going to go to bed. 'Night."

I go to my room, but instead of working on homework, I start packing some things I'm going to need for Wednesday. I grab a couple changes of clothes, extra socks, a spare toothbrush and toothpaste, shampoo, the couple of extra inhalers I have, a blanket, bottles of water, some dried fruit and beef jerky, my jacket, some matches, hand sanitizer, and a roll of toilet paper—a girl has needs! I slip the bag on my back and take a look at myself in the mirror. A wave of excitement hits me, closely followed by terror. Are we really going to be able to survive out there? Is my life really so bad that I am willing to run off into the wilderness with David, leaving behind a relatively comfortable existence...or at least a life with shelter and food?

I close my eyes and imagine what it's going to be like out there. Do I have what it takes? I remember the dream I had of me being in the woods. There was something about all that green and life around me that intrigued me. The woods seemed so wild yet comforting. It's silly to base my judgment of whether this is a good plan or not on a dream, but I can't shake the feeling that there was something more to it than just a dream.

I slide the bag off and shove it as far under my bed as I can. I can't wait to talk to David tomorrow.

■■■■■

I make my way through the thicker-than-usual fog toward the school. The fog is so bad today, you almost run into people before you see them. Once inside, I start scanning for David. I don't spot him before I get to my locker. Victoria stands on the other side of the hallway, laughing. I ignore her while I put my things away. I feel so vulnerable without David standing by my side. After an outburst of roaring laughter, I turn around and see Victoria holding her fingers in circles around her eyes, slumping her shoulders forward, and making a ridiculously stupid face. Clearly, she's trying to impersonate me. I give her as mean of a death glare as I can and then head off to my first-period class in hopes that I can get inside and just sit at my desk until school starts.

I see no signs of David between classes, and by the time lunch comes around, I conclude that he must not be in school today. I hope he's all right. I spend the rest of the day worrying about him instead of paying attention in my classes. There is no doubt that I'm going to fail every single one of them.

I call him as soon as I get home.

"Hello?"

"Hi, Mr. Beckett. Can I speak to David, please?"

"I'm afraid not. He's in the hospital."

"Oh no! What is it this time?"

"He had a severe seizure last night and hit his head on the edge of the kitchen table as he fell down. He cracked his head open pretty good. The doctors say he'll live, but he's got to stay in the hospital for a while so they can find out what kind of damage he did."

"That's terrible! Is there a good time for me to come see him?"

"Uh, I would give it a couple days, Olivia. They are doing some extensive tests to see why his medicine hasn't been working."

"Is there anything I can do?" I ask feebly.

"Just keep him in your prayers and maybe pick up some of his school work for him if you can. You can drop it off here. I'll be stopping at home after work each day to clean up before I go see him."

"Sure. Please let me know if anything changes. I'm so worried about him."

"Of course."

I hang up the phone, bury my face into the pillow, and cry. There is no way we should be running off into the wilderness together. I have no idea how to take care of him if he were to have a seizure! This is a terrible plan. I cry for a while longer and try to compose myself when I hear a light knock on my bedroom door.

"Is everything, okay?" my mom asks.

"No, not really, but come in."

She opens the door slowly, and her face falls when she sees me wiping away a tear.

"What's the matter, Olivia?"

"David is in the hospital again," I sniff.

"Oh, dear. What's it this time?"

"His seizure medication isn't working, and he had a bad seizure while standing. He fell and hit his head on the table. Mr. Beckett said that I should wait a couple of days before I go to see him," I say, tears flowing freely again.

My mom tentatively walks over to my bed, sits on the edge, and stiffly places her hand on my shoulder.

"I'm so sorry, Olivia."

"I just don't understand why David and I have to keep dealing with all of this crap! It's not fair! I just wish we were healthy, normal teenagers. I wish Victoria had to walk in my shoes for a day. Maybe she would stop picking on me all the time."

"Who's Victoria?"

"Victoria is a popular girl in school. She's always telling me she hates me and making fun of me. I actually overheard her say that she wishes I would have succeeded in killing myself."

"That's terrible!" My mom says, aghast.

"Yeah, it is. Sorry, I guess I never told you about it. I just try to ignore her most of the time."

"Well, maybe you need to stand up for yourself. Maybe you need to confront this Victoria and let her know you don't like her treating you that way."

"What would I say? 'Stop it! You're hurting my feelings.' Yeah, that will go over real well." I roll my eyes.

"I don't know, but you need to say something. Tell a teacher. Or the principal. Maybe I should see if I can talk to her parents..."

"No! No, Mom. That would only make things worse. I can handle it myself."

"Okay," she pauses awkwardly. "Well, I guess I'm going to go start making supper. Unless...you needed me to stay and talk a little while longer?" she offers, almost looking worried that I was going to say yes. I can tell she's uncomfortable.

"No, that's okay. I think I need to be alone for a little while."

She exits the room, and I fall back onto my pillow and stare at the wall. It's going to be a rough couple of days.

12

I can already tell that today is going to suck. My mom lectures me all the way to school about having a talk with Victoria. How "being civil and talking through problems can really strengthen a relationship." I quietly stare out the window, watching the endless white haze pass by. I don't think she understands just how much Victoria and I hate each other. She finally forces me to agree to give it a shot. She thinks she's being diplomatic or something, a true employee of the United World Coalition of Peace, just trying to make the world a better place. I think she's being a relentless nag, full of crap and bad ideas.

As I walk into school, I'm more on edge than normal, as if my mother is watching me to see if I follow through with my promise. I really don't need this kind of pressure. I'm guessing that she is just trying to take my mind off from David for a while, but this is definitely not what I want to do instead.

I can see Victoria standing at Marcy's locker down the hall. My chest starts tightening just looking at her. I start to walk over by her when the bell rings. Oh, thank God! Maybe I'll confront her in science class. I have a few hours to think about what I might say.

I make it to science class, where Victoria sits behind me. She has a lovely habit of shooting spitwads at the back of my head when Mr. Schuller is facing the whiteboard. And sure enough, while he writes today's lesson up on the board, I feel something hit me. I turn around to face her, and she gives me a look of disgust.

"What do you want, loser?"

"Stop shooting spitwads at me."

"And why would I do that?" She smirks.

"Why do you hate me so much?" I whisper. My heart is pounding out of my chest.

"Where do I begin? Take a look at yourself! Better yet, don't. We wouldn't want to crack any mirrors."

"Care to share with the rest of the class, ladies?" Mr. Schuller calls out from the front of the classroom.

I turn around and face forward, shaking my head no. Great plan, Mom.

Mr. Schuller gets back to teaching his lesson on atomic mass numbers, and every time he turns around to refer to the periodic table, Victoria shoots a spitwad at me. I start breathing heavy as I fill with rage. I try hard to calm myself down. Only twenty more minutes of class left. After the seventh time, though, I've finally had enough.

"Mr. Schuller! Victoria is shooting spitwads at my head when you aren't looking."

"Is that true, Ms. Campbell?"

"No! Of course not!" Victoria says, placing a hand on her chest and giving him a look of shock.

"She's lying. Look at the floor if you don't believe me."

Mr. Schuller makes his way back to my desk and looks at the small scattering of spitwads on the floor.

"Those were there when we got here, Mr. Schuller. I swear, it wasn't me."

"I think you can collect your things and sit in the principal's office for the rest of the hour, Ms. Campbell." He turns around and makes his way back to the front of the class again. He picks up the phone on his desk to call the office and tell them that Victoria is on the way.

"I'll get you for this. You're dead," Victoria hisses as she gathers up her stuff.

This is not at all what I wanted. Why did I listen to my mom?

I try to keep my eyes on Mr. Schuller, but Marcy keeps turning her head over her shoulder and glaring at me from the corner of her eye, giving me the evilest look she can muster. I will be lucky to make it home in one piece. There's not a lot a toothpick like me can do to defend myself against these girls. Especially if they gang up on me. I wish David were here. He's not exactly built either, but at least he would be there to try to defend me.

Once the bell rings, I slip into the bathroom to use my inhaler and hope that I can hide from Victoria. Once I'm in the stall, I hear someone else come into the bathroom. I can see their shoes as they stop in front of the stall I'm hiding in. Long blonde hair comes into view too as the person outside bends down to look under the stall door. They step away, and suddenly, I hear the bathroom door open again and Marcy yell out, "Victoria! She's in here!"

Crap! I stand at the back of the stall with my legs crammed between the toilet and the wall. The door on the stall next to mine squeaks, and suddenly, Victoria's head pops over the wall.

"Well, well, well. You're going to have to come out of there eventually, and when you do, you're going to pay for getting me in trouble. Principal Meadows called my parents, and now I'm grounded for the weekend. I had plans to go to a party, and now I can't because of you, you freak."

Just then, the bell rings for the next period.

"To be continued." Victoria sneers.

I wait until I hear both girls leave the bathroom before I start breathing again. Crap! Crap, crap, crap! Now, what am I going to do?

By the end of the day, I am shaking from fear. I wish I had never said anything to her. I wish I would have just left it alone. I wish I weren't here anymore. I grab my stuff from my locker and try to walk quickly out of the school before they find me. Hopefully, my mom will be waiting for me in the parking lot. I step outside, and suddenly, a hand grabs me around the waist, and another hand covers my mouth. They drag me around the corner of the school, where nobody will see us, not that anyone could see us through the fog anyway. They let go, and I see that it's

Victoria's boyfriend, Preston. He keeps his forearm pressed against my chest and neck, holding me against the wall.

"Victoria, we're over here," Preston calls out in a loud whisper.

Victoria steps out of the fog and stands so close, I can smell the mint gum she's chewing. Without warning, her hand comes flying up and slaps me hard against my cheek. If it weren't for Preston holding me against the wall, I probably would have fallen over.

"That's what you get, loser," Victoria says, curling her lip.

"I'm sorry, Victoria. I didn't mean to get you in trouble—"

Before I know it, she slaps me again, even harder. I can feel a welt rising on my stinging cheek. My heart is beating out of my chest, and adrenaline starts coursing through my body. The fight or flight response starts kicking in, and I can't think of anything right now but running the hell away.

"Don't talk to me, you little skank. You have no right to even look at me. You disgust me. I wish you were dead."

"Come on, Victoria. We better get going before someone finds us." Preston looks nervous as he keeps watch.

"You go ahead, Prés. Wait for me in the car. I have one last thing to do, and I'll catch up."

Preston pulls his arm off my chest, and I slump over, rubbing my stinging cheek. I hear him walk away, and suddenly, Victoria has a handful of my hair and pulls my head backward.

"If you tell anyone about this, I will do more than slap you."

It feels like my scalp is about to rip open. Rage starts bubbling up inside me, and before I know it, the bones in Victoria's nose are crunching under my fist. Blood gushes down her blouse, and she screams as her hands fly up to her face. She falls to the ground, and I run as fast as I can to the parking lot. I find my mom's car and quickly climb in.

"What happened to you? Why is your face all red?" my mom asks.

"Drive!" I yell.

13

My mom doesn't hesitate and takes off.

"Are you going to tell me what's going on?"

"Can we wait until we get home? My face hurts too much to talk." I gingerly touch my welt.

She huffs but stays quiet for the rest of the drive. Once home, she grabs an ice pack for me and then has a seat on the couch, looking at me with a raised eyebrow, waiting for an explanation.

"Well, I did what you told me to do. I confronted Victoria, but she didn't really have a reason for why she hates me...just that she hates me. Then she kept shooting spit wads at me, and I told the teacher. He sent her to the principal's office, and she got grounded by her parents. So, she had her stupid jock boyfriend grab me when I was trying to leave school, and she confronted me, slapping my face a couple of times, and pulling my hair—"

Just then, my mom's cell phone rings, and she holds a finger up to stop me from talking.

"Hello?... Yes, this is Mrs. Sloane... She did what?" My mom's eyes grow wide, and then she turns her head to glare at me. "I see. Yes, of course. I understand you can't allow that to happen... Did you talk to Victoria's parents about her bullying my daughter?... You did. Okay. I'm very sorry about this, Principal Meadows. I will have a talk with Olivia... Thank you. You too."

My mom hangs up the phone and sets it on the coffee table with a shaky hand. She sits still for a moment, staring down at her phone.

"What were you thinking?" She finally yells, causing a vein to bulge in her neck. "You punched the girl and broke her nose? I told you to talk to her, not get into a fist fight!"

"She was ripping my hair out of my head! What was I supposed to do?" I yell back.

"Well, I certainly don't want you breaking people's noses!" She yells, jumping up on her feet, bearing down on me. "You got yourself suspended for your little stunt! I hope you're happy! You might as well kiss senior year goodbye! You're never going to catch up now!"

"What is wrong with you!" I shout, jumping to my feet to match my mother. She's taller than me, but I want to show her that I'm not going to back down. "She slapped me twice and had my hair in her fist, pulling so hard I felt like my scalp was about to give way! But you don't care about that! No! You only care that I got suspended and might not graduate next year!"

"Of course that's what I'm mad about! If you're going to continue to be so damn reckless, you are *never* going to graduate! You are never going to get a decent

48

paying job and move out on your own! Do you have any idea how all of your suicide attempts and childish antics make me look?"

"Oh, gee! I guess I should have stopped myself from wanting to die because of how it might make *you* look. Mom! You are so selfish!"

"I've had it with you! *Go to your room!*" She screams.

I turn around and storm off to my room, slamming the door hard enough that a picture falls off the wall in the hallway, and I hear the glass shatter.

"Great! Thanks a lot, you little brat!" she yells.

I flop onto my bed, expecting to cry, but I am so angry, I can't. My chest is tight, so I take a dose of my inhaler, cursing my life as I do.

I hear my mother cleaning up the glass and secretly hope that she cuts herself. It'll serve her right. I can't live with her anymore. I hope David gets better soon because I want to run away more than anything right now, with his seizures and all. I hate my life. I hate Victoria. And as of this moment, I hate my own mother.

In the morning, I sneak out to use the bathroom and find a note laying on the floor outside my door.

> Since you got yourself suspended, you also got yourself grounded. Stay in the apartment, and you are not allowed to watch TV. You can use this time to work on catching up on your homework. I will be late for supper. Make it yourself.

I crumple up her note and throw it in the trash. How is she going to stop me from watching TV? I walk straight into the living room to turn it on just to spite her, but the TV isn't there. Where did it go? I see a little slip of paper where it usually sits.

I told you no TV.

Holy crap! She *literally* took the TV away.

I walk past the dining room and see all my homework spread out. She was certainly busy last night. I keep walking and decide that I'm just going to stick it to her by pigging out on junk food for breakfast. I open the fridge to grab a Mountain Dew. It's gone! I slam the fridge and look in the cupboards, only to find all the candy and sweets gone. There's another note on the counter.

You can forget about sweets and junk too. Have a nice day!

I'm a prisoner in my own house because I fought back? This isn't fair!

I run back to my room and start punching my pillow. Once exhausted, I lie down and think longingly about my plans with David. I dig my backpack out from under the bed and go over the things I've packed. I add a couple more articles of clothing and some more food. I can't think of anything else to add, so I shove it back under the bed.

What am I going to do for the next few days? As I pace my room, trying to think of something, I grab the necklace I once found in a box of my Grandpa's old

49

stuff. I like to fidget with it when I'm bored. I didn't show it to Mom when I found it because I knew she wouldn't let me keep it. I was snooping around the apartment one day when I found a box labeled "Dad's stuff," and there it was, rolled up in a pair of socks.

It's a crystal cylinder about two inches long. It has five separate sections that spin. Each section has the same seven weird symbols on them. I like to hold it and spin them around and around, staring at the different symbols, pretending it's some sort of secret key or alien relic.

Suddenly, I get an idea. I put the pendant back in my jewelry box, and I step out of my room. I look down the hallway even though I know she isn't here. I sneak into my mom's room and start looking through her drawers. She likes to keep her secrets? Well, let's just see if we can find some of them.

I search through her end table drawers and find nothing but the usual boring stuff: books, pads of paper, pens. Next, I start at the bottom drawer of her dresser and work my way up. I'm about to call it quits, but then I see something in the top drawer. I move her bras off to the side, and there's a photograph lying on the bottom of the drawer. It's a picture of my mom looking young, beautiful, and pregnant. She's standing next to a man who has his arm wrapped around her. My breath catches in my chest. I think it's my dad!

I rush over to the lamp and turn it on so I can see the photo better. I study his face, and notice that I do, indeed, have the same eyes. Other than that, I look mostly like my mother. He has shaggy brown hair slicked back from his face, a sharp straight nose, full lips, and a broad chin. I can see why my mom was smitten. He's quite handsome. I wish I had gotten to know him.

Even though my dad died before I was born, there is something familiar about him. But it can't be, because this is the first time I have ever seen him.

I hold it with reverence, knowing this is our only family picture, even though I'm technically not in it. I turn it over and stare at what's written.

It's dated five years before I was born.

I place the picture back in the drawer and try to arrange her bras back over it just like it was when I found it. I race back to my room and lie down to process what I just saw.

What is going on? Is there a chance that she is just messing with me? Maybe she just wrote the wrong date down, thinking that I might snoop around and find it, and she wanted to screw with my head.

By lunchtime, I decide that I'm going to work on homework to try to take my mind off the mysterious picture. I'm working so hard that I don't realize what time it is until I hear the front door open and see my mom step in.

"Glad to see you doing your work," she says, attempting to sound nice.

I yawn, nodding my head.

"Did you make supper?" She drops the mail on the table next to the door.

"No. I got so busy working on my homework since there was nothing else to do, thanks to you. I lost track of time and forgot to make supper."

"Well, I have to say, I'm surprised you did what I asked you to do. Keep working, and I'll go make us some supper. Oh, and you got a letter."

She hands it to me as she walks to the kitchen. No return address again. I rip it open hoping to hear from Joselyn.

Olivia,
    Once I'm out of this damn hospital, I'm going to find you, and I'm going to kill you. Stop trying to help Joselyn. You can't. I'm here to stay, and there's nothing you can do about it.
                             Cindy

I shudder. I'm so glad that Cindy is locked up. I hope they can figure out a way to make her disappear for good. Joselyn deserves a better life.

I get back to work on the last few problems of trigonometry, and I can smell that my mom is making tacos again. She's probably hoping to apologize to me by using my favorite supper.

I clear my homework off the table, and my mom starts bringing the food in, giving me a smile as she sets the taco meat in front of me. I roll my eyes as she walks back into the kitchen.

As I dig into my first taco, my mom already starts in on her apology.

"Look, Olivia. I got a check-in call from Dr. Hughes to see how you're doing. I told him about your run-in with Victoria, and he seemed to think that you responded the correct way. That you tried to be civil first and then did what you had to do to defend yourself," she says. "I'm sorry I overreacted. He's right. You shouldn't let people hurt you. I got angry that you were suspended, and I couldn't think about anything other than that. I'm glad she didn't hurt you worse than she did."

I give my head a little nod to acknowledge her. "It's okay, Mom. I'm sorry I broke her nose. I was just trying to get away from her by any means necessary and was shocked when I realized I had punched her."

"Good arm." She winks. We go back to eating, and I can't stop thinking about the photo I found. I really want to know what it means. Maybe she will keep herself from yelling at me since she's trying to be nice again. I decide to take the risk.

"Mom, I have a confession to make."

She sits back and gives me her full attention.

"Go ahead."

"Well...I got bored today and was mad that you took away the TV and everything I enjoy eating, and I decided to look through your stuff. I found a picture in your dresser of you. You were pregnant and standing with a man who, I'm guessing, was Dad? But the date was five years before I was born. Why is the date wrong?"

Her expression is deadpan as she stares at me.

"You snooped through my stuff?" She asks, dangerously quiet.

"Yeah. I'm sorry. I know I shouldn't have. But I did. So, what is up with that picture? I can't stop thinking about it."

"Well. Aren't you a sneaky little urchin. You had no right to go through my stuff, Olivia. Do you ever think before you act?"

"Save me the lecture, please. I know what I did was wrong. I said I was sorry. But you have a lot of explaining to do. Did you write the wrong date on the back just to screw with me?"

"You keep trying to reopen old wounds that I have taken years to heal from. First, you throw your father's death in my face, and now this," she huffs. "Fine, since you brought it up, I'll tell you. I was pregnant before you. I was only seventeen at the time. He was stillborn. I was too young to be pregnant, but I didn't want my baby to die either. It was one of the hardest times in my life. That picture was private, and you had no right seeing it. Now, if you'll excuse me, I need to be alone." she says, a single tear running down her cheek. She stands up, drops her napkin on her plate, and walks back to her room, closing the door with a resounding thud.

Well, now I feel like crap. I had no idea.

I clean up the table as I let it sink in that my mom lost a child before me. That had to be difficult. I guess maybe I mean more to my mother than she lets on.

Morning comes, and my mother doesn't speak a word to me. She goes through the motions of getting ready for her day. I keep trying to apologize, but every apology that gets to the tip of my tongue is evaporated by my mother's icy glare. I'm not sure I'm going to get out of this one too easily. It looks like I have finally hit her last nerve. She leaves for work without a goodbye, and I'm left to figure out what to do with myself for the day.

I grab the phone book and search for the hospital number. I need to see how David is doing.

"St. Mary's hospital. How can I help you?"

"I would like to speak to David Beckett, please."

"I'm sorry. He's not ready to talk to anyone yet. Why don't you try again tomorrow afternoon? Let him rest up some more."

"'Kay. Thanks," I grumble.

I hang up the phone and sigh. Looks like it's homework for me again today. I continue plugging away at it in hopes that maybe I will actually catch up. I keep a close eye on the clock so I can surprise my mom with supper. I make spaghetti and meat sauce, and when she comes home, I stand at the dining room table with our places set, but she just puts her stuff away and heads to her bedroom.

I chance it and knock on her door.

"Mom, I made spaghetti for supper. Want some?"

"No, thanks," she answers. And those are the only words I hear her say for the rest of the night. I really screwed up bad.

By the next afternoon, I'm going stir crazy. I make myself wait until two and then call the hospital again. I get transferred to David's room.

"David!" I yell.

"Ouch, my ear! Hold on while I turn my hearing aid down."

It's quiet for a moment, and I'm almost worried that he hung up on me.

"Hey. How's it going?" he asks weakly.

"Oh man, David, I have missed you so much! I was going crazy waiting to talk to you. I got myself into tons of trouble while you were gone."

"Sounds about right," he says, chuckling a bit. "What did you do now?"

"I punched Victoria and broke her nose, and I got suspended. Then I got mad at my mom and searched through her stuff and found a picture in her dresser that was dated years before I was born, but my mom was pregnant. I asked her about it, and she got totally pissed! Now she won't talk to me! I can't wait for you to come home. Do you know how long you have to be in there?"

"Whoa, whoa, whoa! Back up. You *punched* Victoria? You need to start from the beginning and tell me the whole story."

I take a deep breath and start from the beginning. I try to make sure I tell him every little detail to bring him up to speed.

"Well, sounds like you were busy. You always seem to get yourself into trouble when I'm not there."

"When do you get to come home?"

"They need to run a few more tests, but I should get to come home tomorrow afternoon. I'm feeling miserable, though. They have me on a medicine right now that makes me throw up. Hoping they take me off this one soon."

"I'm sorry, David."

"No worries. Hey, my mom's in the bathroom right now, so I just wanted to apologize quick for ruining our plans. We would be out there right now if it weren't for my stupid sickness. I still want to run away with you once I'm outta here."

"I don't know, David. Are you sure we should even try this? I have no idea how I would take care of you if you had a seizure while we were out there. Maybe we need to reconsider."

"Yeah...maybe..." he says, deflated.

"Hey! Don't you get mad at me now too! I just care about you," I plead.

"I know," he says. "I should probably go. Talk to you later, Liv."

Great! Now he's mad at me too. I can't do anything right!

1 5

It's Friday, and I get to return to school today, but I would really rather not. I want David to be there, but he's not being released from the hospital until this afternoon, and he needs more rest. My mom gives me a ride to school but keeps her cold disposition the whole way, not uttering a single word to me. I try to say goodbye, but she just ignores me, staring straight ahead, and pulls away as soon as I close the door.

I walk to the school, keeping my head down, hoping nobody is staring at me. The fog isn't as thick today, so it's fairly easy to see. I quicken my pace and make it into the school without incident, but as I work on my locker combination, Victoria whispers, "You're dead," behind me. I turn to see her bandaged face glaring at me. Angry bruises leak out from under the bandages and surround the bottoms of her eyes.

"Leave me alone, Victoria," I say vehemently.

"Oh, I'll leave you alone...for now. Wouldn't want to get suspended again. You ruined my life, and I'm going to get you for it. You better watch your back."

I roll my eyes as she walks away. I can just punch her broken nose if she tries to mess with me again. Maybe I shouldn't feel too cocky, though. Next time she tries something, I'm sure she will have her entire entourage with her, and there's no way I will be able to fight a group of people.

My day is going surprisingly well. My classes go more smoothly now that I am almost caught up, and Mr. Schuller moved me away from Victoria in science class too. Now I'm in the front right corner, and she's in the back-left corner. We couldn't be further away. What a relief!

I'm not a people person, but I hang out in the busy cafeteria all lunch period to try to avoid being alone and giving Victoria a chance to attack me. If I'm around a bunch of witnesses, it's less likely that she will try to get me. I take the same approach when leaving school too. I ease myself into the middle of the flow of students leaving for the day. I spot my mom's car and jog over to her.

"How was your day?" I ask.

She shrugs her shoulders in response.

"You can't give me the silent treatment forever, Mom. You're going to have to start talking to me again sometime."

"It's better for us both if I just stay quiet. I have nothing more to say to you."

Yikes. She's still pissed.

I just stay quiet for the remainder of the car ride. Once home, I drop my backpack on the floor and race to the phone.

"Is it all right if I call David?"

"Sure." A fleeting look of compassion softens her demeanor. "Tell him I hope he gets well soon." And with that, she heads to her bedroom to ignore me once again.

"Hey, Liv," David answers after the first ring.

"How'd you know it was me?" I ask, surprised.

"I've been watching the clock all afternoon, waiting for you to call."

"How're you feeling?"

"Still not a hundred percent but better. How about you? Did you go back to school today?"

"Yeah. Nothing to report. Victoria gave me her daily death threat, but other than that, not much. You should see how hideous Miss Perfect looks!" I gush. "Bandages all over her nose and bruises under her eyes. It's fantastic!" We both start laughing hard.

"Ow! My head. Stop making me laugh!" he says, still chuckling.

"Sorry." I pause as I wipe a tear from my cheek. I take a deep breath to try to get serious again. "Look, David. About the not wanting to run away…"

"I understand, Liv. I'm not sure what I would do if the roles were reversed, but I still want to go. I can't live every day in fear of a seizure happening again. What kind of a life is that? I'm not sure how much longer you and I have left to live, to be honest. It's a miracle that either of us is still alive, considering how many times we're hospitalized. And that's why I want to go. Think of it as a major bucket list item. I need to know what's out there."

"You make a good point, but…"

"Don't answer me now. Just take some time to think about it. I know I'm asking a lot of you, to be willing to deal with any of my seizures, but please, just think about it," he pauses a moment. "Ugh! My head is really throbbing right now. I should probably go."

"I'll call you tomorrow."

Once I hang up, I fall over onto my pillow. I just don't know what to do.

At supper, I try to talk to my mom again, hoping I will be able to smooth things over a bit.

"Look, Mom. I'm sorry I snooped through your stuff. It was a bad mix of boredom, anger, and curiosity. I know I shouldn't have done it. Please, just talk to me."

"I don't know what you want me to say, Olivia. You invaded my privacy. How would you like it if I searched through your room?"

"I wouldn't care. I have nothing to hide," I say, but then my cheeks burn as I remember the bag I have stashed under my bed.

"Doesn't matter. I wouldn't do it anyway. I believe in a person having the right to keep some things private. You need to respect that and stay out of my stuff."

We go back to eating in silence. After supper, as I'm cleaning up the table, she drops a paper bag in front of me.

"Here's the extra inhalers you asked for," she says, and then walks off to her bedroom.

"Thanks!" I call out. I go straight to my backpack and stuff them in. She might be mad at me, but I take the extra inhalers I asked for as a sign that she still loves me.

Early Saturday morning, I wake up to my mom knocking on the door. "I have to go into work to get things prepared for a big meeting on Monday. You're on your own. Behave," she says as she leaves.

I lie back down and sleep for a couple more hours. I finally get myself out of bed and see that my mom put the TV back in the living room. I turn it to the Discovery channel to see if there are any old survival shows on that might give me tips on how to survive if David and I do decide to run away. They like to play reruns of old shows that used to be popular before the big war. It's interesting to see what the world was like before: people went into the woods whenever they wanted; they could stand out in the rain and not die; and man, what I wouldn't give to stand in that glorious sunlight that isn't diluted by the fog. I'm just glad that we still have TVs, phones, radios, and stuff like that. The world would be so boring if there weren't any electronics. What did people do before they were invented?

There's nothing good on TV, so I call David.

"Whatcha up to?" I ask as I eat a bowl of cereal.

"About five eleven."

"Har...har."

"Nothing really. My headache went away. I feel pretty good considering, but my mom is making me stay in bed. I'm so bored!"

"I have a pile of homework for you that your dad asked me to grab. Want me to bring that over?" I ask around my mouthful of cereal.

"You can't. Look outside."

I look over and see raindrops sliding down the glass.

"Shoot. I was supposed to drop it off for you earlier. Sorry."

"Not a problem. School won't matter soon. Once we are off on our adventure, homework will be a thing of the past."

"David, I'm torn. I want to go now more than ever since my fight with Victoria and my mom being so cold and distant, but you just got out of the hospital. Shouldn't we take it easy and wait?"

"Wait for what? The next seizure? The next illness? The next cracked skull? We hardly ever have much time between yours or my sicknesses. I say we go while we can still move."

I don't say anything as I think it over.

"Did you hear the news this morning?"

"No. You know I don't watch the news."

"You should," he scolds. "Anyway, our great and wonderful president has decided that 'for the good of the people' everyone is going to get microchips implanted in their arms."

"What? Why?"

"He claims it's a chip that will alert you when the rain is coming, so we can have fewer casualties. Apparently, the government will release a warning signal that will cause the chips to start glowing and grow warm in your arm. They want to put it inside people, so nobody has any chance of losing it, and everyone will have one. That way, there will be no excuse to end up in the rain."

"Hmm...I suppose that might be a good plan..."

"No, it's not, Olivia!"

"What? What's wrong with wanting fewer deaths?"

"They couldn't care less about people dying in the rain! All they care about is controlling people. And what better way to control people than to have every single person microchipped so they can keep track of everyone's whereabouts? They are just trying to come up with a sneaky way to do it so people like you—no offense—will think it's a great and wonderful plan that was set up to protect and save people. But the truth is they are trying to take away our privacy."

"You don't know that that's what they're doing," I say, trying to brush it off. "I think you like to come up with worst-case scenarios and try to make the Coalition look like they are always up to something."

"They are!"

"Whatever."

"Mark my words, Liv. The Coalition is full of bad people, and one day, we will all be brainwashed puppets doing their bidding. I, for one, will not let them put that chip in my arm, even if it means fighting to my death!"

And with that, he hangs up on me.

1' 6

David refuses to answer my calls now, and my mom still won't talk to me. Could I be any more of a screwup? On Sunday, I sulk around the apartment in my pajamas, eating peanut butter out of the jar with a spoon, and watching mind-numbing amounts of TV.

As I'm flipping through stations, I stop on a news report talking about the chip implants David was telling me about. President Turk is standing in front of the Coalition flag, which is a new take on the old United States flag with the original thirteen stripes, but instead of fifty stars, there's ten in a circle—signifying the ten cities that are left—surrounding an olive branch. Kind of lame, if you ask me.

President Turk is encouraging people to "not resist it," that "it is for the good of mankind." What a slimeball. Even his appearance seems greasy: long black hair slicked back, shifty brown eyes adorned with thick, bushy eyebrows, a long hawk nose, and a thin-lipped smile revealing teeth that are so abnormally straight and shiny, I wonder if they're real. I change the channel to old game shows and leave it on that the rest of the afternoon.

I throw a pizza in the oven just as my mom gets home. She walks in the door and gives me a look of disgust.

"What?"

Finally, my schlubby appearance breaks her silent treatment. "What have you been doing all day? You didn't even get dressed?"

"No. Why bother? You're still mad at me, and now David won't answer my calls."

"And why's that?"

Crap! I can't tell her the real reason, so I make something up quick. "Oh, he um...didn't agree with me on which Lord of the Rings movie was better, and I told him he was an idiot, so he hung up on me and won't take my phone calls." Wow, that was a stupid excuse! I hope she buys it.

"Huh. Well, that's not a good way to treat your friend. Doesn't surprise me, though," she finishes with a mumble and walks off to the kitchen to get plates for supper. I flip her the middle finger when her back is turned.

We eat supper in silence, and my mom returns to her room. I don't understand why she is still punishing me over finding a dumb picture.

You know what? I'm done. I'm sick of this! I'm sick of my mom treating me this way. I'm sick of getting death threats from Victoria, not to mention the ones from Cindy too. I'm leaving as soon as she goes to bed. I just hope David isn't so mad at me that he won't carry out our plan.

I wait until her bedroom light goes off around midnight. Taking one last look at the apartment, I secure my backpack on my shoulders and close the door, locking it behind me. The streets are empty as I make my way to David's house. The president has made it clear that it would be best for people to stay inside when it's dark, and like good little sheep, people listen. I sneak around behind David's house and peek through his window. He's lying on his bed, reading a book. I tap on the glass to get his attention, and he starts when he sees me looking at him. I drop my black hood and give him a smile.

"What do you want?" he asks after opening his window.

I lift my backpack up in response. His eyes widen, and a big grin spreads across his face.

"Unless you've changed your mind?" I say playfully.

"No! Nope. Not at all." He walks over to his closet and wrestles a large black bag out. He then pulls an envelope out of the side pocket and carefully places it on his pillow. It reads, "To: Mom and Dad."

Once he has his shoes, a couple of extra layers of shirts, and a coat on, he climbs out of the window and pulls the pane down to hide that we left this way. Excitement is coursing through my body. I feel like I could run all the way there. But we don't run. We walk, carefully staying within the shadows, keeping our heads down. It's going to take a few hours to get to the edge of the city this way, but I don't care. I can already feel a sense of freedom that I have never felt before.

We keep our talking to a minimum so we don't expose our whereabouts. We see a couple of people on the other side of the road, drunk and stumbling their way home. After about an hour, we leave the downtown area, and there are no more streetlights. We can walk freely now, no longer needing to hide in the shadows. The full moon lights up the fog and gives us just enough visibility to not run into anything directly in front of us, but that's about it. David tries to hold my hand, but I give a light squeeze and drop it, sticking my hands in my pockets, pretending I'm cold. I don't know if he thinks I'm suddenly going to start liking him that way since I was willing to run away with him, but I'm not. Ever.

I take to following behind David after I start zoning out and walk into a car parked on the street. Thank God, the alarm doesn't start going off, or we would be done for.

It is eerily quiet out here, which makes me even more nervous. I feel like my footsteps—hell, even my *breathing* is too loud, and someone is going to catch us, but we don't see anyone. After hours of walking, I'm afraid that we are going in circles and will never find our way to the fence. My feet are killing me, and I've needed to take my inhaler every fifteen minutes or so. At this rate, I will be out of inhalers before we even make it to the woods.

Suddenly, David stops short, and I almost walk into him.

"We're here." He slings his backpack to the ground.

I look around him and see the chain link fence looming ahead. I listen intently for guards or anyone who might catch us, but all I hear is David searching his pack for the bolt cutters he brought.

I stand back and keep a lookout while David starts cutting the fence close to the ground. I can't believe we are actually doing this! I cringe with each loud snap of the tool cutting through the wire. I keep glancing over my shoulder to see if anyone is coming, but all I see is poorly lit fog.

"Shh!" I shush nervously. "We're gonna get caught."

"Done," David whispers, pushing the fence to widen the hole. "Ready?"

I nod my head in response.

"I'll go first." He pushes his large bag through the hole. He lies down on his belly and wriggles back and forth until he gets through. He stands up and brushes the dirt off.

"Push your bag through, and then I'll help pull you out."

I shove my bag under the fence and lie down in the dirt.

"Wait! Did you hear that?" David asks.

I freeze. Then I hear it. Footsteps.

"Quick! Pull me through!" I whisper, panicking. I lie down on my stomach and start kicking and wiggling until I'm halfway through, but my pants get caught on the bottom wires of the hole.

"Stop!" someone shouts. I chance a look behind me and see a guard holding a large black gun pointed toward me. I start kicking my legs faster and reach my hands out for David to grab. He takes hold of my wrists and pulls, but at the same time, the guard drops his gun and jumps on my legs, wrapping his arms around them tightly. I feel as though I am going to rip in two.

"Get off me! Let go!" I scream, thrashing around as hard as I can, trying to shake him off. But instead of the guard letting go, David lets go of my hands. I scream as the guard starts pulling me back under the fence. "David!" I grab onto the fence as the guard pulls me out of the hole and back into the city side.

"Let her go!" David yells, and to my surprise, the guard lets go of my legs. I have only seconds to understand what's happening. I look at David, and he has his gun out, pointing through the fence. I look back at the guard.

"Cute gun, kid," he sneers, and I see his eyes go toward his rifle lying on the ground about four feet away. "Do you even know how to use that thing?"

A strange instinct kicks in, and I lunge for the gun, getting to it before the guard does. I pick it up and smash the butt of the gun into the guard's face. He stumbles backward, and I hear a shot ring out. The guard slumps to the ground, holding his hand over the blood gushing out of his chest, right under the Coalition flag patch—a symbol of peace.

"David! What did you do?"

"I didn't mean to!" David says frantically, a pained look on his face as he messes with his ear. "C'mon, Olivia! Hurry up, and get over here before another guard comes to investigate the noise!"

"Shouldn't we help him? David, you just shot him! He's dying!"

"Look, we can talk about this later. Get over here!"

I stand between the guard and David, looking back and forth at them. We are in so much trouble! I finally make my decision and scramble to crawl under the fence as fast as I can to get away from what we just did. What David just did. Just as I pick up my bag and secure it on my back, I hear footsteps running toward the fallen guard. At least, he will be getting help. I turn around and start running behind David, taking cover in the strange, unknown woods. What a great start we're off to.

17

"Just keep running!" David shouts back to me, pointing his flashlight in my direction. The moon no longer lights our way once we're in the woods. Everything is dark. It's risky using a flashlight, but we need to move quickly.

"I can't!" I wheeze, taking another dose of my inhaler.

He walks back to me, grabs my wrist, slings my arm around his neck, and wraps his arm around my waist. Half-dragging me, we continue on. We've been running from the fence for a solid forty-five minutes now, stopping frequently for inhalers. My legs are about to give out, and the stitch in my side feels like I have a knife lodged in my ribcage. I have never run so far in my life. But we have to keep going. If that guard survives, we're done for. He saw our faces, and it's only a matter of time before they start searching for us.

I keep moving my feet, taking step after step, disconnecting my mind from my repetitious movements. I find that I can keep going as long as David continues to help me, but finally, David has had enough, and we have to stop. We fall to the ground, panting. I blindly dig inside my bag until I find a water bottle, and we both take turns emptying its contents. We lie on the ground, quietly catching our breath.

I finally break the silence. "David, why did you shoot that guard in the chest? He's probably dead now."

"I wasn't aiming for his chest. I was aiming for his leg. I told you, I've never shot a gun before," he says, sniffing.

"We're in so much trouble..." I fret.

"Look, it's pitch-black, and we're out in the middle of the woods. We've put a lot of distance between us and the city. We'll be fine. That guard will be fine," David adds with a quiver in his voice. "We need to keep going for a little while longer. The sun will be coming up soon."

We stand up, strap our backpacks back on, and continue trudging along. I follow behind David. He keeps his flashlight shining down at the ground. I keep close watch of where he steps, hoping I don't trip. If I fall down, I'm not sure I will be able to stand back up. Weariness starts to take over, so I mentally go over what I packed for survival to keep my mind occupied. I stop short.

"Shoot! David, please tell me you packed vitamins..."

He drops his bag on the ground and starts digging through it.

"No. I didn't," he says with worry in his voice.

"What are we going to do? I knew this was a bad idea, and now we're going to die out here. We need those vitamins, David!"

"I'm sorry, Liv..."

"We need to go back!"

"Are you serious? We can't go back there. Especially now!"

"David, we are in the middle of the woods that we've been told will kill us, running for our lives because you killed a guard, and now we don't have the vitamins that helped keep us alive when we were home. We're doomed!" My chest tightens as a panic attack rears its ugly head. I can't deal with one of those right now! I take slow deep breaths, trying hard to control it.

"For one, we've been in the woods for a couple of hours now, and we haven't seen or heard a thing, other than one squirrel we startled. Two: that guard might not have died, like I already said. We don't know what happened to him. And three: the vitamin thing is bad luck, but we can't go back to get them. That would be stupid. We'll just have to take it easy and try to survive without them."

I close my eyes for a moment and try to calm down. He's right of course. We can't go back for them.

"Fine." I take one last inhaler dose, and we move on. David scans the area with his flashlight, looking for somewhere safe we can hide in for sleeping. We are both shuffling our feet, barely able to lift them off the ground.

"Look over there!" David shines his light on a pile of rocks.

I step closer and can see a hole in the pile.

"I don't know, David. What if something is living in there? We're going to get eaten."

"Stay here, and I'll check it out." David drops his bag next to my feet. He gets down on his hands and knees and shines his flashlight into the opening. He slowly crawls through the hole, and I lose sight of him and the light. I suddenly feel exposed without his presence. I look around me, trying to keep an eye out, but it's too dark. The silence is heavy in my ears, and I jump about a foot when David calls out my name.

"Olivia! Grab the bags, and come over here. This is a perfect spot," he says excitedly from the mouth of the cave.

I hand the bags to David, and he helps me crawl through a short tunnel that leads to a cave big enough for the two of us to fit in comfortably: tall enough to sit up in and long enough to lie down. We unpack our blankets and start making our beds. I lie in the back of the cave, and David takes the spot closest to the entrance. I am so exhausted, but I lie awake worrying about what kind of creatures are going to crawl on me while I sleep. Maybe this wasn't such a great plan. What were we thinking? I'm already missing my warm bed and indoor plumbing. I sure hope David has a plan or, at least, an idea of what he's looking for.

The mustiness of the cave makes me take a couple extra doses of my inhaler, and David's smell doesn't help. His presence is comforting, but I really wish he would wear deodorant a little more often. After such a long journey, he reeks of BO. Hopefully, he has some packed.

"David?" I whisper. I sigh when he doesn't answer me.

"David," I say louder.

He snores in response.

Great. Guess I'm just going to have to suffer through. I roll onto my side, away from him and bring the blanket to my nose. I breathe in deep and smile. It smells like the cedar chest at home.

"Goodnight, Mom. I hope you enjoy your life without me," I whisper out loud. Before I know it, I fall asleep.

1|8

I wake up to the sound of birds singing. More birds than I ever heard in the city. We get the occasional pigeon looking for food, but they don't sing like this. I sit up and reach for my glasses.

"David! Wake up!" I shout.

He wakes up with a jolt, fists up and ready to face whatever threat there is that made me shout.

"What! What is it?"

"I can't see! My eyes are blurry!" I say in a panic, moving my glasses around, trying to see if adjusting them will help.

"Take them off, and see if they're dirty," he says. He lies back down now that he knows there is no danger.

I take them off to clean with my shirt. I glance my eyes toward David and realize that I can see parts of his face. It's still blurry, but I can actually see his nose and lips. I look out the mouth of the cave and can see tree trunks and rocks.

I shove my glasses on my face ,and the world becomes a blur again. I turn toward David, and I can no longer see the distinct shapes of his face. I slide my glasses down my nose, and his face comes into focus better.

"What the hell is going on?" I ask out loud. I take a deep breath in to try to center myself, and my lungs fill with air without any pain. In fact, I take a breath deeper than any I have ever taken, and it feels *good*. I have gotten used to taking shallow breaths so I don't hurt my airways, never allowing my lungs to fill completely like this.

"David!" I shake his shoulder. "Wake up!"

David grunts and rubs his eyes. "What now?"

"I can breathe!"

"Good for you."

I slap his arm. "Seriously, I can take a deep breath, and my lungs feel great. Try it."

David sits up and inhales deeply. "Holy cow! Mine too." He takes another deep breath and smiles.

"I don't know what I'm going to do about my glasses, though. I can see better without them, but even then, I can't see great. How am I going to make it out there?"

"We'll take it slow."

We eat a quick breakfast of dried fruit and a little jerky. I ask David to leave the cave so I can change out of my dirty clothes. Once he's outside, I hear him call for me.

"What?" I huff, wanting to freshen up.

"Come out here!"

66

I crawl out of the cave and gasp. Although my vision is still blurry, I can see trees. The fog is gone. I look around and see sunlight, pure, bright sunlight streaming through the woods. Lush green leaves are everywhere. All the trees look so healthy and alive. Tears spring to my eyes. This is big. Why would the government be trying to keep us in the city when this gloriousness is out here?

"It's beautiful," I say.

"Where's the fog? See! I told you something amazing was out here!" David says gleefully.

I join him in gazing at the surroundings, but my smile slowly fades.

"Wait a minute, David. We don't have the cover of fog to protect us anymore. If they come looking for us, they are going to be able to find us better now!"

"You're right. Quick, go change and get your stuff packed up. We need to keep moving."

Once we both have all our belongings, we continue our journey further into the woods. I walk behind David and keep my eyes on his feet, glancing up now and again to take in the bright sunlight shining through the leaves. I have never seen pure sunlight before.

"David, can we go over there?"

"Where?"

"See where there is a big spotlight of sun? I want to see what it feels like."

We walk to our right a little and step out of the shade and into the sunlight. I close my eyes and turn my face toward the sky. The warmth of the sun is like a hug for my whole body. I instantly become relaxed and want to lie right down and take a nap in it.

"This is amazing. I have never felt something so beautiful before," David says.

We both stand there for a minute or two, soaking up the sun. I open my eyes to gaze up at it and see its glory. Ow! I cast my eyes to the ground and blink a few times to try to get the bright spot out of my vision. Note to self: don't look directly at the sun.

"Wow, the sun is warm! I'm starting to sweat," David comments.

"Isn't it great?"

"Yes, but we really do need to keep moving, Liv."

I take a deep breath, stretching out my arms as though to embrace everything around me, and let it out with a big sigh.

We continue on our way. With all of this fresh air, I begin to feel clearer-headed and positive. Maybe we are going to be okay. Maybe this is what I needed after all. I continue following behind David, and we walk for a few more hours. The sunshine has done its job of heating up the day, and we are both stripped of all extra clothing by the time we stop for lunch. My t-shirt is drenched with sweat from my backpack holding the heat against my back.

I drop my pack on the ground and rummage through it to find something to eat. I grab a granola bar and pick a spot in the sun to sit.

"How're you doing, Liv? Do we need to find somewhere to camp soon?"

"I'm doing surprisingly well, actually. I have never felt better," I say with a smile.

"Shh! Keep your voice down. You don't need to yell." He looks around.

"I wasn't yelling, David," I snap.

"Okay, maybe not yelling, but you need to be quieter."

"And maybe you need to turn your hearing aid down a little bit," I say.

He takes his hearing aid out of his ear, looking closely at the volume setting.

"It's turned down as low as it will go. I've never had it turned down all the way before. Maybe it's malfunctioning out here."

I shrug my shoulders in response.

We eat in silence for a little while, and I try to strike up a conversation while I'm in such a good mood.

"David, are you scared at all? Being out here in the woods?"

"Well, sure. I have no idea what we are going to find, but I feel good about things. The fog being gone, getting some real sunlight, and fresh air... I think we made the right choice."

"I would feel better about it if my eyesight wasn't freaking out. Everything is still blurry."

David nods his head and continues eating. We share a bottle of water and rest just a bit more before we strap our packs back on and continue.

We walk until the sky turns brilliant shades of orange and pink. I can catch glimpses of the beautiful hues between tree branches, but after I stumble for the third time, I tear my eyes from the sky and keep my focus on David's back. Even though the sky still looks bright, it's dark in the woods, and I have a hard time seeing my surroundings. Everything feels a bit more sinister when you can't see well. I start at every noise and decide I've had enough.

"David, I'm ready to stop for today."

"Me too. I don't see a cave around here this time, but I did bring a tarp and some ropes. I'll set up a shelter for us."

By the time he's done, the sun is gone, and the nightly sound of crickets fills our ears. We eat a small supper, and I fall asleep almost instantly.

I wake up to the sweet sounds of birds again and smile. Stretching out my sore muscles, I sit up and look around, hoping my eyes aren't any worse. To my surprise, they are slightly improved from yesterday. They're still blurry, but I'll take what I can get.

After breakfast, we clean up and continue on our way. I let David lead once again since my eyesight is still poor. As we walk, I watch the sunlight dance through the trees, which are swaying gently in the wind. The cool breeze feels like a soft kiss on the cheek. Suddenly, David holds his arm out to stop me.

"What's up?" I ask.

"I just found a print in the mud," David whispers, staring down at the ground.

"Could it be ours? Are we retracing our steps?"

David kneels on the ground to get a closer look. I would join him, but I wouldn't be able to see it clearly anyway.

"No. These are definitely different. We have on sneakers, and this looks like a boot print." David stands up to look around the forest.

"Crap! How could they have found us already?" I whisper loudly.

We keep trudging along. I glance over my shoulder every thirty seconds to see if someone is following us. David does the same. My feelings of peace have been replaced with paranoia. There's no way they could have found us already.

We keep walking and pass between two boulders covered with a thick layer of moss. I reach my hand out to feel it and smile at the softness of it under my fingers. As we step past the boulders, I look around, and a sense of déjà vu hits me. Since I can't see that well, I'm not really sure why, but I feel like I've been here before.

"David, have we walked this area already?" I whisper.

"No, why?"

"I feel like I've been here before. It seems so familiar."

My instinct tells me to stop moving. I grab David's backpack to stop him.

"Don't move," I whisper with a shaky voice. A chill crawls up my spine.

"What?" David whispers back.

"Tell me, is there a dark figure ahead of us? I can't see," I ask, hoping hard that he says no.

"Holy crap, there is!" David whispers. "What is that?"

My heart starts racing. This is the woods from my dream in the hospital.

"Back up slowly, and try not to step on any branches," I answer.

I grab David's arm as we back up carefully, watching the direction of the beast. Just as we get to the boulder, I step on a stick.

"It's looking at us!" David yells. "*Run!*"

I can see a large black figure start barreling our direction before we turn to run behind the boulders. Before I know it, someone grabs our wrists and pulls us out of the way. A man on the boulder shoots an arrow at the beast. It whines, and he shoots another arrow. There's a crash as the beast falls to the ground. I turn to look at who grabbed us and pulled us to safety, and they are the same startling blue eyes as the guy I saw in my dream.

The other man jumps off the boulder to see if the creature is dead. After a minute or two, he comes back over by us. He pulls a length of rope out of his coat.

"Thank you so much for saving us. You know, it's funny: this happened before in a dream, and I am curious to know who you are..." I say excitedly, and at that moment, the hunter and his young friend who had saved us grab our arms and forcefully push us belly first against the giant boulders.

"Hey! What do you think you're doing?" David yells.

The Rare

The men get to work binding us with their ropes until we can't move our arms. Then, with strips of cloth, they gag and blindfold us. This is not at all how it went in my dream!

The men proceed to pull us along in a tight grip for what feels like hours. They don't talk, not even to each other. What are they going to do to us? Do they work for the Coalition? Do they know who we are and what we've done? I start to cry. This isn't how things were supposed to go.

Even though we walk at a fast clip, my lungs still feel good. At least, I can be thankful for that. Our pace starts to slow down, and my nose fills with the scent of smoke. I hear some chattering coming closer. The man lets go of my arm and pushes me down until I'm sitting. He unties one of my wrists momentarily, slips my backpack off, and then ties my hands around a post. I don't struggle. Although he is firm with me, he never actually hurts me. I can hear them tying David to a post next to me. We both stay quiet.

Since I can't see anything, I try as hard as I can to listen to my surroundings to see if I can figure out where we are. All I hear are our captors' feet walking over stones and leaves as they move away from us, the crackling of the fire that is far enough away that I can't feel its warmth, the breeze blowing through the trees, and birds singing. Nothing significant. And then I hear a quiet conversation begin, and I will myself to breathe shallowly so I can hear every word.

"Where did you find them?" a woman asks.

"'Bout four miles from here. We tracked a Havoc and killed it, but we had to save their sorry asses."

"Are they dangerous?"

"Look at 'em. Do they look dangerous?"

"You never know. They could be spies."

"That's what I'm gonna find out. Fetch me some water, will ya?"

I hear footsteps making their way back toward us. He takes the gag out of my mouth but leaves the blindfold on. I take a moment to try to get saliva back in my uncomfortably dry mouth.

"Who are ya?" the man asks with a gruff voice.

"Olivia. Can you please take the blindfold off too?" I ask innocently.

"Who do ya work for?" he asks, ignoring my request.

"Nobody."

"Likely story. I'm not gonna ask again. You'll answer my questions, or you can forget about the drink of water I have for you."

My mouth is so dry that my tongue feels like sandpaper. I would kill for a drink of water right now.

"I don't work for anybody. I'm a junior in high school."

"Lies!" he bellows.

"Why would I lie?" I ask, trying hard to keep my tone mellow.

"You want me to believe that two scrawny teenagers are trompin' around in the woods on their own? Do ya think I'm stupid?"

"It's true! I-I swear! David and I ran away to the woods because we wanted to see what was out here...what the Coalition was hiding that they didn't want people to see," I finish, biting my lips together. I shouldn't be revealing so much. What if *they* work for the Coalition?

"I see. So, you and your friend here are suspicious of the government, eh? Why?"

I stay quiet, trying to decide how much to give away.

"Speak!" he yells again, kicking the bottom of my shoe.

"W-well, how do I know you guys don't work for the Coalition?" I ask as boldly as I dare.

Laughter fills the camp. After it finally quiets down, he continues. "You don't need to worry about who we are right now, but I can tell ya, we don't associate with the Coalition. Now, answer my question. Why are *you*, a couple of clueless teenagers, suspicious of the Coalition?"

"Well, we were noticing strange things here and there. Like, why are the trees so green in the woods outside of the fence when all the trees inside of the city are sickly yellow? Why are we not allowed to leave the city if we want to? Are the guards stationed at the fence to keep us safe or to keep us inside the city?"

I can hear a low-level buzz of people murmuring about us. It's starting to annoy me. I wish he would take this blindfold off so I could see them.

"What were ya hopin' to accomplish out here? Ya plannin' on runnin' back home when things got tough? Runnin' back to your mommies and hope that nobody noticed ya ran away in the first place?"

"What difference does it make to you?" I ask, trying to keep my attitude in check.

"Makes a big damn difference that you two idiots probably have people lookin' for ya! Within a day or two, we're gonna have Turk's puppet soldiers out here searchin', and we can't let 'em find us."

Suddenly, someone shouts, "Take 'em back out where you found 'em, tie 'em up, and leave 'em for dead! You never shoulda brought 'em here!"

"I brought 'em here to question 'em. What we do with 'em once I'm done, isn't clear yet!" he yells.

My heart is racing. What did we get ourselves into?

I start to speak, my voice trembling, "Look. I don't know what you want us to say that will make you believe we aren't here trying to cause trouble. We don't want to get caught either. If you just let us go, we'll continue on, and you won't have to worry about us anymore."

"I'm not done with you yet," the man says.

I hear his boots crunch on the gravel toward David.

"Well, boy. You got anythin' to add? What're ya two doin' out here that's so important you had to leave the city?"

"Why should I talk? You're not going to believe me anyway."

Suddenly, I hear a hard slap and a groan from David.

"Stop it! What are you doing to him?" I scream, frantically wriggling around to try to break my bonds.

"Henry! Stand down!"

"What? I'm tired of them giving you lip, Pop. Maybe they'll talk if we slap them around a little," I hear a different male voice say.

"I'm the leader here! Go back by the rest of 'em, and let me handle this."

I hear a huff and then footsteps walking away.

"Look now, boy. You need to answer my question quickly, or we're gonna have a problem. Hear me?"

When David doesn't respond, I hope with all my might that he shook his head yes. This is no time to be difficult.

"Did anyone see you leave the city?"

A feeling of dread washes over me as I remember what happened at the fence.

"Sort of," David responds, heavily.

"Sort of? What do you mean, 'sort of'?"

"We shot a guard. And that should answer your question as to whether we work for the Coalition or not."

I hear some low murmurings and a long whistle come from the crowd.

"Well, well. That would change my mind if I thought it were true."

"It is true!" I shout before I can stop myself.

"This is a story we would all love to hear." He chuckles a bit. "Go on. Let's hear this heroic tale of yours."

David doesn't speak right away, so I begin to tell it. "Well, we made it to the fence, and David cut a hole with his dad's bolt cutters. I tried to get under the fence, but my pants got stuck, and a guard found us. He jumped on my legs and started pulling me back. That's when David pulled out his gun, and the guard let go of me. I grabbed the guard's rifle he dropped and smashed his nose with the butt of the gun, and David shot him. I scrambled back under the fence, and we heard someone running toward the fallen guard as we ran into the woods."

Silence. I wish I could see whether he believed me or not.

"Henry!" the man shouts, causing me to jump. "Check their bags for a gun. If we find one, maybe we'll believe this cock and bull story."

I hear the zipper of our bags open and then all the contents get dumped onto the ground.

"It's tucked in a sock," David finally adds. I hear more shuffling of stuff.

"Yup. Yup, here it is, Pop!" Henry shouts.

"Well, well. Looks like maybe you're tellin' the truth about that little pea shooter there. Where'd you get the gun, kid?"

"From my Grandpa before he died."

"That so?"

"Yeah. He didn't trust the Coalition either and hid the gun under a floorboard when they came to search his house. He passed it on to me, and I've kept it secret ever since."

"Okay, say I do believe this story. Ya think you're a tough guy now because ya shot a man? Show your strength, kid. Henry!" he yells out, his voice turning back to the crowd. "Untie him. Let's see what he's got."

Are they expecting him to fight? David doesn't know how to fight. This is bad. This is very bad.

20

I hear him untie David next to me. "You can watch," he says, taking my blindfold off.

I don't want to watch David get his butt kicked. The sudden brightness of the sun blinds me momentarily. After my eyes adjust, I realize that my vision has improved even more. Now I can see things far away, but everything up close is still a tad blurry. What is happening to me?

I watch worriedly as David stands up, rubs his sore wrists, and follows Henry with shuffling steps into an open area. If they are planning on fighting, David is going to lose. Maybe they're trying to embarrass him for fun.

I take a glance at the people standing off to the side. It's an odd conglomeration of people. There is a small group of young children. Their faces are dirty, and their clothes are worn and ratty, but they are smiling away as they scribble in the dirt with each other. Their mothers stand guard next to them, all wearing a look of maternal defiance, daring us to try to harm their little ones. A group of about fifteen men and women sit by the fire, watching us closely. There is an elderly man, sitting on a stump whittling a stick as though nothing strange is happening whatsoever. A tall, scrawny teenaged boy and a beautiful pre-teen girl with wild, bushy hair stand in front of one of the crude shelters, watching David and Henry with wide eyes, not wanting to miss a thing. Standing next to the leader is an attractive middle-aged woman; her skin is darker than any I have ever seen in my life, and she is staring daggers at me. I avert my gaze, feeling extremely uncomfortable with her scrutiny of me.

David stands in the middle of the clearing, keeping his eyes on Henry, who's walking circles around David, sizing him up. After a moment, he stands in front of David and brings his hands up into a fighting stance. David looks scared like he would much rather turn tail and run, but he brings his hands up to match Henry's. Quick as lightning, Henry pushes David's hand down with his left hand, and in one fluid motion, his right is backhand punching him across his face. David drops to the ground with a thump. After a few seconds, he slowly stands up, moving his jaw back and forth. The odd thing is, Henry doesn't goad him. Nobody does. As a matter of fact, the group of people stays oddly silent, watching with reverence and curiosity.

David puts his hands back up in the fighting stance. His jaw is red from the hit. He never takes his eyes off Henry. They stand still for a few seconds before Henry throws a punch just as quick as the last one and hits David in the stomach. David doubles over with a groan. Henry stands back with a slight smirk on his face but waits until David stands up again and faces off. Henry sends his fist flying toward David's nose, but this time, David brings his arm up and blocks it, quickly followed by his other fist, which lands a solid punch to Henry's ribs. The crowd gasps. Henry clutches his side for a moment but shakes it off.

I look at the leader of the group, and he doesn't react. He watches closely, as though studying David's every move.

Henry's face hardens with determination as they face off again. David looks more confident now that he got a hit in. Where did David learn to do that?

Henry sweeps his leg toward David's heels and knocks David onto his back. But David rolls to the side and sweeps Henry's feet out, dropping him to the ground just as fast. They are both on their feet once more, staring each other down. Suddenly, as though a bell sounded that the true fight begins now, their fists start flying in every direction, but none of them hit their target as both boys are blocking and dodging perfectly. It almost looks as though they choreographed this. Sweat starts pouring down David's face as he blocks every punch thrown at him and continues to throw his own at Henry. My jaw drops as I watch David fight as though he's been training for years.

"Enough!" bellows the leader.

Henry immediately stops fighting, and David takes the hint. They both double over, hands on knees, as they struggle to catch their breath after the exertion. David's shirt is soaked with sweat, making it cling to his scrawny frame.

"Not bad," the leader says, as he walks around the two boys. "But it's still inconclusive. For now, you and the girl can sit by the fire while my people and I have a discussion on what to do with you," he says and then turns around. "Cassandra. Timothy. Get these two a jug of water and some food. I'd like you to keep an eye on 'em while the adults talk."

Immediately, the teenaged boy and the bushy-haired girl set off to fetch the stuff the leader said to bring. The adults head to their meeting, and the small children follow their mothers, playing a game of tag as they go. "Come on, Grandpa," I hear Henry say as he helps the old man up off the stump. He leads him to the large shelter made from small logs tied together with ropes and large tarps on the roof to keep out rain.

David walks over to me and unties my hands. He helps me off the ground, but suddenly he starts to sway back and forth looking like he's about to pass out.

"You okay?" I ask, worried.

"Yeah. I'm fine. Just tired and thirsty."

"That was amazing. What you did with Henry. How did you learn to fight like that?"

"I didn't. I have no idea what just happened. It was as though a fog started lifting out of my head; my hands were doing their own thing, and I was just along for the ride."

Cassandra and Timothy come jogging back with a basket of fruits and vegetables and a big plastic jug of water. We have a seat on stumps next to the fire, and they put the food between David and me. I grab an apple and wait my turn for the water, letting David have it first.

"That was pretty cool," Timothy says. "I've never seen anyone match Henry like that. He's the best fighter we got."

"Thanks, Timothy? That's your name, right?" David says.

"You can call me Tim. And this is Cass, my sister." He points to the bushy haired girl. "Only Matthias calls us by our full names."

Cass gives him a stern look and says quietly, "Don't tell them so much! We don't know if the adults are going to decide to let them stay or not."

We sit quietly as David and I eat our fill. I have about a million questions rolling around in my head. It has been at least twenty minutes since the adults left to go talk. Cass and Tim keep staring at us with curiosity as though we're aliens from another planet.

"What?" I finally blurt out, annoyed with the relentless staring.

"Nothing," Tim says, sitting up straight. "Well, it's just...I'm just so excited to meet a Rare."

"A 'Rare'? What's that?" I ask.

"Don't, Tim. You need to wait," Cass warns. I roll my eyes at Cass and stare off at the shelter, waiting for the adults to come back.

Tim leans down and picks a rock up off the ground as I'm finishing the last bite of my apple. Before I know it, my hand is in front of my face, stinging from catching the rock before it hit me in the eye.

"Did you see that?" Tim laughs, nudging Cass with his elbow.

"Wait... Why did you... How did I..." I start to ask, bewildered.

"You're a Rare," Tim says with a huge grin. "I could tell that you were different as soon as you came into camp."

"Cut the crap! How did you know that Olivia was going to catch the rock? And why would you throw it at her face?" David asks angrily. He glances at my hand and gives the red welt a gentle rub.

"Timothy. Cassandra. Don't bother answering 'em. They're leavin'," the leader, Matthias says. We were so distracted, we didn't see that the adults had come out of the shelter.

"Leaving? Wait! We want some answers too!" I say, finding myself not wanting to leave so quickly. I want to know what Tim was talking about.

The lady who was staring daggers at me earlier grips my arm tightly with one hand while holding a knife with the other. She stands me up, directing me out of their camp. "Didn't you hear him? He said you're leaving. Keep your mouth shut and go!"

"We said we came to the woods for answers! We think you could help us!" David pleads, struggling against Henry's death grip.

I stop moving my legs and lock them into place so the lady has to drag me toward the woods. David tries to wrench his arm out of Henry's grip, but his grip is too strong, and David is weak from the earlier fight.

I start to panic. I don't know who these people are, but I think they could help us. They at least have shelter and food and can defend themselves from beasts and other dangers that might be lurking in the woods.

Once they've walked us past the posts they tied us up to when we first got here, they give us a good shove, and I fall in the dirt. Henry and the cranky lady turn around and start heading back to the camp. Rage builds up inside of me, and I start yelling the first threat that comes to my mind.

"Just you wait! The soldiers will eventually find us and take us back to the city, and when they do, I'll tell my mother, Janice Sloane, a *Coalition* employee, that you're out here and where to find you! They'll come arrest you all!"

David helps me up off the ground. We start brushing ourselves off as Matthias comes marching over to us.

"What'd ya say?" Matthias asks, pointing the tip of his knife at my chest.

"I said that if you kick us out, the soldiers will find us, and I'll tell my mom, who works for the government, where you are," I say, immediately regretting it.

Matthias glares at me for a moment, and I'm worried he's going to kill me on the spot.

"Alexandrine! I'm overruling this decision. They stay!" he shouts, lowering the knife.

The dark-skinned lady gives Matthias a look of death, growls, and turns around to head back into camp.

"Timothy. Go grab our guests' supplies. They will bunk up with you and your sister for now," Matthias orders as he turns around and marches away.

"Yes, sir!" Tim says, grinning widely.

"What was that? Why did he suddenly change his mind? You don't think he's going to torture us and kill us now, do you?" I whisper hysterically to David.

David shrugs his shoulders.

"Come on, you two," Cass says. She leads us toward the shelter she shares with her brother.

I keep my head down and look carefully at the people in the camp. The old man—I overheard someone call him Saul—is back on his stump, whittling again. The little children are playing a game of hide-and-seek. The mothers are watching the kids closely and talking quietly among themselves, taking glances at David and me. The men and women are back around the fire, talking intently. Alexandrine and Matthias are standing outside the meeting shelter, having a heated argument. I slow my pace and listen to what they're saying.

"It was agreed that they were to leave our camp! You have no right going against what the group decides!"

"I've every right! Don't forget why we're out here. The only reason any of ya are still alive is because I brought ya here and have kept ya alive!"

"Oh, yes! Heroic Matthias. Our savior. Whoever would have thought that kidnapping would be such a..."

"Yo, Olivia! In here," Cass calls to me, drowning out what Alexandrine was saying. "You coming or what?"

I reluctantly turn and follow Cass's voice. What was she saying about kidnapping? I suddenly have a sick feeling in my stomach.

21

I walk into the shelter and see two piles of leaves and pine needles on the floor with blankets laid on top. Well-worn clothes and threadbare blankets are draped over a line of rope tied down the middle of the room, creating a makeshift wall between the rustic beds. Light streams in through gaps between the logs where they didn't quite match up right.

"I know it's not much to look at," Cass says sheepishly, "but it's all we got."

"No. It's fine." I give her a weak smile.

"You can have a seat anywhere you like," Tim offers, smiling. "Cass and I will go out and start gathering some leaves and stuff for your beds."

"Thanks, Tim," David says.

As soon as Tim and Cass leave the shelter, I start telling David what I just heard.

"David, I don't think we want to stay here. I just hear Alexandrine and Matthias talking, and she said something about 'kidnappings.'"

"Kidnappings?" David says, furrowing his eyebrows.

"What is this place? Who are these people?" I feel the familiar signs of a panic attack starting. I drop to the floor and bring my knees to my chest, rocking back and forth.

"Calm down, Liv. We're going to get some answers. This is why we came out to the woods. For answers. We can always sneak out of here if this place doesn't seem safe."

He sits next to me and puts his arm around my shoulder. He gives me a reassuring squeeze, and for the first time since becoming friends, I welcome his touch.

"Hey, you two," Tim announces his return. His arms are full of dried leaves. "I'm going to put your bed here, David, on my side of the shelter. We'll put the girls together over there on that side."

I watch Tim drop the leaves with a grin on his face as though this is fun, like he's having a sleepover with friends instead of complete strangers. Cass comes in with her load, and Tim explains where she should drop it. They both head back out to get another bunch.

"Tim seems nice," David comments.

"They both do," I agree. "They seem to be the only ones who really want us to be here."

"Well, the old guy who whittles sticks doesn't seem to care about anything but making wood shavings. I'm sure he doesn't care that we're here." He smiles.

I shake my head and give him a small smile back.

"I can't stop beating myself up for what I said to Matthias." I cover my face with my hands. "What do you think he's going to do to us?"

"I don't know, Liv."

"I have so many questions. I hope they are willing to answer them."

"We should probably take it slow. The group of people had decided that we shouldn't be allowed to stay here. I don't think very many of them are going to be forthcoming with answers right away. Perhaps we should keep our heads down and cooperate as best we can to earn their trust."

"Yeah. You're probably right. I'll try my best."

Tim and Cass come back with their second load of leaves.

"Just one more trip, and I think that should do it," Tim says cheerfully, patting Cass on the back.

"Did you want us to go get it?" David starts to stand up.

"Nah! It's no problem. You've had a rough day already, and you'll need your rest before tonight's reckoning. Be right back!" Tim heads back out for the rest of our beds.

David and I both look at each other with wide eyes.

"Reckoning? What do you think that is?" I ask.

"I have no clue. I hope they don't line us up and beat us with sticks to see if we're tough enough to stay in the group or something," David says.

"Matthias already said we're staying. What more do we have to do?"

David and I fall silent as we wait for Tim and Cass to come back. My mind is a whirl of questions and fear.

"That ought to do it!" Tim drops the leaves and wipes his clothes off. "Do you guys have blankets to use?"

"Yeah, in our bags, but mine was dumped out when they were looking for my gun," David says.

"That's right. Sorry about that. The guys can be a little rough sometimes. You want me to go get your things?" Tim offers.

"No. I can do it," David says.

Tim looks down at the floor, dejected.

"But...you can come with me if you want..." David adds slowly.

Tim's face lights right up like a dog who's been asked if they want to go for a walk. They both head out the door, and I call to David to bring my bag back too.

Cass is sitting on the floor next to her bed, looking at me, so I decide to make small talk.

"Your brother seems very...enthusiastic," I comment.

"Oh, yes. He is. Sometimes annoyingly so. He is just so happy to be alive."

"Did he almost die or something?"

"If Matthias hadn't brought us here to live, we would have," Cass says straightforwardly.

I wait for her to continue, but she doesn't offer any more of an explanation.

"Where were you living before that you feel you would have died had he not saved you?" I ask.

"The city."

"The city?" I say questioningly.

"Look. I want to answer all your questions. I really do. But I think you need to save your questions until after the reckoning."

"What is the 'reckoning'?"

Cass bites her lip as she decides whether she should keep talking or not. "All right, everyone who comes to stay with us has to go through a reckoning. You are going to be asked to give all your secrets and knowledge to the group through a series of questions. If they like what you say, then you can be in the group. If not, well..."

"What?" I ask.

"We've had some people go through the reckoning, and they didn't pass. Matthias took them back out into the woods, and we never saw them again. I thought maybe he was releasing them to go back to their lives, but then I saw blood splattered on Matthias's shirt. I didn't say anything, but from then on, I made extra sure I didn't step a toe out of line."

"He killed them?" I ask, horrified.

Cass nods.

"Holy crap! Why does Tim seem so excited about us going through this reckoning?" I ask, my voice shaking.

"Because he's not worried. He believes you two are Rare—"

"What is this 'Rare' you keep talking about?" I interrupt, getting more and more frustrated. But Cass doesn't answer because the boys return with the bags.

"Here ya go, Olivia." Tim hands me my bag. I set it next to me and stare at the floor. I feel like no matter where I go, my life is crap!

"Hey, are you okay?" David whispers in my ear as he takes the blanket out of his bag.

I shake my head slowly.

"You better hurry and finish making your beds. It looked like people were getting things ready for tonight's events," Tim says excitedly. Cass and Tim head outside.

"We're going to die, David," I whisper back.

22

"What? Why do you say that?" David says quietly.

"Cass just told me that they are going to question us, and if we somehow fail, we're going to be taken out into the woods and murdered!" I whisper hysterically. Sure, I tried to kill myself a few times, but the thought of someone else killing me terrifies me.

"David. Olivia. Please join me outside by the fire," Matthias says, peeking his head in the door of the shelter.

I start shaking as we both stand up. I reach in my pocket for my inhaler out of habit but stop when I realize that I don't really need it. This level of nerves usually makes me need at least two doses. I wish I understood what I was doing differently so I would never need an inhaler again.

The daylight is slowly fading as it turns to dusk. The campfire has been stoked, and the wood pops every now and then, causing me to jump a little. We make our way to two empty stumps next to the warm blaze. The group of people sits around the fire, their faces glowing in the soft light. Matthias stands by the stumps, holding two cups in his hands.

"Have a seat."

David and I carefully sit down. My heart is racing out of my chest. My face feels hot after only moments by the flames. I look over at David, wondering if he is as scared as I am. If he is, his expression doesn't show it. He looks at Matthias almost as though he's bored. How can he be so calm?

"Before we begin, I'd like you to drink this, please." Matthias hands us the cups.

"What is it?" David sniffs the contents.

I take a sniff too. It smells like sickly-sweet flowers and overripe, slightly fermented grapes mixed together.

"A little concoction I like to call 'rectitude wine.'"

"What did you say? Rectum wine?" David asks with a look of disgust.

Someone in the group starts to snicker until Matthias shoots a look at them, and they stop immediately.

"I said, 'rectitude.' As in honesty. Truth. You'll drink this wine before we begin the questions."

"What if I don't? Then what?" David asks.

I give him a look to try to tell him to knock it off. What happened to keeping our heads down and cooperating to earn their trust?

"If you don't, you'll be kicked out of our camp, and none of your questions'll be answered. You'll be on your own in the woods at night with the Havoc that like to prowl in the darkness. I suggest you do as I say."

David swallows hard. I don't like the idea of going back out there to try to find a place to stay in the dark. David looks at me and gives a little nod. We both raise the cups to our mouths and drink.

The wine feels thick like syrup, and I have a hard time swallowing it, it's so sweet. I start coughing and wish that I had some water to wash it down. My belly grows warm as it floods into my stomach. After a few moments, I feel a strange tingling sensation making its way up into my skull. It's not an unpleasant feeling; in fact, it's quite thrilling. I find myself suddenly wanting to share my life's story with these people. I sit up tall and wait eagerly for the questioning to begin. I take a quick look at David and see that he is also sitting up straight with a look of rapture on his face.

"All right. Let's begin."

Everyone around the fire grows silent as though they are all holding their breath. I glance over at Tim, and he gives me a big smile and two thumbs up.

"We'll start with somethin' easy. Olivia, what's your full name?"

"Olivia Rosette Sloane," I spew out automatically.

"And David, what's your full name?"

"David Allan Beckett," he answers immediately.

"How old are you, Olivia?"

"Sixteen."

Matthias pauses a moment before continuing, "And you, David?"

"Seventeen."

"What are your parents' names, Olivia?"

"My mom's name is Janice Eve Sloane. I do not know who my father is."

"Why's that?"

"My father died before I was born. My mother doesn't talk about him. She says it's because it hurts too much, but I think she's hiding something." The words flow out of my mouth without me even trying.

"What d'ya think she's hidin'?"

"I don't know. It is just a feeling I have. Something feels off about her and the way she likes her secrets."

"What does your mother do for a job?"

"I don't know what she does exactly, but she works at the United World Coalition for Peace building."

"And she won't tell ya what her job is?" Matthias asks, almost annoyed.

"No. It's just another secret she likes to keep from me."

"Does your mother ever tell you what the government's workin' on?"

"No, sir. She will only tell me when they are having a big important meeting, but she won't divulge any other information."

"I see. How 'bout you, David? Who're your parents?"

"Chloe Jill Beckett and Andrew Curtis Beckett."

"What do they do for a livin'?"

"My father is a mechanic at the Ace Auto Body Shop, and my mother works for Peace Pharmaceuticals, sir."

I hear a few murmurings among the group of people.

"Doin' what?"

"She oversees the sale and distribution of vitamins."

"So, she works for the government too?"

"I guess so, yes." David furrows his eyebrows as though he never realized this.

"Do ya love your mother, David?"

"Of course. She's my mother."

"What if I were to tell ya that anyone who works for the government isn't who ya think they are?"

"I know my mother. She is a good person," David says testily.

"I'm sure ya believe that. Most people who work for the Coalition are excellent liars."

"What is your problem, man?" David jumps to his feet.

"David!" I yell, worried he's going to get us in trouble.

"Have a seat, David. I don't wanna fight ya."

"No! Not until you start telling us what it is you're doing out here!"

"You'll get your answers, but I'm not done askin' the questions yet. Have a seat."

David slowly sits back down, staring daggers at Matthias.

"I'm interested in these vitamins. D'ya know what they do?"

"They're vitamins. They keep us healthy."

"Are ya healthy, David?"

"Well, no. I get sick a lot. But my mom tells me that if I didn't take the vitamins, I would be much worse off than I am."

"D'ya have any vitamins with ya?"

"No. Olivia and I forgot them."

"So, ya haven't taken any in a few days?"

"That's right."

"And how d'ya feel without 'em?"

David pauses with his forehead scrunched as he thinks about this question. "Well, I feel great, actually. The best I have ever felt in my life. But I can't say it's because of the vitamins or lack of vitamins—"

"How 'bout you, Olivia?" Matthias interrupts David. "What's your life been like up to this point?"

"My life is a joke. I am always sick and weak, and I have tried to kill myself on several occasions."

"And now?"

"I feel a lot better."

Matthias is silent for a moment and starts to pace in front of us. David and I wait quietly for him to ask the next question.

"Olivia, tell me what ya know 'bout your father."

"I already told you. I do not know much about him. My mom says he left to go fight in a war, and a bomb dropped on his location, and there was nothing left of him."

Matthias stops pacing and stands next to the fire, stroking his beard, listening intently. "Anythin' else?"

"She had another child with him, but the baby died before he was born."

"Go back to the shelter with Cassandra and Timothy," Matthias says abruptly, turning around and walking away.

"That's it? We're done?" I call out, worried about his sudden dismissal.

David and I both stand up and turn to head back to the shelter. Tim gives me a small smile, but that doesn't stop my legs from shaking uncontrollably.

23

I sit on my bed, picking up dead leaves and ripping them to pieces. Everyone is silent as we wait for Matthias to come back with the verdict on whether David and I passed the reckoning or not. I suddenly have a killer headache, and I no longer want to share my secrets anymore. The wine must be wearing off.

"Did we say something wrong?" I ask, my voice trembling slightly. I look at Cass for an answer. Her face is barely visible in the dim glow of the flashlight sitting in the middle of the floor.

"I don't think so. I really don't know what he was looking for. The adults never let us in on their deliberations," Cass answers.

David looks at me. His eyes reflect just exactly how I'm feeling. Fear. Unbridled fear that we are about to be kicked out or worse.

We wait for what feels like forever. Time only being measured by how many heartbeats I feel pounding in my chest. I start at Matthias's sudden presence in our shelter door.

"Ya two can stay. Rest up. Tomorrow we put ya to work."

And just that quickly, he's gone.

"Thank you!" I yell out but stop as my head feels like it's about to split.

Cass and Tim are on their feet, jumping up and down and smiling like loons.

"You did it! I knew you were going to be fine!" Tim says excitedly.

I breathe a great sigh of relief and smile as Cass and Tim spin each other in circles. David gets off his bed and sits next to me, smiling.

"We get to live for another day," David says quietly.

I lean my head against his shoulder and feel him rest his cheek against the top of my head. I'm suddenly exhausted and want nothing more than to curl up in a nice soft bed. I guess dried leaves and a blanket will have to do.

"Cass. Tim. I think Olivia and I need some sleep. I don't know about her, but I have a nasty headache, and I think I'm ready for bed."

"Yeah! Sure thing! We'll go back out by the fire and let you two get to sleep," Cass offers, shutting off the flashlight and handing it back to David.

I am so relieved that David spoke up first so I didn't have to stop their celebrating. I grab a sweatshirt out of my bag and wad it up to make a pillow. Now that the sun has gone down, there is a slight chill to the air. I fold my blanket in half and lie between the layers like it's a sleeping bag. I'm asleep in a matter of minutes.

I wake up to the sounds of birds singing and the small children giggling outside. The early morning light shines through the walls. I sit up and stretch out my sore muscles. Dried leaves do not give much support while sleeping.

"Good morning, Olivia." David says.

I look over at his bed and see him sitting with his back against the wall, facing me. I suddenly blush.

"Were you watching me sleep?" I ask, embarrassed at the thought.

"Only for a little bit. I just woke up too."

I look at Tim and Cass's beds and see that they're empty. I rub the sleep out of my eyes, and when I look over at David again, I suddenly realize that I can see every detail of his face. His acne seems to be clearing up, his eyes look more alert and hold my gaze confidently, and his jaw is darkening with stubble.

"David, I can see perfectly without my glasses!"

"That's great, Liv! See? I knew there was something to the woods," he says, holding his hearing aid on the palm of his hand, smiling wide.

Odd. His teeth are looking whiter and less crooked. I have to be imagining things.

"I didn't know we would start healing or anything, but I just had this feeling that there was something we needed to come out here for."

"Aha, you two are finally awake!" Tim says brightly, walking through the door. "You were allowed to sleep in this morning because Matthias knew you needed it."

"Why? What time do you usually get up?"

"At dawn. Everyone has chores they need to do in order to get breakfast ready. You'll catch on. Come on! We still have some breakfast for you to eat."

"I'm going to freshen up a bit first, David. Go on without me."

David nods and leaves the shelter. I take in a breath as deeply as I can and let it all out slowly. The lack of pain in my lungs makes me smile. I look around the shelter, taking in every single detail I can: pieces of bark chipping off the logs, a line of ants walking along the dirt floor, sunshine gleaming off an intricate spider web in the corner of the shelter. Out of curiosity, I grab my glasses out of my bag and put them on. I'm suddenly blind. I can't make out a single thing. I toss them back in my bag and get myself ready for the day with clean clothes and a thorough hair brushing. Stepping out of the shelter, I look for David. He's sitting on a stump by the fire, eating food.

"You look nice." David smiles at me as I make my way over to him.

"Thanks. I wish I could take a shower. I'm starting to feel pretty dirty."

"There's a stream not far from here where we bathe," a voice says behind me. A woman with dark hair in a high ponytail steps up to my side and hands me a plate of food to match David's: scrambled eggs, a hunk of meat, and an apple.

"Thank you." I take the food from her. I do a double take when I see her. She looks familiar. I'm not sure where I've seen her before. Maybe not her specifically, but someone who looks like her. She gives me a small smile and walks back to where the children are playing a game of keep away with a weathered volleyball.

"Hmm, she looks familiar," I comment to David.

"Who?"

"The lady who just handed me this food," I say. David narrows his eyes and tilts his head as he looks at her for a moment but then shrugs his shoulders and goes back to eating.

I look down at my plate, trying to decide what kind of meat I'm about to eat.

"Try it. It's not bad. Could use a little salt, though," David says around his mouthful of food. Although his appearance might be changing, his manners are not.

I try the eggs first, wondering what kind of bird these eggs are from. They remind me of regular chicken eggs but are rather tasteless without salt. Once I start eating, though, I find it hard to stop. After I demolish the eggs, I stab my fork into the chunk of meat and take a bite. Warm juice floods my mouth, and I let out a moan.

David finishes his apple and turns toward me. "I don't know if I ever thanked you for running away with me. I'm glad you decided to come."

"Me too."

David is quiet for a moment before he asks weakly, "Do you think my mom is a bad person?"

"No! Of course not, David. She's one of the nicest ladies I have ever met. She's always been nice to me, way nicer than my mom."

"How come I never made the connection that she works for the government? Peace Pharmaceuticals. It was obvious once I said it during the reckoning."

"Maybe it was a truth that you kept hidden from yourself because you didn't want to believe it."

"Maybe, but it was pretty naïve of me. I just always thought she worked at a pharmacy that helped people, never once thinking about the link to the government."

"Look, just because she works at a Coalition pharmacy doesn't mean your mom is a bad person."

"I know she's always been nice, but I feel like she's somehow dirty now. Tainted by her loyalty to the president." David digs the toe of his shoe into the dirt.

"Maybe it's just a job to her. Maybe she just works there but isn't loyal—"

"Whatcha guys talking about?" Tim has a seat on one of the empty stumps.

David looks angry at the intrusion. I take his cue that he doesn't feel like sharing and make something up. "We were just trying to figure out where you got the eggs and meat from."

"Oh! We have chickens that we snuck out of the city. We usually wait until we've collected enough eggs for everyone to have some for breakfast. We also have goats that we get milk from. They live back behind the Commons shelter. The meat we're eating this morning is from some squirrels I shot and killed myself." Tim puffs out his chest a little with pride.

"Squirrel? I just ate squirrel?" I feel sick at the thought.

"Yup. You can't be picky when you live out in the wild. Meat is meat. I'm getting pretty good with my bow. Matthias has been giving me lessons and says it won't be long, and I can hunt Havoc with him," he says excitedly.

"What are Havoc?"

"That's what Alexandrine named the black beasts. I think she said it comes from a line in some old play, 'Cry Havoc and let slip the dogs of war,' or something like that."

"Are there a lot of them out here?"

"I wouldn't say a lot. They mostly stick close to the city's fence, but they wander out here from time to time. We have to stay on alert day in and day out, just in case. The adults take shifts at night, watching over the camp to keep everyone safe. Once I'm old enough, I will be able to take a shift too. That's why training is so important."

"What kind of training?" David chimes in.

"Weapons, hand to hand combat, stealth, balance, and control. Matthias takes it very seriously. And so should you."

"When do we start training?" David asks.

"Alexandrine handles the beginners, and she usually likes to do it in the morning or evenings. Since you guys slept in, it will be this evening," Tim says. "Anyway, it looks like you two are done eating. Come on. I'll show you where to clean your plates."

We follow him through the camp to a path that leads into the woods. I can hear the trickle of water through the trees before we see the river. We walk several yards until we come to a rocky river bank. Smooth stones cover the ground and gently slope down into a wide, slow-moving river. Giant boulders are scattered here and there, and I see articles of clothing laid out on them to dry in the sun.

"This is where we do all of our cleaning and get our drinking water. Wash rags for dishes are over there on that rock. Try to remember to lay them out flat to dry when you're done cleaning up," he adds as though to remind himself as well. "Also, if you are going to take a bath, make sure you tell someone first. I forgot to say something once, and now I can't look Rebecca in the eyes."

"Who's Rebecca?" I ask.

"One of the women with the little kids. She was Saul's live-in nurse back in the city before Matthias brought him out here. He went back and rescued her, and now she's our designated nurse."

"Why did Saul need a live-in nurse?" I ask curiously.

"I was told he had a stroke a long time ago. He couldn't care for himself, couldn't talk, couldn't even swallow food for the longest time, so he had to have Rebecca live with him. He's gotten better in some areas, but he still can't talk. It's a shame because he seems like a pretty cool guy."

I nod even though I don't know enough about him to really agree.

David grabs the plate and fork out of my hand and walks down to the water to clean up. Tim follows him. David looks over his shoulder at me to give me a look of annoyance at Tim's constant presence. I shrug and give him a little smile.

While the boys are washing up, I stand in the shade and look at the scenery. The sun is sparkling off the water. Birds fly overhead, singing beautiful songs. A fish splashes a little way down the river. A cool breeze blows my hair, tickling it against my neck. I stare out into the woods on the other side and wonder what kinds of animals are out there. I've only ever seen wild animals on the TV or in books.

"Aren't you worried about a Havoc coming from the other side of the river and attacking you?" I ask Tim as the boys make their way back over to me.

"Not really. Like I said, they stay close to the city for the most part, and Matthias says that Havoc seem to hate large bodies of water. They can't swim. He said they get most of their water from small puddles after it rains."

"How does he know so much about them?"

"He spends a lot of time studying them. 'Know your enemy' seems to be his mantra. You'll see once you start training with him. He says it at least twice every training session...if not more," Tim finishes with an eye roll.

"Ready to head back, Liv?" David asks.

I nod my head and sigh as we turn away from the beautiful river. I have a feeling I am going to spend a lot of my free time here, thinking. Seems to be a peaceful place for it.

"There you are. Matthias wanted me to take you two out to gather wood," Cass says as we step out of the woods back at camp.

"I was just showing them where to do their dishes."

"Good. You can take the dishes into the Commons shelter over there and then meet us by the fire pit." Cass points to a larger shelter in the middle of camp.

David and I walk together.

"Tim is really getting on my nerves. It seems like I can't do anything without him tagging along," David says quietly.

"Well, look around. Henry is the closest guy to his age, and he doesn't seem very friendly. He's probably lonely."

"I guess," David says reluctantly.

As we head to the Commons shelter, we see Saul sitting on the same stump as before, whittling away at a stick again. He looks up and smiles at me with a twinkle in his eye. I smile back and then look down at the stick in his hand. I see that he's not just whittling, he's carving something. Those symbols look oddly familiar, but before I can figure out where I've seen them before, David grabs my arm and leads me into the shelter.

We walk through the door and see baskets scattered all over the floor, filled with various fruits and vegetables. A few dead turkeys, relieved of their heads, hang upside-down from the rafters by ropes in the back corner. Bags of flour and rice lie in heaps by the walls. A round table made from a giant tree stump sits in the middle of the room with smaller stumps surrounding it. David and I spot a pile of clean dishes stacked on yet another tree stump that has been covered with a white towel. We stack our plates and forks on top and head back out.

"Where did all that food come from?" I ask David as we make our way back to the fire pit.

"I have no idea. Maybe it's time to see if Tim and Cass will answer some of our questions now that we get to stay."

Tim and Cass stand up as we walk toward them. "Ready?" Cass asks.

"We were wondering if you would answer some of our questions for us now?" David asks.

"We can talk while we walk," Tim suggests. He looks around nervously as I watch him slip David's gun into the back pocket of his jeans. Something about his sneakiness puts me on edge.

What if Tim isn't as friendly as we thought. I find myself suddenly worried about going out into the woods with him. What if he was instructed to take us out into the woods and kill us?

2|4

We make our way past our shelter and out into the forest on a narrow path before I call Tim out on it.

"What are you doing with David's gun, Tim?"

"Shh! Strictly speaking, I'm not supposed to have it. I snuck it out of Matthias's hut to bring with us for protection. The last time Cass and I went out to find wood, Matthias wouldn't allow us to bring any weapons, telling us we would be fine and that we needed our hands for carrying the wood. We wandered pretty far away from camp, and suddenly, we heard a few branches breaking in the distance and hurried the heck out of there. We never did see what it was, but I don't want to take any chances."

"Fair enough," David concedes.

I breathe a sigh of relief.

"So, you had some questions for us." Cass stoops down to pick up a few branches lying on the ground.

"I guess the first one on my mind is, where did all of that food come from? Like, where do you get bags of flour and rice out in the forest?" I ask, searching around for pieces of wood to bring back.

"Recon missions to the city. When Matthias goes to see if he can find another person to save from the city, they always swipe food and supplies for the group as well."

"But isn't that stealing?" I ask.

"Sure, it is. But they won't notice a few missing items," Tim says nonchalantly, like stealing is a normal thing around here.

"How does he get in and out of the city when there are guards posted by the fence?" David asks.

"Through the subway tunnels."

"What? What are subway tunnels?"

"Not really sure. I think that's what they brought me and Cass through when they saved us from the city, but I was so young then, I can't remember much about them. I overheard Matthias talking about the subway to Henry once. You'll have to ask him about it."

"Fine," I say, trying to remember some of the questions I had rolling around in my head. "What is the 'Rare' you mentioned?" I ask.

Tim's face brightens right up. "Oh! It's a special group of people who have enhanced abilities. Like how you caught that rock flying at your face, and you didn't even realize it. The Rare have better reflexes, heightened visual or hearing capabilities, and are far stronger than most people."

"So, like superheroes?" David asks skeptically.

"Eh, sort of but not really. The Rare have never been able to fly or have laser vision or shoot spider-webs out of their wrists and things like that. They're just better at all the things normal people can do. Their skills come naturally without much thought or practice. They are better fighters, hunters, scouts...you name it! I wish I were one," he says, childlike.

"You really think I'm a Rare?" I ask.

Tim stops walking and turns around to look at me with scrunched-up eyebrows. He grabs a piece of wood he was carrying and chucks it at me. Before I even give it any thought, I kick the wood out of the air with a perfectly executed roundhouse kick.

"Yup. I believe you are Rare," Tim says, smiling.

I look back at David, and he whistles. I roll my eyes at him and turn forward to continue our search for firewood. My cheeks blush slightly as a smile spreads across my face.

"I wonder what else I can do," I say dreamily.

"You'll find out at your training session," Cass says.

After we all have our arms loaded up with wood, we turn back around to take it to camp.

"So, what is everyone doing out here in the woods?" David asks.

"We are living free, away from the poisonous city," Tim says.

"Poisonous?" I ask.

"Haven't you noticed that there isn't any fog out here?"

"Well...yeah..." I start to say.

"The fog is only in the city," Tim says.

"How can that be true? Where does the fog come from?" I ask in disbelief. We step back into camp with the load of wood.

"Drop your piles over there and follow me."

We drop the wood on the small pile that is already stacked near the fire pit and follow Tim back out of the camp. Nobody calls for us to stop, so we keep walking out into the woods. The trees grow steadily taller and seem to loom overhead. Tim stops abruptly at a tree that has pieces of wood nailed to it all the way up to its branches.

"This is one of our lookout trees. You can see the city from up there. Go ahead. Climb up and see. There's enough room for both of you."

I reach up and grab hold of a makeshift step and start my ascent. I've never climbed a tree before, and I'm a little nervous of heights. After I'm a few steps up, David starts the climb. No turning back now. I make it past the wood steps and up to the branches. I pull myself onto a branch, holding onto the one above me, and feel the one I'm stepping on give a little, making a small cracking sound.

"Keep close to where the branch attaches to the tree!" Tim calls up to me.

I shimmy my way over closer to the tree and can feel that it is much sturdier.

"Thanks, Tim!" I call down to him.

I climb up to the next branch as David makes his way to where I just was. Slowly, I work my way up the tree, placing my hands and feet carefully on the branches. I can no longer see Cass and Tim at the bottom, and I start to shake as I realize just how high I am. I'm not quite to the top when I find a platform nailed up in the tree. I hoist myself onto it, relieved that I made it. There's just enough room for David to join me. I move over and grab his arms to help steady him as he pulls himself up onto the platform next to me.

There is a clearing through the branches that gives us the perfect view. We seem to be in a tree that's up on a hill. I can't believe how far I can see. A valley stretches out below us, filled with trees that come to a stop at the city's fence. Tim is right. The unceasing fog of the city doesn't go past the fence into the forest. I squint my eyes and see the sun shining off water past the city. The ocean. There isn't any fog there either.

"What the...?" I ask.

"How is the fog only in the city?" David asks.

"Better question is: why? Why is the fog only in the city?"

We stand together looking out at the scene in front of us for a few moments longer.

"Liv, there's something I was hoping to talk to you about," David says, shifting his weight back and forth.

"What?"

"Well, I was just, um, wondering if you noticed some chemistry going on between us? I couldn't help but notice you lay your head on my shoulder the other night and stuff like that."

"Oh, David. You never stop, do you? We're friends. Friends. Got it?"

"I just thought—"

"What? That I was suddenly going to want to be your girlfriend? How long have we known each other David?"

"Almost our whole lives."

"Exactly. I wouldn't want to ruin our friendship with a relationship that might not last. We are out here in the middle of nowhere, surrounded by people who hardly know us, trying our hardest to survive. I need you to be my friend, David."

Tears start forming in his eyes. He gives his head a little nod.

Suddenly, our conversation is interrupted by the sounds of a scream and a gunshot ringing out from the ground.

"Crap! What was that?" I ask frantically.

"Let's go find out!" David says, already lowering himself off the platform.

With thoughts of Cass in my head, I climb down that tree faster than I ever imagined I could. Once the ground is in sight, I let go of the bottom branch and fall ten feet, landing with a somersault. David does the same. I look around, desperate to find Tim and Cass. There's blood on the leaves at the base of the tree.

"Let's follow the blood and see if we can find where it came from," David suggests.

I follow closely behind David as he leads us farther into the woods. Splatters of blood can be found every few feet. As we keep going, the blood spots get further apart and harder to pick out. After we've walked about a half mile, I'm starting to feel nervous, being this far away from camp. We hear another gunshot and a whoop of celebration coming from up ahead.

"I did it! I killed one!" Tim yells to us as we run up to where he is standing. At his feet lies a large mass of black fur.

"Are you sure it's dead?" I stare at its body, watching for breathing.

"Yup! I followed its blood trail out here and found it. I shot it in the head to finish it off. I'm a hero! I can't wait to tell Matthias!" Tim beams.

"Good job, Tim," David congratulates him.

I walk slowly around the beast, looking closely at it. Its stench hits me, and I cover my nose with my shirt so I don't throw up. It reeks of sweat, wet dog, and rotting flesh. Its paws are slightly larger than my hands, with two-inch sharp claws. Its tail is bushy like a wolf's, and its fur is long and pitch-black. Even though its hair is long, I can see it has unnatural bulking muscles and an odd hump on its back. Its ears are pointed with long tufts of hair sticking off the tips. Its dead eyes are pools of black like I saw in my dream. Its long pink tongue hangs out of its mouth, past needle-sharp fangs. As I look at the lifeless creature, I feel a mix of relief that it's dead but sympathy also. It's clearly a creature made for hunting prey. Should we really punish an animal for doing what it's made to do?

"Where's Cass?" I ask, looking around.

"She went back to camp to get Matthias and tell him what happened. They should be here soon." Tim smiles.

"So, what happened? We heard a scream."

"Cass and I were standing at the base of the tree you guys were in, and we heard a crack of a branch. I pulled the gun out just as the Havoc jumped out of the woods toward us. Cass screamed and fell to the ground, and I aimed the gun at it, knowing I had to do something, or we were goners. I pulled the trigger and shot it right here." Tim points at the wound on its belly. "The Havoc yelped and turned to run away into the woods. I knew I needed to finish it off so it wouldn't suffer. I told Cass to head back to camp and get Matthias, and I took off into the woods, following the blood trail. I followed it here and shot it in the head to end its misery."

"You've got some balls, kid." We all start at Matthias's voice. He calmly walks toward the dead animal and stops; his facial expression is like stone. "However, if I ever catch ya sneakin' into my hut and takin' somethin' that's not yours again, you'll be livin' out here by yourself. Got it?"

Tim's smile slides off his face, and he looks down at the ground, deflated. "Yes, sir."

"Good. Now, give me the gun."

Tim hands the gun over to Matthias.

"It was stupid to use a weapon ya know nothin' about. What're ya out here in this part of the woods for in the first place?"

"We wanted to show Olivia and David the lookout tree so they could see that the neverending fog stays only inside the city."

"Why does it do that?" I ask.

"I'll answer your questions once we're back in camp," Matthias says.

After we silently make our way back into camp, Matthias sends Tim off to clean the animal pens as part of his punishment.

"Have a seat," Matthias points to the stumps by the fire pit. "So, what d'ya wanna ask?"

"What is the fog in the city? Why does it stop at the fence?" I ask first.

"From what we can tell, the fog's a manufactured poison that dampens the Rares' abilities, but we're not sure how it works...yet."

"If the fog is a 'poison,' then how does it not affect normal people?" David asks.

"As I said, we don't know how the fog works exactly. It seems like we're missin' a piece of the puzzle. Somehow, they've created a way to weaken the Rares and make 'em vulnerable."

"Why would they want to keep the Rares weak?" I ask.

"Do you know why Rares exist in the first place?" Matthias asks gruffly.

"No."

He sighs and pinches the bridge of his nose.

"What do they teach you guys in school?" he whispers to himself. "All right, I'll give you a little history lesson, so listen up. Long before we were born, scientists started messin' with genetic codes. They started tryin' to enhance human genes by pinpointin' the parts of DNA that are responsible for our senses and tweakin' 'em to make our senses better," Matthias says, looking directly at me.

"That's called 'genetic modification,'" David interjects.

Matthias glares at him for interrupting and then continues, "Well, it didn't work the way they thought it would. Instead of curin' problems like colorblindness or hearin' impairment, it created people with hyper senses. They pretty much created a form of superhumans. But not everyone got the changes. Only a small portion of the world got the benefits, and it became a case of immeasurable outrage and jealousy," he continues tensely, his fists balled up.

"There was an uprisin' of people who wanted the scientists to reverse the change, to take away what they'd given. Course, 'The Rare'—that's what they called themselves—didn't want to have their abilities taken away and started fightin' back. Across the globe, people were going crazy and huntin' down the Rares to kill 'em because they were different. It was a witch hunt!" Matthias pounds his fist on his thigh, causing David and me to jump.

"Other people got it in their heads to hide 'em. Well, rumors spread that the US had become a sanctuary for the Rares. Once that got out, the Rares started flockin' here, not understandin' what was gonna happen if they did. They knew that the United States was a powerful country with a strong military, and so they thought they'd be safe here. But the madness had spread throughout the world, makin' everyone believe that they needed to kill all the Rares. It was like Hitler with the Jews all over again, only on an even larger scale. They banded together to bomb the hell out of the US and all the sympathetic Americans. We're talkin' World War III here—"

"I knew there was a war. I just don't know the details. It seems like nobody wants to talk about it," I interrupt.

"People're still skittish 'bout the whole damned thing. But I think it's time we start educatin' ya young people, so ya don't make the same mistakes," Matthias says, pointing at David and me. "Anyway, the US didn't go down without a fight. We shot off a few missiles at China, Russia, Japan, and France. But in the end, we lost..."

"I'm done cleaning the pens," Tim says, walking up behind Matthias. As he gets closer to us, I start coughing at the stench of manure on the bottom of his shoes. I notice David scrunch his nose too.

"Good. Now ya can ask around camp for everyone's dirty clothes and go down to the river to wash it all."

Tim's eyes get wide, but he takes a deep breath to keep himself in check. "Yes, sir," he mumbles as he shuffles away.

"Now, where was I?"

"You said the war happened, and the US lost," David offers.

"Oh, yes. Well, a group of people here in the US got together to surrender and make peace with the other nations in hopes that they would call a ceasefire. They agreed on the terms that all the remainin' US population would be put into cities where they could be monitored, and if any Rares were discovered, they'd need to be 'taken care of.' The group of people agreed and called themselves 'The United Coalition for Peace.' They rounded up the survivors and stuck 'em in cities where they were fenced in and fed lies that the woods will kill ya, and you're not to leave the city at any time. Imprisonin' people and tellin' 'em it was for their own safety."

"Why did people believe them? Why would they allow themselves to be trapped inside the city?" I ask.

"Fear. Fear drives people to do stupid things. They were told that they'd be taken care of in the cities. After the war, people were shell-shocked, and they *wanted* to be taken care of. After a while, they were fed the lies about the dangers that lurked outside the city so often that they started to believe them."

"What made you come out here?" David asks.

"I found out what America was like before the war, that we were a free country once. People used to be able to live wherever they wanted to, own as many guns as they wanted to, and vote for the leaders they wanted instead of leaders bein' appointed to us by other countries. I left because I hate the Coalition and their dictatorship."

"How do you sneak back into the city to get supplies? Tim said something about subway tunnels, but I don't know what those are."

"Before the war, the city was about five times the size it is now. They had underground trains called subways that people used to get around to different parts of the city. After the war, the city as we know it is all that was salvageable. They fenced themselves in the livable part and fixed it up."

"Except for the bad part of town where they let the druggies and homeless people take over. That's still in ruins," I add.

"Correct," Matthias nods. "Well, they didn't think too much about the subway tunnels. They halfheartedly blocked up the entrances and forgot about them. Since the city downsized so drastically, some of those subway tunnels are outside of their fences, and I found one that leads from outside the city, into the 'bad' part of town."

"But going there is almost as bad as dealing with the guards, isn't it? You could get killed, no questions asked, on that side of town," David says.

"It's risky, but I haven't been bothered by any thugs yet. I never go in without a weapon, that's for sure. The tricky part is sneakin' into the better part of town without gettin' caught."

"Matthias! You're needed in the Commons," Alexandrine yells from the doorway.

Matthias stands up with a grunt.

"Wait! I have more questions," I plead.

"They'll have to wait 'til later."

David and I watch as Matthias walks away. After all that information he gave us, I feel like I have more questions than when we started.

"That was not satisfying," I say, frustrated.

"I want to know how all these people got out here. How the fog takes away the Rares' powers. Where the Havoc came from..." David says.

"What part my mom plays in the Coalition," I say darkly. "I can't believe how much my mother has been hiding from me. She's got a lot of explaining to do."

David stands and offers to help me up. I grab hold and feel the comforting warmth of his hand around mine. I look up into his eyes as I stand, and all I see is sadness. He lets go of my hand as soon as I'm on my feet and turns away from me.

"What should we do now?" he asks.

"We could go help Tim with the laundry," I say reluctantly.

"Nah. It's his punishment. Besides, I don't want to wash other people's underwear." He turns his head to give me a half smirk.

"Gross." I give him a shove on his arm.

"Look out!" David shouts, grabbing me and pulling me close to him just as a volleyball goes soaring through the space I just occupied. I look in the direction it came from, and a kid who looks to be about eight years old has his hand over his mouth, looking guilty.

"Sorry!" he shouts and runs after the ball to get it.

I suddenly realize that David is still holding me close, and my cheeks flush. I pull out of his grasp quickly.

"You okay?" David asks.

"Yeah, yeah. I'm fine," I answer, clearing my throat and fixing my hair.

"Hey guys, it's time to get lunch prepared," Cass says from behind us. "Do either of you know how to pluck a turkey?"

"Um...no," I say, slightly disgusted at the idea.

"Well, you're going to learn." She slaps David on the back. "Come on!"

We shuffle behind Cass as she leads us over to the Commons shelter. She ducks inside and comes out with the dead turkeys I saw hanging in the back corner as well as a couple of knives. She hands us the knives and leads us toward the river. We see Tim upstream, crouching down by the water, washing what looks like a bra with a scowl on his face.

We walk over to a long flat rock that stands waist high, and she lays the turkeys down. There are two empty metal buckets sitting on the ground next to the rock.

"What're the buckets for?" I ask.

"One's for feathers, and the other's for guts."

Stomach acid is creeping up my throat. I swallow hard and try to stay focused.

"What do we do first?" David asks.

"You two can work on that one, and I'll work on this one. Just grab a few feathers at a time and jerk them the opposite direction they're lying," she says as she demonstrates for us. "Put the feathers in the bucket as you go. Caroline wants to use the feathers to make a pillow." David grabs hold of the turkey's legs with one hand and pulls a few feathers out of the turkey's back. I watch him do it a couple more times as I work up the courage to make myself help. I grab hold of a few feathers and pull, but they don't come out. I try again, and only one breaks free.

"I can't do this," I say, hoping I can get away with not helping.

"Now's not the time to get squeamish. You wanna eat, right?" Cass chastises.

"Yes. I'm just not used to this. We buy meat from a grocery store. I've never had to pluck my own turkey."

"You'll get it. You just have to do it a few times. It took me a few tries my first time too. Of course, I was only seven when Matthias taught me."

I grab hold and pull again with no success.

"Here." David lays his hand on top of mine. "You have to pull up, against the grain."

The feathers come right out this time, and he gives me a smile. After a while, I've got the hang of it, and we take turns cleaning the bird, filling the bucket full of feathers.

"Now what?" I ask, relieved that we're done.

"Now we take the knives and gut them."

"No way! Nuh-uh. I'm not sticking my hands inside the turkey."

"Hey, you need to learn this stuff out here. This is survival stuff. It's gross, but you have to just shut your mind off to it and get it done." Cass hands me a knife.

I look at David, pleading him with my eyes to help me.

"I'll do it, and Olivia can watch." David takes the knife out of my hand.

"Thank you," I whisper.

I stand off to the side and watch as David mimics each of Cass moves, precisely. I cover my nose with my shirt once he cuts open the turkey. The stench of its insides is enough to make me gag.

His hands move deftly as though he's done this before. I'm amazed at how quickly David has taken to all this survival stuff. We never had to do anything like this in the city, but he's acting as though he's been doing it his whole life.

I follow David to the river's edge to wash our hands.

"Well, that was thoroughly disgusting," David says, washing the gore away.

"What other horrors do you think they have in store for us?"

"I don't want to know."

"Come on, you two. Let's get the turkeys back to camp so we can start roasting them." Cass pats her stomach. "I'm hungry!"

As we follow her, I glance back at Tim and see him violently whipping a shirt against a rock as though he's trying to kill it. I think I like the annoyingly upbeat Tim better.

Once we're back in camp, Cass hands the turkeys off to a man with a bushy red beard and bald head.

"Why don't you go with Frederick, David? You can learn how to properly cook a turkey," Cass suggests.

David gives me a small smile and takes off.

"Now what?" I ask.

"We can go into the Commons and see if they have more work for us to do," Cass suggests.

We turn to walk that way, but I stop short when I see Alexandrine standing next to the shelter, giving me a murderous glare as she spins a knife in her hand.

I grab Cass's elbow and whisper, "I don't think Alexandrine likes me."

"She doesn't. She hates you."

"What? Why?"

Cass shrugs her shoulders. "I don't know. I just overheard her telling Matthias that she refuses to teach you any lessons, and if it were up to her, you would be kicked out of camp."

I look up at Alexandrine and lock eyes with her. She turns her head, spits on the ground, and then walks out of sight.

I better make sure I'm never alone with her.

27

Once the food is ready, I tell David that I want to eat in our shelter, away from everyone. The look Alexandrine gave me put me on edge.

"Oh, this turkey is delicious," David moans as he devours his meal.

"I've never had wild turkey before. This is so good." I take a huge mouthful. I have to swallow a couple of times to get the dry white meat to slide down my throat.

"David, do you feel safe here?" I ask.

"I feel *safer*. These people know how to survive. I'm not sure what I would do if we came across one of the beasts in the woods on our own." He shoves a fork full of food in his mouth. "Why?"

"I don't know. I think Alexandrine is going to try to kill me," I say, paranoia creeping into my voice.

He gives me a quizzical look as he chews his overstuffed mouthful of food.

"After you left to go help cook the turkeys, she was standing outside her shelter, staring at me while spinning a knife in her hand. She had a look on her face that made it clear she doesn't want me here. Cass even confirmed that she doesn't," I say shakily. "Why do I always have enemies? Why does everyone hate me, David?" I start to cry as the all too familiar dark thoughts of suicide creep back up. It's been a while since I've contemplated death. But this time the thought doesn't stick. Things have been better out here, and I'm not ready to give that up.

"She's probably just jealous that she isn't the most beautiful person around here anymore," David says with a wink.

"Whatever." I shake my head at him.

"Look, I don't know why she would hate you. She doesn't know you. Maybe when we do our training tonight, we can ask her."

"Cass said that Alexandrine told Matthias that she refuses to teach me." I shove the food on my plate around with my fork.

"I guess we'll find out tonight, won't we?"

"I'm done!" Tim says, storming into the shelter and flopping onto his bed. He crosses his arms over his chest and stares at the ceiling. "I should just leave. Stupid Matthias and his stupid rules."

"Sorry you got in trouble, man," David says, "but I don't think leaving is the answer."

Tim just huffs and rolls onto his side toward the wall, making the dead leaves spread across the ground with a rustle.

"Is Matthias always harsh with his punishments?" I ask.

"Pretty much, yeah. He tries to keep everyone under control with threats of kicking them out. Most people listen because nobody wants to be kicked out of camp. But I'm close to just leaving and finding a different group to join. Screw Matthias and his dictatorship."

"Different group?"

"Yeah. We're not the only ones out here in the woods. There have to be other camps with other groups of people. I don't know where they would be, though, and that's where the problem comes in. It's dangerous to be out walking on your own in the woods, but I'm so angry right now I think I could kill a Havoc with my bare hands."

"How do you know there are other groups if you've never seen them?" David asks.

"Of course there are other groups. It would be illogical to think that we're the only people who refused to live under the Coalition's rule. Besides, sometimes Matthias and Henry leave for days, even weeks at a time, but they don't come back with stuff from the city. They won't tell anyone where they're going, but he leaves Alexandrine in charge, and she's just as bad as he is."

Just then, footsteps approach our shelter. I hope for Tim's sake it isn't Matthias or Alexandrine.

"Tim, Matthias wants to see you," Cass says, stepping through the door.

"What does he want now?"

"How should I know? He just told me to come fetch you."

He stands up, grumbling to himself. As he walks out of the shelter, David stands and offers to help me up.

"I'm done eating. Let's take our plates down to the river to clean, and maybe we can hear what Matthias is going to make Tim do now."

We walk out past the firepit, where Matthias is standing next to Tim, who's hanging his head like a child, awaiting his fate.

"I was a bit harsh. If ya really wanna learn to shoot a gun, then it would be best that I teach ya. Go get some empty cans from the Commons, and we'll target practice."

Tim's entire demeanor changes instantly. He is back to his bouncy, excited-to-be-alive self.

"Come on. Let's go get the dishes washed quickly so we can watch. Maybe we can pick up a few tips while we're at it," David says, hurrying down to the river.

By the time we're done washing up, Tim and Matthias are done setting up their target practice. There are four empty soup cans sitting on blocks of wood about ten yards away. David and I sit on stumps a safe distance to the left behind Matthias.

"Is it all right if we watch?" David asks.

"Yeah. Pay attention cause ya might learn somethin'," Matthias says gruffly.

"Now, you already know a thing or two 'bout guns, but since we got people watchin', I'll go over the safety tips for their sake."

"Yes, sir," Tim says.

"Your gun should always have the safety on until you're ready to shoot. Never point a gun at a person, even if you think the safety's on. Keep your finger off the trigger. Your finger should only be on the trigger when you're ready to shoot."

"Got it," Tim nods seriously, giving Matthias his full attention.

Matthias hands Tim the gun. "Ya wanna have a sturdy stance. Bend your knees slightly; ya don't want 'em locked."

"Like this?"

"Yup. Now, hold the grip, keep your trigger finger off the trigger, and keep your thumb away from the slide, or you'll be regrettin' it."

I glance at David, and he has his hands positioned like he's holding an imaginary gun, following Matthias's every instruction. Meanwhile, I have to force myself to pay attention. Guns hold no interest for me.

"Bring the gun up; arms should be straight but elbows slightly bent, not locked."

"Should I take the safety off?" Tim asks.

"Not yet. Are ya left-eye dominant or right-eye?"

"Right, I think," Tim answers.

"Ya think, or ya know?"

"I know. I did the test you showed me."

"Good. Close your dumb eye, and line up the sights just under where ya wanna shoot. Once you have it right, take the safety off."

Tim lowers the gun to locate the safety. I find myself yawning loudly, but David keeps watching them like a hawk as though this is the most interesting thing he has ever seen.

"Line it back up, and squeeze the trigger."

BAM!

I start from the noise and cover my now ringing ears. I don't remember the gun being that loud.

The soup can is still on the stump.

"I missed," Tim says disappointedly.

"Yeah, well, a soup can's a lot smaller than a Havoc. Try again."

"Aren't we going to run out of bullets?" David asks.

"Don't worry about that. We have ammunition." Matthias never looks away from his student. "Timothy, bring the gun back up like I showed ya. Focus down the barrel at your target. Hold steady when ya squeeze the trigger."

BAM!

I was ready for it this time. The can tipped over and rolled off the stump.

"Better, but ya just grazed it," Matthias grunts. "You need to work on holdin' still."

"Can I try?" David asks.

"I'm teachin' Timothy right now," Matthias scolds.

"No, it's all right. He can try." Tim puts the safety on and hands the gun over to Matthias. Tim walks over to me, looking slightly disheartened. "I thought I would be better at this since I can shoot squirrels. But a rifle and a bow are a lot different from a pistol." He plops down on David's empty seat.

David stands confidently next to Matthias.

"I assume you were payin' attention?"

"Yes, sir," David replies.

Matthias hands the gun to David, who is already standing the way Tim was taught. He brings the gun up and aims it at the targets.

"Good, now you'll wanna—" Matthias starts.

BAM!

The can goes flying backward.

David turns slightly to the can on the right. BAM! That can goes flying too.

I look at Matthias, and he seems just as surprised as I am. He's watching David with his eyebrows raised and his mouth slightly open.

David moves again to the next can. BAM! Direct hit. BAM! BAM! All five cans are now lying out in the woods.

David puts the safety on and turns to look at Matthias.

"Helluva good marksman. Let's see whatcha can do from back there."

I glance at Tim, expecting to see him jealous or mad at David, but I couldn't be more wrong. Tim is sitting on the edge of the stump, smiling like a goon with tears sparkling his eyes.

"I knew it!" Tim whispers excitedly.

I watch as Matthias and David put the cans back on the stumps and walk away to about twice the distance as the first round. Tim and I move to a safer spot.

"Do your thing, and I'll help if ya need it." Matthias steps off to the side.

David sets himself back up, takes a few deep breaths, and starts shooting them down, left to right. Every single can is hit dead center. Tim jumps off his seat and shouts in jubilation.

"Impressive." Matthias slaps David on the back.

David beams. "Liv's turn," he says, looking at me.

"Nah, you guys go ahead. I don't want to waste any bullets and have you laugh at me," I say dismissively.

"It's important to know how to use a gun properly. Get over here," Matthias says sternly.

I stand up and give David a death glare.

He winks at me in response.

I can feel my hands shaking from nerves. I really don't want to do this.

"Shouldn't I be closer for my first time?" I ask once I see how far away the cans are.

"Fine. Move up."

Once I'm in place, I start shifting my feet around until I'm standing how David was. Matthias hands me the gun. It feels heavier than I expected. I try to mimic everything David was doing, hoping I can avoid too much scrutiny. Matthias moves my thumbs around into position and takes the safety off for me. His hands feel rough and scratchy from the years of living out in the wild. I wonder if mine will eventually become like that.

"Remember what I told Timothy: aim down the barrel at the target, and squeeze the trigger," he says calmly, removing his hands from mine.

The gun shakes slightly in my hands. I take a couple of deep breaths and try to focus on the can. I let out my breath and squeeze the trigger.

BAM!

The can sits in exactly the same spot.

"Try again," Matthias says.

My heart is pounding so hard in my chest, my hands move slightly with each beat. I focus back on the can and take position. Deep breath in, out, and...

BAM!

The can on the stump next to the one I was aiming at falls over.

"What happened?" I ask.

"What do you mean? You hit the can," Tim pipes in.

"I wasn't aiming for that one. I was aiming for the one right in front of me," I say, embarrassed.

"What're ya lookin' at when ya pull the trigger?" Matthias asks.

"Nothing. I aim and then close my eyes as I pull the trigger..." I mumble.

"You should never close your eyes when shootin' a gun," Matthias scolds. "That's a good way to get somebody killed!"

"Okay, I'm sorry," I say bitterly. "I didn't even want to shoot a gun in the first place. I don't like guns."

"It's important to learn how to defend yourself, guns included. Since ya don't like guns, what weapon do ya like?" Matthias asks.

"I don't know. I didn't exactly train in combat when I was in and out of hospitals."

Matthias turns abruptly. "David, watch 'er while I go grab somethin'. Maybe ya can give 'er a few pointers." Then he turns back to me, "Keep practicin'. And for goodness' sake, keep your eyes open."

I huff as he strides away. David stands behind me and grabs my shoulders, turning me toward the cans.

"I thought for sure you were going to nail them like David did," Tim says contemplatively. "You know, being Rare and all."

"Not helpful," I mutter.

"Here, let me help you," David says. "Stand like this."

I copy his stance.

"Now, bring the gun up, and look through this sight with your right eye, and line it up with this sight on the end of the barrel. Move the gun until you have the sights aimed for a spot right beneath where you plan on shooting. Try not to move the gun when you squeeze the trigger." He steps back and to the left. "Okay, go—no, wait!"

BAM!

"Ow!" I scream as pain rips through my hand. I reflexively drop the gun and grab hold of my throbbing thumb. I can feel the warmth of blood wetting my palm.

David stoops down and picks up the gun, putting the safety on before handing it to Tim. He returns to me and wraps his arm around my shoulder. "I'm so sorry, Liv! I didn't see that your thumbs were wrong until the last second. Have a seat." He leads me to the stump.

"I'll go get Rebecca," Tim offers and runs off.

Hot tears are streaming down my cheeks. I hold my thumb tight, afraid to look. David squats down next to me, rubbing my back.

"Here, let me see it," David says, taking my hands gently in his own.

I squeeze my eyes tight, and little white dots dance beneath my eyelids. I feel lightheaded and take a deep breath, realizing I've been holding it in. I slowly let go of my thumb, and the air stings the wound.

"How bad is it?" I squeak.

"Well, you tore a good chunk of skin out, but I think you'll be okay," he says.

I feel his lips press gently against the back of my hand. I open my eyes and meet his apologetic gaze. I give him a small smile through my tears.

"I'm so sorry, Liv. I should have protected you."

"It's okay, David. But I never want to touch a gun ever again."

"What happened?" a voice says, followed by the crunch of footsteps on the gravel and dried leaves. I look up and see it's the same woman who brought us our breakfast the first morning. There's just something so familiar about her, but I still can't place it.

"The pistol bit her," Tim answers from behind her, breathing hard from running. "I don't like seeing people bleed. I'm gonna go find out what Cass is up to. Hope you feel better soon, Olivia."

"Thanks," I say as he runs off toward our shelter.

Rebecca takes my hand and pours a bottle of water over the wound. The blood washes away, and we see that I have about a one-inch cut on the side of my thumb.

"It's not too bad, but we'll need to get it bandaged tight to stop the bleeding."

She pulls her long black hair up into a high ponytail and sets to work wrapping the wound with gauze from her first-aid kit and then securing it with tape. I watch her as she's doing it, trying to figure out why she seems so familiar. I sense a sadness in her, a sort of sadness that's rooted deep in her pale blue eyes...

Then it hits me like a slap across the face. Pale blue eyes? Long black hair pulled into a ponytail? Cindy!

No, not Cindy...Joselyn. Yes, I can see it now. I stop myself from blurting out the question that is now stuck in my throat. I need to be careful how I word it.

"You're a mom, right?" I ask feebly. I'm such a moron.

"Yeah, why?"

"Oh, I was just wondering who your kids are."

She gives me a strange look but answers, "The twin boys over there." She points to two little boys wrestling on the ground, who look to be about four years old.

"They're cute," I say. Crap, she's almost done. Spit it out, Olivia! "Do you have any other children? Like, maybe ones that aren't here?"

She furrows her eyebrows, snaps the first-aid kit closed, and walks away. Smooth.

"Oh, and, um, thank you!" I say as she storms away.

"What was that about?" David asks me. "Why were you so interested in her kids? You came off as a weirdo."

I huff. "I know. I suddenly realized why she seemed so familiar to me. I think she might be Joselyn's mom. Or at least, related somehow. Her eyes are exactly the same."

"Joselyn? You mean like the girl in the loony bin you told me about?"

"Yup. That's the one," I answer. "But it can't be. Can it? Why would she be out here instead of in the city with her daughter?"

But before David can answer, Matthias comes back, holding a bundle of something wrapped in a blanket. He bends down and sets it on the ground carefully.

"Stand up," Matthias directs.

"What now? You're not going to make me shoot another gun, are you?" I ask worriedly.

I watch as Matthias starts unwrapping the blanket. He stands up, holding a sword. "Here, take this," he commands.

"I can't. I hurt myself on that stupid gun while you were gone," I answer.

"So what? Pain ain't an excuse for laziness. In a fight, you're gonna get hit once in a while, and you gotta learn to push through the pain if you wanna keep your life. Now stand up, and let's see whachya can do with a sword."

I reluctantly stand up and grab the sword hilt with both hands.

Matthias bends down and grabs another sword. He plants himself in front of me and looks at me expectantly. "You ready?"

"Um, no. You don't expect me to fight you with real swords, do you?" I ask, swallowing hard.

"You gotta learn somehow. Now turn sideways so there's less target for me to hit," he commands and waits for me to obey.

I reluctantly shift my body around.

"Good. Right foot forward, sword held up to protect your face, and remember to move your feet."

Matthias makes an exaggerated strike at my head with his sword. I awkwardly swing to block it. Our blades connect with a metallic clang that vibrates through my arms, making me almost lose my grip. He swings his sword around and tries to slice my stomach. I step backward and block it just in time. I take the chance and go for a blow to his neck, but he's too quick for me and knocks the sword out of my hands.

"Pick it up. Quickly," he says.

I bend down to pick up my sword, and he kicks me behind my knee. I topple to the ground and just barely catch myself before face planting.

"What the hell was that for?" I yell.

"Ya never turn your back on your opponent when in a fight. Ya need to be on guard at all times."

Rage from being humiliated is pumping through my veins now. I stand back up and face off with Matthias. I stare into his eyes, hoping he will feel my anger.

"Ya want to study your attacker. Learn his moves. Does he have a tell before he's gonna strike? Maybe he looks where he's gonna hit before swingin'. Maybe he steps to the side when he's gonna swing at your stomach. Ya need to know your enemy."

He goes to swing at my stomach, and I block it confidently. He picks up the pace and tries to strike at my head, but I duck and go for a knee shot. He moves just before I make contact. Something seems to click, and I can block every strike he makes and fluidly make my own attack on him. The clanging of our swords rings loudly throughout the camp.

I continue to concentrate on every move Matthias makes, mirroring much of what he does. Sweat starts dripping down my neck, tickling as it snakes its way along my back.

Block, strike, block, strike.

Our feet are in constant motion as though we are dancing: a warrior's dance. Matthias picks up the pace again, and I find that I'm not even thinking about my moves anymore; I'm just reacting. Adrenaline courses through my body, fueling me until I'm not holding back. A part of me wants to defeat Matthias, even if it means hurting him. As he pushes me harder with his attacks, I become more determined to end this with me as the victor. I crave to take him out.

It barely registers that we are surrounded by people. I'm so focused on what I'm doing, I don't even care that the sweat is dripping into my eyes, and my injured thumb is stinging with pain. I just keep pushing.

As Matthias makes a wide sweeping arc toward my neck, I shift my weight and block upward with all my might. His sword slips out of his hands and goes flying. That's when I make my move to end this. Dropping my sword, I close the gap between us, wrap my arms around his, and hip-toss him, dropping him on the ground. He lands with a thump. Before I know it, my right hand is wrapped around his throat. His eyes are wide with surprise. I quickly let go when I realize what I'm doing.

I hear a catcall from behind me, but I just keep staring at Matthias, afraid he is going to counter-attack and continue the sparring match. Or worse, he is embarrassed that I bested him, and he'll want me out of camp. He reaches his hand up to me, and I cautiously grab it to help him up.

"You're one helluva fighter, Olivia. I think ya could be better than any of us." Matthias gives me a slap on the back.

I smile at the compliment.

"Next time, ya fight David."

"Wait, what?"

"It's clear now that both of you are Rare. Nobody else in camp is, so you're gonna train against each other," he answers, turning abruptly and walking toward his hut.

I look at David, and he winks at me. My stomach drops as I remember when we first got here, and I watched David fight against Henry. He was good.

The group of onlookers starts to disband and head back to whatever it was they were doing. I start when I hear a voice behind my right shoulder.

"That was some fight," Henry says. "I've never known my dad to train one-on-one like that. He always delegates others to fight. There's something special he sees in you." And with that, he turns and stalks away.

David steps up to me and wraps his arm around my shoulder. "Good job, Liv!"

"I don't want to fight you, David," I whisper.

"What are you worried about? It's not a real fight."

"You don't understand. While I was sword fighting with Matthias, I had this sense of pleasure at the thought of besting him. In fact, I needed to win. And I remember seeing that kind of determination on your face when you first fought with Henry."

"True. But I would never hurt you, Liv," he says.

"I'm worried I'm going to hurt you," I say sheepishly.

"Ha! You can't hurt me." David smirks. I punch his arm playfully, and suddenly, I realize just how fatigued I am: my muscles ache from the sword fight, my thumb is throbbing, and my eyelids weigh about ten pounds. Plus, I'm dirty. I need a bath. I head back to our shelter and find Cass sitting on the floor, writing in a notebook.

"Hey, Cass. How come you didn't watch your brother shoot?" I ask, rummaging through my bag, looking for a clean change of clothes.

"I needed some alone time. Sometimes I need to write out my thoughts to keep my head straight." She closes the notebook. She sits there watching me with a hint of annoyance. I must have interrupted something important.

"I need to get cleaned up. What's the best way to get some privacy?"

"If you head up the river a little way, there's a spot where some branches hang down to the water. That's usually where I go."

"Thanks."

"You're welcome. Oh, and keep an eye out for the mukduks. They have a nest in that area, and I watch them whenever I take a bath."

"Mukduks? Will they attack me?"

"Nope, they're not menacing at all. They have shiny blue feathers, long bright orange beaks, and are about the size of an apple. They're so cute!"

"I'll see if I can spot them," I say with a quick smile.

I make it to the place Cass directed me to. The branches hang down low and gently touch the flowing river, creating a rustic wall. As I walk to the shore to lay my clean clothes down, I hear a small cheeping noise. There on a low branch of a pine tree is a nest with three baby birds. Cass wasn't joking; they are adorable. Their bright orange beaks are so long, it's almost comical. They are nearly the length of the bird's body. Even though the sun isn't shining on them directly, their feathers shimmer sky blue.

After watching them for a few moments, I force myself to get back to the task at hand. I lie down in the water and hold on to one of the branches so I don't float away. I shiver as the slow current of cold water flows around my aching body. A hot bath would feel so good right now, but I'll take what I can get. After lying in the water for about a minute, my skin prickles from goosebumps. I get washed up and grab my sweaty clothes to clean while I'm at it. Looking around to make sure nobody will see me, I stand up and walk to the river bank. I get dressed quickly and make my way back to camp, feeling refreshed but frozen.

After I hang my wet clothes up in some tree branches to dry by my shelter, I join David at the firepit. He's sitting alone, hunched over. As I sit down next to him, he turns his face away from me and rubs his eyes with the heels of his hands.

"Are you okay, David? What's wrong?"

"You weren't supposed to see that," he says, sniffing.

I reach my hand out to place on his arm but hesitate. I don't want him to read into my friendly gesture as an act of romance. But he looks so sad, I decide it's worth the risk. I lay my hand on his forearm and relish the warmth seeping into my frozen fingers. He looks at my hand touching his arm and grabs it with both of his hands, squeezing gently.

"What's wrong, David?"

"I miss my parents," he mumbles, staring at the ground.

I place my other frozen hand on top of his.

"I just hate the thought that they might be angry with me."

"What did you write in the letter you left them?"

"Not much. I just explained that I loved them, but I was tired of being a burden. I was going to go find some answers, and I would be back after I found what I was looking for." He sniffs. "I wish they could see me now."

He glances at me sideways, and I notice his eyes have changed. They used to be a muddy brown, but now I see flecks of green and a rich golden color surrounding his pupil. His skin has changed up too. His once ruddy, pimple covered face is now clear and slightly tan. Reddish brown stubble is growing along his jaw, making him look more like a man than a teenager.

"They love you, David. I'm sure they're sad, but I don't think they'll be mad at you. You're seventeen. You'll be an adult in just a couple of months. I think if they saw you, they would be happy that you left the city," I say with a small smile.

He lifts his hands up and kisses the back of my hand that's resting on top. A jolt shoots through me. I'm not sure if it's embarrassment, pleasure, or fear. I pull my hand away and pretend to scratch my nose.

"To be honest," I say, "I miss my mom too. I know we fight, but she's still my mom."

"Maybe we could talk Matthias into a recon mission to bring our parents out here. The city is a poisonous place to live. I would love to get my mom and dad out here where it's healthier."

"I doubt he'll agree to it, but I guess it wouldn't hurt to ask."

We hear the footsteps of someone walking up behind us, and I pull my hand out of David's grasp quickly. Frederick walks around to the fire pit and drops a bundle of sticks on the ground.

"Hey, kids. We're getting supper started. Go see what jobs are needed to be done," he commands as he starts breaking up sticks and putting them in the fire pit.

We stand up, and I grab David's bicep when my legs buckle, and I almost fall. His muscle feels well defined, not big by any means, but solid.

We start heading for the Commons when David grabs my elbow and stops me.

"What—"

"Shh!"

I stand there listening but hear nothing except some faint sounds of conversation coming from one of the buildings. I look at David, and he has his eyes closed and his head cocked to the side.

"Tell me what they're saying," I whisper.

He squeezes his eyes tighter as he concentrates and starts saying, "You need to tell her... No, I don't... If you don't tell her, I will... To hell, ya will. Ya tell her, and I'll take ya out to the woods and make ya disappear... I'm not scared of you, Matthias..." and suddenly, David opens his eyes wide, and his mouth drops open. "Let's get out of here."

"What?"

"Quick! Get into the Commons, now!" David insists, pulling me.

Once we're in the Commons shelter, we see some of the women and their small children getting supper ready. One lady has her son and daughter peeling carrots as she chops up miscellaneous vegetables. Another woman has her little one help count out silverware. Rebecca watches her twin boys take turns stirring a big pot of boiling water. One of them scoops the spoon up and almost spills what looks like potatoes on his brother. She snatches the spoon away and scolds him. He furrows his brow at her but then lowers his chin to his chest at the reprimand, his bottom lip sticking out.

"Anything we can do to help, ma'am?" David asks the lady cutting vegetables, with a slight tremble in his voice.

"Don't bother with the ma'am stuff. My name's Caroline, but you can call me Carol. Those two women over there are Rebecca and Suzanne."

David and I look to where she's pointing, and both women give little waves in response to their names.

"Why don't you grab a bag of barley from the back corner and take it over to Rebecca?" She points with the knife.

Her two kids look up at us with shiny, curious eyes. I smile at them, but they just go back to peeling the carrots. I follow David to the back corner.

"What did you hear out there, David?" I whisper.

"Later, Liv. For now, let's just be as helpful as we can."

David heaves a large white bag labeled "barley" up onto his shoulder and carries it over to Rebecca.

"You can set it down right there," Rebecca directs.

David drops the bag gently. "Anything else we can help you ladies with?"

"Umm, it looks like we pretty much got things covered in here, thanks."

As David and I go to leave the Commons, Alexandrine storms in, holding a wet cloth on her face. The murderous look she's wearing makes the hairs on the back of my neck stand up. She looks at me, and her expression darkens even more. She turns to Rebecca and lifts the cloth off her face, saying something indistinguishable. David tugs on my shoulder and leads me out of the shelter and down to the river. The early evening sun is sparkling off the water, and a cool breeze picks up, giving me chills once again.

"So, are you going to tell me what's going on?" I ask.

"I wasn't a hundred percent sure I heard what I thought I did, but Alexandrine just confirmed it," David says. "He hit her."

"What? Are you serious? Is that why she had a cloth over her eye?"

"I think so," David says.

"So, Matthias is a woman beater? Maybe we shouldn't stay here."

"Maybe we shouldn't jump to conclusions. Perhaps she was trying to hit him first, and he was just defending himself—" David starts.

"What does that matter? He shouldn't be hitting women."

"Are you saying that a man should take a beating from a woman anytime, no questions asked, but a woman should never have a hand laid on her, even if she's the one who started attacking first? What if she pulled a knife on him? Or a gun?" David asks, eyebrows furrowed in angry confusion.

"I guess there are times when it would seem appropriate," I concede. "Do you think she attacked Matthias first? From what you were hearing, it sounded like Matthias was threatening *her*. Who do you think she was threatening to tell his secret to?"

"I guess we'll never know because I'm certainly not going to ask, and neither should you. I want you to watch yourself around him, Liv," David says, staring directly into my eyes.

I nod my head in response. The chilly air seems to have settled all the way in my bones now. I start shivering uncontrollably.

"Let's get you back up by the fire," David says.

I try to speak, but my teeth chatter instead. We shuffle our way back to camp. Frederick and another man are sitting next to the firepit, laughing.

"Is it all right if we sit by the fire?" David asks. "Olivia is frozen and needs to warm up."

"Help yourself," Frederick says. "Not sure if you've been introduced to my brother, yet. This is Markos."

I never would have guessed they were brothers by looking at them. Frederick reminds me of a Viking: bald, burly, and has a large red beard. Whereas, Markos is about half his size in body mass and has a short pointed red beard on his narrow chin. His eyes are sky blue, but Frederick's are dark brown. Looking at him closer, I can see the resemblance in their noses, broad with large nostrils. It fits Frederick's face but looks way too big on Markos.

"Hi, I'm Olivia," I say, lamely holding out my hand.

Frederick takes it in both of his and bows his head. "Brr, he wasn't kidding. You're like ice. Here let me move a stump closer to the pit so you can get warmed up," he offers.

"Thanks. Sorry for interrupting your conversation," I say, holding my hands out toward the fire.

"Not at all. Markos was just telling me that Alexandrine went and got herself in trouble again. She needs to learn when to quit, that one," Frederick says with a chuckle.

"Does she get hit a lot or something?" David asks.

"Matthias has to put her in her place from time to time."

Scandalized, my jaw drops, and I glare at Frederick.

"Look. She's a firecracker, that woman. Maybe if she would stop trying to kick us guys in the balls every time she disagrees with us, we wouldn't have to resort to hitting. She gets real physical real fast, and it takes a good lickin' to get her to stop."

"Why is she so violent and angry?" I ask.

"Well," Frederick says, shifting around uncomfortably, "She was 'attacked' by one of Turk's soldiers, if you get my drift. She ended up getting pregnant, and when the kid turned out to be a Rare, they took it away from her. If anyone has grounds to hate the president, the Coalition, or anyone who works for them, it's her."

My heart skips a beat as though it's breaking for her. How terrible! I guess I can see why she hates me now. I was quick to throw my mom's connections to the government at them when I thought they were going to kick us out. Not my finest moment.

A memory of the conversation I overheard after Matthias decided to let us stay slips into my brain. These guys seem pretty forthcoming with information; maybe they'll answer my question.

"I overheard Matthias and Alexandrine arguing once, and she said something about kidnapping. What was she talking about?"

"Well, first of all, kidnapping is a pretty strong word." Frederick shakes his head. "Leave it to her to make a rescue sound negative."

"Okay, what happened?"

"On one of the recon missions, Matthias came across Alexandrine fighting with a coalition guard. She had pulled a knife out and stabbed the guy in the neck while screaming, 'Give me back my daughter!' Matthias was drawn by her hatred of the Coalition and knew she was done for if he left her there in the city. So, he approached her while she continued to stab the guard and decided it would be safer for him and Henry to bring her out here unconscious."

"Once in camp, it took a very long time to convince her that it was for her own good; that had they left her in the city, she would either be in jail or dead," Markos adds.

"I can hear you idiots talking about me," Alexandrine says, startling us all. I was so involved in their story, I didn't notice her walking up behind them. She abandoned her wet cloth, and I can see the dark bruise forming around her right eye. "What do you think you're doing telling *her* information about me?"

"Sorry, Alex. We didn't mean nothing by it," Frederick says soberly.

"I want you guys to get lost. I'd like to have a little girl talk with Miss Priss here."

Markos and Frederick obey immediately. David stays where he is.

"Did I not make myself clear, boy? Get. Lost."

"I'm not leaving you here with Olivia alone. I've seen the way you look at her."

"If I were going to kill her, I would've done it already," she admits, stone-faced. "Now, give us a minute."

David stands up, gives me a worried look, and heads to our shelter.

My knees are visibly shaking, so I clench them together. We both watch David until he makes it inside. Then she turns to me with an ugly scowl on her otherwise beautiful face.

"I don't like you. I probably never will. I knew immediately who you were when you stepped foot into this camp." She points her finger at my chest.

"H-h-how do you know who I am?" I squeak.

"Just looking at you I could see it...the family resemblance."

"L-look, Alexandrine. I'm not my mother. I never—"

"I'm not talking about your filthy government-loving mother," she pauses, giving me a significant look. When I don't respond, she huffs, "Are you really this dense?"

My face grows hot as the rage starts bubbling up in my chest again. I'm getting real sick of her dancing around what she wants to say.

"Family resemblance? Are you going to tell me what you're talking about, or are you going to keep playing with me?" I ask, losing my temper.

"You moron," she mumbles to herself. Then looking straight into my eyes, she says, "Matthias is your dad."

30

"Bull." I shake my head at her. "That's impossible. My mom said my dad died in the war."

"Your mother is a liar," she spits out.

I continue to shake my head, glaring at her.

"Why do you think Matthias decided to let you stay here when you mentioned your mom's name? Did you actually think he was worried about Turk's disposable heroes coming out to get us?"

My head is buzzing. What is she trying to do? Why would she make this up? I'm not sure what to say to her, so I just keep staring in disbelief, hoping she shouts, "Gotcha!" or something. She stares right back.

"Whatever," she huffs. "I told Matthias I was going to tell you if he didn't. Now you know. Secret's out. Do us both a favor, and stay away from me. This will be the one and only civil conversation we have."

She stands up and stomps back to her shelter. I watch her, shell-shocked. What am I supposed to do with this? If it's true, if Matthias really *is* my dad, then he better have a really good explanation for abandoning my mom and me. I stare at the fire as a mixed concoction of emotions is saturating my mind. I'm feeling so many things right now, my stomach starts to cramp, and I'm afraid I'm going to throw up. I'm relieved when David has a seat next to me by the fire.

I reach out and grab his hand to stabilize myself. I feel as though everything I thought I knew is suddenly fake. At least, David is a constant I can depend on. He squeezes my hand gently in return.

"She just told me Matthias is my dad," I whisper, still in shock at the thought. Tears are stinging my eyes.

"I heard," David says with a look of pity. "Why wouldn't he have told you as soon as he figured out who you are? And why would your mother lie?"

"Good questions. If you find out the answers, let me know," I snap. "Sorry."

"It's okay. I'm frustrated, and it has nothing to do with me," he says. "Are you going to confront Matthias with this? He didn't want Alexandrine to tell. He might get mad."

"I don't know." I cover my face with my hands. "I don't even know if it's true. But my mom has kept a lot of secrets from me, so I wouldn't be surprised if this is just another one."

My mind is filled with so many questions, I feel I could scream from frustration. Just as I'm about to lose it, David puts an arm around my shoulder. That calms my mind momentarily, at least, stops me from releasing the scream that is hanging in the back of my throat. We sit quietly by the fire, watching the flames dance and the smoke swirl. A slight wind blows and carries the smoke right in my face, stinging my eyes. I close them, waiting for it to move, but it's getting hard to breathe. The all too familiar feelings of my airways constricting forces me to get up. I soon find myself pacing, agitated once more.

How could he? How could Matthias have left my mom and me? How could he not tell me that he was my dad as soon as he found out? If I tell him that I know, will he be willing to rescue my mom and David's family? Will he be willing to right the wrong he made so many years ago? What if he's not my dad? What if Alexandrine is messing with me?

Before I know it, I'm marching toward Matthias's hut. Blood is pounding in my ears as I lose myself to rage. David calls my name, but I keep walking. Like an unfinished melody, this needs to be resolved.

"Is it true?" I ask, barging into his hut.

He spins around as he's pulling a shirt on. Before he tugs it down all the way, I see a number of scars etched across his well-defined abdomen.

"Ever heard of knockin'?" he growls.

"Is it true? Are you my father?" I ask loudly. My face is radiating heat from embarrassment and anger.

His face hardens, and he looks like he's about to start yelling, but he keeps his composure. "Yes. As soon as ya said your mother's name, I knew it."

My heart drops into my stomach. I liked it better when I thought Alexandrine might be lying to me. This is so much worse. Tears flood my eyes as my mind tries to make sense of this information.

"How could you? Why did you abandon my mom and me?" I ask as a lone tear runs down my cheek.

"I'm sorry, Olivia. I never meant to hurt ya. I never meant for your life to be hard like it was," he says, reaching out to touch my arm.

I reflexively pull away.

He makes his hand into a fist and drops it to his side. His face hardens a bit more as he looks into my eyes. "Look, I had to do what I had to do. The Coalition was gettin' too damn powerful. They took away our guns; they took away our rights; they took away our freedom; hell, they even took away the sun! It didn't sit right with me. Any of it. Every day I stayed there, it kept eatin' away at me 'til I thought I was gonna snap and kill someone. I knew we had to get out, but your mother was in too deep with the government."

He drops his gaze and starts pacing his hut. "I pleaded with her to come with us, but she refused. Stubborn woman! So, one day while she was at work, I packed up what I could carry and brought Henry and my dad out here to survive. It killed me to leave your mother pregnant and alone, but I knew she would never be swayed."

"Why didn't you come back for me?" I ask. "Didn't you care about my existence?"

"Of course, I cared. But it was too dangerous to go back and take ya away from your mother."

"Why? If you're not afraid of Turk's soldiers, why would you be afraid of Mom?"

"She's more powerful than ya think."

I give him a cocked eyebrow. "Is she a Rare too?"

"I'm not talkin' physically. She's Turk's right-hand woman."

"No way! What a bunch of bull!" I yell, my anger rising again. "First, I find out that you're my father, but you were keeping it a secret. And now you're trying to feed me lies about my mother to turn me against her? You're a real piece of work, aren't you?"

"Listen here!" Matthias steps closer to me, and for a moment, I'm afraid he's going to hit me, but I stand my ground. "I didn't tell ya I was your father because I was scared. That's right. Matthias, the fearless leader of a rebellion group, was afraid of a teenage girl. I knew I'd made a mistake, not comin' to get ya, and I was afraid of how you'd react. I figured it was better for me to just play the role of father figure as your leader. I didn't want your judgment and hatred, knowin' I'd abandoned ya."

A fresh tear leaks down my cheek. My thoughts are screaming inside my head. I've wanted to know who my father is for so long, and now I stand in front of a man I hardly know, who's claiming to be him. Things were easier when I thought my father was dead. At least, his absence from my life was for a reason. This is just painful. He's right about the judgment and hatred part. I feel nothing good toward the man in front of me.

"You're wrong about Mom," I growl. "She likes her secrets, but she's definitely not 'Turk's right-hand woman.'"

"What makes ya so sure? Ya told me yourself she never lets on what she does at the government building."

"I know my mother."

"Do ya?" He asks with a scowl. "I knew 'er once too. At least, I thought I did. Her love of secrets, long hours at work, and outright refusal to leave proved otherwise."

Confusion is taking over my senses. I don't want to believe a word Matthias says to me, but he has a point about me not really knowing what my mother does.

"Fine! Then, let's go rescue her now! Maybe if she left the city, she could change too."

"She's not a Rare. She won't change out here." Matthias shakes his head at me.

"Well, maybe knowing that you and Henry are alive will make a difference," I say, grasping at straws.

I don't know why I want my mom out here so badly. We fight all the time, but maybe we could patch things up and be a real family someday. Maybe.

"No! Now, I want ya to drop it!"

I hear a call from outside, "Supper's ready!"

I turn to storm out of his hut, but he steps in front of me. Pointing a finger at my chest, he says, "Nobody needs to know that you're my daughter. Not yet. Keep it to yourself for now."

"What...are you ashamed?" I ask, glaring.

"Not at all. But it might ruffle a few feathers from some other members of the group. Alexandrine knew that. Just keep quiet 'bout it, and I'll break the news on my own terms." And with that, he allows me to go.

I'm seething with anger, so I choose to go to my shelter instead of joining everyone for supper. I walk past Saul and take another glance at what he's carving. I manage to get a better look at the symbols, and suddenly, I know where I've seen them before.

My necklace.

The box marked "Dad's stuff" wasn't my mom's dad, but my dad's dad. Matthias's dad, Saul. It must have belonged to him. I wish I would have brought the necklace with me. It seems like it was important to him since he keeps carving these symbols. I wonder what they mean. Maybe I'll ask him or Matthias someday, but not right now. I'm too angry.

I march back into my shelter and flop down on my bed. After ten minutes of sitting there, trying to figure out what I'm going to do, David comes in carrying a plate of food for me. I grab it from him and eat quickly, hardly tasting anything.

"So, it's true, huh?" David asks, watching me stuff my face.

I nod my head in response. I swallow hard, almost choking on the mouthful of potatoes.

"I don't know who I'm madder at: my mom or Matthias."

David gives me a sympathetic look and has a seat next to me. "I know this situation sucks, but..." he grows quiet, hesitating to finish what he was going to say.

"But, what?"

"You just found out your Dad's alive! And you have a brother and a grandpa! You should be happier than this. Sure, he didn't tell you right away, but it was probably a shock that you suddenly showed up out of nowhere, and he didn't know what to do."

"He abandoned me! He took my brother and left me to live with my mom alone! I spent all these years thinking my father was so brave to go fight in a war and that he died with respect. Instead, I find out he was more of a coward than anything!" I yell.

"I blame your mom," David says matter-of-factly.

"What?" I ask incredulously.

"Your mom refused to go with your dad when trouble started. Then she lied to you and told you that your father was dead. She could have said he left her and that you had a brother."

I stay quiet, staring moodily at the opposite wall. He's right. I'm back to not knowing who I'm more pissed at. I wish my mom were out here so I could lay into her.

"I'm sorry. I don't mean to make things harder for you," he says calmly. "Here, let me take your plate. I'll leave you alone so you can think about things. If you need me, just let me know."

As I sit, thinking about how screwed up everything is, an unrelenting desire to confront my mom has taken hold of my mind. I need to talk to her. I need answers. I just hope I can sneak out without David noticing. And maybe I can grab the necklace while I'm back.

31

I decide the best time to leave would be in the middle of the night. I pretend to be asleep when David comes in to check on me. I hear him kneel next to me and whisper, "I'm sorry," as he runs his hand over my hair a couple of times. It takes everything I have in me to not move a muscle. He quietly stands back up and leaves the shelter.

I must doze off at some point, though, because now everyone is back in the shelter sleeping, and it's pitch-black outside. I sit up, cringing at every leaf that rustles under my weight. I grab my blanket and the sweatshirt I use as a pillow and stuff them in my bag. I sneak out the door, taking a look at David before I go. I know he's going to be mad at me, but I need to do this. If I told him I was going, he would only try to talk me out of it or insist that he goes with me. I can't risk his life by going back into the city. He's safer here.

I peek my head out of the shelter to make sure nobody is sitting by the fire. I blink a couple of times when I realize I am seeing perfectly in the darkness without any source of light helping me. It must be another benefit of my Rare abilities. I smile at how far I've come since stepping foot into the woods. I can breathe easier, see better, and even though we haven't been out here that long, I've actually started putting some meat on my bones. At least, something is going my way. I head to the Commons to see if I can find some food to take with me for the journey.

I grab as many apples as I can as well as some carrots and a few strips of dried meat. I think I still have a couple bottles of water at the bottom of my bag I never finished before Henry and Matthias found us, so I should be okay there. I spot a big filet knife in its sheath lying on the table and take that too. I'd rather have a sword, but Matthias keeps those in his hut.

Once my bag is full, I head to the river. I'm going to have to walk on the opposite side of it for a while to avoid the two people who are on guard duty for the night. Since Matthias believes the Havoc are afraid of water, they don't keep watch over the river, so this is the safest way out. I pull my socks and shoes off, stuff my socks in my pocket, and tie the shoelaces together so I can sling them over my shoulder to cross the river.

The water is frigid. I'm glad I don't have to walk in it for long. Once I'm on the other side, I sneak along the river bank, making as little noise as possible. I'm sure the water current would cover any sounds my feet make, but I can't take the risk. Once I'm confident I've made it far enough out of camp, I cross back over the river and find a fallen log to sit on so I can get my socks and shoes back on my frozen feet.

I keep going downriver, thinking it has to lead to the ocean by the city. I'll climb a tree once the sun starts to come up and get my directions right. I need to keep moving, and this seems like the logical choice.

Every owl hoot and cricket chirp draws my attention, and fear begins to needle its way into my brain. I listen closely for any signs of Havoc, praying hard I don't run into one. I feel so lonely and exposed without David by my side. Perhaps I should have brought him with me. He might have agreed to it if I explained how important it was for me to talk to my mom. I'm pretty sure David would do anything for me if I asked him, but I can't put him in danger just because I'm too chicken to be alone. This is for his own good.

I'm slowing down as I continually step over fallen logs and underbrush. After a couple of hours of plodding along, I sit down for a break. The night sounds are giving way to the sweet sounds of morning. Birds have become alert and are singing in the trees. The darkness is fading away to the soft light of dawn. I need to find a tree that's tall enough to allow me to see the city.

I climb a tree I think is tall enough, but once I make it to the top, I can't see past the other trees in the forest. I'll need to keep searching. I walk downriver until the sun is up fully, and the air is growing hot. I spot an oak that towers over all the surrounding trees. The problem is, the branches are about twelve feet from the ground. How am I going to reach those to climb?

Next to the giant oak is a smaller maple with branches closer to the ground. I pull myself up and climb until I'm level with the oak's branches. Taking a deep breath, I let go of the maple tree and jump to the oak. I manage to grab hold of a branch, but the rough bark skins the palms of my hands. Now my hands and injured thumb pulse with pain. I almost let go, but I keep my grip and swing my leg up on the branch. I straddle it and lean my back against the tree so I can take a look at my hands. Huge chunks of skin are peeled off, and blood has made its way to the surface. They sting bad enough to make my eyes water. That was a stupid thing to do!

I carefully pull my bag off my back and search for something I can use to wrap my hands with. I find a clean pair of socks and tie them around my injured palms, pulling the other end with my teeth. It's going to be much harder to climb the tree now, but I have to do it. I secure my bag on my back and carefully climb the rest of the way up. The socks make it harder to grip the branches, but I manage to make it to the top. The sun shines down on me with blistering intensity. I hold on to the tree with one hand and use the other to shield my eyes from the blinding sun.

I can see that the river does, in fact, flow to the ocean, but it's miles away from the part of the city I'm trying to get to. I need to make my way to the far side where the subway tunnels are. Matthias never gave me an exact location of the entrance he uses, but I know the general area I need to be. By the looks of things, I still have at least a day and a half of hiking to go. I'm already feeling exhausted from hiking all night after such a short nap in the evening. I'll try to make it a little farther, but I'll need to find a place to camp out for the night soon.

I methodically work my way down the tree, supporting most of my weight with my legs to save my hands. Once I'm on the ground, I head east away from the river. I hate the idea of leaving the safety the river can give me from the Havoc, but I need to keep going.

After a few more hours of walking, I can barely lift my legs anymore. I come across a rock outcropping with a hole at the base big enough for me to lie down in. I'll be guarded on three sides, so it seems as good of a shelter as any. It's only early afternoon, but I can't walk anymore. I squeeze in the hole and stuff my bag in the opening I crawled through so I can at least feel somewhat hidden. Even though I'm hot, I cover up with my blanket out of habit and fall asleep almost instantly.

I snap awake when I hear a snuffling sound right outside. It's dark now, and I can't see anything other than the rock walls of my hiding spot. I don't know whether I should lie still and hope whatever it is goes away or try to sneak my way out. Not knowing exactly where it is makes the sneaking out part pretty much impossible.

A branch snaps not far from my bag, and I pray hard that it's not a Havoc. Adrenaline is coursing through my veins, and I try to keep my breathing shallow. I grab hold of my bag and slowly slide it to the side so I can get a glimpse of what's out there. I'm greeted with two glowing eyes only a foot away, and I stifle a scream with my sock wrapped hand. I lie still, gathering up the courage to look again. When I take a closer look, I realize it's far too small to be a Havoc. This creature is black with a stripe of white down its back and is about the size of a cat. It's sniffing at my bag and I realize it probably smells the food I brought.

I slowly spin my bag and take out an apple. I awkwardly toss it out past the critter, hoping he will chase after it. He takes the bait and follows the apple. I crawl out and stuff my blanket in my bag, watching the direction of the animal. Now that I can get a better look at the creature, I realize it's kind of cute. It has such a bushy tail, I almost want to pet it, but I know better than to touch a wild animal. As I swing my bag up to slide onto my arms, the animal gets spooked by my sudden motion. It lifts its tail, sprays something at me before running away, and I find myself covered in the most foul-smelling stench I have ever experienced.

I cover my mouth and nose with my hand, but that doesn't help one bit. My eyes are watering, and I fall to the ground, retching. I stand back up and try to run, hoping it didn't get too much on me, but the smell doesn't go away. I stop and start ripping my clothes off, anything to get away from this horrifying odor. Once stripped, I realize it's on my skin too. I start to cry at the ridiculousness of my situation. I'm standing alone in the middle of the forest at night, completely naked, and I smell horrendous. I need to find a way to wash this off.

I'm miles away from the river now, and I have no idea if there is any other water source to bathe in. I take the bottle of shampoo out of my bag and start rubbing it vigorously all over. My flowery shampoo does nothing to mask the stink. I keep scrubbing, scratching with my fingernails until my skin turns red and raw. I use a bottle of water as sparingly as I can since I will still need drinking water on this quest. The smell continues to permeate off my skin strongly. I yell out in frustration but clap my hand over my mouth when I hear it echoing throughout the woods. I'm going to have to just keep going and hope this stench fades away quickly.

I grab a clean outfit and get dressed. I decide to ditch the stinky clothes I tore off. I don't need them to make everything else in my bag reek.

Once I start walking again, I think about David and what he's doing. I wonder if he'll come out to try to find me. I hope not. I probably should have left a note or something. Too late now. I walk until the sun starts to show itself through the trees. I made it through another night alive. I go to yawn, and I realize I don't smell as bad as I did when I first got sprayed. Either that, or I'm getting used to it.

I hike for a few more hours, stopping to stretch every now and then. I'm not used to getting this much exercise, and my hips are aching with each step I take. Either I've pulled a muscle, or I'm not getting enough water. Probably both. But I need to keep going. If I continue walking, I should be able to make it back to the fence by nightfall.

By mid-afternoon, I'm exhausted. I wanted to ration my water so I would have enough to make it all the way home, but I couldn't help myself. I finished the last bottle about an hour ago when I felt like I was about to pass out from the heat. I would give anything to have a drink. I munch on an apple, sucking at the flesh to quench my thirst with as much juice as I can get. I can't keep going on in this heat. I'm going to have to make camp until it gets dark and cools off.

I look around for anything that might work to hide me. There aren't any rock outcroppings or caves, but I do find some underbrush that could work. I push my way through some thorns and branches until I'm in the center of it. I crouch down, and I can't see anything. This is as good a spot as any. Taking my knife out, I hack away at the plants to make a place big enough to lie down in. It's not going to be overly comfortable, but it'll do. I stretch out on my back, using my bag as a pillow. I hope I'm almost back to the city. I'm not sure how much longer I will make it without water.

I toss and turn, trying hard to adjust to a spot that will allow me to sleep. This is miserable! I don't know how I can be so physically and mentally tired, and yet I can't fall asleep. I lie there for hours, getting more and more angry. As the sky starts to darken, I can't take it anymore. I feel more sore and tired than when I started. I curse loudly as I grab my bag and start marching out of my hiding spot.

A low growl stops me dead in my tracks. I'm not quite all the way out of the bushes, so I crouch down as quietly as I can. My hands are shaking as I pull my bag in front of me and try to find my knife. I don't know what direction the sound came from. I slow my breathing so I can listen. I hear it again off to the right, not far from where I'm hiding.

I remember seeing a guy on one of the survivor shows make himself as big as he could when a black bear crossed his path. It scared the bear away, and he never had to hurt it. I weigh my options. I could try to do what the guy did and make myself as large and noisy as I can, but at a whopping height of five-foot-one, I doubt

I would ever scare whatever is out there. More like annoy it enough to make it want to eat me as an hors d'oeuvre. Or I could continue to cower here in the bushes and hope it passes by quickly. I decide to continue crouching and hope it passes.

After a minute or two of sitting back on my heels, listening to where the creature went, my calf cramps so hard, I cry out in pain before I can stop myself. Out of reflex, I stand up and stretch my muscle out. I look over to where I last heard a noise, and there stands a Havoc about twenty feet away, staring at me.

32

I stand as still as I can, watching the Havoc slowly stalk closer to me, never taking its eyes off me. I want to run, but I don't think I could move even if I tried. Matthias isn't here to save me this time. I'm going to die, and I never said goodbye to David or to my mother. I inhale a shuddering breath, and a tear leaks down my cheek. My entire body trembles as the Havoc is now only a few steps away, moving slowly as though he's hunting me.

I can't take the suspense. I wish he would just get this over with quickly. Hopefully, he bites my throat and kills me instantly. I can't even fathom being eaten one leg or arm at a time—or worse yet, starting at my stomach and eating my insides first. I whimper as it takes the last step to close the distance between us. It stretches its neck out and sniffs at my pants. Exhaling hard and shaking its head as though it's trying to fend off a pesky bee, it turns around and trots away.

I collapse on the ground, crying tears of relief. I have never been more happy to smell bad in my life. I sit in the bushes for a moment, catching my breath and thinking about what just happened. It was looking right at me, so how come it didn't attack me? Perhaps it can only see movement. Maybe it saw me stand up, but since I stood still, it couldn't see me anymore? I guess it doesn't really matter. What matters is I'm alive.

I carefully stand up, looking around for any more threats. The coast is clear, so I step out of the underbrush, moving as quietly as I can. My calf is still hurting from the cramp, but I limp away from the area quickly. I've got to keep going while it's cool out.

Every single muscle and injury aches. I'm beginning to wish I had just stayed with David at camp, but the anger I have toward my mother's deceit drives me on. She has a lot of explaining to do. I hope she doesn't try to stick me in the looney bin for running off. I'll fight her tooth and nail to never enter that cursed place again. And now that I'm stronger and know how to handle myself, I bet I could win a fight with her if she tried to do that.

As I continue on, one thing becomes clear: I need water. My brain is sluggish. It's hard for me to even finish a thought. My muscles are shaky, weak, and keep cramping up. My tongue feels like sandpaper, and my lips have started to crack. I haven't peed since yesterday morning, and when I did, it was dark brown. If I don't get water soon, I think I'm going to die.

I keep trudging forward, one step at a time. I eat the last of my apples slowly, allowing the fruit to stay in my mouth longer than normal in hopes that I can produce saliva and alleviate this dryness, but there's no saliva left. I want to cry, but I would hate to waste any remaining fluid on tears.

As I try to step over a fallen tree, I trip and land on the ground. This is it. This is how I'm going to die. I think it would have been better to have been eaten by that

Havoc. At least being eaten would have been quick. This is torture. I don't have enough energy to sit up, so I just lie here with my face pressed in the dirt.

I close my eyes. Once more, I find myself wishing for the sweet release of death. Anything to bring an end to this pain. And that's when I feel it. A drip. I open my eyes, wondering if I was just imagining it. And then another one hits me on the cheek. I hear the soft patter of raindrops falling on the leaves above me and all over the ground. I start to panic and force myself to get up, every muscle protesting and shaking from use. I need to find shelter somewhere away from the rain, or my flesh is going to melt off. A drop lands on my arm. I go to brush it away, but out of morbid curiosity, I lift my arm up to eye level to see if I can watch it melt through my skin.

Nothing.

The rain starts to pick up, and soon, drops are falling steadily through the trees. I hold my hand out in front of me and feel the rain tickle my skin as it lands. It doesn't hurt. In fact, it feels quite refreshing. I tilt my head back and open my mouth. A few drops fall on my tongue, and it tastes sweet, but there isn't enough landing in my mouth to quench my thirst. I look through my bag to see what I can use to catch some rain with. Other than the empty water bottles, I have no containers. The water bottles' openings are too small to catch anything.

It starts to pour, and I'm desperate to collect some of it to drink. I leave the bottles open on the ground anyway, but the fat raindrops keep knocking them over. I get frustrated as I keep standing them back up just to have them fall again. Soon, rain is dripping off my hair into my face, and my clothes are soaked. Then I get an idea.

I can suck the water out of my clothes.

It probably won't taste good, but water is water. I start sucking on my shirt, and I'm able to get a little out. I need more. I pull out every piece of fabric I brought with me and lay it out in the rain. I grab the bottom of my shirt and hold it out to catch more. Once my shirt's soaked, I bring it up to my mouth and suck every last drop out of it. I'm rewarded with two swallows of water. I grab my sweatshirt, which is lying in front of me, and draw every bit of moisture I can out of it as well. My head is starting to clear up a bit as I slowly rehydrate myself.

The rain continues to fall, and I keep drinking as much as I can, laying the pieces of clothing back out in the rain so they can get wet again. My muscles stop shaking, and my strength is returning to me. I've never really had much experience with God, but I lift my head up to the sky and thank him, anyway.

I realize that I should probably start trying to fill some of my bottles so I can have some water to keep going. I shouldn't be that far away from the city by now, but I don't ever want to be without something to drink again. I hold a bottle between my legs, and wring little sections of material over it, trying hard to not spill any. Once that shirt is wrung out, I lay it back down and grab another one. After I've gone through all the clothes and the blanket I have laid out, I start over again.

When the rain finally stops, I have two water bottles filled. I can't wring any more out of the material, so I suck out any moisture that might still be there and then pack it all back in my bag. I'm ready to find that subway tunnel and get back to my apartment.

The sun starts to come out once again, and I head in the direction of the sunrise. I walk at a slower pace, trying to keep myself from sweating as best I can. Two bottles of water are not going to last me long with how hot it has been lately. I'm so focused on watching the ground for tree roots sticking up or rocks that I might trip on that it takes me a little while to realize that it's starting to get foggy. I look up and see that the city fence is only about ten yards to the right from where I'm walking. I made it! I quickly get myself back into the shelter of the woods. I don't want a guard to see me. I must have passed where David and I came out of the city a while ago because where we exited, we went straight into the wilderness. Here, I'm finding city ruins I've never seen before.

Keeping a close eye on the city fence, I search for any sign of the subway tunnel. I have no idea what I'm looking for, though. I pick my way through overgrown piles of rubble from the war-strewn remains that once were part of the city. Half-erect buildings still stand, being swallowed up by nature. I pass between rows of dilapidated structures, assuming I must be walking on what was once a street. Now, it's covered in layers of dead leaves and dirt that plants have used to take root.

I get an eerie feeling from all this wreckage. People once lived here. Moms, dads, sons, daughters, brothers, sisters. It's surreal to think humans used to occupy this space. I pass by cars now rusted and covered in vines; a bicycle half-buried in bricks from a broken building; a baby stroller, turned onto its side, covered in dirt and mildew. I close my eyes and picture what this city must have been like filled with people. People driving, walking to work, going to school, hanging out with friends and family, having dinners and parties, shopping, kissing, fighting, yelling, laughing.

A tear rolls down my cheek as I think of the fear and loss that happened during the war. Loved ones being torn apart by death and destruction. Children crying for their mommies and daddies as bombs dropped on the city. People's homes being destroyed—all because of intolerance. I stand here now, weeping for the lives of the people who just wanted to give the Rare a chance at life, who wanted to give people like *me* a chance at being accepted.

I wipe my tears away and get ahold of myself. Until now, I have never truly thought about what sacrifice really is. What it means to stand up against the world to do what is right. I will never be able to thank the men and women who tried to fight for good. I hope one day, I will be able to repay them in some small way, but for now, I need to find that tunnel.

I walk up and down streets, completely guessing at where I should be going. Even though the fog here isn't nearly as thick as it is in the livable part of the city, it still makes me feel disoriented at times, losing track of where I've been and making me walk in circles. After at least an hour of winding my way around the fallen city, I finally find something promising: a stairway that leads down into the ground. Matthias said the subways ran under the city, so I think this might be it. A sign hangs above the stairway, but it's unreadable. I'm just going to have to take the chance.

I cautiously work my way down the stairs, worried about what I might find down here. I make it to the bottom and stand still while I allow my eyes to adjust to the darkness. The air is stale down here, and the dust my shoes kick up threatens to choke me. I look around in the dim light and see an area that looks like little gates. I walk over to them and try to lift one, but it won't budge, so I climb under it. Standing up and brushing the dirt off my jeans, I keep walking farther away from the stairs I came down. I sure hope I'm going the right way.

The walkway I was on suddenly disappears, and I stop just in time. Crouching down, I see the tiniest glint shine off something metal in the hole. I carefully lower myself down off the sidewalk. Running my hands along the metal that was on the ground, I feel that it's a long narrow strip. They told me subways were like underground trains. I bet this is the track! Now, which way should I go? I pull my bag off my back and grab the little waterproof capsule of matches I brought with me. I use the patch of sandpaper that's glued to the outside to light it. Holding it down by the railway, I search for footprints that Matthias would have left if this is the subway he uses. It takes three different matches, but I finally find what I'm looking for. I set off down the tunnel and wonder just how much longer this is going to take.

I continue down the dark track, occasionally stumbling on fallen bricks and rocks. The air down here is musty and unmoving. I imagine this must be what a tomb feels like. The thought makes me shiver. A constant drip echoes down the tunnel, putting my nerves on edge. I begin to feel panicked as the darkness closes in on me. I'm not sure how long I've been walking down here, but it feels like an eternity. Every step I take just leads to more blackness. I start to question whether I'm even moving at all. Are my eyes even open? I hold my hand up in front of my face, and I can't see anything. I was able to see in the darkness at camp, but down here, it's like I'm blind.

Just breathe, Olivia.

I stop walking for a moment and take a deep calming breath before a panic attack hits me. This would not be a good place to have one. I allow myself to drink a mouthful of water, to clear my head and some dust out of my throat.

Once my bag is settled back on my shoulders, I trudge on in hopes of finding the exit soon. Up ahead, I see a tiny pinprick of dim light come to life. It moves upward, holds still momentarily, and then is shaken out. I move cautiously, taking care to make as little noise as possible. As I get closer to where the little light was, I see a small red dot grow larger and then fade away to almost nothing. The air changes as I get closer to that glowing red dot. I take in a breath, and my lungs are filled with smoke. I cough involuntarily.

Suddenly, I'm blinded by a bright light shining directly in my eyes.

A guard found me!

33

I hold my hand out in front of my eyes to shield them from the headache-inducing beam.

"Who're you?" I hear a voice bark.

Should I lie? I don't know who they are or what they want. I wish David were here.

I stay silent.

"Wha'chu doin' down here, girlie?"

I squint at the source of light to see if I can spot the guy talking to me, but I can't see anything. He doesn't talk like I imagine a guard would.

"I got lost. I'm headed back into the city," I answer.

I hear him make a tsking sound.

"This ain't no place for playin' hide-'n'-seek. Why don'cha come closer, and I'll show ya why pretty little girls like you ain't 'spose to be down here."

He shuts the flashlight off, and I hear the swish of clothing as he comes toward me. I can't see a thing, but as soon as I feel his hand on my shoulder, instinct kicks in. I grab his hand and twist his arm behind his back into a wristlock. Now with just a small amount of pressure, I can lead him anywhere. I kick where I guess his knee would be, and he falls to the ground. I shove him forward and hear his head hit a rail. I stand over him, keeping pressure on his wrist.

"Ugh! You stink!" he says in disgust.

I guess the stench didn't wear off, I just got used to it. I bend his wrist harder, and he cries out in pain.

"Where's the exit? How do I get out of here?" I ask.

"Le' me up, an' I'll show you," he says.

He struggles to free his arm, but I step on his back and use both hands to apply force to his wrist. I can feel a bone crack and wonder if I've broken something.

"Ow! Ge' off me!"

"How much further until the exit!" I yell.

"A'ight, a'ight. You ain't that far. There's a hole in the wall up ahead. Go through, and then you at the platform to get out."

"How do I know you aren't going to try to attack me as soon as I let you go?"

"I guess you don't."

"Then I guess we're stuck here." I push as hard as I can on his wrist.

"Ow! You gonna break my damn wrist! Get off me, an' I'll let'cha go!"

"Give me your flashlight."

"Take it! Take wha'ever you want. Just stop breakin' my wrist!"

I reluctantly let go with one hand and grab the flashlight he's holding. I put some distance between us and turn on the flashlight, shining it right at the guy. The sight of him shocks me. His long stringy hair frames his gaunt face. His eyes are sunken and bloodshot. His ragged clothes hang loosely off his skeletal body. He cowers on the ground like a rat, no longer pretending to be a tough guy. He's still bigger than me, but I could easily take him down if he tried to hurt me. As he shifts his weight, he exposes his forearm momentarily, and I see a line of marks from the crook of his elbow, down his arm.

I momentarily shine the light toward the wall he mentioned and spot the hole. I point the light at him again and slowly back up toward the exit. He keeps his tired eyes on me but never makes a move in my direction. Being bested by a girl that he should easily have been able to subdue must have been sobering. Now he looks lost and defeated as he holds his injured wrist tightly against his abdomen. I scramble through the opening and use the flashlight to figure out where to go next. I see a platform up ahead, and I drop his flashlight, feeling guilty at the thought of stealing something from someone needier than me.

I pull myself up onto the platform and quietly walk toward the door, hoping to get out quickly. I crawl under the little gates just like the ones from where I entered the subway and climb the stairs slowly. The light streaming down the stairwell is the same hazy, half-light I've lived with my whole life. Once I'm almost to the top, I peek my head around the corner to make sure I'm not seen. I haven't been out in the woods for long, but I forgot how terrible it is to be surrounded by this thick fog. I can barely see anything.

I step out of the stairwell and start walking in what I hope is the right direction. The city is a little better here than it was on the other side of the subway, but I would hardly deem it livable. Most of the buildings have sections still standing, but I can't see a single one that is completely whole. It looks as though most of the windows are missing, and the walls that are still standing have been adorned with colorful graffiti.

I stride down the sidewalk, keeping a close eye out for guards—or any human for that matter. Anyone willing to live in this dump is probably just as much of a threat as a guard. I give a wide berth to a few people curled up in doorways who appear to be sleeping. A burly, unkempt man wearing a patched-up leather jacket over a stained white undershirt and camouflage pants stands in a doorway, looking in my direction. On the front of the door is a picture of a blonde woman holding a mug of beer, and I assume he must be in front of a tavern. He watches me as I get closer and blows a cloud of smoke in my face as I'm about to pass. From the smell of it, I don't think that was cigarette smoke. He guffaws as I run down the sidewalk away from him, coughing and hacking on the fumes.

The road up ahead is blocked by a fallen building, so I turn down a side street, feeling like I'm in some sort of messed up maze. I don't want to make too many turns, or I'm going to end up going in circles. I pass by a woman rummaging through a garbage can as her two little girls stand close to her, eyeing me with sullen, dead expressions. They look like they haven't had a decent meal in their entire lives.

I stop walking, unstrap my bag, and dig out the dried meat strips I had grabbed from camp. I hold it out to them, and their eyes brighten, but they don't take it.

"Here you go," I offer. "Go ahead. Take it."

The older of the two girls slowly reaches out her dirt-crusted fingers, but just as she's about to grab the meat strips, her mom turns around and slaps her hand. The little girl recoils, and tears spring to her eyes.

"Don't you dare take food from some stranger! We ain't no beggars!"

"Excuse me, ma'am, but aren't you rummaging through the trash for food?" I ask in shock.

She quickly stuffs a little bag of white powder into her jeans pocket. "It ain't yo' business what I'm doin'. We ain't no charity case. You best keep walkin' if you know what's good for you." The mom's eyes are wild and threatening.

I give a sympathetic look to the little girls, who meet my eye for a second, and then I walk away. I turn my head and see that the mom has gone back to looking for whatever it is she's looking for. The girls glance in my direction, and while they're watching, I toss the meat strips behind me. I hope they will be able to sneak the food. A little dirty meat is better than no food at all.

I quicken my pace, but there is no way to tell if I'm even going in the right direction. My head starts to feel funny as though the fog is seeping into my brain. My thoughts are sluggish again, and I'm getting lightheaded. I need to get home. I spot an overweight woman with a head of bushy gray hair, shuffling her way down the sidewalk toward me, muttering to herself.

"Excuse me, ma'am. Do you know what direction the main part of the city is?"

She points to her right and continues shuffling along, having a one-sided conversation. I call out a thank you, but I don't think she heard me. I walk to the next block and turn the way she pointed. My feet ache from all this walking. I can feel the blisters forming, but I try to ignore it the best I can. I just hope I have enough to make it back to my apartment.

As I walk, I go over what I might say to my mom once I get home. I stop short when I hear a voice up ahead. It's garbled as though it's coming out of a TV or a radio.

A guard!

I scramble into an alleyway and hide behind a pile of bricks, listening to where the guard is.

"Hold on, Camden, I thought I heard something," the guard says.

I scoot down as low as I can and pray he doesn't find me. I hear his shoes scraping against the cement as he turns the corner into the alleyway. A beam of light cuts through the fog overhead, moving from side to side. My heart is pounding in my ears, but I can still hear his slow, calculated steps coming closer to my hiding spot. My sluggish brain is trying to come up with an escape plan. Other than chucking bricks at him, I'm not sure what else I can do. He's got a gun, and I can't dodge bullets. I chance a look to the side and see the barrel of his gun and the flashlight he's holding come past the brick pile. I rest my hand on a brick, ready to do what needs to be done in order to get away.

This is it. He's only one step away from finding me. Just as I'm about to draw the brick back, getting ready to throw it, a loud crash comes from down the alley, followed by a cat yowl.

"Damn cat!" The guard yells. I hear him slide his gun back in the holster and turn around to head back to the street. "Never mind. It was just a damn cat in the alleyway," he says. A staticky voice responds as his footsteps recede.

I let go of the brick and catch my breath. That was close. Too close. I stay hunkered down for a couple more minutes, trying to work up the courage to continue on. I must be getting close to the main part of the city if a guard is here. After I'm sure the coast is clear, I stand up with a groan. My muscles have seized up, and now, it's hard to move. I carefully make my way out of the alley, looking both ways down the street, but with the fog, I can't tell if there is anyone there anyway. I can't hear anyone, so I keep moving.

As the sun starts making its way to the horizon, I take notice in the dimming light that the buildings are starting to look nicer. I think I made it. Now, I just need to figure out where I am. Keeping an eye out for guards, I try to search for a street sign. I'm not entirely familiar with the streets of the city, but maybe I can figure it out. At the next intersection, I discover that I'm only a couple blocks away from my school. I'm almost home.

I start to get chilled as the sun is going down, and my clothes are damp from the fog. I pull out my sweatshirt and hide my face in my hood, hoping nobody will recognize me. As a couple of cars drive past me, I start to worry that this was a bad idea.

Finally, after another hour of cautiously making my way back home through the darkening fog that's intermittently lit with spotlights from the streetlamps, my apartment building stands before me. Keeping my head down so nobody can see my face, I walk up the stairs and to my front door. The ever-present smell of disinfectant and stale cigarettes that lingers in the hallway is even stronger than I can remember. I fumble with my keys and hope I can get inside before one of the neighbors spots me. I swing my door open and freeze when a gun barrel is shoved in my face.

34

I drop my bag and hold up my hands. I slowly move my right hand to my hood and pull it back.

"Olivia?" I hear my mom say in disbelief.

Before I know it, she's embracing me in an awkward hug. She lets go and tightly holds onto my shoulders at arm's length.

"Where have you been? Are you hurt? I was worried sick! Where are your glasses? Why didn't you leave a note? I thought you had finally succeeded in killing yourself! You have a lot of explaining to do!" She spits out, her concern turning to anger.

I take a deep breath and push her hands off me.

"I'm fine, Mom. But it's you who has a lot of explaining to do."

I step around her and walk into the living room. She follows close behind.

"What is that smell? Don't sit on my couch smelling like that. Go take a shower, and then we'll talk."

A shower sounds amazing right now, so I oblige. I relish the warmth of the water running over my sore muscles. I missed this. I open my mouth under the water, ignoring the taste, and drink until my belly feels full. After scrubbing three times with a loofa until my skin is bright red, I'm finally finished. Once I'm dressed in a change of clean clothes and fresh bandages, I go back to the living room where my mom has set out cold bottles of water and a bowl of chips. She looks at me with worry, but if I'm not mistaken, there seems to be a hint of contempt there too.

"So, explain yourself," she says.

"First, I want you to answer some questions. That's why I'm here." I sit down on the couch and grab a bottle of cold water. I have never been more grateful to have an endless supply of drinking water than I am right now.

"'That's why you're here?' You left without telling me where you were going. I've searched for you for over a week, trying to find you. I got the police involved! And you come back here as though you're perfectly innocent and demand answers from *me*?"

"I'll explain everything. Just let me start with some questions."

She glares at me, flips her long dark hair over her shoulder, and sits up straighter.

"Fine. Go ahead."

"Why did you lie to me about Dad?"

"I don't know what you're talking about," she starts to say, shifting in her seat.

"Cut the crap. You told me Dad died fighting in the war. That was a lie."

"What makes you so sure?"

"I met him," I say, watching her reaction closely.

Her eyes grow a little larger before she narrows them again, frowning. "I don't know who you met, but it wasn't your father. He died." She shakes her head at me.

"No, Mom. Matthias is alive. And so is your son, Henry."

Tears well up in her eyes. She looks down at her lap and picks a piece of lint off her pants as she gathers herself. "Where have you been, Olivia?"

"I'm still asking the questions. Why did you lie to me and let me believe my father was dead all this time?"

When she doesn't answer me, I lose control of my anger.

"Tell me!"

I can tell her patience is growing thin.

"I told you your father was dead, because by the time I had you, he was as good as dead. Especially to me. He left me! And he took *my* son with him!"

"He said you wouldn't run away with him. That you staked your allegiance with President Turk instead of him."

"Unbelievable. Of course, he would say that." She shakes her head in disbelief. "I was four months pregnant with you. Why would I want to go run out into the wilderness in my condition? I pleaded with him to just stay here, to try to make things work, for the safety of you and your brother. But that son-of-a—" She stops and collects herself before continuing. "He pretended to agree with me, but then, when I came home from work the next day, he was gone. He packed up and took Henry."

"So, why didn't you follow him? Or call the police and have him brought back?"

"I was going to call the police to find him and bring them back, but I still loved him." She pounds her fist on her leg in frustration.

I give her a quizzical look.

"I was afraid that if I got the police involved, they would kill him for being a traitor of the Coalition."

I grab a handful of chips and eat them while I let what she said sink in. Something about this seems off. Why wouldn't she go out of her way to get her child back? If she loved Matthias so much, why wouldn't she take a chance and join them? Then I remember my conversation with Matthias.

"Are you sure you weren't just trying to save face in front of President Turk, being his right-hand woman and all?"

"What are you talking about?"

"Matthias said you wouldn't go out in the woods with him, not because you were pregnant, but because you were in too deep with Turk."

She gives me a shocked look, but I can tell it isn't genuine.

"Are you part of the reason that the Rare are being kept weak?" I jump to my feet. Anger is rolling off me like waves.

Next thing I know, she's on her feet, pointing her finger in my face. "You've got a lot of nerve! You leave and don't tell me where you're going. You then come back and start accusing me of being a liar. And now, you think I'm Turk's right-hand woman, whatever that means."

"Answer the question!"

Her nostrils flare, and her chest is heaving as she breathes heavily. She stares into my eyes, hardly blinking, and I stare right back.

"You owe me," I say with as much anger as I can put into three words.

"Damn you, Matthias," she mutters under her breath and then sighs. "Sit down so we can talk."

Once we're sitting, she begins, "Fine. Yes. I play a part in the Coalition that keeps the Rare weak and monitored."

She pauses and takes a drink, never taking her eyes off me.

"I have never fully understood why the world freaked out like they did. Personally, I think it was amazing what the scientists had accomplished and what the Rare were able to do. With the heightened senses, there were some amazing detectives, scientists, athletes, musicians, you name it. But I guess that was part of the problem. Regular people were losing jobs and positions of power to the Rare because there was so much more that they could do, and it made people outraged and jealous."

"If you think we're so great, then why are you trying to keep us weak?"

She lets out another big sigh. "I take it you discovered you're one of them?"

I nod.

"Your grandmother told me that at the beginning of the peace deal, when the Coalition was first put into place, they didn't try to keep the Rare weak. Everyone just coexisted inside the city for a while. But foreign extremists were sneaking over here, hunting the Rare down, and killing them. Well, a couple of the extremists were killed by some of the Rare who found out what they were doing and fought back. Word got out about what happened, and the foreign countries demanded that something be done about it, or they were going to 'finish the job.'"

"'Finish the job'? They're the ones who kept starting it!" I interrupt.

"I know. Originally, the way they kept the Rare weak was to inject them with a DNA alteration, but it didn't always turn out right. Instead of dampening their heightened senses, it took them away completely."

"It took away their senses? You mean, they blinded people or caused them to be deaf?"

"Yes." She nods solemnly. "A lot of people had a psychotic break or died from it too."

"What?"

"The Coalition was in its early days, scrambling to find peace between the world and the United States. Over the years, we have been able to find a suppressant that does less damage. Of course, it comes with its downfalls too, but I have hope that we'll be able to create the perfect solution."

"The perfect solution would be for the world to stop being bigots and let us Rare exist without trying to kill us or control us!" I jump to my feet.

"Settle down, Olivia."

"The Coalition isn't any better. They set themselves up to keep the peace between the world and the US, and yet they give in to the demands that essentially wipe out the Rare; the very people the US was trying to protect in the first place."

"Lower your voice," she hisses.

"They are only looking out for themselves. They don't give a damn about the Rare. And you're in on it!" I spit out, marching off to my room. I slam my door, lock it, and then flop on my bed, seething with anger.

I hear my mother's footsteps stop outside my door. Her muffled voice says, "You don't understand anything. Nothing is black and white like you want to believe it to be. We have to do something, or they'll start up the war again, and there'll be nothing left!"

"Whatever. Leave me alone!" I yell into my pillow.

"Open this door so we can talk. I still have questions for you, young lady!" She rattles my doorknob. "You were gone for over a week. Where did you go?"

I say nothing.

"Where did you find your father? Did you leave the city?"

I lie on my side and stare at the door, wondering how long she's going to stand out there, asking questions.

"What...what did Henry look like?" she asks sadly.

This question tugs at my heart a bit. I'm about to stand up and let her in when I hear a sob, and her bedroom door thumps closed.

It was a mistake to come back here.

3|5

I lie on my bed, listening to my mom cry in the other room and then get herself ready for bed. I expect her to come talk to me, but she doesn't bother me again.

As I'm lying there, I suddenly remember the other reason I came back. I was going to grab the necklace. As I search my dresser for it, I see another letter addressed to me with no return address. I open it with a slight tremor in my hand, expecting it to be another threat from Cindy. I can just make out the water-splotched writing:

Olivia,
    HELP ME!
        Joselyn

Come on! What does she expect me to do? There's nothing I *can* do.

I pace back and forth in my bedroom, holding the letter in my hand. I glance at those two words, crying out for help, and I start wondering what would happen if Joselyn escaped from the city. Would she get better like I did? How could she? I only got better because I'm a Rare.

I set the letter back down on my dresser and open my jewelry box. I pick up the necklace and smile. I was right. The symbols match Saul's carvings exactly, but I can't remember the pattern he made. I spin the different sections around, but nothing happens. I'll have to wait until I can look at Saul's carvings again. I stash the necklace in my bag where I won't lose it.

I continue pacing my room for a while, but exhaustion wins out, and I get myself ready for bed. Oh, sweet, comfortable bed. How I've missed you!

My mother wakes me up before she heads off to work in the morning.

"I suppose you think you're skipping out on school?"

"I'm never setting foot in that building again." I yawn.

She makes an exasperated sound. "Fine. I'll let it go this time, but you've got to promise me you're not going to leave again. I want to talk to you, but I have to go to work today. I can't miss."

"Mom, why don't you come with me?"

"I can't."

"You can't, or you won't? We could be a family again."

"Olivia, I don't have time to have this conversation right now. I promise we'll talk when I get back. I'll bring home some pizza tonight. See you later."

I hear the front door close, and her keys jangle as she locks it. I'm not waiting around for her to give me lame excuses for why she won't come out to the woods with me. If she wasn't willing to run away with Matthias when she was still in love with him, she's not going to be willing to go out there now after years of being devoted to the Coalition. I plan on getting out of here well before she gets home, but my bed is so warm and comfortable, I allow myself to sleep for a couple more hours.

Once awake, I take another long hot shower and then bandage up my hands with extra layers of gauze. I grab all the remaining bandages from the medicine cabinet, a bottle of vitamins, and the painkillers my mom hides in her room and stuff them in my bag. I fill all my empty bottles with water and grab extra unopened ones. My bag is getting so heavy, I'm afraid the straps are going to rip off. After I've stuffed a flashlight and as much food as I can fit into my bag, I search the apartment for some rope or bungee straps that will allow me to attach my pillow to my bag. I've decided I can't live without it. A wadded up sweatshirt just wasn't cutting it. I stuff my pillow in an empty garbage bag to keep water off and use an old bathrobe belt to strap it on.

I'm about to head out the door when a wave of guilt stops me. My mother hasn't been a very good mom, but she deserves to have some reassurance that I'll be okay. I drop my bag and sit down at the table with a sheet of paper.

Mom,

I know you're going to be pissed that I took off again, but I don't belong here. I found a group of people who have accepted me and are helping me to find my true potential. After leaving the city, I got so much healthier. The healthiest I have ever been in my entire life! I don't need my glasses or my inhalers anymore, and David has seen amazing improvements too.

I really want you to come with me, but I know you would never agree to, so I'm making things easier on us both. I'm going back to where I was, and I want you to know that I'm okay. I'm sure I'll be back to see you again someday. Please, don't try to find us. Just enjoy your life without all the hospital stays and fights we have.

I know I don't say this, like ever, but I love you. Thank you for taking care of me. Now, it's time for me to take care of myself.

Olivia

P.S. Henry is handsome and looks just like Matthias, but he has your smile.

I fold the letter and leave it on the table. The time is closing in on noon, so I grab a quick lunch of sandwich meat, a cheese stick, and an orange, and I head out. I throw my hooded sweatshirt back on so I can conceal my face, but once I step outside, I realize it's going to be too hot for it. I take it off and tie it around my waist. The fog seems thinner today, which means I'm going to have to be extra careful not to be seen.

I begin walking down the street, back the way I came when a car slows down as it gets near. I glance over my shoulder and recognize the car. I quicken my pace, keeping my head down and turned slightly away from the road.

"Olivia? Olivia, is that you?" I hear Mrs. Beckett call from her open window.

Crap!

Just as I'm about to turn down a side street and start running, she cries out, "Please! Just tell me David is okay. I'm not mad at you, Olivia. I just need to know my son's okay."

I stop walking, close my eyes, and take a deep breath, knowing I should just make a run for it, but I can't. She's always been so nice to me, I can't just run away without saying something.

"Yes, Mrs. Beckett. David is more than okay. He's the healthiest he's ever been," I say at my shoes, not wanting to make eye contact. "His seizures have stopped, and he doesn't need his hearing aids anymore." I chance a look at her and see tears rolling down her cheeks.

I turn and run down the alleyway to my right, making my way between foul-smelling garbage dumpsters and piles of wet cardboard boxes until I get to the next street. Glancing both ways before stepping out, I continue my way to the bad part of town. Every time I hear a car, I find a place to hide until they're out of sight. I'm afraid Mrs. Beckett is going to try to talk to me some more. I can't be seen and recognized again. I need to get out of here.

Walking as quickly as possible, I'm able to make good time. I can see the change in the buildings up ahead through the haze. I stop walking momentarily so I can listen for any guards. All I hear are some distant traffic behind me, the beating thump of some music being played loudly, and the wail of a baby. Everything seems to be okay, so I slip my way back to the dangers of the rundown part of the city.

I wind my way through the rubble-scattered roads, searching for the subway entrance. I stop when I get an uneasy feeling like I'm being watched. I look around but can't spot anyone through the mist. I decide to take a side street to try to shake the feeling. I really don't like being here. I wish I were back in camp now, but I have a long way to go.

I'm suddenly aware of how quiet it is. I no longer hear the baby crying, and the bass thumps from the music have faded away. All I can hear are my own breathing and the steady rhythm of my steps pounding on the concrete—that is, until I hear a brick clatter on the road behind me.

"Hello?" I squeak. I try to keep my breathing even. "Is someone there?"

No answer. I strain to hear any noise I can as I stare into the fog behind me. After a minute or two of hearing and seeing nothing, I continue on a little faster than before. That feeling of being watched comes back, and I whip my head around trying to spot the source of my uneasiness. I start to panic as the smell of the city's decay fills my nostrils with its unpleasantness: a mixture of rotting garbage, mold, and sewage. I don't remember things smelling this bad on my way through the first time. Then again, I smelled bad on the way through the first time.

I cover my nose with my shirt and take deep breaths to calm myself down. Up ahead, loud music and laughter flood the street and then muffle again. As I walk closer, I realize it's a tavern full of people. There's a picture on the door of a blonde lady holding a mug full of beer. I remember seeing that picture when that creepy guy blew smoke at me on my way to the apartment. I'm almost to the subway tunnel.

I run the rest of the way and stifle a cry of relief when I see the steps leading down to the subway. I pull out the flashlight that I remembered to pack and make my way into the darkness of the tunnel once again. I sure hope that nasty guy isn't still there.

Once I'm back on the railway, I push myself through the hole in the wall and shine my flashlight in every direction before I take any more steps. A pair of eyes catch in my beam, and it startles me enough to almost drop my light. I shakily move my light back to where the eyes were. A mangy gray cat with bright yellow eyes stares at me, then hisses and runs away to hide in the darkness once again. I clasp my hand over my heart as I catch my breath. I continue to sweep the area with my light until I'm certain no one's there. The coast is clear, so I cautiously make my way back to the other entrance, keeping the flashlight shining toward my feet.

After trudging on for what feels like hours, I finally see the platform up ahead. Just as I'm about to climb up, a scuffling sound comes from down the tunnel behind me. I shine the flashlight around to search for the source of the noise, but nothing's there. It was probably that stupid cat again. I climb up the platform and head out of the subway tunnel, happy to be away from the dangers of people. Now, I just have to worry about the Havoc again.

By the time I get out of the ruins and back into the cover of the woods, the sun is setting. The fog is fading away, the farther I get from the fence. The scent of trees and dead leaves helps me to clear my head and feel calmer. I realize I feel more at home in the woods than I ever did in the city. The cool night breeze rustles the leaves above my head, making it sound like rain falling momentarily. A distant owl hoot reminds me that the night animals are on the prowl. I should probably find somewhere safe to spend the night.

I recall reading a book a couple of years back where a girl strapped herself to a branch up in a tree so she could sleep. I wonder if that would actually work?

I look around me and find a tree with thick branches. I climb my way up about fifteen feet until I find a branch that has enough room for me to get comfortable. There's a nub of a branch not far from where I'm sitting, so I hang my pack off it and untie my pillow. I try to use the bathrobe belt to tie myself to the branch, but it's not long enough. I pull a long sleeved shirt out of my bag and tie the belt to one of the sleeves, then wrap it around the branch and tie the other end to the other sleeve. It's long enough, but now I worry whether the knots will hold. I place the pillow behind my head and try to get some sleep.

I sleep lightly all night, waking up to every strange noise. I hear some odd howling in the distance and pray hard that Havocs can't climb trees. As soon as the sun comes up, I decide I've had enough and want to keep moving. My stiff muscles make it hard to climb back down the tree, but I manage to make it without falling. I eat a granola bar for breakfast and stretch out before continuing.

Excitement for getting back to camp makes me walk faster than I should. I force myself to keep my pace slow and steady so I can conserve as much energy and water as possible. I lose myself in thought as I look around at the beauty of the woods again. I wish I could have known about the healing powers of nature a long time ago. And not just healing for my body, but psychological healing as well. My thoughts were always so dark when I was living in the city. There wasn't a day that went by where I didn't contemplate dying. Those thoughts haven't gone away completely, but I feel more hope out here, more purpose. Maybe someday, I'll finally stop wanting to die and find some real joy in living.

Suddenly, a branch snaps behind me. I quickly hide behind a tree and peek around it to see if I can find the source of the noise.

Nothing.

The wind shifts the shadows around, making my eyes play tricks on me. Every little movement causes my breath to catch in my chest. I drop my bag on the ground and rummage around for the knife. Cautiously, I move on, holding the knife in my hand as I go. A sense of danger tickles the back of my mind. Is there a Havoc stalking me that I can't see?

As the sun makes its way across the sky, I'm grateful that the temperature is rather mild compared to my journey to the city. I stop occasionally for a drink of water, but otherwise, I move as quickly as I can. I want to be at camp, where I can be protected. I hope they'll let me back in. What will I do if Matthias is pissed at me and won't allow me in? What if he decides to punish me for leaving?

I can't worry about that right now. I snack on some dried mango as I work my way through the wilderness. I want to make it to the river before nightfall. The niggling in my brain that's telling me I'm in danger never goes away. I can't figure out what's causing it, but it feels like I'm being hunted.

Daylight is slowly fading away to dusk. My hair is dripping wet with sweat, and my backpack weighs a ton. I've rationed my water, only allowing myself a drink every half hour or so. I stop to take another drink and eat some cashews for supper when a flock of birds starts and flaps out of the trees behind me. I crouch behind a fallen log and watch to see what caused the sudden upheaval.

I can't see anything, but I hear the rustle of leaves in the distance. I stare at the spot I thought I heard the sound come from, watching for what made the sound. After staring for about five solid minutes, my eyes start to lose focus, and my muscles cramp up from holding still. I slowly stand up and stretch out. The sun is close to setting, and I still haven't found the river yet. I change my direction and head northwest instead of heading straight west.

After another hour of walking, the sun is gone, and the woods are dark and ominous. I pull out my flashlight to keep myself from falling over branches. I occasionally stop and sweep the area around me with my light, trying to catch whatever it is putting my nerves on edge. I would almost welcome a fight at this point if it meant getting rid of the panic-inducing feeling of danger. But there is never anything there.

Finally, sweet relief fills me when I hear the sound of rushing water. I run the rest of the way, tripping occasionally on sticks and rocks. I stop at the water's edge and plunge my hands into it, scooping up handfuls of refreshing, cold water to wash my face with. I try hard not to drink any of the river water. I learned on one of the survival shows that you could get sick and die from drinking unclean water. The cool water is so tempting, but I'll just stick to my plastic-flavored bottled water.

I followed the river downstream when I left, so I make my way upriver to get back to camp. It shouldn't be too long now. I walk as fast as I safely can and finally start to recognize where I am. I see a dark figure stand up from a boulder as I work my way to the rocky riverbank.

"Olivia? Is that you?" I hear David call out in hushed tones.

"Yeah! It's me!" I call out and run the rest of the way to where David stands.

He stoops over to drop something from his hands, and we fall into an embrace, squeezing each other hard. Suddenly, David tenses and lets go.

"Did you bring someone with you?" he asks, quietly.

"No. Why?"

David bends over and picks up what it was he had dropped.

"Get down!"

I obey immediately and watch as he nocks an arrow and shoots toward a tree. I hear a voice yell out a curse and watch in horror as a man stumbles and runs away, holding his injured arm.

"Who was that?" I squeak.

"I don't know, but I'm going to go see if I can catch him. Wake Matthias!" he orders as he turns to run after the man.

"No, David! Don't..." I call helplessly after him, but he's already gone.

I run down the path to camp and barge into Matthias's hut. He's fast asleep on his back, gripping the handle of a knife lying on his chest. Thank goodness, it's sheathed. I drop to the ground next to his cot and shake him awake.

"Matthias! Matthias wake up!"

His eyes snap open. He pulls the knife out and has it up to my throat before I can utter another word. The cold, sharp edge of the blade rubs against my skin and cuts a line ever so slightly before Matthias realizes he's in no danger.

"Olivia? What are ya doin' in my hut? Never wake me up like that again. I could've hurt ya."

"David told me to come get you. He took off after some guy who followed me here."

"What?" Matthias jumps off his cot and throws a shirt on. He grabs his boots and pulls them on his bare feet. "Which way'd they go?"

"After he shot the guy in the arm, he took off downriver, and David ran after him. Please, you gotta help David."

"I'm on it. And when I get back, we're gonna have a long talk." He glares at me.

I watch as he runs to another hut to wake up Frederick and Markos and then heads off in the direction I mentioned. It takes only a minute before the brothers come rushing out of their hut and follow behind Matthias, carrying bows.

I go to my shelter to drop my backpack off. I move as quietly as my adrenaline-filled muscles will allow me so I don't wake up Cass and Tim. I don't need a barrage of questions at the moment.

I slip out and pace back and forth next to the fire pit. My neck stings where the knife cut me. That was a close call. I nervously pick at the dry skin around my nails. What was I thinking? Why did I feel the need to talk to my mom so badly? I hope the necklace was worth going back for.

My legs begin to get shaky as I keep walking the same track over and over again, searching every direction for any sign of their return. Maybe I should try to get some sleep. I'm not sure I will be able to sleep with David out there in potential danger, but I'm exhausted.

"Olivia. Get outside now. We need to talk," Matthias says sternly. I snap awake as soon as I remember the events of last night. I dig around in my bag until I find the necklace and slip it around my neck as I head outside.

"What happened? Did you catch him? Who was he?" I blink profusely in the bright sunlight. I look over to the fire pit and see Rebecca bandaging up a long gash on David's temple.

"David!" I cry. I try to check on him, but Matthias grabs my shoulder and spins me around.

"What the hell were ya thinkin'? Where'd ya go?" Matthias growls. He looms over me, making me feel like a small child.

"I-I needed to talk to Mom. I needed her to answer some questions. It was stupid, and I'm sorry," I say, staring at the ground.

"You're damn right it was stupid. You're a part of this group now. We look after each other. But if you're gonna be so damn foolish and run off to the city, maybe ya need to leave for good."

I glance to the right and see Alexandrine with a small smirk. I glower at her and turn my attention back to Matthias's angry face.

"Here." I remove the necklace and hand it to him. "I also went back to get this. I don't know what this is, but it has the same markings as the sticks Saul carves."

He grabs it from my hand and shoves it in his pocket without even looking at it.

"Did you catch the guy?" I ask.

"Not yet. We didn't know where David had run off to, and by the time we found 'im, he was unconscious, and the guard was gone."

"How do you know it was a guard?"

"David saw a tattoo on his forearm of the Coalition flag before he was knocked out."

"Well, what's the plan now?" I ask.

"We hope the guard either bleeds out before he can get back to the city, or Markos and Frederick find him. In the meantime, we prepare for battle."

"Do you really think they are going to come out here?"

"He knows where our camp is. If he makes it back to the city, they're comin', and we have you to thank for it."

"I said I was sorry, Matthias. I had to know why Mom didn't come with you. Why she lied."

"Yeah, well, your little honesty quest could mean a war for us. Ya didn't think. Ya only cared 'bout your hurt feelin's, and now we have to pay the price."

"Lay off, Pop. We've been found before, and we kicked their asses. We can do it again," Henry says, walking close to where we're squared off.

"Disrespect from you now too? Like two peas in a pod. I blame your mother for this."

"Well, I don't remember her so—" Henry starts to say.

"Animal pens. Both of you. Now!" Matthias storms off to his hut.

Henry huffs and swears under his breath. I look over at David, who now has white gauze wrapped around his head to keep the bandage in place, and give him a little apologetic wave as I turn to follow Henry to the animal pens.

"Thanks for sticking up for me back there," I say, breaking the silence.

"Don't mention it. Pop can be uptight, and sometimes he needs a reminder to cool it."

Silence falls between us again as we set to work. I watch as Henry grabs two shovels and hands me one, catching my eye. He looks so much like Matthias with the bushy facial hair, broad chin, straight nose, and muscular stature. However, his mouth is so much like my mother's, it makes me think of her just by looking at it.

"So, I guess you're my brother," I say lamely.

"Yup. Guess so." He scoops up a shovel full of manure and dumps it into one of the wheelbarrows.

"What's Matthias like as a dad?" I ask, trying to keep the tone light.

"Strict. Disciplined. Rigid. He wasn't exactly the perfect Dad, but he respects me, and he's taught me a lot."

I nod as we keep working.

"What's Mom like?" Henry asks hesitantly.

"Um, she likes her secrets. We don't exactly get along that well, but she tries to be a good mom, occasionally. Her taco making skills are excellent, though."

"Tacos? What are those?" Henry asks with a quizzical look.

"Oh, wow! I guess you probably wouldn't have had tacos out here in the woods. They're deliciousness wrapped up inside a soft flour tortilla."

"What's a tortilla?"

"It's like a really thin circle of bread," I start to say, but I can tell he still has no clue what I'm talking about. "You know what? Never mind."

The two wheelbarrows are full, so I follow Henry down a trail leading outside of the camp to dump it in the manure pile they save for fertilizer. I'm having a hard time coming to grips with the fact that this man in front of me is my brother. I'm not even sure how brothers and sisters are supposed to behave around each other. Henry seems too cool to be related to me. I feel the sudden urge to apologize to him.

"I'm sorry I left to go confront Mom. It was really stupid. I was just shocked when I found out Matthias was my father. I needed to know why Mom had lied to me my whole life."

"It's okay. Just don't do it again," he warns.

I nod.

I follow him back to the animal pens, and we finish cleaning up what's left. Henry makes a couple of noises as though he's going to say something but then stops. We work in the heat of the day, sweat glistening on our arms and faces. Henry seems to be troubled about something, but he doesn't speak. We take the rest of the filth out of camp to the dump pile, and that's when Henry finally says something.

"Hey, um, did Mom ever mention me?" Henry wipes the back of his neck nervously.

"No. I didn't know you existed until I found a picture of her pregnant, and it was dated five years before I was born. Her explanation for it was that she had a stillborn."

Henry narrows his eyes and shakes his head slightly.

"She did, however, ask me what you looked like when I was back in the city."

"What did you say?"

"That you're handsome like Matthias, but you have her smile."

He chuckles a bit at that. "Thanks."

As we take our wheelbarrows back to camp, Henry says, "I'm going to see if Pop will let me work with you and David for a while on your combat training."

"Okay."

"We should probably get started right away, so go get changed and meet me by the fire pit."

I throw on some sweatpants and a plain gray t-shirt and head back to the campfire. David is still sitting there, cradling his chin in his hands, staring down at the ground. I have a seat next to him, and he gives me a sad look.

"I'm sorry I didn't catch the guy. I feel so embarrassed about getting knocked out by him."

"It's okay, David."

"Why did you leave without me?" he asks. "You know I would have gone with you if you had asked me."

"No, you would have tried to talk me out of it."

"Probably." He nods. "We're not part of the city anymore, Liv. We belong out here."

"I know. I got confused with this whole Matthias thing, and I wasn't thinking rationally. It won't happen again, I promise."

"Good."

"I also grabbed the necklace from home that I'm pretty sure belonged to Saul."

"How do you know it belonged to him?"

"Saul carves symbols on the sticks he's always whittling, and I recognized them as the same ones that are on the pendant I once found in a box marked 'Dad's stuff.' 'Dad' meaning Matthias's dad, Saul."

"Cool! Can I see it?" David's eyes light up with intrigue.

"Nope. I gave it to Matthias."

"Why'd you do that? You probably won't get it back now."

"Maybe I can ask for it back once he's cooled off."

"Maybe," David says with disappointment. We fall into a moment of silence, and then I remember something else.

"Your mom spotted me while I was back."

"What? What did she say? Is she mad at me?"

"No. I told her how you're doing so much better, and it made her cry."

David reaches out and puts his hand on top of mine.

"What did everyone do when they found out I was gone?" I ask.

"Nothing," David starts to say. I give him a shocked look, and he quickly adds, "Well, Tim, Cass, and I were dead set on going out there to search for you, but Matthias forbade it. He was pissed at you and said you deserved whatever you got."

"How fatherly," I mutter.

"He talked some sense into us that we probably wouldn't find you anyway since the woods are so big, and we didn't know which way you headed. I was so worried something bad was going to happen to you, I couldn't eat or sleep until you got back."

I give him a small smile just as Henry comes back with a bundle of weapons in his arms.

"He gave me the all clear. Let's get started."

We begin with sword fighting, but he isn't as good as Matthias, and I beat him within thirty seconds every time we start.

When it's David's turn, they seem to be a little more evenly matched as they fill the camp with metallic clangs from their blocking and striking. David taps out when his head injury starts to bleed through the bandages, and he almost throws up from the pain. I run to the shelter and get him some of the medicine I brought with me.

Tim and Cass join us as Henry and I are about to start hand to hand combat.

"Now, how much do you know about sparring?" Henry asks.

"She punched a bully in the nose and broke it," David says with a smirk.

"Nice," Henry chuckles. "Anything else?"

"Only what I saw you and David doing when we first got here. I don't know anything about it otherwise."

"All right, Tim and Cass, why don't you two pair up over here next to us and practice while I teach Olivia. You can show her how some of the moves look."

Tim and Cass quickly take their place next to us, and Cass whispers, "I'm glad you made it back, Olivia."

I smile at her.

"Okay, what you want to do is stand with your right foot forward. Your legs should be about shoulder-width apart. Hands up, protect your jaw. Tim, I want you to throw a slow punch at Cass's head. Cass, block, and punch to his ribs."

I watch as they do what Henry says with exaggerated movements. Looks simple enough.

"All right, good. Olivia, your turn."

Henry throws a slow punch at my head. I block it and land a punch to his ribs.

"Perfect. Now Cass, I want you to come at Tim with both hands toward his neck. Tim, you're going to block her hands and knee her in the groin."

They both nod, and Cass starts toward Tim with both hands. He steps forward, brings both hands up with a circular motion and blocks them outward, then lifts his knee up to her groin without making contact.

"Yup. Now you try, Olivia."

Henry comes at me, and I mimic everything I just saw Tim do. It feels so natural like I've been doing it my whole life.

"Great. Now we're going to try—"

"Enough!" I hear a voice yell. I look up just as Alexandrine steps behind Henry. "Stop babying her. It's time to show her what real combat is like."

My heart starts to race as I look at the anger that borderlines insanity in her dark brown eyes. Her hands are up, and she's bouncing back and forth on her feet, itching to fight. Henry steps off to the side with concern on his face. I bring my hands up and shuffle my feet, trying to stay light on my toes. She throws a fast punch and lands it right in my stomach. All the air is knocked out of my lungs, and I drop to my knees as I gasp for breath.

"Come on! You're gonna have to do better than that!" Alexandrine goads.

Once I manage to breathe again, I stand back up and get ready for the next blow. She throws a punch toward my head, but I block it and punch her in the stomach. My fist hits solid abs, and I think my hand hurts more than her stomach does. She seems angered by the punch I got through, and she starts throwing strikes at me rapidly. I block and dodge the best I can, but some of them land their mark, and I'm momentarily stunned. She takes advantage of this and continues to punch me in the ribs or the stomach.

I'm having a hard time staying on my feet each time she lands a punch, but I'm determined to not let her win. My body feels like it's being tenderized. I can already feel bruises forming on my ribs. I start to tighten my muscles every time she throws a punch, and it helps.

"Show me what you've got, oh, great Rare one!" She takes a break from punching me and instead dances around me.

I decide to make a move and lunge at her, but she's too quick, and I'm suddenly lying flat in the dirt. My head swims from the sudden fall, but I stand up and wait for her next attack with renewed determination.

She stares me down for a while as we stand off, and I begin to wonder if maybe she's ready to be done, but then she charges at me. It's like a slow-motion movie playing before my eyes. I watch as she cocks her right arm back, takes a step forward with her right foot, and then brings her fist toward my head. I easily block it and sweep her leg out from under her, knocking her on the ground. Before I know what I'm doing, I drop to the ground too, wrap my legs around her torso, lock my feet together, and squeeze her ribcage. Her eyes bulge as the breath is being squeezed out of her body. She taps my leg with her one free arm, but I keep squeezing. It isn't until I hear everyone around us telling me to stop that I snap out of it and let her up.

"Where'd you learn that take-down?" Alexandrine asks, bent over as she tries to regain her breath. She doesn't seem at all angry that I almost killed her.

"I didn't learn it. It just felt right," I answer truthfully.

"You need to learn to block punches."

"Maybe if you hadn't insisted that I take you on without proper training, I could be working on that," I say, getting angry.

"You wouldn't have known that was something you needed to work on unless we had a sparring match. Now you know."

"What is your problem? Why do you hate me so much?"

"I don't have time for this. I need to go help Matthias get ready for when the guards come out here because of you."

I watch as she storms away. I want to pick up a rock and throw it at her head, but I keep my cool and mutter curse words at her instead.

"Don't let her get to you," Henry says. "She's not an easy person to get along with."

I smile a little at him.

"She is right about you learning to block better, though. That was kind of brutal."

"So, teach me."

We spend a good portion of the afternoon learning combat moves and strategies. I teach everyone the take-down I used on Alexandrine. When David performs it on me, he loses his balance, and his face comes within inches of mine. He pauses a moment as though he's considering kissing me, his breath hot on my face, but I roll away from him to stand back up before he has the chance.

We are all sweaty and tired by the time Caroline tells us it's time to prepare supper. Once we're eating, I can't help but notice everyone seems to be on edge. Markos and Frederick haven't returned yet, and I can only hope that's because they've caught the guard's trail and are close to finding him. Nobody else asks me where I went or why I left, and I'm grateful for it. The young children whisper to each other while eyeing me once in a while, but they never say anything to me. I'm happy to be back out here, and I hope to never set foot in the city again.

I go to bed before the sun even sets. It's been a long day, and I'm exhausted. I wake up to Cass shaking my shoulder.

"Olivia, you need to get up. We have to get breakfast ready. You and I are on food prep duty."

I groggily roll off my leaf bed and feel as though I were hit by a truck. Yesterday's sparring match with Alexandrine has taken its toll. I can barely lift my arms without pain ripping through my ribs and stomach. I gently lift my shirt up and see dark purple bruises dotted across my torso.

"Ouch! Alexandrine wasn't pulling her punches with you. Maybe you should take another soak in the river to help with the swelling."

"No, I'll be all right. As long as we don't have to do any more training today."

I'm not so lucky. Henry insists that we keep on it. Injured or not, we need to prepare. I take some medicine, and it helps take the edge off, but the bruises make me slow. We do some target practice with the bows, and David is a natural with it.

"I practiced while you were away," he admits.

I take a shot at it, and I manage to hit most of the cans. At least, I'm better at shooting bows than I am at shooting guns. Maybe I can get even better at this once my bruises heal, and I'm feeling good again.

Alexandrine hasn't said a word to me since our sparring match, but she isn't giving me death glares either. She seems to have moved to ignoring me. I'm okay with that.

Another day of physical training has exhausted me, and I sleep like a rock. It's just before dawn when everyone in my shelter wakes up to the sound of Frederick's voice calling out for Rebecca. We all rush out to see what's going on.

"Frederick, what happened to Markos?" Rebecca asks as she runs to his side. Markos is slung over Frederick's meaty shoulder, unconscious.

Matthias runs out of the woods from where he was keeping watch over camp. He helps Frederick get Markos off his shoulder and down on the ground.

"What happened?" Matthias asks, staring down at the bloody wound in Markos's chest. Rebecca lifts his shirt, and we can see a two-inch stab mark close to his heart. Markos's skin is pale, and his chest is just barely rising as he breathes.

"We were hot on his trail, tracking his bootprints and the blood streaks on the trees where he rubbed up against them. But then we lost sight of any traces, so we decided to split up and search the area. I hear Markos yell, and I run to where I heard him, thinking he had picked up the trail. Instead, I come to find him lying on the ground, bleeding. I hear the snap of a branch and just catch sight of the guard running again toward the city. I had to make the choice of hunting him down or helping my brother before he dies. I couldn't just leave him. I'm sorry, Matthias!" Frederick wipes snot off his nose with the back of his hand.

Matthias sighs deeply. "Ya did the right thing, Frederick. But this means we need to relocate camp. We can't stay here."

"What? How are we going to move everything?" I ask, bewildered.

"We're not. We take the essentials and find a new place to build a camp."

Everyone is quiet as we all watch Rebecca clean Markos's wound and hold pressure to stop the bleeding. Frederick pulls a stump over from the fire to sit on and watches helplessly, exhausted from carrying his brother back to camp. His shirt is soaked in Markos's blood, but he doesn't seem to notice.

"What do you think, Becky? Is he going to make it?" Frederick asks.

"I don't know. He needs a hospital," she says, worry etched on her brow.

"Do what ya can," Matthias grunts, and then turns to address everyone else. "Y'all should be preparin' for the move. Rebecca's got this under control. Get to work!"

Guilt weighs heavily on my mind. I did this. I got Markos stabbed. I made it so everyone has to abandon their home. I look around at the group, and they all look sad or worried. David and Cass give me small sympathetic smiles.

Tim leans in and whispers, "It's okay, Olivia. We've had to move camps before."

"Really?" I ask, slightly relieved.

"Yeah. Alexandrine tried to go find her daughter once, and she had a group of guards after her. They followed her, and we managed to kill the guards, but we changed locations before people came out looking for the missing men."

"I just hate that it's my fault."

"We all make mistakes." Tim pats my shoulder.

David and I follow Cass and Tim to our shelter. I haven't taken much out of my bag since I've been back at camp, so it doesn't take me long to pack. I search around for anything more I can do.

I walk past Rebecca as she's stitching the hole in Markos's chest.

"I don't know if this is going to work. If the knife cut something on the inside, he's going to die from internal bleeding," Rebecca frets.

Frederick covers his face with grimy hands. I'm not sure I will ever be able to look him in the eyes again if Markos doesn't make it.

I step into the Commons shelter, where two other women are gathering up cooking supplies and food.

"What can I do to help?" I ask feebly.

"We're going to need the wheelbarrows to move all this stuff, but you guys used them to haul manure. Take them down to the river and wash them out as best you can," Suzanne says.

I don't let on how disgusted I am. It's payment for the mess I got us all in. I just nod and set to work. I pull the two wheelbarrows down to the river and tip them on their sides so the current can do most of the work. Meanwhile, I look around at the morning sun shining on the trees across the wide river. It's so peaceful here. I close my eyes for a moment and listen to the Mukduks up river chirping their happy song, the trickle of water over rocks, the creaking of trees swaying in the wind.

I grab a cloth off the boulder that is supposed to be for dishes, but I've got nothing else to use. I start scrubbing the smelly remains of animal waste out of the wheelbarrow when I hear a sorrowful cry from camp.

"*No!* No, please, God! Don't die, Markos! Don't leave me!" Frederick cries.

Tears spring to my eyes, and I start weeping with him. I want to run back to camp and tell Frederick how sorry I am, but he needs this moment to himself. I'm not sure he's ever going to forgive me. I wouldn't if I were him. Markos seemed like such a nice guy, and I killed him. I killed his brother.

My sadness turns to anger toward myself. I'm an idiot. Maybe I should be kicked out and eaten by a Havoc. Maybe I should have died a long time ago. Maybe I should die now. I focus my anger toward the cleaning job. I start scrubbing the wheelbarrow so hard, I rip one of the scabs open on my hand, and it starts bleeding. I relish the pain. I deserve pain.

The sound of Frederick's sobbing continues. I finish one wheelbarrow and start on the other. David joins me by the river bank and crouches next to me.

"It's not your fault, Liv."

"Yes, it is. It is entirely my fault. I'm the one who ran back to the city. I'm the one who was followed. I'm the one who got Markos killed!" I know David is trying to make me feel better, but that just makes me angry. Denying the fact that it is all my fault is foolishness.

"All right. It was your fault," David says. "What are you going to do about it?"

"I don't know. Stop breathing?"

David slaps me on the shoulder. "Knock it off, Liv. I'll tell you what we're going to do. We're going to honor Markos's death by helping the group in any way we can, and we're going to keep training. We'll pour ourselves into our lessons and make ourselves useful. You and I are Rare. If we focus on becoming the best versions of ourselves we can be, I don't think we'll have to worry about the stupid guards anymore. They won't stand a chance against us."

I stare at the cloth in my hand, waiting for David to finish his lecture. I feel like crawling into a hole and never coming out again, and here he is, full of enthusiasm, making it sound like we are prized members of the group. Like I didn't just get a fellow member killed. Like I deserve to be here. Alive.

David puts his hand on my shoulder. "Hey," he says calmly, "I know you're upset, and I can't say I wouldn't be if the roles were reversed, but you are not in control of other people's actions. You didn't make Markos run after the guard and get himself stabbed. It sucks what happened, but none of that was in your control." David stands back up and walks to a boulder nearby to have a seat.

I really wish he would leave me alone.

"You can go back to camp, David. I'm almost done."

"I'm not leaving you here by yourself, Liv. I know how you can get when something bad happens, and you feel guilty. So, I'm going to stay right here until you're done cleaning those wheelbarrows, and then I'll help you take them back."

I huff angrily at him and get back to scrubbing. Suddenly, David starts singing, and I stop to listen. He's been tone deaf ever since I've known him, and it's always been painful to listen to him try to sing songs. He was so bad, most of the time you couldn't tell what song he was trying to sing unless you listened to the lyrics. But now his voice is so clear and beautiful, goosebumps pop up on my arms and the back of my neck. I close my eyes as I listen to the lilting beauty of his melancholy song that echoes through the trees. His voice is rich and deep as he sings the haunting lyrics of love and loss. I've never heard the song before, and I'm not sure I will ever hear it's equal again.

"How was that?" he asks once he's finished.

A tear runs down my cheek. I clear my throat, and all I can say is, "Wow."

"All right, all right. I'll stop distracting you. Get back to work," he says with a wink.

I turn my attention back on the wheelbarrow and hurry up to finish. It suddenly seems so quiet, and it takes me a moment to realize I don't hear Frederick crying anymore. I pull the wheelbarrow out of the water and scrub my hands extra hard, wishing I had my soap with me, but it's all packed up. I don't feel like going back to get it.

David and I take the wheelbarrows back to the Commons and help the ladies load it up with supplies. Cooking utensils, dishes, and tools go in one, and the bags of food go in the other. They use ropes to strap it all down, and David helps to get it tight. Carol's son comes walking over to us, leading two of the camp's goats, and Carol places something across their backs that looks like two bags attached by a strip of cloth in the middle. She then proceeds to fill the bags up with loose foods like apples, onions, and carrots.

"I had no idea you could use goats to haul stuff," I comment.

"Yup. They're smart animals. You just have to train them up a little bit," Carol answers.

"Do we really have to leave, Momma?" the boy asks with sad eyes.

"Yes, Noah, we do," she answers calmly, ruffling his hair.

"How is Daddy going to find us if we move?"

I suddenly feel uncomfortable listening to their conversation, but I can't seem to walk away either. I know very little about these people, what their stories are, and I'm curious.

"Baby, he isn't coming. I know you miss your Daddy, but he signed up to work for the bad man," she says gently, wiping a tear off his cheek. "Now I need you to be strong for your sister and me. You're the man of our family. A little bit of crying is okay, but then you wipe those tears away, and you get back to doing what needs to be done."

"Yes, Momma." Noah sniffles. He tries hard to wipe the tears away and stand a little taller, but his chin quivers, and it makes me want to cry along with him.

"Go help your sister get her stuff packed up. I think we'll be leaving pretty soon."

Noah turns around and shuffles back to their shelter.

"He seems like a good boy," I comment.

"Most of the time," Carol says. "He's only eight, but he's had to grow up really quick living out here."

"You said your husband works for the 'bad man.' Do you mean Turk?"

"That's right. He signed up to be a guard, even though he knew how I felt about it all. I want nothing to do with Turk and what he's doing to people."

Just then, Rebecca staggers by, looking shell-shocked and covered in blood.

"Excuse me." Carol runs over to Rebecca to help her down to the river to get washed up.

The other women are finishing up with the rest of the food, so David and I head back toward our shelter. As we walk past the fire pit, we see Frederick walking into the woods, carrying Markos's body. Matthias is walking next to him, carrying a shovel with one hand, and his other hand is on Frederick's shoulder. My heart drops again, and I feel like I'm going to be sick.

Tim and Cass have the shelter emptied of their things, and we all sit by the firepit, waiting for the rest of camp to be ready. Henry leads Saul out to the firepit and has him sit down. He looks at me and smiles with a twinkle in his eye. I wish I could have gotten to know him better before he got to be this way.

Everyone waits by the firepit for Frederick and Matthias to return. The chickens have been caught and put in cages made from sticks and twine. They voice their displeasure at being trapped by clucking frantically and flapping their wings. The goats don't seem to care what's going on as they munch on apples that Noah gave to them.

Nobody talks as we wait patiently for the men to return. It feels like we are paying our respects to Markos with a long moment of silence. Even the young children sit quietly with their mothers. Finally, Frederick and Matthias come back to camp, arms and clothes covered in dirt, and walk solemnly down to the river to clean up. We wait some more as the men go back to their shelters to change clothes and gather up their things. Nobody dared go into Matthias's hut to grab the weapons, so it takes a little while for Matthias to get everything together.

Matthias hands out the weapons to everyone, except the children. I'm given a sword, and I strap it to my back and then put my bag over the top so it's mostly hidden, but I can reach it easily if needed. It's not very comfortable, but my safety is more important.

Frederick joins the group, and the women take turns hugging him and expressing their condolences. I feel like I should say something, but I also feel like I should just keep my mouth shut and never talk to him again. I don't deserve to even look at him. A tear slides down my cheek, and I feel about one inch tall right now.

"All right, group," Matthias says. "I'll lead. Saul will stay by me. Henry, ya take the back, and everyone else can fall in line. Let's go!"

I take one last look around at our camp, and a feeling of loss hits me. I haven't been here that long, but I feel like I'm leaving home and never going to see it again. It must be so much worse for everyone else. With a heavy sigh, I follow behind David as we head off into the unknown once more.

38

Our pace is set at the speed of Saul, which is about as slow as you can get. We are heading northwest from our camp, putting as much distance as we can between us and the city. We walk in the water up the river for a little while, so we can hide our footprints, but the current gets to be too strong for Saul and the children, so we move back to dry ground.

We stop periodically for water breaks and snacks. Suzanne's little girl, Sonya, has had enough already, and she falls asleep in her mother's arms. Suzanne asks for the other women to help by taking turns carrying her. The weight of their bags, plus a sleeping child, is a bit too much for hiking out in the woods, and they have to pass her around before someone accidentally drops her from fatigue.

The sky is cloudy today, which keeps the temperature mild in the forest. There isn't much wind, so the woods seem extra quiet. Other than goat bleats, chicken clucks, and the occasional whispers and giggles from the children, our group moves as silently as we can through the woods.

David glances back at me occasionally to give me a small smile or an eye roll from our turtle like speed. It's going to take forever to make it a safe distance, but I don't complain. We find a small clearing and stop for the night. After a supper of dried venison, apples, and raw carrots, Matthias and a few men set to work hanging all the bags that have food up in trees a safe distance outside of our camp so they don't attract bears. The rest of us set up the sleeping arrangements. We put the small children together in the middle, their mothers and Saul around them, then the rest of us on the outside perimeter. Matthias tells Frederick to take the night off and that he and a few others will take turns keeping watch.

I lie awake for a while, listening to Frederick quietly crying himself to sleep. The only other sounds we hear that night are the sounds of the nighttime animals looking for food. Hopefully, none of them will have a taste for goat or chicken. By sunrise, Alexandrine is waking the group up so we can get started on the day.

"This is kind of exciting, isn't it?" David asks quietly as we eat breakfast away from the rest of the group.

"It would be if it weren't my fault we're doing this."

"You're going to have to forgive yourself, Liv."

"I can't, David. Markos is dead because of my actions."

"I think you should talk to Frederick. At least, tell him you're sorry. Distancing yourself and staying quiet isn't helping anyone."

"I will. I'm just waiting until the time is right."

"Don't wait too long."

After everyone is finished eating, we gather up our things and burden ourselves with our heavy bags once again. I hear the bottle of vitamins I grabbed from the apartment rattle. I should probably give them to Matthias sometime since he seemed so interested in them. I'm curious to know what he thinks is wrong with them.

The walk is rather uneventful, other than the constant potty breaks the kids keep having to make. Who knew children needed to go to the bathroom so often?

We stop a little early to set up camp because Saul's feet are swelling from all the walking. Matthias sends Tim and three men out to hunt for some meat. Cass and I set to work collecting wood so we can cook the meat once they're back. Wood isn't hard to find, and soon, we have a nice pile.

I look over and see David talking with Frederick. Frederick is nodding his head somberly, and then they both look over at me. My cheeks turn red, and I quickly look away.

"Olivia, come here," David calls.

I give him a quick death glare but make my way over to them. How dare he put me on the spot like this.

David whispers, "Now's the time."

I take a quick glance at Frederick, and he's looking right at me. I gaze back down at the ground, and tears start to well up in my eyes.

"Frederick, I am so sorry for what happened to your brother. It's all my fault!" I say as I start ugly crying. "I never should have gone back to the city. I'm an idiot. Please, forgive me."

I feel his big hand rest gently on the back of my head, and he starts stroking my hair. That makes me cry even harder.

"Markos died with honor. He gave his life to protect those he loved. And since he was always willing to give people a second chance, I think he would want me to forgive you. And I do. Don't be too hard on yourself, Olivia. Markos is in a better place, and one day, I will be with him again."

With that, he puts his big arm around me and pulls me into a hug. I hug him in return but hold my breath because he smells like BO after a long day of hiking.

"Touching. Now let's get camp finished up," Alexandrine cuts in.

"She's right. It will be dark before we know it," Frederick comments with a small smile.

I feel like a weight has been lifted off my shoulders. It feels so good to have apologized and made things right with Frederick. Now, I need to work on forgiving myself.

After another hour, the hunters come back with a big doe and a few squirrels. The men set out to clean it away from camp, taking the shovel along to bury the entrails, and Cass works on starting a fire. The little children are playing a game of hide-and-seek in the trees around camp. Their laughter helps lighten the mood a bit. Everyone is still mourning the loss of Markos, and I think it will be a while before people get back to normal.

It's well after dark by the time we finish cooking the meat and eating. As we start to lay out blankets, David stops and shushes everyone.

"There's something out there. I can hear it breathing."

We're all quiet, and everyone jumps a little when we hear leaves rustling.

"It could just be a squirrel," Tim offers.

David pulls the flashlight out of his bag and shines it in the direction of the noises. Two eyes glow from close to the ground, and that's when I see it: a white stripe down its black body.

"Nobody move," I whisper frantically.

Everyone stands still. Suzanne scoops Sonya off the ground and holds her tightly.

"I don't know what they're called, but they spray stinky stuff out of their butt that's hard to wash off," I say, and I hear Noah giggle.

"It's a skunk," Matthias says. "Henry, fetch me the bow, will ya?"

Henry carefully shuffles his way to the back of the group to find the bow. David keeps the flashlight shining on the skunk.

"You're not going to kill it, are you?" Noah's little sister, Emily, asks.

"Yes, I am."

Emily starts to whimper, and Caroline slowly drops to her knees to hug her. Henry returns with the bow and hands it to Matthias. The skunk has moved farther away from camp, but we can still see it with the flashlight. He takes aim, careful with his movements, and fires. He misses but spooks the skunk enough that it takes off into the dark woods. We all relax and start getting back to what we were doing, and then the smell sets in. Not again!

Pandemonium erupts as the kids start squealing about the stench, jumping up and down with their noses pinched.

"The skunk must have sprayed as it ran away," Henry says, covering his nose with his shirt.

Everyone is coughing and complaining all at once. Let's hope there aren't any Havoc nearby to hear us. And then I remember my first run-in with a skunk.

"Well, one good thing about this is we're less likely to be attacked by a Havoc," I say and tell them my encounter with the skunk.

"Great. We'll just all die from the stench instead of being eaten." Alexandrine scowls.

"We're not gonna die from the smell. Now, everybody, settle down, and get some sleep," Matthias orders.

It's a restless night for everyone. Once we get the kids settled down, we all try to get some sleep, but the smell is just too much. By morning, everyone is cranky and ready to move out.

For four more days, we plod along through the woods. Luckily, we found a small pond yesterday, and everyone took turns bathing in it, in hopes of washing the lingering smell of the skunk off. Thank God, nobody was directly sprayed by the skunk this time.

After walking all morning, we come to a large clearing, and Matthias has everyone rest while he, Frederick, and Henry scout the area. They climb trees to see what they can find. About forty-five minutes later, they come back to the clearing.

"This is as good a place as any to set up camp. There's a small stream not far from here for our water needs. Let's begin," Matthias announces.

We spend the first day clearing the area of rocks, sticks, and other debris. We let the chickens out of their cages, and they happily strut around the place, letting us know they're here. The children run around, keeping them near camp. Everyone seems to be in a better mood knowing that we finally found a place to make home.

The next day, the men go out to the forest to find wood for making shelters. The women build a nice-sized fire pit that will allow everyone to fit around it comfortably. The kids run around having sword fights with branches, and Saul has found a fallen log to sit on to whittle sticks again. I asked Matthias if I could have my necklace back, but he was too busy to dig it out of his bag at the time. I didn't dare ask him if I could look for it.

As I help the women plan out our camp, I start to feel a sense of hope and belonging. The sadness of Markos's death is still there, but I'm slowly letting go of the guilt. I'm not sure if I will ever let go of it entirely, but starting somewhere fresh will be helpful. Alexandrine gives me the cold shoulder now and again, but she seems to enjoy having something to do, and I catch her smiling occasionally.

I sleep soundly after a hard day of work. I'm feeling so much closer to everyone in the group. Matthias, Henry, and Saul may be my family by blood, but everyone in this camp is my family by choice. Even Alexandrine.

The next day, the men head back out to find more building materials. Rebecca, Caroline, and Alexandrine are discussing where gardens should be planted while Suzanne keeps an eye on the kids. On one of the last recon missions, Matthias was able to get his hands on some seed packets. According to the packages, we will be able to grow radishes, spinach, broccoli, green onions, and baby carrots in about a month. In the meantime, we have to scavenge for food so our supply doesn't run out too quickly. That's what I'm doing today.

I head out with some bags to find anything that might be considered food. Suzanne gave me a book with pictures of edible plants. Let's hope I can identify them correctly.

After walking only five minutes away from camp, I come across a bush with thorns and fat berries. I open the book and flip through the pages until I find a picture of it. The book says it's safe to eat, so I pull one off and smell it. It smells sweet and makes my mouth water. As I bite into it, the berry bursts in my mouth, flooding my taste buds with sweet juice. I have never tasted something so good. Being careful of the thorns, I set to work filling the bags full of them.

We have a tasty supper of berries and venison from another deer Tim was able to shoot. Everyone seems content with a full stomach, and we start to get settled in for the night. I can't wait to have shelters built again. I don't like feeling exposed while sleeping.

Tim pleads to take first watch, telling Matthias that he's gotten so good with the bow now, he feels like he should be able to keep watch like all the other adults. Reluctantly, Matthias agrees to it, and we all settle in for a good night's sleep. I stare up at the stars contentedly and say a little prayer to ask God for forgiveness for Markos and to thank him that I'm here—stronger, healthier—and that my life is better than I ever could have imagined it. Then I close my eyes and drift off to sleep.

I wake up in the middle of the night, needing to go to the bathroom. I look over at Tim, who's supposed to be keeping watch, but he's fast asleep. I'll wake him up when I come back. I carefully step over people and walk a good distance away from camp for privacy. The night is still and peaceful, and I can see stars shining through the forest canopy. As I'm finishing, I hear footsteps coming from the direction of camp. I wonder who's up. I start to head back, but I'm stopped in my tracks by a gunshot ringing out through the forest.

I start to panic, wondering what's going on. I run a short distance but quickly hide behind a tree when I see a group of government soldiers surrounding the camp. They're wearing gas masks and pointing guns at everyone, who are now awake and on their feet. How did they find us so quickly?

"Which one of you is Olivia?" A soldier says through his mask, making his voice muffled.

My heart is racing out of my chest. What do they want with me? I carefully look past the tree to see if anyone was shot, but everyone seems to be okay. Nobody in camp moves. They all stay quiet except for small sobs from the children. A huge soldier has his arm wrapped around Tim's neck and a gun pointed at his head. Tim looks scared out of his mind with tears streaming down his face.

"Maybe you didn't hear me. Which one of you is Olivia?" The soldier yells. "Give her to us, and maybe we'll let you live."

I stay hidden behind the tree, terrified to move. I watch as Matthias slowly reaches behind his back to grab the handgun he has stashed in a holster on his belt, but a soldier notices and marches up to him, pointing his gun in Matthias's face.

"Give me the gun."

Matthias glares at him but puts his hands in the air. While the soldier reaches around Matthias's back to grab it, Matthias locks eyes on Henry and gives a nod ever so slightly. Henry gets the message, and they start fighting with the soldiers to disarm them. All hell breaks loose as every able-bodied adult in our group starts fighting tooth and nail to disarm the soldiers. Suzanne yells for Cass to gather up the children and run for cover, but Cass gets pulled into the fray.

I hear guns firing, and I can't just leave everyone to fight these soldiers just to save me. I race to the nearest one and pray that I don't get shot. I kick his legs out from under him, and he falls to the ground. I rip his gas mask upward and punch him in the nose as, hard as I can, feeling the bones crack under my knuckles just like

Victoria's did. He points the gun at me, and I grab the barrel, shoving it away as I kick him in the ribcage. Finally, his gun falls on the ground when I stomp on his male parts. He curls up in a ball and I search around for the next opponent.

I look over at Cass, who's biting the hand of the soldier she's fighting. I watch as another soldier grabs her hair and rips her head backward, bringing a knife to her throat. Without thinking about it, I dive at the soldier who's about to kill my friend and send his knife flying.

I start hand-to-hand combat with this guy who appears to be only a few years older than me. He knocks me to the ground and before I can stand back up, he lifts his mask and shouts, "I found her!"

I watch in horror as a few soldiers pull canisters from their belts and drop them on the ground. Smoke spills out of the canisters, filling the camp quickly. I try to cover my nose and mouth with my shirt, but it doesn't do any good. I see my friends dropping to the ground like flies. David gives me a fearful look just before his eyes roll back, and he falls to the ground.

God, my friends need me! Please, don't let me die!

I land on the ground with a thump, and everything goes black.

A continuous rhythmic beeping pulls me from my dreamless slumber.

Oh, thank God! I'm not dead.

THE
REMNANT

DIANE ANTHONY

1

As I lie in the hospital bed, my mind races to figure out what just happened to me. The last thing I remember, I was fighting for my life and the life of my friends and family out in the wilderness. I think they knocked us out with some kind of gas, but how did I get here?

Where is "here," anyway?

Nothing looks familiar, but then again, my eyes are blurry from having just opened them. I try to rub the gunk away, but my hand stops only inches off the bed.

Not this again.

I blink, trying to get my eyes to adjust, but they won't. Panic starts to rise in my chest, and I squeeze my eyes shut. Taking a deep breath, I open them again and squint around the room, trying hard to recognize anything that will give me a clue as to where I am. I start to tear up at the thought of needing to wear my glasses again. What's happening to me?

It's hard to tell, but the counters over by the wall reflect the fluorescent lights like they're metal. I don't remember ever being in a hospital room that had metal counters. Am I in some sort of laboratory?

Voices start coming from the hallway. I slow my breathing so I can listen. They are standing outside the door, and I can just barely hear what they're saying.

"She should be awake by now. Do you want to be the first person she sees?" a low male voice asks.

"Yes, thank you."

That voice was my mom's. What's going on? Does she know I'm strapped down to the bed? Why would she allow this to happen?

I have only seconds to decide how I want her to find me. Maybe I should pretend to be asleep. Or maybe I should give her a glare that lets her know I'm pissed. Before I make my choice, she swings the door open and catches me before I close my eyes.

"Oh, good. You're awake."

"Where am I? And why am I strapped down to this bed?" I ask as calmly as my rage will allow me to.

"Nope. You'll be answering my questions this time."

"No, I won't!" I yell.

"Your cooperation is what stands between you and your release."

"No, you are what stands between me and my release. Unstrap me!" I scream, flailing my arms around, rattling my restraints.

"No. Now calm down, or I'm leaving!"

"Good! Get out!"

She huffs, pushes open the door, and a nurse steps in, holding a syringe.

"Olivia, calm yourself down now, or we'll give you something to knock you out."

I close my eyes, calculating my options in this situation. I should cooperate. It would make things go more smoothly, and it might mean my release. I don't know where my friends are. They could be strapped down to beds here as well. If I get released, maybe they will too. I look at the cold expression on my mom's face as she waits for me to give her an answer.

"Screw you!" I scream, thrashing around.

My mom nods to the nurse and leaves the room. The nurse steps forward, grabs my IV line to inject the syringe into it, and leaves as I continue to scream swear words at my mother. My head is pounding from the exertion, but I don't care. How dare she do this to me! I feel my muscles weaken and go slack as my head falls to the pillow and everything goes dark.

▪▪▪▪▪

My mother returns the next day just as I'm waking up. At least, I assume it's the next day since she's wearing a different outfit than she was before. I have no way to tell time in here.

"Water," I manage to croak out of my tight throat.

"Not until you answer some of my questions," she says, retrieving a cup from the sink and filling it up with water. She sets it down on the table next to me, taunting me with it. "Where were you going, Olivia?"

"Why should I tell you?"

"I need to know where you were going," she presses.

"Why?"

She glares at me for a moment. "Where's Matthias?" She grabs the cup of water and takes a sip.

My mouth drops open slightly at the audacity of her drinking my water. Wait, if she's asking me where Matthias is, then maybe everyone in camp wasn't taken. Unless she's just screwing with my head. "Why do you want to know that?" I mutter, my throat so dry, I can barely swallow.

"You need to answer my questions!" she yells, slamming the cup down on the table, splashing it everywhere.

"This is a fun little game we're playing, Mom, but I'm not telling you anything," I say as calmly as I can. My desperation for a drink of water is making it hard to keep my secrets.

"Damn it, Olivia! I am your mother. You need to obey me and answer my questions. If you don't answer me, we're going to have to take other measures to get the information out of you. I don't want it to come to that," she says, pinching the bridge of her nose. "Where is Matthias?"

"Why do you want to know? What difference does it make where Matthias is? Why didn't the soldiers take him when they took me?"

"Their orders were to find you and bring you back. Once you were brought back, President Turk decided he wants the rest of them brought in for being traitors of the Coalition."

"Oh. Well, why didn't you say that? In that case...go to hell!" I scream, injuring my throat in the process.

"Nurse!" my mom yells, slamming open the door and storming away.

The same nurse as before steps into the room and injects the sleeping drug once again.

■■■■■

A tapping noise wakes me up, but I don't open my eyes right away. My head aches, my throat is raw, and my lungs are on fire. I feel like garbage.

"I know you're awake," I hear a deep voice say as the tapping stops.

I lie still but open my eyes to see who's speaking. There's a blurry form sitting on a chair in the corner of the room. He stands up and walks toward me, his shoes clacking on the hard floor. As he gets closer, I see he's a tall man, with muscles bulging under his fitted dark blue three-piece suit.

"It's in your best interest to cooperate and tell us what we want to know."

"And if I don't?" I ask, my voice cracking from disuse.

"I've been given permission to make you talk."

I swallow hard but keep my eyes locked on his. "And how exactly are you going to make me talk?" I cough at the end to cover up the quiver in my voice.

"I have my ways. Don't worry. I'll start small and work my way up until I have the information I need from you," he says, putting blue latex gloves on his slender hands.

I turn my head to the side and see my glasses sitting on a little table next to me. "Can I please have my glasses?"

He reaches next to me for my glasses and slides them on my face gently. His cologne lingers in the air for a moment, making me wonder who he's trying to impress. Does he always dress nice and wear cologne for the people he's about to interrogate?

Once my glasses are in place, I look at him closer and see that he's quite attractive for someone in their mid-thirties: brown hair styled into a fauxhawk, sharp jawline, straight nose, groomed beard, full lips, and stormy blue eyes. Then I glance around the room. My heart sinks as I realize I can see perfectly with my glasses again. What happened to my Rare abilities? Where did my amazing eyesight go?

"All right, Olivia. Let's start."

Sitting next to him is a small tray of syringes. He picks one up, flicks it with the tip of his finger, and squirts out a little liquid to remove any trapped air.

"What is that?" I ask, unable to look away from the syringe.

"This is a little cocktail I came up with. Once I inject this into your IV, you will start to feel a stinging sensation throughout your body that will grow until you feel like every nerve in your body is on fire. I'll start with a small dose. I think that's all I'll need before you tell me what I want to know."

I try to say something, but my throat has closed off, and all that comes out is a squeak.

"Unless, of course, you want to cooperate with me now. You can save yourself a lot of pain if you choose to be forthcoming."

I glare at him as I weigh my options. Of course, I don't want him to inject me with that stuff, but I'm also not telling him a thing about the camp. I wish there was some way I could get my hands free and give him a taste of his own medicine.

"No comment?" he asks, grabbing my IV line. "Fine. Let's begin, then."

I start breathing heavily as he slides the needle in and pushes down the plunger about halfway. He steps back, drops the syringe on the metal tray, and watches me. I refuse to make eye contact, so I stare at the ceiling, waiting for the pain.

The liquid feels cold as it flows into my veins. A tingling sensation begins in my fingers, slowly creeping upwards until it spreads throughout my chest and down my legs. It almost feels like the same sort of pins and needles feeling you get when your foot falls asleep and starts to wake up again. Maybe this won't be so bad.

Suddenly, the tingling turns to a burning so intense, I start to scream at the top of my lungs. It feels like lava is flowing through my veins and melting my insides. Every nerve in my body is firing off in pain.

My voice gives out from the screaming, so I silently sob as the pain rips through my body. I thought I had felt pain before, but this is a new kind of horror. I'm having a hard time catching my breath, and I start to hyperventilate.

"It should be wearing off anytime now, Olivia. Take a deep breath."

My muscles are shaking uncontrollably, but I feel the pain starting to fade away back to the pins and needles sensation. I take a deep breath to try to slow my heart down and get oxygen back in my lungs.

I'm internally panicking as I realize that I won't be able to withstand that torture again. That was only a half dose? What happens when he gives me a full dose?

"I imagine you're feeling pretty terrible right about now," the man says with a stony face. "I'll give you a moment to gather your strength before answering my questions."

I squeeze my eyes shut and swallow the lump that's lodged in my throat. I know David wouldn't be mad at me if I give in and tell them what they wanted to know. He understands pain and the need for it to stop.

Suddenly, Markos's face flashes through my mind. I didn't know him for very long, but he gave his life trying to protect everyone in camp. It was my fault that the guard had found the camp in the first place, resulting in Markos's death. If I tell these people what they want to know and they capture my family and friends, then I'll be a traitor who deserves exactly what I'm getting.

No, I have to be brave. I have to endure this for them. They deserve their freedom. They don't deserve to be caught just because I was too weak to face the pain and ratted them out.

I take a shuddering breath and resolve myself. I'm going to do what needs to be done, even if it kills me. At least I'll die with honor, just like Markos did.

I open my eyes and see that the guy is still watching me.

"Ready to answer my questions now, Olivia?"

I respond by staring back at him tight-lipped.

He lifts an eyebrow at me. "Where were you headed?"

"The north pole. I wanted to see if Santa would give me my present early."

"Very funny," he says as his expression hardens.

"I'm not answering your questions. How about you let me go, and we can forget this ever happened?"

"Nice try. Where were you and your group headed, Olivia?"

"An alien landing site. We wanted to know if their world is better than this one."

"Cut the crap, and answer my questions properly. If you don't, I'll inject you with more pain."

I swallow hard and glance at the syringe on the tray.

"Where were you and your group headed?" he asks with a sharp edge to his voice.

I make a big dramatic sigh. "Fine. I really shouldn't tell you this. We were on our way to an Entmoot."

"What is an 'Entmoot'?"

"I can't be sure. I was told it's where the wisest come together to discuss things. They say it takes a really long time for anything to be resolved."

He furrows his eyebrows for a moment. "Where is this Entmoot happening?"

"Fangorn Forest," I say, holding in a laugh. He can't possibly be buying this.

"Why does that sound familiar?" he mutters to himself as he stands up and walks to the door. "You better not be lying to me, or you're in for a world of hurt."

After he steps out of the room, I burst into a fit of giggles.

I stop when I hear raised voices from outside my room.

"You idiot! She's pulling your leg. She's referring to some old books or the movies," a different male voice says.

"What?"

"Ents are tree creatures that live in Fangorn Forest, and when they get together to discuss things, it's called an 'Entmoot.' She's making fun of you. Get back in there, and get some real answers!"

The door slams open, and fauxhawk stomps back in, his face red from either anger or embarrassment. Maybe both. He doesn't say a word as he grabs my IV line

173

and injects the remainder of the contents into it. Then he grabs another syringe, and before I can get a word out, he injects the entirety of that syringe as well.

21

"Olivia? Olivia! Can you hear me?" my mom's voice calls out.

As I wake up, it feels like I'm being sucked out of a dark tunnel. All my senses start slowly working again. I hear a heart monitor beeping and the whiny hum of the fluorescent light. I can smell a strange metallic scent that seems familiar, but I can't quite figure out what it is. And unfortunately, I feel every part of my body aching. The worst pain is in my chest. It feels like I was kicked by a mule.

I open my eyes but can't see a thing. It's all just colorful blurs.

"Mom? Where are you?" I ask in a strained voice.

"Oh, thank God!" my mother cries out. "Eva, you're a miracle worker."

"Thank you, ma'am," a gentle female voice responds.

"Mom?" I say again, my voice still weak.

"You better get out of here before we get caught," my mom says quietly, but I don't think she's talking to me.

I hear footsteps and then the door opening and shutting. Then my mom is at my side, sliding my glasses onto my face. As soon as they're in place, I take a good look at her and see that she has blood splattered on her face and down her shirt.

"Mom? What's going on?" I squeak.

"Shh! Take it easy," she says, unstrapping the velcro bonds that are holding down my wrists.

I sit up, look at the floor, and see fauxhawk guy lying in a pool of blood. That must be the metallic scent I couldn't quite place.

"What happened?"

"He killed you, Olivia. He gave you too much of that stuff, and your heart stopped. And when I came in here to save you, he pushed me away, saying you got what you deserved. So I shot him."

I slide off the bed and try to stand, but my knees buckle, and I fall. My mom catches me before I land on the floor and helps me sit back down on the bed. Fatigue is setting in, but I have to stay awake long enough to talk some sense into her. "We need to get out of here, Mom. You're going to be in big trouble! They probably heard the gunshot and are on their way now!"

"I used my silencer, but I'm sure someone still heard it. You need to leave quickly."

"What about the guy in the hallway?" I ask, remembering the guy who told fauxhawk what an Entmoot was.

"I don't know who you're referring to. Nobody was out there when I got here. Now, hurry up!"

I have mixed emotions running through me as I look at my mother. All the anger at her keeping me tied up here fades away as I think about how much trouble she's going to be in once they find out she killed someone. She is still my mother, and I love her.

"Come with me, Mom. Help me escape, and we can go find Matthias and my group. We can be a family again."

My mother locks eyes with me as she takes my face into her hands. "I can't. I have to face the consequences of what I've done."

"No, Mom. You can't do that. They'll lock you up in jail. You have to come with me. Please!"

She ignores me as she walks to the door and peeks her head out, looking both ways. "The coast is clear. Do you think you can walk?"

I push myself up off the bed and sway a little, trying to get my balance. I glance at the pool of blood surrounding the man who tried to murder me, and my sight starts swimming as the blood drains from my head, and I flop back onto the bed.

"Come on, Olivia!" My mother's voice sounds distant. She starts patting me on the cheek, slapping me a little harder than I think she means to. The stinging on my cheek pulls me from my stupor, and her face snaps into focus. Her eyes are shining with tears as she looks back and forth from me to the door. "Olivia! You need to get out of here. I'll take care of everything, but you need to leave. Now!"

I blink slowly, feeling the weight of what has happened to me turn my limbs to stone. I can't believe I died. And now she wants me to escape alone? I don't feel like I can even lift my head off the bed.

She pulls on my arms, lifting me up to a sitting position. As she's struggling to help me up, I see the door open. I want to scream, to tell mom to turn around, but I can't. I can hardly keep my eyes open long enough to see who's coming in. My breath catches in my chest when I see who it is.

Matthias. Followed closely by David. They're both dressed head to toe in soldier uniforms, but I can see their faces through their masks.

My mother notices I'm looking toward the door. She lets go of my arms, and I flop back on the bed, unable to keep myself upright. Before she turns all the way around, Matthias shoots her with a stun gun, shocking her until she goes stiff and falls over backward. He then drops to his knees and shoves something small in her mouth. I'm about to ask what it was, but David rushes past him.

"David!" I cry out as he runs to me and gives me a hug.

"Are you all right? What happened here?" David looks at the body lying in a pool of blood and then back at me, worry etching his brow.

"Never mind the small talk. We need to get out of here," Matthias says gruffly. He stalks to the bed and grabs my upper arm tightly as he tugs me to my feet. David takes the cue and wraps my other arm around his shoulder.

"How did you guys find me? How did you get in here without getting caught?" I ask as they help me walk toward the door.

Neither of them is answering me.

I look down at my mom. "We need to take Mom with us!" I say, locking my knees and digging my heels in the ground so they stop.

"No," Matthias grunts as he struggles to get me moving again.

"Come on, Matthias! She's going to be in a lot of trouble when someone finds out what she did. She was just trying to protect me, and now she's going to go to jail...or worse! You have to take her with us!" I plead as I thrash around.

Matthias stops moving and faces me; a tendon in his neck spasms. "I don't have to do nothin'! I came to rescue ya, and that's what I'm doing. Now ya better start walking, or I'll knock ya out and drag ya back to the woods!"

"David! Please! Help me here! We need to take Mom, or she's going to be in a lot of trouble."

"Keep your voice down, Olivia!" Matthias spits out and re-tightens his grip as he starts pulling me toward the door again.

I can feel my energy draining as I struggle to stop them from moving, and I just can't keep it up any longer. I go limp, and David almost drops me. We're at the door, and I realize this is my last chance to get Matthias to take my mom. I know it's risky, and we might get caught, but I can't think of anything else other than what's going to happen to her when someone finds out she killed this guy.

I fill my lungs with air and start screaming. Matthias lets go of my arm and puts me in a chokehold, squeezing both sides of my neck with his arm. I stop screaming as everything fades and I pass out.

3

I can feel my feet dragging behind me as I come back to consciousness. I'm being pulled along by two people who have my arms wrapped around their shoulders; their sweaty palms are gripping tightly on my arms so they don't drop me. They reek of dirt and sweat, and I wish I could walk on my own so I wouldn't have to smell them anymore.

I groggily open my eyes, and the light causes a wave of nausea so strong, I just about throw up. All I want to do is lie down and go back to the sweet oblivion of unconsciousness, where there were no pain or worries.

I suddenly remember why I'm in this situation and snap back awake.

Mom!

I tense up, getting ready to fight with Matthias again. I lift my head and see him in front of me, carrying my mom's limp body on his shoulders. Her head is bobbing with each step Matthias takes.

If Matthias is ahead of me, who's carrying me, then? I look over and smile when I see my brother's face. "Hi, Henry."

"Hey, Olivia," Henry answers. "Pop, Olivia's awake. Mind if we take a rest?"

"Not until we get back into the woods."

"Hang on. Stop for a second, guys. I can walk on my own," I say.

David and Henry stop walking, and I plant my feet on the ground. As they let go of my arms, I lurch a little as my vision swims. My head throbs with pain, and my thoughts feel fuzzy. What did Matthias do to me?

David wraps his arm around my shoulder and props me up again. "Steady, Liv. You okay?"

The pain abates some as I take a deep breath. My airways are tight, and I find myself wishing I had an inhaler. "Yeah. I'm okay. Just stay close to me so I can grab your arm if I feel like I'm going to fall."

"You got it."

Matthias didn't stop when we did, so now we have to try and catch up to him. As we hurry after Matthias, I take a look around and can see piles of rubble and war-torn buildings through the fog. We are at the edge of the city, outside the fence. I was unconscious for that long?

I have so many questions running through my head, I'm not sure what to ask first. They just start spilling out. "How did you find me? How long was I gone? How did you get soldier uniforms? What happened to everyone else at the camp? Is everyone okay?"

"Whoa! Slow down." David smiles. "One question at a time."

We've almost caught back up to Matthias as we make our way over brick-scattered roads. My legs are like lead, but I don't want to be dragged along anymore, so I push myself to keep up. I can feel my every footstep throb in my head.

"How did you find me?"

"The soldiers who came to our camp were looking for you, so Matthias knew it had to be your mom's doing. He then figured that you wouldn't be taken back to your apartment since your mother used government forces to search for you, so they probably took you to her government facility. He assumed you would be questioned about your motives for escaping the city."

"That's some good guesswork," I say.

"Not guesswork. I know your mother. I know how Turk operates. If he catches wind that someone might be a traitor, he either has that person killed or, in your case, tries to use ya to gather as many traitors as possible," Matthias says as he keeps walking.

At that moment, Matthias stumbles over a brick and almost drops Mom. He starts swearing loudly as he repositions her back over his shoulders.

"Pop, do you need me to take her for a while?" Henry offers.

"No. I got 'er." Matthias gives me a glare before turning around.

We continue trudging on. Soon the bricks and fallen-down buildings are replaced by moss-covered trees and wet decaying leaves. I already start to feel at home.

"How long was I gone?" I ask David.

"It's been about eleven days since the attack."

"Eleven days?" I ask, trying to decide whether I feel as though the attack happened just yesterday as memories of the event flood my mind or whether I feel like I was being held prisoner for more than eleven days because that also feels true. "Was anyone injured?"

David and Henry exchange a grim look.

"David, was anyone injured?"

"Suzanne didn't make it," David answers, his voice barely louder than a whisper.

"What? What happened?"

"She hit her head on a rock. We're not sure if it happened when we all got knocked out from the gas or if it happened during the fight."

"She had a little girl, right?" I ask, trying hard to remember.

"Yeah—Sonya. The other moms are taking care of her. She's too young to really understand what's going on, but she cries for her mom at night," Henry answers somberly.

"Was anyone else hurt?"

"Not really. Tim's mind might need some healing. He's blaming himself for the attack and Suzanne's death because he fell asleep on his watch. I tried to say something encouraging before I left to come get you, but he wouldn't listen. He looked pretty down," David says.

"As he should be," Matthias growls.

I look up, surprised.

179

Matthias continues walking forward, eyes trained on whatever is in front of him.

I glare at the back of his head. "How can you be so mean?" I spit out.

"He asked to take a watch. He wanted to prove that he could do what the adults do, and he failed."

"He made a mistake, and he feels terrible about it. Maybe you should try a little compassion," I say in disgust.

I know how Tim's feeling. I still blame myself for Markos's death. I would hate for Tim to fall into the pit of self-loathing that I often find myself in.

Matthias stops suddenly and turns around to face me, my mom's head swinging back and forth from his quick movements. His face is red, and his eyes are narrowed to slits. Henry is at his side in moments, with his hand resting on Matthias's shoulder, concern etched across his face.

Matthias glances at Henry and takes a deep breath before talking. "I ain't gonna coddle someone who made a mistake that cost someone their life. I'm in charge. It's my responsibility to keep people safe. Tim's lucky I didn't kick him out into the woods."

"As someone who also made a mistake that got somebody killed, I can tell you that it doesn't do any good to make him feel worse. The guilt is enough punishment on its own. You have no idea how badly I wanted to be the one who died instead of Markos. I would trade places with him in a heartbeat," I choke out as I start to cry.

"No. You're right. He shouldn't spend time feeling bad," Matthias says.

I breathe a small sigh of relief.

Then he continues, "He should stop acting like a damn baby and learn from his mistakes, like a man."

My sadness turns back to rage, and I want nothing more than to punch Matthias in the nose. My heart pounds in my chest, causing my head to throb so severely that my vision pulses red around the edges with each heartbeat. I take a step toward Matthias, but before I'm able to take another step, I pass out.

■■■■■

I wake up to the sensation that I'm drooling, but before I get too embarrassed, I realize that there's something pressed against my lip. I open my eyes slightly and see David's concerned face hovering over mine. He has my head resting on his lap, and he's trying to give me a drink of water.

"Come on, Liv," he says with a slight quiver in his voice.

I open my eyes all the way and make eye contact. A grin spreads across his face, and for a moment, I hardly recognize him. The David I once knew is gone. All the little changes I noticed when we first went out to the wilderness suddenly hit me as I gaze up at him. His skin is smooth and completely clear of acne, his teeth are still slightly crooked, but they're white now. His eyes are a rich golden color with flecks of green instead of muddy brown, and his black hair looks thick and healthy. And since when did his lips get so full and soft?

"Liv, are you okay?" he asks, concern creeping back into his voice.

My cheeks blush as I realize I was staring at his lips a little too long. He helps me sit up, and I rest my head in my hands, waiting for the dizziness from changing positions to go away. "Yeah, I'm fine, I think."

I go to stand up, but I hear Henry say, "Stay sitting. Jeez, Olivia. You scared us!"

I look around to find Matthias, but I don't see him anywhere. "Where's Matthias?"

"After he tied up your mom, he left to scout the area, make sure it's safe for us to stay here for the night," David answers.

"Sorry I made us have to stop," I say sheepishly.

"Nah. Pop was getting exhausted. He's just too stubborn to admit it." Henry smirks.

I gaze around and see my mom leaning against a tree with her hands tied behind her back and her ankles tied together. Her head is lolled back, and I'm starting to get a kink in my neck just from looking at her. "Any idea how far away from the city we are?"

"Too close for comfort. We're all going to have to take turns keeping watch tonight, just in case someone comes looking for you and your mom," Henry answers.

"Our mom," I respond, watching him to see how he reacts.

He gives a quick dip of his chin, and his eyes flit to where Mom is tied up, but he turns his back to her and scans the area, deliberately looking anywhere else.

"Here, drink this." David offers me some water.

I know that I should conserve our water, but as soon as I swallow the first drink, I find that I can't stop myself, and empty the entire bottle. "Sorry," I say, trying to catch my breath. "So, how did you guys get the uniforms and get inside the government building to rescue me?"

"Well, let's just say that Pop is a man who likes to live inside the gray areas of life, sometimes stepping over the line into the black," Henry answers.

"What does that mean?"

David looks at the ground and won't meet my eyes.

"David?"

"He took them off some soldiers who died."

"How did they die?" I ask, unsure I want to hear the answer.

"I broke their necks to save yours," Matthias says, startling us all. "Now, stop your yapping, and everyone get some sleep. I wanna start moving before the sun comes up."

[4

I can't sleep. I know I should be getting rest so I can regain some of my strength, but I can't stop thinking about how both of my parents murdered people to save me. Should I be grateful that I'm no longer strapped down to a bed, being tortured, when my freedom cost other people their lives? Should I feel happy that my parents care about me enough that they would do anything to ensure my safety?

I look at David, who's sitting with his back to us, keeping watch. Does he agree with what Matthias did? He shot a guard to help us escape the city. How do we know that guard didn't die? Am I the only one here who believes murder is wrong?

I roll onto my back and look up at the sky, glad that I still have my glasses on. Between the blackness of branches and leaves, I spot a star in the inky sky. I continue to stare at it until it's the only thing I see, and I let my mind wander.

Maybe this is what life is: you'll always be surrounded by darkness in one way or another, but you have to keep your eyes trained on the light—the good in this world—or better yet, be the light in this dark world. I may allow myself to get angry. I've punched people and even squeezed the breath out of Alexandrine when sparring, but I will never kill someone. Matthias can train me in combat all he wants, but I will not kill. I will not allow him to turn me into a murderer.

Then my mind turns to Markos again and how I was part of causing his death. Who am I kidding? My hands are not as clean as I would like them to be. I led that guard right to our camp, and Markos was killed because of my mistake. Matthias is right. I was only thinking about my hurt feelings.

I can feel the darkness closing in around me. My chest suddenly feels heavy, as though the depression has manifested itself into a tangible entity that can hurt me physically. A tear trails across my cheek onto my ear, and a sob escapes my lips.

"Liv? You okay?" David whispers.

"Y-yeah. I'm fine," I lie.

"No, you're not. Come over here."

I stand up and quietly make my way to sit by David.

"What's going on?"

I don't answer him at first, embarrassed that he caught me crying. He puts his arm around me and gives me a gentle squeeze, reminding me that this is David I'm talking to. I can tell him anything.

"I was just staring up at a star, resolving myself to focus on the small points of light in this dark world, but then my mind went directly to Markos, and the darkness overtook me again, and I fell." I sniff.

He understands what I'm referring to. I've used the imagery of me standing on the ledge of a pit, and when depression takes me, it's like I'm falling into the abyss of darkness, emptiness, and sadness. He always jokes that he'll carry around a rope so he can help me back out, and he seems to know just the right things to say to make me feel better. I don't know what I would do without him.

"Liv, you can't keep blaming yourself for Markos. Everyone else has forgiven you. You need to forgive yourself and let it go, or you'll drive yourself crazy."

"I don't think Matthias has forgiven me," I say, being stubborn.

"Matthias can be a prick, but I'm pretty sure he's forgiven you too."

I pull my knees up to my chest, wrap my arms around them, and bury my face as I try to hide from the world.

"C'mon, Liv," David tries again, rubbing my shoulder gently. "Remember that time when we were in second grade, I kicked the soccer ball too hard, and it hit you in the nose? I thought for sure I had broken it. You bled so much."

I nod, remembering how the pain caused starbursts in my vision, and my mom was angry that my new dress got blood all over it.

"Remember how I wouldn't let it go? I was so afraid that you were never going to talk to me again that I kept apologizing to you over and over for days until you finally yelled at me to stop?"

"Yeah. I was angrier with you for repeatedly apologizing and bringing it up than I was that you hit me with the ball in the first place."

"Think of this as me yelling at you," he says gently. "Everyone has forgiven you and wants to move on. Not that they want to forget Markos, but they want to mourn him or remember him in their own way. But if you keep sulking around, wallowing in your guilt, it's like bringing up what happened over and over again."

"You're right, I guess." I sigh, letting his words sink in.

"Of course, I am," David says with a sly smile. "Now, you need to get some sleep. I think we only have a couple more hours before Matthias will want to head out."

"What about you? Have you gotten any sleep?"

"I'll be fine," David says, and I hear some shuffling around. "Here, take my hoodie. It's a little chilly out tonight."

I grab the hoodie and pull it on. It smells like campfire smoke and David's deodorant. I find the scent comforting. "Thank you, David," I say, pouring as much meaning behind my words as possible.

Then I crawl back to my spot and lie down. I pull my hands inside the sleeves and tuck them under my chin. His words roll around inside my head, and I feel the darkness ebb away. As I start to fall asleep, I realize David is my light. I need to be more like him.

■■■■■

Matthias wakes me with a hard shake. I open my eyes and see that it's still dark out, and I wonder how long I actually slept.

"I want to head out in five. Eat quick, and let's go," Matthias says gruffly, handing me an apple and a strip of dried meat as I slip my glasses on.

I sit up and stretch out my stiff back. My body still aches from yesterday, but my head feels clearer. My eyes turn to Henry when he flips on a flashlight momentarily to search for something in his bag, and I sigh when I realize I can't see with my glasses again. I really didn't like being unable to see with or without my glasses the last time. Hopefully, I'll get my vision back faster since I wasn't in the city for too long.

"How're you feeling?" David asks as he stuffs a few things back into his bag.

"Better. Thank you for last night."

When David says, "Anytime," I know he means it.

I had barely finished eating when Matthias began moving. It's going to be tough trying to keep up since it's dark and I can hardly see. After tripping over a stick and almost face-planting on a fallen tree, I hurry to catch up to David so I can follow him like last time. "I can't see. My eyesight is changing again, and everything is blurry," I say to David in a slightly panicked voice as I stumble over another branch.

"I got you," David says, reaching out and grabbing my hand.

At one time, I would have been repulsed to be holding hands with him, but his touch is comforting, and I thread my fingers with his so my hand won't slip as he leads me through the woods.

We march on, putting as much distance between ourselves and the city as possible. The forest around us comes to life as the sun begins to rise. Birds sing out their cheerful songs as they search for their breakfasts, and squirrels scamper through the dead leaves, chasing one another around the trees. I inhale a deep breath and smell the pleasant scent of dirt and leaves. My chest still hurts from the nurse restarting my heart yesterday, but my lungs have opened up again, and I can breathe freely.

My hand's getting sweaty, and I let go of David before he gets grossed out. Instead, I hold onto a strap on his bag and follow behind him. I peer around David and spot Henry just up ahead, scanning the area with his bow out and an arrow nocked, ready to fight off any Havoc or people that might get in our way. Farther past him, I can see what must be Matthias carrying my mom on his shoulders again.

"David? Is my mom still unconscious?"

"Yeah."

"How?"

"He's been giving her something to keep her asleep."

When I scoff, he quickly adds, "Just until we get back to camp."

"I hope it was the right choice, bringing her along. I pushed him into it, but now I'm starting to wonder what's going to happen when she wakes up."

We stop to eat lunch by a little stream. Matthias props my mom up against a tree and disappears into the woods without a word. I look at Henry questioningly, and he just shrugs. After eating a couple of carrots and a handful of sunflower seeds, I check on Mom to see if she has any injuries. There's a small cut on the back of her

184

head from when she hit the floor after being stunned, so I grab a water bottle, fill it in the stream, and carefully wash away the dried blood.

I sit next to her and look at her closely. This woman raised me, provided for me, worried over me, and now killed to save me, and yet, I can't help but feel like I don't really know her. She tries so hard to keep her distance, to keep her secrets. And we fight so often, I feel like she's more of an older sister than a mom. A mom is supposed to be warm and loving like David's mom, not harsh and argumentative.

The sound of footsteps behind me pulls me from my thoughts. I whirl around and catch Henry standing a short distance away, watching me with her.

"So, this is the woman who abandoned me?" Henry asks coolly.

"I guess you could argue that Matthias abandoned her...and me," I shoot back, his accusation rubbing me the wrong way.

"Matthias wanted to leave the city and the tyrannical government that was holding people prisoner. He was trying to protect us. She," Henry says, jabbing his fingers toward her, "refused to come. I had to grow up without a mother because she was too stubborn to leave."

"She might not have been the greatest mother in the world, Henry, but she's a better parent than Matthias."

"You have no idea what you're talking about! Pop has worked hard to raise me with very little help. He provided for all my needs and taught me how to survive."

I start to speak, but he interrupts, "How about you? She did such a great job of raising you that you wanted to kill yourself!"

His words cut deep, and I can feel my cheeks grow hot from embarrassment.

Just as I'm about to lay into him, Matthias returns with a bundle of wood in his arms. "Knock it off! Ya two want to get us caught?"

"Sorry, Pop."

"What are ya fightin' about, anyway?" he asks, as he builds a fire ring from some rocks by the stream.

"You and Mom and who was a better parent," I say with a glare.

"We both suck. There. Argument over. Now Henry, fetch the pot outta my bag, and let's get some drinking water made up so we can move on."

We trudge on as day turns to dusk. I move on autopilot, stepping in rhythm to David's footsteps as I replay the argument with Henry over and over in my head, feeling guilty that I raised my voice at him. It was unfair of me to accuse Matthias of being a bad parent. I've hardly known him. I don't know what made me defend my mom so hard. In all honesty, she's not great either. But she's all I've had.

We find a thick patch of trees and settle in for the night. The air is starting to get cooler as we head into early fall. David lets me borrow his hoodie again, which I'm grateful for.

I'm told to take a watch tonight so the others can get some sleep too. I choose to take the first watch, that way I can get it over with quicker. It seems silly that I should be keeping "watch" when I can't really see that well, but my hearing is just fine. Before he lies down, Matthias hands me his gun. I try to protest, but he says he doesn't have any swords with him, so I'm going to have to make do. I stick it inside the pocket of the hoodie and try to forget it's there.

I keep watch while standing up, bouncing back and forth to try to stay warm. The woods always seem a little eerie at night, and tonight is no exception. The steady sounds of breathing from everyone sleeping makes me feel lonely. They're all right here, but they might as well be miles away.

An owl hoots in the distance, setting my nerves on edge. I don't like to think about what kind of creatures are out at night. After a while, my legs grow weary from being on them all day, so I sit down with my back against a tree. It's not long before my eyelids grow heavy, and I struggle to keep myself awake. I don't blame Tim for falling asleep the night I got caught. It's not easy being the only one awake.

My eyes snap open when I hear some leaves rustling a short distance from behind the tree I'm leaning against. I carefully peek my head around the tree and see a dark shape walking on all fours.

Oh, crap! Not another Havoc!

5

"Matthias!" I whisper-shout. "Matthias, wake up!"

He doesn't stir. I want to slap him awake, but I'm afraid to move away from my hiding spot. Last time I came face to face with a Havoc, the skunk stench saved me. I don't have that to save me now. I'm going to have to face it.

I slowly stand up, careful to not make any noise. Leaning against the tree, I peek my head around until I can spot it again. The creature is darker than the nighttime, making it just visible. Now that I'm standing up, I realize it's smaller than I was expecting. Maybe it's a baby Havoc? In that case, where's its mother? I scan the trees but don't spot anything.

This creature's making a lot more noise than I remember Havoc making. It's shuffling the leaves around and making snorting sounds. I jump when I hear a twig snap farther away in the woods. Crap! Maybe if I shoot at it, it'll run away, and its mom will too. I pull the gun out of my pocket and flip the safety off. I can hardly see, but I don't need to kill it. Just the sound should scare it away. I hope.

I point the gun up toward the sky above where the creature is standing, and right before I pull the trigger, I shout, "Matthias, wake up!"

Bang!

The men are on their feet in an instant, drawing their knives, ready to fight. Henry and David have their flashlights out and are shining them all over the woods, looking for the attacker. I breathe again when I hear the creature running away from us.

"What the hell was that?" Matthias yells.

"There was a black creature making its way toward us. I thought it was a Havoc, so I shot at it to scare it away."

"Well, ya coulda gave us a warning!"

We both stop talking immediately when we hear footsteps approaching.

"You idiot! You scared away our food," a cranky voice accuses.

I already know who it is before I see her.

Alexandrine.

"What are ya doin' way out here?" Matthias questions, sliding his knife back into its sheath.

Henry and David relax and do the same.

"Hunting. And we're only about a mile away from camp," she says, pulling something off her head. "Aww. Did the mighty Matthias forget where camp is now and get lost?"

"I was following the stream. I knew we were gettin' close," he answers defensively.

"Why were you hunting in the dark?" I ask.

187

"One of the soldiers dropped a pair of night vision goggles during the attack. It's the only good thing that's ever come from you being here."

I give her the finger, and she sneers at me.

"What were you hunting? Was it a Havoc?" Henry asks.

"No. Wild boar. They live around this area, but they're nocturnal, so we never see them. I was on watch tonight when I just happened to spot one way out in the woods. I woke someone else up to take my place so I could hunt it. I needed to get away from the incessant sniveling anyway. I swear the kid never sleeps."

"If you're referring to Tim, it's because he feels guilty and needs time to heal," David interjects.

"He needs to man up and move on," Alexandrine says.

"You are such a—" I start to spit out.

"Enough," Matthias interrupts. "Since we're close to camp, let's get moving so we can get some proper protection and sleep tonight."

Everyone but the people on watch are sleeping when we get to the camp. While Matthias figures out a place to tie Mom up, David spots Tim curled up in the fetal position about twenty feet away from everyone else. We quietly make our way over to him and lie down. David shuts off his flashlight, leaving me squinting in the dark. Before I close my eyes, I let out a happy sigh, knowing that I'm home again.

■■■■■

I wake up to the sound of quiet muttering. It takes me a moment to remember where I am. I open my eyes, sit up to stretch, and am relieved when I can see everything clearly again without my glasses. I look to my right and see David sitting next to Tim, facing away from the camp. They're talking low enough that I can't hear what they're saying. I look to my left and see a head of bushy hair.

"Cass!" I call out involuntarily. I'm so happy to see her.

She spins around, and her face lights up when she sees me. "Olivia!" she squeals, coming over to give me a hug. "I thought I was never going to see you again. You have no idea how hard it was to let you sleep. As soon as I saw you, I almost screamed!"

We both giggle, and I look over at Tim, who's still facing away. "How's Tim?" I whisper soberly.

"Not good. I've tried talking to him, but he just ignores me. So I make sure I stay close to him in case he needs anything. Maybe you could talk to him sometime."

"I could try."

"All right, gang, listen up," Matthias calls out. "Now that everyone's awake, I thought it'd be a good time to fill y'all in. First off, we found Olivia and were able to bring her back."

A few people clap, while others look at me indifferently.

"We also brought her mother with us," Matthias says, pointing to my mom, who's still tied up and asleep.

"What?" a few people proclaim.

"Why would you do that? She works for the government! They're gonna send soldiers out to find her, and we're gonna lose more people!" Rebecca shouts.

"Fool!" Alexandrine pipes in. She already knew that Mom was with us. I think she just wanted to call Matthias a name.

"I know! Shut up, and listen!" Matthias yells. "This woman was in trouble. She killed a soldier to save Olivia, and Olivia didn't want her mother to die. I have control of the situation. Y'all need to trust me."

Some people nod, while others shake their heads.

"Now, another thing. While I was in the city, I got to talkin' to a guy. He gave me more information on the Haven."

A few loud groans echo through the camp. I wish they would stop. I want to hear what he's talking about.

"Give it a rest, Matthias!" Alexandrine growls. "The Haven doesn't exist!"

"Ya don't know that! I've heard enough rumors goin' 'round that I think it's true. We know it's out west somewhere, but this guy told me that there's someone the next city over who can get us there, who has connections."

"Great. Another wild goose chase," Alexandrine scoffs.

"Let the man talk!" Frederick scolds.

"No, forget it. I'm done talkin'. Get to work."

Everyone starts chatting amongst themselves as they get up to do chores.

"Alexandrine, I want a word with you," Matthias snarls and stalks off.

Alexandrine groans and turns to follow.

"What's 'The Haven'?" I ask Cass as I stand up and brush off my pants.

"Oh. It's supposedly a city where a bunch of Rares live in secret. He's talked about it before, but everybody's skeptical."

"What about you? Do you think it exists?"

"I think it would be great if it did. But I've learned long ago to not get my hopes up. It seems a little far-fetched that a place like that would exist undetected."

I don't know Matthias that well, but I don't take him for a liar either. Maybe there's something to this. I just shrug as we head out to help with chores.

As I'm walking back to camp with an armful of wood, I hear Matthias's raised voice. I step around a tree and see him squatting down in front of my mother, who's now awake. She has tears streaming down her face as she looks at him. I quickly hide behind the tree to eavesdrop.

"Bull! I did not abandon ya, Jan. Ya refused to do the right thing!"

"It wasn't like that! You were asking me to leave the safety of the city while pregnant so we could go live out in the woods. What was I supposed to do?"

"Listen to reason, for one thing! Ya've always been so damn stubborn. Can't ya see what the government's doin'? They're lockin' people inside the city and tellin' them that they're safe. It's not safety, it's imprisonment! People should be allowed to leave if they want."

I hear my mom sob out, "I loved you, Matthias. You left me to raise Olivia alone. You took *my* son away. I wanted to find you. I wanted to send soldiers after you to bring you back, but I was scared. I was scared they were going to kill you!"

They both go silent, and I start to wonder if Matthias left. I'm about to peek around the tree when I hear Mom ask in a whisper, "How is he?"

"What?" Matthias grunts.

Mom clears her throat and asks a little louder, "Henry. How is he?"

"He's fine. He's a smart young man. Strong. He's got a good head on his shoulders."

"I'm sorry..." she starts to say, but her voice cracks. And then she starts crying again.

I hear Matthias mumbling as he stomps off, "I don't have time for this."

I come out from my hiding spot and carry the wood to the firepit. I turn toward my mother, and she's sitting against a tree, with her face buried in her hands. It looks like Matthias cut her hands free but bound her ankles and legs with zip ties. I grab a cup and fill it in the pot of clean drinking water to take to her.

"Here, Mom," I say gently, offering her the cup.

She wipes her eyes with the heels of her hands, spreading mascara across her cheeks. She takes the cup and drains it, her bloodshot eyes never leaving mine. "What are you doing, Olivia?" she asks, handing me back the cup.

"What do you mean?"

"You should never have had Matthias take me. I would have been fine."

"You would have been killed or thrown in jail!"

She shakes her head. "Is this really better than being in jail?" she asks, holding up her raw wrists. "You've only made things worse. I told you I had it under control. I told you to leave, but once again, you didn't listen to me."

I stare at her with my mouth hanging open in disbelief.

She sighs dramatically. "But I guess you did it with good intentions, so I should say, 'thank you.'"

I stand waiting for her to say, "thank you," but when she doesn't, I realize she's too proud to actually say the words. "Mom, I was afraid of what they would do to you. I thought you would be better off leaving the mess you made behind and coming out here with me, to be with your family."

I grow angry as she stares at the ground and doesn't respond to me.

"You know, maybe this is your chance to prove that you don't value yourself and your secrets over the wellbeing of your children. This is your chance to redeem yourself from being a terrible mother. I suggest you take it."

I storm away before she has a chance to talk. I can't help but feel like this was a bad idea.

190

6

I spend the next few hours circling around the camp to pick up any fallen branches or dead logs I can find for firewood. It hasn't been decided whether this is the new permanent camp location, but for now, we are trying to make it as livable as possible. Everyone has chores to do to get supper prepared for tonight. David got put on hunting duties since he's such a great shot. I wish he could have come with me. I'm bored without him.

I venture out a little farther from camp on my fifth trip out into the woods. As I bend down to pick up a large stick, I hear a primal yell coming from farther out. I drop the branches I'm holding and run toward the direction of the yell. I hope nobody is injured. I'm bad with injuries. Maybe I should have run back to camp to get Rebecca, but it's too late now.

I continue running until I hear someone wailing loudly up ahead. I take a few more steps and see Tim on his knees, curled over, holding his face in his hands. His body shakes violently as he sobs. I stand there for a moment, unsure of what to do. Should I give him his privacy or try to say something to help? Before I've made my decision, he turns his head and looks at me. He quickly wipes his eyes and nose, trying to hide the fact that he was crying.

"Tim? Are you okay?" I ask tentatively.

"I'm sorry you saw that," he says, embarrassed.

"Don't be. It's okay. Do you wanna talk about it?" I make my way over to where he is and sit down beside him.

"Not really," he sniffs, avoiding eye contact.

"You know, sometimes it helps to talk about it, especially to someone who understands."

He picks up a stick and starts breaking it into pieces. I sit quietly next to him and wait. I grab a stick and break it into little pieces too, tossing them at a hollowed-out stump. He notices what I'm doing and joins in. We make it through about six sticks each before he finally starts talking again.

"I just can't stop thinking about what I did," he says, voice quivering. "It was my responsibility to keep everyone safe, and Suzanne died. It should have been me."

"I get it. I really do, Tim. I led a guard to our camp, and Markos died because of me."

Tim shakes his head and is silent for a moment. "How do you make it stop?"

I think I know what he's talking about, but I ask anyway, "Make what stop?"

"The guilt. The pain. The feelings of worthlessness that seep from your brain down into your chest and fill you with an ache so powerful, it feels like it's suffocating you. It feels like you're dying, but you're not. And then, after a while, you find that you wish you were."

"I don't have the greatest track record to be giving you advice on not wanting to die, but I can tell you that things will get better. I'm glad that I didn't succeed in my attempts now. I never would have found you, this camp, or my Rare abilities had I died," I say, starting to tear up. "I can also tell you that there are a lot of people who would miss you if you died."

"Yeah, right. Like who? Matthias gives me an accusing look every time I'm near him. The women seem to busy themselves whenever I'm nearby so they don't have to look at me. Little Sonya cries for her mom at night. She's going to learn what I did and hate me too."

"No, she won't. It was an accident. You're going to have to learn to forgive yourself, or you will drive yourself crazy. Remember what you once told me? 'We all make mistakes.' Well, you made a mistake. But you didn't make Suzanne hit her head. It just happened," I say, paraphrasing what David said to me when he tried to make me feel better.

He shakes his head, and I start to get frustrated. He's completely unwilling to listen. Maybe this is how David feels when I won't listen to him. I start to feel guilty about that but force myself to stop. I do not need to be pulled down into the pit with Tim.

I stand up and brush myself off, then offer my hand to Tim to help him up. "We should really be getting back, Tim. Will you walk with me? I need to bring another load of wood back to camp, and I could use the company."

He grabs my hand, and I pull him to his feet. I keep pace with his slow shuffle as we silently make our way back to camp, picking up any pieces of wood we can find.

The people at camp have started a fire by the time we arrive. We drop the wood on the pile, and Tim disappears back to where he slept last night, turning his back to everyone. I miss the Tim I got to know, the bubbly, overenthusiastic Tim. But I will never say that to him. That would break him even further. I know that the best thing to do is exactly what Cass said she's doing: to just be there for him when he needs us and to check in with him from time to time.

As I'm trying to decide where I can help out, David comes trooping back with the other hunters, who are pulling along a deer, two turkeys, and a couple of squirrels. He gives me a proud smile. I'm glad to see him being able to contribute to the camp.

While David and the others prepare the meat for cooking, I take Mom another cup of water. They have her set against a tree close to the fire so they can keep an eye on her. She rubs absentmindedly at her wrists as she silently watches what everyone is doing.

"Are your wrists okay?" I ask as I hand her the cup of water.

"I'll live." She takes the cup and drinks. "So, this is what you all do every day? Just gather wood and hunt so you can have a meal? Then what? You do the same thing all over again? Doesn't seem like a good way to live life. At least in the city, you can have access to all the food and comforts you need."

"Sure. You can have all the comforts you want—for the price of your freedom." She begins laughing.

"I don't see what's so funny."

"You sound just like him. The government is not imprisoning people, Olivia! They are protecting people. Your father is just a paranoid conspiracy theorist hellbent on fighting against the government for no reason. There are no enemies."

"If there are no enemies, then why do they need a fence?"

"The fence is to keep predators out. And traitors like your father who can't be trusted!" she shouts as Matthias walks closer.

"I'm not the one around here who can't be trusted," Matthias growls.

"Why did you bring me here, Matthias? Huh? Am I your prisoner?" Mom asks, pulling on her the zip ties to try to get her legs free.

"I brought ya because Olivia was worried about ya. If it were left up to me, I would have been more than happy to see ya get what ya deserve!"

She scowls. "And what exactly would that be?"

Matthias looks like he's about to go over and smack her, but then he glances around and notices everyone is silently watching them. Instead, he heads over to his bag and pulls out a length of rope and a strip of cloth. He marches over to Mom and forces her arms behind her back.

As he's tying her wrists together, she yells, "If I'm not your prisoner, then release me! You have no right to imprison me like this! Let me go, Matthias!"

He finishes binding her wrists together and then gags her mouth with the cloth. She continues yelling even though it only comes out as a muffled grunting sound.

"This was a mistake, Matthias!" Alexandrine shouts out at Matthias as he storms away. "You need to fix this fast, or I will."

Matthias just continues walking, heading out into the woods. Alexandrine turns and gives me an evil glare. She spits on the ground, right next to my mom's feet, and then disappears into the woods, opposite the direction Matthias went. Everyone in camp seems to have snapped out of their trance and goes back to what they were previously doing.

I had no idea bringing her out here was going to be such a train wreck.

"Why are you acting like this, Mom? Can't you be happy just being here with me?"

She stops yelling and looks at me, deadpan.

"Please, Mom," I plead. "Please cooperate. I love you."

She closes her eyes and leans her head back against the tree.

I feel like I'm about to cry, but then I see Henry walking past, keeping out of Mom's sight, and I have an idea. I get up and catch him before he disappears into the woods.

"Hey, Henry," I whisper. "I need you to help me with Mom. She's angry with me because I didn't listen to her and let her stay in the city. She won't cooperate with Matthias and keeps being a pain in the butt. Will you please come talk some sense into her? I want her to choose to stay here with us. It would mean a lot to me."

"I don't know, Olivia..." He shifts his weight back and forth while scratching at his head.

"Please?" I ask, giving him big pathetic puppy dog eyes. "C'mon, big brother. Pretty please?"

He smirks a little and then gestures with his hand for me to lead the way. I have a seat in front of her, and she opens her eyes to glare at me. Her stony expression melts off her face as Henry steps around the tree she's tied up to. He kneels beside me and reaches over to remove Mom's gag.

"Henry?" she whispers.

"Yeah. It's me."

"Look at you! I never thought I would see you again." She sobs.

Henry takes a seat next to me on the ground facing our mother. His blue eyes are cold and calculating as he looks at her. I nudge him a little with my elbow, worried that he's not going to get her to stay by glaring at her.

"I'm so sorry, Henry. I'm so sorry for not trying harder for you."

"I managed. Pop took good care of me."

"I see that. Oh, Son! I can't believe I'm looking at you. You've turned out to be so handsome," she gushes. She makes a motion with her arm as though she wants to reach out and touch him, forgetting momentarily that she's tied up.

Henry scratches at his head awkwardly. "Look, this is uncomfortable for me. I don't know you. Clearly, you're happy to see me, but from where I stand, you abandoned me, and now you're nothing but a stranger."

Mom cringes as though he just slapped her with his words. I feel a slight sense of contentment knowing he just hurt her a little.

"We can get to know each other now," Mom offers. "I'm sorry you feel like I abandoned you, Henry. Not a day went by that I didn't think about you."

194

"If you want to get to know me, then you're going to have to get along with Pop. I know you two have a bad history, but we need everyone to live peaceably for survival."

"I will do whatever it takes. But you're going to have to tell him that."

My mom continues to stare at Henry in awe. I start to feel a little jealous. I don't think she's ever looked at me with that much love in her eyes.

"Okay, then. I guess I'm going to go help get supper going. I'll talk to Pop about having you released," Henry says, looking at me with a raised eyebrow as though questioning whether he's done enough.

"Thanks, Henry," I whisper.

He nods at me, then gets up to leave.

I look at Mom, and she's still smiling as she watches Henry walk away. "You were right. He's handsome, just like your father was at that age. I can't believe that's my little boy," she says quietly, still wonderstruck. "Did you know his very first word was 'Mama'?"

"Yeah...that's great," I say, a little annoyed. "Henry's right, you know. About you getting along with Matthias. If we cut you loose, you have to behave yourself."

"I get it," she snips. "Who was that woman who tried to spit on my shoe?"

"Oh, that's Alexandrine. You'll want to stay away from her."

"Why?"

"Because she hates you."

"She doesn't even know me!"

"You work for the government. Around here, that's enough reason to hate you."

She scowls. "Great. Am I going to have to watch my back every second of every day?"

"It depends. If you pitch in and help around here, I'm sure you can be adopted into the group eventually."

She looks around camp, scrutinizing everyone, and gasps.

"What?" I ask.

"Saul?" she calls out.

I look behind me and see Saul sitting against a tree on the outskirts of camp. He looks up from his whittling when he hears his name called. His eyes narrow; then he goes back to whittling.

"Hmm. He must not recognize me. I can't believe he's here. I honestly thought he had died. I'm glad to see he's doing okay," she says, but for some reason, I don't believe her.

"I should probably go see if there's anything for me to do. Are you going to be okay here?"

"I'd be better if you cut me loose."

"I can't do that. I have to okay it with Matthias first."

"Of course," she mumbles and rests her head against the tree again.

I sure hope Matthias lets her loose. If he doesn't do it soon, I think I might just so we can start working on getting along.

Before I go check in with the camp ladies to see if there is any food prep for me to do, I make my way over to Saul. He's carving the same symbols as he always does. He hears me as I step closer to him, and he looks up at me with a twinkle in his eye.

"Hey, Saul. How're you doing?"

He smiles at me and nods. I interpret that to mean "good."

"Did you see that my mom is here with us?" I ask, wondering how he will react.

His smile falters a little when he glances her way, but then he looks at me, and his smile returns as he nods.

"She's agreed to cooperate. She wants to get to know Henry, so she's decided to stop fighting with Matthias. We might actually get to be a family again."

He puts down his stick and pats me on the cheek with his soft hand. His eyes have a look of pity as he pulls his hand away.

"You don't think it's ever going to happen, do you?" I ask, deflating.

When he sees that I'm sad, he grabs my hand and places the stick he was whittling on my palm.

I look down at it and run my thumb over the carvings in the wood. "Thank you," I say, putting it in my hoodie pocket.

Saul leans over and grabs a different stick to start working on. I take that as my cue that he's done with our little conversation, and I turn to find where I'm needed. I scan the camp and realize that Tim is gone.

Something about his absence puts me on edge. I check with David first, in case Tim decided to help them. "Hey, have you seen Tim?"

"No, sorry. We've been busy with this," David answers, tossing a chunk of meat into a bucket. "Do you want me to come help you find him?"

I take a look at his bloody hands and shake my head. "You can finish with what you're doing. I'll go see if Cass knows where he is. I don't think we should let him out of sight for too long," I whisper quietly so the other men can't hear me. I don't know why I'm being secretive, but this feels like a personal matter.

I go to the spot that Tim usually sits and scan the woods to see if I can find him. Nothing. I try to tell myself that maybe he went out because "nature called," but something is needling me in the back of my mind. I know the terrible place Tim is in mentally, which means I need to find him before it's too late. I can't find Cass in camp, so I decide to search for him myself. I head toward the stream and see Tim leaning over the water, washing his hands and arms.

My hand goes to my chest as I blow out the nervous breath I was holding. "Hey, Tim."

He whips his head around to look at me, and his eyes widen a bit, but he gives me a little smile as he finishes up and rolls his sleeves down. "Hey, Olivia."

"I didn't see you in camp, so I got a little worried. You okay?"

"Yeah. I'm fine. I thought about what you said earlier, about working on forgiving myself and how people will miss me if I...you know," he says, looking down at his feet. "I think it'll take some time, but I'm not ready to give up on life yet."

"I'm so glad to hear that, Tim. If you ever need to talk to someone, I'm here for you. Anytime," I say, patting him on the shoulder.

We walk together back toward camp, and as I step out of the tree line, I see Matthias cutting the zip ties that are holding my mom's legs together. Henry is standing next to them, and my mom is smiling up at him. Tim heads off toward David, and I go to see what's going on.

"You're on a very short leash, Jan. The only reason I'm cuttin' ya loose is because Henry asked. Any funny business, and I'm tyin' ya back up," Matthias threatens, pointing the knife toward her face. "Got it?"

"I wouldn't expect anything less from you," she says through a fake smile.

Matthias slams his knife back in the sheath and turns to leave.

As he's walking past me, I mouth, "Thanks."

He nods curtly and heads over toward Saul.

Henry offers a hand to Mom to help her up.

She takes it with a smile, genuine this time, and he pulls her up. "Thank you, Son."

"You're welcome. Now, my help is needed elsewhere. Olivia, you wanna keep her company?"

"Sure. And thanks, Henry."

I take her over to where I have my stuff and help her find something she can wear. We didn't have time to bring a bag of clothes or blankets for her, so she'll have to borrow some. I pull out a pair of athletic pants and a T-shirt, and I keep watch while she hides behind some trees to change. While she's changing, I put my hands in my hoodie pocket and find the stick Saul gave me. I slip it into my bag so I won't lose it. I really want to go ask Matthias for the pendant, but he just did a favor for me by letting Mom go. I better not push it.

We walk down to the stream to wash her clothes out, and I find that I'm feeling cautiously optimistic. I can't believe I have my whole family in one place. A small flicker of hope blossoms in my chest. It'll take some time, but maybe I can start to think of Matthias as a dad, and Henry can finally have a mom.

"I'm glad you're here, Mom."

"I never thought I would say this, but I am too. I'm looking forward to spending time with Henry."

"And me."

"Of course," she says, her voice a little too high.

As I'm stepping up to the stream, I stop short when I see a large rock with drips of blood on it. How did that get there?

8

For the next week, my mom upholds her end of the deal by helping wherever she can. I've never seen her put forth so much effort to make anyone else happy. It's kind of surreal. Anytime she can assist Henry, she does, even if it means getting her hands dirty. The other camp members are still uneasy around her, but she doesn't seem to notice. She only has eyes for Henry.

He's been warming up to her a bit. He's even included her in some of our combat training. We watch in awe as she performs a perfect roundhouse kick and knocks the volleyball out of the air. Henry and I both clap for her, and she beams brightly as she does a playful curtsy. I wish I could've had these sorts of moments my entire life.

Tim seems to be doing better. I caught him whistling the other day, and it made Cass and I look at each other and smile. She's relaxing a bit now that his mood is shifting, and we've been hanging out a little more.

I want to hang out with David, but he's always dragged away to do some type of chore, and I only ever see him at mealtimes. At lunch today, Matthias sits by the fire with David, Henry, Mom, and me, which is a rare occasion. We eat in awkward silence until Henry starts telling Matthias about earlier.

"You should have seen it, Pop," Henry says, swallowing a bite of venison. "Jan just did a roundhouse kick and knocked the volleyball right out of the air. It was pretty cool."

"Huh. Ya've come a long way since I last knew ya. This is the woman who couldn't even walk and chew gum at the same time when we were together."

"Oh, shut it, Matthias," she says around a mouthful of food.

My muscles tense as I feel a fight coming on.

But then she swallows and chuckles a bit as she says, "That was one time. I stumbled over a patch of grass, and the gum fell out of my mouth."

Matthias smirks a little.

"My coordination has improved a lot over the years. One of the many things I've had to work on for my career."

"Don't mention working for the government, Mom!" I whisper-yell.

She swallows a bite of food and side-eyes me. "Every employee is subjected to target practice and martial arts training."

"Is that so?" Matthias grunts. "You and your government buddies get to practice with the very weapons they stole from civilians. Sounds about right."

"Oh, get over yourself, Matthias! Not everything is some evil conspiracy or plot. The government is put into place to protect the people. And that's what we're doing."

David and I exchange a worried look that this is about to go south.

"Oh, is that what they were doin'? Stealing our weapons and then protectin' us? I don't need some pencil pusher who takes a few target practice lessons to protect me! I can protect myself!"

"Prove it! I bet I could outshoot you any day!"

"Don't make me laugh! All right. Let's have a little competition. If ya outshoot me, I'll allow ya to ask me any question ya want, and I'll answer it truthfully. And vice versa," Matthias offers.

I look at mom as she thinks this over. She loves her secrets, so these are pretty high stakes.

"Deal!"

Matthias raises an eyebrow at her. "Okay. We'll get things set up after lunch."

Word travels fast through camp, and soon everyone crowds around as Matthias sets up the cans. Excited whispers come from the crowd. They all want to see Matthias put a government worker in her place.

Matthias finishes and shoos people back to give my mother and him room. My mom is stretching her arms out, and Matthias chuckles a little at her. I stand between Henry and David, watching with butterflies in my stomach.

Alexandrine stomps up to Matthias and says in a not-so-quiet voice, "Do you really trust her with a gun? What are you going to do if she turns the gun on you, Matthias? This is idiotic!"

"Ya don't know her like I do—"

"Did."

Matthias huffs, "She was one of the most competitive women I've ever known. She never backed out of a challenge. I trust that she'll follow the rules for this. Now ya need to trust me."

Alexandrine scowls but turns around and stands next to Frederick to watch.

"Ya ready?"

"Yes, I'm ready to win," she smirks.

If I didn't know any better, I would think she's flirting with him. This is so weird to watch. I'm feeling nervous, so I reach over and grab David's hand to keep me grounded. From the corner of my eye, I see him glance at me, then down at our hands, and then back at my mom and Matthias as a smile spreads across his face.

"All right. Two cans, four shots total. I'll go first and show ya how it's done." Matthias gets himself set up and starts shooting. He shoots the first can, knocking it over, and then shoots it again as it's rolling away. He does the same thing with the second can. He has a smug look on his face as he turns to look at Mom.

"Not bad."

Matthias puts the safety on and then goes to set the cans up for her. He looks the cans over to see where he shot them and nods. He places them in the same spot they were in and walks back to Mom, handing her the gun. A heavy silence spreads over the camp as everyone has their eyes on her.

She gets herself in her shooting stance, turns the safety off, and aims at the cans. She shoots the first one, and it pops up into the air, and then she shoots it again before it hits the ground. She does the same with the second can.

I look at Matthias, and he's still staring at the cans, his cheeks turning red under his beard.

My mom puts on the safety and hands the gun back to Matthias. "I told you so."

"Yeah, yeah. I ain't too stubborn to admit that that was some pretty good shootin'."

My mom smiles at that. "I do believe you owe me a truthful answer to any question I ask."

"Those were the terms. Go ahead. Let's get this over with."

I look around at everyone to see how they feel about this deal. Some people look scared. Some are shaking their heads slightly in disapproval. Alexandrine looks like she wants to take the gun away from Matthias and shoot my mom.

"I'm not ready to ask one yet. I need to think about it first."

A collective sigh seems to escape the crowd. I let go of David's hand as everyone starts to disband now that there isn't anything to watch.

"That was some really good shooting, Mom. I didn't know you knew how to do that," I say.

"There's a lot you don't know about me," she mumbles as she steps past me to catch up to Henry.

I stare at her in disbelief.

"Well, what do you think, Son? Was that some good shooting?"

"Yeah. You'll have to teach me how you get the cans to pop up in the air like that."

"I'd love to. But I was thinking about something when Matthias was loading the gun. How do you guys have enough bullets for target practice?"

"Pop knows a guy."

"That's it? 'Pop knows a guy'?" she says, nudging him with her elbow. "C'mon, Henry. You can tell me."

Henry scrunches his eyebrows at her and shakes his head slightly. "Look, the bet for a secret was between you and Pop. If you want to know, ask him."

Henry walks off, leaving Mom behind looking disappointed. I want to go talk to her, but she keeps giving me the cold shoulder. She can't still be mad at me for making Matthias take her from the city. She seems so happy to be spending time with Henry. I need to know why she's treating me like this.

Just as I'm about to go talk with her, I hear Cass yell, "Tim! Tim, get back here!"

I look over to where she's yelling, and I see Tim running away from her out into the woods. I take a closer look at what Cass is holding in her hand, and my breath catches in my chest. It's a shirt I've seen Tim wear, but the sleeves are bloody.

9

I hurry over to Cass, forgetting about my questions for Mom. I'll talk to her later. David must have heard her yell, because he's right behind me.

"Cass? What's going on?" I ask.

"Everything okay?" David questions.

"No. Everything is not okay," Cass spits out in hushed tones. "I caught Tim trying to hide this shirt," —she shows us the bloody sleeves— "and when I asked him what was going on, he told me to leave him alone and took off running."

"Is he hurt?" I ask, hoping the blood is from hunting or something, although I already know that it can't be from that because he's refused to have anything to do with hunting or meat prep since I've been back.

"I don't know," Cass says, voice shaking. "You guys have to help me find him. Please?"

David and I nod, and we take off running the direction Tim ran. I want to run at full speed, but the underbrush is too thick. Sure enough, I trip over a stick, but I tuck and roll, coming back up onto my feet in one fluid motion. I love having these reflexes.

"You okay?" David asks.

"Yeah, I'm good."

We both stop for a moment so Cass can catch back up.

"Can you hear anything?" I whisper to David. His hearing is now better than mine. I can't believe he used to wear hearing aids.

"Hold on," he says, scrunching up his face and turning his head to the side. "There! I just heard some leaves rustle in that direction."

We take off to the left where David heard the leaves. It doesn't take long, and we find Tim sitting against a tree, hugging his legs, with his forehead resting on his knees.

"Tim?" David says cautiously. "What's going on, man?"

Tim lifts his head and glares at Cass. "Cass is sticking her nose in my business. That's what's going on!"

"I'm worried about you! Where did that blood come from, Tim?" Cass quavers.

Tim rocks back and forth, looking down at the ground. "It's nothing. I just tripped out in the woods and cut my arms on some sticks. I didn't want to worry you, so I was trying to hide my shirt until I had a chance to go wash it."

"Let me see your scratches, then," Cass says.

"No! Leave me alone!"

David gives me a quizzical look.

"Tim, you should probably have Rebecca look at them," I offer.

"It's not that bad. Really."

David kneels next to Tim and places his hand on his shoulder. "Look, I know you're hurting, but we all care about you," David says, gesturing to Cass and me. "What's really going on?"

Tim continues to stare at the ground, refusing to make eye contact.

David grabs Tim's arm and pulls it away from his leg. Before he's able to pull his arm free, we see fresh blood staining his clean long-sleeved shirt and his pants where his arms were resting.

"Holy crap, Tim!" Cass shrieks.

"You need to get that bandaged up," I say, biting my bottom lip.

"Look, guys. I don't really want to talk about it anymore," Tim says, getting frustrated.

"I don't care! I'm your sister, and you need to tell me what's going on. I think you're lying about tripping and scraping yourself on sticks. Now spill it!"

Tim glares at her again but then starts to cry.

I sit next to him and wrap my arm around him. Cass kneels in front of him and rubs his knee gently.

"Tim, you don't have to suffer alone. We are all here for you," I say. "I don't know about Cass, but David and I both know what it's like to be depressed. We can help you, but you have to talk to us."

"Please, Tim. Please." Cass sniffs. "I love you. What happened to your arms?"

"I don't want to tell you, because I'm ashamed," Tim says through his fingers.

"Ashamed? Of what?" Cass asks quietly.

"I found a way to cope with my guilt. I found a way to release my misery. For a little while, anyway."

The silence hangs heavy in the air as we wait for him to tell us what he's talking about.

Tears are rolling down his cheeks as he presses his lips together. Finally, he sighs and hangs his head. "When I do it, I feel lighter, more relaxed. It makes me feel in control of myself," Tim says weakly.

David gently grabs Tim's wrist and unbuttons the cuff of his shirt. This time, Tim doesn't pull away. He squeezes his eyes shut and shakes his head in shame. David carefully rolls Tim's sleeve up until his forearm is exposed. Cass gasps in horror and starts bawling.

His forearm has a number of angry red cuts from the crook of his elbow to his wrist. Some of them are scabbing over, while others are deep enough that the skin is gaping open and bleeding.

"Why would you do this to yourself?" I hug myself, rubbing my hands up and down my arms.

"I told you. When I do it, it makes me feel better. Like I'm in control. When I make a cut, it's like the guilt seeps out along with the blood."

"This isn't okay, Tim," David says firmly. "You need to figure out some other way to cope."

Tim's face screws up with anger, and he pulls his wrist out of David's grasp. "I didn't expect any of you to understand! This is why I didn't want to tell you! Just leave me alone, and let me deal with my problems how I want."

Cass stops crying when Tim raises his voice. She wipes her tears away angrily, then points a finger in his face, "No! This is insane! *You're* insane! How could you do this to yourself? How could you even *think* about doing this to yourself?"

I stand up and grab Cass's arm, dragging her away from Tim. I pull her up to her feet and walk her away so I can talk to her for a moment. "Cass, that isn't helping! I know you're concerned about your brother, but he's hurting inside, and yelling at him is only going to make it worse. We need to handle this calmly."

"I can't be calm," she says, shaking. "He's going to kill himself."

"I don't think he plans on going that far. But if he doesn't get those cuts taken care of, he could get an infection. We need to go back there and gently persuade him to get Rebecca to stitch some of those deep cuts up."

"How could I not have known this was going on? I thought he was getting better," Cass says, distressed.

"I thought so too, but we've been doing our own things or helping around camp; none of us have been paying much attention to him."

"I blame Matthias for this! He's been so hard on Tim, he's caused Tim to do this to himself!" Cass says, still shaking.

"He has been hard on Tim, I'll give you that, but this isn't anyone's fault. Tim is doing this on his own. We need to figure out a way to help him, a way for him to deal with his pain without hurting himself," I say. "Let's go get Tim to Rebecca."

We make our way back over to the boys, and I see that David has wrapped Tim's arm with some cloths to stop the bleeding.

"Where'd you find something to wrap his arms with?" I ask curiously.

David lifts his sweatshirt up, exposing his abdomen. "I used my T-shirt."

I blush slightly. I can see his training sessions have been paying off as he flexes his stomach before pulling his sweatshirt back down. He used to be so scrawny, but now he looks healthy and strong.

"C'mon, Liv. Help me with Tim."

David grabs Tim's upper arm, and I go to Tim's other side and grab the other. We help Tim up and walk him back toward camp.

"You guys can't tell Rebecca how I got these. I don't want anyone else to know."

"How are we going to hide it?" David asks. "She's going to see that they are clean lines cut with a knife."

"I don't know. Tell her we were sword fighting, and it got carried away?"

"We're not going to lie for you, Tim," Cass says. "We'll just take you to her and ask her to help. If she asks how you got them, tell her you cut yourself. If she asks you how, tell her you're an idiot."

"Very funny," Tim responds.

10

Rebecca stitches the deeper cuts and gets Tim bandaged without asking too many questions. I could tell she wanted to, but David took her to the side and whispered something to her when we got there. She looked at Tim with motherly concern but got to work.

When she's done, we all follow Tim to his sleeping spot. Cass grabs her notebook out of her bag and has a seat facing Tim.

"Let's make a list."

"Of what?" Tim asks sulkily.

"Of things you could do instead of that," she says, pointing the pen at his arms.

"I think that's a good idea," I say.

Tim just shrugs.

"You could have my notebook and start writing in it. Write about how you feel. Or why you're hurting," Cass offers.

"You could whittle on a stick like Saul does. Maybe cutting a stick would help," David suggests.

Cass writes both things down in the notebook.

"You could go for a walk," I say.

"Talk to someone when you're feeling the urge."

"Pray."

"Let your emotions out. Cry or scream."

"Ask me for a hug," Cass says sweetly.

"Skip stones in the stream."

"Okay, guys! I get that you want to help me, but you're kinda stressing me out right now. I need to think for a moment."

We all sit quietly next to him. I get distracted by the snippets of conversations I hear as people pass close to where we're sitting. A couple of people accuse us of being lazy, just sitting here making everyone else work.

Then I catch Henry's voice in the mix and focus my attention on him. "She wanted me to tell her how we have enough bullets for target practice, but I didn't tell her anything, Pop. All I said was that the bet was between you and her, and if she wanted to know, she should ask you," Henry says.

"So, you didn't mention anything about the bunker?"

"Of course not."

"Good. I'm going to have to head over there and get some more ammo soon. I don't want anyone but us to know about it."

He found a bunker with ammo? Where did that come from?

I focus my attention back to Tim and see him staring down at the ground, almost in tears. He's rubbing at his arm, and I suddenly have an idea. I stand up, run

204

over to my bag, take out my hairbrush, and pull off a hair tie that I have twisted on the handle. I run back over to Tim, who's now watching me with a questioning look.

"Here, try this. You can wear this hair tie on your wrist, and when the emotions start overwhelming you or you start thinking about hurting yourself, you can snap this hair tie on your wrist. Maybe the sting will be enough."

"I can try," Tim says, putting it on.

"But he's still hurting himself," Cass points out. "Shouldn't we think of something that doesn't cause pain?"

"I think Liv is on the right track. I don't think Tim is going to heal overnight, but this is at least something he can do in the meantime that won't be dangerous."

We all look at Tim, and he nods as he snaps the hair tie on his wrist.

"Were you just thinking about cutting again?" Cass asks worriedly.

"No. I just wanted to see what it felt like. I think this will help. Thanks, Liv."

I give Tim a hug, and Cass and David join in, making it a group hug. We go off balance and all tip over, laughing. Even Tim. David helps me back up, letting his arm linger around my waist for a moment longer than natural. I give him a smile while nervously running my fingers through my hair.

What is happening to me? I told David we were only ever going to be friends, and I meant it. So why do I suddenly find myself so awkward and nervous around him?

"C'mon guys. We should probably go help everyone else out." Cass grabs Tim's hand to drag him over by Frederick, who's piling wood up in the fire pit to get a cooking fire going.

"We're going to go get some firewood," David calls out to no one in particular.

I follow him out of the clearing, but I turn to spot my mom before I do. I see her helping Caroline peel vegetables for our next meal. They're both laughing about something. Maybe Mom is going to be okay here after all.

David and I walk about a quarter of a mile away from camp before he starts talking. "I'm glad to finally be hanging out with you again."

"Me too. It was beginning to feel like they were keeping us apart on purpose or something."

"So, how are you, Liv?" David asks, eyebrows furrowed.

"I'm okay. Why?"

"Just all this stuff with Tim got me thinking about how important it is to be there for each other, to check in once in a while." He stops and grabs my arm, pulling me to a fallen tree to sit down.

"I'm doing a lot better now that I'm back out here."

"I've been meaning to ask, what happened in the city before we rescued you? You looked pretty rough."

I grind the toes of my shoes in the dirt before answering. I try to not think about what happened—or what could have happened if my mom wouldn't have saved me. "They tortured me to try to get answers about where Matthias was or where we were going."

"They tortured you?" David asks in disgust. "How?"

"Some guy injected me with something that made my insides feel like they were melting," I say, my voice quivering. "He told me he would do it again unless I told him what he wanted to know. I had a moment where I didn't think I could go through it again. And I thought about how you would understand if I gave in to avoid the pain."

David reaches over and wipes a tear away with his thumb.

"But then I thought about Markos and how he died protecting everyone. I wanted to do the same, so I gave him fake answers. He got pissed and injected me with three times as much as the first injection, and I guess I died," I say quietly.

David shakes his head slowly. "I almost lost you again? I am never letting you out of my sight."

I smile a little at him. "Mom shot the guy who injected me and had a nurse restart my heart. Once again, my death was thwarted."

"Thank God for that," David says softly. "I honestly don't know what I would do without you, Liv."

"You'd survive."

"No. I don't think I would."

I look up at him, and he is looking at me so intensely, I blush and look away.

"Liv, I can't help but notice some changes between us," he says, gently grabbing my hand and cupping it between his.

Crap. Here we go again. "If you're referring to when I held your hand, that was because I was nervous when my mom and Matthias were about to shoot. I needed to hold your hand to ground myself," I say defensively.

"So, nothing's changed, then? Between us?" he asks, looking at our hands instead of my eyes.

I stop and think about how to respond. He has been pursuing a relationship with me for so long, and I keep rejecting him. I hate to think that I'm causing him pain.

"I wouldn't say that, David. Some things have changed," I start to say, and I see his face light up. I need to keep going quickly so he doesn't get the wrong idea. "I care so much for you, but our situation hasn't changed. We are still out in the middle of the wilderness, trying to survive. Your friendship has been my only saving grace. You have helped me to keep going, to not want to give up on life—"

"And if you give me the chance, I could love you like you deserve to be loved, Liv. I would treat you like the warrior princess that you are, and you would never have a doubt in your mind that you are desirable or wanted," David interrupts, lifting my chin to face him. "You are the most important person in my life. Please, Liv, give us a chance."

A wave of emotions comes crashing over me: anger that he keeps doing this to me, that he keeps trying to be more than friends; frustration that he can't just leave good enough alone; sadness that I am about to hurt him once again; flattery that he cares about me enough to want to be in a relationship; confusion that a little part of me is curious to see how it would go. "David...I—"

He stops what I'm saying with a gentle kiss on my lips. I'm about to pull away, but this is the first kiss I've ever had, so I allow myself to go with it. His lips are soft and warm against mine, and I find that I actually enjoy it.

He pulls away and rests his forehead against mine. "I love you, Liv."

I jerk my head back and look at him to see if he's serious.

Love? What does he know about love? How does anyone know if they love someone? I suddenly feel sick to my stomach. I pull away from him and scoot over a little to put some space between us. I can feel his eyes on me, but I can't look at him, so I just stare at a leaf on the ground as those words keep rolling around in my head.

He loves me? What is there to love?

"Liv? C'mon. Say something."

I finally get up the nerve to look at him. My heart drums in my chest as I stare into his golden-brown eyes. "I love you too, David," I say slowly, shaking my head. "But I'm not *in* love with you."

I watch as his entire demeanor shifts. His loving gaze turns stony after I say those words. He stands up abruptly, back straight and chin held high. "Fine. I get it."

"David, please, I—"

"I should get back to camp."

"No, David, please!" I stand up and grab his arm. "Don't do this! I need you and our friendship!"

"I'm not going anywhere, Liv," David says with a pinched voice. "If you need me, of course, I'm still here for you. But I'm done trying to convince you that we would be perfect together. I'm done getting hurt." He pulls his arm out of my grasp. "I'll see you back at camp." He turns and walks quickly away.

I sit back down on the tree and stare out into the woods. Why do I always make such a mess of things?

11

I sit out in the woods until the sun starts going down, and a chill fills the air. I pull my arms into my sweatshirt and rub the goosebumps away as I walk back to camp. My mind is numb as I plod along. I should be more nervous about a Havoc or some other wild animal picking me off before I make it back, but with the way I'm feeling, it's almost a welcoming thought.

I can smell the food cooking well before I get back to camp. My mouth waters, even though I don't feel hungry. As I enter camp, I see David sitting by the fire. A part of me wants to talk to him some more, but instead, I just go back to my sleeping spot and curl up on the ground. I lie there sulking, thinking about things, about how I made David feel. I'm so deep in my wallowing that I jump about a foot off the ground when I hear a voice right behind me.

"Here, Olivia. I brought you some food."

I sit up and see my mom offering me a plate of meat and boiled veggies. She has a concerned look on her face as she passes me the food.

"Thanks."

"Are you okay?"

I take a moment to see if she really cares. She continues to look at me with concern, so I take a chance and tell her what's going on. "Well, actually, no. I just hurt David's feelings, and I feel terrible about it."

"What did you do?" she asks, sitting down next to me.

This is weird. She's trying to be nice. Why is she trying to be nice? "He kissed me and then told me that he loves me."

"Well, that sounds wonderful! What did you do?"

"I told him that I love him but I'm not in love with him."

"Ouch."

"I keep telling him that I need him to be my friend. What happens if we try to do the relationship thing, but it doesn't work out? Then I'll have nobody. Why can't he just leave good enough alone and keep our friendship the way it is?" I ask, getting angry.

"I get it. Commitment issues run in the family," she says, nodding knowingly.

"Really?"

"Before I met and married your father, I was in love with someone else. I was afraid to be in a relationship at the time, so I kept him at a distance. It stems from my upbringing."

"What happened to you when you were a kid?" I ask, knowing I'm pushing my limits.

She looks up at the trees as tears brim her eyes. "My father was verbally abusive. On particularly bad days, my mom would turn around and take it out on

me. She'd tell me it was all my fault. That he wasn't like this before I came along."
She stops talking and takes a moment to collect herself.

I wipe away the tears that are forming in my eyes as well.

"I don't have any memories of my parents ever telling me they loved me. Sure, they gave me what I needed to survive—food, shelter, clothes—but that was it. It took me a long time to believe I was worthwhile. So, when a boy started showing interest in me, I thought it was a trick, that he was going to treat me just like my father treated me."

"So, what happened?" I'm shaking slightly from nerves at my mom actually opening up to me and telling me about her past. I don't know what she's playing at, but I'm going to see how long I can keep her talking and relish this moment. I've always wanted my mom to have heart-to-heart talks with me. I wonder what's changed?

"We hung out, spent time together, flirted, even kissed a few times. Eventually, he told me he loved me, and he wanted to be with me forever. I told him I wasn't ready to be in a relationship for what felt like the hundredth time, and he finally gave up. I was crushed. Looking back at it, it was foolish for me to think he would wait forever. Teenage me was smitten with him but too afraid of getting hurt. In the end, I hurt us both."

"What was his name?"

She chews on her bottom lip for a moment as though deciding whether she should tell me or not. This must be hard for her. She's never told me anything about her past life. Or current life, for that matter. "We all called him Arty."

"Arty? Was he good at painting or something?"

"No." She chuckles a bit. "His initials were RT, so people called him Arty."

"Ah. That makes sense."

We're both quiet for a moment. I grab the plate of food I had set down, stab a chunk of carrot, and pop it in my mouth.

"I'm sorry I haven't always been there for you, Olivia."

I turn and look at her with furrowed eyebrows. I swallow and ask, "Where is all of this coming from? Don't get me wrong, I'm really enjoying talking to you, but this is strange. You've never wanted to open up and talk about feelings."

She shrugs and tucks her hair behind her ear, looking self-conscious. "I know," she whispers. "I was talking to Caroline, who, by the way, has been the only one that's even talked to me like a normal person since I got here."

"Sorry about that, but you are a government worker in a camp of anti-government people. Give it time. I think they'll come around."

She gives me a skeptical look but continues on, "Anyway, she was giving me some parenting advice. I guess I've always been so focused on my work, I never stopped to try to be the mom I never had and always wanted. I honestly didn't know how to be a loving mom, and so I just threw myself into my work and told myself that I was providing for you, and that should be enough. Now that I'm out here, I realized that I missed so much. I never got a chance to know Henry, and I never tried to get to know you."

"You've been kind of cold to me since you got out here."

"I'm sorry about that," she says.

We sit in comfortable silence while I eat the rest of my food. I mull over what my mom told me about her childhood. If what she told me is true, I can understand why she struggled so much to show me love. It's a foreign concept to her. I look over at her and see her watching the birds in the trees, and my heart breaks a little for her. Our relationship is not even close to perfect, but she's never made me feel completely worthless. I've felt that all on my own.

When I'm done eating, she takes my plate to wash up, saying she volunteered to be on dish duty.

Now that I'm alone again, a part of me wants to continue sulking over here away from everyone, but I look over by the fire and see that almost the whole camp is sitting together, Tim included, and I suddenly feel lonely. I can hear the children playing a game of keep away, and their giggles send a wave of longing through me.

I want to be happy. I want this ever-lingering darkness to go away. I want to feel hope and contentment. I'm the healthiest I have ever been in my life. I can see better, hear better, breathe better. I even have amazing reflexes with my Rare abilities, and yet there is a darkness in my mind that just won't let go, won't allow me any peace. Maybe I'm broken and will never be free.

I can't stand being alone with my thoughts anymore, so I make my way over to the group and see David sitting between Tim and Alexandrine. Tim's nervously fidgeting with the hair tie on his wrist like he wants to snap it but doesn't want to bring attention to himself. Alexandrine is cleaning out dirt from under her fingernails with a knife.

David looks up at me as I come closer but then looks back at the fire quickly. The pain in his eyes is heart-wrenching.

I find a spot next to Cass and sit on the ground. "What did I miss?" I whisper to Cass.

"Everyone is telling stories about things they witnessed in the city that didn't sit right or that made them wonder if there was something going on."

I sit up a little straighter and listen in.

"The rain. The rain is what got me questioning things. Has anyone actually seen the effects of the rain on a person?" Caroline asks.

I look around, and everyone is shaking their heads.

"Rebecca? You worked in the hospital. Did you actually see anyone with their flesh melted off after a rain?"

"I can't say that I did."

"See? I knew it!"

A few people around the campfire are nodding.

"I was chopping wood one day," Frederick says, "and I got it in my head to do a little target practice with the ax. I enjoyed it, so the next day, I set out to do it again, but a guard just 'happened' to be passing by and took my ax, claiming I was a danger to the neighborhood." He scoffs. "More like I was becoming a danger to the government by learning how to fight. Jokes on them, though. Markos brought his ax over, and we spent hours practicing in my basement."

A little shock of guilt runs through me when he mentions Markos's name. I glance at Frederick, and instead of the sadness I was expecting to see, I see a small smirk of amusement at the memory. That makes me feel a little better somehow.

Nobody else is talking, so I decide to say something, "I never really had any feelings of my own that something was going on until David started questioning things, and it put it in my head." I give him a little smile when he looks up at me. "There was one weird incident that happened in the psychiatric ward, though. A young girl named Charlotte told me about 'the magic within.' At the time, I just assumed she was crazy, considering where we were. But now I'm wondering if she could have known about Rare abilities."

I look around at everyone and see that Alexandrine's giving me a weird look.

Just then, my mom comes back from dish duty, and the conversation dies out. Apparently, nobody wants to continue talking about the government being shady around her. I don't blame them.

"I think I'm ready to ask my question now," Mom announces to Matthias.

Matthias shuffles around on his seat and crosses his arms over his chest. "Shoot."

"It was difficult to figure out what I wanted to ask since there are so many questions I have for you, but I think I'm most curious about where you get enough ammunition to do target practice."

Henry looks worriedly at Matthias, but he just shrugs. "Why do ya care?"

"I'm just curious."

"There's a bunker with ammunition and a few weapons hidden to the northeast of the city," Matthias answers, annoyed.

"Hmm. So, you don't know about the weapon cache on the west side of the river then?"

"No?" Matthias uncrosses his arms and leans forward.

My mom glances at Henry and smiles mischievously. "It's big enough to arm a sizable militia."

"Why are ya telling me this?" Matthias asks distrustfully.

"Because I want to help," she says, winking toward Henry.

Alexandrine stands up abruptly and storms away.

"What's her problem?" Mom asks, her smile fading.

"You. Alexandrine trusts ya about as far as she can throw ya. To be honest, I'm feelin' the same way. What's your objective here, Jan?"

Mom scoffs and shifts her weight back and forth for a moment, looking both embarrassed and angry. "You're a real piece of work, aren't you? You're the one who brought me out here, Matthias! 'What's my objective?' How about the fact that I can't go back now? The fact that you kidnapped me, brought me out here, and I haven't shown back up yet? That tells them that either I'm dead or I've become a traitor. They don't think very kindly toward government workers leaving to go hang out with rebel groups. If I waltz back in there, telling them that my estranged husband kidnapped me and I stayed because I wanted to spend time with my son, they would put a bullet in my head for misconduct. I swore an oath to my position, and now I've not only killed a fellow comrade, but I've been cavorting with their enemy." She takes a deep breath to try to calm down. "No. The only way I can go back now is if I have you in custody or I kill you all. And I'm not willing to do that."

"But why tell us about the secret weapons? What do ya have to gain?"

"Henry is my son too, Matthias! I haven't gotten to be his mom. Maybe this is my way of trying to make up for that!" she yells, crossing her arms over her chest and scowling.

Matthias puts his hands up as though surrendering. "All right, all right. I'm standin' down. Tell me what ya know, and then we'll make the decision."

"Why don't you give her some rectitude wine? Then we'll know whether she's lying or not," one of the men shouts from the crowd.

"Can't. I haven't made a new batch yet."

I shiver as I remember how it made me want to divulge all my secrets. Mom would hate that stuff.

12

"Hey, have ya seen Alexandrine around anywhere?" Matthias asks me.

"No. Why?"

"I wanted her to be a part of the discussion on the weapons cache."

"I'll let her know if I see her."

I watch as he goes back to a group of people, and they look around the camp once more before heading out into the woods. I'm so happy that my mother decided to help us all out. I'm hoping to start fixing our relationship now. It's never too late to start over.

My good mood is making me antsy. I spot the kids' volleyball, and I get an urge to play. "Hey, Cass!" I yell out. She's sitting next to a tree, writing in her notebook. "Wanna play?"

She looks up from her notebook, and when she sees me holding the volleyball, she drops the notebook and pen on the ground. She comes running over and tries to grab the ball out of my hand while giggling. "Tim! Get over here!" Cass shouts.

Tim has been sitting by the firepit, staring at the ashes, for a better part of an hour. I think this will be good for him.

He looks over his shoulder at us, and his eyes light up a bit. He makes a big show of reluctantly standing up and shuffling his way over slowly, but once he's about five feet away, he lunges at the ball in Cass's hands and knocks it out of her grip.

"Hey!" Cass laughs.

Tim picks it up and holds it over his head, well out of Cass's reach. She jumps a couple of times, but it's no use, so she starts tickling his sides. He drops the ball, laughing, telling her to stop.

As they're goofing around, I see David and skip my way over to him. "Hey, David. I know you're mad at me, but Cass, Tim, and I were about to play a game with the ball. Would you like to play?"

"I'm not mad at you, Liv," David says, exasperated. He looks over at Cass and Tim and smirks. "Sure. Let's play."

We team up to play a game of soccer, girls against boys. David's and my reflexes are so fast, Cass insists that he and I have to play against each other; otherwise, it isn't fair. It's a little awkward since we have to be so close to each other, but we just play the game as best we can. I've never been good at sports, but I find myself really enjoying this: the competitiveness, the skill and coordination involved, and running around getting the blood flowing.

We attract the attention of the small children, and before we know it, they're all running around with us. Rebecca and Caroline stand off to the side, watching us with amused looks. Little Sonya pulls her hand out of Rebecca's grasp and runs over to play too. Tim's smile fades a bit when he sees her. He stops what he's doing and hands the ball to her. She gives him a big smile and takes off with the ball toward the goal we made with some sticks. We all cheer for her when she throws it and scores. She turns around and hugs Tim's leg before running off to get the ball again.

I watch Tim stand still for a moment.

"See? It's going to be okay, Tim," I say.

He nods, and we go back to the game. We play until the adults come back from having their discussion.

"So, what did you decide?" I ask Henry, a little out of breath.

"Pop's going to announce it at supper. You'll just have to wait like everyone else." He winks, and I punch his arm playfully.

I worked up a sweat while playing, so I decide to take a quick bath in the stream before we work on supper. When the weather gets cooler, we're going to have to boil water and do sponge baths or something, but today is still mild, so I'm just going to do it the quick way.

As I'm heading over to get some clean clothes, I see Mom lying down on the ground, facing away from camp. I tiptoe my way to my bag, and as I get closer, I hear her talking, but I can't quite figure out what she's saying. I try to sneak up so I can hear her, but my shoe catches on a rock and sends it clattering.

She rolls over, eyes wide.

"Who were you talking to?" I ask lightly, walking normally to my bag so it doesn't look like I was spying on her.

"Oh. I was just praying," she answers in that high-pitched voice again, fixing her hair as she sits up.

"I didn't realize you believed in God enough to pray," I say slowly.

"Of course I do."

I raise my eyebrow at her. "You never took me to church or anything."

"That was some game you guys were playing over there! Who won?" she asks, clearly trying to change the subject.

I try to let it go. She's putting forth the effort to be better; I shouldn't push her too hard. "We weren't really keeping score, but I got more goals than David did, so I'd say that Cass and I won."

"Sounds like fun," she says distractedly. She keeps playing with her hair. I've never seen her so fidgety.

"It was. Anyway, I'm going to go take a bath before we get started on supper."

"Okay, sweetheart."

Sweetheart? She's acting so strangely. I wonder what she's hiding now.

13

After my brisk bath, I bundle up and head over to where I see a group is gathered. They're standing around Matthias, so I hurry up to hear what the decision was.

"I'll need volunteers," Matthias says.

"Volunteers for what?" I whisper to David as I step over to where he's standing.

"They've decided to check out the weapon cache."

A few men raise their hands, Henry included. Before I know it, David volunteers too.

"Are you sure you want to go?"

"It's better than sitting around here day after day. Besides, they could use my help," he answers without looking at me.

"...four, five, six. Good. We'll start planning and head out in a few days. We're gonna need supplies for the trip there and back, but we'll need to pack light so we have space for bringing as much ammunition back as possible. It's gonna be heavy, so ya better be ready."

Everyone disbands, and I follow David back to his bag.

He opens the zippers and dumps his belongings out onto the ground without saying a word to me. He starts sniffing his clothes to figure out what's clean and what needs washing. "Will you watch my stuff while I'm gone?" David asks as he makes a pile of dirty clothes.

"Is it going to do a dance for me?" I ask in a lame attempt at humor.

He gives me a halfhearted smile as he continues to add clothes to the dirty pile. By the time he's done, he only has one change of clothes left. "Huh. I guess I should go do some laundry. I really miss washing machines."

"What would you know? Your mom used to wash your clothes for you," I tease.

He throws a balled-up dirty sock at me, and we both laugh.

■■■■■

The entire camp is together having supper the night before the group leaves to get extra ammunition. That is, everyone except Alexandrine. She still hasn't shown up yet, and nobody knows where she went. Matthias seems a bit on edge with her absence, but he carries on with the planning anyway.

We're all sitting around the fire as my mom and Caroline hand out bowls of the stew they prepared. Mom walks over to Henry and me with two steaming bowls, and my stomach rumbles in anticipation. I reach out to grab one from her, but she pulls it away from me and hands it to Henry.

"This one's for Henry. I picked the peas out of it for him since I remember he hates peas." She gives a knowing smile.

"That was when I was like two. I don't mind peas now."

Mom's smile fades, so I elbow Henry, who's completely oblivious to how he just made her feel.

"Ow. What?" he says through a mouthful of food.

I jerk my head toward her and give him a look.

He swallows quickly. "I mean, thanks for thinking of me. I appreciate it. The stew's good with or without peas."

Her eyes brighten a bit as she turns back to the pot to dish up more.

After supper, everyone decides to turn in early so the group can get up with the sunrise and head out. I can't seem to slow my mind down to fall asleep, so I just lie there, listening to the deep breathing of those who are already sleeping.

I keep hearing Tim snap the hair tie on his wrist, and my soul aches for him. I can't imagine being tempted to hurt yourself like he did. I know I tried to commit suicide a couple of times, but I was trying to escape pain, not inflict it. I have spent so much of my life being in pain and miserable, I can't imagine the place you have to be in mentally to want to hurt. Before I fall asleep, I say a little prayer for Tim in hopes that if there is a God, he will be able to help Tim through it.

Morning comes, and I wake up to voices murmuring nearby.

"I need to go, Pop. You need my help," Henry says weakly.

"You're sick as a dog. Ya ain't comin', Henry. You'd only slow us down," Matthias scolds but then changes his tone. "Ya need to stay here and get better. We'll manage without ya on this one."

Just then, I hear Henry retch, and Matthias pats his back.

"Rebecca. Ya got anything that could settle his stomach down?" Matthias asks with a touch of worry in his voice.

"I'm afraid not. He's going to have to just ride it out. I'll make sure he stays hydrated."

I turn over and see that David has his bedroll all packed up, and he's sitting by the fire, ready to go.

"Well, we're down a man. Anyone else wanna come?" Matthias calls out.

I watch as Cass runs up to Matthias and whispers at him. Matthias looks toward Tim, then back at her and sighs.

"Timothy? How 'bout you?" Matthias asks.

Tim lifts his head to look at Matthias. He's silent for a moment as he fidgets with the hair tie. "Sure." He shrugs. Before the accident, Tim would have jumped at the chance to go along with the guys, but now he seems reluctant.

"Okay, grab your stuff. We're gonna head out soon."

I join David by the firepit as Tim gets his bag ready. "Stay safe out there," I say, poking the side of his leg.

"I'll try."

"Promise?" I ask nervously.

He reaches over to wrap an arm around me but stops before he touches me. A painful look crosses over him as he takes his arm away. I find myself longing for the comfort of his touch, but I'm the one who made it weird between us.

"I'm sorry about the other day. I pushed too hard," David finally says after a moment of awkward silence.

"No, I'm sorry I hurt you."

"It's my own fault. You've told me how you feel. I was asking to get hurt again. I just hope that maybe someday we can get settled enough that we could give it a try."

"Maybe. Perhaps if we ever find the Haven, we could focus more on us than on survival."

"So, you believe Matthias? That the Haven is a real place?"

"Maybe...?" I say, suddenly self-conscious.

"Look at you. It took me forever to get you to leave the city, and now you believe that there is more out there all on your own."

"Yeah, well, it's like Tim had said once, it's foolish to think we're the only ones who don't trust the government. The more I'm out here around 'rebels,' the more I realize how blind I was while I was in the city. No pun intended." I chuckle. "Sure, we had access to food and hospitals and all that, but what were they really doing for us? I think I feel safer out here in our camp than I remember feeling in the city."

"Me too. It doesn't hurt that you and I can kick some serious butt now. I would give anything to see you fight Victoria."

I laugh. "She wouldn't stand a chance! I'm glad I'll never see her stupid face again. Or Cindy's. Did you know that she wrote me letters from the looney bin?"

"Who? Cindy?"

"Yeah, she threatened to kill me if she ever got out of the hospital all because I was trying to help Joselyn. Thank God she's stuck in there! Cindy...not Joselyn."

"I knew what you meant. Poor Joselyn. Some of the people who were in there didn't seem like they deserved to be locked up. Did I ever tell you about one of the people I met when I was in there?"

"Bartholomew, your imaginary friend?"

"No. Not him." David scoffs. "There was this guy who was in there for only a little bit. He wasn't suicidal or anything, so I have no idea what his deal was. Anyway, I sat at the same table as him for lunch once. He was chatting away, keeping those around him captivated. He seemed to know things before they happened. It was weird."

"Like what?"

"While we were eating, right before the alarm started sounding, he told us it was about to start raining. Then, midsentence, he turned around and caught a fork someone accidentally dropped before it hit the floor. Also, before he finished eating, he got up and left abruptly, and just as he walked out of the room, one of the other patients had a violent meltdown and had to be restrained. It was nothing big, but it was like he was clairvoyant or something."

"Do you think he had some sort of super-level Rare reflex abilities?"

David shrugs. "How could he if he was living inside the city? Any of his abilities would have been dampened just like ours were."

"True."

"Ya ready, David?" Matthias calls from the group that gathered while we were talking.

"Yup!" he calls back, then turns to me. "Stay out of trouble, Liv."

"Of course. You know me."

"Exactly. You always manage to get into trouble while I'm not with you."

"I'll be fine."

"Good. See you soon." He straps his bag on his back.

I glance over at Henry, and he's watching them all with envy on his pale face. Mom is sitting next to him, patting his arm gently. I hope I don't catch whatever he has. He looks miserable.

I stand and wave to David as he heads off on this adventure. I'm kind of jealous, but I think this will be a great opportunity to spend some time with Mom. Tim looks nervously around camp once more, waves to Cass, and then turns to follow the men. I hope this trip helps him.

1 4

I feel like I'm slowly going crazy. Mom spends most of her time helping Rebecca nurse Henry back to health, which doesn't give us much time to do anything together. Chores seem so much more tedious, knowing that David is out there doing something adventurous without me. Cass isn't a whole lot of fun to be around, because she keeps fretting over Tim. I understand her worry, but every time I try to strike up a conversation, she only talks about whether I think Tim will struggle and start cutting while he's away. I just sigh and reassure her once again.

It's been a day and a half since the men left, and now that Henry's almost back to normal, he keeps trying to tell us he can catch up if he leaves now. He won't listen to us when we tell him he can't.

Finally, Frederick has had enough and scolds him. "Sit yourself down, Henry, and stop acting like a fool! They left yesterday morning. They're probably almost there by now."

Henry glares at Fredrick with his fists balled at his sides, but after a moment, his shoulders drop, and he relaxes. "You're right. I'm just not used to sitting around."

"Well, if you're feeling up to it, let's go get some food for supper."

Henry nods, and they take off into the woods. Finally, Mom and I have a moment together.

"I hope Henry will be okay out there," Mom worries.

"He'll be fine. You and Rebecca did a good job taking care of him."

She looks me dead in the eyes and says gravely, "I just want what's best for you and Henry. Always remember that."

A chill runs up my spine as she turns and walks toward the stream. "Where are you going?" I call after her.

"I've got something to do."

"Need any help?" I ask, confused.

She turns and looks at me. "No, I need a little time to myself to collect my thoughts. I'm tired," she says, stroking her forehead. "Why don't you go help Caroline and Rebecca with the kids? They could probably use a break." She gazes at me for a moment, then turns back toward the stream and walks away.

My mind immediately plummets into thoughts of being unwanted and unloved, but I refuse to entertain them for more than a few seconds. She just spent the last couple of days doting on Henry, and sometimes you just need to be by yourself.

After about five minutes of sitting here, I can't shake this uneasy feeling I have after that interaction with my mom. Something is niggling me in the back of my mind. I consider following her to see what she's up to, but I stay put. I decided that I would try harder to get along with her, and following her would just make her mad.

I don't feel like hanging out with little kids right now, so I head over to where Cass is sitting doodling in her notebook. I take a seat against a tree and listen to the birds sing, mulling things around in my mind.

"My mom's acting weird again," I blurt out.

"Was she ever normal?" Cass smirks as she continues drawing.

"I'm serious. Something seems wrong. I can't shake this feeling that something is about to happen."

I look over at Cass and see that I have her attention now. She puts down her pencil and sits up straighter. "Why? What do you think will happen?"

"I don't know," I mumble, shaking my head.

"Maybe you're just nervous because David went with Matthias."

"Maybe," I say skeptically, but in my gut, I know that isn't it.

"I'm sure they'll be fine. Matthias is in charge. He's too stubborn to let anyone get hurt on his watch. I'm sure that Tim will be fine too," Cass says, reassuring herself more than me. She gives me a smile and then picks her pencil back up to continue working in her notebook.

I decide to lie down and take a nap. Being temporarily unconscious sounds amazing right now. I slow my breathing down and tune out all the different noises coming from camp. I let my mind wander, feeling sleep tugging me down into its comforting embrace. My muscles relax, and it's as though I'm sinking into the ground. As I'm just about to fall asleep, a surge of adrenaline rushes through my body and pulls me awake with a painful jolt. I sit up and look around for the imminent danger.

"What's the matter?" Cass asks, looking at me with worry. "Did you have a bad dream?"

"No," I answer, breathing heavily. "Something's wrong. I need to find my mom." I frantically stand up and am heading the direction my mom went when, suddenly, a faraway boom echoes through our camp.

My heart immediately drops into my stomach.

Cass is up on her feet, looking as scared as I feel. "What was that?" she yells.

Everyone in camp has stopped what they're doing and are all looking around at each other questioningly. My entire body shakes with fear of what that explosion could have been. I need to get higher so I can see what's going on.

I run out to the woods and pick the tree that seems to be the tallest in the area. I get a running start and use one foot to kick off a nearby tree's trunk, which pushes me toward the one I want to climb. I jump back and forth, kicking off each tree as I climb higher and higher toward the branches. I give one last hard push and grab onto the bottom branch. I swing myself up and take a moment to catch my breath. I can't believe I can do things like that!

I quickly climb my way to the top of the tree, and even though it's not a clear view, I can see a thick column of black smoke swirling up from west of the river, right from the direction David was heading.

15

I find myself on the ground, but I don't remember climbing down the tree. I'm on my hands and knees, breathing fast and hard. My vision fades black around the edges as terror rips through my body. I look up as I hear footsteps crashing through the trees and see Henry and Frederick running back to camp. I push myself up and stumble my way back. I have just enough sense not to take off by myself to find David, even though I desperately want to. My head is fuzzy as I try to process what's going on. I finally make it back and see everyone in camp flocked around Henry and Frederick.

"I have no idea what that was," Henry says to Cass, who looks white as a ghost.

"It came from where David was going. West of the river," I choke out, my throat tight with emotion.

"Are you sure?" Henry asks.

"I climbed a tree and saw smoke billowing from there."

Henry lets out a frustrated yell toward the sky.

"We don't know that anything bad has happened to the group yet. We need to keep our heads. Henry, take a seat before you pass out," Frederick says.

Henry plops down on a tree stump, bracing his head in his hands.

"Did Matthias mention anything about blowing the cache up after they got the ammo?" I ask, hoping with all my might that that's the case.

"No. Why would they do that? That would announce their location and bring attention to themselves," Henry answers in a condescending tone.

"Okay. I'm sorry. I just don't want it to be the alternative."

Henry rubs at his face with both hands, letting out a frustrated groan. "Where's Janice?" he growls, standing up abruptly. "She did this. She had to have had something to do with this!"

"After you went off to hunt, she said she had something to do and wanted to be alone," I answer. "But why would she do something like this? She said she wanted to help us. Especially you."

Henry stands there thinking for a moment and then looks straight at me with his piercing blue eyes. "I don't think it was a coincidence that I got sick the night before we were supposed to leave for this. She didn't want me to go, because she knew there was going to be an explosion. That's why she insisted I get the bowl of stew you had grabbed. She poisoned it to make me sick!"

My stomach does a flip when I realize he might be right. But why would she do this?

"Let's stop standing around talking about the whys and why-nots. What are we going to do about it?" Frederick asks.

"We're going to go save whoever might still be alive," Henry replies. "Who's coming?"

Frederick and Henry look around camp to find any volunteers.

"Rebecca, we're going to need you to come with us. You're the best at this kind of thing. Bring your medical kit," Frederick says.

Rebecca nods and runs to grab her equipment.

"I want to come," I say because I need to know David is okay.

"No. You're part of the reason this happened. We just had to bring her out here because of you. You better hope to God that Pop is all right," Henry barks angrily, pointing a shaky finger at me.

I take a couple of steps back, stunned at the venom in his voice. He's right. If mom did cause the explosion and anyone died because of it, it would be my fault.

"Cool it, Henry!" Frederick yells. He gives me a sympathetic look before grabbing Henry's shoulder and dragging him off to gather supplies.

I glance around at everyone in camp, suddenly feeling vulnerable. I don't want to be standing here in front of everyone. I spot Cass, who's rocking back and forth, hugging her knees and crying. I have a seat next to her and wrap my arm around her shoulders.

She leans into me, sniffling. "Do you think anyone died?" she asks with a shudder.

"I don't know."

"Is this the bad feeling you were having? Did you know this was going to happen?"

"I had no idea about the explosion. I just felt a weird sensation that something bad was coming."

"I hope Tim is okay. I'm the one who told Matthias to take him along. If something bad happened to him, it was my fault," she blubbers.

"We need to stop blaming ourselves for everything. You didn't make Tim go. You only suggested that he did. Everything else was out of your control. I made Matthias bring my mom out here, but I didn't make her do this, and how do we even know this was her doing? Henry might be right, but he could be wrong too."

"True. But you said it yourself that your mom was acting weird."

I nod reluctantly. We sit together, watching the group of people gather up their things and get ready to head out to find the survivors. Rebecca heads over to where we're sitting.

"Please help keep an eye on my boys for me," Rebecca says as she straps her bag on her back. "Caroline already has enough on her plate with taking care of her kids and Sonya. Oh, and make sure you help Saul out too. We'll be back as soon as we can."

We watch as a group of people set out toward the explosion. I don't know what I'm going to do for the next couple of days before they get back. I wish they would let me go with them. I want to know if David is okay, and it's going to drive me crazy until I do.

"What are you going to say to your mom when she comes back?" Cass asks.

"I'm just going to ask her if she had anything to do with this. I can sometimes tell when she lies to me," I say weakly. "Do you think I should go out and try to find her?"

"No. I think you had better stay put here and help out as much as you can. Henry seems pretty angry with you. You wouldn't want to go get lost or something."

I'm so full of nervous energy that I can't just sit still anymore. I get up and start walking laps around the camp, chewing on my fingernails. Some people have suggested that we start packing up our stuff in case we need to leave as soon as they get back, but I'm not in the mood.

What am I going to do if David died? I can't imagine my life without him. I would never survive, and not just physically, because he is always there to help me out of the mental darkness. Without him, I don't stand a chance.

Cass is right. What am I going to say to Mom when she gets back? I really hope Henry is jumping to conclusions. Maybe he just got a stomach bug. It happens. She's not the greatest mom in the world, but I could never imagine her doing something like this, poisoning him to make him sick.

Maybe Matthias decided to take what he needed from the weapons cache and destroy the rest. Sure, it would have alerted people from the city, and it might mean their capture, but I can't live with the idea of the cache being rigged. That would definitely mean my mom had something to do with it.

I pace and pace, getting more agitated as I mull these things around in my head. I need to figure out a way to keep my mind occupied and away from these thoughts.

I find Caroline and have her point out where the peeler and carrots are. I might as well do something useful. I grab a bowl and start peeling carrots for supper, saving the scraps for the animals. There's something therapeutic about mindless repetition, and I suddenly understand why Saul whittles sticks. I think he's onto something.

After a while, though, my mind goes back to David, and I can't stop thinking about him. I wish I would have tried to talk him into staying here with me. If I had told him I love him and left it at that, maybe we would be here, making out or whatever it is couples do, instead of him possibly lying dead somewhere.

I look down at the carrot I'm peeling and realize I scraped it away to a nubbin. This is no use. I'm going to end up hurting myself because I'm not paying attention. I abandon the carrots and pace around the camp some more. Cass is curled up into a little ball on her bedding, shaking from her sobs. Everyone else in camp is somber as we wait to find out what happened. Even the little kids are quietly doodling in the dirt.

Saul is whittling as usual, but I can feel him watching me as I pace past him. I stop and take a seat next to him. "It seemed like you were not happy that Mom was here. Do you think she's capable of poisoning Henry so he wouldn't go with the group because she knew there was going to be a trap?"

Saul looks at me and nods.

My breath catches in my chest, and I want to be alone. "I'm going to go into the woods for a little bit," I mumble as I get up.

If anyone around here knows Mom, it would be Matthias and Saul, and now Saul just let on that my mom is capable of doing something this evil. I certainly hope she comes back soon. She and I need to have a serious talk.

Sleep was agonizing. I tossed and turned all night, with visions of exploded body parts raining from the sky. I'm thankful when the sun starts to come up. At least I can stop being angry that I'm not sleeping.

I sit up and look around to see if Mom came back during the night. It's still pretty dark despite the dawn light filtering in, but my enhanced eyesight allows me to see with very little light.

Once again, there's still no sign of Mom. I'm so angry at her right now. She better hope that she had nothing to do with this, or she's going to regret it. I don't care if she's my mother. She tried to hurt people I love, and she's going to pay for it.

I shiver as I crawl out of my blankets into the cool morning air. I start to wonder what I'm going to do once winter comes. I didn't pack anything heavier than a hooded sweatshirt. Maybe Matthias will go on a recon mission to get some winter gear. If he's still alive, that is.

I'm one of the first ones up, other than the two men keeping guard. I throw on an extra layer of clothes to try to stave off the chill and go over to relieve Stan of the last hour or so of his duty. He seems like a nice guy, but I haven't really gotten to know him that well. He's a middle-aged man who mostly keeps to himself. He always seems to have a sad expression on his face and hardly ever smiles. He gratefully accepts my offer and heads off to rest.

I sit with my back leaning up against the tree, staring out into the woods when I realize that Stan never handed me the guard weapon. I look around the ground to see if maybe he set it down, but there's nothing there. No gun, no sword, no knives. I just shrug it off because I won't have to keep watch for much longer.

To stop myself from thinking about David, I run songs through my mind, bopping my head along to the beat. I quit when I see movement out in the woods. I stare at the spot where I thought I saw it, but nothing else happens. Maybe it was a tree that seemed to move weird because I was bopping my head? Or a bird that flew through the trees and now is gone? I watch for a little bit longer but then go back to keeping my mind occupied with music.

There! I see something again. This time it was closer. It looked like someone's head peeking around the tree and then disappearing behind it once more. I start to panic as I remember that I don't have any weapons. I stand up, my muscles tensing in preparation for a fight. Just as I'm about to alert the camp, I watch Alexandrine step out from behind a tree with her arm around Charlotte, the girl from the hospital. And hidden behind them trails someone I can't quite make out.

"Hey, Olivia," Alexandrine calls out as they walk closer to camp.

"Alexandrine! Where have you been?"

"Finding Charlotte." She smiles. She looks like a completely different person. Her eyes are bright and cheerful as she looks down at the girl.

"Hi, Charlotte." I acknowledge the girl with a smile. Then I turn back to Alexandrine, "Is she— Is this your daughter?"

"Mmhmm! I also brought along her friend," Alexandrine says, looking back at the person trailing behind them.

When I see who it is, my heart leaps into my throat, and I instinctively put up my fists in self-defense.

"Olivia!" Joselyn squeals and runs over to give me a hug.

"Joselyn?" I ask, hugging her back.

She nods as she pulls away, smiling.

"Joselyn! I'm so happy to see you!" I half lie. "How are you? How did you get here?"

I glance over at Alexandrine, who has her arm wrapped protectively around Charlotte's shoulders as she watches Joselyn and me. She tenses a bit when I ask how they got here.

"I'm fine. Alexandrine brought me along when I asked if I could go too. After you left, Charlotte and I got to be friends, and I didn't want to be alone again. I'm feeling so much better out here. It's beautiful."

"Good," I say through a forced smile. I really need to talk to Alexandrine alone for a moment, but I know she's not going to want to be away from Charlotte for long since she just got her back. I go for the easier questions first. "How did you know where to find Charlotte?"

"It was what you said that night around the fire that made me realize where she was. A girl named Charlotte in the mental ward who said something about 'magic within.' I knew it had to be her. They took Charlotte from me because she had Rare abilities, so I knew it was possible that she would wind up in the psychiatric hospital since that's what often happens to Rare people."

I nod, even though it still seems like a stretch that she would go waltzing back into the city on so little.

"Where's Matthias?" she asks, craning her neck to try and spot him.

"Did you hear the explosion on your way back?"

"Yeah. We picked up the pace once we heard it. What was it from?" Alexandrine asks as she plays with Charlotte's hair.

Charlotte looks unsettled, like she's not sure of Alexandrine, but she doesn't pull away either. I can only imagine what she must be feeling right now. A woman who claims to be your long-lost mother finally shows up to rescue you after years of being abandoned.

"Matthias went on a mission to gather weapons and ammo from a bunker my mom told him about. But then the explosion happened. Smoke was billowing up from the location my mom said the bunker was in, so Henry gathered a crew to go rescue any survivors," I say as a fresh wave of fear crashes down on me.

Alexandrine's eyes no longer sparkle with happiness. Her chest heaves as her face grows dark. Before I know what's happening, I'm on the ground with her knife against my neck. I grab Alexandrine's wrist that's holding the knife and thrust my hips up to knock her off balance, careful not to let her cut me. I spin myself out from under her and am up on my feet in seconds, ready for her next attack.

Charlotte's hiding her face, peering between her fingers to watch. Joselyn suddenly has a twisted smile on her face and claps her hands as she watches Alexandrine come at me again. Looks like Cindy's back.

I dodge Alexandrine's swipe at my abdomen and grab onto her wrist, spinning it behind her back into an arm lock, making sure I keep the tip of the knife away from me. I make sure to lock her wrist as she bucks around to try to free herself.

"What is wrong with you?" I scream in her ear.

"We never should have let your mother into this camp! I should've put a bullet in her head the first moment I saw her!" she grunts as she struggles to get free.

I let go of her and put distance between us, holding up my hands in defense. "I'm sorry! Okay? I just wanted my mother with me like you want Charlotte with you!" I yell, tears stinging my eyes.

Alexandrine glares at me for a moment, but then the hand holding the knife toward me drops to her side, and her shoulders slump as the fight seems to leave her.

"C'mon! Kill her!" Cindy shouts to Alexandrine.

"Oh, shut up!" she snaps back.

My words seem to have had an effect on her. She slides the knife back into its sheath. As she does, I notice that it has dried blood on it and cringe at the thought of her having cut me with that thing.

"Fine. You want to be with your mom. I get it. But that doesn't mean I'm letting you off the hook if Matthias is dead," she says, walking toward me, pointing her finger at my chest. "And if your mother had something to do with this, I'm going to put a bullet in her head right here," she growls, poking me in the forehead between the eyes.

"Fair enough," I concede.

She raises an eyebrow at me in surprise.

"What? That's it?" Cindy sneers. "If you don't kill her, I will!"

Cindy starts running toward me, but Alexandrine steps in front of me and knocks Cindy to the ground.

"What is wrong with this chick?" Alexandrine asks as we watch Cindy stand back up and brush herself off.

"This girl's name is Joselyn. She's a sweet kid with DID, but one of her personalities is named Cindy, and Cindy hates me."

"Why?"

"Because she wants to get rid of me, that's why!" Cindy yells and tries to get to me once more, but Alexandrine stops her again.

"Cool it! I brought you out here because you're Charlotte's friend, but if you become a threat to this camp or anyone in it, Olivia included, I have no problem killing you. Got it?"

Cindy hesitates a moment but then nods, which appeases Alexandrine. But not me. I know she's going to try to kill me. It's just a matter of time.

17

Alexandrine and Charlotte head off to go get something to eat, leaving me with Cindy. Before she leaves, Alexandrine hands me a spare pocketknife and whispers, "Do what you have to do."

I slide the knife into my pocket and hope to God I won't need it. Cindy stands still, her pale eyes boring a hole into mine.

"I wanted us to be friends, Olivia. But you had to ruin it by trying to get rid of me."

"We've been over this, Cindy. You're just a personality trapped in a little girl's body. It's not fair to Joselyn."

"Fair? What the hell do you know about fair?" Cindy yells, gesturing to her body.

"You're right! Okay? The entire situation sucks. Now that you're out here, though, there's no medication for Joselyn to take, so I won't be trying to get rid of you or anything. Can we please just try to get along? Everyone relies on everyone else for survival out here. We need to have each other's backs."

Cindy pulls her ponytail over her shoulder and twirls it around her finger as she thinks about what I just said.

I watch awkwardly, never taking my eyes off her.

"Okay," she says, tossing her hair back over her shoulder. She thrusts her hand out in front of her. "Let's shake on it."

I furrow my eyebrows at her as I slowly reach my hand out to shake.

She grabs my hand and rakes her fingernails down my wrist.

"Ow!" I scream, holding my wrist tightly. "What the hell, Cindy?"

"There. Call us even. For now, anyway." She smiles wickedly.

My hand starts going for the knife in my pocket, but I take a deep breath and remind myself that I would be hurting Joselyn. I look down at my wrist and see that she didn't draw any blood, thankfully. Just red marks.

"What do you guys eat around here?" she asks in a friendly tone as though she didn't just attack me.

"We hunt animals and gather any food we can find. We also grow our own crops."

"Hunt? So, you guys have weapons?"

I ignore her and lead her to the basket of apples. "Here. You can snack on some apples. We also have that pot of drinking water. Just grab a cup from over there if you want a drink."

As I'm watching Cindy sort through the apples to find one that appeals to her, Cass cautiously steps up behind me and whispers, "Who's that?"

"That's Joselyn. I think I might have mentioned her before. Anyway, she's a girl with DID. This is one of her personalities, Cindy. You'll wanna stay away from her. She's crazy."

"DID?"

"Dissociative Identity Disorder. She has multiple personalities."

"What? Really? That must suck."

Before I know what's happening, I reach out and catch an apple that's flying at my head.

"I know you're whispering about me," Cindy says around a mouthful of apple. "I don't like being whispered about."

"Sorry. Cass, this is Cindy. Cindy, this is Cass."

"I like your hair! Can I brush it?" Cindy gushes.

Cass looks at me quizzically.

I shake my head slightly.

"Um...no?"

Cindy shrugs and goes back to eating her apple. She twirls in a circle on her toes a few times and then starts moseying around the camp, checking things out. I follow closely behind to try to keep her out of trouble. I can't believe Alexandrine brought her out here. We make a few laps around camp. I introduce Cindy to a couple of people, but she decides to take over the introductions and bounds up to everyone with so much enthusiasm, it puts them off. They look confused as they shake her hand reluctantly.

Alexandrine and Charlotte are down by the stream, washing some laundry together. They're not talking, but they seem to be content in their silence. I'm happy for Alexandrine. Hopefully, she'll be nicer now that she has her daughter back.

We make our way over to the firepit and have a seat.

"So, Cindy? What do you think of our camp?" Cass asks, trying to make conversation.

"It's crap," she answers, picking at her teeth. "But it's better than the nut house, so there's that."

Cass seems insulted, but I put my hand on her shoulder to warn her to let it go.

We're quiet for a while as Cindy looks around at the colored leaves that still remain on the trees. She should have been here a couple days ago. It was like the woods were on fire with all the warm-colored hues. I couldn't stop staring at them.

"I will admit that the scenery is nicer," she says, smiling at a red maple tree.

"I couldn't agree more," I say, watching her.

She closes her eyes and shakes her head like there's a bug bothering her. She stops abruptly and looks at me with a kind expression. "Oh hey, Olivia!" she says. "Who's this?" She points at Cass.

"I'm Cass..." Cass says slowly.

"I'm Joselyn. It's nice to meet you."

I hear Cass whisper, "Whoa!" quietly to herself.

"So, what is this place?" Joselyn asks.

"This is a rebel camp full of people who got tired of living in the city and following the government rules."

She nods as she looks around at everyone. "How long have you been out here? Is that why you stopped answering my letters?"

"Yeah. I'm sorry. My friend David and I escaped a while ago. I've gotten a lot better since I've been out here. It's been really wonderful."

Cass stands up and starts pacing around, worry etched on her brow. It brings the fear for David and the others back to my mind, and I start bouncing my knees up and down.

"What's the matter?" Joselyn asks, noticing our nervousness.

"We think some of our friends and family might have gotten hurt or killed in the explosion. Now we have to sit around here and wait until people come back before we can know anything." Anger bubbles up in my chest towards my mom. It's been a couple days now since she's left. At this point, I have no doubt in my mind that she must have had something to do with the explosion.

"What are their names?"

"What does it matter to you?" Cass asks. "Sorry. That came out meaner than I meant. I guess I was just wondering why you care. You wouldn't know who we're talking about anyway."

Joselyn looks down at the ground, fidgeting with her fingers. She glances up nervously at me and then looks away again.

"Joselyn? You okay?" I ask. "Is there something you want to tell us?"

"You're going to think I'm crazy," she mumbles. "I think I'm crazy."

Cass and I both hold still as we wait for her to spit it out. I'm not sure I want to know what could make her feel crazier than she already is.

"I've been told that one of the people living inside me can talk to the dead," she says, blushing with embarrassment. "I just thought that if I knew their names, maybe he would be able to know if they were...you know."

Cass takes a step back, hugging herself. She rubs her arms briskly with her hands.

"Landon?" I ask, remembering the goth guy I met during one of the group meetings.

"No," she answers, shaking her head, making her ponytail wave back and forth. "His name's Jack. He doesn't show up very often, but I've had nurses tell me that he freaked them out, talking about their loved ones who died recently. The nurses sometimes come around looking for him, saying his name at me, in case Jack has taken over."

I can't believe what I'm hearing. The nurse did mention that there were more personalities, but I thought she meant Landon. I feel even more sorry for Joselyn now.

"You think I'm a freak, don't you?" she asks, her face scrunched up with anguish.

"No. No, of course not. I just feel bad for you, is all. I never met Jack while I was in the hospital with you. To be honest, I'm kinda glad I didn't." I chuckle.

She nods knowingly.

"Girls, we need help getting supper done," Caroline says tiredly, holding Sonya on her hip. She does a double-take when she sees Joselyn looking up at her. "You know, you look a lot like someone here at camp. What's your name?"

"Joselyn, ma'am."

"Hello, Joselyn. Anyway, it looks like the woodpile could use a bit more. Cass, maybe you could help me peel some potatoes while Olivia and Joselyn go get some wood?"

We all nod and stand up.

I can't help but feel uneasy about going out into the woods alone with Joselyn. This ought to be interesting.

18

I lead her out into the woods along a deer path. We pick up whatever sticks we can find as we make our way farther away from camp. Farther away from safety. I toss around the idea of keeping the knife in my hand the whole time, but that would make it harder to hold the gathered wood.

No. I need to just calm down. Cindy was civil after she scratched me. Maybe things won't be so bad.

"What did she mean that I reminded her of someone?"

"Oh. Just that you have the same shade of blue eyes and black hair as someone else from camp."

"What's her name? Where is she?"

"Her name's Rebecca. She took off to go find the others after the explosion."

Joselyn stops walking and stares at the middle distance for a moment. She looks at me with a sad expression. "Could it be?" she whispers to herself.

"What?"

"Never mind." She goes back to collecting sticks

I want to ask her what she was talking about, but the poor girl has had enough difficulties for one day. I have no idea what Alexandrine was thinking, bringing her out here. So what if she said she was Charlotte's friend? Why would you break a person out of the mental hospital? Her daughter...sure. That makes sense. But some strange girl who asks to come? I'm seriously questioning Alexandrine's judgment.

We both have an armload of branches and head back to camp. I suddenly have an urge to talk to David, and my stomach turns sour as soon as I remember that he's not at camp.

That he could be dead right now.

Damn you, Henry! I really wish I was with them so I could know what happened sooner. Waiting is torture.

"Branches aren't going to cut it, girls," Stan comments when we return. He's at the firepit, trying to get a fire going. "We're going to need logs of wood. Take the hand saws, and see if you can find a fallen tree to block up."

"I've never used a saw before," I say. "Isn't there someone else who could do it?"

"No. We're down too many people. You're going to have to learn."

I turn around and see that Joselyn retrieved the saws already. I'm filled with dread as I look at her innocently holding a potentially dangerous weapon. I don't want to be alone in the woods with a girl whose alternate personality would love the chance to kill me. I involuntarily shiver at the thought of having that toothed blade run across my skin.

"You ready?" Joselyn asks.

"Yeah. Want me to carry the saws?" I ask as nonchalantly as I can.

233

"I've got it," she says, shrugging. "C'mon, let's go."

Before we go, I pat my pocket just to reassure that I still have a weapon to defend myself. The knife's presence is only slightly comforting.

We hike through the woods, making circles around the camp, moving farther away as we go. We want to find a tree that's close so we won't have as far to haul the wood. After going around about three times, we find a tree that's tipped over, its roots pulled up out of the ground. I think this might be the tree I sat on when David told me he loved me. The thought brings a pang of grief.

"I think we should cut off the branches first before we start trying to cut it into chunks," I say, trying to figure out what would be the best way to do this.

Joselyn nods, and we start working. "You know, this survival stuff is kind of fun. It's at least more fun than group time or the lame arts and crafts they made us do. I felt like I was going crazy in there."

I laugh.

"What?" she asks, stopping to look at me.

"You just said you felt like you were going crazy...in a psychiatric hospital."

"Oh, yeah. I guess that is kind of funny," she says, smirking a bit. She goes back to sawing while she continues talking. "You know, when I'm me, I don't feel crazy. I feel like I don't belong with all the other people who have serious problems. I don't think I'm a squirrel or that I have magical powers or have an irrational fear of spiders. I'm just me. A normal twelve-year-old girl."

"But you're not," I let slip.

She stops sawing again and looks at me, taken aback. "What?" she says, clearly offended.

I stop sawing too and look at her as I answer quickly, "I just mean that you're not a normal twelve-year-old. When you're you, you're amazing! Sweet, kind, friendly. But your other personalities are not so nice. So even though you—Joselyn—are great, you have lived an abnormal life. You've experienced things not very many other twelve-year-olds have experienced, and that makes you different. Special," I add, hoping I defused the situation. I'm kicking myself for having even said something. If she wants to feel like she's a normal kid, then I should let her. She deserves that much.

"You're right. Who am I kidding? Even if I got rid of all the extra personalities, I would still be messed up." She starts sobbing, and now I feel like a jerk.

I take a step toward her, but she stops crying abruptly. I watch as she wipes the tears off her cheeks with her hand and looks down at them, confused.

She then looks at the saw in her hand and up at me with a malicious grin. "You made the kid cry. I thought you were friends."

"We were—are. I mean, we are."

"Tsk, tsk, tsk. Then why're there tears on our face?" she accuses, pointing the saw at me.

"I might have said something that made her cry. Why do you care?"

234

"I protect her. That's what I do, silly Billy. That's why I'm here," she says, spreading her arms theatrically.

"You protect her? But you told me yourself that you tried to commit suicide. How is that protecting her?"

Cindy rolls her eyes and huffs. "You wouldn't understand. It's a secret."

"I wouldn't understand, or it's a secret?" When she doesn't answer, I decide to just let it go. I would really like to know what triggers Cindy's return so I don't have to see her anymore. "Why don't you take a little break? I'll work on it for a while."

She places the handle of the saw in my hand but doesn't let go when I grab it. I tug a few times, and just when I'm about to get angry at her, she releases it with a smirk.

I put her saw on the ground and position myself so I can see her in my peripheral vision as I work on the branches. At first, she just stands around looking at the trees, but then she starts doing ballet poses. Pretty soon, she's twirling and leaping her way around the woods. I consider complimenting her on her form to be nice, but honestly, I'm sick of talking to her. I wish she would go away for good, and I worry that if I keep engaging her, it will somehow make her stick around.

I choose to ignore her and throw myself into a particularly thick branch, sawing back and forth until my arm starts to ache. Sweat droplets run down my face and into my eyes. I stop for a moment so I can wipe them away, and then pain explodes on the back of my head, and I black out.

I wake up to the sound of someone humming "Mary had a Little Lamb." I let out a groan as I try to open my eyelids, but the sunlight burns, and I squeeze them shut again. What happened to me?

I go to sit up, but as soon as I lift my head off the ground, a wave of nausea hits me hard. Saliva pools in my mouth, and before I can try to stop it, hot bile rushes up my throat, and I turn to the side as I spew it out onto the ground.

The pain in my skull is so intense, I'm certain my head is about to explode. I honestly think drilling a hole in my skull would make me feel better right now. It would at least release some of the awful pressure. I try to sit up again, and this time I can without feeling sick. I shield my eyes from as much light as possible and crack my eyelids so I can see where I am.

"Wakey, wakey, Olivia!"

I whip my head around to where I heard the voice come from. Bad idea. Another wave of nausea hits me, and I throw up again. "Cindy?" I say, wiping the drool from my mouth. "What happened to me?"

"I told you I was going to make you pay. Ka-ching, ka-ching! It was only a matter of time."

I know I should stand up and face Cindy, but another wave of agony crashes through my head, and I lie down, unable to sit up anymore. "What did you do?" I whimper.

"I found a thick stick and hit you quick, chick. Haha! I'm a poet, and I didn't even know it," she giggles to herself.

"You're insane," I groan.

"Now, now, Olivia. There's no need for name-calling," she says in a mock scolding tone.

"I'm so tired..." I say as everything fades away again.

"You can rest when you're dead! Now it's wakey-wakey time," she says chipperly.

My head throbs where she hit me, and I find myself wishing she'd leave me alone so I could either go unconscious or die. I start to dream about smoke billowing in the distance and a feeling of terror pressing down on me. Suddenly, I'm back awake, and someone's slapping my face.

"Ow! Stop hitting me," I say and crack my eyelids open. Panic rises up as I look at who's hitting me, and I can't remember who she is. She seems familiar, but the thought just won't come. "Who're you?"

"Methinks I might've hit you too hard," she says, tapping a finger on her temple. "Whoopsie!"

"You hit me? Why? Is that why my head hurts?"

She sneers. "Ugh. You're starting to get annoying."

I watch through my eyelashes as she stands up, looking in every direction around us. She licks her finger and holds it straight out in front of her. She spins around a few more times and then kneels down by my head again.

"All right, here's the thing. I mighta, sorta got turned around, and I need you to take us back to camp."

"Camp?"

"Yes. Camp. El Camperino. La Campitan."

Nothing she says makes any sense to me. I close my eyes again, desperate for the sweet oblivion of sleep.

"Wake up!" I hear Cindy say, but her voice sounds distant. "Whatever. Joselyn, it's your turn."

I'm just about asleep again. Images of a gentle kiss and how soft it felt on my lips play through my mind, but I can't tell if it's a memory or a dream. Who would have kissed me?

David!

I sit bolt upright, panic spreading through my body with a jolt. Everything around me starts spinning, but I force myself to stay sitting as I squeeze my eyes shut again until it subsides.

"Olivia! Are you okay?"

I open my eyes back up and see those pale blue eyes staring at me with concern. Looking at Joselyn, I suddenly remember who she is. "Hey, Joselyn. Where's David?"

"I'm not sure, but I think he was one of the people in the explosion..."

"Explosion?"

"What's wrong with you, Olivia? You seem confused."

I stand up slowly, grabbing onto a tree to steady myself. My ears start ringing, drowning out the sounds of the woods, which just makes me more off balance.

Joselyn wraps my arm around her shoulder to help me. "Okay, Olivia. I need to get you back to camp. Do you remember what direction camp is?"

I hold my hand up to my forehead to block the sun and look around. I slowly spin in a circle, but everything looks the same; nothing stands out. That is until I see the fallen tree and the saw still stuck in the branch where I was cutting it. "I remember! I think camp is back that way," I say, pointing. "Grab the saws, and let's get out of here."

By the time we make it back to camp, I'm feeling nauseous again, and I beg for her to let me lie down.

"Hold on, Olivia. Not yet."

We stumble our way to where my stuff is, and she helps me sit. She then goes to find someone to have a look at me. The ringing in my ears has become a deafening roar, and I just can't take it any longer. I lay my head on my pillow and immediately start to drift off.

■■■■■

"Olivia? Liv!"

I wake with a start when I realize I recognize that voice. "David?"

"Holy crap, you had me scared to death!"

It takes me several seconds to remember where I am. David comes into focus, and I gasp when I see the state he's in. He has scratches all over his face, a white bandage soaked with blood right above his eye, and his arm is in a sling. I sit up and wrap him in a hug before I realize I shouldn't have sat up so quickly. My head pounds, and I lie back down before I throw up again.

"Whoa! Take it easy, Liv."

Suddenly, I feel the need to explain why I'm acting this way. "I was out getting wood with Joselyn, and Cindy hit me in the head with a branch."

"Cindy? Like, crazy hospital Cindy?"

"That's the one."

"Where is she now?" David brushes a lock of hair out of my eyes before looking around camp to spot her.

I stare up at him, unable to comprehend what he just asked me. Why is the ringing in my ears so loud? I can't think straight. I close my eyes again and feel the weight of sleep taking me under.

"Stay with me, Liv." I hear David say. I open my eyes when I feel him stroke my cheek with his thumb. "Why do you always get yourself in trouble when I'm not here?"

"Hey, David! Do you know what I got on my history test? Did you see my grade?"

"History test?" he says, furrowing his eyebrows while shaking his head.

"Yeah, the one were you going to help me study for," I say.

"Liv, we haven't gone to school for weeks now," David says slowly. "I think Rebecca better take a look at you. You're acting weird."

"No, don't go," I say weakly as he stands up. Before I can stop myself, I fall back to sleep.

■■■■■

I wake up to a bright light shining in my eye as someone holds my eyelid up. Then they do the same to the other one.

"She's got a concussion. By the knot on the back of her head, I'd say it's a pretty severe one."

"What can I do for her?" David's voice asks.

I groggily open my eyes and see Rebecca, David, and Cass all leaning over me.

"You shouldn't be doing anything, David. You need to get some rest and heal yourself," Rebecca answers sternly.

"Not when Liv's hurt," David responds defiantly. "I'll be fine."

A happy sigh escapes my lips. Leave it to David to put my needs before his own.

"Do you know what happened to her?" Rebecca asks Cass.

"Cindy hit me over the head with a stick," I say.

"Who?" Rebecca asks, confused. "Where is this Cindy now?"

"She started acting crazier than before and took off down by the stream," Cass answers. "She's been sitting down there talking to herself since before you guys got back. I check on her every now and then to make sure she's still there."

"Can you tell her to come up here? I'd like to talk to her," Rebecca asks tiredly.

Cass nods and heads down to the stream.

"Olivia, we're going to have you sit up for a while. Sleep is good, but you need to drink something." Rebecca has David grab my other arm, and together, they help me up and set me against a tree.

As Rebecca is tipping a cup for me to take a drink, I see Cass walk back to camp with Joselyn. Rebecca notices me staring and glances over her shoulder to see what I'm looking at. Suddenly, she drops the cup of water, soaking my pants, and gasps loudly. "Joselyn?" she whispers.

"Mama?"

A warm feeling spreads through my chest as I get ready to watch this heartfelt reunion. Joselyn deserves this.

"Stay away from me! Just stay right there!" Rebecca yells as she takes a step back.

2 0

I look between her and Joselyn in disbelief. Joselyn looks like Rebecca just slapped her hard across the face. Anguish washes over her, and she lets out a sob.

"Who let her in here? Who brought her here?" Rebecca is yelling, panicked.

I stand up between Rebecca and Joselyn, my head swimming in the process. I start swaying slightly as the pain pulses in my skull. David's at my side in an instant, holding my arm to steady me.

"What's going on, Rebecca? Why are you acting like this?" I ask calmly.

"You don't know what she is. I put her in that hospital for a reason. How did she get out? How did you get out?" Rebecca asks Joselyn angrily.

"I brought her out here," Alexandrine says, walking back from the stream. "What's going on?"

"She's a lunatic!"

I hear Joselyn lose it and start bawling loudly.

"David, Cass, would you guys please help with Joselyn? I need to talk to Rebecca," I say.

"Are you sure, Liv?" David asks, concerned. "You need to take it easy."

I just nod in response, and he reluctantly lets go. I make my way over to Rebecca, and the exertion causes me to see stars in my vision. I grab a hold of her upper arm to stop myself from falling headfirst. I wish I wasn't feeling so crappy.

"Would you guys mind keeping an eye on Charlotte for me too?" Alexandrine asks reluctantly. I can tell she doesn't want to be away from her.

Cass nods, and we walk a short distance away from everyone.

"What is going on?" I ask once we have a seat on some moss outside of the camp.

"She is not who you think she is," Rebecca says, her eyes flashing with fear.

"I know that she's a twelve-year-old girl who's lived a hard life, dealing with different personalities and being stuck in a mental hospital..." I start to say but stop when Rebecca shakes her head vigorously.

"She hasn't been Joselyn since...I don't even remember. I'm not a hundred percent sure she's ever been just Joselyn."

"She said Cindy took over once her dad died when she was young," I say, holding my head in my hand to try to stop the pain that's throbbing in my brain.

"She's a liar. Cindy was around a lot longer than that, Joselyn just doesn't remember because she blacks out when another person takes over. Did she happen to mention how her dad died?" Rebecca asks, her face ashen.

"No."

I look at Alexandrine, who meets my eyes for a moment, and I can feel the dread passing between us as neither of us are ready to hear what she's about to say.

"He 'fell' down the stairs," she scoffs, making air quotes. "When I came running to see what the noise was, I saw him lying at the bottom of the stairs, blood pooling on the floor and his neck at an odd angle..." She stops to let out a sob before continuing, "And there she was, standing at the top of the stairs, staring down at us. She didn't look sad or scared. In fact, she looked—I don't know—pleased? Curious? Nothing you would expect from a four-year-old."

I cannot believe what I'm hearing.

"Of course, I couldn't prove anything. I wasn't there to actually see it happen. Whenever I asked her about it, she would shrug." Rebecca stops to wipe her nose on her sleeve.

"C'mon, Becca. A four-year-old pushed a grown man down the stairs? He must have just tripped, and she was standing at the top of the stairs because she heard the commotion," Alexandrine proposes. "What makes you think she pushed him?"

"Well, as I said, there's always been something...off...about her."

"Of course there was something off about me, mommy dearest."

We all jump a little at her voice. Rebecca's eyes are wide as she scoots back away from where Joselyn is now standing. I look up at Joselyn's face and see she's got a wild look to her. Cindy.

"Sorry, ladies!" David apologizes as he comes running up to Cindy, panting. "She started going nuts and slipped away before we could catch her."

Cindy just ignores him and keeps talking. "You blame me for Dad's death, but did you ever stop to think about why I killed him?"

Rebecca looks horrified. "I knew it!"

Cindy gives a wicked smile that turns to a sneer. "I didn't show up when he died. I showed up when he started hurting Jossy."

Rebecca angrily shakes her head. "You're lying. Samuel wouldn't have done that."

"Guess again! Didn't you ever find it odd that he was always willing to give Joselyn a bath every night?"

"He just wanted to help. He knew I was stressed by the end of the day, and he wanted to give me a hand with her," Rebecca says desperately.

"Wrong again! He hurt her. Every. Time."

Rebecca buries her face in her hands.

"Didn't you see the signs? Didn't you hear me start yelling before he would cover my mouth with his big hand? I would take over because even though I wasn't strong enough to stop him, I was strong enough to shield her from the trauma."

She turns to me and says, "You asked me earlier about my suicide attempt. Secret's out! After a particularly bad night, I didn't think I could keep protecting her. Dying seemed like a good way to protect her from him."

"That was you? I thought she cut her wrists on the broken fence she tried to climb," Rebecca shrieks.

"I had to make it look like an accident," she scoffs as though it were obvious.

"She was only three and had to be hospitalized for a week!" Rebecca yells.

"Whoops," Cindy says with a halfhearted shrug.

I feel like I'm about to throw up.

"I finally got to the point that I knew I had to stop it from happening to her again. So, when I saw him standing at the top of the stairs, I ran and shoved him as hard as my little four-year-old body could. I wanted to hurt him. I didn't realize it would kill him. I'm not sorry it did. He couldn't hurt her—us—ever again."

Hot tears roll down my cheeks. Poor Joselyn! Crying is making my head throb, and I realize I need to stop. The pain is becoming too much.

"Liv? You okay?" I hear David ask as I tip over to the side and pass out.

21

Voices whisper around me as I come back from the darkness. It takes me a moment to understand what's happening. My ears stopped ringing, and the throbbing in my head is mostly gone, but a feeling of sorrow still presses down on me. I begin to cry before I remember why I'm feeling so sad. The memories of what Cindy told us trickle in, and I'm distraught all over again. I may not like Cindy, but I respect her for taking over during those bad times to shield Joselyn.

I look up and see David next to me. A shock runs through me when I realize he's back, and I have no idea what happened to him and the group. I was so out of it, I never thought to ask.

"David," I croak out, then clear my voice and try again. "David. What happened?"

"You blacked out..."

"No. I mean, the explosion. What happened?" I ask as I sit up.

A grave look crosses over him, and I'm afraid of what he's about to tell me. I'm not sure I'm ready for more sadness.

"The bunker was rigged. Jeffery, Andrew, and Ryan volunteered to go in and retrieve the ammo. Matthias insisted he go too, but Ryan told him no, that if anything happened, the camp needed to have their leader. It was like he knew something was going to go wrong," David says, rubbing his hand over his face.

"Or maybe he didn't trust my mom," I say darkly. I'm embarrassed that I vouched for her. She hasn't shown back up yet, which just proves that she had something to do with the explosion. I should have followed her when I had the chance.

"That too. Anyway, Tim, Matthias, and I were positioned in the tree lines around the building to keep an eye out for soldiers. I heard one of the men inside yell 'Run!' just before the explosion happened," David says, stopping to look up at the trees as he clenches his jaw a few times.

I lay my hand on his bicep. "What happened then?"

"This is where it gets a little weird. Don't judge," he says, rubbing the back of his neck awkwardly. "Do you remember Bartholomew?"

"Your imaginary friend?" When he gives me a glare, I put my hands up. "Sorry. I mean your guardian angel..." I say, keeping my tone in check.

"Well, just as I heard them yell, 'Run,' Bartholomew materialized in front of me and shoved me as hard as he could. I was already on the ground when the explosion happened. And a good thing too, because when I finally came to my senses, I stood up and saw a piece of the steel wall from the building lodged in a tree right where my head would have been. Bartholomew saved my life."

"Thank you, Bartholomew," I say, playing along.

"Anyway, I realized we needed to get out of there, quick. I found Matthias with blood running down his face from his eye, but he didn't seem to care too much as he was cinching his belt around the remaining part of Tim's arm."

"What?" I whisper. "Tim lost his arm?"

"Yeah. We were in rough shape. I was the luckiest one. I only came away with some cuts that needed stitches and a broken wrist."

"A broken wrist still sucks, though."

"It does, but at least I'm alive and I still have my arm."

I nod, which was a bad idea as everything starts spinning uncontrollably. I hold still and close my eyes until the vertigo passes.

"We did a quick check to see if any of the men survived the blast, even though we knew they didn't. There's no way they could have. The building was completely destroyed. But we had to check...you know, just in case," he adds weakly.

"Well, where's Tim and Matthias now? Did they make it back to camp?"

"They made it because of Rebecca. It was a miracle when she showed up. She's a badass, by the way. I know we just found out some terrible stuff about her with Joselyn and all that, but I'm glad she's a part of this camp."

I'm not so sure. How could she have not known what was going on with Joselyn? You would think her motherly instincts would have kicked in or something when Joselyn started acting weird.

"She didn't have the right stuff to handle a missing arm, so she did something she had seen on an old tv show once. She had Matthias pull open some bullets and dump out the gunpowder onto Tim's bloody stump. Then she lit the powder on fire, cauterizing the wound."

"That actually worked?" I ask incredulously.

"Yeah, for the most part. It at least stopped the heavy bleeding. I didn't really understand why she had asked me to find a stick and remove the bark until I saw her stick it between Tim's jaws just before they lit the gunpowder on fire. I thought he was unconscious and would be fine, but as soon as the gunpowder ignited, his eyes bulged open, and he clamped down on the stick hard while screaming. I felt so bad for him."

"How about Matthias's eye? Was Rebecca able to save it?"

"No. His eye's gone. He's walking around with an eyepatch now, which just makes him look even tougher. Missing an eye has made him pretty cranky, though. Understandably."

"Crankier than he's already been? I can't even imagine."

David smirks at me, then sighs.

"So, all this happened, and yet you came to my side to help me feel better from my concussion?"

"What do you expect? You were hurt. Of course I'm going to worry about you." He leans over and kisses the side of my head, then pulls back quickly and apologizes.

"I'm so glad you made it back to camp." I ignore the kiss and the apology about it.

"Me too."

"Oh, good. You're awake," Henry stops to say as he's passing by. "Start packing your things up. We're heading out soon."

"What's going on?" I ask, realizing everyone around us has been bustling about getting things packed.

"Pop decided that we have to leave. For good. We gave as much time as we could for healing, but we can't afford to wait around any longer."

"Where are we going?"

"To the next city over. It's going to be slow, so we need to get started."

David stands and helps me up off the ground. A wave of pain spreads through my skull. I thought I was doing better, but standing up just made me realize that it will take a while to heal from this.

"David, what if my mom comes back here to explain what happened? If we leave, she's not going to be able to find us."

"It's probably better that way. I have a feeling that if she ever shows her face again, it's not going to end well for her," David says darkly.

I nod. "I know I'd like to give her a piece of my mind. What she did..." I stop as the emotions form a lump in my throat.

David pats my shoulder. "Let's get packed and get out of here."

I follow behind him to where my stuff is piled. I check my bag to make sure I have everything packed up. I tie my pillow back on and go to see if Caroline needs any help with the kids. As I'm walking back toward her, I overhear Alexandrine talking with Matthias. I stop to listen, pretending to tie my shoe.

"Where are we headed?"

"We're headin' west to the next city over."

Alexandrine huffs. "You really think that's a good idea? Winter is imminent, and moving away from the ocean is going to make the temperatures colder."

"We don't have a lot of options. We've survived the winter before. We can do it again."

"But not like this," she says, gesturing to Matthias's eye and then over to Tim.

"We need to get movin' before the troops get out here. Ya know as well as I do that that explosion means they're comin' to see who set it off. We don't have the manpower to fight 'em. Our time here is done," Matthias says gruffly.

"Okay," Alexandrine concedes.

"Okay? Ya ain't gonna fight me more on this?"

"My priorities have changed." She looks over at Charlotte, who's getting her hair braided by Joselyn.

"Huh. We should've rescued your daughter a long time ago. You're a lot more agreeable."

"Oh, shut up, Patches," she says with a smirk playing at the corners of her mouth.

"Don't," Matthias warns.

"What? Too soon?"

He answers by turning around and storming away from her. I watch her snicker to herself for a moment before heading over toward Charlotte.

■■■■■

Rebecca gives me a tablet of painkiller for my head before we take off. She says she would have given me two, but we have to ration them. I feel bad for even taking one when Matthias, Tim, and David need them more than I do.

I look around camp one last time, but I don't feel as much attachment here since we haven't stayed as long. I'm nervous about leaving, though. The days are getting shorter and a lot cooler. I've always had a nice warm apartment to live in during the winter months. I don't know how I'm going to survive this.

I follow behind David as we all take off in a line through the woods. I'm beginning to grow accustomed to the back of David's head and his backpack. It's almost a comforting sight at this point. I feel safe when I'm with him.

"Hey, Olivia?" I hear Tim's voice say over my shoulder.

"Yeah?"

"I'm sorry I lost your hair tie."

I turn and look back at him, confused.

He motions his head at his missing arm.

"Are you serious? You lost your freaking arm, and you're apologizing for my hair tie being on it?"

His eyes twinkle a bit with humor before turning serious again.

"How are you doing?" I ask.

"Okay, I guess. I mean, this sucks pretty bad. It hurts, and I find myself missing my arm. But I feel like I've paid up a debt. I know it might not make sense, but I feel at peace about it. I'll have to live the rest of my life without my arm, and that seems like a just punishment for what I did."

I stop walking and face him so he knows I mean what I'm about to say. "Tim, you didn't owe anything. It wasn't your fault," I say, looking into his eyes seriously. "But I'm glad you've found some peace."

He nods, and I pat his good arm before turning around and hurrying to catch back up with David.

The day started off mostly sunny, but as we walk, dark clouds roll in and bring an uncomfortable chill to the air. When we stop for a water break, I pull out a couple extra T-shirts to throw on under my hoodie. It's not much, but it's all I have.

We continue walking until it grows too dark for Matthias to see, and we stop for the night. Finding a comfortable spot to sleep is near impossible. Rocks poke into me wherever I try to lie. We finally get everyone settled in, but by the shuffling noises and heavy sighing, it sounds like nobody is sleeping well.

By morning, everyone is awake and cranky. I stretch out my sore muscles and look around to see what's being decided for breakfast. We missed supper last night, and now my stomach is growling loudly. A pot of water is heating over a fire to make it safe for drinking, but nothing is cooking from what I can tell.

"What's for breakfast?" I ask nobody in particular.

Everyone looks around at everyone else, waiting for someone to have the answers. Eyes turn toward Matthias, who's glowering at the fire. He doesn't give us any indication that he heard us. He just keeps staring at the fire as though he wants to kill something or someone.

Finally, someone suggests that we eat the chickens so we have less to carry. We take a vote, and all the adults agree to it, but the kids are sad.

"I don't want to eat Henny Penny!" Caroline's little girl whines.

"I know, baby, but they're starting to get old, and we can always get new chickens once we find a different place to live."

Emily starts wailing loudly, which sets off Sonya. The noise echoes through the woods, and everyone looks around at each other nervously.

"Shut them up!" Cindy growls, holding her hands over her ears.

"You can't just make a kid stop crying automatically," Caroline says, exasperated as she hugs the girls.

"There was a song her mom used to sing to help Sonya stop crying, but I can't remember what it is," Rebecca adds, picking a red-faced Sonya up off the ground.

Caroline shrugs in frustration.

This commotion can probably be heard for miles. If there were any soldiers following us, this is going to tell them exactly where we are. I hear someone whisper that maybe now's not the time to eat the chickens. Minutes tick by, and the noise is starting to give me a headache.

"I don't know that one." I hear Cindy say in a deep voice with an English accent. I turn my head in surprise and see her looking up at something, but I don't know what she's looking at. "Okay. I'll try, but go slow."

We all watch as Cindy stands up, walks over to Sonya, and begins singing in that oddly deep voice, "*Hush little one, with a face so sweet.*" She pauses, turning her head to the side, then nods and continues singing, "*A precious little girl, I was blessed to meet.*"

I glance over at Rebecca and Caroline, and they are both staring at Cindy in shock. Sonya has stopped crying loudly and is watching Cindy with big tears on her cheeks.

"*Ten perfect fingers and ten tiny toes,*" Cindy sings, pausing as she looks over her shoulder and nods again. Her low voice is soothing as she continues, awkwardly touching the parts she's singing about. "*Brown curly hair and a cute button nose.*"

The entire camp is silent as we watch what's going on. Sonya smiles and reaches out for Cindy to hold her. Cindy takes her in her arms uncertainly but smiles when Sonya lays her little head on her shoulder.

"Mommy's little angel sent from heaven up above. A perfect, joyful life because it's you I get to love," Cindy finishes.

She stops singing, and the camp is silent.

"How did you..." Rebecca starts to ask, but Cindy holds up a finger to stop her from talking.

She closes her eyes as though listening to something, then turns toward Tim. With the same deep, accented voice, she says, "It wasn't your fault. You need to stop blaming yourself for what happened. It's time to heal and come back to the Tim we all love. Your enthusiasm helps everyone to stay positive. You are important to these people."

Tim's eyes are wide with shock at her words, and his mouth hangs open slightly. He drops to his knees as what she says sinks in. He covers his eyes with his hand as he rocks back and forth on the ground, overtaken with emotion. Cass goes to him and pats him on his back, hushing him. I get goosebumps up my arms that aren't from the cold.

Cindy's eyes grow wide, and she spins toward Matthias. "You need to leave. They're coming."

22

I watch as Joselyn staggers backward, holding her hands to her head. Everyone is on their feet and all speaking at once.

Matthias claps his hands loudly to get their attention. "What do ya mean 'they'? Soldiers? Havoc? What?" Matthias asks her.

She looks at him, confused. "I don't know what you're talking about," she says with a tremble in her voice. She cowers away from Matthias's stern look.

"Stop playin' around! You just said they're comin'!" Matthias barks out, pointing a finger in her face.

"Leave her alone," Alexandrine says, stepping up to Joselyn. "She's confused. Let's just pack up and leave now. We were going to be leaving soon anyway."

Matthias looks between her and Joselyn with a look of annoyance. "Fine. Everyone get yourselves ready."

"What about breakfast?" Noah asks him timidly.

"Grab an apple to eat as we walk. Let's move!" Matthias answers for her.

Matthias heads over to Saul to help him get ready. I shove my blanket into my bag and strap my pillow back on. My stomach growls as I grab an apple. I know this isn't going to be enough, but I take what I can get. The drinking water is still boiling hot, but we try to fill up our bottles and cups as much as we can. Water is water, whether it's hot or cold. Frederick takes the pot down to the pond to cool the metal before packing it up.

Matthias sends Henry and David to the back of the line with guns to keep watch. Luckily for everyone, it wasn't David's shooting wrist that got broken. I'm sad that I don't get to be by him, but now's not the time to be picky. We walk at a faster pace than we usually do. I can't see ahead of me to know how Matthias gets Saul to walk this fast, but I'm grateful to be moving quickly.

Joselyn is just ahead of me, and I can't help myself from asking her about what happened. "How did you do that?"

"Do what?"

"Sing that song? How could you have possibly known the words to a song that Suzanne made up for her daughter?"

"I have no idea what you're talking about. I sang a song?"

"Oh, right. It wasn't you. But I still don't know how Cindy would have known that song."

"This Suzanne person wouldn't happen to be...you know...dead, would she?" Joselyn asks hesitantly.

"Yeah, she died not too long ago."

"Then it must have been Jack. Remember? I told you about him. Jack can talk to the dead."

"Oh, yeah. I remember you mentioning him." I shiver at the thought of being able to talk to dead people. I didn't believe her when she told us about Jack, but I don't know how else she could have known that song.

We finally stop for a break, but Matthias insists it needs to be a short one.

"I'm sorry, Pop. We need to keep going." I hear Matthias say to Saul.

Saul looks worn out, and I start to worry about him. Is he going to be able to survive the journey?

"David? Did ya hear anything followin' behind us?" Matthias asks.

"No, sir. My ears are still ringing from the explosion, but I don't think I heard anything."

"Good. Let's hope it stays that way."

All this walking makes my skull ache. I want to hold out from taking painkillers, but I don't think I will be able to handle it much longer. I get some from Rebecca, who I noticed is staying as far away from Joselyn as possible.

"You know, it's not her fault she has DID," I say gently. "She doesn't like it any more than you do."

"I just can't live with what she did to Sam," Rebecca replies.

"You heard Cindy. He was hurting Joselyn."

"I don't believe her," Rebecca says stubbornly. "That's not the Sam I knew."

"We all have demons we deal with, Rebecca, secrets we keep hidden away. Do you really think Sam would tell you he's the kind of guy who wanted to do those things to your little girl? Maybe you should try believing your daughter," I say as anger bubbles up to the surface.

"Cindy is not my daughter," she says, pointing in my face.

"But Joselyn is! And right now, she has different personalities living inside of her that she can't control! She's scared, lonely, and believes she's a freak. She could use her mother. Aren't you a nurse for Pete's sake? Shouldn't you know about mental illnesses?"

Rebecca stares at the ground, shaking her head.

"What's goin' on over here? We need to get movin'," Matthias says, but I don't acknowledge him. I'm so angry right now.

"What if Cindy was telling the truth? Your little girl was being hurt by a man she should have been able to trust, and now her mother won't believe her or support her? In my mind, that makes you just as bad as he was," I spit out before turning and storming away while everyone in the vicinity watches.

I head straight over to Joselyn and give her a big hug. I don't care if she's Joselyn or Cindy or any of the others. She deserves some support. She gives me a confused look and a small smile.

"I believe you," I whisper. I glance back at Rebecca, and she's glaring at me with her hands on her hips.

I look around and see that everyone is on their feet, ready to leave, so I hurry over to my bag. I make sure I'm as far away from Rebecca as possible, staying close to the back by David. I don't think I'll be getting any more painkillers from her.

It's a good thing Matthias has a compass. The clouds are so thick that there's no way to tell the direction from the sun's positioning. I hate days like today because I'd rather take a nap than do anything else when it's so dreary. It reminds me of being in the city with the fog that blocked out the sun. I shudder at the memory.

A strange rumbling sound snaps me out of my stupor, and I look around to figure out where it's coming from. I see that David is looking around the woods too, but nobody else around us seems to be bothered. It must be something only we heard.

"Did you hear something?" I whisper to David.

"I did," he says, looking up at the sky that can be seen between the branches. "It could be thunder. Maybe a storm's moving in."

"Should we tell Matthias?"

"It sounded far away. Let's just keep walking, and if we hear it again, we can tell him."

David and I never hear the sound again. I decide that it must have just been a passing storm cloud.

Day turns to dusk, and my stomach feels like it's digesting itself from hunger. I also ran out of water about two hours ago, and I'm really feeling it. Everyone is tired as we start to set up camp. There is barely enough energy to go around to prepare supper, but the thought of food gives people a second wind. Much to Emily's displeasure, we decide it's time to eat the chickens tonight. There's just enough for everyone to have some but not enough to fill anyone up. We top it off with some rice and boiled carrots.

Frederick heads off to get some water for everyone. Henry volunteers to go along, taking David's flashlight and a gun.

No one talks as we all huddle together by the fire to stay warm. Rebecca refuses to look at Joselyn or me. I don't care if she's mad at me, but I really wish she wouldn't treat Joselyn this way.

I watch as Alexandrine wraps a blanket around herself and Charlotte. She looks so much happier than she did before. Charlotte is starting to look more comfortable around her too. A pang of longing runs through me at that moment. Even before Mom's recent betrayal, she was never a loving mother. I wish I had what Charlotte is experiencing right now. I think that's why Rebecca's behavior bothers me so much. She has an opportunity to have a relationship with her daughter, and she's refusing to take it.

After about an hour, Frederick is back with the pot of water. By the looks of him, it was a long journey. The bottom of his shirt, his pants, and his shoes are soaked, and he's staggering under the weight of the pot. Henry comes into view, holding the flashlight as best he can for Frederick. With a grunt, Frederick places the pot on the hot coals and slumps down in an open spot by Matthias.

"What'd ya do? Fall in?" Matthias asks with a hint of amusement.

"It's dark out there. I stumbled over a few sticks and splashed myself. Enjoy your water. I hope you choke," Frederick grumps, staring at the fire with a scowl.

"Thank you for getting the water, Frederick," David says.

"Yeah, thanks." I smile at him.

People around camp take the hint, and soon everyone shows gratitude to Frederick. Even Matthias pats him on the shoulder and says thanks. I watch Frederick's icy demeanor melt, and he's back to the warm, friendly guy we all know.

"Rebecca? You need to come check on Tim," Cass says worriedly.

Tim is leaning against a tree, wrapped up in a thick blanket, shivering, and even though the light from the fire is dim, he looks pale to me. I watch as Rebecca hurries over to him and places her hand on his forehead.

"Someone got a flashlight?" Rebecca asks with an edge to her voice.

Henry brings over David's flashlight. He shines it at Tim as Rebecca removes the blanket. The whole camp is silent as she pulls the bandage off Tim's wound. I immediately cover my nose as a rank smell hits me. I see that David does the same.

"I was afraid of this," Rebecca says gravely.

23

"What? What is it?" Matthias asks.

I scoot closer to Cass and put my arm around her. She's hugging her knees and rocking back and forth as she cries silently.

"He has an infection," Rebecca says. "If we don't get him the proper treatment, he could get sepsis."

"What's sepsis?" I ask.

"It's something like blood poisoning. If he gets that, he will most likely die," she says matter-of-factly.

Cass starts bawling, and I hold her tighter.

"Well, what does he need?" Henry asks.

"A hospital."

"That's not an option," Matthias says. "Do ya have anything in your medical kit that could help?"

"I have one bag of IV fluids and a small tube of antibiotic cream, but I'm afraid that's not going to be enough."

"Well, we have to try," Matthias says, going to grab the medical kit for her.

"What about plants? Could we find some kingsfoil in the woods and heal him with that?" I ask desperately.

"What's kingsfoil?" Rebecca asks, confused.

"Liv, that's a plant from a movie. It's not real," David says.

I feel my cheeks burn from embarrassment. "Sorry. I watched it so many times, I forget that it's not real."

In this moment of urgency with Tim, Rebecca seems to have forgotten that she's mad at me and smiles. "Your natural remedy idea reminds me of something. I remember seeing a honey bee hive about a quarter mile back."

"Okay?"

"Honey has been used as an antibiotic for centuries. Is there anyone willing to retrace our steps and go get it for me?" she calls out.

"I will," David offers.

"I'll go too," I say, not wanting to stay behind again.

"I'll get you a bag to carry the honeycombs in. It's been getting cooler at night so, I'm not sure if there will be any bees still alive in the nest. Are either of you allergic to bees?" Rebecca asks.

"I don't think I've ever been stung in my entire life," I admit.

"I have. I was fine," David says.

We hear Matthias clear his throat, and we look over to see him looking uncomfortable. "I'm allergic to bees. It's possible that Olivia could be too," he says.

"I never knew that. You should have told me," Rebecca scolds. "As the camp nurse, it's my job to take care of you all. We only have one EpiPen in my kit, and even that is expired."

She shakes her head as she turns back to us. "David, you do most of the bee handling, then. I'll send the EpiPen with you, in case Olivia gets stung and needs it. An expired dose is at least better than nothing."

"How will I know if she needs it?" David asks, holding the EpiPen carefully as though it's a bomb about to explode.

"Difficulty breathing. Hives. Throat or tongue swelling." Rebecca ticks off on her fingers. "Trust me, you'll know."

Rebecca shows him how to use it as I go grab a knife from my bag. My nerves are on edge at the thought of walking off into the darkness, but having David with me helps.

He gets the flashlight from Rebecca and the handgun from Henry. As we get ourselves ready, I hear Joselyn say, "Careful, Olivia. Wouldn't want that pretty face ripped off by any wild beasties!"

"Thanks, Cindy. I'll keep my eyes open."

I'm nervous about leaving Cindy here at camp alone, but Tim needs us to hurry. Let's hope she behaves herself while I'm gone. We take off in the direction we came earlier today.

I follow behind David, watching his feet in the glow of the flashlight. "Do you think this is going to work?" I whisper to David.

"What?"

"The honey."

I hear him sigh. "I hope so."

We walk for a little while more, focusing on keeping our footsteps and breathing as quiet as possible. It's not easy with all the dead leaves covering the ground. David stops abruptly, and I run into his back, grabbing onto his shoulders to catch myself from falling.

"Did you hear that?"

"No, what did you hear?" I ask, looking around at the darkness.

"I heard a small buzz sound, and then it was gone."

We stop and listen, waiting to hear it happen again. The dead leaves rustle as a small breeze blows through the woods. An owl hoots off in the distance, but I don't hear a buzz.

"It's nighttime. If any of the bees are still alive, would they be asleep?" I ask.

"I have no idea. I feel like we're on an impossible search since Rebecca couldn't give me very good directions," David says, frustrated.

We stand quietly, waiting for another buzz. My teeth start to chatter now that we stopped moving. I clench my jaw to keep them quiet.

As I'm about to ask whether we should search the area with a flashlight instead of standing around, I hear a rumbling noise off in the distance. The same noise we heard earlier today.

I look at David, and his eyes are wide. "I heard it," David whispers before I ask anything. "Let's hurry up and find the beehive so we can get back to camp. We should probably tell Matthias about it this time."

I nod, and we start shining the flashlight up in the trees. I grab onto David's arm when a pair of eyes catch the light and shine down at us momentarily.

"Don't worry. It's just a raccoon," David says, slightly out of breath. I think it scared him too. He just wants to seem brave.

I never really cared that much about animals to devote my time to learn about them. I begin to wish I would have paid more attention when they taught us in school. Especially after that run-in with a skunk. It would be really handy to know which animals are dangerous and which ones aren't.

We continue walking for at least a half hour, circling the area David thought he heard the buzzing sound. The rumbling noise we heard doesn't happen again. My curiosity is getting the better of me. I almost want to take off and see what's making the sound, but I've already learned my lesson about leaving camp alone.

After walking another fifteen minutes or so, I hear David whisper-shout, "There!" He points the flashlight at a tree up ahead.

Dangling off a branch is a nest about the size of a basketball covered with bees, but they're hardly moving.

"How are we supposed to get the honeycomb when it's covered in bees?" I ask, exasperated.

David walks around the hive, staring at it with his face scrunched up in thought. "Either we grab the whole thing in the bag, bees and all, or I scrape off as many bees as I can before taking the honeycomb. Either way, you should probably get away from here while I do it."

"We can't take the bees back to camp. Matthias said he's allergic," I whisper, dread filling me at the thought of the other option. "But if you try to scrape the bees off, you're going to get stung."

"If I get stung, I get stung. We need to help Tim. What's a few bee stings if it means saving Tim's life?" David says bravely. "I have on a thick layer of clothes. We'll just hope they don't go for my hands or my face."

"I don't like this, David. How are you going to do this alone with a broken wrist? I have to help you..."

"No, Liv. You could be allergic. I'm not taking the risk. It'll be harder, but I'll figure it out. Now, go stand out there away from me. I need to do this before I lose my nerve."

I give him a worried look before turning around and walking about twenty paces away. I twist back around to watch, and I see David shoo me farther with his hand. I go another twenty paces until I'm just still able to see David.

I watch as David tucks the flashlight in a branch so it's pointing at the nest and then spreads the plastic garbage bag open on the ground beneath the hive. I have a bad feeling about this. But what can we do? Tim needs it.

David takes off one of his extra shirts and ties it around his good hand, using his teeth to pull it tight. He lifts his wrapped hand up slowly toward the hive and carefully scrapes a handful of bees off the nest and bends down to put them on the ground, but by the looks of it, they aren't letting go of his hand. He's bent over, shaking his hand slightly, and that's when I hear it, an angry buzzing sound as the nest of bees start swarming.

David rips the shirt off his hand and jerks upright, swatting at the back of his neck. He spins and looks at the nest for one second and then starts running toward me.

"David!" I yell.

"Run!"

I turn and run as fast as I can. My legs have never moved at this speed before. I feel like I'm flying through the trees. Luckily for us, the clouds broke this evening, and the moon makes it so I can see every tree or branch coming toward me. I dodge them swiftly, never losing speed. I hear the swarm of bees angrily buzz as they chase us. I try to focus on what's ahead of me, hoping I don't trip over a branch and get attacked. Even if I'm not allergic, being stung that many times can't be good.

We run for so long, I'm dripping with sweat. My head is pounding with pain, and I want to stop, but the flight response mixed with adrenaline keeps me moving.

I listen to the sounds behind me; other than David's heavy breathing and footfalls, I don't hear the bees anymore. I duck behind a big tree, crouching into a little ball, with my arms over my head to protect my face. David takes a seat beside me, and we both try to breathe as quietly as we can, listening for the bees.

"I think we lost them," David whispers.

I'm too afraid to lift my head and look to see if he's right, but I'm finding it hard to catch my breath curled up on myself. I finally straighten so I can stretch the cramp out that I'm getting in my ribs. I look around above where we're sitting and don't see any bees. My muscles relax a bit now that the threat is gone.

"Are you okay, Liv?"

"My head is throbbing, but otherwise, I'm fine. How about you? How many stings did you get?"

"I think just the one on my neck. It's a good thing I was wearing so many layers of clothes, or it could have been a lot worse."

We both quiet as we catch our breath. I wish we were back at camp. I look around us and realize I have no idea where we are. We wandered so far away from camp to find that nest and then ran to escape the bees. We might have to wait until morning to find our way back.

"Did you hear that?" David asks, suddenly going still, snapping me out of my thoughts.

"No..." I say, listening hard.

"There! That. It sounded like a popping sound," he whispers.

I turn my head to the side and listen for a moment. Then I hear it. "I think it's a campfire. You don't suppose we ended up making it back to camp, do you? I'm not sure what direction we were even running."

David holds his finger up to his mouth, and I nod as I follow behind him, walking carefully to avoid as many sticks as we can. My concussion makes it difficult to keep steady, but I push through the pain. I can hear the fire popping louder as we get closer.

After taking about fifty slow, meticulous steps, David holds his arm out to stop me. He immediately crouches down, and I match his movements. He holds his finger to his lips again and then points straight ahead.

I move a branch that's blocking my view and see five soldiers camped out around a fire, eating supper.

2[4

I carefully put the branch back in its place, scared to make any noise at all. David starts crawling backward, and I follow. I want to run out of there as fast as possible, but they'd hear us. We make it behind a tree, and both stand up, facing each other.

"What do we do?" I whisper as quietly as I can.

"We have to find camp and tell Matthias."

I nod as I panic internally. Even if we make it back quickly, there's no way our camp will ever be able to outrun healthy soldiers. We walk away slowly to avoid making any noise, but all this exertion is too much for me with my head injury, and I lose my balance, stepping on a stick with a loud crack.

We both stop moving immediately. I plead in my mind that the soldiers didn't just hear that. A few seconds tick by that feels like hours as we listen.

"Did you hear that?" a deep voice asks from the soldiers' camp.

"Probably just an animal," another voice answers lazily.

"We should check it out. It could be a predatory animal."

"Go for it. But if it's a deer or something, kill it so we can eat it. I'm tired of eating this slop."

David grabs my hand, and we take off running as fast as we can once again. I'm not sure I'll be able to keep it up for long this time. I really need some water. David hangs on tightly as we wind our way through the trees. My legs are starting to give out, but I push on. Footsteps are closing in, and I'm beginning to wonder if David and I should stop and fight. With the two of us, maybe we could take them down.

I'm just about to ask David whether we should when I see a light up ahead. It takes me a moment to realize it's the flashlight David had stuck in the tree to see what he was doing with the bees.

The bees!

I turn my attention toward the nest and see them flying around, agitated. David circles wide around the area, and we make it to the opposite side, where he ducks down behind some brush and pulls me down with him. I watch as he picks up a big rock off the ground and keeps his attention on the bees. I try to stifle my heavy breathing as we watch a single soldier come crashing into the clearing, looking up at the flashlight wedged into the branches. He pulls his rifle up to his shoulder and starts scanning the area through the scope.

When the soldier's back is turned, David throws the heavy stone at the nest, and I gasp as the honeycomb breaks free from the branch and falls to the ground. It's like I'm watching the scene in front of me in slow motion as the swarm of bees flies upwards from the ground in a dark, angry cloud. At the same time, the soldier whips around to see what the noise was. It takes him only a second to register that he's in danger before he starts running away toward his camp. A couple of bees manage to get him on his exposed skin, and we hear him swear loudly as he gets farther and farther away.

David quickly runs over to the honeycomb and stuffs it in the plastic garbage bag, tying the top tightly. He shakes his hand violently to get the bee that's stinging him off. I don't think the honeycomb was clear of all the bees before David tied it up, but we can't stay here any longer.

He grabs the flashlight out of the tree and signals for me to follow. We don't run this time, but we walk at a brisk pace. My balance is still poor, and I keep tripping over sticks, which starts to irritate David. He keeps shushing me every time I make a noise.

"What do you want from me, David? I don't feel well," I mutter.

He stops and looks at me, his face a mix of concern and annoyance. "Do you think you'll be able to make it back? We still have a little way to go."

My head gives a nasty throb that darkens my vision momentarily. I rub my forehead, trying to think, and before I know it, David sets the bag with the honeycomb down and squats to the ground in front of me. "Hop on."

"What?"

"I'll give you a piggyback ride to camp. Hop on. We need to move quickly."

"David, this is ridiculous. You don't need to give me a ride back to camp. You're tired too."

"I'll live. Probably a better chance of survival carrying you than having you stumbling your way through the woods, making such a racket. Now get on my back, or I'll throw you over my shoulder like a fireman."

I hesitate for a moment, but this is probably our best option. I climb on his back and wrap my legs around his waist, hooking my feet together. Then I wrap my arms over his shoulders and hold onto his chest.

"Here. I'll need you to carry the bag. Just hang on tight to this and to me, and I'll get us to camp."

I feel so awkward clinging to him like this. It takes him a moment to get used to my weight, but once he finds his center of balance, he hurries off as though I'm nothing more than a backpack.

My muscles start to ache, and I realize I'm holding on stiffly, trying to take as much pressure off him as possible, which suddenly seems silly, since he's carrying all my weight whether I'm relaxed or not. I loosen up a bit and rest my throbbing head on his shoulder, our cheeks brushing against each other. His stubble feels rough on my skin, but it's not unpleasant. I take a deep breath, and the scent of sweat with a hint of vanilla fills my nostrils. Again, not entirely unpleasant.

The bag of honeycomb grows heavy in my hand. It swings back and forth with every step David takes, making it hard to hold onto with my almost numb fingers. I grip it tighter, trying hard to keep it from bumping into David as he goes.

"Thank you, David," I say in his ear. "For everything."

He nods but stays focused on the task. His pace is slowing down, and I can feel him shaking slightly from fatigue, but he never stops. His transformation from the weak, seizure-ridden boy to this strong, healthy man is incredible. I can't believe how far we've come.

Voices pull me from my thoughts, and I look up to see our camp ahead of us. David crouches down so I can slide off his back. He staggers a bit when he stands back up, and I grab his arm to steady him. We quickly make our way into camp, waving at Stan, who's on watch duty.

I walk over to Rebecca and hand her the bag with the honeycomb.

"It might still have bees on it. You'll probably want to take it out of camp a little way before opening the bag."

"Thanks," she says as she stands up to take the bag out into the woods immediately.

I glance at Tim, who's asleep on the ground. His skin is a sickly gray color and covered in a sheen of sweat even though he's shivering violently. Cass is at his side, looking terrified.

"We need to leave. Now," David announces.

"Why?" Matthias asks.

"Liv and I just stumbled on a camp of soldiers a few miles back."

David has everyone's attention now. Cass starts crying as she looks down at Tim.

"Can we take them on? We have weapons. Maybe we could stand our ground and fight." Alexandrine asks.

"Look around. Half this camp is in no position to even run away, let alone fight," Matthias growls, clearly frustrated. At that moment, the campfire reflects in his good eye, making him look wild and dangerous. "We're gonna have to move."

Just then, Rebecca comes back to camp, carrying the bag of honeycomb. "I got the last few bees off. Someone want to hold the flashlight so I can see what I'm doing with Tim's arm?"

"It'll have to wait. We're leavin'."

"Leaving? If Tim doesn't get treated, he's going to die," Rebecca says, scandalized.

"There's a group of soldiers camped out a few miles from here. If we don't leave now, we're all gonna die!" Matthias barks.

"You don't know that! I have a duty here as a nurse. Tim needs treatment!"

"I have a duty here as well, Rebecca. I'm not gonna let everyone get killed just so you can try to save the kid!"

Both of them are glaring at each other, breathing heavily with anger. Everyone else stays quiet as we wait for a solution to present itself.

Finally, Cindy, of all people, stands up and breaks the silence, "This isn't getting us anywhere. We're running out of time. Let's give Rebecca a chance to treat his infection with the honey and get it redressed. While she does that, how about other people make a stretcher from some wood and a blanket."

"That's a good idea," I pitch in.

"Fine. Ya got an hour. Whoever's not ready by then will be left behind. Move!"

Everyone starts working. It doesn't take long to have the bags and supplies ready since there wasn't enough time to unpack anything.

"I don't know how we're going to do this. The kids need sleep," Caroline complains. "Sonya and Emily are already asleep. I can't carry them all."

"Carry Sonya. The others will have to walk," Alexandrine answers as she helps slide a backpack on Charlotte's back. "Our survival is more important than our comfort."

Caroline grumbles but starts getting the children ready. Rebecca's twin boys, Joey and Isaac, blink heavily as they look around at all the commotion. It's going to take a miracle to get us out of here.

2 | 5

The hour flew by quickly, but everyone is ready to move by the time it's over. Once the fire is put out, we immediately feel the temperature change. I have on every shirt I own, hoping it will be enough to keep me warm. I don't know what Matthias has planned, but I hope we find somewhere safe to camp soon so we can get another fire lit.

A couple of the men place Tim carefully on the stretcher. He looks as sick as ever. They wrapped an extra blanket around him, and it seems like his shivering calms down a bit, but by the look on his sleeping face, he's in a huge amount of pain. Frederick and Stan take opposite ends of the stretcher to carry between them, being extra careful not to tip Tim off it.

Caroline came up with a smart way to keep the children together in the dark. She got a length of rope for the children to hold onto to help them stay in a line. She tied the front end of the rope to her backpack so she can use both arms to carry Sonya, who's still asleep, and Alexandrine is holding the back end of the rope, right behind Charlotte.

It's going to be slow moving since it's not only dark, but everyone is exhausted. Once again, Matthias takes the lead with Saul by his side. Henry is put on the end with a gun to keep watch. I make sure I'm right behind David this time. I feel better knowing I'm following him.

The moon gives barely enough light for those who don't have Rare abilities to see. We're moving almost half as fast as we normally would in the daylight, which is probably a good thing since my head is still aching.

After an hour or so of steady walking, we stop to take a bathroom break and to switch up who carries Tim. Henry swaps places with Frederick, handing Frederick the gun to protect us from behind, while another guy from camp, Leroy, takes the back of the stretcher. Really, Leroy should be the one to take the front, since he's almost twice the size of Henry, but from what I've seen of him around camp, he's rather lazy. He's one of the more recent additions from what I've heard, joining the camp right before David and I got there. You'd think his beer belly would be gone after eating smaller amounts of food and having no access to alcohol, but his gut hangs out over his belt in an unhealthy way.

"Mama, I'm cold," Isaac sniffles to Rebecca just before we're lined back up and ready to move.

She kneels down and gives him and his twin brother, Joey, a big hug. "I know, baby. But we need to keep moving. Moving will help you stay warm."

"He can have one of my extra shirts," Joselyn offers timidly.

Alexandrine must have taken the time to pick up some spare clothes for Charlotte and Joselyn before leaving the city. I don't remember seeing Joselyn wear

262

anything other than pajama pants and an oversized white T-shirt while I was in the hospital with her. That must have been all the hospital was willing to buy her since she was in there for so long.

"That's very—kind—of you, Joselyn," Rebecca says hesitantly.

Isaac looks at his mom, and she nods to let him know it's okay. He grabs the shirt and pulls it on over his jacket. The shirt hangs down to his knees, and it's unlikely that it will actually do anything to help him stay warm, but a smile spreads across both their faces.

We continue on, marching through the night. It doesn't take long before I hear Leroy huffing and puffing up ahead of me. I hope to God he doesn't drop Tim. I think Cass is worried about it too, because I keep hearing little nervous moans coming from behind me.

"You've got to lift him up, Leroy." I hear Henry grunt.

"I can't do it, man! I'm too tired."

"We're all tired, but we need to keep moving. I can't carry Tim by myself. Help me out."

They stop moving, and I almost run into David's back.

"Nah, man. I can't do this anymore."

"Matthias, hold up!" I hear Alexandrine shout from up ahead.

After a minute, everyone gathers around Tim's stretcher. Matthias pushes through the crowd to see what's going on.

"What's the problem?" Matthias asks, irritated.

"I can't do this. I'm sick of it!"

"Sick of what? Carryin' Tim?"

"No. This. All of it," he answers, gesturing around himself. "I just can't do it anymore. At least I had a warm house in the city. And food. It was stupid to leave that all behind to follow you. And for what? Freedom? Is this what you call freedom? What a joke."

"Ya wanna leave? Then get the hell outta here. We don't need ya holdin' us up."

"Fine. Give me a weapon so I can get back."

"No."

"I'll die out there!"

"That's your problem. Ya wanna leave this camp, then leave, but you ain't takin' any of our stuff. You're on your own."

A feeling of danger needles my mind as I see the venomous look take over Leroy's face. I watch in horror as Leroy pounces on Frederick, wrestling the gun out of his hands, and then points it at Matthias. The momentary shock wears off, and I'm about to step in and take Leroy down, but Joselyn's suddenly on him like a crazed cat, clawing at his face and hands. She bites his ear, and Leroy drops the gun with a yowl. Matthias picks it up and points it at Leroy's head.

I glance over at Joselyn to see if she's okay, and she's grinning wide with blood dripping down her chin. Looks like Cindy stepped in again to help.

"You gonna shoot me, Matthias? Hmm?"

"Do it!" Cindy giggles.

"I want everyone outta here. Henry, help your Granddad."

"What are you going to do?" David asks.

"I'm gonna have a little chat with Leroy here, and then I'll catch back up with y'all."

Everyone stands around, looking at one another.

"I said go. Now!" Matthias shouts.

We all obey reluctantly. I have a sick feeling in my stomach at the scene before me. Cass had told me once that he shot people who didn't make it through the reckoning. Is he going to kill Leroy?

"You know the gunshot will be heard by the soldiers if you shoot him," I say, but Matthias ignores me, so I let it go.

I take the back of the stretcher, even though I shouldn't because I'm the one with a concussion, but we need to move. My hands are shaking with adrenaline as I lift him up. David pulls up the back of the line with one of the rifles from camp. I can tell he wants to be the one carrying Tim instead of me doing it, but he can't with a broken wrist.

I hear Frederick mutter from the front of the stretcher, "Goodbye, Leroy," as the group takes off into the darkness once again.

I have to remind myself to breathe as I wait for the gunshot to ring out through the woods. But it never does. I try to relax, but my arms are going numb from carrying Tim. I dig deep inside myself to keep going.

After a while, I hear footsteps coming up quickly behind us, and my heart almost stops. Even though I knew Matthias was coming back, he still scares me half to death, thinking the soldiers caught up to us. Matthias passes by in a blur as he trots toward the head of the line. I couldn't get a good look at him, but I have a sick feeling things didn't end well for Leroy.

What would make Leroy suddenly act out that way? Just because he was tired and miserable? I shake my head in disgust. I really hope Matthias didn't kill him. I hope he just let him go to head back to his life in the city.

I'm starting to get hot from the effort of carrying Tim's weight. My hands are losing their grip on the sticks, but I can't let go. Frederick needs my help. He's got to be getting tired too. He's doing most of the heavy lifting.

I need to focus my mind on something other than the pain in my head and arms, so I start counting our footsteps, but after I reach five thousand, I decide to give up. The tediousness of counting isn't helping.

The kids are whining up ahead again, and I feel like we're not going to make it far enough to avoid getting caught. They're getting tired, and we can't expect them to walk all night.

"Take a break." I hear Matthias call out from up ahead.

Frederick and I carefully lay Tim down on the ground, and I immediately stretch out my hands, arms, and shoulders.

"We can't keep going. We need to find a safe place to sleep, Matthias," Rebecca pleads.

Matthias looks around at everyone and nods tersely. He looks worn-out, but he holds out his hand to David. I look closer at his hand and see that it's covered in dried blood. My stomach gives an uneasy churn. We never heard a gunshot, but Matthias must have killed him some other way. He's a murderer.

"Flashlight," he barks.

David pulls the flashlight out of his pocket and gives it to him.

"Want me to come with you, Pop?" Henry offers.

"Nah. Stay with the rest of 'em. I'll try to be quick."

Everyone stays quiet as we rehydrate ourselves and attempt to stay warm. I sit up close to David and whisper, "Does it bother you that Matthias just killed Leroy?"

"A little. But I understand Matthias's position. He couldn't just let the guy go and hope that he doesn't tell anyone about us. Leroy was already proving that he wasn't trustworthy and had a grudge against Matthias."

"But he killed someone. That's not okay," I whisper a little louder than I mean to.

Alexandrine must have heard me. "Matthias has to make decisions for the safety of the camp. He feels responsible for everyone's survival. If our survival is threatened, he does what he feels he must to keep us safe. If that means killing a traitor, so be it."

"'Killing a traitor?' Sounds like Turk," I mutter but realize my mistake immediately.

Alexandrine is on her feet, pointing down at me, her hand shaking with anger. "Don't you ever compare Matthias to Turk."

"You're right. I'm sorry," I say sheepishly. "I'm just not okay with ending someone's life."

"That's not really your call, now is it?"

I blow out a big breath trying to control myself. "No. I guess not."

Everyone is quiet for the moment. The children have all laid down and are now fast asleep.

"Hey, guys? Why is there blood around my mouth?" Joselyn's voice squeaks.

"You attacked Leroy and bit his ear," Cass answers.

"What?" she says, horrified. "Why?"

"To save Matthias from getting shot," Rebecca responds.

"That must have been Cindy," Joselyn mutters in disgust as she scrubs her chin clean.

"Either way, it was very brave," Rebecca says.

This is the first kind thing Rebecca has said to Joselyn since Joselyn got here. Maybe there is hope that they could repair their relationship. I'm not sure they'll be able to if Cindy keeps making an appearance, but she is a part of Joselyn, whether we all like it or not.

The sweat I worked up carrying Tim wears off, and I start to shiver. I try not to think about how miserable I feel, but my stomach gives a loud growl, and I become aware of just how hungry I am. We hardly had anything to eat for supper, and we've been walking for hours. I don't know how much food we have left, but I'm worried that it's getting pretty low. When we were eating the chickens, someone had commented that the goats might be next, but they have been carrying heavy loads for us, so I'm not sure how we'll get by without them.

My fatigue sets in, and I start to nod off. Before I think about what I'm doing, I lay my head on David's shoulder and immediately start to dream about bees attacking me while being chased through the woods by an army of soldiers. In front of them is Cindy, with blood dripping down her chin.

I wake up with a start and realize David was resting his head on top of mine. He quickly sits up, clearing his throat and shifting away from me a little.

"You okay?" David whispers.

"Yeah. Just a bad dream," I say, slightly embarrassed. "Has Matthias come back yet?"

"Not that I know of. I kind of dozed off there for a bit."

We sit quietly and hear the heavy breathing of sleep around us. I look around and see Frederick and Henry keeping watch, but their heads keep bobbing like they're falling asleep too. Saul snores loudly. We need to find a safer place for us to camp out. Hopefully, Matthias will come back with good news.

Leaves rustle out in the woods, and I watch as a deer plods along past us. I momentarily consider taking Henry's bow and shooting it for a meal, but I know I could never kill it. Not that I couldn't hit it—I'm actually getting pretty good since I've been practicing—but that I could never take its life. I can't help but put myself in its place, and it makes me sad at the thought.

Finally, my ears pick up someone coming toward us. This time, I don't panic, knowing Matthias was bound to return sooner or later.

"Everyone up. I found a spot. It'll be rough goin', but it's safe."

Sounds of moaning and grunts come from all around as people stand up to move again. The kids whine that they don't want to walk anymore, but Caroline bribes them with a pinch of sugar from the small bag she has in the supplies. I secretly wish I could have a pinch of it too.

We switch up positions again. Nathaniel, a guy in his mid-thirties with curly blond hair and light green eyes, who I just recently found out is the father of Rebecca's twin boys, offers to take my spot carrying Tim. Which means I get to take the goats that he was in charge of. They're tired too, but you can usually keep them going with bits of food.

Before too long, a tall wall of rocks stands before us.

"Is there a cave or something?" Alexandrine asks with a yawn.

"There's a secluded area at the top, surrounded by trees and boulders. We can all tuck in there nicely and stay hidden."

I look up, my head tipped back as far as it will go. He expects us to climb to the top?

"How are we going to get up there?" Alexandrine asks what everyone's thinking.

"I told ya it'll be rough goin'. There's a bit of a trail, but at some points, there'll be some climbing to do. We're gonna have to help each other out."

I look around at everyone's expressions of displeasure. Nobody looks happy to be tackling this near-impossible task. It would be hard enough in the daytime, but now we're doing it in the dark while having to carry Tim, push wheelbarrows, lead goats, and help small children. Not to mention, Saul looks pretty worse for wear. But the thought of being able to rest safely once we make it up there pushes us forward.

The sun starts to rise by the time everyone is at the top. We inched our way up by having an able-bodied person climb a little, then stop and reach down to help pull up a child, a wheelbarrow, or Tim. Luckily, the goats took climbing with stride. Even being weighed down with our stuff, they climbed the rocks easier than any of us humans. They were almost pulling me up the rocks at some points.

There were a couple of rough patches. Saul lost his footing and hit his shin hard against a rock. He didn't cut himself, but it has already started to bruise. He had to go even slower after that. And at a particularly steep spot, Nathaniel and Frederick had to tie ropes around Tim and the stretcher, climb up to a safe place, and then pull Tim up to them. Tim had a moment of alertness before they were tying the ropes on. He told them he could climb it himself, but just as he got the words out, he turned and threw up. Frederick told him to lie down and shut up, which Tim did.

As soon as I'm at the top, I find a tree to tie the goats up to, remove the bags off their back, and give them what little water I can find. Everyone is working as quickly as their tired bodies can to lay out their sleeping gear and finally rest. The clearing is a bit small, so we're all tucked up next to one another.

Even though my concussion makes my head throb, I can tell I've gotten through the worst of it. It's not nearly as painful as it was before. I don't think I could have made that climb if I wasn't feeling better. I'm thankful for that.

I lay my bedding down by David's and stretch a little before going to sleep. I can see the sun turning the sky orange as I gaze down at the treetops below us. Many trees have lost their leaves, and now they look like giant sticks stuck in the ground.

As I take one last look before lying down, I spot a small column of smoke in the distance. The soldiers must be awake.

27

"Matthias," I whisper. He lifts himself up on his elbow to look at me with annoyance.

"What?"

"I just saw smoke coming from out where I think the soldiers' camp is. They're awake."

Matthias sits up, looks around at everyone for a little while, and finally says, "There's nothin' more we can do. We all need to recharge and gain our strength. I suggest ya lay down and put it outta your mind. We should be safe up here."

I nod reluctantly. I lie down on my side, facing David, who's lying on his back with his good arm resting under his head. He has his eyes closed, but I can tell he's not quite asleep yet.

"I'm scared, David," I whisper.

"Don't be. I got you," he whispers back without opening his eyes. He rolls to his side and puts his arm over me protectively. I snuggle in a little closer to let him know I'm okay with this. The weight of his arm feels comforting, and I can immediately relax my mind. Sleep finds me quickly.

■■■■■

I wake up to the sound of distant voices. The sun is now up and shining directly on us. I look around and see that everyone is still asleep. Did I really hear voices, or was I just dreaming?

I slide carefully out from under David's arm. He grunts a little, then rolls over to continue sleeping.

"Their footprints stop here."

"They must have climbed."

"Do we wait down here, or should we climb up and see if they're still there?"

They found us.

I scramble my way through the sleeping bodies to get to Matthias. I make sure I stay down by his feet when I shake him awake to avoid a knife to my neck like last time.

"Matthias!" I whisper.

He snaps awake and sits up in one fluid motion. His green eye locks onto mine, going from kill to confusion in a blink of his eye.

"They found us," I whisper fearfully.

"Where are they?" he asks, seeming to know immediately what I'm talking about.

"On the ground. They haven't climbed up yet."

"Wake everyone up. Be quiet about it. We gotta move."

I nod and start shaking people awake, holding my finger to my lips when their eyes open and they look to see who woke them. Once everyone is up, Matthias fills them in on what's going on.

"The soldiers are comin'. Pack your stuff, and get ready to move. We're gonna head that way and see where it leads," Matthias says, pointing at the trees opposite of the way we came up. The wall of rocks we climbed brought us to this plateau that stretches on through the trees for who knows how long.

"Come on, Matthias. We can't keep running. We have a position of power, let's use it." Alexandrine protests quietly.

"She's right. We could hide everyone out in the woods, have a few of us stay put here, and shoot the soldiers as soon as they make it up," Henry suggests.

Matthias strokes his beard as he looks around at all the eyes watching him. "Fine. David, Henry, and I will stay behind. Everyone else, head out into the woods at least a half-mile, and hide. Olivia, ya listen and wait until ya hear me whistle this." He stops whispering and whistles a three-note tune. "If ya hear that, ya know it's safe to come outta hidin' and that we're on our way. If ya hear gunshots and ya don't hear my whistle, somethin's gone wrong, and the rest of ya will have to take out any soldiers that are left."

"Matthias, do you want me to stay, and you can lead the rest of them?" Frederick offers.

"Nah. I can still shoot usin' my good eye. Ya need to help carry Tim."

I look over at Tim and see that he's still asleep. His skin color looks a little better, but not by much.

I give David a worried look. I wish he wasn't such a good shot. I don't want him to keep being chosen to do dangerous things.

"Matthias!" I hear Rebecca call out in a hushed yell.

I look up to see Rebecca supporting Saul as he tries to take a step but stumbles and falls. Matthias rushes over to him, and I start to panic at how much time we've wasted already. The soldiers could be here at any minute.

"Pop! What's goin' on?"

Matthias helps lay Saul down on his back, and Rebecca lifts his pant leg to look at where Saul had bruised his leg.

I gasp when I see it. His calf is swollen to twice its size, the bruise where he hit against the rock is dark purple, and the surrounding skin is an angry shade of red.

"This isn't good," Rebecca says, tenderly poking around the injury. "I think he's got deep vein thrombosis."

"English, please," Matthias grunts.

"It's a blood clot in a vein deep in his leg. I don't have the blood thinners needed to treat this," she says, her voice shaking.

"What's gonna happen if it's left untreated?"

"Well, a piece of the blood clot could dislodge and travel up his bloodstream into his lung, causing a pulmonary embolism." She looks up from Saul's leg to see

Matthias giving her a look of annoyance. "In other words," she breathes out heavily, "he could die."

"Uh, guys. I don't mean to interrupt," Nathaniel says, "but we need to get moving before the soldiers get here."

Matthias covers his face with his hands, rubbing his fingers on his forehead, thinking. "You're right. Can you help Saul outta here?" he asks Nathaniel.

Nathaniel nods, as he and Rebecca work together to help Saul up off the ground.

"Get yourselves to a safe place, and find something comfortable for him to rest on. We'll catch up as soon as we can," Matthias says as the hand holding a rifle shakes a bit.

"Be careful," I mouth to David, and he winks at me.

I untie the goats and follow behind everyone as we make our way into the woods, taking one last look at David before I'm too far away. They are placing themselves behind boulders that will allow them to hide while keeping watch for the soldiers to make their appearance.

The goats are being uncooperative this time, and it takes a lot of tugging and treats to make them move. After we walk for about fifteen minutes, Rebecca decides that's as far as Saul's going to make it.

We all scatter out, taking shelter behind trees or rocks that are big enough to conceal us. I find a fallen tree with its roots pulled up out of the ground, making a natural wall to hide the goats with me.

As we all sit there, quietly waiting to hear the gunshots, I shake my head in disgust that we're having to kill people again to assure our safety. Will David really be able to do it? I know I wouldn't. Why are our lives more important than the lives of the soldiers? Even though they've given their allegiance to Turk, does that really mean they deserve to die? What if those men have families back home? What about them and their lives that will be messed up because of us? Anger bubbles up inside my chest at my mother. We wouldn't be in this terrible situation if it hadn't been for her. Now because of her, more people have to die.

My muscles start shaking from the constant tension I'm holding. I hear someone humming "London Bridge" not far from where I'm hiding, and I immediately know Cindy is back.

"Shh! Cindy, be quiet!" I hiss.

"How'd you know it was me?"

"Wild guess," I say. "You have to stay quiet so we can hear what's going on."

"Okalie dokalie."

The minutes tick by, and I start to worry about what's going on. A fleeting spark of hope ignites in my mind that maybe the soldiers decided to turn around and head back to the city.

That's when I hear the distinct sound of a gunshot. I squeeze my eyes shut, praying hard that it wasn't from a soldier's gun. I hear another one, followed closely by another. The goats don't seem fazed by the noise. Meanwhile, I'm barely keeping it together.

Five shots are fired in total, with the last two being a little quieter and spaced farther out than the others. Now the silence feels thick as I listen closely for Matthias's whistle. My muscles are so tense, I feel like they could snap. A crow caws loudly above where I'm hiding, and I just about scream, letting out a weird squeaky noise instead. The goats bleat in response, watching me with their alien eyes. I hold a shaky finger up to my lips at them in vain.

After waiting for what feels like forever, I finally hear Matthias whistle. I collapse on the ground with relief.

2'|8

I let everyone know I heard his whistle, and we all gather together close to where Saul and Tim are lying. It doesn't take long before the men find us, carrying extra weapons that they must have taken off the soldiers. Matthias heads straight for his dad without a word to anyone else.

David comes over to me with a look of concern.

"What happened? What's wrong?"

"Matthias took them all out himself. I think he was getting revenge for what happened to Saul or something. Only three of the soldiers climbed up, while two stayed on the ground. As soon as he killed the three, he muttered 'know your enemy,' then he climbed halfway down the rocks and sniped the other two. I've never seen him so crazed before. It was kind of scary."

"Apparently, killing people is fun for him or something."

He ignores me and goes on to say, "He took an earpiece out of one of their ears and heard someone on the other end asking if they were okay and whether they knew where we were headed next. He thinks these soldiers weren't hunting us down to kill us, but following us to see where we were going and then reporting back."

"Well, that's good, isn't it?"

"Not exactly. They know where we are right now, and you can just about guarantee they will be sending a larger group out next time. We can't keep this up forever."

At that moment, we hear the rumbling sound again. It's a little louder than before. It's a cloudless day, so there shouldn't be any thunder. I look around to see if anyone else heard it, and Charlotte and Cindy are looking up with confused looks. They heard it too.

"Do either of you know what that was?" I ask.

They shake their heads.

"You hear it too? I thought I was going crazy," Cindy says, tipping her head off to the side and crossing her eyes.

"That's a short trip," Charlotte teases, and Cindy sticks her tongue out at her.

"Let she who hath not been thrown in thine nut house cast thine first stone," Cindy responds in a mock dramatic voice. And they both erupt in a fit of giggles.

I look at David, who's watching them with furrowed eyebrows. He hasn't experienced Cindy's brand of craziness much, and it shows.

"I'm going to go tell Matthias about the noise. Wanna come?" David asks.

The girls start playing a game of thumb war, and I decide to follow him.

Matthias and Rebecca are separated a bit from the group, having an intense conversation. Matthias has a desperate look on his face as he listens to Rebecca telling him that she can't fix Saul.

"There's nothing I can do. I want to. Believe me. I love him too, but this is just out of my hands. I don't have the skill or the equipment to treat him."

"Is there a chance that the blood clot won't break off? That it'll just go away?"

Rebecca looks over at Saul, who's lying on a pile of blankets. His face looks ashen, and his breathing is labored.

"I think it's already happening," she says with a catch in her voice.

Matthias looks at his dad and rushes to his side. He grabs Saul's hand with worry etched on his face.

David and I decide that now is not the time to be bothering him. We quietly back away and have a seat next to Henry, who's sitting against a tree, watching.

"Pop might be a tough and fearless leader, but when it comes to family, he's a big softy. Don't tell him I told you that," Henry whispers to me, then turns back to watch Matthias sadly.

"I'm really glad I found you guys," I say. "I wish I could have known Saul while he could still talk."

"I wish I could have too. But he was able to teach me a lot without having to say a thing. He'll be missed greatly," he says, his voice thick with emotion. "I'm just glad I didn't have to live with Janice. It's a miracle you turned out as decent as you did."

"Thanks, I guess. I often wonder what life would have been like if Matthias had come to rescue me when I was little. Maybe I would be a superpowered Rare by now or something, never having had my abilities suppressed."

"Sorry it didn't work out that way," he apologizes sincerely.

We are quiet for a while, watching Rebecca as she applies fresh honey on Tim's infected stump and then bandages it with a clean cloth. She sorts through her first aid kit with a shake of her head. I have a sinking feeling that her supplies are running dangerously low.

My stomach growls loudly, and David hears it.

"Has anyone figured out what we're doing for a meal yet?"

"I don't think so. I think everyone's still exhausted," I say, feeling tired myself.

"I saw some fresh deer droppings on our way out here," Henry pipes in. "I'll go hunting. I need to clear my head anyway."

■■■■■

The afternoon passes by quickly with people resting and taking much-needed naps. Frederick was able to find a pond of water for us to drink. It has an unpleasant taste even after boiling it, but nobody complains.

Matthias had taken a moment from his dad's side to inform the camp on what's going on. "We got at least two days before we're in any real danger of a new squad of soldiers catchin' up. Everyone needs to take this time to rest and regain your strength. Help out where ya can, and be ready to move when I say it's time."

Henry returns, dragging a deer with him. He looks worn out, so Nathaniel and Frederick offer to prepare it for supper.

Cass has been sitting by Tim's side since his bandage was changed. She's kept herself busy writing in her notebook, but when nature calls, she asks me to stay with him while she's gone.

I agree, and I take a seat next to his good arm. I stare up into the trees, watching a squirrel hop around when I hear Tim make a small noise in his throat. I look down at him, and he has his eyes cracked open. My first instinct is to call out for Cass, but she's in the middle of going to the bathroom.

"Hey, Olivia," Tim grunts.

"Hi, Tim. You okay?"

"I've been better. Why do I feel sticky?" he asks, looking toward the bandage.

"Rebecca is using honey to try to cure your infection."

"Honey?" His brows furrow.

"Yeah, she says that honey has been used as an antibiotic since ancient times."

Tim just nods and blinks his eyes tiredly. "Do you think this is God's way of punishing me for what I was doing? You know, for cutting myself? I was misusing my arms, so he took one away?"

I absentmindedly rub the knot on my head as I try to figure out how to answer his question. "I don't have a lot of knowledge when it comes to God, but I don't think he would take an already broken person and punish them. So, no, I don't think this is a punishment for your cutting. You losing your arm is just a crappy thing that life threw your way."

He nods. "Well, I'm sorry I ever did that in the first place. I would give anything to have my arm back," he says, bowing his head and looking away from me.

We already gave him lectures about cutting, so me saying more negative things about it isn't going to help. I take a different approach. "We all love you, Tim, whether you have one arm or two. Whether you're depressed or annoyingly happy. You're an important part of this camp, and we're all here for you."

Cass comes bounding back and squeals when she sees that Tim's awake. I leave them to have a little sibling time. I go help David with the fire he's building.

"I heard what you were saying to Tim. Those were some important points you should keep in mind next time you're suffering from a bout of depression."

"Yeah, yeah," I say, brushing it off. It's been a while since I've had a struggle with my depression. I don't think I'm completely healed yet, but I think I'm getting better.

"Pop? Pop, please don't go." I hear Matthias plead.

"I'm sorry, Matthias," Rebecca says, and then steps away to give him his privacy. Henry went running as soon as he heard Matthias cry out, but I'm rooted in place.

"You should go over there, Liv. He was your grandpa too. Even though you didn't get to know him for that long, you're still family."

I stand up hesitantly. This feels like an intimate moment, and I haven't been here that long to deserve to intrude on it. I walk up slowly to Matthias and lay my hand on his shoulder. He reaches up and puts his warm, rough hand on top of mine. We all look down at Saul quietly. His mouth is slack, and his eyes are slightly open. His labored breathing has stopped, and now he's lying there motionless. Henry reaches out and gently closes his eyes.

"I'm sorry, Pop," I whisper to Matthias, feeling that the moment calls for sentimentality.

"That's the first time I heard ya call me that." Matthias sniffs.

"I know. I'm sorry about that too. It takes me a while to deal with my feelings."

We're quiet again as we mourn Saul's passing. I can hear sniffles coming from where the rest of our camp is sitting. They are being respectful and giving us our space.

"Guess I should find a place to bury him," Matthias says, standing up abruptly. He rubs his eye quickly as though he hopes nobody knows he's crying.

"Want me to help, Pop?" Henry asks, wiping his tears away with the heels of his hands.

"I need to be alone for a bit. Go help supper get done. I'm hungry," he says quickly, then turns to head out into the woods to find a resting place for Saul.

Matthias insists on burying Saul on his own. It takes him a long time since all he has is a small camp shovel to work with. Once he's done, he comes to get us so we can all say our goodbyes. Then we head back to camp to have dinner.

Frederick starts a toast in honor of Saul, and everyone goes around saying something nice about Saul. Matthias keeps his gaze on the fire but nods with each sentiment.

It comes around to me, and I try hard to find something profound to say. "I didn't get to know Saul for that long, unfortunately. He seemed like a kind man. He always had a twinkle in his eye when he looked at me. I was intrigued by the way he kept carving the same symbols over and over again on sticks. They matched up with a pendant I once found in a box in my old apartment, and that makes me feel somehow connected to him."

Matthias's head snaps up, and he looks at me when I say that. He gets up and walks over to his bag, pulling out his belongings until he finds the pendant he took from me. He walks back, staring at the symbols. He holds it out to me, and I take it gently. The firelight sparkles in the crystal, making the black symbols stand out more.

"Do ya remember what he carved?"

I try hard to think about the sticks I always saw him whittling, but I can't remember the exact sequence. I roll the tumblers around with my thumbs, hoping to land on the right ones, but nothing happens. I can feel everyone's eyes on me, and I don't like it.

I start to shake my head no when I remember the stick Saul gave me. I race to my bag and dig around until I feel the smooth, slender stick with the symbols carved on it. I want to try setting the symbols in order over here, where nobody is watching me, but everyone wants to see what's going on.

I walk back to the fire, holding the stick and the pendant with reverence. Excitement is blooming inside my chest. What's going to happen when I line up the right combination of symbols?

I sit next to David and Cass while everyone continues to watch me. David holds the stick for me to look at while I twist each tumbler into the right place. Holding my breath, I slowly slide the last one into its spot.

Nothing.

I tug on it gently. Nothing happens.

"What's it doin'? Anything?"

I shake my head and hear people letting out disappointed sighs. "I put the symbols in the right order, but it's not doing anything."

"Mind if I try?" Matthias asks.

I hand the stick and the pendant to him, and he sets to work, rolling the tumblers around to reset the combination, then slowly puts them back into order, but once again, nothing happens.

"Maybe it's like a locker combination. Maybe you need to turn them in the right direction too," David suggests.

"David's probably right. Why don't ya fidget with it, Olivia. Let me know when something happens. I'm goin' to sleep." Matthias hands me the pendant and slumps away heavily.

A somber quiet falls over the camp. The chill in the air has us all huddled close to the fire, cocooned in blankets and warm clothes. Rebecca, Caroline, and Alexandrine work on getting the children put to bed, snuggling them up close to one another. Being that close to each other makes it difficult for them to stop goofing around and go to sleep, making bedtime take twice as long as normal.

I offer to take a watch tonight. That way, I can play around with the pendant while listening for danger. As I sit and twist the symbols around, trying multiple combinations, I start to wonder: what if it doesn't open? What if it's a secret code that spells out a word, and I don't know how to decipher it?

After about the fifteenth time of trying and getting frustrated when it doesn't do anything, I hang it back around my neck and take a break. Now that I don't have anything to occupy my mind, I notice just how cold the night is with this constant wind blowing. The chilly temperature seems to go right through me down to my bones. I lay Henry's bow on the ground close by and wrap my blanket tighter around me.

With summer over, the woods are unnervingly quiet. I miss the sounds of crickets chirping at night. A lonely owl hoots off in the distance, but that's the only sound I hear while I keep watch. I guess I'm grateful for that. We don't need any more excitement right now.

I check the wristwatch Frederick gave me and see that my shift was done an hour ago. I wake Alexandrine up to take my post, trying hard to not wake Charlotte too, who's wrapped in Alexandrine's arms. Once again, a wave of longing washes over me. I will never feel that kind of love, and it makes me sad.

She stands up and catches me watching them with a sad expression. "What's wrong with you?"

I don't want to tell her that I'm feeling jealous of her and Charlotte, so I go a different route. "I'm sorry about my mom. For her betraying us all. You were right to not trust her. I was foolish to believe that she could be different. I was blinded by my own longing for a happy family."

"It was foolish," she says bluntly. And just as I'm starting to get angry, she adds, "But I don't blame you. Having Charlotte here with me is everything. You wanted to be with your mom. I get that. Maybe you should focus on getting to know the family you have here with you instead."

I nod as I look at Joselyn lying next to Charlotte.

"Do you think Rebecca will ever believe Joselyn—I mean, Cindy—and forgive her?"

"I hope so. If Cindy was telling the truth about her dad..." she stops as a dark expression crosses her features, making her look like the Alexandrine I first got to know, "then he got what he deserved, and she deserves all the love she can get."

She turns away and stalks over to the lookout spot. I think this topic hit a sore spot with her, and with good reason. I can't even imagine the long-lasting mental anguish a person deals with after going through abuse like she's been through, like Cindy took on for Joselyn. It's no wonder Cindy acts crazy.

I get myself settled next to David and try hard to put those terrible thoughts out of my mind, grateful that I have the option to do that.

●●●●●

When I wake up in the morning, everything is covered in a sparkly layer of frost. I'm one of the last ones to wake up, surprised that I slept so hard. The children giggle as they melt little handprints in the frost on a large boulder.

I run my hand through my hair and realize that it's been a long time since I've washed up. I pull out the collar of my shirt, tuck my nose down in it, and sniff. I almost gag from the stench. What I wouldn't give for a hot shower right about now. I miss the comforts of home, but I know I'm in a better place, even if it means smelling rank and using leaves as toilet paper. Caroline was kind enough to teach me what poison ivy looks like so I don't make a horrible mistake.

I head over to Matthias and take a seat next to him as he tries to build a fire. "How'd you sleep?" I ask kindly.

"'Bout as well as I expected," he answers. "Did ya get anywhere with the pendant?"

"No, but I'll keep trying."

He pokes at the fire with a long stick, causing embers to float up with the smoke. The wood is damp from last night's frost, so there's more smoldering going on than actual fire.

"What are our plans now?"

"We keep movin'. Once I have a fire built, we'll eat lunch, boil up some drinkin' water, and head out."

"Any chance of bathing? I'm filthy."

"You're more than welcome to go with Frederick to the pond. Ya can take a bath after he gets the pot of drinking water out. But it's gonna be cold," he says, slightly amused.

I shiver at the thought. "Can't we just boil up some water, and everyone can take turns washing up?"

"We don't have time for that."

"Don't we want to give Tim more time to heal?" I ask, looking around to see where Tim is.

When I finally see him, I'm shocked. He's sitting up next to Cass, smiling at something she's saying to him. He still looks paler than normal, and his eyes are sunken and dark, but he seems to be a lot better than yesterday.

"I think he'll live," Matthias grunts but then looks away quickly, still upset about Saul's passing.

"What's for lunch?" I ask, changing the subject.

"Goat."

"What? Really? Aren't they carrying our extra supplies?"

"We're runnin' low on food supplies. The goats slow us down. We'll have to distribute the supplies amongst ourselves to carry and get some new animals once we find a place to settle."

Just then, I hear the rumbling sound once more. I look up at Matthias, but he doesn't give any indication that he heard it. "Did you hear that rumbling?"

Matthias looks up at the sky and then back at me, shaking his head. "What rumblin'?"

"David and I have been hearing a rumbling sound a couple times a day for a few days now. We haven't had the chance to mention it to you. It's weird because it sounds a little like thunder off in the distance, but there never seem to be clouds in the sky when it happens."

"Ya hear it twice a day?"

"Yeah."

"Is it around the same time of day?"

I scratch at my lump, which has shrunk down to about half its size, and think. "Now that you mention it, yeah, I think so. Usually once in the morning and once in the evening."

"It's a train." He stands up and starts pacing. "Which direction is it comin' from?"

I think about it for a second and point to my right.

"West. Good," Matthias mutters almost more to himself than to me.

"If I can hear it, does that mean we're getting too close? Will they see our smoke?"

"Nah. We're not that close. Plus, they're fast trains, so by the time they spot our smoke, they'll be speedin' away."

I nod, relieved that there isn't something else we need to worry about.

After lunch, we all get packed up and ready to move. I get in line behind David, both of us weighed down with some extra supplies the goats were carrying. I'm sad about the goats, but I think we'll move a lot faster without them.

We all wait as Matthias and Henry stop by Saul's grave one last time before we take off. I hold the pendant tightly in my hand while they're gone. I hope I can figure this thing out soon. I had a moment of frustration earlier and thought about smashing it open with a rock but decided that wouldn't be a good idea. Not only is it sentimental, but what if there's something valuable inside?

Once the men return, we finally set off again.

"Matthias thinks the sound we've been hearing might be a train," I say to David as we plod along.

"Really?"

"Yeah, but he said not to worry about it. That we're a safe enough distance away."

David's quiet a moment then turns his head to say, "Too bad we can't hop on the train and make our trip quicker."

"I don't think the train would lead to the Haven."

David shrugs and continues following the line of people.

Tim is a little ahead of him, walking on his own now, but Cass is at his side in case he needs help. We make good progress today. The plateau we were on eventually comes to an end, and we climb our way back down. It's not as steep as going up, so it doesn't take too long, especially since the kids seem to think it's fun climbing on the rocks. They get way ahead of their moms and find themselves in trouble once they reach the bottom. Much to everyone's surprise, Matthias tells the women to lighten up, smirking at the children's antics.

Once we're all on the ground, we walk about a mile before we reach an abandoned road. I knew we couldn't stay in the wilderness forever before finding remnants of civilization. The pavement is all broken up where plants have pushed through, making it look less like a road and more like a strange stony garden.

There are a few cars on the side of the road that are nothing but shells. All the engine parts have been stripped, leaving just the body of the car. Even the wheels are gone. The gas tanks are open, and Matthias says that's because the gas was siphoned out. Too bad we couldn't hop into the cars and drive. I would love to crank the heater on full blast and fall asleep.

We walk by the road, keeping ourselves hidden in the woods just in case, until the sun starts to go down. Matthias finally leads us away from the road, and we come to a house that's half standing. The left side of the two-story house has been destroyed by something, leaving a giant pile of debris, while the right side is still in relatively good shape. The paint is chipping away, and a few of the windows are broken, but the rest of it seems intact.

"Everyone, wait here. I'll go check it out," Matthias says.

As we watch Matthias walk stealthily to the abandoned house, I hear the rumbling again. This time, it's loud enough for everyone to hear.

"Sounds like a storm's coming. I hope we can sleep inside tonight," Caroline comments, looking at the cloudless sky.

"It's not thunder. Matthias thinks it's a train," I say.

"Well, let's hope he's right. I'm not feeling like getting soaked through with these cold temperatures. I'd never be warm again."

I watch as a flashlight beam passes by an upper window, then disappears again.

The wind picks up and seems to blow through every layer of clothing I have on. I shiver, hoping along with Caroline that we can sleep inside tonight.

Finally, Matthias is back out, walking toward us. "Looks safe enough for the night."

A few cheers erupt, and the kids go racing toward the house. Their happy giggles mimic what I'm feeling inside. I wonder if the plumbing still works.

30

We walk into the house, and by the light of the flashlight, we see that we're not the first ones to have been here. The living room walls are graffitied with all sorts of anti-government propaganda: Turk's name crossed off inside a circle; the words "The Coalition are liars!" and "Long live the Rare!" in giant red letters as well as other assorted phrases. I hope the kids can't read or at least don't recognize the swear words painted up there.

I look around at the rest of the room and see that the furniture is moldy and moth-eaten. The carpet isn't any better. It's filthy and full of dead bugs, which is probably not unrelated to half the house missing. We keep walking, and I spot a torn coalition flag lying in a heap in the corner. Whoever was here better hope they don't get caught doing this stuff. They'll more than likely be killed for it.

"It's a dump, but it's shelter. The rooms upstairs aren't as bad as this."

"Anything in the kitchen?" Rebecca asks as we walk through the doorway leading to a ransacked kitchen. The cupboard doors are all open, and some of them are hanging by one hinge. The white refrigerator is rusty and has more swear words scratched on the surface. I walk to the sink and pull up the faucet handle. It gives a few sputters, and then rusty brown water trickles out slowly.

"The plumbing still works. Maybe there's a bathroom," I say hopefully.

Stan heads through a door, and we hear him say, "Bathroom's in here, but I don't think this toilet's working. Yuck!"

"Hey, I found some canned food. They're expired, but maybe we could open them and see if they're still good," Rebecca says. She has climbed onto the counter and searched the top cupboards for anything that might have been left behind.

Matthias hands her a knife, and she cuts the tops open. "They look fine," she says while Matthias shines the flashlight at the food. "Smells fine too."

"Everyone, grab one and dig in," Matthias says.

I end up with green beans that taste like the can they're in.

David takes something I've never seen before.

"What is that?" I ask, slightly disgusted.

"I don't know. It says 'Spam,' but I have no idea what it is. I think it might be meat." He digs a chunk out with his fingers and sniffs it before putting it in his mouth. He chews a few times, then nods a little. "Not bad, actually. Want some?"

"No, thanks. I'm good." I wrinkle my nose at him.

We all pile our empty cans on the table and head up the stairs to see what other wonders await us. The stairs creak under everyone's weight, and I start to worry whether the second floor will support us all. I reach the landing and see the hallway end abruptly with a tarp covering the hole where the other half of the house collapsed. The wind blows, making a howling sound that sets my nerves on edge.

I've only ever seen a couple of horror movies in my life, but this is definitely how one would begin. Matthias points out the two bedrooms, and we split up into groups.

"Which room do you want to sleep in?" David asks me.

"Well, Joselyn is in with the kids, which means Rebecca is in there too. Maybe I should stay close by to support Joselyn if she needs it."

"Lead the way."

I step through the door and see that this must have once been a little girl's room. The pink walls are now dirty, but the vibrant hue peaks out beneath the grime in various spots. Lacy curtains are hanging in front of a window seat lined with dolls, a zoo of stuffed animals, and fluffy pink pillows, all covered in a thick layer of dust. The four-poster queen bed is a mess, but the mattress looks intact.

Caroline and Rebecca get busy stripping the dust encrusted bedding off the mattress and throw it into the closet. They lay out the children's blankets and have them sleep across the width of the bed so they can all fit. Once they're settled, Caroline and Rebecca take opposite sides of the bed on the floor. Charlotte, Joselyn, and Alexandrine settle in by Rebecca, leaving a space at the foot of the bed where David and I can lie. Cass and Tim tuck themselves on the other side of David, against the wall. It must be hard for Tim to get comfortable with his injury, but luckily, the infection is almost gone. Rebecca has been treating it every day with honey, and surprisingly, it's working.

"No kissy facing, you two," Joselyn says, and Charlotte giggles.

"Oh, knock it off, Cindy," I say.

"No, it's me. Joselyn. I was just kidding, Olivia."

I'm taken aback slightly. That seemed like something Cindy would say. "Sorry. I just assumed. Goodnight, Joselyn."

I lay out my bedding and get comfortable next to David. It's still chilly, but it's a definite improvement to sleeping outside. I fall asleep with thoughts of how glorious a shower would feel on my sore, aching muscles.

We're running with all our might. The broken-down buildings and destroyed roads pass by in a blur as we run to our only hope of survival. The kids can't run as fast as we can, so I scoop Emily up into my arms, her weight making me slow down more than I care to. The sense of impending doom keeps my legs going, though, so I push through.

I look behind me and see the soldiers coming up quick in a military truck. We're far enough ahead of them that they can't use their weapons yet, but it won't be long.

"Matthias!" I shout with what little breath I have left in my lungs. "We need to get off the road! They're getting too close!"

"We're almost there! Follow me!"

We turn off the road and start running through the woods. I hear the truck come to a stop. I chance a look behind me and see at least ten soldiers hop out and start chasing us on foot.

"There it is! It's starting to move. Hurry up!"

I look up and through the trees and see a rectangular metal box moving slowly forward. Then another right behind it. And more after that.

A train!

We reach the train, and Matthias pulls the door open. He jumps into one of the boxes and then leans out the edge to grab our hands. We all have to run next to the moving box to get in. Once the children have been pushed up into it, the adults start climbing on. David gives Tim a hard shove, making him faceplant on the floor, but there's no time for apologies.

I look behind me, and the soldiers are just coming to the tracks. They're close enough to use their guns now, and a loud gunshot rings out behind me as a bullet hits the track next to me with a spark. I jump up and catch the edge of the platform. Hands immediately grab onto my arms and shirt and pull me to safety.

I lean my head out and see David has fallen behind a bit. He's holding his arm as blood seeps through his fingers. He puts on as much speed as he can, barely able to keep up with the train that's moving twice as fast as before. With a giant leap, he belly flops into the car, and Frederick drags him in just in time. A soldier comes into view outside of the box we're on, and Matthias shoots him in the face without hesitation.

The train has worked up its momentum, and we speed off, leaving the rest of the soldiers behind.

■■■■■

I'm awakened by a loud voice shouting from below us: "You ate all my food! You kids better hope to God you're not still here, or I'll kill you!"

Everyone is sitting up, looking wide-eyed at each other. The sun is just starting to come up, making the room bright with the early rays of sunshine. Rebecca holds her twins tightly as we hear heavy footsteps on the stairs. David gets up, grabs the lamp by the bed, and stands next to the door.

"Hey, mister," I hear Matthias's gruff voice say outside the bedroom. "We don't want any trouble. We just needed a place to sleep for the night."

"Who're you?" the stranger asks. His voice sounds a bit wavery, like an old man.

"The name's Tom," Matthias lies. "My friends and I are travelin', and we found your house. We thought it was abandoned. Sorry for intrudin'."

"You ate my food," he accuses.

"I'm sorry, sir. We helped ourselves, and we shouldn't have. I'll have my group pack up, and we'll be out of your hair."

Silence follows, and I hold my breath as I wonder if the guy is going to make trouble or not.

"Eh, stay as long as you like. I could use the company," the old man says tiredly, and then we hear him stomp back down the stairs.

Everyone in the room lets out the breaths we were all holding. David puts the lamp back on the table and then opens the door slowly.

"It's safe to come out," Matthias says. "Let's all head downstairs so we can thank him for lettin' us stay here."

David swings open the door, and we all shuffle our way downstairs.

"I thought you were the damn hooligans who destroyed what was left of my house. I leave for a few days to see if I can find some food, and I come back to this," the old man calls from the living room as we all troop downstairs.

"No, sir. We're just passin' through."

The old man whistles as we pile into his living room. "There sure is a lotta you. Where are you all headed?"

I step in behind Cass and get a good look at the old man. He's bald on the crown of his head but has long gray hair on the back and sides pulled into a ponytail. He's thin and fragile-looking; however, his eyes hold a fire that lets us know he's not one to be messed with. He's wearing a red flannel shirt with brown patches on the elbows and a pair of well-worn jeans. His boots look like soldiers' boots, which make me suddenly worried that maybe he's hiding something.

"West. We outstayed our welcome at the last place."

"You friends of Turk?" he asks, picking at a hole in the couch.

"No, sir," Matthias answers.

The old man squints at him, waiting for him to continue, but when he doesn't, the gentleman looks around the room at each and every one of us. His eyes linger on me and then David for longer than I like.

"Well, Tom. I know I said you can stay as long as you like, but I can't be found housing a bunch of Rares, so you're going to have to keep your visit short."

"How do you know some of us are Rare?" Alexandrine asks, glancing at Charlotte with a look of concern.

"Just putting two and two together, darling," he says with a wink.

"Don't...call me darling," Alexandrine growls, balling her fists up.

I watch as Matthias lays his hand on her shoulder, and she pulls away from his hand, giving him a glare.

"Sorry, Margarite's a little feisty," Matthias says, trying to defuse the tension. "We're just curious how ya could know just by lookin' at us?"

The man's eyes sparkle a bit as he looks around at us again. His gaze lands on Joselyn, and his eyes widen slightly. "I can sense it. It's one of my gifts. This girl here is powerful. You'll want to keep an eye on her," he says, pointing at Joselyn.

We all look over at Joselyn, whose cheeks are turning bright red.

"One of your gifts? Are ya Rare too?" Matthias asks.

"You got that right. Though I'm not as strong as I once was, I'm still sharp as a tack," he says, tapping the side of his head.

"What do you mean by 'one of your gifts'? Rare people only have heightened senses and reflexes..." I begin to say.

286

"Ah, I can see they brainwashed you too," he says, clicking his tongue, "Do you really think people having good eyesight or hearing was the cause of the war? Think! The Rare are more powerful than you can imagine. Especially untainted ones."

We all stand there staring at him in stunned silence.

"Haven't there been things you've done that you can't explain?" he asks impatiently. "That would be your Rare abilities shining through. 'Course if you've been unlucky enough to be living in the city, then your abilities were most likely tampered with."

"Could that be what the vitamins do?" David asks.

"I don't know, Son. I'm just going off what I've heard. I've never set foot in any of the cities, and I don't intend to either. I like my freedom, and I'm keeping it that way."

"You sound like Matthias," Alexandrine mumbles.

"Who's Matthias?" the old man asks.

Matthias gives Alexandrine a quick look of annoyance but lies for her. "Her ex-husband." He quickly changes the subject. "Once again, I'm sorry we ate all your food. Is there anything we can do to repay ya?"

"Don't worry too much about it. I was beginning to wonder if that food was good anyway. Hope none of you got sick from it."

We all look around at each other and shrug.

"We have some good hunters here. We'll get some meat, and I'll show ya how to dry it out so ya can have better eatin' than outdated canned food."

"Much appreciated."

"Mind if we use your shower, sir?" I ask with some slight desperation.

"Sorry, you can't. The septic's backed up since there's nobody around to pump it out. I just heat up buckets of water I pull up from the well and use that to clean. You're welcome to it if you like."

I slump my shoulders a bit but remember to say thank you.

"Well, I reckon I better get to my chores. I could use some help around here if anyone's willing. Oh, and a word of advice to you hunters: don't go off that way," he says, pointing to the west. "Train's that way. Wouldn't want you to be killed or, worse, caught."

31

By the time evening rolls around, we're all exhausted. We helped the old man with numerous chores as a way of saying thank you for letting us stay. I didn't envy Caroline as she scooped the backed-up toilet's nasty contents out with a big empty can and took it to his makeshift outhouse. I gagged a little just at the thought of doing it. The old man said the mess was from those hooligans who wrecked his house and that he was going to get to it someday, but he just didn't have the stomach for it. How he could live with the stench of it in his house, I have no idea.

The dream I had last night has been running through my mind all day. What if what the old man said was true? What if Rares have more gifts than just reflexes and better senses? What if I'm dreaming about the future? Before I even set foot in the woods, I had that dream about Matthias and Henry finding me and killing the Havoc. Reality didn't play out exactly as the dream had, but it was close enough. What if this dream is the same? I see Matthias outside chopping wood with the old man's ax in the evening's fading light. I decide to tell him about it.

"So, ya had a dream that we hopped on the train?"

"Yeah, because the soldiers were chasing us."

"And from your dream, it sounds like we got on a boxcar, which is made for carryin' cargo, not people."

"So?" I say stupidly. I don't know much about our modern-day rail systems.

"The trains have been revamped since the war, made to reach high speeds to travel faster between the cities. The front of the train has enclosed cars, fit for carryin' passengers, while the back of the train has boxcars for supplies. Ya get on one of those goin' up to speed, it would be one helluva ride."

"Why?"

"They just took the old boxcars, modified the running gears, and threw on airfoils for aerodynamics. They're either lazy or cheap. Most likely, both."

I want to ask what airfoils are, but I already look like a moron, so I don't bother. "I think we could handle it," I say stubbornly.

Matthias lets out a breathy laugh, shaking his head slightly. "Well, did ya happen to see why the train was stopped?" Matthias continues on skeptically.

"No, just that it was starting to move by the time we got to it."

"Well, trains don't stop in between cities, so I'm not sure how much weight ya should be putting into this."

"But the old guy said Rares have special gifts..."

"If ya ask me, the old coot is a little off his rocker. He's talkin' about people havin' superpowers, Olivia," he says, shaking his head in disbelief as he picks up his ax to continue chopping. "And hoppin' on a train would be foolish and dangerous."

"But it would also get us to the Haven faster," I say, getting frustrated with him. How can he be dismissing the idea of the Rare being more powerful than what we previously thought?

"We're headed to the next city over, which ain't the Haven."

"Well, if my dream is right, the train stops at some point, and we could get on it!" I shout, letting my anger get the better of me.

He stops chopping and points the ax at me, "If ya figure out some way to make the train stop, let me know. In the meantime, we keep doin' what we're doin'."

"What? Continuously walking and hoping we don't all die?" I mumble as I turn and storm back into the house. I head over to the old man, who's sitting on his couch reading in the candlelight. "Excuse me, sir," I say meekly and wait until he looks up from his book. "Has the train nearby ever stopped for any reason?"

He puts a strip of paper in his book to mark his place and sets it down beside him. "There have been a few times. There's a cliffside nearby that crumbles from time to time and leaves a mess on the rails. They usually slow down through here because of it. Wouldn't want another derailment like they had about ten years ago," he answers and then furrows his eyebrows. "Why do you want to know?"

"Oh, just wondering. I want to make sure my friends are safe in case the train does stop. We'll want to steer clear of it," I lie on the spot.

"That'd be wise," he says. "Now, you got anything else to ask? I'm getting to a good part in my book."

"No. That's all."

I head off to find David. Maybe he'll see things my way. I don't know why boarding a government train seems like such a good idea to me. It's really not. We could get caught and thrown in jail or killed. But after that dream, I can't seem to let it go. I find David out back, building a fire.

"You know he's got a wood-burning stove inside the house, right?"

"I prefer campfires now," he says and then adds quietly, "Plus, his house gives me the creeps."

I nod as I take a seat next to him on the cold ground. "David, do you think he was telling the truth? That Rares have more power than what we thought?"

David stares down at his hands and clenches his jaws a few times as he thinks. I take notice of the facial hair that's starting to fill in on his face. His hair is black, but his facial hair has highlights of light brown and red. It looks good on him.

"I think I do. Bartholomew saved my life, Liv. I'm not sure who Bartholomew is or what he is or how he showed up when he did, but I can't stop thinking about him. I would have died if he hadn't saved me."

"You think Bartholomew and your Rare abilities are connected?" I ask, confused.

"Maybe? I haven't figured out how yet, but I'm leaning that way."

"I think I might be able to dream of the future," I say, wanting to impress him.

"What makes you think that?"

"Well, I had that dream while I was in the hospital about Henry and Matthias saving me from a Havoc, and then it came true. And last night, I had a dream that felt real, like the one in the hospital. We were running for our lives and got on a train that had stopped nearby. We all made it, but you got shot in the arm," I say, giving him an apologetic look.

"Why would we get on a train?"

"So we can travel faster? I don't know. We were being chased by soldiers, and it seemed like the best way to escape," I say, annoyed.

"But wouldn't the soldiers chasing us just radio in that we got on the train? Then we'd be caught."

Anger bubbles up inside of me. "I don't have all the answers, okay? All I know is what I dreamed."

"Calm down, Liv. I'm sorry. I was just trying to understand," David says, bumping his shoulder into mine.

We sit quietly next to each other, and I think about what he said. He's right. My dream was probably nothing more than just a dream. There are so many bad consequences that could happen if we boarded a government train. But then something clicks.

"What if my dream is just one possible outcome? What if my dream shows what could happen unless we change things?" I say excitedly. "What if we somehow made the rocks crumble onto the tracks on purpose, and while they cleaned it up, we got on the train? You know, before we're chased by any soldiers. Then we're getting on the train on our own terms."

David stares at the firepit, thinking. Then he finally says, "But how would we make rocks fall onto the tracks? You would need some dynamite or something, and the last I checked, we aren't carrying any of that around with us."

I instantly deflate when he points that out. "You're right. I'm an idiot."

"No, Liv. You're not. I'll mull it around in my mind for a while and see if a solution comes to me," he says supportively.

We go back to sitting in silence for a little while. The cold evening air makes me shiver, and David notices. He puts his arm around me, rubbing my shoulder to help warm me up. I lean into him, resting my head on his chest, and I feel him sniff my hair. I close my eyes, relishing the touch.

What am I doing? I shouldn't be toying with him like this. I told him no to a relationship, yet I can't deny that I like this. Maybe it's time I give him a chance. But just not yet.

■■■■■

A few days pass, and I'm starting to get the itch to keep moving. I hate to admit it since he's been kind enough to let us stay in his house, but Mr. Wick gives off a vibe I don't like. I can't really put my finger on why, but I don't like being around him. Maybe it's the way he seems to watch me whenever we're in a room together. He watches Joselyn and Charlotte that way too. He's sneaky about it. You can't usually catch him doing it, but you can feel his eyes on you when you're around him. Maybe he doesn't trust other Rares? Either way, I make sure I'm never alone with him.

I talk David into ducking out of doing chores today, and we venture our way over to look at the rocks. We wait until after the morning train goes through so we know we'll be safe to search around for a while.

The rock face is steep, but we manage to climb it. David has to be careful since he can only use one hand, but I stay close behind him and offer help where I can. Once we reach the top, we're able to see the surrounding area better. With the leaves gone off the trees, we can spot about a hundred houses that have either been destroyed completely and are being reclaimed by nature or are in far worse shape than Mr. Wick's house. By the looks of things, I think this area used to be a small town before the war. Once again, those feelings of gratitude toward the people willing to stand up and fight for the Rare overwhelms me. So many lives lost or ruined because people had to be bigots and try to get rid of other people who are different from them. And even though the war is over, the government is still trying to control the Rares and make our lives miserable.

"Liv, look over there," David says, snapping me out of my thoughts.

I look to where he's pointing and see a giant boulder about the size of a car, sitting ten feet away from the edge. "What about it?"

"Maybe we could push that boulder onto the train tracks," David says with hope in his voice.

"I know we're stronger than we once were, David, but you and I can't possibly move that thing ourselves..."

"We'll get Frederick and others to come here with us and push the boulder onto the tracks after the evening train goes through. Then we wait until the morning train has stopped. While they're busy cleaning it up, we can sneak everyone onto the train and make our way to the next city."

"Let's go run it by Matthias," I say, high-fiving David.

32

"I suppose it could work," Matthias says, stroking his beard. "At least the boulder part, but I just don't know if it's worth the risk of bein' caught."

"I'm ready to leave this place. I don't like it here."

Matthias takes a deep breath and blows it out slowly. "Let me talk to Alexandrine about it first."

■■■■■

Alexandrine is on board with the train idea. I think everyone is getting tired of staying here.

Mr. Wick has been getting crankier since we arrived. It doesn't help when the children complain about being bored and make a ruckus with the volleyball by dribbling it upstairs over the top of him as he's trying to read. He doesn't say anything, but you can see it on his face.

A heavy frost set in overnight while we were sleeping. I wake up to Emily squealing with delight when she looks outside from the upstairs window. I get up and take a peek too. The morning sun is shining brightly on the frost, making it sparkle like diamonds. It's quite beautiful.

Today, David and I are taking a group of able-bodied people up to see the boulder and get a better plan on how to do this. By the time everyone is up and ready to go, the morning train has already gone through, and the frost is almost completely melted. Only the frost in the shady areas remains, making parts of the climb a bit slippery.

"That's a big rock," Frederick says, walking around it. "You guys really think we have enough man-power to push that thing over?"

"Accuracy of getting it on the tracks would be nearly impossible," Alexandrine says, peering over the cliff's side.

My shoulders drop as they make these observations. I had my hopes up that this would work, but now I realize it's probably not going to. I look over at David, and he's got a stony expression.

"We're going to at least try, right?" David says.

"I think it'd be a waste of time," Nathaniel says. "A boulder this size doesn't just tumble off a cliff. The conductors would catch on that this wasn't a natural occurrence, and they'd send someone to look for whoever did it."

"So, what's your solution, then?" David asks, getting worked up.

"Calm down, David," Matthias growls. "Nathaniel is right. I say we find some hammers and chisels and hack this boulder into smaller rocks. Then we can toss 'em onto the tracks, make it look like a rockslide."

"Let's get started then," David says.

"Hold on. We didn't agree to it yet," Nathaniel says. "Tell me how this isn't a really bad idea again."

"In my dream, we were being chased by soldiers and got on the train. I think we should take matters into our own hands and not wait for the soldiers to be chasing us before we hop on the train to get to the next city. Winter's coming, and we are dangerously low on supplies. We need to get there fast."

"So now we're following dreams? Last night I dreamed I could fly. Think I should throw myself off this cliff?" Nathaniel goads.

"Go ahead. Rid us of your stupidity," Matthias snaps, wiping the smirk off Nathaniel's face. "Since ya don't have Rare abilities, keep your mouth shut."

Nathaniel gives Matthias a threatening glare but then drops his gaze, surrendering.

"You think the old man has the tools we need?" Frederick asks.

"If he doesn't, one of the surrounding houses might."

■■■■■

To nobody's surprise, the old man does not have the tools we need. Matthias doesn't divulge why we need them, and I think it's because he doesn't trust Mr. Wick much either. It's not hard to miss the way Mr. Wick watches us Rares like a hawk. I don't understand why, though. He has Rare abilities too, so why would he act as though we're untrustworthy?

We pair up and start searching houses in the area. David and I head up a side street that's more vegetation than pavement now. The bare tree branches reach overhead, entangling with each other from opposite sides of the road. A breeze blows, causing the branches to click together eerily, setting my nerves on edge. I've come to notice that there aren't as many birds singing anymore. The sounds of summer are gone, leaving just crow caws and the calls of a few hardy birds that stay for the winter.

We come to a small house that's still standing. The paint is faded and peeling, and all the windows are broken, but it seems to be in okay shape otherwise.

We walk to the garage and see that the door is slightly ajar. David pushes the door open slowly while staying outside. His muscles are tense as he prepares himself for whatever might be hiding inside. He shines his flashlight in every direction, and I can see his muscles relax as he rules out any threats. I peek my head inside and see that whoever lived here was a neat freak. Every tool is hung on the wall in a perfectly organized manner. David hands me the flashlight and walks into the garage.

As David steps over the threshold, we hear a strange whiny buzzing sound. I look around the rafters for bees, even though it sounded different than bees buzzing, but I don't spot any. I follow David over to a hammer that's bigger than I have ever seen before. Its wooden handle is almost as long as my leg, and the head is a black barrel shape that's bigger than my hand.

David picks it up with a grunt. "This thing is heavy!"

He hands it to me, and I almost drop it. It has to weigh at least twenty pounds. I carry it up against my shoulder, balancing the weight so it's easier to hold.

We look at the rest of the tools, but none of them look like they would help us break apart a rock, so we leave them. As we walk back to the door, we hear that buzzing sound again.

I look up and see something black and round mounted up in the corner of the wall. "David? What's that?"

David looks up to where I'm pointing and swears loudly as he grabs my free hand and pulls me outside quickly. "That was a camera, Liv. We have to warn the others," David says worriedly. He keeps a hold of my hand as we trot back to the house.

"A sledgehammer? Nice," Frederick says, giving us a thumbs-up as we hurry past him to find Matthias.

We find him out by the firepit, arranging some tools he must have found.

"We need to leave now," David says as we get closer to him.

"What's goin' on?"

"The house we went to had a surveillance camera in the garage."

Matthias scratches at his beard. "So?"

"It was still working!" David says urgently.

"Ya sure?" Matthias asks seriously.

David nods.

"Couldn't it just be an old camera the owners put there to protect their stuff?" I ask.

"We can't take the chance. It could be a government camera watchin' for traitors," Matthias answers while gathering up the hammers and chisels from the ground. "Let's get this plan into motion and get outta here."

■■■■■

We spend the night hacking away at the boulder. By morning, Matthias, Henry, Frederick, Nathaniel, and I have a pile of sizable rocks tossed down on the tracks, and sore, tired arms to show for it. I pushed it a bit too hard, and now my head throbs, but I keep that to myself, not wanting to seem weak. David won't let me hear the end of it if I push myself too hard. He was reluctant to let me go without him, but with a broken wrist, he wasn't able to help.

We told everyone else to have our stuff gathered up and to be ready to go when the train comes through. Now I'm hoping we have enough time to get back down off the cliff before it gets here. I hope David packed my stuff for me.

We are almost back to the house when I hear the familiar rumbling sound off in the distance. A jolt of nervous energy courses through me as I think about what we are about to do. Is this even going to work? Horrible images run through my mind of us being caught, tortured, or killed and how it would be all my fault. I'm already starting to feel guilty, and nothing has happened yet.

As we walk down the driveway, I see everyone waiting for us outside, but something seems off.

"Where's Joselyn?" I ask Charlotte.

"Mr. Wick wanted to show her something. I asked to go too, but he wouldn't let me," she says sadly.

"She's alone with him?" I ask frantically.

People nearby us glance around at each other, shrugging as though this was news to them. David gives me a worried look.

I race into the house, heart pounding. She should not have been left alone with him. I run upstairs, hoping she's still packing or something, but a terrible feeling is needling at me.

I punch the wall in frustration when I see the empty rooms. Where could she be? I hurry back downstairs, almost running into David. He grabs ahold of my shoulders, steadying me, and I hear a faint scream come from the woods. David's eyes widen, and I know he heard it too.

We rush out of the house and sprint in the direction we heard the scream. I hear footsteps behind us and glance back to see Matthias and Henry are tailing us with weapons drawn.

I frantically scan around the area, looking for any sign of where Joselyn could be. Some of the wet leaves have been disturbed, as though something was dragged across them. They turn off to the right, through a thick tangle of underbrush. We follow the drag marks that come to a weather-worn shack up ahead. The boards are grayish brown and covered in splotchy moss. The roof's shingles are curling up on the edges with an even thicker layer of moss.

Anger courses through my veins, and I can feel heat radiating up my neck from beneath my sweatshirt. As I start to step toward the shack, David holds out his arm to stop me. I give him a glare, wondering why he isn't charging in there himself, but he holds up a finger to his mouth to warn me to be quiet.

"Wait for Henry and Matthias. They're the ones with the weapons," David says smartly.

After a few moments, Henry and Matthias come charging in behind us, and David waves at them to be silent. We all creep up to the building, listening for any signs of life. I hear muffled yelling, and my fists ball up at my sides. Joselyn doesn't deserve this. Mr. Wick better not have hurt her, or he's going to regret it.

"I know you're out there. I can sense Rare abilities, remember?" We hear Mr. Wick's voice call out.

Matthias marches over to the door and tugs it open with a creak from the hinges. I follow right behind him and see Joselyn tied to a rickety wooden chair with a gag in her mouth, eyes wild. Cindy's come back to save Joselyn from the trauma again.

"Let her go!" I shout.

"Why would I do that? I told you she was a powerful one. She's going to fetch me a pretty price," he says, running the back of a blade down her cheek. "I'm going to be set for a while once I turn her in."

"Turn her in? I thought you were a Rare, a traitor just like the rest of us," Henry says.

Mr. Wick laughs coldly. "My Rare power benefits both the government and myself. I made a deal. I'm allowed to live on my own, and I'm rewarded with things I need if I turn in any other Rares I find. I think I'm going to ask for double what they usually give me for this one." His eyes shine greedily.

Matthias points the gun at him. "How're ya gonna do that with a bullet in your brain?"

The old man's smugness falters a bit at the sight of the gun. He ducks down behind Cindy, and all we see of him is his arm holding the knife against her neck. "Shoot me, and I'll make sure the last thing I do is slit her throat."

Cindy rolls her eyes and yells angrily into her gag. She doesn't even look afraid. She looks annoyed.

"Ya don't need to do this," Matthias says calmly, nodding slightly at Henry. "We're gettin' ready to leave. Just let her go, and we'll pretend none of this ever happened."

"Why? The soldiers are almost here. I called them as soon as you fools showed up."

As the men talk, I watch Henry nock an arrow and take aim at the old man's exposed elbow. I want to yell at him to stop, that it's too close to her face, but he pulls back the string and lets the arrow fly, hitting his target with perfect accuracy. Mr. Wick yells out in pain, dropping the knife. Matthias marches up to the old man and shoots him through the temple without a second thought.

33

After I untie Cindy, I see the wildness in her eyes disappear, replaced by a look of terror and confusion. That's the first time I've seen Cindy give control back to Joselyn so quickly. I want to ask about it, but we don't have time. I grab on to Joselyn's hand, and we all head back to the house, where everyone is nervously watching the direction we ran.

To my surprise, Rebecca is the first one to come rushing toward us. "Are you okay?" she asks, stopping a few feet in front of us. Her eyes are misty and full of concern.

"Yeah, I think so," Joselyn replies shyly.

"Good." Rebecca reaches out and rubs Joselyn's arm tentatively.

Joselyn starts weeping and steps forward, wrapping her arms around Rebecca. She looks uncomfortable at first, but after a few seconds of Joselyn sobbing into her shirt, Rebecca wraps her arms around Joselyn and holds her close.

"We need to go. Soldiers are on their way," Matthias says, stomping past them.

"They're almost here!" David shouts. "I can hear them. They're about a half a mile that way," he says, pointing to the east.

Everyone scrambles to collect their things, and we take off running toward the train tracks. Let's hope they're almost done cleaning up the rock mess we made.

The small children are falling behind, so I scoop Emily up in my arms and run with her. Her weight slows me down more than I like. I chance a look behind me, and I can see the soldiers approaching in their vehicle with remarkable speed. They're still too far away to shoot at us, but fear of being hunted makes me dig deeper for the strength to run faster.

I suddenly realize that things from my dream are playing out. I look ahead for the train, and sure enough, there it is, and it's just starting to move. We run alongside the train car as Matthias hops up, grabbing onto the lever, which he pulls up, sliding the door open. I pass Emily to Caroline, and she hands her up to Matthias, then climbs on. The other adults do the same, passing the children up to the train and then climbing on themselves. It takes a few tries for some to make it as the train steadily speeds up. David gives Tim a push to help him, and Tim ends up face planting, just like in the dream. All that's left is David and me. I look behind us, and there are the soldiers coming up to the train now.

"Hurry, David!" I scream, just as a bullet ricochets off the track. I shove off the ground with my right foot and just barely flop into the train, the edge of the platform bruising my rib cage. Hands immediately pull me in, and I turn right around, reaching my arm out toward David, hoping I can be quick enough to stop what's coming next.

But I'm not. David is already holding onto his arm, and I groan as I see the blood seeping between his fingers. He's fallen behind too much, and I worry he's not going to catch back up. I'm just about to hop back off the train to help him when he pushes himself harder and jumps onto the car just as a soldier comes into view. I grab ahold of David and drag him inside, then cover my ears. Matthias shoots the soldier directly in the face.

The train speeds off, leaving the rest of the soldiers behind. The wind howls in the open door of the train car, setting my teeth chattering. I pull David to the back of the car and help him sit up against the wall. Matthias calls Henry over to help him slide the door back shut. The speed of the wind makes it nearly impossible to push the door forward, but they finally do. The sound of the wind continues howling through the crack in the door. Matthias was right about how uncomfortable this ride will be.

"Rebecca! David's been shot!" I yell over the racket of the train and the wind combined.

She crawls her way back to us with her medical kit. "Help me by getting his shirt off," she says as she digs in her bag for supplies.

He's been shot in the same arm as his broken wrist, making it difficult to get his arm out of the sleeve. I fumble around, trying to pull the sleeve out straight so he can slip his arm down out of it. When that doesn't work, I grab the bottom of his shirt and start sliding it up.

"You know," he says, a mischievous glint in his eye, "I've had dreams that started like this."

I laugh. "What? Being shot in the arm and bleeding all over?"

"No, you pulling my shirt off..." he says just loud enough for me to hear, and my cheeks grow hot.

Rebecca shuffles up to me, startling me out of the moment. "What are you doing? I need to see his arm. Here, let me." She pulls out a pair of scissors out and carefully makes a cut in the shirt over the wound. "Good. This is what I hoped for," she says, poking around on his arm, making David wince in pain. "The bullet went clean through your muscle. I won't have to dig the bullet out. It's going to hurt, but it should heal up nicely."

She gets to work bandaging his arm up, and I look around at the rest of the group. Matthias is standing closest to the door, keeping watch out a window. His shoulders are slumped, and his face is sullen as he watches the landscape pass by in a blur. I wonder if he's thinking about Saul. He hasn't talked about him since it happened, but I've seen him lost in thought from time to time, always with a sad expression on his face.

Everyone else is tucked up against the walls, silent and alert. We still don't know whether this is going to work or not. If one of the soldiers radios in that we hopped on a train, we're doomed.

Rebecca finishes up and turns her attention on Tim, whose nose is bleeding from smacking it on the floor.

I wedge myself in between David and Cass, grateful for the body heat. "Sorry about your arm."

"Eh, it's just a flesh wound," he says in a terrible British accent. We both laugh at the quote.

The vibration of the train starts to lull me to sleep. I lay my head on David's shoulder and close my eyes, grateful to finally rest after staying awake all night. The heaviness of slumber starts tugging at me, but then my mind becomes alert again when I hear Cass ask over my head, "Are you two boyfriend and girlfriend now?"

She must think I'm asleep, so I keep my eyes closed and my breathing steady, wanting to hear what David has to say.

"No. She said she's not interested."

"Could've fooled me." Her voice sounded playful.

"I don't know what this is, but I'm not going to spoil it. If she wants to hold my hand or lay her head on my shoulder, I'll let her. I'll take what I can get."

"I hope she comes around. You two would make a cute couple."

They both go quiet, and David rests his cheek against the top of my head. Their conversation makes me feel awkward, like I'm using him or something, but before I start to feel too bad, I fall asleep.

■■■■■

"Wake up! The trains slowin' down," Matthias calls out.

My eyes pop open as what he says registers through the fog of sleep. I scramble to my feet and help David up. Everyone else straps on their bags and looks around with worry.

"Are we at the next city?" I ask, looking out the door at the passing trees and fields no longer blurry from speed.

"It feels like it's been long enough," Matthias answers, peering out the window. "But we're not. It's just trees outside."

"What are we going to do?" Alexandrine asks, holding Charlotte close.

"We're gonna have to fight," Matthias says, opening the bag of weapons he carries.

"Can't we just hop off the train and run?"

"As soon as this train stops, there's gonna be soldiers on top of us. Our best bet for survival is to kill every last soldier we come across," he says with hatred in his voice.

He hands out the weapons, giving me a sword. I've practiced with it enough times that the weight of it is familiar in my hand, but the heaviness of what he's asking from me turns my arm into lead. I know we need to fight for our survival, but my stomach turns sour at the thought of killing someone. Maybe I can just wound them without taking their life.

Matthias instructs the women and children to get up against the wall, as far out of the way as possible. Alexandrine looks torn between wanting to help Matthias fight and wanting to join the women in protecting the children. In the end, she swallows her pride and stands in front of Charlotte, shielding her from the train car opening.

"Everyone, stay quiet, and wait for my signal," Matthias says.

I take a deep breath to gain my courage. I look over at David, wondering if this will be the last time I see him. He has a handgun in his good hand, and when he catches me looking at him, he winks at me as though this is just a minor setback. I wish I could have some of his bravery.

The train slowly stops. Without all the noise from the train moving, it seems eerily quiet. Matthias gets into position, wearing a look of murder, and I start to wonder if he actually likes killing people. He doesn't seem at all bothered by it, and that bothers me. His intentions may be good, but his actions are not.

The seconds turn into minutes as we wait for the soldiers. Maybe we're overreacting. Maybe the train just stopped for maintenance. But just as I'm about to let my guard down, I hear the crunch of boots on gravel about five train cars ahead.

They're coming. My muscles turn rigid, and I grip my sword handle harder.

"Get ready," Matthias says deadpan.

Henry is next to Matthias, an arrow nocked on his bow. "How long do you want to wait before we start taking them out?"

"We'll wait for 'em to come to us."

Everyone stays as quiet as they can, but little Sonya, unaware of the dire situation, starts squirming away from Caroline, screeching to be let go. Caroline grabs her around the waist and covers her mouth with her hand, but it's too late.

"Got 'em. They're in the last car," a soldier calls out.

The older children cling to their moms in fear. Everyone waits with bated breath, listening to the footsteps coming closer and then stopping right outside the train car.

This is it. Time to fight for our freedom.

The latch starts to turn, and Matthias holds his rifle up to his shoulder, ready to shoot, but the door never makes it open. Instead, we hear gunshots and shouts as though a fight has broken out between the soldiers. What is going on?

After about a minute, it's quiet, and we all look around at each other in confusion. We wait, listening for any noise. When we don't hear anything, Matthias holds his finger to his mouth and slowly slides the door.

The scene before us is ghastly. A dozen soldiers lie on the ground in pools of blood. Some have their heads turned at impossible angles, necks obviously broken. Standing by the tree line is a group of men, easily outnumbering us two to one. They're wearing black ski masks and leather jackets with various scraps of metal strapped on as makeshift armor over their chests, arms, and legs. They are each armed with guns, some with two, and they're pointing them directly at us.

34

"Off the train," one of them barks.

We look to Matthias for our next move. He grabs his bags and hops off the train. Everyone follows. The adults try to shield the kids from the grizzly surroundings, but there's nowhere to turn without seeing it, and I hear Emily whimper.

Once we're all down, they order us to hand over our weapons, shoving them in Matthias's weapon bag as we do.

"Who are you?" Alexandrine asks as they start pulling out lengths of rope.

"We call ourselves the Metal Militia," an enthusiastic voice answers from a scrawnier looking rebel. At least, I presume they're rebels since they willingly killed the soldiers.

"Shut up!" another one shouts at him. The scrawny guy hangs his head from the scolding. "There'll be no more talking from anyone."

The militia members get to work tying everyone's wrists together, even David's, causing him to wince in pain. I look around to see if anyone dares to resist, but Matthias stands tall, with a look of annoyance on his face. He doesn't seem fazed by their antics. In fact, he looks at them as though they're a bunch of amateurs.

"What do I do with this one?" someone who's standing in front of Tim asks.

"Uh, tie his wrist down to his thigh," another answers, improvising.

"Please, I have to carry her. You can't tie my wrists together," Caroline says, holding Sonya.

A husky militant looks at her, stroking his chin through his ski mask, thinking. "Our orders were to tie everyone up," he says uncertainly, looking at Sonya, who's wiggling in Caroline's arms to get down. "I'll carry her."

He takes Sonya from Caroline. Holding her in one arm, he starts playing peek-a-boo with his free hand. After a few times, she giggles. Whoever these people are, they don't seem overly threatening.

"Who's the leader?" asks a man with two handguns strapped to his side and a belt full of bullets slung across his body like a sash.

Another one scoffs, "Isn't it obvious?" while holding his hand outward toward Matthias.

"Orders are to blindfold and gag you," he says, taking out two strips of black cloth from his pocket.

"You can't..." Henry starts to say, but Matthias lifts his bound hands up to stop him, and Henry backs down.

It's rather odd that Matthias seems to be going along with these people. Maybe it's because they just killed the soldiers, so he trusts them. It almost seems as though he knows these people.

"All right, let's move!" the guy who blindfolded Matthias shouts as he grabs Matthias's upper arm, leading him toward the woods.

Apparently, the orders to blindfold and gag were only for Matthias. I'm grateful that I can still see.

We all stay quiet as the Militia escorts us through leafless forests and open fields. There doesn't seem to be a rhyme or reason behind any of the twists and turns these men take us on, and I start to hope that they know where they're going.

Hours slip by as we march out of the woods and through what used to be suburbs. I worry that we'll be spotted, but the militia people just keep guiding us along as though it's no big thing.

I look around and shake my head at the aftermath of the war that happened so many years ago. Abandoned cars are parked in driveways, slowly rusting away, never to be driven again. The houses look like they were once nice places, but since they've been deserted, the elements have had their way with them, leaving them to rot. Trees have overtaken yards, turning them into forests.

We continue on through various neighborhoods, sometimes passing under huge roads lifted up into the air. I've never seen this before, and it kind of scares me at the thought of being in a vehicle so high in the air, especially since sections of the roads have now collapsed. We walk by large forsaken stores and restaurants, some with their brick walls crumbling, leaving gaping holes that allow anyone or anything to enter with ease. I hate to think of what kind of animals could be calling them home now.

The last neighborhood we pass through has an old elementary school in its midst. I have to say, the long-forgotten playground kind of creeps me out. The wind's blowing just enough to make the swings move back and forth on squeaky chains, and the merry-go-round seems to be spinning on its own accord. My brain starts imagining ghosts of the children who died during the war playing on this equipment, forever stuck between worlds. I don't like it.

The sun hangs low in the sky as we leave the remnants of humanity and come to a vast forest of towering pine trees. I'm staring up at the impossibly full branches of these green giants when everyone stops walking abruptly, and I run into David, who's right ahead of me. I peek my head around him and see that we've come to a large encampment. Shelters with mismatched siding and different colored roofing tiles are built just inside a perimeter of a barbed wire fence that seems to encircle the entire area. In the center is a big barn with a rusting silver roof and a patchwork of multicolored wood. It looks like they replace the boards as they rot out with whatever wood they can find. The barn's windows are still intact but dirty, leaving them more brown than clear. A brick building is behind the barn, and in the very back of the encampment is a large greenhouse. I've never seen one this close before. They had greenhouses in the city to help grow our food, but they were in a part of town I never visited.

People of all kinds mill around inside the encampment, some going about their business, completely oblivious to our arrival, while others stop to watch as we are all ushered through the narrow gate into their territory.

The men lead us straight into the barn. At the end of the building is a massive fireplace built with smooth rocks with a cheery fire roaring in its depths, giving the building a warm stuffy feel. Two lines of various dining room sets are placed along the sides of the structure, leaving an open aisle down the center of the room.

A man wearing jeans and a tight gray wool sweater stands facing the fire with his hands clasped behind his back. After everyone has been brought into the barn, our escorts close the doors once again, making the already dim light even darker. With the sun almost gone and the pine trees blocking any of the feeble light it's still giving off, our only source of light is the blaze coming from the fireplace. The flickering flames send shadows dancing on the walls, which keep catching my eye, making me think someone's there.

"Here they are, boss," says the man holding Matthias's arm.

I watch as the guy rocks up and down from toes to heels a few times, then slowly turns to face us. He almost looks like Matthias, but it's hard to tell because this guy's beard and hair are shorter and better groomed.

"Well, well. Look what the cat dragged in. What do you have to say for yourself?" the man goads Matthias by turning his head and putting his hand up to his ear as though trying to hear Matthias's answer.

Matthias grumbles something through his gag, and I'm pretty sure it wasn't a nice word.

The man nods at the militant, who takes his cue to free Matthias.

"Still one for the dramatic flair, huh, Eli?" Matthias says as soon as he's free.

The man named Eli smiles big and pulls Matthias into a bear hug. They both slap each other's backs hard, almost as though they are trying to hurt one another.

The rest of the men untie us all, and I watch in confusion at the scene playing out before my eyes.

"What are you doing all the way up here, Matt?" Eli asks as he lets go of Matthias.

"Matthias," he growls. "Ya know I don't like bein' called Matt."

"I could call you Fury." Eli laughs, pointing to Matthias's eye patch.

"Ya haven't changed one damn bit, have ya?" Matthias shakes his head.

"What would be the fun in that? If I lost my sense of humor, I would become you, and that's just terrifying," he says with a mock shiver.

"Care to explain to us what's going on?" Alexandrine asks.

"This is my brother, Elijah," Matthias answers.

"You can call me Eli." He holds out his hand for a handshake.

Alexandrine stays put, looking him up and down with an expression of distaste.

Eli holds his hand out for a few awkward seconds, then lets it drop, taking a look around at the rest of us. "Henry, my boy!" Eli says warmly, stepping up to Henry for an embrace.

"Hey, Uncle Eli." Henry returns the hug.

"Let me have a look at you!" Eli steps back with his hands up on Henry's shoulders. "I see you've been blessed with the same handsome gene I have. Too bad your father missed out on that one." He winks.

"We're twins, ya idiot," Matthias grunts, not appreciating being the butt of his brother's jokes.

"Shh! Don't tell people that. I have a reputation to uphold." Eli pretends to be scandalized.

"Cut the crap," Matthias huffs. "How'd ya'll know where we were gonna be?"

"Nice southern accent you got there." A playful smile tugs at Eli's lips.

"Ya know I lived in the south for years. Ya pick up on it after a while. Now answer my question."

"We found a few government radios, and we leave them running so we can know our enemy and what they're up to."

Know our enemy? He sounds just like Matthias. They look similar, but their personalities are like night and day. I wonder what the story is between them.

"We've been tracking you for a little while now. They've given a description of you a few times. I hear you blew up a military weapons cache. I didn't realize you'd be dumb enough to try to start a war. You're being called a terrorist now," Eli accuses. "What were you thinking?"

"We didn't blow it up," Matthias growls. "I wasn't tryin' to start anything. We were given a tip that it was there, and it ended up bein' rigged."

"Uh-huh." He pauses, giving Matthias a look, then moves on. "Then we heard that a group of rebels hopped on a train headed west. I knew right away it was you, so we decided to come get you."

"Thanks," Matthias mumbles while clearing his throat. "Did ya really need to tie us up, though?"

"No. That I did just to annoy you." He guffaws. "I gave them orders not to tie up Dad, though. Where is the old man?" He searches our group for Saul.

"He's gone," Matthias answers, voice thick, unable to look Eli in the eyes.

"What'd you do?" Eli asks seriously, his jocular demeanor changing so quickly, it's like he's a different person. Now the resemblance to Matthias is uncanny.

"It wasn't my fault," Matthias says, getting defensive.

"Everyone out!" Eli yells. "Horace. Benjamin. Take the rest of them to their shelters," Eli says, staring daggers at Matthias while he addresses his men.

Why is he so angry with Matthias? What happened to Saul was an accident. I want to stay and hear what his problem is, but David grabs my hand, leading me out of the barn and back into the chilly, pine-scented air.

3 5

The men take us to a few empty shelters with cots for us to sleep on. We hear some muffled shouts coming from the barn, but neither David nor I can distinguish what is being said. After a while, I stop trying and fall asleep easily.

I'm the first one awake in the morning. I sit up and look around at the building we're in, impressed by its quality. There's a small wood-burning stove on the back wall that keeps out the chill, there aren't any gaping holes between the wood plank walls, there's an actual floor instead of just dirt, and they even put in a door and windows. It's like a little house instead of a crude shelter. If they put so much work into it, that must mean they don't have to move as often as our group. I'm looking forward to hearing more about Eli and his camp and what makes their camp different from ours.

Once everyone is awake, we head outside to find the rest of our group and see what's expected of us. We're handed plates of steaming eggs and fried potatoes for breakfast. It's the best food I've had in a long time. Is that salt I taste? I haven't had food with salt since I lived in the city.

As I eat, I observe the people who live here and notice that they are all clean and well-dressed. Their clothes are washed and hole-free. Their hair isn't greasy and matted down. I start to feel self-conscious about the way I must look and smell. I anxiously run my fingers through my hair and then take a whiff down my shirt to see how bad it is. I cough at the stench of BO and sweaty clothes. I'm suddenly worried that David has smelled me and hasn't said anything just to be nice. I'm so embarrassed.

I turn my thoughts away from myself and realize I don't see Matthias. I wonder what happened between him and Eli last night. As I'm about to ask David what he thinks, Matthias steps out of the other shelter, his bottom lip fat and bloody.

Someone hands him a plate of food, which he takes with a grunt; then he plops down next to Henry.

"What happened to you?" Henry asks.

"Eli and I worked out a problem."

"Men," Alexandrine mumbles.

"What was the problem?" I ask, swallowing my last bite of potato.

"Pop was in my care, and I was supposed to protect him," he answers, stabbing at his eggs.

"But you were. We were getting away from the soldiers. What happened was an accident," I say, confused at what the problem was.

"He sees things my way now." Matthias looks up from his plate at Eli, who's approaching us. "With one eye anyway."

Eli steps up to our group, his right eye swollen shut and bruised.

"Mornin'!" Eli says brightly. "My people and I had a discussion this AM, and before we ask you to pitch in around here, we're going to give you a day to rest and to wash up. We'll show you how to fill the cistern atop the wash house, and you'll have showers and sinks available for you to use."

"Really?" I jump to my feet.

"Yes, really," Eli laughs. "We have a wood-burning stove to heat up the water too, so you can have hot showers."

Tears, real tears, spring to my eyes at the thought of a hot shower. Everyone around me mutters happily.

"We have two shower stalls and two sinks, but since it takes a while for the stove to heat up the cistern of water, you'll want to be conservative with how much you use. You won't want to just stand with the shower running constantly, or you're going to run out of hot water quick."

I nod, not really listening to what he's saying as I daydream about how good it's going to feel.

"I don't suppose you have working toilets too?" David asks.

"No, sorry. We have a few outhouses, though."

"Toilet paper?" Caroline asks hopefully.

"Yes, ma'am."

Everyone seems to be cheerful at the thought of having some real creature comforts.

"You look familiar," Eli says to me as everyone stands up to get started on laundry and showers.

"I'm Olivia, Matthias's daughter."

"Ah, yes. The spitting image of Janice. You anything like your mother?" His features darken a bit as he mentions Janice's name.

"No, sir. Not at all."

"Good." He pats my shoulder. "Welcome to the camp and the family, Olivia."

■■■■■

We spend the majority of the day taking turns with showers and washing the laundry. We're shown how to get water from a spigot that has to be pumped by hand, collecting it in buckets that we carry up a ladder to the cistern on the second story. I didn't know what a cistern was until this day. It's a big metal tub placed high in the building with a pipe to let the water flow out by gravity to the first floor. I'm tempted to hop in it and take a bath in the hot water, but that would be terrible of me.

We work at keeping the woodburning stove fueled as well. It's a long day of tedious work, but everyone stays in chipper moods as we all clean up. When it's finally my turn in the shower, I let out a moan as soon as the warm water hits my body. It's so hard to make myself shut the water off while soaping up, but I remember what Eli said and try to conserve the water for other people. I scrub myself until my skin turns pink and slightly raw. I feel like a whole new person by the time I'm done. I had chosen an outfit that was the least smelly to put on after my shower, but after getting all scrubbed up and smelling nice, these clothes feel dirty now. I hate doing laundry, but I'm excited to have clean clothes again.

I eventually get my turn to wash laundry sometime after lunch. Eli has ropes tied up for us to hang our wet clothes on. I don't like the idea of my underwear being out where everyone can see, but this is survival mode. The day is just warm enough that our clothes don't freeze, but it will take them a while to dry. As I'm hanging up the last of my laundry, I see a girl with shoulder-length dark brown hair, wearing a black leather jacket and jeans ripped at the knees, approach David. She has a big smile, which David returns easily. I hurry up, throwing my last two shirts on the line haphazardly, and fast-walk over to them.

"I could show you around, handsome," the girl says as I get closer. She links her arm with his just as I step up to David's other side.

"Hi," I interrupt. "What'd I miss?"

"She was just going to show me around camp," David says.

"Is this your girlfriend?" The girl looks me up and down.

"No," David answers quickly. "We're just friends."

Ouch. A pang of jealousy tears through me as I see the girl tighten her grip on David's arm. "Who're you?" I ask, keeping my tone in check.

"You can call me Angel."

"Angel?" I give an involuntary small, breathy laugh.

"Well, my real name is Angelina Maria Raquel Consueala Tomasine Yolanda Esperanza Lola Martinez," she responds with attitude.

"Angel it is," I say.

"Do you mind if Olivia comes with us?" David asks.

"I guess she can tag along." Angel winks at him.

They turn and start walking arm in arm, and I follow behind, biting my tongue. I see David glance over his shoulder at me a couple of times, but he lets her lead him around the camp. She shows him where she stays first, much to my annoyance. Is this chick for real? She's coming on a little strong.

"So, Angel," I interrupt her story about how she once got caught skinny dipping in the nearby lake. "How old are you?"

"I just turned eighteen. How about you, handsome?" she asks David.

"I'll be eighteen in a few months."

"Sweet! Legally an adult. That means you can do whatever you like," she says flirtatiously. "I'm a bit of a troublemaker around here."

"You got that right." A man with the same colored hair and skin ruffles her hair as he passes by.

"Hey! Watch the hair!" she yells, her cheeks turning red as she smooths it back out.

"Who was that?" David asks.

"That's my big brother, Jesús."

"I have a big brother too. Of course, I didn't know that until recently," I say lamely, trying to remind them I'm still here.

Angel raises an eyebrow at me, then links arms with David again and leads him on. I reluctantly follow. She points out different cabins and who sleeps where, listing off names I only half hear. I'm not really paying attention to what she's saying. I'm more concerned about how cozy she seems to be getting with David. Now not only is her arm linked with his, but she has her other hand resting on David's forearm. I want to force my way in between them, but I would look like an idiot, so I stay behind, repeating to myself, *You told him you were just friends. It's okay for him to like other people. You told him you were just friends. It's okay for him to like other people...*

"And this is the kitchen." She stops in front of the large brick building behind the barn. "We do all our food prep and cooking here. No one's allowed in there unless you're helping with the meals, but I like to sneak in and snitch food when nobody's looking."

David peeks his head inside the building. "Wow, you guys have a lot of food."

"Yeah, well, we have a lot of people." She laughs at David's shocked expression. "I'm guessing your camp never had this much?"

I peek my head inside and see shelves full of canned goods, baskets of seasonal produce, bags of rice and beans, fresh bread laid out on a counter, boxes of snack foods... "Holy crap! Is that soda?" I ask, my mouth watering at the thought of drinking a can of it.

"Yeah, that's for special occasions, or when Eli gets a migraine."

I look closer, and what I thought was Mountain Dew actually says "Mello Yello."

"What's Mello Yello? Don't you guys have any Mountain Dew?" I ask.

"What's Mountain Dew?"

"You don't know what Mountain Dew is?" I ask incredulously.

"Isn't that what I just said?" Angel snaps.

"Sor-ry," I mutter childishly.

"How do you guys have so much good stuff here?" David interjects, trying to calm the tension.

"We get it from the city. Eli's got some good connections," she answers David with her sultry tone once again. "Basically, once a week, we send some guys in to get the stuff they've collected for us."

"What does Eli have to offer them in return for all that?" David asks the same question that has come to my mind.

Angel looks around conspiratorially and then leans over to whisper, her lips almost touching his ear lobe. She doesn't keep her volume down enough, and I hear her say, "Eli grows weed in our greenhouse and trades it for supplies."

"Why would he grow weeds? And why would anyone want them?" David asks, confused.

Angel laughs loudly. "Oh, aren't you cute! Don't you know what weed is?"

We both shake our heads no, but she only has eyes for him.

"Weed, as in marijuana," she says quietly, still laughing.

David looks at her blankly.

"Have you two been living under a rock?" She looks at us, her brown eyes wide in surprise. "Marijuana is a drug. It's illegal to possess any in the city, so it's highly valuable."

"What if the guards find out?" I ask, horrified.

Angel laughs again. "Some of the guards are his biggest customers. As long as we keep a low profile, we can basically come and go as we please in the city."

I shake my head in disgust.

"What?" Angel asks.

"I can't believe my uncle is a druggie," I say.

"He's not a druggie; he's a dealer," she says with a temper. "And it's how we're able to have so much."

"Great. Your leader's a criminal."

"Nobody asked you for your approval. If you don't like the way we do things around here, you can leave," Angel says, taking a threatening step toward me.

David reaches out and grabs her shoulders to stop her. "Whoa, whoa, whoa. Settle down," David says to Angel and then turns to me. "Liv, Matthias's ways weren't exactly innocent either. We stole things from the city, which is also a crime. In survival situations, sometimes you gotta do what you gotta do."

"So you're taking her side?"

David looks at me uncomfortably but doesn't respond. Angel glances at him and then back at me with a smug smirk on her face.

"Fine." I turn around and storm away from them.

"Liv!" I hear him plead.

But then Angel says, "Let her go. C'mon, I'll show you my favorite spot to hide when I want to be alone."

I stomp my way back to the shelter I slept in last night and see Cass doodling in her notebook again. I flop down on the cot, wiping away angry tears.

"What's up?" Cass asks.

"Angel." I put as much disdain in my voice as possible.

"Who's Angel?"

"She's a stupid girl who has the hots for David."

"Uh-oh. Is someone jealous?" she asks playfully.

"Ha! Hardly." I avoid making eye contact. "It's just sick that she's all over him, and she doesn't even know him. And he doesn't seem to mind. We don't know these people. She could be a Coalition spy or a mass murderer, and he's letting her hang all over him!"

"Uh-huh," Cass says. "I don't get you. You have a cute boy who's madly in love with you, and you keep friend-zoning him. Of course he's going to be interested in a girl who's giving him attention. Maybe you should just go out with him already!"

"She also told me how Eli can get all this good stuff," I say, changing the subject quickly. "He grows marijuana and trades it."

"Marijuana?" Cass asks, just as confused as David and I were.

"Apparently, it's a drug."

Cass looks up at the ceiling for a moment in thought, then back at me. "Smart."

"What?" I ask, shocked.

"Well, the drug part isn't great, but growing something that's valuable and making trades is smart. Matthias was able to steal us stuff, but nothing like what these people have. Plus, Eli seems to be..." She pauses, snapping her fingers as she thinks. "What's the word? Charismatic? Yeah, that's it. He's more charismatic than Matthias."

"I got a tiny glimpse of another side of Eli that made him more like Matthias. He asked me if I was anything like my mother, and he suddenly seemed dangerous. Like someone you wouldn't want to mess with."

"That must be how he's the leader. Friendly but tough."

I nod, thinking about the nut job family I belong to. My mom's a liar, a traitor, and a murderer. Matthias is a murderer and a thief. And my uncle is a drug dealer. It's no wonder I'm messed up.

Speaking of messed up: "Where's Tim?"

"Some geeky-looking guy started asking him about his missing arm and took him off somewhere. I don't know what they're doing now."

She goes back to her notebook, so I lie down facing the wall, wondering what Angel and David are doing. I get more and more agitated as I think about how cozy she was getting with him, but once I picture them kissing, I can't take it anymore. I get up off the cot and pace around the room.

"Why don't you go find him and tell him how you feel?" Cass thrusts her hand out toward the door.

"No. I already made a mess of things."

"Fine, but could you at least do your angry pacing outside? You're distracting me."

I head outside, the temperature shocking me slightly after being inside the warm shelter. I decide to check on my clothes, knowing they're still going to be wet, but I don't know what else to do with myself. As I'm checking them, Matthias steps up next to me with his laundry.

"I've been meanin' to ask ya if ya've cracked the code on the pendant yet?"

"No. I kind of forgot about it with everything that's been going on," I admit sheepishly.

"Keep workin' on it. I'd like to know what Pop thought was so important."

I nod and start to walk away, but I turn back toward him and say, "I found out today how Eli has so much stuff. He grows drugs and trades it for things."

"I know," Matthias says.

I wait to see if he's going to say more, but he just keeps hanging up his clothes. "You knew? Are you okay with it?"

"Of course not. That's why I'm not part of his camp. When I first found out what he was planning to do, we got in a fight, and I told him to leave."

"That must have been hard, fighting with your twin brother."

"It hurt him more than me. Pop refused to go with him because he disapproved of Eli's choices too. Eli was crushed but too stubborn to give up on his plan, so he'd send a guy to check in now and again to see how Pop was doing."

"Is that why he was so mad when he found out the news about Saul?"

Matthias stops hanging his clothes for a moment, his jaw flexing as he stares at the flannel shirt in his hands. I recognize it as one Saul used to wear.

"Yeah," Matthias says distantly.

"It wasn't your fault," I remind him.

"I made some bad choices. The injury was an accident, but the reason he got the injury was my fault."

"But you shouldn't blame yourself," I say, trying to help.

"When ya make a mistake, ya own up to it, then ya get over it. Something you should keep in mind." He gives me a significant look. He turns back to his laundry and hangs the last few things on the line. Once he's done, he pats me on the shoulder. "Let me know if ya crack the code, hmm?"

I nod and watch him leave toward the barn where Eli hangs out. Now that he mentioned the pendant again, I decide that I want to work on it some more. I'm desperate to get my mind on something other than what David is doing, but as I get closer to the shelter, I spot Angel and David standing right outside the door. She's holding onto his hoodie strings, looking up into his eyes with a smile.

"Thanks for showing me around," David says politely.

"Anytime, handsome."

I watch as she pushes up onto her tippy toes and plants a kiss right on David's lips. My face turns hot as my stomach does a flip from the sight of them. I immediately spin around and walk the other direction, not sure where I'm going to go, just knowing I don't want to be here.

I can't leave the compound, so I find a building by the fence and hide behind it. Hot tears burn my eyes, but I force myself to not cry. I slide my back down the wall until I'm sitting on the ground with my knees to my chest. I wrap my arms around my legs and stare out at the woods, seething.

Why am I so angry? I should be happy for him. He's finally found a girl who's showing interest in him. Am I mad at the thought of him spending more time with her, which means less time with me? Maybe I'm afraid that I'm going to lose him as a friend.

Geez. I'm lying to myself now.

I'm so lost in my thoughts, I don't hear someone approaching.

"What are you doing back here, Olive-uh?" someone says, getting my name wrong on purpose.

I jump a little at the voice, but when I see it's Cindy, I go back to staring at the woods. "Leave me alone."

"Sheesh. What's got your knickers in a twist?"

"Nothing," I snarl.

"Liar." She matches my tone.

"I'm not in the mood right now." I glare. "Why are you even around? Did something happen to Joselyn?"

"I don't have to have a reason to come out and play. I can be here if I want."

"Whatever," I say. "So, are you on your way somewhere?" I ask, hoping she'll keep moving along.

"As a matter of fact, I am. But I saw you sitting here like a lump and thought I would come see why."

"Well, that's very—thoughtful—of you," I say as evenly as possible, hoping she doesn't pick up on my sarcasm. My head still hurts at times from when she hit me, making me highly skeptical of her "concern."

"Yes, well, I am known for my rational thoughts and empathy," she says airily.

I start chuckling, and she joins in. Soon we're both holding our stomachs as a wave of laughter washes over us. Am I having a moment with Cindy?

Once we both settle down, Cindy grows serious. "Sorry I tried to kill you."

"No, you're not." I wipe the laughter tears off with the heels of my hands.

"I am."

I look up at her and see that this is the most sincere I've ever seen her. "Where is this coming from? I thought you hated me."

"I did, but I don't anymore."

I lift an eyebrow at her. All those death threats, then she actually tried to kill me, and now she's saying she doesn't hate me?

She sighs dramatically. "You believed me when nobody else did. Then you gave me a hug without knowing whether it was Joselyn or me. I always knew we were going to be best friends!" Her face splits in a creepy smile.

"I wouldn't go that far." I give an unsettled laugh. "But I'd be willing to be your friend as long as you're done hitting me with sticks."

"Promises, promises." She puts her fists on her hips. "Fine. Just don't piss me off."

I nod. I think that's about as good of a deal as I'm going to get.

Just as she's about to leave, I say, "I hope you don't mind me asking, but what did Mr. Wick mean when he said you're a powerful one?"

"He must have been talking about Joselyn." She shrugs, then skips away.

"Thanks for clearing that up," I mumble. The talk with Cindy distracted me enough that I'm ready to go work on the pendant now, even if it means facing David.

37

David isn't in the shelter when I get back, and Cass is gone too, which I'm grateful for. I just want to be left alone. I retrieve the pendant and Saul's stick out of my bag and set myself up against the wall, trying to get comfortable. I spin the tumblers around randomly as a way of resetting it. I'm not really sure if that's how it works, but I do it anyway out of habit from when I had a locker.

I try to mentally keep track of the different combinations I use, but after a while, I just can't anymore. I need a piece of paper, but the only paper around is in Cass's notebook. I know she would be outraged if she caught me messing with it, but desperate times call for desperate measures.

I slide off the cot and look out the window, checking to see if she's back yet. I don't see her, so I quickly open her bag and pull the notebook out. All I need is a clean piece of paper, so I flip to the back of her notebook, expecting to find an empty one there. Instead, I find a tear-stained letter addressed to her mom. I hear my conscience screaming, *Put it away! Don't look!* but I can't seem to stop myself from reading it.

> Mom,
>
> I know you won't ever see this, but I need to write it. It's been 7 years since you sent us with Matthias. You told us you'd come find us as soon as you could. LIAR! I was only 6 when you sent us away. Tim told me why, and I hate you for it. How could you do this to your own kids? How could you choose that loser of a boyfriend over us? You wanted to start a new family with that jerk, so you got rid of us?
> Now that I think about it, I guess I'm glad you gave up on us. I'm glad you're not my mom anymore. The people in this camp are better parents than you ever were. They taught us how to survive, how to look out for ourselves, how to be good people, things you never would have been able to teach us. The women in camp have been teaching Tim and me the important stuff we've missed since leaving school, like reading and writing. I'm glad about that too because now I can write this letter to tell you how much I hate you and that I hope I never see you again.

Poor Cass! I quickly flip through her notebook, trying not to pay attention to anything else until I find a clear page. I rip one out and stuff her notebook back in her bag. I take the blank page and pen back to my cot, still shaken by her letter. I

314

guess I never really thought about where their parents were. I just assumed they had died or something. That would have been easier than abandonment. I know that from experience.

I try to put the letter out of my mind as I work on the pendant. I write *L* or *R* in a column to signify which tumbler I turned left or right. After about twenty columns, I start to wonder again if this thing actually opens or if these symbols are a kind of code instead.

I decide to give it one more try before putting it away for the day. I haven't spun them all in the same direction yet, so I reset it and spin them to the right until the correct symbols line up. I hear the tiniest click as the last tumbler is set into place. My hands are trembling as I grab the very top and the bottom of the cylinder and pull gently. It slides apart, revealing a USB stick at the top of the pendant. I'm not sure what I was expecting it to be, but this wasn't it. I tip the bottom part of the pendant over, shaking it to see if maybe there's a secret note or something stuck inside. Nothing. We're going to need a computer. Let's hope Eli has one.

I hop off the cot and race toward the barn to find Matthias. I see him lounging at the head of the table with Eli next to the fireplace.

"I got it!" I shout as I run up the aisle. "I finally got it open!"

Matthias pushes up out of his chair so quickly, he almost knocks it over. I've never seen him excited about something, and the sparkle in his eye reminds me of Saul for a moment. I hold it out by the chain, and he takes it gently into his palm.

"It's a USB stick. Do you have a computer, Uncle Eli?" I ask.

"No, sorry," he says.

My shoulders slump, and I hear Matthias make a frustrated noise.

"But I know where we can get to one."

"Then let's go," Matthias says eagerly.

"Hold on. It's not that easy. It's inside the city," Eli says. "You can't just run in, guns blazing, like some sort of cowboy."

"Fine, O mighty wise one, then how do we get in?"

They glare at each other, and I almost chuckle when I realize Eli's black eye is the same as the one Matthias lost.

"We're going to need to put together a team—"

"I'll go," I interrupt. "I should get to go since I figured out how to open it. It's kind of been my project this whole time." I'm desperate to get away from David and Angel. If this mission turns out to be dangerous, all the better.

"Sure," Eli says. "We're going to need to collect supplies."

"Ya mean drugs?" Matthias says testily.

"How else do you think I get into the city?" Eli's voice is dangerously low. It's clearly not the first time they've had this argument.

"Criminal," Matthias grumbles.

"Idiot," Eli responds.

"Guys! Let's get back on topic. When can we go?"

"Give me a couple of days, and I think I'll have the stuff we need by then."

"So, where is this computer?" Matthias asks.

"It's in one of the towers. There are four of them on the outskirts of the city, and one of them is close by. I can get us inside easily, but getting our hands on a computer is going to be a challenge."

"We'll figure it out," Matthias says with hope in his voice.

We're interrupted by someone knocking on the door to be let in. The doors open, and a procession of people enter, bringing in steaming bowls of food and dishes. Supper time. Eli slaps Matthias on the back, and they move their chairs up to the table.

I watch as David walks in with Angel still hanging on his arm. He makes eye contact for a split second, and I see guilt written all over him. I turn away and find that the seats are filling up quickly. I don't want to be stuck next to them, so I pick a spot between Stan and Cass.

Cass and I sit on tall padded chairs where my feet can't even touch the ground. The table is a tall dark brown wooden square that only seats four people. I have to look down to see Stan, who's sitting at a formal oak table made to seat six. It has beveled edges and decorative chairs with cream-colored upholstery that look like they belong to someone with lots of money.

The barn grows loud as everyone from the camp comes in to have a meal together at the mishmash of tables. The noise is a little overwhelming, but I remind myself that I can't run off and be alone every time I'm sick of the noise. I watch as Angel pulls David over to the other row of tables to sit next to her brother.

"I figured out the pendant," I say to Cass, turning my attention away from them.

"Really? What happened?" she asks excitedly.

"It opened up, and there was a USB stick inside." I beam.

"A what?"

"A USB stick. It's something that holds information that you plug into a computer. Eli said he knows where we can use a computer to find out what's on it. It's inside the city, and I told him I'm going."

"Cool! So, how did you figure out the code?" She reaches for the bowl of green beans. Someone sets a plate of grilled chicken breasts on the table in front of us.

My face flushes as I try to decide whether I should be honest about the notebook or not. I dish up some food as I work up the courage to spill my guts, but just as I'm about to say something, Tim and the geeky guy Cass told me about show up and take the seats across from us. I do a double-take when I see a strange metal hook sticking out from Tim's sleeve.

"What's that?" Cass asks, dumbfounded.

Tim's face lights up. "Denis made this and gave it to me to wear. It's a prosthetic arm. Here, watch this."

Tim sets the forearm down on the edge of the table and screws up his face as he makes the hooks open and close a little. Denis strokes his goatee deep in thought as he watches Tim intently. He wouldn't look that geeky except for his clothes. He had removed an olive-green tweed jacket with brown suede patches on the elbows so he could eat. Now he sits at the table with black suspenders, a black and green striped bow tie, and a white dress shirt with a pocket filled with small screwdrivers and pens.

"It's going to take me some time to figure out how to work it," Tim says.

"That's so cool!" Cass says. "You made that?"

"It was quite simple, really," Denis starts to say. "Finding the right materials was the difficult part."

"Denis is a genius," Tim gushes.

Denis beams a bit from the compliment, nudging Tim with his elbow. "I wouldn't say genius, but it's definitely a passion of mine. I had a best friend who was missing an arm, and his family couldn't afford to buy him a prosthetic, so I learned all about them and vowed to make him one."

"I bet he was grateful." I take a bite of chicken breast.

"I'll never know. He was killed before he got a chance to try it out." Denis rakes his fingers through his brown curly hair.

"I'm so sorry." Cass's eyes grow misty.

"Yeah, well, it turns out he and his brother had been plotting to kill President Sawyer. They were caught with blueprints of the Coalition headquarters and a gun."

"Wait...did you just say, 'President Sawyer'? Don't you mean Turk?" I ask, confused.

"No. President Sawyer is the leader of our city. Each remaining city has its own leader. Didn't you know that?" He stuffs a forkful of green beans into his mouth.

Tim, Cass, and I all shake our heads.

Denis looks at us, surprised. "There's so much distance between the cities, they appointed a president for each one. Honestly, the term president is a bit pompous if you ask me. It's more logical to call them 'mayors' like what city leaders used to be called back before the war. I guess they want to feel more important."

"So, what's President Sawyer like?" Tim asks.

"Well, he's somewhere in his fifties, balding, fat, and he's about as smart as a bag of rocks. It's his wife you need to watch out for. She's a conniving, cold-hearted witch. I'm almost certain she's the one who ordered John and his brother to be killed." His blue eyes fill with hate.

"I'm sorry about your friend, Denis," Tim says.

"Yeah, well, that was a long time ago. C'est la vie." He sighs. "Anyway, the prosthetic Tim's got on is the one I was going to give to John. I saw Tim and knew the fit would be a close match. He's just about the same size as John and everything. There's more tweaking we're going to have to do to get it just right."

"It hurts a bit to wear right now since I still have some healing to do, but I'm excited for when I can use it regularly. Thank you, Denis."

"Of course." He waves Tim off.

We all finish eating and help clear the table. Denis tells us to stack the dirty plates at the end table by the door, where the people on dish duty can grab them easily.

We follow him into his shelter. It's stacked high with tools, metal parts, and books. Loose papers with drawings and notes are scattered everywhere. There is only one bed in the room, and it's piled high with more notes and schematics. He grabs it all and stacks it into a pile on the floor next to a red wingback leather chair. He motions for us to sit on the bed as he throws a fresh log in his wood-burning stove. He then takes a seat and pulls a pipe out of his jacket pocket. I've never seen one in real life. I recognize the pipe from watching a movie about a detective who used one. He pulls out a little cloth pouch and stuffs something inside the end.

"That's not weed, is it?" I use the term I heard Angel use.

Denis shakes his head. "Nah, I don't go near that stuff. This is just some dried up flowers and herbs. I find it calming to puff on a pipe. I hope you don't mind."

I shake my head. "So, what's it like around here? What's your city like?" I make conversation.

"I imagine the city's like all the other cities. It's only about a quarter of the size it used to be."

"Is there fog?" I ask.

"Sometimes it's fog. Sometimes it's radioactive dust clouds." He puffs out a smoke ring.

"What?" Tim watches the ring drift upwards with fascination.

"It's pretty windy in the city for the most part. Fog will be present some of the time, but it gets blown away by the wind and isn't a big deal. However, the land to the west of here was decimated by nuclear bombs. When the wind blows from the west, clouds of dust come swirling in carrying radioactive particles. So, as a precaution, mandatory shots are given to the citizens to keep people from getting radiation poisoning. If you guys plan on staying here for long, we're going to have to use our stock of shots we keep around for new members and babies."

"Holy crap," Tim says quietly.

"I don't know if we're staying that long. I really don't know what the plan is. We're headed to a place called 'The Haven.'" I watch to see how he responds.

He just nods, taking a puff of his pipe.

"So, you've heard of it?" I ask.

"Heard of it? Yes. Do I know where it is? No."

"Well, if it's a wasteland to the west of here, it probably isn't that way. Could it be north?" Cass asks.

"You don't want to be going north," Denis says seriously. "There are rumors of terrible creatures up there."

"Really? What kind of creatures?" Tim asks.

"They say it has large claws, a long tail with spears at the end, huge fangs, and two horns sprouting from its temples. It supposedly breathes fire and smoke, and smells terrible, like a combination of buzzard meat and skunk perfume."

"Sounds fake, but then again, we had beasts called Havocs outside of our city. Do you have any of those around here?" I ask with a yawn.

"No, can't say that we do." He puffs on his pipe again.

The shelter is filling up with hazy smoke. That, combined with a full stomach and the stove's cozy warmth, makes my eyelids grow heavy.

I shuffle behind Matthias down a narrow alleyway. The smell of rotting garbage and stale urine assaults my nose, making me pull my shirt up over my face so I don't lose the contents in my stomach.

We come out to a street that's identical to the one we left: tall buildings still mostly intact, shop signs promising low prices, office buildings with windows glinting in the fading sunlight. I never got to see the buildings in my city this well because of the never-ceasing fog. But just as Denis said, there's a breeze blowing here from the east that clears the fog away. When the wind isn't blowing, the streets fill up with fog again, only to have it blow away once more. Clearly, it's not a natural fog.

The street is empty of people, except for one old man standing on the corner, holding a cardboard sign with a word written in black marker. The sign reads: "BELIEVE!"

Eli turns right, heading down the street toward the tower. As we pass by the old man, he starts preaching: "The world is actually on our side! If we would just go to them, they would accept us. Listen to the voices from above. They tell me encouraging words."

I grab Joselyn's hand and drag her faster past the crazy guy.

FLASH!

I'm inside a room, surrounded by guards with guns, but they're not pointing them at us. They have their hands gripping the sides of their heads, and their faces are twisted in pain. The overhead lights and computer screens are flashing on and off like strobe lights as the sirens blare from the tower's security system. I see Joselyn screaming at the top of her lungs just before I feel an unbearable squeezing pressure inside my brain. My hands fly up to my head too in some sort of lame attempt to stop the agony that's going on inside my skull. It feels as though someone has my brain in their hand, and they're squeezing it like they would a wet sponge that they're trying to get every last drop of water out of. I succumb to the pain and pass out.

FLASH!

I'm being dragged outside the tower by my arms. My shoulders are on the verge of dislocation, but the pain in my head seems to have lessened. I look to see who's pulling me, and it's Joselyn.

"Ugh. Why are you so heavy, Olive-uh?" she grunts when she sees me looking at her.

"Cindy? What are you doing?" I start coughing.

"Saving everyone's asses," she says as she stops and lets go of my arms.

I look over and see Matthias, Eli, and Charlotte lying in the grass. Alexandrine's sitting next to Charlotte, stroking her hair.

"Saving us from what? What happened in there?"

"From Joselyn's drama and the fire she caused. I told you not to let her go on this mission. I warned you this would happen, but did you listen to me? No. Crazy Cindy doesn't know what she's talking about," Cindy scolds.

I look back at the building, and sure enough, there's smoke coming from the ground floor window. "You dragged everyone outside all by yourself? Do you have super-strength too?" *I ask, confused.*

"No." *She looks at me like I'm a moron.* "I got the fire under control long enough to start pulling Charlotte out. Alexandrine woke up before any of you did and helped me with the guys. I left you in there for last," *she says with a hint of amusement.* "Sorry. Old habits."

I start coughing again as a response.

"I can't remember what happened in there. Did we find out what was on the USB stick?" *Matthias asks.*

"No. We didn't have time before the guards showed up and Joselyn went berserk." *Cindy wipes sweat off her forehead.*

"Then this was all for nothing." *Eli groans as he sits up.*

"Hold your horses, Mr. Mary Jane. I might have swiped something that could be useful," *she says, picking something up off the ground. She turns around and has a laptop in her hands.*

"A laptop! Smart girl." *Eli holds his hands out for her to give him the computer.*

"Tut, tut, tut. Back off there, grabby. I just saved your lives. What's in it for me?"

"Let's talk about this back at camp, shall we?" *Alexandrine looks around.*

The sky has turned a pale orange on the horizon as the sun lets off its final rays. I notice that all the surrounding buildings are dark. Even the streetlights are void of their usual golden pools of light. I look back at the tower, and the only light I see is from the fire Cindy saved us from. Whatever knocked us out knocked the power out too.

"Wake up!" *Cass yells, shaking me awake.*

I sit up with a jolt when I realize I have fallen asleep, and now Tim, Denis, and Cass are all staring at me.

"Oh, thank God! You had me scared!" Cass's hand is on her heart.

"I'm sorry. I must have fallen asleep." I sit up, rubbing my eyes.

"You weren't sleeping. It's like you were in a trance. You looked like you were in pain, with your hands to your head, and you kept opening your eyes looking at us...but not looking at us," Cass tries to explain, looking spooked.

"I think I had one of my dreams again. I better go talk to Matthias."

3|8

"Why would Joselyn even be there with us?" Matthias asks.

I found Eli and Matthias still in the barn, sitting by a roaring fire. They have a couple of chairs pulled over to the fireplace, one for sitting and one to rest their feet on. They each have a glass of wine in one hand and a chunk of chocolate in the other. Unfortunately, neither one of them offers me any chocolate. Rude.

"I have no idea. I'm just telling you what I saw. This dream was different. It was longer, and it kept skipping ahead. Just showing me pieces of events."

"So, ya didn't get to see what was on the USB stick?" Matthias asks once more.

"No, like I already told you," I say, getting annoyed.

"It would have been convenient if you had. Then we wouldn't need to track down a computer," Eli chimes in airily, taking a sip from his glass.

"When should we have a meeting about this mission?" I'm anxious to get started.

"The sooner, the better," Matthias answers at the same time as Eli says, "No need to rush into anything."

They both look at each other with their eyes narrowed and lips tight.

"I'm with Matthias on this," I say. "Especially after what Denis said about radiation poisoning."

"What about it?" Matthias asks.

"Denis told us that if we don't leave here soon enough, we'll all need to get shots to stop us from getting radiation sickness."

"Denis is a bit of a drama queen." Eli waves me off. "I'm not sure I buy into this radiation nonsense. I think it's just the government using scare tactics."

"So, ya haven't taken one of the shots then?" Matthias challenges him.

"No. I did," he says, taking a bite of chocolate. "Better safe than sorry."

"You're so full of crap. Maybe ya should step out to your garden. I'm sure the plants would love the BS that's constantly spewin' outta your mouth."

"What?" Eli gives a confused laugh.

"Ya talk big, but when it comes to actually standin' up for your beliefs, ya fall right in with the rest of the sheep."

Eli gives Matthias a hard punch on the arm, which Matthias is about to return, but I clear my throat loudly, and they stop.

"I think we should have a meeting soon to get this computer plan hashed out," I say, interrupting yet another squabble between these two.

"Fine. We'll set up a meeting for tomorrow at noon. I don't think we'll need that many people for the mission, though. I know a few guys who're willing to look the other way for us to do what we need to get done."

Matthias heaves a big sigh.

"Knock it all you want, Brother. At least I get results." Eli raises his glass toward Matthias, who doesn't return the gesture.

"Okay, tomorrow at noon. In here?" I ask. I'm getting antsy to get out of here and head to bed.

"Sure. After lunch." Eli says.

I head back outside and see David leaning against the side of the barn alone. "Liv. I want to talk to you." He pushes off the wall toward me.

"Go talk to your girlfriend." I start walking quickly toward the shelter.

"She's not my girlfriend," he says defensively. "C'mon. I've only known her for a day."

I laugh mirthlessly. "I saw you guys kissing."

He grabs my wrist to stop me from walking away from him. "No, you saw her kiss me. I never asked for it. In fact, if you had been watching closer, you would have seen me push her away. And what difference does it make if I kiss someone else or not? You shouldn't care, remember?" he says angrily.

"You're right. I don't. Go ahead and kiss whoever you want." I twist to get out of his grip.

"Why are you so mad at me?" he asks with pain in his voice.

I stop trying to get away and face him. He has a desperate look in his eyes, and I realize I have the power to hurt him with how I respond at this moment. I stare into his eyes, seeing the boy I've come to rely on, the boy who's always been there for me whenever I needed him, the boy who has proclaimed his love to me, and it finally hits me.

I love him too.

The thought terrifies me, and I suddenly don't want to be here. I feel vulnerable and confused standing in front of him, feeling how I'm feeling. "Can we talk about this tomorrow?" I ask quietly. "I need some time to think about things."

"Sure," he says, releasing his grip on my wrist. As I slide my wrist out of his grasp, I grab onto his hand momentarily, giving him a light squeeze before walking away to the shelter.

3|9

The next couple of days pass, and David doesn't hold me to the talk I promised him. It almost seems as though he read my thoughts that night, because he's been even sweeter than normal, if that's possible. He asked Angel to cool it and told her that he's more than happy to be her friend. She bristled a bit at first but backed off. She still calls him handsome, which annoys me, but I try my best to ignore it.

The meeting we had about the computer mission didn't go over too well. Some of Eli's group seems to think it's an unnecessary risk and use of their resources. In the end, we took a vote and got enough people to agree to it. Finding people to volunteer for the mission was a different story, though. I already knew who would be in the group, so I wasn't surprised by the lack of volunteers.

It did surprise me, though, when Alexandrine suggested Charlotte go with us. It didn't make sense to me that she was there in my dream, but apparently, Charlotte has the ability to make people fall asleep by singing. Alexandrine prompted her to show us while plugging her own ears. It took Charlotte a while to get brave enough to sing, but once she did, the effect was immediate. My entire body went slack, and I started dreaming within moments of my eyes closing. When I woke up, I had no idea what time it was or how long I was out. Alexandrine told us it had only been ten seconds. I was dumbfounded.

Charlotte agreed to go, but only if Joselyn could go too. We tried to talk her out of it, but she folded her arms over her chest and refused to speak to anyone until Alexandrine finally caved. David looked like he was going to raise his hand, but I shook my head at him to remind him of the conversation we'd had earlier in the day:

"It's a dangerous mission, David."

"Exactly why I want to go. I want to be there to protect you."

"I'll be fine. I saw what happened in my dream, and you weren't there with us. It was Cindy who saved everyone, if you can believe it."

"Liv, I—" David starts to protest, but at that moment, I grab his face gently and kiss him to stop him from talking. I'm just as surprised at what I was doing as he is.

"As you wish." He leans his forehead against mine, and I smile at the quote. "But don't get it in your pretty little head that you can kiss me to get me to do what you want."

"Of course not." I give him a flirty wink.

He wraps his arms around me, pulling me in for a hug. I could feel him turn his face toward my neck and breathe in deep, sighing as he let it out.

An unspoken change is happening between us, and I think I'm finally okay with it.

■■■■■

"Everything's ready for the mission," Eli announces at supper a couple days after the meeting. "We'll be leaving tomorrow after lunch."

"Are you sure you don't want the Metal Militia to escort you?" a young man asks eagerly.

"I appreciate your enthusiasm, Edward, but I'm afraid that would draw too much attention."

I see Edward's shoulders slump in disappointment.

"I still don't get why this is so important," an angry-faced old woman asks.

"What's on the USB stick seemed important to my dad, so it's important to me. It's not for you to question my decisions," Eli says with utmost authority. His casual attire of a soft dark blue sweater and brown skinny jeans seems to clash with the powerful tone in his voice and the threatening way he's holding his body. A vision of him welcoming someone in for an embrace only to snap their neck once they get close pops in my head and makes me shiver.

"You guys shouldn't be letting Joselyn go. You have no idea what kind of power she has when she gets scared," Cindy says.

"She's going because it's what Charlotte wants," Alexandrine says firmly.

"Do you always give your kid everything she wants?" Cindy asks in a bratty tone.

"When we're asking her to do something special for us, yes." Alexandrine glares.

Cindy puts her hands on her hips and says to Charlotte, "That was a stupid use of a favor. Why didn't you ask for your own shelter? Or a unicorn or something cool?

Both the girls giggle, and everyone directs their attention back on Eli.

"We'll make sure everything is under control while you're gone," someone says reassuringly.

"I appreciate that." Eli nods and dismisses everyone to go about their business.

I head back to the shelter to check over my bag again. I had it packed up yesterday, but I just want to triple check that I'm not missing anything.

"Are you absolutely sure I can't talk you out of this?" David asks again.

I sigh and grab his hand. He lifts my hand up to his lips and presses them against my knuckles.

"I need to do it. The pendant was obviously important to my grandpa," I say, stumbling a bit over the word "grandpa." I feel sadness settle in a bit when I think about Saul and how I wish I could have been his granddaughter for longer.

"Just promise me you won't get yourself into trouble like you always do when I'm not around." He nudges me with his elbow.

"I can't promise anything, but I'll try my hardest," I say.

He raises his eyebrow and gives me a look of frustration.

"Hey! Things just kind of happen to me. It's not my fault."

David rests his hand on the back of my neck and rubs my cheek with his thumb, sending goosebumps down my body. Just then, Cass comes barging in the shelter. I quickly move away from David, uncertain whether I want people to know we're becoming something more than friends, but the smile that spreads across Cass's face makes me relax a bit.

"It's about time!" she squeals. "Sorry to interrupt. I'll just go find somewhere else to be."

"No, Cass. It's okay…" I try to say, but she gives me a wave and closes the door behind her.

I can't quite meet David in the eye when I realize what Cass thinks we're doing. She's acting more mature about all this than I feel, and she's three years younger. I'm just so far out of the loop with what couples are supposed to do that I think my maturity is more like a ten-year-old.

"Tell me again what happens after you get the computer," David says, knowing full well I don't know.

"We skip our merry way back out of the city with the laptop in hand. The guards happily open the gate for us, saluting us as we pass by, and once we get back here, we plug the USB stick in to find that it's a map leading us to a buried treasure." I laugh.

"Very funny," David says with a half smile. "What if something bad happens after Cindy saves you? What if you guys get caught and are thrown into jail? Or worse?"

"I'll be with Matthias and Eli. They wouldn't let something like that happen." I rub his arm.

"You're right. They'd probably shoot you and themselves to avoid being captured," David says darkly. He looks so concerned that my resolve wavers for a moment.

"What if the information on the USB is the location of The Haven?" I challenge. "Don't you think that's worth finding out?"

David chews on his inner cheek a moment and finally agrees. "Fine. You're right. Just don't lose the pendant while you're in there. It would be bad if the Coalition got their hands on that information."

I nod. His concerns have me a little worried now. I didn't think much about what happened right after Cindy saved us from the tower. I hope what's on the USB stick is worth the risk.

[40

After a secret farewell with David, I found it hard to leave, but now that I'm outside the compound, the excitement of adventure draws me forward.

Eli leads the way, while Matthias takes up the rear. We wind our way for hours through empty streets and eerie subdivisions. The vacant houses seem to peer at us with dark windows, giving me the unsettling feeling of being watched. I focus my attention on Charlotte and Joselyn, who walk ahead of me with their arms linked, whispering secrets to each other. It gives me a pang of longing for David to be here with me.

"We're almost there," Eli announces.

I look up and see a city encompassed by a fence. There's a thin cloud of fog, but you can still see the buildings for the most part. There are houses on the outskirts surrounding the tall skyscrapers that are still standing. As we get to be about a hundred yards from the fence, Eli tells us to wait in the wreck of a building, out of sight.

"Ya sure about this?" Matthias asks uncertainly.

"Of course. Just stay put. They can get a little suspicious if a group of people is standing outside the gate."

I listen to his boots crunch on the gravel as he approaches the city gates. His footsteps stop, and when I don't hear anything else, I go to peek my head around the corner, but Matthias grabs my arm and shakes his head. He mouths, "wait," and I hold my breath as I try to listen to what's going on.

"Hey, hey! Bryce, my man!" Eli's voice calls out.

After a beat, I hear some hand slapping and a deep voice answer, "Yo, Eli. You looking to get in?"

"That I am, my friend. Got a small group of people looking to gather supplies."

"Small group?" Bryce asks.

"They're back there. I didn't know whether Godzilla was working this afternoon or not. You know how he is."

"Sure do," Bryce answers knowingly. "Coop's got the day off, though. You're safe. So," —Bryce pauses, lowering his voice to where I can just barely make out what he's saying— "you got the goods?

"Of course," Eli says. There's another pause and I assume he's handing off the drugs.

I can hear Bryce take a deep breath and say, "Ahh! That's some good stuff."

Matthias looks like he wants to murder his brother and this Bryce person. His disdain for the way his brother conducts business is clearly showing as he curls his lip and balls his hands into fists. If it weren't for the laptop, I wouldn't be going along with this either.

326

"Pleasure doing business with you, Bryce," Eli says. Then we hear a whistle signaling it's safe to come out.

As we walk through the gate, Bryce nods to each of us but does a little double-take when Matthias steps past. Even though Matthias keeps the hair on his head and face vastly different from Eli's, their similarities are still noticeable. Bryce locks up the gates behind us and gets back to his post. We continue to follow Eli as he leads us toward the tower, trying to blend in as much as we can, but I notice the few people on the streets watch us walk past, and I don't like it.

We make it through the residential area and come to roads lined with businesses. I take a deep breath and almost shout in jubilation when I recognize the smell. I keep sniffing until I'm lightheaded, and my mouth waters.

Tacos!

"Eli, please tell me you have some money or something to buy tacos," I plead.

"We don't have time for that," Alexandrine answers, and I whip my head toward her and give her a shocked look.

"There's always time for tacos! C'mon, Uncle Eli. Please," I beg. "Please, please, please!"

Eli laughs a little. "Yeah. I have a pouch of Coalition coins. We'll get you some tacos."

I jump while clapping my hands. I haven't been this excited in a long time. Everyone's looking at me strangely, so I stop and try to control myself. We look up and down the road and spot a truck parked on the street with a big window open on the side and a menu posted next to the window.

"Why is there a truck selling tacos?" I ask.

"You didn't have food trucks in your city?" Eli asks, surprised.

"No. This is weird. Can you trust it?"

"Honestly, some of the best food I've ever had came from a food truck. It must be a city ordinance thing. Maybe your president didn't allow it."

I shrug, and we walk closer to the truck, the scent getting stronger until it's the only thing I can smell. "Street tacos?" I read. "I've never had these before, but if they taste as good as they smell, I'll try them."

They have ground beef, chicken, and steak. I order one of each and an extra ground beef one to take to Henry. We'll have to reheat it, but since he's never had a taco before, he won't notice it's not quite as good as when it's fresh. I suspect he'll like it anyway. Everyone else only orders one, making me look like a pig, but you know what, I don't care. These tacos are so much smaller than the ones I'm used to, and they don't have salsa, but as soon as I bite into the chicken one, I close my eyes and moan. I try to make them last as long as I can, but it's a struggle. I'm tempted to eat the one I got for Henry too, but with a huge amount of willpower, I wrap it up in the foil they came in and stuff it in my bag, sighing.

Once everyone is done, we walk down the sidewalk until I recognize the area from my dream. Sure enough, Eli leads us down an alleyway connecting the streets.

327

The smell of rotting garbage and stale urine causes my stomach to churn. I quickly pull my shirt over my nose so I don't have to taste the tacos again.

We come out to a street like the one we were just on. I look around with a feeling of déjà vu as I see the tall buildings still intact, a store selling clothes with a sign in the window promising "Low Prices!" and office buildings with windows glinting in the fading sunlight.

I take notice of the fog—or rather, the momentary lapses of fog—just like in my dream. Then I remember the old guy on the corner. I check the direction where I remember seeing him, and I spot him holding the cardboard sign that reads, **"BELIEVE!"**

His appearance is off-putting: ratty clothes, hair matted with dirt, and crooked black teeth. He sees us coming and turns his sign toward us. "The world is actually on our side! If we would just go to them, they would accept us. Listen to the voices from above. They tell us encouraging words."

"Nut job," Eli mutters so only we can hear.

We stay on the opposite side of the street, trying to ignore him as we make our way toward the tower that's straight ahead.

Out of the blue, a voice rings in my head as clear as someone speaking directly to me. *Please, listen to me. They want to find us. We'd be set free. I hear their voices at my home. Come with me. You can hear them too.*

I peer in the guy's direction and see that he's staring straight at me with a curious look. I purposefully look away and pick up my pace, blowing past Eli in an effort to get away from his unsettling stare.

Carl. My name's Carl. You don't have to be afraid, girl. I won't hurt you, the voice says inside my head.

"Hey. Slow down, Olivia. We need to keep it cool, or people will take notice of us, and we don't want that." Eli grabs my arm to slow me down.

"Sorry. I just wanted to get away from that guy. Anyone else hear him talking inside their head?" I say quietly.

"Oh! That was him? I just thought I was hearing voices again," Joselyn says with a nervous laugh.

"What are you girls talking about?" Alexandrine asks.

"I think that guy's a Rare, but he's insane. He told me to come to his home to hear the voices. That the voices tell him the world is on our side," I say.

"Ignore him. Keep walkin'," Matthias grunts.

The guy stops trying to talk to me, and I'm relieved, but I'm also kind of interested in what he was talking about. What if he's not completely crazy? Clearly, he's a Rare, but what happened to him? He must have telepathic abilities, so who's he talking to? Voices from above?

I'm so lost in thought, I don't notice we're about half a block away from the tower until Eli shows us where we should keep out of sight again.

"Are you ready, Charlotte?" Alexandrine asks.

Charlotte nods slightly.

"Sing loud!" Joselyn gives Charlotte a hug.

"I'll be watchin' the whole time," Matthias reassures Alexandrine. "If anything seems to be goin' wrong, we'll come get ya."

"Make it convincing," Eli throws in.

We watch as Alexandrine and Charlotte move toward the tall gray cone-shaped building with metal poles that stick up into the sky. As they get closer to the entrance, Charlotte puts her hands between her knees and crosses her legs, bouncing up and down as though she has to go to the bathroom. She says something to Alexandrine, who does a show of looking around for somewhere to go, just like they rehearsed. They need to make it convincing, in case there are cameras or someone watching from the narrow windows.

She grabs Charlotte's arm and pulls her toward the entrance. Charlotte continues to dance around as Alexandrine knocks on the door. The door stays closed, but Alexandrine leans toward the wall.

"I'll bet they use intercoms," Eli comments.

The door suddenly pops open, and a Coalition guard steps into the doorway, holding a rifle in his arm. I see Alexandrine lift her hands up to her ears and stick in the earplugs she was carrying.

Within a few seconds, the guard drops to the ground like a marionette whose strings were just cut. I can hear a faint melody, and even from this far away, I begin to feel the effects. Alexandrine sways a little on her feet, but she manages to stay standing.

"All right. Put your earplugs in, and let's go get this over with," Eli says.

I take the squishy earplugs out of my pocket, roll the tip of it between my fingers until it's thin just like I was shown, and then stuff them in my ears. The ambient sounds of the city are instantly muted.

We walk to where Charlotte is still singing. The earplugs work but just barely. I'm finding it hard to keep my eyelids from closing. We step past the sleeping guard and into the tower, where the polished tiled floors reflect the fluorescent lights, and the scent of cleaning solution burns my nose. There's a desk by the wall where several monitors show what's outside the tower, but unfortunately, there's no computer here.

We walk along the corridor as quietly as we can, while Charlotte continues to sing. We're getting far enough away from the sleeping guard that I'm worried Charlotte's singing won't affect him anymore. If he wakes up now, he'll probably find us.

Finally, Eli peers into a window on one of the doors and motions for us to stop. He holds his finger up to his lips at Charlotte so she'll stop singing. He takes an earplug out and gestures for us to do the same.

"There are computers in there, but there's also about five guards sitting around those computers. So here's what I'm thinking. We'll crack the door open just enough for Charlotte's voice to get in. Then, once they're all asleep, we'll go in and use the computers."

"I already told you we never get a chance to use one. Cindy steals a laptop."

"It'll have to be one of us who takes the laptop," Joselyn says quietly.

"Why's that?" I whisper.

"I made Cindy promise to leave me alone on this mission," Joselyn says. "I wrote her a note and told her I wanted to try to handle things myself. That I'll never be strong if I don't try. She promised, 'crosses her heart and hopes to die.'"

This bit of information helps me to understand my dream now. I couldn't figure out why Cindy would allow Joselyn to stick around long enough to freak out.

"Let's not even bother with pluggin' in the USB stick here. Someone should grab the laptop, and we'll take off," Matthias says, and everyone nods.

"Earplugs back in. Charlotte, are you ready?" Eli asks.

Charlotte looks frightened, but she whimpers a yes.

After everyone replaces their earplugs, Eli puts his hand on the door handle, ready to start our plan, but at that moment, a guard comes marching around the corner and catches us. "Stop right there! Hands up where I can see them!" the guard yells.

"Sing!" Eli shouts, but Charlotte seems too scared. Her voice cracks, and she starts bawling instead.

Eli puts his hands up in the air, stepping in front of us. "We're so sorry. My friend here needed to use the facilities. The nice guard at the front door let us in, but we got lost trying to find the bathroom," Eli lies as the guard moves in closer, pointing his gun at us.

Charlotte continues to cry, unable to use her abilities.

"Put your hands behind your head, and turn around," the guard barks, obviously not believing the lie.

The guard is now right behind Eli, pushing him up against the wall. He grabs ahold of his radio to call in backup, but Matthias takes this moment of distraction to pull out the handgun he had tucked in his belt and shoot the guard. Sirens start blaring throughout the building, and I look back toward the entrance and see the guy who opened the front door awake and talking on his radio as he walks toward us.

Alexandrine is trying to soothe Charlotte to get her to sing again, but Charlotte just looks at her in terror. We push our way into the room with the computers, desperate to get it and go. The five guards who are in the room are grabbing their guns to respond to the alarm system going off. Matthias has his gun drawn, but he never gets a shot fired.

Joselyn starts screaming at the top of her lungs, and everyone in the room immediately grabs hold of their heads. The lights flicker as though someone is playing with the light switch. The computer screens are flashing too. The pressure inside my head is unbearable. I feel like my brain is about to pop. Everyone around

330

me drops to the floor like flies, and right before I pass out too, I see sparks shooting out of the wall sockets, catching the desks and nearby wastebasket full of paper on fire.

[4 1

I wake up to my wrists and shoulders feeling like they are about to dislocate. My shirt has pulled up a bit, and my back is getting scratched from sharp rocks and rough concrete that I'm being dragged over. My head is still throbbing from whatever happened in there. I take notice that the sounds of the siren have stopped, and it's ominously quiet, except for Cindy's grunting.

"Ugh! Why are you so heavy, Olive-uh?" she says, pulling me up next to Matthias.

"Cindy? What are you doing here?" I ask groggily, forgetting my dream for a moment. I start coughing and can't seem to stop.

"Saving everyone's asses." She lets go of my arms.

"Saving us from what? What happened in there?" Eli asks.

"From Joselyn's drama and the fire she caused. I told you not to let her go on this mission. I warned you this would happen, but did you listen to me? No. Crazy Cindy doesn't know what she's talking about," Cindy scolds.

I look back at the building to watch the smoke coming from a ground floor window. "You're the one who promised Joselyn that you'd leave her alone. You could have jumped in to stop her from freaking out," I challenge.

"A promise is a promise is a promise. I at least had the sense to take over right before everyone's heads exploded and you all burned to a crisp."

"Seriously? Is that what would have happened? Our heads would have exploded?" I ask, horrified.

"Did you get the laptop?" Eli interrupts.

"Yes, indeedly doo, Mr. Mary Jane," Cindy says, picking the black computer up off the ground.

Eli reaches out to grab it, but she pulls it away from him. "Tut, tut, tut. Back off there, grabby. I just saved your lives. Well, me and Alexandrine. What's in it for moi?"

"Let's talk about this back at camp, shall we?" Alexandrine looks around.

The sky has turned a pale orange on the horizon as the sun lets off its final rays. I notice that all the surrounding buildings are dark, just like in my dream. The streetlights aren't working either, leaving us in the convenient veil of darkness. I look back at the tower, and the only light I see is from the fire Cindy saved us from. Joselyn's ability not only knocked us out, she knocked out the power too.

Now that every part of my dream has played out, I'm suddenly nervous. I don't know what's going to happen, and I don't like it.

"Is Charlotte okay?" I ask Alexandrine, who's on her knees, holding Charlotte.

"She feels guilty."

"I'm s-so, so s-sorry guys," Charlotte squeaks.

"Shh. It's okay," Alexandrine shushes Charlotte, then says to us, "Let's get moving."

Eli leads us as fast as he can to an alleyway out of sight of the tower. The guards will be waking up soon—that is, if they haven't died in the fire. A pang of guilt washes through me at the thought. We should have tried to save them, but then again, that would mean our capture. I feel like Matthias making the choice to kill someone just for our sakes. I feel dirty.

Once we're safely out of sight, we slow down a little since it's dark and hard for those without Rare abilities to see. I can hear people on the streets murmuring about the power outage and making wild guesses about what's going on. Some are worried that the city has been attacked, while others blame the president for using too much power for his estate.

We quietly work our way up and down sidewalks and alleyways, trying hard to stay unseen. As we're coming out of an alley, Eli peeks his head around the corner and throws his arm out to stop us. He guides us back behind a dumpster. We squat down to keep out of sight. I peek my head out to see what we're hiding from, and a guard steps into view, shining a flashlight down the alleyway. I whip my head back just as the beam of light scans back and forth a few times. He must not have seen me, because the light disappears, and the guard's footsteps move on. I blow out the breath I was holding in, willing my heart to settle down.

Where are you going? a voice echoes inside my head. *Come hide at my place. Then you, too, can hear the words of comfort.*

That weirdo is trying to communicate with me again.

I don't know you. Leave me alone, I think as clearly as I can. I don't know whether he can read my thoughts or how his abilities work.

If you ever want to listen, remember: QRP 14.060. You're not alone.

I try to ignore what he's saying and focus on following behind Cindy. The man doesn't say anything more, and as we get to the subdivisions again, I can feel myself breathe. I just want to be back at camp with David.

The houses in this part of town still have their electricity. It appears that Joselyn's abilities only work in a certain radius. We have to be more careful to stay in the shadows now. I don't know if the residents know what's happening downtown, but we can't take any risks.

Eli must have taken a wrong turn and struggles to remember his way back to the gate. We stop a few times as he spins around in circles, trying hard to spot something that will spark his memory. I offer to climb up on the roof of a dark house to see if I can spot our exit. He refuses at first, but after walking in circles a couple of times, I get fed up with him and pick out a tall tree instead.

I almost yell in frustration once I'm high enough to see the gate. It's lit up with floodlights. There's no way we're going to be able to leave without being caught.

Even if the same guard is still manning the post, he's going to know we caused the trouble, and I doubt he's going to just let us go scot-free.

I climb back down and give them the bad news.

"What do we do?" Alexandrine asks.

Eli strokes his beard, a lot like Matthias does while thinking. "Well, we have two girls with us who have some serious powers. I hate to ask you to use them again, but it might be the only way."

Cindy lets out a laugh. "You really want to unleash Joselyn's power again?"

"Like I said, it might be the only way."

"Whatever. It's your funeral," Cindy mumbles.

"Do ya have a better plan?" Matthias barks.

"How did you and Loverboy escape the city?" Cindy asks me.

I frown at her. "*David* cut a hole in the chain-link fence, and we climbed under it. We were skinny back then, so we didn't need to cut much."

"That's not going to work here. The fence has hot wires," Eli says. He looks at our confused faces and explains. "They're wired with electricity."

"Really? That seems extreme," I say.

"That's why I had to work so hard to make connections with some of the guards. The only way into the city is through the gate or across the lake, but even that is monitored pretty heavily."

"Charlotte, do you think you could sing our way out?" I ask.

Charlotte looks at me uncertainly, shaking her head slightly. "I can't. I'm too scared."

"Baby, there's nothing to be scared of. You have a wonderful gift!" Alexandrine throws in.

"I know, Mama. But it makes my throat hurt."

"Oh, for Pete's sake! You're gonna have to sing, or we're stuck in here," Matthias says callously.

"Don't talk to my daughter that way, Matthias."

"Then ya better explain to her she can't chicken out now." He and Alexandrine stand almost toe to toe.

"You all better calm down, or we're bound to be heard." Eli looks around nervously.

"While you idiots were arguing, I hashed out a plan." Cindy picks at her teeth. We all watch her as she impolitely finishes picking out whatever it was stuck in her teeth and sucks it off her fingernail.

"Care to share your plan?" Eli says impatiently.

"Huh?" She glances around at us, confused.

"The plan! The plan you said you hashed out to get us out of the city!" Eli says loudly but then bites his lips together.

"Oh, right. That," she says as though she suddenly remembers.

The adults throw their hands up in exasperation.

"It's simple. You people will stay put out of range while Jossy does her power surge thing and knocks the electric fence offline. Bada bing, bada boom! We cut the fence and escape."

"I don't know. What if the guards hear her screaming and come check it out while we're trying to cut the fence?" I interject.

"She doesn't have to scream to use her powers. She just keeps them buried deep down until she has a freak-out and loses control of them."

"Well, what do we use to cut it?" Alexandrine asks.

"I don't have all the answers here, people," Cindy replies. "If you don't like my idea, come up with one of your own."

"It's not a bad plan, Cindy. We just need to figure out the details," Eli says.

I watch as Cindy gets her twisted smile again, the one she uses when she wants us to be "best friends." Looks like Eli made her best friend list.

"I don't suppose anyone has a tool for cuttin'?" Matthias asks.

"I have a multipurpose tool, but there's no way it's going to cut through a fence," Eli says.

We stop talking for a moment when we hear a strange siren. The sound is coming closer, and I see flashing red and blue lights down the street. We all duck down quickly behind a bush and watch as it turns onto a different road.

"What was that?" I ask.

"An old police car that the guards use from time to time," Eli answers.

"Police?" Cindy asks.

"Back before the Coalition was put into place, police officers used to keep the peace. Law and order," Eli explains.

Cindy nods as though she understands, but her expression reads otherwise.

"If your multitool has pliers, then I have an idea of how we can get out," Alexandrine says, getting back on topic. "Joselyn will knock the power out, and as soon as she does, we'll use the pliers to untwist the top and bottom connections and then unweave the fence. I've done it before at our old city."

"That fence is at least twelve feet tall. How are you going to reach the top?" Eli asks skeptically.

"I'm a good climber. I'll climb up there and do it," I offer.

"Fine. Let's go. We've been standin' here yackin' for too long," Matthias says.

[4 2]

We head off to a part of town far enough away from the gate that we should be safe. It's mostly rundown buildings over here, making me think of the bad part of my home city. Let's hope it's empty and not full of criminals.

Matthias picks a building that still has all four walls, and we tuck ourselves inside it while Cindy reassures us she's got this. I don't like relying on Cindy with something this important, but we need Joselyn.

"I'll make Jossy come out, and then you guys will have to explain what to do."

"Should we plug our ears or something?" Eli asks.

"Her powers don't have anything to do with sound," Cindy answers condescendingly, as though it were obvious. Then she turns and walks a few paces away. "Jossy. We need you to do this thing for us. Pretty please, come out and use your 'knock out' power to cut the electricity. The peeps need you."

Quiet.

"Don't be such a baby! You could actually help people this time."

Silence.

"If you don't come out now, I'll punch you in the face!" Cindy threatens.

It is so strange seeing Cindy talking to herself. Her face darkens as she stands around, waiting for Joselyn to show up. Without warning, Cindy punches herself right across the chin, hard.

"Ow!" she says, tears forming in her eyes as she holds her face. "What just happened to me?"

"Joselyn?" I ask.

"Yeah. What's going on?"

We explain the plan to her, and she seems reluctant to help.

Charlotte steps up to her and gives her a hug. "It's okay to be scared about your power, but if you don't do this, Joselyn, we aren't going to make it out of here."

Joselyn seems to understand what Charlotte's saying but still looks unsettled.

"This is the last time we'll ask you to do this," I say. "You're not hurting anyone anyway. Just knocking out the power so we can get out of here."

Joselyn looks around at us for a moment and then seems to make up her mind. "Okay. I'll do it," she says, voice quivering a bit.

We watch from the doorway as she works her way to the chain-link fence. Matthias keeps the gun out and ready in case she needs help. Joselyn holds her hands out in front of her, standing with her legs shoulder-width apart. Her back is turned to us, so I can't see what she's doing, but suddenly, the fence starts sparking and making loud snapping noises. Then it stops just as quickly as it started. I could feel the pressure inside my head while she was using her ability, but it was more like a bad headache than intense squeezing.

We race over to the fence to get started before anyone notices. Charlotte gives Joselyn a high five once we get to her, and I rub her arm a little, giving her a thumbs up.

"You did great!" I whisper, and she smiles proudly.

Alexandrine holds a flashlight for Matthias to see, keeping her hand over the end to conceal most of the beam. Matthias pulls a long weed out of the ground and holds it against the fence to check if it's still live. He seems satisfied.

"Hand the tool here, Elijah," Matthias says.

Eli pulls the multitool out of a pouch that's hooked on his belt and slaps it onto Matthias's outstretched hand. Working quickly, Matthias undoes a couple of wires that hold the fence to the metal frame at the base. Then he untwists two wires of the fence that are twined together at the bottom.

"How will I know what ones to untwist at the top?"

Matthias strokes his beard a moment as he thinks of a plan. "Anyone have a length of rope?"

I pull the bag off my shoulders and dig out the paracord roll I have and hand it to Matthias. He crouches down and ties the cord to the fence where he just untwisted it.

"Now, climb up to the top, pull the cord straight, and ya should have the right spot to untwist." Matthias hands the tool to me.

I slip it into my front pocket, feeling nervous about this. Everyone is relying on me, and I'm afraid to mess this up. Matthias gives me a gentle pat on the shoulder. I throw the cord over my shoulder before grabbing on to the fence to start my climb. The toes of my shoes are too round to fit in the links, so I do the bulk of the climb with my arms while pushing my feet hard against the fence. By the time I reach the top, my hands are so sore, I can barely hold on any longer. Climbing trees is far easier than this.

I make it to the metal bar at the top and wrap my arm over it to hold myself up. The twisted sections of the fence dig into my armpit, making me work as quickly as I can to get this over with. I pull the cord straight until I find the connection I need to untwist. Fumbling around, I try to dig the tool out of my right pocket with my left hand since my right arm is holding me up. My hand is so slick, I almost drop it. My pulse is racing, and my hands are trembling so bad, I can barely manipulate the tool to do what needs to be done. I recognize these as the symptoms of a panic attack, and that makes me freak out just a little bit more. I really can't have one right now. I close my eyes, trying to focus my mind. After a few breaths, I've calmed down enough to get back to what I was doing.

With a lot of effort, I untwist the top part of the chain and put the tool back into my pocket, where it's safe. I glance down at the faces looking at me and give them an okay gesture. I decide I can't climb back down because my hands are still sore, so I drop and do a roll once I hit the ground. Joselyn and Charlotte clap enthusiastically until Alexandrine shushes them, and they do a silent clap instead.

I put my bag back on as the two men get to work, twisting a piece of the fence like it's a screw. It looks like a loose spring as it comes unlinked with the rest of the fence. I watch as the top parts fall open now that they're no longer being held together. Excitement courses through me until I hear light footsteps coming toward us.

I look to the right and see guards wearing night-vision goggles headed our way. They've got their guns pointed at us, and I put my hands up to show them I'm unarmed.

"They found us!" I alert everyone.

Matthias immediately stops what he's doing and goes to pull his gun out.

"Hands where we can see them!" a guard yells, training his gun on Matthias.

It looks like Matthias doesn't want to comply, but he seems to think better of trying to take on that many guards and puts his hands up slowly.

The guards march over to where we're standing, and I hear Joselyn whisper, "You got this."

Charlotte lets out a little whimper, but then Joselyn takes her hand and squeezes. That seems to give her courage.

"Ears!" Joselyn shouts, and we all cover our ears.

As the guards try to understand what's going on, Charlotte starts singing, and they crumple to the ground. All except one guard. Why didn't he fall like the rest of them? As he turns his head, I notice the hearing aid stuck in his ear. He turns his gun toward Charlotte, and in the time it takes me to register what's happening, Joselyn steps in front of Charlotte just as the guard pulls the trigger.

I let out a scream, but surprisingly, Joselyn seems unharmed. The guard hesitates too long, confused by why Joselyn is still standing, and Matthias takes that pause to shoot the guard, showing no mercy once again. Charlotte is still singing quietly, but her voice is wavering. If she can't keep it up, the other guards will wake up and catch us.

I desperately want to ask Joselyn if she has bulletproof abilities too, but we need to get out of here. The men work even faster at untwisting the fence until it finally falls open. Alexandrine guides the girls through the fence, and I jump when I hear sirens coming our direction.

"Hurry!" I shout as I climb through the fence. Once we're all through, we take off at a fast run through the city ruins.

Eli leads us down roads I don't remember walking on when coming to the city, but I trust he knows his way back to his compound. We take breaks to catch our breath, hidden in copses of leafless trees that used to be manicured parks or large yards, now overgrown and wild. I listen for sirens or footsteps, but from what I can tell, there's nobody following us.

Hours pass by as we hurry our way back to the compound, my fingers frozen from the chilly air. With temperatures like this, it feels like it won't be long before the first snowfall happens. I wonder where we will be when winter finally comes. Does Matthias have a plan?

It seems like we've been running all night, and just when I start to worry that maybe we're lost, the towering pine trees that hide Eli's compound come into view. I almost cry in relief at the sight. He leads us through the fence and guides us to the barn, promising a roaring fire and hot chocolate to drink. I'd like to wake up David, but it's only a couple more hours until sunrise. I'll just let him sleep.

We all wait around patiently as Eli sets to work building a fire. I take this moment to ask Joselyn the question that has been burning the back of my mind. "Joselyn, are you bulletproof?"

"What?"

"You stepped in front of Charlotte just as the guard shot at her, and nothing happened to you."

"I did?" she asks, confused.

"Yeah! It was really cool of you," Charlotte says.

"Very brave," Alexandrine says, not unkindly. "Thank you for that, by the way."

"I have no idea what you guys are talking about. I was shot?"

I watch her to see if she's pulling our legs, but she seems sincere. "You black out when someone takes over. Maybe it's Cindy who's bulletproof," I suggest.

"I think each of my personalities have a different ability, but only one each," Joselyn says thoughtfully.

"Well, let's go through them then. You have knock-out power that affects both people and electrical things," I begin, listing them off with my fingers. "Cindy can handle trauma and shields you. Jack can talk to the dead..."

Joselyn nods.

"But there's one more. Who am I missing? I feel like I'm missing someone."

Joselyn scratches at her head as she tries to remember who I'm talking about. She runs her hand over her hair and feels the fly-aways from her ponytail. She pulls the hair tie out and shakes her head, finger combing the snarls out. Her long black hair momentarily falls over her face, covering half of it. Then it hits me.

"Landon! What about Landon?" I ask. "Maybe he's the one who can dodge bullets," I say excitedly.

"What do you mean 'dodge'?" Alexandrine asks. "She was standing still when they shot."

"You're right," I say, absentmindedly rubbing the still-present lump on my head.

"Maybe," Charlotte begins meekly, "he's not dodging them but making them move through the air to avoid hitting their target?"

"You know what? You could be right," I say, thinking about what I had seen earlier. The guard shot right at Joselyn, but the bullet never hit her. "That would be so cool!"

339

Eli has the fire lit, and I can feel the warmth radiating from it, taking the chill out of the air. "All right, let's see what's on the USB stick."

Cindy sets the laptop on the table, and everyone gathers around as Eli pushes the power button. The screen lights up, and we watch as it goes through its power-up process. Finally, a picture of the coalition flag shows up on the login screen with a spot in the center to type in the password.

"Crap! Anyone have any idea what the password could be?" I ask.

"The battery isn't going to last forever, so we can't spend too much time trying to figure it out," Eli says wisely. "I may have to see if I can do a factory reset, but let me just try something first." We watch as he types something into the box. He hits enter, and the screen changes to the desktop screen. "Idiots," Eli says, shaking his head.

"How did you do that?" I ask. "What did you type in?"

"'adminadmin.' It's a default password that, apparently, these morons were too lazy to change. Or too cocky, thinking nobody would ever get ahold of their computer."

"How do ya know so much about computers?" Matthias asks.

"I meet people inside the city, Brother. Some of those people are beautiful women who take me back to their place and teach me a thing or two." Eli smiles slyly.

Alexandrine curls her lips at him in disgust.

I pull the USB stick out from under my shirt and unhook the chain. I hand it over to Eli, who plugs it into the computer. A little alert shows up in the bottom corner, prompting us to click it to open. Eli clicks it, and we watch as a screen comes up with a list of files. Some of the files have names, while others are just gibberish.

"What the heck are those?" I point to the files that make no sense.

"Those are encrypted files. We're not going to be able to look at those right now," he says, clicking on a file that reads "Entry1."

I try to read it, but I don't quite understand what it says.

"You've got to be kiddin' me," Matthias mutters in shock. He's up on his feet, shoulder to shoulder with Eli as they click on another file.

"What?" I ask.

"You gonna tell us what's going on?" Alexandrine snarls.

"The Haven isn't a city," Matthias starts to say, and I fall back into my chair, disappointed at the news. Matthias continues, "The Haven is the United States. The US still exists out there."

At that moment, Matthias is interrupted by someone slamming the barn door open. "Someone's here to talk to you, Eli."

"Who could it be at this hour?" Eli says, frustrated at being pulled away from what he was doing.

Two of Eli's men walk in, leading someone who has their hands up in surrender. The two men move to the side, revealing who it is. I let out a gasp.

"I'm alone and unarmed. I've just come to talk," Janice says sincerely.

As Eli is about to respond, Matthias turns from the laptop, pulls out his gun, and shoots her.

THE
RETURN

DIANE ANTHONY

1

The gunshot echoes in my ears as I stand frozen by the sight in front of me. A thin tendril of smoke curls up from the barrel of the gun in Matthias's hand. My mom hits the floor with a thud.

"You shot me!" she screams, holding pressure on her bleeding thigh.

"Ya deserved it," Matthias growls. "Ya got a lot of nerve, showin' back up after what ya did."

"What'd she do again?" Eli asks curiously, showing little emotion for Janice's pain.

"She lied, got a few of my men killed. I lost an eye, and Tim lost an arm, all because of her," Matthias answers, still aiming the gun toward my mom.

"I know a 'sorry' won't cut it, but I had my reasons for what I did," Janice groans.

"I don't want to hear it," Matthias snarls.

I watch as my mom tries to stem the blood flow with her hands, but a sizable pool is gathering under her, and I start to worry she's going to bleed out.

"Uh. Matthias? I think we better get Rebecca in here to fix her leg before she dies," I say meekly.

"Nothin' less than what she deserves," Matthias says.

"True, but I think we might want to find out why she's here before we let her die."

"Thank you, Olivia," my mom mutters.

"Don't," I say angrily, but seeing the blood under her leg and her face twisted up in pain gives me mixed feelings. I'm not sure I'm willing to forgive her for what she did to our camp, but I don't want her to die either.

"I'm going to go get Rebecca." I hurry past my mom and out to the frigid air. I wrap my arms around myself as I rush over to Rebecca's cabin.

It takes me a couple of tries to convince her to patch my mom up. She's still upset about the carnage the explosion left, but her sense of duty as a nurse kicks in, and she agrees to help. As I go to follow her, David calls my name. I turn toward our shelter and watch as he closes the door behind him, wrapped in a blanket, his shaggy black hair disheveled from sleep. I race toward him as he holds out his good arm, bracing himself for impact. He folds me up in his blanket, and we stand holding each other, rocking back and forth gently.

"I'm so glad you came back to me," David whispers.

"Me too." I let out a sigh as he kisses the top of my head. "I should probably get back to the barn, though."

"Why? What's happening in the barn?" David reluctantly lets me go. The chill of the air bites into my hands and face.

"My mom showed up, and Matthias shot her. I'm afraid he's going to kill her if I don't get back in there."

"She deserves it," he says coldly.

I furrow my eyebrows at his harshness. I watch to see if he's going to start smirking because he was joking, but he never does.

"What?" he asks, confused.

"She's still my mom, David."

"She killed Ryan, Jeffery, and Andrew while almost killing Matthias, Tim, and me. Are you really standing up for her after what she did?" Anger starts to creep into David's voice.

"I'm not standing up for what she did, but I'm not okay with killing her either."

He looks at me with uncertainty, as though he wants to argue but doesn't want to fight with me.

"Are you saying you'd be okay with killing her?" Goosebumps run down my arms that have nothing to do with the cold air.

"I believe in justice being served when it's necessary. The fact she's your mom makes it more complicated. If she were any other person, I think I'd be fine with Matthias giving her what she deserves."

I can't believe what I'm hearing. My sweet, gentle David is suddenly showing a side I don't think I like.

I turn around without another word and start for the barn.

"Hey, Liv—wait. I'm sorry, okay? I don't want Matthias to kill your mom." David grabs my wrist and pulls me back toward him.

I can't look him in the eye, so I stare at the ground.

He lifts my chin and says, "It was just a terrible thing she did. I care about you, though. So, if you want me to forgive her for what she did, I'll try."

The tenderness in his voice and touch puts me at ease. I know he wouldn't lie to me. All I'd have to do is ask him to forgive my mom, and I know he would. But that's not what I'm asking for. What she did was unacceptable. I just don't want them to kill her.

"You have every right to be mad at her. *I'm* mad at her. Let's just give her a chance to explain herself, and then we can figure out what to do with her."

"Fair enough," he whispers, then kisses me gently before letting go of my chin.

"Why don't you head back to bed. You still have a couple of hours before we have to get up."

"Okay." David yawns. "But I'll walk you to the barn first."

We make our way to the barn slowly, enjoying this moment alone before everyone else wakes up and the camp bustles with people once more. Before I open the door, I kiss David again, savoring the way it makes me feel. Each time I kiss him, it's like the darkness that lives inside of me fades away and is replaced by a warm glow. It doesn't last forever, but it's enough to remind me that there are good things in this life worth holding on to.

I push the door open and see they have my mom tied down to a cloth-covered table and Rebecca is working on her leg.

"You know, if you shot her in the arm, it would have been less flesh to dig the bullet out of," Rebecca mutters as she moves her surgical tool around inside Mom's wound.

My mom squeezes her eyes shut and bites her bottom lip as she tries to hold still. Her skin is pale, and she's sweating profusely.

I almost ask why they didn't put her to sleep, but I leave it.

Matthias grunts. "I could've shot her in the head, and then there wouldn't have been anything to fix."

I give Matthias a dirty look, but he's focusing on what Rebecca is doing. Eli is still sitting in front of the computer, looking over files from the USB stick.

"Did you find anything else important?" I ask as I walk over to the laptop.

"Not a lot. Most of the files are encrypted. I would love to see what's on those, but I don't have the skill to open them. According to one of the files I was able to read, there's a large DMZ—demilitarized zone—to the west of here. It's the part of the country that got hit with nukes, so they left the uninhabitable land as a buffer zone between the Coalition and the Haven."

"So, are we going to leave for the Haven as soon as possible?" I ask.

"I have no interest in going," Eli says.

"Seriously?" I ask. "Why?"

"I have things pretty good here. I'm not sure I want to give it up," Eli says airily.

"I always knew ya were an idiot," Matthias says.

"Tell me, Brother, how do you plan to get across the DMZ and over to the Haven?" Eli asks.

"We just found out it's there. I haven't come up with a plan yet," Matthias answers.

"Well, let me know once you figure it out. Then I'll decide if it's worth it or not."

"Are you sure you're going to be allowed back in the city after what just happened? People saw you. That guard knows it was you," I point out.

"Eh. Things will blow over. I'll give it a little time, make them live without my product for a while. They'll be begging for me to come back for a visit."

"Like I said. Idiot," Matthias grunts.

Eli makes a rude gesture at Matthias, but Matthias ignores him.

"Got it." Rebecca holds up a bloody bullet fragment.

"Good. Patch her up, and get her outta here." Matthias turns his attention to the laptop.

"Don't you want—" Janice stops, scrunching her eyes tightly as Rebecca gets to work stitching the bullet wound.

"You said there was a reason you led our camp members to their deaths," I say, anger bubbling over. "Explain."

Matthias turns his head slightly so he can hear better.

"Can you unstrap me first?" she asks weakly.

"No. Answer the question," Rebecca responds, finishing the last few stitches.

"Remember the day you caught me talking to myself and I told you I was praying?" she asks me.

"Yeah?"

"I had an ear bud Matthias failed to notice. I was still in contact with my people."

"With your people?"

"Yes. I have my own team. I worked hard over the years to earn Turk's trust. I did some things I'm not proud of, but it was necessary for him to finally put me in charge of my own team at a different facility."

"What does that have to do with ya blowing up some of my men?" Matthias asks.

"My team informed me that Turk was orchestrating a manhunt with at least a hundred of his soldiers to come out and find whoever abducted me. The orders would be to kill you on sight. I had to think fast, and the weapons cache seemed to be the quickest way to not only get you to leave, but get me back into the city and into good graces with Turk."

Matthias starts to yell a profanity, but Eli slaps his hand over Matthias's mouth. Matthias shakes his head back and forth until Eli lets go. "Because of you, three of my men were killed!"

"I'm sorry. Casualties were inevitable. I needed a good cover, and it seemed like the best one."

"How'd you know Matthias wouldn't be blown up too?" I ask.

"I didn't. It was a calculated risk. I know he's more of a look-out guy, so I figured he'd be safe."

"So, let me get this straight. You work for Turk, but you have your own team? What does your team do?" I guess I was wrong to think she was nothing but a secretary.

"Turk thinks my team captures and tortures spies for Haven secrets. Instead, we trade secrets and give Turk just enough information so he thinks he's ahead of the game, but never enough for him to actually do any harm. Meanwhile, we give the Haven dirt on Turk and the Coalition. Then we help them make it back out of the city."

"So, you're a double agent?" Eli asks.

"A double agent would imply she's one of the good guys, and we all know that ain't true," Matthias growls.

"Can it, Matthias!" Janice says.

"And you've never been caught?" I ask to get the conversation back on track.

"Well, almost. He once sent someone over to watch me work, and I happened to be in the process of helping the Haven spy leave when Turk's guy showed up. He saw that the spy was in perfect health so I had to kill Turk's man, claiming it was the spy who got ahold of his gun. That was right before the whole mess of a situation with you. He put me to searching for you, but when I brought only you back, he questioned why I didn't capture everyone else, and sent someone over to interrogate you on Matthias's whereabouts."

"You mean torture me," I snarl.

"Yes, and I'm sorry about that. I had to play along, or I would have blown my cover. But then his henchman killed you, so I killed him, which has only made Turk more suspicious. I'm not sure he trusts me as he once did."

"Lying and murdering. Sounds about right." I shake my head.

"Judging me with your black and white view of the world is unfair. Just wait until you have to make life-or-death decisions that could cost people their lives. It's not as easy as you'd like to think it is," she snaps, face wincing in pain from getting worked up.

"Why are you here?" I try not to cry as memories of Markos flood my mind. I made the choice to go back to the city, and was followed by a guard, who killed Markos, one of our camp members.

"I guessed Matthias would make his way up here to see Eli, so I came to warn him and Henry to never come back to the city. You were caught on camera, and now you have a bounty on your head. They even put up posters in the bad part of town. Now your druggie friends will turn you in for a price."

"Waste of time. We weren't planning on setting foot there ever again anyway."

"Yeah, well, my conscience wouldn't rest until you were warned. Henry can never come back to the city." Her chin quivers.

"So, what are you hoping for by giving the Haven information? Are they preparing to go to war against the Coalition or something?" Rebecca asks, changing the subject. She tosses the bloody gauze into the fire, then resumes cleaning up after the operation.

"Whispers of war are spoken by both sides, but nothing is in motion. The Haven doesn't have enough manpower to defeat the Coalition, and the Coalition isn't really that interested in going to war. Turk's happy with his rule and wouldn't want anything to infringe on it," my mom answers.

"I hope we don't go to war. It would be bad for business," Eli comments.

"It could mean the end to Turk's tyranny and the oppression of the Rare!" Matthias shouts.

"I get it, but how could the Haven have enough manpower to win against the whole world? Think about it, the world has a stake in the Coalition and would not easily give it up. They appointed Sawyer, Turk, and all the other presidents to run things exactly how they want to. They ship Rares over *here* to be dealt with under the guise of sanctuary, but we all know that's hogwash. And they support the cities with all the products and finances they need so everyone will continue to do their bidding. This part of the world is their baby, and they'll fight tooth and nail to defend it. If the Haven was strong enough, wouldn't they have done something already?"

"Ya think the *whole* world is in on it? I bet there are countries who don't know what's really going on. If we could somehow let them know how things actually are..."

I storm out of the barn before Matthias finishes what he's about to say. All this talk about war is making me sick to my stomach. I need to lie down.

The sky is lightening from black to a royal blue as I push the door to the cabin open. David is curled up on his side, asleep. I'm still feeling down in the dumps after thinking about Markos and decide I would like a little comfort. I grab my blanket, wrap it around myself, and wriggle my way onto the cot with David, careful not to bump his broken wrist or gunshot wound. He groans sleepily as he wraps his good arm around me and holds me tight. His warm presence relaxes me, and I fall asleep immediately.

David and I stand facing each other in a dimly lit room. I can see the glow of a computer screen in my peripheral vision, but everything else in our surroundings is blurry as I stare into David's eyes. I feel a sense of uncertainty, and I don't know why.

"David, you're going to kill Olivia for what she's done," a deep, shaky voice says from behind me.

David's looking at me, but his eyes are unfocused, as though he's looking through me.

I try to move, but I'm frozen in place by an invisible force. My breathing is rapid as fear takes hold of me. The man who spoke rolls around me in a wheelchair and stops in front of David. He holds a gun out with a frail, quivering hand. David looks at the gun quizzically before reaching out and taking it. He waits for the man to roll back out of the way and then points the gun at my chest.

I try to scream, to cry out to David, but I can't seem to form the words. They're lodged in my throat. All I can do is plead with my eyes. For one brief moment, I see a flicker of recognition on David's face. He looks terrified.

"Kill her now, David," the man says.

I watch in horror as David's eyes glaze over once more, and his finger starts to squeeze the trigger.

"Breakfast time in fifteen minutes, you two lovebirds," Cass calls out.

I jolt awake as a sob escapes my lips. I sit up and cry as the feeling of fear and hopelessness tears at my mind.

2

"What's the matter, Liv?" David's voice is full of concern.

He wraps his arm around my shoulder, and I reflexively cringe away. The image of him about to shoot me clouds my mind from rational thought.

I look around the shelter, but it's just David and me. "I had another dream. It was real like my visions, but it can't be..." My voice cracks. I hold my head in my hands as a headache starts pulsing in my skull.

"What happened?"

"You were going to kill me. There was an old guy telling you to do it, and he handed you a gun. You were about to squeeze the trigger when I woke up."

"I would never ever kill you, Liv. It was a dream. Nothing more," David reassures me, stroking my face with his hand.

"I don't know, David."

"Well, if we ever meet someone who looks like the guy in your dream, let me know, and we'll kick his butt."

"He's an old man in a wheelchair, David," I say.

"Then we'll kick him in the shin and run away." David laughs, coaxing a laugh out of me as well. "There could never be a force more powerful than my love for you." David gives me a hug, which I return, and find the tension melting away. His sappiness can almost be too much at times, but I just go with it.

We make our way to the barn after taking turns changing clothes in the shelter. As we step out of the crisp, cold air and inside the stuffy barn, we see almost the whole camp gathered in here, sitting at the tables, facing the fireplace. In front of the fireplace is my mother, strapped down to a chair with a gag in her mouth and a blindfold over her eyes. Matthias and Eli are standing on opposite sides of her, facing everyone.

"This USB stick showed us that the Haven is a real place, that it's the remainder of the US as it once was," Eli says.

"How do you know it's not a trap to weed out enemies of the Coalition? Anyone who dares to leave and try to make it to the Haven gets killed in the process!" Caroline shouts.

David grabs my hand and leads me to an open table where Tim and Denis sit pouring over notes instead of listening.

"Morning," David says and gets a halfhearted wave as Denis shows Tim something.

I turn my attention back to my mom.

"It just so happens that Eli still has a batch of the rectitude wine I once gave him. How about we get some straight answers?" Matthias asks, and a cheer rises from the tables.

I shudder at the memory of that stuff. It was thick like drinking syrup and made me want to divulge all my secrets. I watch as my mom's muscles stiffen up. This is probably one of the worst tortures they could have come up with.

Matthias removes her blindfold and takes the gag out of her mouth.

"I'm willing to talk if you just give me the chance. You don't have to do this." Frustration drips from her words as she looks at the goblet in Matthias's hand.

"Oh, but I do. After what ya've done, this is the only way I know you'll be tellin' the truth."

I expect her to yell, or swear at him, but she holds still as he raises the goblet up to her lips. Everyone in the room is silent as he nods to indicate that she drank some. I watch her back straighten just as mine did when the wine kicked in.

"We'll start small and work our way up. What's your name?" Matthias asks.

"Janice Eve Sloane."

"Do you work for the Coalition?"

"I am employed by President Turk, but I don't work for him."

Matthias pauses waiting for her to say more, but she stops there.

"Who do you work for?"

"Myself."

Even with the rectitude wine, she's still as cryptic as ever with her "truths."

"Do you help spies from the Haven?"

"Yes."

"How?"

"I give them Turk's plans, help them gather any information they're looking for, and then help them leave the city."

Matthias paces next to her, stroking his beard as he thinks of his next question.

"Did you lie to me about the weapons cache because you knew it was the only way to get me to leave?"

"Yes."

"Did you poison me so I couldn't go?" Henry shouts from a nearby table.

She scans the crowd of faces until she spots Henry, and that sparkle of love shows up again. "Yes. I'm sorry about that, Henry. I knew it was dangerous, and I didn't want you to get hurt," she says, opening up more for Henry.

"But you were okay with anyone else dying?" Matthias growls.

"Yes."

"How many people have you killed?" I ask in disgust.

She looks at the ground as though she's calculating it. "Too many to count."

Bile rises in my throat at her answer.

"How do we get to the Haven?" Matthias asks.

"That I don't know. I only help the spies get safely out of the city. They have their own means of transportation that I have nothing to do with."

Matthias's shoulders slump at this. It would be nice to have a plan of action to get ourselves to the Haven.

Matthias continues stroking his beard as he paces. He leans down and whispers a question so nobody else can hear, but I can, and I'm sure David can too. "Did you ever love me?"

I'm taken aback by his question. I wasn't expecting him to ask something like that.

"Yes, and I still do. It's just different now."

Matthias turns and walks toward the fireplace for a moment.

I think of a question and head over to them so I don't have to shout. "Did the vitamins you give me dampen my Rare abilities?"

"Yes."

"Why did you give them to me?"

"It is Coalition orders to report Rare abilities, and if they aren't useful to Turk, then they are put on the vitamins. Most people don't know what they are actually for."

"Did my mom know what the vitamins did?" David asks, his face like stone.

"Yes," Mom starts to answer, but I interrupt as my anger bubbles over.

"Is that why I was sick a lot?"

"Sickness was a side effect, yes."

"Why didn't you come searching for me?" Henry asks, now interrupting my line of questions.

"I couldn't leave, or I would have destroyed all the progress I had made earning Turk's trust."

"So, your work was more important than me?" Henry asks, stiffly.

"Yes," she answers matter-of-factly. "I knew that Matthias would take good care of you, but I never stopped loving you. I just needed to keep up what I had started."

"What is Turk working on now?" Matthias asks.

"He's finishing up the mandatory chip implant project, and then he's beginning to work with scientists to screen babies to know whether they will be born Rare or not."

"What for? To kill them before they even get a chance at life?" I ask.

"No. I believe he's searching for a specific Rare ability, but no one knows which one. He has become paranoid and suspicious—almost desperate in his search."

"What does he want with Rares, anyway?" I ask. "I thought his plan was to keep us weak."

"The majority, yes. But he has a few Rares in his pocket with specific skillsets that benefit him."

"Rares are not tools for Turk or anyone else to use. They are gifts given to us, and we have every right to use them how we please!" I hear some whoops of agreement come from behind me.

"I never said otherwise."

"But you kept me weak with the vitamins!"

"That's because your heightened senses would have given you away. People are told to report any signs of Rare abilities. So, I did the only logical thing that would keep you safe. I figured illness was easier to deal with than servitude. I just wished I could have figured out a way to stop you from trying to kill yourself."

"Perhaps, after realizing shame and guilt trips didn't work, you could have tried a different approach," I bite back.

"I never claimed to be a good mom. Just a protective one." She rubs her forehead with a grimace.

It looks like the wine is wearing off. I remember the headache well.

"How could you go along with all of this? How could you know what was happening to Rares and keep working for Turk?" I blurt, losing my cool.

"I'm done answering questions now," Mom says curtly. "My head feels like it's about to split, and I'm exhausted. Can I have a place to sleep, Matthias?"

"She can have my cot," I offer, waving her off. I want her out of my sight as fast as they can move her.

3

While my mom is taken to my shelter to get some sleep, David and I sneak off to get away from all the people.

"If my mom knew what those vitamins did, why would she continue distributing them? They watched me have seizures and still kept me on them!" David kicks a stone toward the fence.

I grab him and hold him tightly, my heart aching with him. "I'm sorry, David. My guess is they were doing what they were told by the people in charge."

He shakes his head in anger.

I rub his back, searching for the right words to say to him. I'm not good at this like he is.

"Hey. All that is in the past. Look at you now. Strong, healthy, ridiculously attractive." I get a breathy laugh out of him.

"My bad health did play a part in my desire to leave the city, which was one of the best decisions I've ever made." He strokes the back of my head as I bury my nose into his neck and sniff.

"I believe your parents love you, David. I think people just get mixed up on politics and worry about following rules. Good thing you're a rule-breaker, or we never would have made it out here. You rebel," I say with a wink.

David kisses my head again, then sighs.

"Do you miss them?" I ask.

"Of course, I miss them. Not a day goes by that I don't think about them. Especially my mom's cooking."

"I think about your mom's cooking too." I laugh.

We're silent for a moment as we hold each other's hands tightly, both lost in our own thoughts.

Finally, David breaks the silence, "Want to head over to Denis's shelter and see what he can make of the USB stick?"

"Sure. We'll have to get it from Uncle Eli." I say, then give a fake shudder.

"What?"

"It's so weird calling him Uncle when I barely know him."

Eli allows us to use the computer and USB stick, claiming he's gotten about as far as he's going to get with it. He warns us the battery is less than fifty percent and we should try to conserve as much as we can.

We knock on Denis's door and are greeted with, "Hold on a minute!"

David raises his eyebrows at me as we hear some clattering and muffled grunts coming from inside.

Finally, Denis opens the door, slightly out of breath.

I peek inside and see Tim sitting in a chair next to the woodstove, looking down at a sheet of paper.

"What are you guys up to?" David asks.

"A project." Denis steps out of the way for us to enter.

"What is it?" I ask curiously.

"Can I tell them?" Tim asks.

Denis looks us up and down, as though he can tell whether we're trustworthy just from our appearance. "Fine, but it doesn't leave this cabin," he says, taking a seat on the edge of his cot.

"Denis and I are working on weaponizing my prosthetic. I'll have a hidden knife here," he says, pointing at the top of the forearm, "and we're still working out the kinks, but I'm going to have a gun that shoots when I straighten out my arm fully."

"Are you sure it's safe?" I ask.

"Of course. We're putting in a safety that he'll have to turn off with his good hand before he can use it," Denis responds.

"I mean accuracy. Will he really be able to shoot straight if he's moving his arm around to make it work?"

"He'll have to practice, but I think it'll be fine."

"Where are you getting all the parts for things like this?" I ask.

"Eli has a junk shed. It's full of spare parts and things that could be useful."

"Did you get it from Eli's drug trades?" David asks with a slight edge to his voice.

"No. We scavenged most of it from nearby houses. You'd never believe the kind of stuff you can find. Want to go check the shed out?"

David and I both nod. Tim joins us, and we all follow behind Denis. As we're walking, I look over at Tim and see him smiling, which makes me smile. Just then Tim notices me looking at him.

"What? Do I have something on my face?"

"Yeah. A smile. It looks good on you." I bump my shoulder into his.

"It feels good to smile again. Denis has given me hope," he says, raising his prosthetic arm, "and I feel like I fit in here. I like working as his apprentice. I've learned so much."

"That's great, Tim. I'm happy for you." I'm a little jealous that he seems to have found some peace, but I won't allow myself to dwell on it, and I'm definitely not going to say anything negative to Tim. He deserves to be happy.

Denis leads us to a building a little cruder than the rest. There are gaps between the weathered boards, the roof has curling shingles, the door is almost falling off its hinges, and there's a dirt floor. I walk in and see there are shelving units jammed-packed with miscellaneous stuff. I immediately start looking around, captivated by all of it. There are some things I recognize, like toasters and microwaves, and other things I don't.

"Why do you have so many electronics when this camp doesn't have electricity?" I pick up a Blu-ray player to examine it.

"For the parts. There might be a screw or a spring that we need for a project, and we can salvage them from here."

David and I head down different aisles, taking it all in. I spot something interesting on a bottom shelf and crouch down to see it better. It's a rectangular electronic device with six knobs, seven buttons, and a little blank spot I assume would display something if it were turned on. I take it over to Denis.

"What's this?"

"Oh, that's a ham radio."

"A what?"

"A ham radio. It's a radio that people used to use to communicate with one another. They could be used for emergency purposes, or just to talk with someone on the other side of the planet."

I click the power button, and the little screen lights up with some green numbers, and it makes static sounds. "It's broken."

"No, you need to hook it up to an antenna and then tune it to a working channel, but it won't work because the cities' towers suppress radio waves."

"Do you have an antenna?" I'm curious to try it anyway.

"I putzed around with making one for it—you know, just in case the Coalition ever collapsed and we could use the radio again—but it was unsuccessful. You're welcome to give it a try if you want."

"Sure."

He leads me to the back wall, where he has a little table set up with some wire that's fished through the wall to the outside. He takes the radio from me and hooks it up.

"This ham radio doesn't have a microphone, so you wouldn't be able to talk to anyone anyway, just listen." Denis hands the radio back and then gets called over by Tim.

I start turning the dial and watch the numbers change. For some reason, a memory hits me as I'm looking at the numbers and letters being displayed.

The crazy guy from the city.

What if he wasn't crazy? What if he was talking about a radio station? What were those numbers he said again?

"What'd you find, Liv?" David asks.

I look up and see he's holding a boom box complete with a cassette player. He has it up on his shoulder like we once saw someone do in an old 1980s movie, and he starts bopping his head around as though he's jamming out. We both laugh.

"Denis said it's a ham radio. There was this guy in the city who told me voices speak to him and told me to remember some weird letter and number combination. I thought he was nuts, but looking at this, I think he might have been giving me a ham radio station, or whatever they're called. I just can't remember the combination."

"QRP 14.060," I hear a voice say behind me.

I spin around, startled. "Cindy? What are you doing in here?"

She sneers. "I can do whatever I want."

"Sorry. I just meant, what are you up to?"

"I like to come in here and look around. I feel like I'm prying into people's personal lives. It's fun." She smiles wickedly.

"How'd you know what the crazy guy said?" I ask, ignoring her personal brand of creepiness.

"He wasn't crazy, for your information, and I heard him." She taps her head with her finger.

Of course, *she* wouldn't think he's crazy. Her standards are pretty low.

"How come you didn't say anything?"

"Tell you I heard a voice in my head? Would you like me to report to you every time I hear a voice? I hear one now." She covers her mouth and giggles. "Would you like to know what they said? It wasn't very nice."

"No. Spare me." I roll my eyes. I turn the knob until it displays QRP 14.060, holding my breath in anticipation.

Static.

I sigh, but as I'm about to turn it off, I think I hear something. I turn the volume up.

"*...are here for you. If there are any Rares hearing this, we want to remind you that the US is still here, and we care about you.*"

Tim and Denis drop what they're doing and come over quickly to hear what's being said.

"*We've received word that Turk's next project will be the screening of babies for a specific ability. Yes, you heard that right. Turk is looking for something, folks. Let's hope he doesn't find it. In other news, Canada's Prime Minister declared March to be Rare Awareness month in hopes that...*"

The radio cuts out and goes back to static.

"Boring," Cindy declares, then shuffles her way back out of the shed.

"What happened? I thought you said it wouldn't work?" I mess with the dial to get it going again. Hearing someone talk positively about Rares sparked hope. I want to hear more.

"It's possible some radio waves got through because of the damage Joselyn caused at the tower in the city. Perhaps they have things shut down for maintenance." Denis scratches his head as he thinks.

"Well, that verifies what was on the USB stick. The Haven is a real place," David says excitedly.

"The laptop," I say, snapping my fingers. "Eli let us borrow it so you could take a look at the files on the USB stick. Do you know anything about encrypted files, Denis?"

"I can take a look."

14

"Sorry. I just don't have the skill set to decrypt them, and I don't want to run the battery out trying." Denis hands the laptop to me.

My shoulders slump in disappointment.

"Thanks for giving it a shot," David says. "We'll let you get back to your project."

Denis nods, his curly hair bouncing slightly as he does. He turns his attention to the schematics laid out on his cot. Tim gives us a bright smile as we turn and head out the door.

"Where should we go now?" David holds his arm out for me.

I thread my arm through his, and we start walking without a specific direction. "Should we go tell Matthias we can confirm the Haven is real?"

"Sure."

As we walk past our shelter, we spot Frederick standing guard with a gun.

"Think he's protecting my mom, or protecting everyone else from her?" I whisper.

"Maybe a combination of both."

Frederick gives us a wave, which we return as we continue to the barn.

The late morning sun peeks through the clouds, providing moments of glowing warmth. It's a nice reprieve from the constant frigid air. I'm grateful to have shelters and wood burning stoves to keep us warm now that winter is officially here.

David drops my arm so he can hurry to the barn door to open it for me. "M'lady."

"Thank you, but shouldn't I be opening doors for you since you only have one good arm?" I ask with a smirk.

"What kind of gentleman would I be if I made delicate hands such as yours do manual work like opening doors?"

I playfully punch him in the shoulder, and we both enter the barn, laughing.

Matthias and Eli are camped out by the fireplace again. Their appearances are in stark contrast to each other. Eli is wearing a light blue button-down shirt with a dark blue sweater vest and a pair of clean jeans. Matthias has on an oversized gray T-shirt covered with a ripped-up red flannel and dirt-crusted sweatpants. His hair is greasy and pulled back into a messy ponytail, which accentuates his scruffy overgrown beard. If I didn't know them, I would easily choose Eli as a leader over Matthias by appearance alone.

"Hey, guys," I say, announcing our presence.

"What do ya two want?" Matthias asks with a touch of annoyance in his voice. For some reason, it rubs me the wrong way, and I have to bite my tongue to not throw attitude back at him.

"We just got confirmation the USB stick wasn't a hoax," David says.

"How?"

"We found a ham radio and were able to pick up a channel where someone from the Haven was broadcasting that they are there and care about Rares."

"Good. Well, that settles that part of this debate," Matthias says resolutely. "It wouldn't be a 'fruitless endeavor,' because now we know the files weren't fake."

"All right, but we still have no idea how to get you across the DMZ. From what I know, the radioactivity is still strong over there since we're told the dust blowing over here is radioactive."

"Isn't that what your supply of radiation medicine is for?"

"Yes, but who said I was going to give you my stock of it?"

David and I stand by awkwardly, listening to them bicker. I feel like we're prying into a personal conversation, but they never told us to leave. I'd like to hear what their ideas are for getting to the Haven.

"If ya share it, you'll get us out of there faster."

Eli strokes his well-groomed beard, thinking about what Matthias said. "True, but now we're back to how do we get you to the Haven."

"If only ya had access to a plane or helicopter," Matthias grunts.

Eli laughs. "My product will get you high, but not like that. You know as well as I do that there are no planes or helicopters allowed in the city anymore. Only trains."

"And ships," Matthias adds.

Eli nods.

"Do you think there are any trains connecting the Haven to the Coalition?" David asks.

"I'm going to take a wild guess and say no." Matthias sulks dismissively.

David's cheeks redden for a brief moment, but he seems to get over it quickly. Everyone is silent as we think.

"Could we find a car and drive there?" I suggest.

"A car?" Matthias scoffs. "For driving fifty or more people?"

This time, my cheeks blush while anger bubbles up inside my stomach. Matthias is being a real jerk today.

"Fine. A bus, then," I snap.

Matthias huffs in exasperation, and is about to say something, when Eli interrupts, "I know someone who has a bus, but we had a bit of a falling out, so he probably won't let us have it."

"You could give it a try," I suggest.

Eli looks at me skeptically.

"What was the falling out about?" Matthias asks.

Eli clears his throat in embarrassment. "He caught me in bed with his wife."

"Ya dog." Matthias shakes his head in disgust.

"I didn't know she was married. And besides, it turns out they had been separated for a while."

"Separated ain't divorced." Matthias angrily points his finger at Eli.

I stare at Matthias in shocked disbelief. He can kill people without giving it a second thought, but he's angry at Eli for causing a woman to cheat on her husband? His priorities are completely messed up.

"I didn't ask for your approval, Brother." Eli scowls. "It was a long time ago."

"If it was a long time ago, do you think they guy's over it now?" David interjects.

"I don't know. I might be able to smooth things over if I bring a peace offering."

Matthias rolls his eyes and shakes his head.

"Okay, but how would you get a bus out of the city? I think the guards would notice," I say.

"He doesn't live in the city. He's got his own camp on the northern outskirts. We were doing trades for a while before the falling out. None of us have been there since. It's possible they aren't even there anymore."

"It's worth a shot though, right?" David asks.

Eli looks at his brother, then back at David. "Yeah, it's worth a shot." Eli stands to stretch. "I'm going to need to collect some supplies before I take off."

"Do you need someone to go with you?" David asks. "If the guy's still pissed, you might need back up."

"You offering?" Eli asks with a raised eyebrow.

"Um," David says, looking uncomfortable. "I don't think I would do much good with just one arm."

"How about you, Brother?" Eli asks with a hint of amusement.

"I'd rather skinny dip in piranha-infested waters," he says. His response pulls a chuckle out of Eli.

"I'll go ask around to see if anyone wants to come with me," Eli says as he heads out of the barn.

As Eli closes the barn door, I ask Matthias, "Why are you so mean to Uncle Eli? He's doing us a huge favor by letting us be here and sharing all his stuff."

Matthias looks at me deadpan. "Because every day we stay here is an assault to my conscience. I swore off my brother long ago because of the way he does business. The sooner we can get out of here, the better."

"C'mon! Aren't you overreacting a bit? He grows and trades marijuana. It's not like he's murdering people," I finish with a mumble.

He lifts his head and glares at me with his good eye. "Murder? I kill people who're a threat to me or my family," Matthias growls. "Why don't ya ask Eli how he got into his line of business in the first place." He stands up abruptly, knocking over his chair in the process, and storms out.

"Am I missing something?" I ask David.

"I have no idea, but I think it would be best if we drop it. It seems like a sore subject."

5

Eli announces his plans at suppertime. Matthias is nowhere to be seen, which makes me feel guilty. "If anyone's willing to join in with some weapons to help protect me, I'd greatly appreciate it."

A couple of Eli's men raise their hands.

"Thank you. Gather up your supplies, we leave in the morning."

Eli's camp disperses, while everyone from our camp sticks around for the meeting Alexandrine called.

Alexandrine looks around. "Anyone seen Matthias?"

"He's mad at me for questioning his methods," I say.

"What methods would those be?" Alexandrine asks.

"Murdering people. Sorry, I mean, 'killing threats.' He's angry with Eli for doing something that I don't see as being as bad as killing."

"Typical," Alexandrine says.

"What?"

"Flapping your gums at Matthias, throwing accusations around, when you don't even know the whole story."

"It's hard to know the whole story when nobody's willing to talk about anything," I fume.

"Fine. I'll give you a quick history lesson. This camp wasn't Eli's to begin with. He weaseled his way in, getting people to like him, then led a mutiny. The original leader was lynched, and anyone who opposed Eli was taken out as well. Not by Eli, of course. He had other people do his dirty work for him. Then he started growing marijuana, figuring out a way to lace it so it would have a more potent effect and be addictive."

My face grows hot as what she says sinks in.

"So I suggest you stop accusing Matthias of wrongful behavior when Eli's whole sordid operation is far from innocent."

"I'm sorry. I didn't know," I say angrily. "I guess I didn't realize the men in my family were so evil."

"Leave me out of it," I hear Henry say from a couple of tables away.

"Did you know about all this?" I call out to Henry.

"Bits and pieces. Pop didn't talk about Eli much. I only met him a couple of times in my life and never really cared enough to get to know him," Henry says without emotion.

"Well, this will make leaving for the Haven easier," I say.

"Speak for yourself," Stan says. "We never had it as good as this with Matthias in charge. I think I'd rather stay here than go on some wild goose chase."

I look around, and there are other people nodding their heads.

"It's not a wild goose chase," I say, getting defensive. "We heard someone from the Haven talking on the radio."

"Doesn't matter. I'm tired of being on the run. I'm ready to settle somewhere, and this seems like a good place to do just that."

"But you just found out that Eli is dirty." I can barely hide my disgust.

"How he got this camp doesn't concern me. That's in the past. I'm more concerned about how he runs it, and from what I can tell, he's a good leader."

My jaw drops slightly. I can't believe what I'm hearing.

"All right. Since almost everyone is here," Alexandrine says, looking around, "let's take a vote. Who wants to go with Matthias to the Haven?"

I raise my hand and look to see who else has their hand up. David and Cass have theirs raised, but Tim, who's sitting by Cass, doesn't. Maybe he doesn't want to participate in the vote. I turn back to Alexandrine and watch as she finishes counting.

"Okay, hands down. Now, who wants to stay here?"

I'm surprised at how many hands are in the air. I'm even more surprised when Tim slowly raises his.

Cass looks at him, horrified. "Tim?" she squeaks.

I turn my attention to them and what they're saying.

"I'm sorry, Sis. I belong here. I've been learning so much from Denis. I don't want to stop now."

"Matthias saved us. How could you turn your back on him?"

"I'm not turning my back on anyone. If Denis decides to go, then I'll go too, but I want to stay with him and keep learning."

Cass starts to cry angry tears. "I'm your sister. You're the only family I have left."

"I know, and I'm sorry, but I finally found somewhere I fit in."

"Well, that settles that. We've got a bunch of ship jumpers." Alexandrine turns her attention to the barn doors and says loudly, "What do you make of that, Matthias?"

My heart skips a beat. I had no idea Matthias had snuck into the barn and was listening. The scowl on Matthias's face speaks loud enough on its own.

"I guess I'm not surprised. I'll be glad to be rid of the dead weight," Matthias growls. "Y'all can leave and never darken my doorway again." He spits on the floor with finality.

There's an uncomfortable silence, and then Stan speaks up, "But that's just it. You don't *have* a doorway to darken. Even when we were in our camp, we all knew it wasn't permanent."

"Ya want something permanent, do ya? All the more reason to go to the Haven."

"I'm tired of running. If Eli is willing to let me stay, then I'm staying here." Stan crosses his arms over his chest. Other people seem to agree with Stan.

"It would be just one last trip, and then we would be free," Matthias says through gritted teeth.

"You can't guarantee that we would even make it. You have no plan on how to reach the Haven," Stan replies. "No. I'm out."

Matthias looks as though he's about to say something else but bites his lips together and leaves the barn.

"You're a bunch of heartless jerks," Henry says. "Pop has done nothing but keep you all alive, and this is the thanks he gets? You're willing to throw away your chance at freedom for some sense of comfort?"

Stan can't seem to meet Henry's eye line. In fact, everyone seems to be looking anywhere other than at Henry.

"Well, this has been fun and all," Cindy chimes in, "but I'm ready to hit the sack. Why did you call this meeting in the first place, Lexi?"

Alexandrine glares at Cindy for calling her Lexi. "I just wanted to see if anyone was interested in starting back up our combat training sessions. Nobody at this camp seems to view combat training as important, but I still think it is and was willing to start it up again." She looks at Stan. "But under the recent turn of events, I think I'll wait."

That's the cue that we're finished here. I grab onto David's arm, and we head back outside. As I zip up the coat I got from Eli, I suddenly find myself hating everything he's offered us. I want to rip the jacket off and toss it in a fire, but I can't deny I need it. It's too cold to make a stand right now.

We walk past Matthias's shelter, and I hear muffled voices. I stop walking and almost knock David down.

"What?" David asks.

"Shh!" I pull him to the back of the shelter, tiptoeing in the snow to make the least amount of crunching as possible.

"What are we doing?" David whispers.

I crouch down behind the shelter under a window and listen. My breath catches when I hear my mom's voice.

"It doesn't matter how good you are to people, there will always be someone who's dissatisfied. You can't please them all," Mom says.

"But how have I been so blind? I've been offering them the hope of freedom, thinking that was enough." Matthias sighs.

"It is enough. At least you've weeded out the people who don't really care about your goal. Consider it a blessing. Less baggage."

"I guess you're right. I still have some people who're willing to follow me."

I'm so shocked at the civil conversation I'm hearing, I've forgotten to breathe. My head starts spinning, and I grab ahold of David's arm for balance.

"Ya sure you're okay with Olivia coming with me? I don't want ya thinkin' I took another one of your kids away from ya."

364

"She's better off with you. My line of work is too dangerous, and if you do manage to make it to the Haven, she'll be safer there."

"When are ya planning on headin' back to the wretched city?"

"I have to give my leg a couple more days to heal, thanks to you," she says, accusingly. "I can't believe you shot me."

"Do ya really want to go there?" Matthias growls.

I start to worry they're going to fight and there's nobody there to stop them, but my mom laughs instead.

"Nah. I suppose I deserved it." She pauses. "Take care of yourself, Matthias. Our kids too."

My leg starts cramping from crouching for so long in the cold. I straighten as pain shoots through my calf. Before I remember I'm in front of a window, I catch a glimpse inside and gasp.

My parents are standing in the middle of the room, kissing.

6

David pulls me away from the window before I get caught and drags me to our shelter. My heart is fluttering in my chest.

"Did you see that?" A mixture of excitement, confusion, and disgust courses through me. Once we're inside, I pull my jacket off and toss it into the corner.

"Yes, but we shouldn't have. You need to forget what you just saw," David says seriously.

"Why? There's a chance my parents could get back together." Hope pushes its way to the top of my emotions.

"No, Liv. Your parents are not going to get back together. It was just a kiss. A moment of passion in a moment of weakness."

"You don't know that."

"Do you really want your parents to get back together under these circumstances? He just shot her in the leg, then forced her to drink rectitude wine to divulge her secrets." He huffs when I give him a shrug. "She tried to blow him up—well, not him specifically, but she blew up some of our camp members to try to manipulate Matthias into leaving the city. This would not be a healthy relationship. And from the sounds of it, it never was."

"What are you, the relationship whisperer?"

David throws his hands up and scrunches his eyebrows at me.

"Okay, okay. I get it. You're right. I was just caught up in the moment. I wish I had a big happy family, but I never will." I flop onto the cot and throw my arms over my face, exhausted from the emotional rollercoaster.

"That's not true. We can change that." David kneels on the floor next to the cot. He gently pulls my arms off my face. "Someday, we could get married and start our own family."

I look him in the eye and see so much love pouring out, it calms me. "I'm not sure I could ever be a good mom, David." The weight of this conversation is overwhelming since I'm only sixteen.

"You have a good start since you know what *not* to do. Just love our children how you always wanted to be loved."

"You're assuming we're going to get married someday."

David smirks. "Of course you're going to marry me."

"Oh? And what makes you say that?"

"I got you to be my girlfriend, didn't I?"

I laugh. "Yeah, after four years of begging me."

"See? I wore you down. I still have time to trick you into marrying me."

"Trick me? How?" I ask, amused.

"All I have to do is wink and flex my bicep, and you'll be all over me," he says, laughing.

"Won't work. I'm not that superficial."

"Watch this." David winks and then flexes his bicep and as he does, I see he's holding something in the hand of his injured arm.

It's a ring box opened to reveal a small silver ring with a round green jewel.

I try to speak, but shock has closed my throat. I swallow hard to clear it. My heart is hammering in my chest as I look into David's eyes. "David, I—" I start to say, shaking my head.

"This isn't an engagement ring," he says calmly. "This is a promise ring. I love you, Liv, and I promise that someday I'm going to ask you to marry me. Someday when you're ready." He tucks my hair behind my ear.

The shock wears off, and I nearly knock him over as I lunge for a hug, tears of joy and fear seeping out of my eyes.

"See? I told you you'd be all over me."

We both laugh, and he kisses me deeply. I sit back down on the cot, wiping the tears off my face. He pulls the delicate ring out of the box and slides it onto my finger.

"It's a bit big," I say, sliding it on and off easily.

"We'll fix it."

"Where did you get this?"

"I found it in Eli's shed. I'm not even sure it's real. I would love to give you real jewelry. Maybe someday." A wistful look fills David's eyes.

"No, it's perfect." I look at the small jewel as it reflects the shelter's dim light.

He kisses my forehead and then has a seat next to me on the cot, wrapping his good arm around my shoulders.

I wish I could freeze this moment, stop time and live inside this happiness forever, but my bubble bursts when Cass comes crashing through the door.

"I've had it! I can't talk to him," she yells.

"Who? Tim?" I ask, stupidly.

"Yes! His mind is set on staying with this Denis guy. He doesn't even know him that well." I can almost feel the anger radiating off her. "Why would he abandon me for him?"

"I don't think it has anything to do with you, Cass. I think it's just that Denis has given him hope, and he's been in short supply of that lately, so it makes him feel good. It feels good to have a purpose." David grabs my hand and squeezes.

"I'm his sister. His family." Tears roll down Cass's face.

I pull out of David's grasp reluctantly and head over to Cass's cot. "Well, the alternative is you could stay here with him."

"I couldn't do that. Not when we know the truth." She sniffs back another sob. "David, could you please talk to him? You are so good with words."

David gives me a pleading look while Cass rubs the tears away.

I just shrug.

"Uh, sure. I can try."

Cass breathes a heavy sigh of relief as though he's already convinced Tim to go. Let's hope he's able to, or Cass may never forgive him.

17

A week has gone by, and there's still no sign of Eli. Matthias is on edge, waiting for word on whether we have a way out or not. He's been calling meetings to discuss other options, but nobody has any new ideas.

My mom left a few days ago to head back to the city. Like David told me, that kiss between Matthias and her was a one time thing. The very next day, they fell right back into their old ways of snarky comments and shared disdain for one another. I had hoped to witness a heartfelt goodbye, but Matthias disappeared as she was saying her goodbyes to Henry and me.

David tried to talk to Tim about leaving, but Tim just seemed so happy, David didn't have the heart to push the matter. Cass is in a surly mood and won't listen to reason. I tried to explain to her we're her family too, but it didn't help.

The camp has been doing a good job at keeping things running smoothly during Eli's absence. Today is an exceptionally cold and snowy day. Almost everyone decides to stay inside their shelters to wait it out, but a few camp members brought peanut butter sandwiches around to everyone for lunch.

I kind of wish Cass didn't share a shelter with us. Her bad mood is killing what could be a romantic day for David and me. We try to make the most of it anyway, wrapped up in a blanket together, cuddling on a cot with our backs against the wall. The heat of the stove keeps the chill out of the air for the most part, but when the wind picks up, the icy breeze creeps in through the cracks. I occasionally lean into David's neck, warming my cold nose on his skin. He takes those moments to sneak kisses when we think Cass isn't looking.

"What do you think the Haven will be like?" I ask, breaking the silence in the room.

Cass looks up at me from her notebook with bloodshot eyes. "I have no clue. Hopefully, it'll be better than this place. Then Tim'll be sorry."

"Well, technically, he won't know what he's missing," David says, and I elbow him in the stomach. He gets the hint and adds, "But you'll know, and that'll be satisfying."

"I hope they have indoor plumbing," I throw in with a sigh.

"What's your obsession with indoor plumbing?" David asks with a laugh. "You seem to think about it a lot."

"Well, if you had to sit down every time you went to the bathroom, I think you would miss it too. I just went after breakfast, and I almost froze to the seat," I say, only slightly exaggerating. "Have you ever gotten to use a flush toilet, Cass?"

She stops to think for a moment. "I think I did when I was little, before I went with Matthias, but I don't remember them. I don't remember much about my life before Matthias. All I have left of it is Tim." Her chin quivers, and she goes back to writing in her notebook.

David and I exchange exasperated looks.

"Well, I hope the Haven is full of Rare people and soldiers that will lead us into victory against the Coalition. Maybe then we can be free," David says.

"So, you think we should go to war?" I try to hide the tension in my voice.

"I think it's the only way to end the Coalition."

"I disagree. I think there are other ways. More civil ways to end it." I pull away from him, rubbing my arms reflexively.

"I think you two are getting ahead of yourselves. How about we find out what kind of people are in the Haven before we decide to team up with them," Cass throws in.

"She's right." David kisses the top of my head.

We sit in peaceful silence, only getting up once in a while to throw another log in the stove. I would normally be bored out of my mind, sitting around not doing anything, but being with David is pleasant. The secret kisses help pass the time too.

We are pulled from our stupor when we hear children giggling outside.

"Should we go see what's going on?" David asks.

I nod, and we bundle up in our borrowed winter gear before heading outside. The snow has stopped falling, and a quiet calm fills the air. We hear the children giggle again as they come racing around one of the shelters. Noah throws a snowball at one of the twins but misses and hits David's face instead. He stops short, eyes fill with trepidation, worried that David is going to be mad.

David keeps his face expressionless as he wipes the snow off his skin. "You're gonna pay for that!" He bends over, scooping up a handful of snow. His wrist must be feeling better because he's not wincing as he works the snow into a ball. He throws it at Noah's stomach.

Pandemonium breaks out as all the children start throwing snowballs at David and me.

I let out a playful scream as one hits the back of my head. A chunk of it falls into my coat and down my shirt, leaving a trail of icy water as it melts down my back. I start packing snowballs quickly so I can get some shots in, being careful to not hit the kids in the face.

I laugh as I dodge their assault, rolling in the snow for dramatic flair. Some of the adults decide to join in on the fun, hiding behind shelters waiting for the little ones to run past before biffing them with snow. The laughter echoing all around is intoxicating, leaving my heart feeling light and happy.

My hands grow numb as I pack snowball after snowball, throwing them at whomever I see. I hit David with one, and he comes running at me, playfully tackling me into the snow. I get caught up in the moment and kiss him passionately. I hear one of the kids yell, "Ew!" as they run past us.

My cheeks grow warm momentarily, as I push myself back up off the ground. I reach down to pull David up, but he starts sweeping his legs and his good arm back and forth in the snow, making a snow angel.

I laugh, flop down next to him, and do the same. After a while, I stop moving and stare up at the gray sky, listening to the commotion going on around us. I don't know what the future holds, but for the first time in a long time, I feel at peace.

David's hand comes into view, and I grab onto it. He pulls me up, allowing me to stand without destroying my snow angel. I turn around and chuckle a little at David's angel only having one wing.

"So, did it hurt?" David asks.

"What? Making a snow angel?" I ask, confused.

"No. Did it hurt when you fell from heaven?" he asks with a flirty smirk.

I shake my head at him and laugh.

"You two are adorable." Cass walks toward us.

"Um, thanks." I study her attempted smile. Her eyes are still sad. "Want to make a snow angel?"

She fidgets with her coat sleeve. "Nah. I'm headed off to talk to Tim."

"I don't know if that's such a good idea, Cass. Maybe give yourself a little time to sort out your emotions," I suggest.

"No. It's okay. I figure I should patch things over with him before we leave."

"That's very mature of you." Something seems off. She was distraught only a half an hour ago, and now she's suddenly ready to patch things over with him. I have a bad feeling, but I'm not sure why.

David tugs on my arm to lead me back to the shelter, but I plant my feet as I watch her walking away. She has her right hand clasped around something, and as she makes it to Denis's cabin, I see the glint of metal.

She has a knife tucked in her sleeve.

8

I race after her as she opens the door to the shelter. I ignore David calling me, asking what's wrong. I have a feeling Cass is about to do something terrible, and I need to stop her. I put on as much speed as I can and catch her right before she's over the threshold.

"Cass, stop!" I grab whatever I can get ahold of, tugging her coat hood to pull her backward out of the shelter, slamming the door behind us.

"What are you doing?" Cass turns to glare at me.

"What's in your sleeve?" I ask in hushed tones.

I hear Tim and Denis inside the shelter asking each other what that was all about.

Her cheeks turn bright red, and she looks down at the ground. "None of your business," she mumbles.

"It is my business when my friend is about to make a big mistake," I whisper-yell. "Come back to the shelter, and let's talk about this."

Cass hangs her head and follows behind me. I see David watching us with concern, so I hold up my hand and give a little head shake to tell him to leave us be for a moment.

Once we're back in the shelter, I sit her on her cot and kneel to be eye level. "What were you planning on doing, Cass?"

She lets out a big sigh and pulls a hunting knife out of her coat sleeve.

"Were you going to try to kill them?" I ask as calmly as I can, even though my heart is pounding.

"No. I was going to tell him that if he doesn't come with me, I would start cutting my arms like he was doing to himself. And to show that I was serious, I was going to pull out the knife and do it in front of him."

"Cass! This isn't like you. You hated that Tim was doing that to himself, and now you were going to do it? What's gotten into you?"

"I don't know. I'm just desperate! I couldn't think of any other way!" She hides her face in her hands.

I wrap my arms around her and hold her tight as she sobs. As soon as I can get her to settle down, I'm going to have to talk to Tim about this.

"Cass, it's going to be all right." How do I deal with this?

She continues to cry into her hands as I awkwardly hold onto her, patting her back. Minutes tick by, and I struggle to know the right thing to do.

"Hey, guess what?" I say, thinking of something that might take her mind off Tim for a moment.

"What?" Her voice is muffled in her hands.

"David gave me a promise ring."

She uncovers her face, sniffling.

I hold my hand out for her to look at the ring, and she smiles a little.

"A promise ring?" She takes my fingers in her hands so she can see the ring closer.

"He promised that he's going to ask me to marry him someday. When I'm ready." I smile down at the green jewel.

"What? In another five years?" She says with a little laugh, wiping a stray tear from her cheek.

"Har. Har," I say. "There's no point in getting engaged when I'm only sixteen—well, almost seventeen. We can't get married yet anyway."

"You could if Matthias gave you permission." Cass lets go of my hand and readjusts herself on the cot.

"Really? And how do you know that?"

"It was in a book I once borrowed from Alexandrine. A book about Coalition custody laws and parental rights."

"That sounds exciting," I say sarcastically.

"I was looking for an answer to a question that popped up in my mind once about whether Matthias could be considered my adopted father after taking care of me for so long. Turns out, he can't." She sighs and looks down at the floor as she grinds the toe of her shoe in the dirt.

"You wanted Matthias to be your dad? Having a family must be very important to you."

"It is. Family is the *most* important thing."

"That seems like a strange book for Alexandrine to keep around."

"Not really. I'm sure she was trying to figure out how to get Charlotte back. I'm glad that she finally did."

"Even though she might have killed people to do it?" I shiver as I remember the blood on the knife when she got back to camp with Charlotte.

"Yeah, that part wasn't good, but if I were locked up in a mental institute, I would want someone to do whatever they could to rescue me."

"I suppose," I concede. "Are you going to be okay here if I go talk to Tim?"

"I'll be fine." She gives me a sheepish look. "Thank you for stopping me from what I was about to do."

I nod and grab the hunting knife she was going to use, putting it back into its sheath. I stuff it into my jacket pocket, barely fitting it in.

I step outside to the fading light of day and see David pacing in front of the barn, waiting for me. When he sees me, his whole face lights up, and I can't help but smile.

"Everything okay?" He bounds over to me. His cheeks are rosy from being in the cold, and I feel a little guilty for asking him to stay outside.

"It is now. I stopped her from doing something she would regret." I leave it at that. "I'm going to go have a chat with Tim. Wanna join me?" I hold my gloved hand out for him to take.

"Of course."

We walk toward Denis's shelter, and David squeezes my hand, pulling me from my thoughts. "Are you okay, Liv?"

"Yeah. I guess I'm just not sure what to say to Tim. Or how to say it. Cass is pretty shaken up that Tim wants to stay. Family is very important to her, but I also understand Tim's point of view. He finally has hope, and I think that's something worthwhile too."

"It's not your job to convince anyone of anything. Just help them to understand each other's side of things, and then the choice is up to them."

"I suppose. I just wish there were a way to make both of them happy."

"Perhaps we need to convince Denis to leave," David says quietly as we step up to the shelter.

"That's asking a lot. He seems happy to be here." When David lets out a sigh, I realize I'm being difficult. "But we can definitely try."

We knock on the door and wait for an invitation before entering. Denis is crouched by the chair Tim is sitting in, adjusting the prosthetic on Tim's missing arm.

"Hey, guys. What's up?" Tim flinches a little when Denis shifts the prosthetic.

"We wanted to talk to you about Cass," I say.

"What about her?" Denis asks around the pen stuck in his mouth. He pulls it out and makes a mark on Tim's skin.

"She's pretty shaken up that Tim's not willing to come along to the Haven. Family is important to her."

"If family is so important to her, then she should stay here, where Tim's happy. Why should Tim have to leave if he doesn't want to?" Denis argues.

"Because she believes that freedom in the Haven is important too," David says.

"Maybe you could come along with us, Denis," I say.

"Why would I do that? I don't know you people that well, and I have everything I need here. Eli has been good to me. I don't see a reason to leave." Denis turns to take the prosthetic off Tim.

"Maybe the Haven would have laboratories full of tools and spare parts for you to work with and you could build even better stuff than you can right now," David says.

"It's not a guarantee, though, and I don't like to gamble." Denis tinkers with the prosthetic on his table.

"Tim, Cass is in a bad way right now. She was going to threaten to cut herself if you didn't agree to come." I wish I didn't have to bring Cass's moment of desperation into this conversation. I feel like I am somehow betraying her trust.

He looks up at me with concern, about to say something, but he's interrupted by Denis.

"Manipulation by threat of self-harm. Stupid, but effective," Denis quips, and Tim furrows his eyebrows at his insensitivity.

"Denis, I really enjoy working with you and all, but if my sister is this upset about me staying, then I think I should go," Tim says.

"Then go. I'm not going to stop you." Denis waves his hand dismissively.

I glance at Tim and see his shoulders drop a bit.

"Would you please consider coming along, Denis?" I ask.

"I'll consider it, but don't get your hopes up," he says. "If you don't mind, I'd like to finish up here before supper is ready. I'm on dish duty tonight."

I give Tim a sympathetic look as David ushers me out of the shelter.

"Well, that didn't go as well as I had hoped," I say.

"What do you mean? You got Tim to agree to come," David says.

"Yeah, but at the cost of his happiness."

"Liv, you can't win them all. And why are you so invested in this decision, anyway? You have your own happiness to care about."

"That sounds a little selfish." I cross my arms over my chest. "I guess I want others to be happy and not suffer from depression like me. I know how it feels, and if I can help someone else to not feel that way, then I'm going to try to do whatever it takes."

"And I'm going to do whatever it takes to save you from it as well, even if that means persuading you to stay out of other people's drama."

We're interrupted by the shouts of "dinnertime" as the camp kids go knocking at shelter doors to inform everyone the food is ready. I immediately turn to walk away from this conversation, but David grabs my arm and pulls me back to him. "We'll talk about this some more after supper. I'm not going to stop fighting for your happiness."

I let out a frustrated huff, and we make our way to the barn.

"Wanna join me for dinner, handsome?" Angel asks David. "She can join us too if she has to."

David glances at me, and I shake my head slightly. We walk through the barn and scan for a better place to sit, but the only open spots are two seats by a morose-looking Cass or two seats over by Cindy. I can tell it's Cindy and not Joselyn, because she's twirling her ponytail around her middle finger with a mischievous smile on her face.

"Fine. We can sit by Angel." I roll my eyes to myself.

We follow Angel over to a glass table surrounded by plastic lawn chairs. She sits across from David, giving him a wink as he settles into his chair. What I wouldn't give to punch her in the face right now.

Someone sets a bowl of stew on the table in front of us and a plate of bread slices.

"Thank you." I reach for the ladle, but Angel grabs it first. She leans over the table to retrieve David's bowl, showing David a lot of skin with her low-cut blouse. I catch David glancing before lowering his eyes to his lap.

"You realize David and I are a couple now, right?" I say as she sits back down to serve herself some stew.

"So what?" Angel plops the ladle back into the bowl.

I growl a bit as I grab the ladle to dish up my own bowl of stew. "So, stop flirting with him."

"Just because you nabbed him, I don't get to have any fun?" She lifts a finger to her lips to suck some gravy off, eyes focused entirely on David.

"He already asked you to cool it and told you he wants to just be friends." I clink the side of my bowl a little hard with my spoon, momentarily allowing my temper to get the better of me.

David reaches over to my knee and gives me a calming squeeze.

"Fine. Prude."

I take a bite of the stew and chew slowly, forcing my tongue to be too busy to say what I would love to say in response.

"So, you guys are planning on leaving soon?" Angel asks David.

"Yeah, well it all depends on what Eli says when he gets back."

"Oh, he got back earlier this afternoon. My guess is he's resting before telling everyone what he found out."

I look over to where Matthias is sitting and see Eli's empty chair. Matthias doesn't look the least bit anxious. Maybe he doesn't know Eli's back yet.

We finish our supper, with Angel attempting to flirt with David a few more times, putting me in an even worse mood. I'm ready for this day to be done now.

The crowd starts to thin out as people finish their food and head off to their shelters again.

"Want to come back to my place for some dessert?" Angel asks David with her sultry tone again.

"No, thanks," David dismisses her.

Angel glares at me as she throws her coat on and heads out the door.

"We're never sitting by her again." I cross my arms and let out a huff.

At that moment, the barn door flops open, and Eli comes storming in, a dark cloud hanging over his head.

Matthias stands from his chair. "Eli. What did ya find out?"

"Sorry, Brother. No deal." Eli says tiredly.

19

"Ya couldn't find him, or he wouldn't let ya have the bus?" Matthias asks as Eli dishes up some stew.

"Oh, I found him all right. Hasn't changed a bit either." Eli rubs at a bruise on his cheek I hadn't noticed before. "The price for the bus is too high. You're going to have to find another way."

"What did he want for it?" Matthias asks, taking a seat across from Eli.

"My crop." Eli shoveles a spoonful of stew into his mouth.

"So? This is important," Matthias says, angrily.

"You don't understand. He doesn't just want the product; he wants the plants. If I gave him every last ounce of weed I have, I wouldn't have anything left to make trades with to provide for my camp."

"Think of some other way to get supplies."

My jaw drops a little at Matthias's audacity. Even though I don't agree with Eli's way of trading, Matthias can't really be asking for so much just because he wants to get to the Haven.

Eli slams his fists on the table. "Why should I put my camp out and make them suffer just for you? Huh, Brother? What have you ever done for me?" Eli's face is red with anger.

"What about in the fifth grade when I saved your life?"

"Oh, come off it. That was a long time ago!" Eli shouts. "I wouldn't have died."

"Ya almost got trampled by a herd of cows because of your stupidity!" Matthias yells back, receiving an eye roll from Eli. "And what about the time ya were arrested? Who got ya out?"

"You did. But you didn't give me enough time to figure out how to escape. I'm sure I could have found a way."

"This is just like ya. You've always been so ungrateful. I want to do something good for me and my people. To get us somewhere better, and unfortunately, I need your help in order to do it."

"At the cost of my livelihood," Eli growls.

"Ya don't have to give it all to him. Take half, and tell him it's the whole crop."

"Nah. He said the only way he'd follow through with the deal is to send some of his men to collect it. If they find that I'm hiding some, then the deal is off."

"This is ridiculous," Matthias mutters. "Did ya even see the bus to know he still has it?"

"Yes. I insisted he prove that he still has it. It works, but it's old. He also has a few barrels of fuel in the back that he's collected from the city." Eli rubs his forehead with the heel of his hands.

Everyone's quiet for a moment.

"What if we stole it?" David asks.

"How are you going to steal a bus right out from under their noses? The bus is parked next to their camp," Eli says.

"What is their camp like? Shelters? Tents? Old houses?" Matthias strokes his beard.

"They fenced in part of an old subdivision where people bunk up to sleep, and then they gutted out a house to turn into their 'mead hall,' as he likes to call it, for their dining area and kitchen." Eli draws it out with his finger on the table. "The bus is parked right inside the fence."

"It'd be a shame if their mead hall caught fire," David says mischievously.

"David!" I scold.

"What? If we snuck into their camp at night and lit their kitchen on fire, it would cause a diversion as they all worked together to put it out. Only one person needs to do the lighting. The rest of the group can be hiding by the bus and load up during the diversion. The person who lit it would just have to figure out how to get themselves over to the bus."

"They have guards watching the place just like we do. They'd see a group of people waltzing up to the camp," Eli says.

"Alexandrine and I could take care of the guards," Matthias offers.

"Stealing, arson, and murder. Great plan," I say disgusted.

David turns to me and cups my face in his hands. "Liv, this is survival. We can't ask Eli to give up his crop for us, and I don't see any other way to do this. I think it'll work."

I stare down at the floor, thinking. "What if we had Charlotte help again?"

"We can't rely on her. She messed up last time," Matthias says. "Plus, her voice wouldn't be loud enough to work on everyone."

Eli snaps his fingers. "I think I might have something in the shed that could help with that." He throws his coat on and heads out of the barn without another word.

"Are we supposed to follow him?" I ask.

David shrugs.

Matthias glares at me with his one eye. "Ya know, Oliva. You're going to have to get off your high horse at some point."

"What do you mean?" I ask, annoyed with his criticism.

"Someday, ya might end up having to make a hard choice about whether a person needs to be killed for your safety or the safety of someone ya care about. If ya let every bad guy go, it'll come back to bite ya."

"Ugh! Not this again. At least I can live with my own conscience."

"Not if you're dead," Matthias growls.

"So, what are you suggesting? I start killing every person who looks at me the wrong way?"

"No, I'm suggesting ya keep an open mind and stop judging other people for making the choice to do things differently than you."

"Whatever," I mumble under my breath. "I just think it would be better to find solutions to problems that don't involve death."

"Ya won't always have that luxury. Some solutions are spur of the moment, and ya need to be willing to do what needs to be done."

"I happen to like that Liv chooses to be a good person," David says, holding my hand.

"It's not good to choose the life of a bad guy over the life of your friends and family."

"Well, let's just hope I never have to make a decision like that. Once we're in the Haven, maybe our lives can be less murdery."

At that moment, the barn door pops open, and Eli comes waltzing in with a white cone-shaped device. He holds it up to his mouth with the attached handle and says, "Found it!" His voice is so loud, it hurts my ears.

"Where'd you find a megaphone?" David asks.

"In one of the nearby houses. We have no use for it, since we'd really like to keep the attention away from camp." Eli hands it off to Matthias. "This will amplify her voice enough to make the whole camp sleep like babies."

"Yeah, and us too. Ear plugs aren't gonna be enough to keep her voice outta our heads with this thing."

"Guess we'll have to see what we can use to block it." Eli taps his chin. "I'm sure we can figure something out. I like this plan a lot better than giving up my crops."

"Of course, ya do. But what do ya think is gonna happen when he comes here lookin' for his bus? He's gonna know you had somethin' to do with it. You were just up there askin' about it."

"I'll have my men be ready with extra protection. If he comes here to make trouble, then that's what he'll get."

I scoff quietly to myself. "And then we did nothing to solve this problem without death."

"What's with her?" Eli asks Matthias.

"She doesn't believe in killing people, even if it means protecting people ya care about." Matthias looks at me as though I'm an idiot.

"Ah. I used to be like you. Then my girlfriend died because I was only willing to shoot the guard to maim not kill, which didn't stop him from shooting her in the head. That was the first time I killed someone. Now I don't mess around. You threaten my friends or family, you die."

"As it should be." Matthias nods.

"Fine. All right? I get it. You've made your point," I say grumpily. "Now we better hope Charlotte is willing to help us again."

10

"I don't know..." Charlotte says at breakfast. "What if I get scared just like last time?"

"Then we'll go with plan B, I guess," I say.

"What's plan B?" Alexandrine pulls Charlotte's thick wiry hair into a ponytail.

"We light the mead hall on fire and steal the bus while everyone's trying to put the fire out."

"Not a terrible plan if you could guarantee that everyone in the camp would pitch in to help. Some people would probably choose to stay out of the way. Then we'd be caught."

"That's why I figured Charlotte singing them all to sleep would be a better plan."

"How does the megaphone work?" Charlotte asks.

"You just have to speak into the mouthpiece like this, 'Hello, Charlotte! See how loud my voice is?' Here. You try." I hand it over.

"Everyone's going to look at me." Charlotte glances around the room with wide eyes.

"It's good practice. Maybe if you can get used to using it in front of people, you won't have any trouble when we go to get the bus."

"Give it a try." Joselyn takes a bite of her eggs.

Charlotte's cheeks turn red as she lifts the megaphone up to her mouth. She looks around the room to see if anyone is looking at her. Satisfied, she clears her throat, and I hear one note reverberate around the room before I pass out.

I wake up with a gasp. How long was I asleep? I blink my eyes lazily as I sit up in the chair, my back stiff. I look across the table and see Charlotte cowering against the barn wall, looking terrified.

"You weren't supposed to sing in it, Charlotte! I meant try it by talking into it."

I glance around the room and see people asleep in awkward positions all over the place. Some fell asleep while sitting. Others were walking around when they passed out and are sprawled out on the floor. There are a few broken dishes scattered amongst them, their food spilled all over the dirty floor. Alexandrine is slumped over the table, face down, nose squashed against the wood. I shake her shoulders, and she snaps awake, grabbing my wrist tightly in one fluid movement.

"What happened?" Her voice is thick with sleep.

"Charlotte misunderstood what I meant and sang through the megaphone instead of speaking."

"Charlotte, that was very dangerous!" Alexandrine scolds.

"I'm sorry, Mama," Charlotte wails.

I better say something before Charlotte gets too upset and never wants to use the megaphone again. "No, this was good. Now we know it will work perfectly. Charlotte was very clever to test it out, but maybe a warning next time though, okay?" I give her a wink when she scrunches her eyebrows at me.

"How long were we out?" Alexandrine asks.

"I don't know," Charlotte sniffles. "Like, maybe five minutes?"

"How long did you sing?"

"I only sang two notes. When everyone started falling over, I got scared and stopped."

Slowly people around us wake up, asking what happened.

"We just demonstrated how we plan on getting the bus that will take us to the Haven," Alexandrine says.

People start muttering; some are smiling, while other's eye up Charlotte like she's a threat.

"C'mon, Charlotte. Let's go talk to Matthias." Alexandrine holds out her hand to her daughter. She pulls her up off the floor and wraps an arm around Charlotte's shoulders protectively. As they walk out the door, David comes trudging in, holding a towel to his mouth, his wet hair plastered to his forehead.

"What happened to you?" I ask, concerned.

"I was taking a shower and I suddenly blacked out. I must have smacked my lip on the wall before I went down," he says, removing the towel from a bloodied, swollen bottom lip.

I cringe.

"I don't know what happened to me. The water ran out by the time I woke up, and I was lying on the shower floor, just about frozen to death."

I wrap my arms around him, rubbing his back to help warm him up. "You must have heard Charlotte singing. I had her try the megaphone, but instead of just talking into it like I thought she was going to do, she decided to sing. I only heard one note before I blacked out."

David winces as he licks his injured lip.

"Let's go get that lip checked out." I lead David out of the barn.

■■■■■

"Doesn't look like you'll need stitches, but we do need to put some ice on it." Rebecca grabs a clean cloth and heads outside.

David shivers under the blanket Rebecca gave him, even though I'm nearly sweating from the heat in her shelter. She threw some extra logs into the wood stove to try to warm him up. By the iciness of his fingers wrapped around mine, I'd say it's going to take all day to thaw him out.

"Here." Rebecca walks back into her shelter. "I couldn't find any ice, so I wrapped up some snow. Just lean forward so it doesn't soak you as it melts."

"Thanks." David gingerly presses it up against his lip.

"While you're here, I'm going to check your other injuries." She leans in and looks at his forehead closely. "The gash above your eyebrow's gone now, so that's good."

She helps David remove his coat and pulls up his sleeve.

"The bullet wound is almost healed as well. How does it feel when you lift your arm?"

David lifts his arm and responds, "It's still a bit sore, but not too bad."

Rebecca nods as she presses her thumbs around the area. "If you take it easy for about another week, I think it'll be completely healed. How about your wrist?"

"The throbbing is gone," he says as she removes the brace.

"That's a good sign." She holds David's hand and moves it around. "Does any of this hurt?"

"Barely."

"A couple more weeks in the brace, and I think that'll be healed too." She helps David get the brace back onto his wrist.

"So, you're coming along to the Haven, right?" I ask.

"Yeah, I think I'll tag along. Eli tried to talk me into staying, telling me he could use a good nurse like me, but I couldn't abandon Matthias like that." She starts packing up her medical kit.

"I think your kids would be better off with us. Joselyn included," I say.

Rebecca gives me an uncertain look as she zips up her bag. "You've put a lot of stock into the Haven, haven't you? What if it's nothing like what you hope for?"

"I don't really know what I'm hoping for. Some place better than the Coalition cities. If they're cool with Rare, then I think it's the place to be."

"Let's hope you're right."

"Let's hope Matthias is right," I say, and Rebecca nods agreeably.

"You two are welcome to stay here by the fire, but I need to go check on my boys. When that snow has melted," she points at the makeshift ice pack, "wait about an hour before putting some more on it. I'll come check on you later."

"Thank you, Rebecca," David says as she steps out the door.

She nods and then closes the door, causing a blast of cold air to hit us.

"We're alone." He wiggles his eyebrows at me.

I laugh. "You are in no condition to be doing any kissing."

"I can dream," he says.

I sit down next to him on the cot and rest my head on his shoulder. We're silent for a moment, listening to the crackle of the fire and the distant voices of people going about their business.

"What do you think would be strong enough to block Charlotte's singing so we don't fall asleep? As Matthias said, ear plugs aren't going to cut it," I ask David.

"Maybe Denis could come up with something."

I shrug, unsure of whether I want to ask any favors from Denis right now. "I think Eli was going to check his shed to see if he had anything. Wanna go take a look?"

"Sure, after I'm done icing my lip."

We grow quiet again. As I trace his knuckles with my fingertip, a dark cloud of self-doubt edges its way into my thoughts, completely out of nowhere. Ridiculous thoughts of David deciding he would rather have Angel than me, or David dying and me being alone for the rest of my life. Of failing to get the bus and people being killed by the other camp, of never finding the Haven, or worse, not being accepted in. Of Cass doing something horrible to herself and I should have stopped her. I know all these thoughts are irrational, but they inadvertently fill up my mind until I feel weighed down with anxiety and fear that's so overwhelming, I let out a sob.

"You okay, Liv?" David asks in surprise.

"I thought I was done with this. Why can't I be better?" I hide my face with my hands. I hear David let out a little sigh, and now I feel even worse that I'm being a burden.

"We'll get through it." David wraps his arms around me, holding me tightly.

My entire body feels heavy, like I've spent the entire day shoveling snow and now every muscle aches and I can't move. I start to panic because I don't want to fall into the pit again. I don't want to spend my days feeling like there is no happiness to be had.

I force myself to take ten deep breaths. And then ten more. Each breath helps my mind stay focused on what's happening around me. None of the things my anxiety wants me to focus on are actually happening, and it's important I remember that.

David hums a calming song as he strokes my hair gently. I can feel my muscles relax slightly from his touch.

David's right. I'm going to get through this. I've gotten through this before. I can't succumb to the darkness, but I also can't snap myself out of it immediately. I know it's an illness, and I need to treat it as such. I wish I didn't have it.

"Ready to go check out Eli's shed?" David asks, holding the wet rag that was his ice pack.

I rub my hands over my face and take one more deep breath, digging deep to find the strength to stand.

"Yeah, let's go."

When we get to the shed, Eli, Denis, Tim, and Matthias are already here. I want to turn right back around so I don't have to be around people when I feel like this, but our quest to find a solution keeps me in place.

"We found a couple pairs of earmuffs." Eli grins. "They're for blocking sound while target practicing."

"Nice. Will they block out sound entirely?" David asks.

"That's impossible," Denis throws in. "We don't just hear sounds with our ears. The vibrations of sounds can also be picked up by your cranial bone, which transmits it to your eardrum. It's called bone conduction. You'll never be able to block out sound completely unless you're deaf."

"So, whoever wears them could still end up hearing Charlotte?" David's eyes grow wide.

"Yes, I believe they will," Denis answers.

"The only way we are going to know if they work is to test them. We also need to figure out who's going to go with Charlotte and drive the bus out of there."

"I'll do the drivin'," Matthias offers.

"Alexandrine's not going to allow Charlotte to do this unless she's there too," I add quietly.

"You guys know you can't just drive across the DMZ, right?" Denis asks.

"Why not?"

"Because there's a giant river separating this side of the country from the other side."

"The Mississippi River," Matthias says.

"Aren't there bridges?" I ask.

"Scott—the guy who's got the bus—said something about a bridge that nobody knows about. It was made after the war," Eli says.

"Oh, yes. That's not shady at all." Matthias rolls his eyes. "I'm not taking any advice from a guy ya screwed over back in the day. I'm not even that comfortable taking a bus from him."

"Options are limited, Brother." Eli pokes Matthias in the shoulder.

Matthias slaps Eli's hand away.

I huff and look around at the shelves as they continue to talk. I spot a baseball bat. An unpleasant memory strikes me at the sight of it. We were lined up outside in the hazy fog for a baseball game in gym class. I didn't really want to play, but Mr. Crenshaw was forcing me to. I was the last one picked, as usual, and was somewhat relieved I wasn't on Victoria's team. I learned quickly that wasn't a good thing. When it was my turn to bat, she happened to be the pitcher and chucked the ball at me as hard as she could, hitting me in the leg. I had a huge black-and-blue bruise for weeks afterwards. Of course, she didn't get into trouble, but I was scolded by the gym teacher for not paying attention.

"Liv? You okay?" David asks.

"Sorry. Just daydreaming," I mumble.

"The others left to go test the earmuffs with Charlotte. Did you want to go check it out?"

"There aren't enough earmuffs for everyone, so we wouldn't be able to watch," I point out. "I kind of just want to take a nap."

"That's not a good idea. It's better for you to stay awake," David says calmly.

He's right. If I lie down when I'm feeling like this, I usually sink further into my despair.

"Want to take a walk?" David asks.

"Around the compound so people can look at me? No, thanks," I mutter.

"No. Let's slip out and go look around the area. We'll be leaving soon. I thought it might be nice to take a little time to ourselves." David gives me a winning smile, and I cave. Some alone time sounds nice.

We head back to our shelter to bundle up in all our warm clothing and pack some snacks and water into our coat pockets. As we're about to slip out, Cass walks back into the shelter.

"Where are you guys headed?" she asks.

"We just wanted to go check out some nearby houses to see if we could find more earmuffs for the bus plan," David says on the spot.

"Can I come?" Cass asks.

David and I exchange a look, and she picks up on it.

"Never mind. You guys don't have to lie to me if you want to go somewhere to make out or something."

"No, that's not it," I say, getting defensive.

"Relax. I'm kidding." She chuckles. "Go have some alone time. You won't get much once we're driving on the bus for who knows how long."

I nod. David bumps my shoulder and jerks his head toward the door, and I turn to follow him but then stop. "You know, if you ever want to have a girl day, I can tell David that's what I want, and he'll leave us alone," I say after David walks out the door.

Cass smiles but doesn't say anything. There's still pain in her eyes.

I should tell her Tim said he'd go, but I don't feel like explaining right now that it's at the cost of his happiness.

I head out the door, and David grabs my hand as we walk toward the gate.

"Where do you think you're headed?" one of Eli's men who are on watch duty asks.

I recognize him as the metal militia guy who offered to carry Sonya when we were "captured."

"We're checking out nearby houses to search for more earmuffs for the bus mission," David says once again.

I'm beginning to wonder if that's what we're actually doing.

"You have protection?"

David blushes but then stammers, "Um, I have a couple of hunting knives on me."

It takes me a moment to realize why David seemed embarrassed, and now I have a sudden urge to hide my face.

The guard pulls a handgun out of his coat and hands it to David.

"Here. I keep an extra one on me when I do watch duty. My shift's almost done. Be careful out there."

David takes it and puts it inside his inner coat pocket. The guard opens the gate, and we slip out quickly, hoping to get away before someone else stops us.

We walk for a while in silence, taking in the billowy snow piled up on the tree branches. The snowy pine trees look like the pictures that are always out around Christmastime. I never got to experience the beauty of snow while living in the city. Sure, it snowed. But with the constant fog, it made things look even whiter, and it was blinding.

We make it to the elementary school that creeped me out the first time we walked past it. The playground equipment is also covered in a layer of snow and no longer moves in the wind, so it seems a little less scary now. David pulls me toward a swing and has me sit down. He pushes my back with one arm, and I start pumping my legs. I get going fast enough, I feel that strange sinking sensation in my stomach as I swing back and forth. I tip my head back and laugh as I get dizzy.

After a couple of minutes, David stops pushing me and has a seat on the swing next to me. He hooks his arm with the broken wrist around the chain and holds on with his good hand. He tries to pump his feet to get going, but he's unable to swing straight. I slow down to a stop, and we sit next to each other, kicking our feet against the ground.

"I'm scared, David."

"Scared of what?"

"Everything. The mission to get the bus. The drive through the DMZ. Meeting everyone at the Haven. What if they're not nice people? What if they don't accept us and they throw us in jail or kill us?"

David looks at me. "That's part of the adventure, isn't it? We don't know what's going to happen, but the chance of good things happening outweighs the bad. And as long as I have you by my side, I'm happy."

Tears spring to my eyes. "Why? I'm terrible company."

"I would rather spend a lifetime with you than spend one day with someone else who's quote-unquote 'happy.'"

I close my eyes and try to let his words sink in. I want to believe him. I want to feel like someone worth loving. But every time I think about myself, all I feel is disgust. David deserves someone happy, and I don't believe I will ever be what he deserves.

It's almost like he can read my thoughts, because he kneels down in front of my swing and grips my hands firmly in his. I open my eyes and look at him staring up at me with concern in his beautiful golden eyes. I'm about to tell him I love him when I hear something strange in the distance.

"Do you hear that?" I ask as the noise gets steadily louder. It sounds like a vehicle but different.

David's up on his feet, looking around to try to pinpoint the direction it's coming from. "We need to hide. C'mon!" He pulls me off the swing, and we run toward the abandoned school building.

12

"Our footprints!" I yell as he drags me through the snow. "They're going to know where we are."

"There's nothing we can do about it. Run!"

We head to the back of the building, moving slower than I would like. Our bulky winter clothes and the deep snow make running harder than it should be. Once we're around the building, we find one of the padlocks on the doors has been cut. Probably by someone from Eli's camp looking for materials.

David yanks the door open, and we dart inside. It's dark in here with the limited windows, almost too dark for me to see even with my Rare eyesight. We sprint down the dirty hallway, leaving behind more footprints and clumps of snow as we go. There's no way we're going to hide from whoever that was. Let's just hope they don't see our tracks, and if they do, they don't care and keep going.

David pulls me into an empty classroom. There's nothing in here but an old dry-erase board on the wall and some blinds on the windows. Everything else has been cleared out. He closes the door and locks it, then leads me to the window facing the front of the school. We crouch down and pull two of the blind slats apart just enough to peek out.

The strange sound we heard grows louder until we finally see the cause. It's a machine with two skis on the front and a track on the back that makes it move on top of the snow. The driver straddles a seat behind a tiny windshield, steering the machine with handlebars.

The driver cruises past the swing set, but I see his head turn as he spots our footprints. He does a loop and comes back to the swings, stopping his snow machine. He climbs off it and starts following our tracks. David tugs on my arm to pull me to the floor. Before I let go of the blinds, I spot a coalition patch sewn on his jacket.

"That's a soldier. What are we going to do?" My breath comes heavy, making me feel like I might choke.

"We're going to stay put in this room with the door locked, and if he breaks in, I'll shoot him."

"Can't we break through the window and run?"

"With what? There's nothing in here to break the window. If I try to break it with the gun or something, I run the risk of getting hurt. No. We have to hide in here and hope he leaves."

We hurry over to the wall by the door. I try to stay as quiet as I can, but we kicked up some dirt from the floor when we ran over here, and now I have a tickle in my nose. I pinch my nostrils closed and try hard to make the sensation go away.

The soldier is in the school now. I can hear his boots squeaking on the floor.

The tickle seems to have subsided, and I let go of my nose. As soon as I take my next breath, I unexpectedly sneeze, not able to cover my mouth in time.

David whips his head around with an exasperated expression.

I mouth an apology, and we stand still, listening. Maybe he didn't hear my sneeze. These walls are made from thick concrete; it might have been enough to muffle the sound.

But my hopes shatter as the door handle jiggles.

David raises the gun, ready to shoot the soldier if he gets in.

A loud thump rattles the door, and my heart leaps into my throat. Why won't this guy just leave us alone? He bangs against the door again and again, but the lock holds firm.

After two more thumps, it grows quiet. I let out a breath of relief when I hear his footsteps heading back toward the exit.

"Is he giving up?" I whisper as quietly as possible.

David shrugs and motions for me to follow him. Staying low, we hurry back over to the window to watch. I huddle on the floor, waiting for David to tell me what's going on.

"He's walking back to the machine," David whispers. "He's not getting on it, though."

I squeeze my eyes shut. "What's he doing?"

"He grabbed something, but I can't make out what it is." David drops down quickly next to me, face ashen.

"What?"

"He turned to look at the school, and I think he might have seen me."

I reach out and put my hand on David's leg, squeezing. It's unnervingly quiet as we wait.

A loud bang comes from outside, and the window shatters above our heads, raining glass down on us. I instinctively cover my head, and a small shard of glass slips down the back of my shirt, cutting into my skin. I try to move, but it cuts deeper.

"David, help me!" I panic as we listen to the crunch of snow as the soldier gets closer to us.

"With what? We need to get out of here!" David says, grabbing my bicep to pull me toward the door.

"I have glass down my back, and I can't move."

David reaches his hand down my shirt and feels around until I wince with pain when he bumps into it. As he's pulling the glass out of my shirt, we hear the soldier breaking what was left of the window. He pushes the blinds forward and starts to climb through.

David reaches for the gun in his pocket, but I tug on his arm to run. I don't want David to become like Matthias. We race to the door, unlock it, and make it out as the soldier shoots at us, missing David by an inch.

I find it odd the soldier hasn't uttered a single word to us. It makes this whole situation more terrifying as we run down the dark hallway from someone who means to kill us.

David grabs my wrist and pulls me down another hallway. There are no windows in this part of the building, making it pitch black, forcing us to slow down so we don't run into anything. David tugs at a set of double doors, and we slip inside just as the soldier comes around the corner.

I blink in the darkness of the room, trying to make sense of where we are. It smells of moldy bread. I reach out in front of me and feel around as I take tiny steps, not wanting to get hurt again. The cut on my back stings as my shirt clings to my skin, wet with sweat and blood.

"I think we're in the kitchen," David whispers from in front of me. "Come over here."

I hurry as fast as I can to where his voice is coming from, and as soon as I get next to him, he pushes me into a small space. He closes the door behind us.

"Where are we now?" I ask, my breathing ragged.

"The freezer, I think," David says uncertainly.

I'm so scared, I feel like I'm about to throw up. We stand still, waiting to see if the soldier will find us in our newest hiding spot; waiting to see if he's going to find a way to kill us.

"How much longer do we stay in here like sitting ducks?" I ask once my breathing has returned to normal.

"I don't know. I thought I had heard the door open shortly after we got in here, but I haven't heard anything since," David whispers.

As soon as David finishes his sentence, the freezer door handle turns, and the door swings open. The soldier has a flashlight pointing toward us which blinds me momentarily, but David doesn't hesitate for a second.

He leaps out of the freezer with a guttural yell and tackles the soldier before he can get a shot fired. The soldier drops the flashlight, and it goes spinning across the floor. I race for the flashlight as David knocks the soldier's gun out of his grip, and it comes sliding my direction. The flashlight stops against the wall behind me, shining enough light that I can see with no problem.

I stare at the gun, stunned for a moment, trying to figure out what to do.

A shout from David snaps me back into the moment, and I look over to see the soldier lying on top of David, trying to cut his neck with a knife. David has his hands on the soldier's arm, pushing with all this might, but the soldier's knife is slowly lowering toward David's neck.

I pick up the black handgun and point it at the soldier. My hands are shaking so much, I'm not sure I could even hit him if I wanted to. "Get off from him!" I yell with as much authority as I can.

The soldier looks at me for only a second, obviously not scared of the small girl who can't hold the gun still.

390

David takes that moment of distraction to give a big shove on the soldier's arm, knocking him off balance, allowing David to get out from under him. But while David stands up, the gun he's carrying falls out of his pocket and clatters to the floor.

The soldier grabs the gun before David knows what happening.

It's as though I'm watching in slow motion as the soldier brings the gun up toward David, pointing it at his head. I don't wait to see whether he's going to try to manipulate me into dropping the gun in my hands or not. Adrenaline kicks in at the thought of him harming David, and I squeeze the trigger, desperate to save David.

I watch as the soldier's eyes bulge in surprise before he falls to the ground. I stand rooted in place, my ears ringing from the gunshot. I stare down at the puddle of blood forming underneath the soldier's lifeless body, unable to look away.

David rushes over to the soldier, placing his fingers against the guy's neck to check if he's still alive. After a few moments, he calmly removes his fingers. He pulls the gun out of the soldier's hand, puts the safety on, and places it back into his coat pocket.

I realize I still have the gun pointed toward the soldier, and let my arm drop to my side, staring at the body.

"Liv? You okay?" David's voice sounds far away.

I feel him gently grab the gun out of my hand. I don't respond. I just keep staring.

"Liv. Hey. Olivia!" David snaps his fingers in front of my face.

The dreamlike state I was in lifts, and the reality of what happened hits me like a ton of bricks. I turn away from David as the contents of my stomach comes rushing out in a burning stream. I wipe the bile from my lips and crumple to the floor, barely missing the rancid puddle.

"What did I do?" I squeak.

"You saved my life, that's what you did." David kneels next to me, rubbing my back.

I cringe as he unknowingly rubs against my cut, but the pain sharpens my mind again, breaking through the fog of disbelief settling in once more. I start panting as I look at the body again.

"Let's get out of here, Liv. At least, away from this room." He retrieves the flashlight, then reaches his hand out toward me.

I grab onto it, my body feeling like lead as he pulls me up off the ground. He wraps my arm around his shoulder and holds on to my waist, dragging me away from the mess I made.

13

I have no idea where we are, or that I'm even moving, until David pushes on my shoulders to get me to have a seat on the merry-go-round out in the playground. I blink slowly in the sudden brightness of daylight as my senses come back. The air smells crisp and clean compared to the staleness of the air in the school, and I take a deep breath, filling my lungs with as much of it as I can.

"How did we get out here?" I wonder how I walked through the snow and didn't realize it.

When David doesn't answer me, I look up and find he's over by the snow machine, tinkering with it. He yanks on something, causing the machine to sputter to life and then motions for me to join him. I stumble my way to the loud machine and stand next to it, wondering what David's plan is.

"I'm going to get you back to Eli's camp faster. Climb on behind me and hold on tight," David shouts over the engine.

I swing my leg over the seat and slide as far forward as I can, wrapping my arms around David's stomach. My coat pulls tight against my back, making me wince in pain, but I ignore it and rest my head against David's back.

After a few choppy movements forward, David seems to figure out how the machine moves, and we take off through the snow. The speed is exhilarating, but my mind is too numb to enjoy it. We whip through the trees, the sound of the engine bouncing off the trunks as we drive by. Before I know it, we're slowing down as we come into view of Eli's encampment. I feel David's shoulder blade move, so I lift my head up and see he's waving to the man on watch.

"Where'd you get that?" the guy yells when David pulls to a stop by the gate.

"A Coalition soldier. We need to speak to Eli immediately."

The guy lets us through, and we slowly drive the machine to the barn, people staring at us as we go. David parks it and shuts off the engine. The change in sound makes my head buzz.

I reluctantly let go of David, nervous to not have the comfort of his presence right next to me, but it's only for a moment, because he grabs onto my hand as soon as he's off the machine.

Eli and Matthias come striding out of the barn, looking at us curiously.

"Where'd you get this?" Eli asks.

"From a Coalition soldier." David grips my hand firmly in his, which I'm grateful for.

"What'd ya do? Ask him for it, and he let ya have it?" Matthias crosses his arms over his chest.

"No, sir. After the soldier tried to kill us, Liv shot and killed him." David smiles at me proudly.

392

I let out a whimper as the weight of what I did settles in my chest. I killed a man.

Matthias looks at me with a raised eyebrow and says, "Let's go inside. This is a story I need to hear."

David has to tug on my arm to get me to move. I don't want to listen to him tell the story. I want to go hide in a dark hole, where I belong.

After David relates everything that happened, Matthias and Eli look between him and me, speechless. I shift around on my chair, uncomfortable in my own skin. I don't want them to look at me, so I stare down at my hands as though they are the most interesting thing in the world.

"Good job..." Matthias starts to say, but I can see in my peripheral vision that David is motioning for him to stop. I'm grateful for that. "Why are ya tryin' to stop me from sayin' what I need to say? Olivia did the right thing. Had she not, you'd be dead. Both of ya would. This is exactly what I was talkin' about, and she made the right choice."

"I know it was the right choice, but that doesn't mean I feel good about it." My voice catches on the lump in my throat.

"Are ya glad David is alive?"

"Of course, I am," I grumble.

"Then I suggest ya put it out of your mind. That soldier meant to kill ya. He wasn't a good guy. Ya just rid the world of a bad guy, so good job."

His words hold truth. I don't know what I would do without David. It was a choice that had to be made, and even though I don't like it, I made it.

"What was a soldier doing out this far?" Eli strokes his beard. "I've never had a soldier out here before."

"I think we'd better get our plan into motion now, before it's too late," Matthias says. "He might have contacted some of his buddies before he got himself killed."

I sink lower into my chair. The soldier's face is engrained in my mind's eye, and I shiver when I see his dead, glassy eyes staring at the ceiling. I don't think I'm ever going to get that image out of my mind.

"And just leave me here to deal with the soldiers on my own?" Eli asks.

"Come with us, then." Matthias turns and throws his hands in the air.

"No. It was probably just someone going for a joy ride." Eli waves Matthias's offer away with his hand.

I watch Matthias ball his fists at his side in frustration.

"But I agree that we should get you out of here. The sooner, the better."

"We're going to need the radiation prevention shots before we go," David interjects.

"Yes, yes. Of course. It'll take my whole stock, but I'm sure I can get more at some point." Eli stands. "I'll go grab it while you gather up your people in here, Matt."

"I'll follow ya out, Elijah," Matthias growls, and Eli chuckles.

"C'mon, Liv. Let's go help Matthias." David grabs my hand and pulls me out of the chair.

I pull my hood up, hiding inside of it as much as I can, and shuffle my way behind David. The coldness of the wind sets my teeth chattering.

"We'll go to Rebecca's shelter first so we can get that cut looked at." David's comment jerks me from my thoughts of warmer weather.

"What is it with you two?" Rebecca asks after David explains what happened to my back. He mercifully left out the part of the story where I killed the soldier. "All right. Take off your coat, Olivia, and let's have a look at it."

David averts his eyes like a gentleman when Rebecca asks me to lift my shirt.

She uses alcohol wipes to clean the blood off, and it stings like crazy. "No stitches required, though it looks close. You lucked out." She places a bandage over the cut.

"We're also here to tell you to head to the barn. We need to get our radiation prevention shots because Matthias wants to leave as soon as possible. He's worried that the soldier could have contacted someone else and told them he saw us."

"Where's this soldier now?" Rebecca finishes up with the patch job and pulls my shirt back down.

I stare at the floor numbly. "He's been taken care of."

Rebecca doesn't ask for more details. "Okay, I'll go help Eli with the injections."

We make our rounds, telling everyone we can to get to the barn. We have one awkward incident when Cindy opens her door wrapped in a blanket, and from what we can tell, she has nothing on underneath it. David turns right around and walks away.

"What? I sometimes take a nap naked. It's very liberating," Cindy says with a yawn.

"Just get to the barn," I say. "Preferably, with clothes on."

David and I finish up and make our way inside. We spot Denis standing next to Tim, and I get what little hopes I have left up that maybe Denis changed his mind.

"Are you coming with us?" I ask, momentarily snapping out of my funk.

"I haven't decided yet," Denis answers. "I'm just here for support."

Tim looks up at me bashfully. "I'm not a big fan of needles."

I hold in a laugh. The same guy who was cutting his arms with a knife is scared of a needle poke. Kind of ironic.

"All right, everyone. Listen up!" Matthias yells over the din. It quiets immediately. "Once ya have your injection, ya need to head back to your shelter and start packin'. We leave at dawn."

"Why so sudden?" Caroline asks, holding Sonya on her hip.

"Ya may have spotted that machine outside the barn. That belonged to a

Coalition soldier. We don't know if there's gonna be more comin' out here, so I want to get goin' as soon as possible."

"Do we have a plan figured out?" Alexandrine asks.

"We'll meet up after supper and go over our options," Matthias says with finality.

Rebecca and Alberto, a man from Eli's camp, set up a small table with two chairs on either side at the front of the room. They lay out the boxes of needles and call people forward to get their injection.

I stand in front of David, and he massages my shoulders as we slowly step our way up to the front of the line. He's doing everything he can to help me relax, but my mind keeps replaying the squeeze of the trigger and the face of the dead soldier.

After David and I are done, we go back to the shelter to pack up our stuff. Cass is there, whistling while she puts her clothes in her bag.

"Hey, guys!" she says with a smile.

"What's got you in such a good mood?" I ask.

"Tim got a shot. That means he's planning on going with us."

"Do you know whether Denis has decided to go or not?" I ask, even though I doubt she knows.

"Who cares. In fact, I'd be happier if he didn't." Her smile slips a bit as she shoves the clothes into her bag a little more forcefully.

"But Tim wouldn't be happy. Don't you care about that?" I don't know why I'm trying to pick a fight. In fact, I'm not even in the mood to talk, but something about her jovial behavior at the expense of her brother's happiness rubs me the wrong way.

She huffs. "Of course, I care. I'm not heartless."

David lays his hand on my arm to signal me to stop, so I do. I'm irritated with her, but I don't have any fight left in me anyway. After I zip up my backpack, I lie down on the cot and cover myself, head to toe, with a blanket.

"Liv, come on. We have to head back for sup—"

He's interrupted by the same sound we heard by the school—the snow machine. I sit up, breathing hard. By the sound of it, there's more than one.

"Cass, get down!" I grab onto her and pull her under the cot.

David goes to the door and opens it a crack to peek out. We can hear the sound grow louder as the machines get closer.

"They found us! Everyone, grab your weapons!" We hear Eli yell from outside, followed by guns firing from over by the gate.

I hold my breath, hoping the men standing guard killed them, but my hope fades quickly as the machines come charging into the encampment.

1|4

Gunshots explode around us. I cover Cass's head with my arms as we huddle together on the floor. Screams of women and children can be heard between shots.

"David? Are you still in here?" I ask, scared he went out to help.

"Yeah. Shh," he says.

A cold draft hits me, and I chance a look to see what's going on. He's crouched, holding the gun with the door slightly open.

"Are we going to die?" Cass's voice trembles.

"I hope not." I want to comfort her and say "no," but I don't want to lie.

The gunshots come from every direction. I close my eyes and pray, hoping this will be over soon. I jump when I hear some shots right outside our shelter. Cass is shaking uncontrollably, and I hold onto her tighter.

A bullet hits our shelter, and I realize they could easily shoot Cass and me if they shoot low enough. The thought makes me cringe, but a little part of me almost hopes for it. For a release from this terror. After what feels like an eternity, the sounds of gunshots stop, and a voice rings out, "Clear!"

I push myself out from under the cot, trembling. I help Cass stand, and we both throw on our coats to go outside and see what happened.

The smell of gunpowder hangs in the air. As we walk around the shelter, we see the bodies of soldiers as well as camp members lying in the snow, red mixing with white. As we get to the barn, Eli is hunched over the snow machine and then stands up, fury written across his face.

Eli storms over to Matthias. "This is all your fault!"

"My fault?"

"They had a tracker on that thing! Your daughter led them right to us."

David and I exchange a worried look.

"How could we have known that there was a tracker? Ya didn't think of it either, Eli!" Matthias yells right back at him.

"What is that?" I interrupt, pointing to a mangled metal contraption laying on the ground.

"It looks like one of their new military drones I've heard about." Eli kicks at it. "I shot it down before it had a chance to kill anyone, but this looks like a camera here at the front, so now not only do they know where I live, but they've seen my face."

"Eli—" Matthias starts to say.

"I want you out of here. Now." Eli's voice is dangerously low.

"Fine. But can I at least find out who died before ya kick me out?"

Eli doesn't answer, walking toward the closest body. Matthias does the same.

The men of the camp work together to move all the bodies into a row by the gate. Five soldiers came here in total, and they were able to kill nine people before they died. All of them were Eli's people, including that nice guy who carried Sonya when we first met them.

"When you go, take those machines with you, and leave them somewhere far away from here." Eli refuses to even look at Matthias.

"I will. For what it's worth, thanks for everything ya've done for us." For once, Matthias's voice is soft and meek.

Eli doesn't answer. He just turns and walks away.

"All right, people. Grab your stuff, and let's go," Matthias shouts.

I hold onto David and Cass's hands as we walk to the shelter to grab our bags. "How are we going to know where this guy's camp is without Eli?" I ask.

"We know it's north, on the outskirts of the city. I think that's as much information as we're going to get from him."

"This is all our fault, David." I cover my face with my hands and try to swallow the lump lodged in my throat.

"Not now, Liv. Okay? We couldn't have known. It's not worth beating ourselves up over. Let's focus on the task at hand."

I don't know how he does it. How can he put what just happened out of his mind? He's always been more stable than me.

We stand outside with our stuff, waiting for everyone to finish collecting their things. I check to make sure I have Saul's USB stick and find it in a pocket on my bag. I wonder if the people at the Haven will be able to open the encrypted files.

As I stand thinking about what the Haven will be like, a crowd gathers around us, waiting for Matthias to leave. Tim and Denis stand next to Cass, both holding multiple bags.

"Does this mean you're coming to the Haven, Denis?" David asks.

"Yes. I've decided to take my chances elsewhere."

I watch Tim grin at Cass, but her returned smile doesn't quite reach her eyes.

My attention shifts to Alexandrine, who's standing with her arm around Charlotte. She doesn't look happy. "What's wrong?" I ask after working up my courage.

"I don't like leaving before we have a plan set up. Eli is overreacting, kicking us out so suddenly. I suppose we have you to thank for that."

My stomach drops.

"Mama!" Charlotte says, shocked.

Alexandrine sighs. "But I guess you couldn't have known there was a tracking device. And they would have just followed your footprints and found us anyway if you had left the snowmobile there."

"Snowmobile?" David asks.

"That's what those are called. I had an uncle who owned one once. He'd let me ride it around his backyard." A smile tugs at the corner of her mouth at the memory. "I almost crashed it into a tree because it was so foggy, and I was going way too fast."

I try to picture a small Alexandrine zipping around on one of those, having the time of her life. What kind of person would she have been had she not been attacked and had her daughter taken away? She seems like she could have been a nice person. I see it in her when she dotes on Charlotte. I guess that's what makes us who we are—our experiences. Good and bad, they shape us into the people we become.

Matthias comes marching up to the group, his bags slung on his back. Henry follows, a tightness on his face.

"Is that everyone?" Matthias asks.

We all look at each other and nod. Our group is too big to use the snowmobiles to travel to the Haven. They would have been a lot easier than this mission to the bus, but a lot colder too.

"Anyone who's comfortable driving a snow machine can follow me. The rest of ya, follow behind us on foot. We'll come back to get ya. Stay out of sight. Let's go."

"I don't think it's a good idea to leave Eli on these terms," Henry says under his breath. "You should apologize, Pop."

"Apologize for what?"

"Maybe not apologize but give him your condolences. Say goodbye. I don't know. He's your brother, and he's done a lot for us—"

"I already said thanks," Matthias says stubbornly.

"You may never see him again."

"As he wants it. Now, let's go."

"We need more food, Pop," Henry says even quieter. "We need to ask him to let us have some food, or we're not going to make it very far."

"I'm not askin' him for anything more. We're just gonna have to hunt."

"Hunt while we drive on a bus?"

Matthias ignores Henry and starts toward a snowmobile.

I look longingly at the shower house before strapping my bag onto my back. I don't know how long it's going to be before we make it to the Haven. If only I had taken a shower this morning.

"Hey, Handsome, wait up!"

I turn my attention from the showers and see Angel running up to David with a bag in her hands. "This is for you. Good luck out there." She plants a kiss on his cheek and then runs back to her shelter.

David opens the bag and finds food and soda stashed inside. "See? She's not all bad," David says, zipping the bag back up.

"She kissed you again. She's lucky she ran away."

David just sighs, takes his jacket off, and slings the bag onto his back to keep the sodas from freezing.

Not enough people feel comfortable driving the snowmobiles, so David has to drive one, even with a broken wrist. I would ride with him, but we wouldn't both fit with our bags, so I'm left to walk through the cold, deep snow.

"Goodbye, Uncle Eli," I say under my breath, fear and excitement filling me for what's ahead.

15

"Where are they?" I look around, turning in a full circle, even though we are following their tracks.

"Keep walking. They'll find us," Alexandrine growls.

I let out a frustrated grunt.

Charlotte and Joselyn walk directly behind Alexandrine, holding hands quietly. Sonya has to be carried through the snow, her little legs unable to take big enough steps to keep up.

The full moon shines brightly against the snow, lighting up our surroundings without the need of a flashlight.

"Everyone be quiet." Alexandrine stops to look at the twins, who are making farting noises at each other and then giggling.

"Yes, ma'am," Joey and Isaac respond with a snicker.

"Boys, this is serious," Rebecca scolds.

The twins hang their heads. "Sorry, Mama."

"That's better. Now, let's keep going," Rebecca says softly.

The line starts moving again. I actually didn't mind the boys goofing around. It brought a little lightness to our situation and helped me ignore that my feet are so cold, they're numb. My backpack keeps bumping into the cut on my back, making it sting constantly. I can't wait to be riding on a bus. I just hope it'll be able to drive through the snow.

We continue on for another hour, stopping for an uncomfortable bathroom break when Noah says he has to go and can't hold it anymore. The temperature is so much worse when you're not moving to stay warm.

"The kids are getting heavy." Caroline shifts a sleeping Sonya in her arms.

"Give her here," Frederick calls from up ahead.

I let out a breath I didn't realize I was holding when we turn to see the men trudging toward us down the snowmobile tracks. I run for David and wrap my arms around him, burying my nose in his neck.

"All right, it's gonna get rougher now because we're gonna have to blaze a new path. Let's go," Matthias says.

"Is there a way we could camp out in an abandoned house for the night?" Joselyn asks Alexandrine.

"The sooner we get that bus, the better."

"But what if we don't get to the guy's camp until daytime? Then we're going to have to wait until night anyway. Everyone is cold and tired. Can we just take a break and then continue walking in the morning?"

"She makes a good point, Matthias," Alexandrine says, to my surprise. "Maybe we could hole up in one of these houses."

I glance around and see houses standing in the moonlight. Their dark windows stare back forebodingly. I'm tired, but the vibe the houses give off makes me wonder if I will even be able to fall asleep inside any of them. Especially with the dead soldier's face constantly popping up in my mind's eye.

"We'll vote. Those in favor of camping out for the night and picking up the trek in the morning, raise your hands," Matthias says.

Almost everyone raises their hands.

"What happens if someone comes out this way and sees footprints leading to a house?" Henry counters.

"We're going to have to take shifts keeping watch. Two people will watch for two hours and then switch. I'll start. Let's go."

We choose a house with only one story. Once everyone is inside, we lock the door behind us, even though it's not going to serve as much protection. It's the principle of the thing. Someone turns on a flashlight to look around and the dread I had from the outside appearance melts away. It seems like it was once a nice house, but unfortunately, it's falling to the decay of time and the elements. The damask wallpaper is peeling off the wall in strips. The furniture is covered in plastic that has a thick layer of dust and dirt, making it impossible to tell what the color the couch is. The kitchen has a large marble-topped island and stainless-steel appliances. The two bedrooms have queen-sized beds and large walk-in closets. If only this place had electricity and heat, I would be happy to stay here for a while.

We pile our bags in the kitchen, and everyone lays out their bedding in the living room or in one of the bedrooms. The carpeting throughout the house is dirty, but it's soft, so maybe sleeping won't be too bad. I lie down between David and Cass, ready to be unconscious. Matthias doesn't choose me to be one of the lookouts this time, so I'm looking forward to a full night of sleep. The only trouble is, my mind keeps replaying the look on the soldier's face when I shot him. I continually remind myself that if I hadn't, David could be dead right now. I could too, but that seems less important.

I toss and turn, bumping into David and Cass over and over again, drawing out frustrated sighs. Finally, David turns to his side and wraps his arm around me, holding me close. The weight of his arm has a calming effect, and I stop rolling around.

"It's going to be all right, Liv. You did the right thing," David whispers in my ear.

"If it was the right thing to do, then why do I feel so bad?"

"Because 'right' isn't always easy. Now, take some deep breaths, and let's get some sleep."

I still question if it was right at all. It doesn't feel right, but I know I didn't really have an alternative.

David kisses my forehead, careful not to hurt his busted lip, and I relax. Before I know it, I fall asleep to his calming rhythmic breathing.

■■■■■

"All right, everyone. Time to get up and get movin'." Matthias's growl wakes me from a dreamless sleep.

After a scant breakfast, we head out the door to find a snowstorm moved in overnight. All we see is white flakes falling at a steady rate. Our footprints from last night have been covered, which means we need to figure out which direction is north. Matthias is certain it's to the left, while Alexandrine insists we need to head right from the house.

"Should we stay another night and figure it out once the snow has stopped?" Caroline asks, clearly unhappy at the thought of carrying Sonya through the blinding snow.

"No. I think this is the perfect time to go. It's unlikely the soldiers will be drivin' around in this, and the snow will fill in our tracks. We're gonna head left, and if I'm wrong, Alexandrine has the right to punch me," Matthias answers.

"Wait up!" we hear Frederick call from the house. "Look what I found in the garage." He holds up three plastic sleds with a smile. "Now the kids won't have to walk in this."

Frederick and Henry work together to tie longer ropes to the sleds so the adults pulling them can wrap the rope around their waists instead of tiring out their arms.

We start marching through the deep snow, my thighs burning from having to pick my feet up so high in order to follow the footprints. I pull the hood of my jacket as far forward as I can to keep the snowflakes out of my eyes. It leaves me unable to see any of my surroundings as I stare down at the ground, trying to stay on the path.

I grow sweaty from the effort of walking in the snow, making my cut sting. Meanwhile, my face stays uncomfortably cold. When we stop for a break, I sit down and pull my coat and shirt up over my face, trying to warm up. I probably look like an idiot, but it works. I savor the feeling of solitude in here, knowing it's going to be a while before I can be alone.

"David, can I have one of your sodas? I ran out of water about an hour ago," Cindy asks.

"How do you know I have soda?" David asks with suspicion.

"I saw your side chick give you a bag with snacks and sodas. Totally unfair to the rest of us, by the way," she accuses as though it's David's fault.

"She's not my 'side chick,'" David snaps. "And how could you be out of water already?" David asks the question in my head. One of the first things David and I did when we heard we were leaving Eli's was fill up all our water bottles from the hand pump.

"Snippy, snippy." Cindy frowns. "We left in such a hurry, I forgot to fill a couple of my bottles. What's it to you?"

"What's it to me? You just asked me for one of *my* sodas."

"Oh, right." Cindy wipes the sassy scowl off her face and then switches over to puppy dog eyes. "C'mon. Pretty please, David. I could use a sugar buzz right about now, anyway."

David breathes a heavy sigh and zips open the bag. I watch as he pulls a Mello Yellow out and hands it to her, and before he zips the bag up, I see a note tucked inside.

"Looks like you've got mail." I point at his bag. My mood darkens even more at the thought of what's written in that note.

"Yeah, I saw that. I'll read it later." David shrugs.

"You should just burn it," I mumble, but David hears me.

He sits next to me. "Liv, we need to talk."

I groan internally. Nothing good ever comes from those words. I can't quite look him in the eye.

"I was flattered by your jealousy at first, but now it's just becoming insulting. I told you that I love you and even gave you a promise ring. I would never do anything to hurt you, but you keep getting jealous every time Angel even speaks with me. You act as though I'm going dump you and run off with her just because she flirts with me a little." David grabs my face and holds it up so I look him in the eyes. "You are the one I want to be with, and no amount of batted eyelashes or sultry tones from some other girl is going to change my mind. Now, could you please trust me and my feelings for you and stop getting so angry every time another girl talks to me?" He kisses me on the forehead and then stands to slide his bags back on.

I hold my tongue from the barrage of excuses as to why I'm not wrong to be jealous. His words cut, but as I quietly sit there and let them sink in, I realize he's right. I'm being unfair to him, although, in my defense, I'm not good with this whole relationship thing. I've never done it before, and I've never been around a healthy relationship in my entire life. As I stand to strap my bag back on, I make a silent vow to be better for David. He deserves my trust.

"Everyone ready?" Matthias asks.

After a few responses, he turns and starts marching on.

The snow stopped falling about a half an hour ago, but now a cold wind picks up and swirls the powdery snow around in blinding white clouds. I keep my focus on my feet, watching carefully for footprints to follow. It would be easy to get lost in these conditions.

It doesn't take long before the children get too cold to keep going. Since they're being pulled on sleds, they aren't producing body heat by moving, and their little bodies can't take this biting wind.

"Matthias, we need to stop," Caroline announces as Sonya starts to cry again. "The children can't be in these conditions."

"But we're almost there," Matthias argues.

"How do you know that?" Caroline sweeps her arms out toward the snowy surroundings.

"I've spotted a few landmarks I remember Eli mentionin', and from what I remember him tellin' me, we're only about two hours away. The sun's goin' down soon, so this is the perfect time."

"But the kids are shivering so much, they can barely walk," Caroline says over Sonya's screeching.

I'm with Matthias on this one. I want to get on that bus and be on our way as soon as possible. But we'll be caught if we get anywhere near their camp with Sonya screaming like she is.

"If we're only two hours away by walking, how about a few of you go on ahead and get the bus while the rest of us wait in one of these houses? Then you can come get us?" Caroline asks.

"How do you plan on driving a bus in these conditions?" Denis chimes in.

"Eli said it's not a typical bus. They jacked it up and put chains on the wheels. It should be able to handle the snow."

"That's going to make it less fuel efficient." Denis strokes his beard. "But I guess we just make it as far as we can and then walk from there. It's better than nothing."

I look around and see a bunch of people nodding.

"All right. Let's figure out who's gonna retrieve the bus. Charlotte has to go, so I'm assumin' you'll be goin' too, Alexandrine?" Matthias asks.

"Obviously."

"Count me in!" Cindy says enthusiastically, as though they are headed to a candy store instead of into a dangerous situation.

Matthais raises his eyebrow. "Why you?"

"I go wherever Charlotte goes." Cindy's smile turns to a scowl, and her fists ball at her sides.

"Fine." Matthias holds his hands up in surrender.

"I'll come, Pop," Henry offers.

"I think you'd better stay here with everyone in case something happens to me." Henry scoffs, but Matthias continues, "Besides, it's probably best to have fewer people for this because of the way we're gettin' the bus. Less people to fall asleep from Charlotte's singin'."

As we stand here talking, the snow keeps whipping around. We better find shelter soon, or we're going to be buried in a snowdrift.

"Let's get y'all settled into a house and get this over with."

16

It's only been a couple of hours since they left, but I can't stop staring out the window into the darkness, nervously waiting for the headlights of the bus. I wish I could have gone with them, because not only do I hate waiting to find out what's going on, but this place is a nightmare.

Matthias holed us up in a two-story Victorian house with a giant dragon weathervane at the top of a tall spire. He wanted to put us in an easily recognizable house, and I'd agree that this one stands out from all the others with its green accents on a black house. It looks like a villain's castle from children's movies. I've only seen a handful of them, but I know bright green signifies evil, and this house definitely exudes those characteristics. I'm hoping Matthias comes to get us soon before the ghosts do.

"Liv, come check this out!" David calls out.

I shudder. David has been searching the house out of curiosity, and so far, he's found a collection of creepy old dolls with missing eyes and cracked porcelain faces. After that, he found a room of taxidermized animals, including a black cat in mid-stretch and a giant bat hanging from the rafters with its wings folded over itself, and then a room full of scary, impractical weapons, including one Frederick identified as an iron maiden. Whoever lived here was twisted.

"Let me guess," I say, trudging reluctantly to the hallway toward his voice, "you found a mummy?"

"Close." He shines his flashlight out of a doorway three doors down. "A skeleton."

"Jeez! This place is like a house of horrors." I cross my arms tightly around myself. "Matthias should have come inside to look around before he stuck us in here. We're going to get some sort of curse put on us."

"Don't be silly. This stuff is really interesting." David grins as he opens a desk drawer full of tiny corked jars. He picks one up that's half full of white powder and shines his flashlight at the little label. It reads, "Cyanide" in swirling black calligraphy letters.

"Put that back!" I yell.

"Relax, Liv. I doubt these are real."

"Take a look around you, David. This place gives me the creeps. I don't doubt that they would have poisons sitting in a drawer. You need to wash your hands now."

David sighs, but puts the jar back in its place, then heads to the bathroom with a bottle of water to rinse his hands off.

I stumble my way through the dark hallway and back to the room with the window seat I was sitting on before David's morbid discovery. I plop down on the lumpy cushion and continue staring out the window. The wind occasionally blows

405

the snow up against the glass, obscuring my view. The house does a good enough job at keeping us sheltered from the wind, but without heat, it's still freezing in here. I put my feet up on the window seat and wrap my jacket around my knees, pulling the zipper up to my chin.

Everyone else is camped out either in the living room or the dining room next to it. I would probably feel safer being around a bunch of people, but I also want to be alone with the mood I'm still in. Well, mostly alone, with David dropping in and out of the room as he tours the house. The depression hasn't released me from its death grip yet. With visions of the dead soldier's face and the bodies of Eli's campmates lying dead in the snow because of David's and my actions, I'm not sure how soon I'll be able to shake out of this.

David shines the flashlight at my face. "I'm going to go check out the basement. Wanna come?"

I hold my hand up to block the light from my eyes. "No! Are you nuts?"

"Not nuts, just curious," he says, turning to leave me in the dark once again. Only now the dark seems darker after being blinded by the flashlight.

"Hey, do you have another flashlight I could use?" I call after him.

"Yeah, there's one in the side pocket of my bag. See ya later," he yells back from down the hallway.

I opt to crawl around the floor as I try to find his bag, being careful not to run into the gaudy four-poster bed set up in the middle of the room. I let out a squeal when I slide my hand over a furry lump. I finally find his bag next to the doorway and pull out the flashlight, shining it toward the floor where the lump was. I let out another squeal when the beam lands on a dead mouse. Even though I know it's not going to get rid of any germs, I immediately rub my hand on my pants.

I shine the flashlight back toward our bags and pull out a water bottle so I can clear away some of the dust in my throat. As I go to put the bottle back, I see David's bag is open slightly, and Angel's note is lying at the top. I instinctively reach out to grab it but then freeze. This would be a violation of his trust. He asked me to trust him, so wouldn't reading the note without his permission be a betrayal of that trust?

I stare at it for a moment, torn between my curiosity and my conscience. I huff as I zip his bag up and go back over to the window seat. I know I would have read that note in a heartbeat before our little talk, but now I want to be better. I stare out the window for a little while longer, fighting temptation, until I finally can't stand it anymore. I grab the bags and head downstairs by everyone else.

I drop our stuff on top of the pile of everyone else's bags. "What are you guys up to?"

People are gathered around the fireplace, where a cheery fire is roaring in its depths. Frederick figured it would be safe to have smoke coming out of the chimney since it's dark outside. The warmth of the fire is comforting, but the long, eerie shadows it's casting around the room are not.

"We're just twiddling our thumbs as we wait for our ride." Henry crosses his arms over his stomach and slumps deeper into the couch.

I take a seat next to him. "You really wanted to go along, huh?"

"Beats sitting around here, worrying about what's going on. What if they get caught and killed? How much time do we give them before we assume the worst?"

"It's going to be fine, Henry," Rebecca reassures him. "Just get some rest so you can be ready to lend a hand once they get here."

It grows quiet in the room, and soon people start to drift off to sleep. The children have already been put to bed in the corner, all sharing an unzipped sleeping bag to keep them warm. Soon Rebecca and Caroline join them. The men who aren't on watch take the dining room so the women and children can stay warm by the fire.

After I've stared at the fire for about ten minutes, David is finally back from his basement excursion and takes a seat by me, pulling me from my thoughts of doom and gloom about what could be happening to Matthias.

"What'd you find?" I ask as he stretches out his legs with a groan.

"Not much. They had it decorated as a dungeon down there, you know—chains, whips, shackles, a whipping post—nothing too unusual," he whispers casually.

I glance at him, and he's smirking, the fire reflecting in his eyes. I laugh a little and rest my head on his shoulder. Frederick stokes the fire again, and after staring at it for a while, I can't keep my eyes open anymore. David and I join the rest of the group and lie down to get some sleep.

■■■■■

A honking sound jolts me awake. I sit up and see everyone else looking around at each other, trying to make sense of the sound. The morning sun shines through the stained-glass picture window, throwing splashes of colors all around us. Before anyone has quite figured out what we heard, someone comes crashing through the front door.

"Out! Out now! We need to go!" Matthias yells.

A loud rumbling sound is coming from in front of the house. Panic sets in as everyone's up on their feet, scrambling to collect their stuff.

"What's going on, Pop?" Henry slings his bag onto his back. His blanket is hanging half out of the zipper, and a dirty sock falls to the floor. Henry reaches down to snatch it up and stuff it in his pocket as he rushes to follow Matthias out the door.

"Don't worry about whose stuff is whose. Just grab what you can carry and get on the bus. We'll sort it out later!" Rebecca commands.

David and I grab as much as we can carry and head out to the bus. The bright sun shining on the fresh snow is blinding. I squint as I run out to the old school bus. Its dirty yellow paint is chipping away, leaving spots of ugly brown rust. The oversized bus tires are wrapped in chains like Eli said. I follow behind David as he climbs up the bus steps. I notice the back window is broken, letting in cold air and exhaust fumes. It gives me a headache almost immediately. I spot the barrels of fuel sitting in the back and wonder if it's really safe to be traveling with them there, but I don't think on it too long.

David takes a seat, and I slide in next to him, sighing at how hard and uncomfortable the seat already is. We're sitting behind a heater vent, but it's only warm enough to take the edge off the frigid outside air. I remind myself that it's still better than walking. I look to the right and find Joselyn and Charlotte asleep in the seat across from us, both wrapped up tightly in their blankets. I can't believe they can sleep through all this commotion.

"What's going on, Pop?" Henry asks again from the front seat.

"Is that everyone?" Matthias asks as Frederick climbs the stairs.

Henry throws his hands up in frustration.

"Yup. I double-checked the rooms. That's everyone."

Matthias takes his place behind the wheel and pulls the doors closed. "Take a seat, and hang on!" He puts the bus into gear and stomps on the gas.

17

"Alexandrine! You mind filling us in while Pop drives?" Henry calls back to Alexandrine, who's sitting in front of the sleeping girls.

"We snuck up on the camp, and Charlotte did her thing. Unfortunately, covering our ears wasn't enough, and we all fell asleep, waking up only five minutes before people in their camp woke up. As we were driving away, they fired shots at us, breaking the back window, but otherwise, we got away unharmed."

"Then why all the panic and rushing around?" Henry asks.

"Because Matthias took a wrong turn and got too close to the city. We weren't sure whether we were spotted or not until Cindy swore she heard the siren of an old police car in the distance. They're going to be able to follow us because of our tracks, but we have the advantage with our big chained tires."

"How long do you think we have until they catch up?" Caroline asks.

"There's no way to know. We're just hoping they can't drive in this snow, but we have to keep going as fast as we can, just in case."

I look down in my lap and remember I have someone else's bag.

"Hey, whose bag is this?" I call out holding it up.

We all get busy sorting out whose stuff is whose, giving us something to do. Joselyn and Charlotte wake up in the bustle and are now playing pat-a-cake with each other, adding to the noise of the already raucous bus.

The clamor starts to weigh on me. It feels like an angry nest of hornets buzzing in my brain. The mixture of exhaust fumes and the overwhelming sound is starting to make my stomach upset, so I cover my ears and squeeze my eyes shut, trying to block out the sound, but it's no use. I'm grateful to be on our way to the Haven, but I didn't realize just how miserable this ride was going to be.

"You okay, Liv?" David rubs my back, careful to avoid my cut.

"It's loud in here."

"Yup, and it seems worse with our Rare hearing. I almost miss the days when I could turn off my hearing aids," he says.

After a few more minutes of chaos, everyone finally has their bags, and it quiets down. I rest my head against the back of the seat and stare at the roof, lost in thought. I jump a little when Matthias accidentally grinds a gear, but otherwise, the rumble of the bus has lulled me into a semi-relaxed state now. I grab David's hand and thread my fingers through his, wanting the comfort of his touch.

"Do you hear that?" David whispers.

"Hear what?" I whisper back.

"There's a weird 'wop-wop' sound that I can't place."

I close my eyes and tip my head to the side to see if I can pick out what he's hearing, but all I can hear is the bus engine, Joselyn and Charlotte giggling, and the sounds coming from the broken window in the back. Concentrating as hard as I can, I finally catch it. My heart starts racing right before I realize what it is.

"Helicopter!" David and I both yell at the same time.

"Matthias, we hear a helicopter!" I jump to my feet with difficulty as the bus bounces around. "We need to hide somewhere!"

"Hide a bus? How're we going to do that?" Rebecca grabs hold of her twin boys protectively.

"We can't exactly hide when the tire tracks give our location away," Henry adds.

"We can't stay out in the open either!" Caroline throws back, her brows furrowed in concern as she holds Sonya tightly on her lap while her other two children hug each other.

"Everyone quiet! I think I see a warehouse up ahead. We'll pull in there and figure out a plan!" Matthias barks.

I look out the windshield, and he's right. There's a big building up ahead. As we get closer, we can see part of the roof has caved in and the doors are hanging off their hinges, but we should be able to pull the bus in and keep it out of sight. The helicopter sound is getting loud enough that I don't need to strain to hear it anymore. Matthias maneuvers the bus through the doorway, but the metal doors are not quite open wide enough, and it makes a sickening screech as we drive in. He parks the bus as far away from the hole in the roof as possible and turns off the engine.

"All right, here's what I'm thinkin'." Matthias stands to face us all. "We need to grab our stuff and get as far away from the bus as we can before the helicopter shows up. They could have weapons to shoot at us, and we don't want to be here when they do."

"But they could see our footprints," someone from behind me chimes in.

"It's not a perfect solution," Matthias growls, "but if we sit here arguin', that chopper is gonna be here in the next minute or so, and we won't have a choice to get away. So, grab your stuff and move!"

Everyone obeys, and we climb off the bus, huddling together as a crowd. Matthias leads us to a side door and wrenches it open.

"This way," Matthias orders.

He heads outside, and there's another building right next to this one only a short distance away. Matthias runs through the snow to the side door and tries to open it, but it's locked. The helicopter is almost here. Matthias gives the door a hard kick, busting the door frame away from the crumbling bricks. Everyone hurries to get inside, and I watch in horror as the helicopter comes swooping into view.

"It's here!" I yell as David pulls me into the building.

This place seems to have been an office building. The cubicle walls are still standing like ghostly sentries protecting the long-abandoned computers. We all head to the back of the room and gather around Matthias as a voice echoes around us from outside.

"*By order of President Sawyer, surrender yourselves.*"

"What do we do?" Henry asks.

Matthias pulls at his beard and then looks at Joselyn. "Think ya could use your power to knock these guys out?"

"Sorry, Jossy's not available right now. Please, try again later," Cindy says, impersonating a voice mail message.

"Cut the crap, Cindy! Give control back over to Joselyn so we can get out of here," Rebecca says, exasperated.

"*We repeat, by order of President Sawyer, surrender yourselves now!*"

"If she does her thing, she'll cut the power to the helicopter, and those men will die," I point out.

"That's the idea." A hard edge fills Matthias's voice.

I look around at all the scared or angry faces staring at me and realize this is one of the moments Matthias was talking about. Choosing between the soldiers' lives or the lives of the people I love.

"Cindy, you need to force Joselyn out here. We need her," I say as calmly as I can, even though I know the weight of making the choice to kill someone is a heavy burden to bear, whether there's ever a right thing to do or not.

Matthias gives me a pat on the shoulder, and I fight the urge to jerk away. The helicopter noise continues to pound in my ears, making me anxious.

Everyone turns their attention from me to Cindy, and she doesn't take too kindly to that. She scowls and as she's about to say something—more than likely something sassy from the way her hands are now on her hips—she's interrupted by a spray of bullets hitting the building next to us. The building where we parked the bus.

We all instinctively drop to the floor, covering our heads. The kids start to cry, except for Noah, who puts on a brave face as he holds his little sister's hand.

"All right, all right," huffs Cindy. Then closing her eyes, she says, "Joselyn, your services are needed!"

"*Come out with your hands up, or we'll shoot again!*"

"What's going on?" Joselyn squeaks.

"We need you to do your thing again," Alexandrine answers.

Joselyn's eyes grow big, and she starts shaking. "I-I can't."

Another round of shots fire at the building, drawing screams from Emily and a few of the adults.

"Come on, Jos. You can do it," Charlotte encourages with a quiver in her voice.

"Wait! If she does her thing here, we're all going to get hurt," Alexandrine warns. "Take her out of here, Matthias! Get her closer to the helicopter!"

Another dozen or so bullets are fired, and this time, a few hit the roof of the building we're in, leaving small beams of sunlight filtering in through the holes.

"We gotta go, now!" Matthias pulls a handgun out of his jacket. He grabs Joselyn's arm and drags her toward the door.

I grab onto David's hand and squeeze. They're going to get shot, and I just talked Cindy into it! I listen to their footsteps grow farther away. How are they going to get to the other building without being spotted?

"It's going to be okay. Shhh, quiet down Sonya," Caroline soothes, holding a now screaming Sonya.

"Try singing the song to her again," Frederick suggests.

"Hush little one, with a face so sweet," Caroline sings frantically. "A precious little girl, I was blessed to meet."

Just then, more bullets are fired, and we all freeze in fear that they killed Matthias and Joselyn. I let out a sob as fear wracks my brain. Sonya is still screaming, so Caroline snaps back into the moment and tries again.

"Ten perfect fingers and ten tiny toes," Caroline sings, voice catching. "Brown curly hair, and a cute button—"

An extreme pressure builds up in my skull, and the last thing I see is the pained faces of everyone around me. I try to hold on as long as I can, but I can't take it anymore as my brain feels like it's being crushed in a vice, and I fade to black.

1 8

I inhale sharply as I come to. It takes me a few seconds to remember where I am and that I need to find Matthias.

There's something heavy on my back. I reach my hand around me and feel someone's head. I wiggle back and forth, trying to get out from under them, desperate to know what's going on. I'm finally free, but my head aches, and my lungs work double-time trying to catch my breath, leaving me disoriented. After the room stops spinning, I look over and see it was David on top of me. In fact, everyone is lying on top of each other in a big pile.

I check on the children to make sure they aren't being squished, and it looks like they're fine, so I leave them where they are. Once my heavy breathing has subsided, I suddenly realize how quiet it is. I don't hear the helicopter anymore, and although that's a relief, the silence is also terrifying. I shake David's shoulder, desperate to have him by my side again. He groans a little, so I shake harder.

"David! David, wake up!"

He snaps awake and sits upright. "You okay, Liv?" David says with concern, but then stops to hold his head as he takes a moment to gather himself.

"I don't know. We need to find Matthias," I mumble as I turn to leave.

"Wait, I'll come with you." He holds his hand out to me so I can help him up.

We stumble our way to the door, and David grabs my jacket to pull me back before I carelessly walk outside.

"We need to make sure the coast is clear before you go waltzing outside!" David scolds.

My first reaction is to get mad at him, but he's right. That was foolish. I wait as he carefully looks out the door and then beckons me to follow him. We run as fast as we can to the building where the bus is parked. Once inside, I spot Joselyn cowering in the corner and Matthias passed out on the dirty floor in an awkward position.

"Check for a pulse, I'll help Joselyn," I say to David. I run over to Joselyn and wrap my arms around her, rubbing her back. "Shh. It's going to be okay, Joselyn. Are you all right? Do you know where the helicopter went?"

She looks up at me with red rimmed eyes, a clump of her long hair is stuck to the snot running out of her nose. "They crashed it, but I don't know whether they're dead or not," she says miserably.

"Matthias is alive," David calls out to me.

"You did a great job, Joselyn. Stay here, though, while David and I go check on the soldiers."

She nods and hides her face in her knees again.

David grabs the gun still in Matthias's hand, and we head over to the front doors, pressing our backs to the wall. David slowly peers around the corner out the doors, then quickly pulls back in and whispers, "It looks like the helicopter hit a tree on the way down, breaking off the blades or whatever those things on the top are called. The helicopter is laying on its side facing away from us. I can't see the soldiers."

"Let's go check it out. We need to make sure they can't follow us." I swallow hard. My shoulders slump as the weight of what I'm insinuating hits me.

David takes the lead, holding the gun out in front of him as we go. We crouch as we run to the bottom of the damaged machine, instinctively trying to stay low. David puts the gun's safety back on and sticks it in his back pants pocket so he can climb on top of the helicopter. Once he's up, he immediately takes the gun back out again. He pulls the door open with one hand while pointing the barrel into the cockpit.

I cover my ears, waiting for him to shoot, but he doesn't. In fact, he turns his face away, grimacing, and shoves the gun into his jacket pocket.

"What? What is it?" I ask. "Are they dead?"

"Yeah." He nods slowly. "Definitely."

As David climbs down, curiosity gets the better of me and I walk around the helicopter to peek through the windows at them. One glance and I turn away, unable to look at the gruesome sight for more than a second.

David wraps his arm around me. "Liv, you shouldn't have done that."

"Let's get back to the others." I automatically move that direction.

As we step back into the warehouse, we see Matthias sitting up, holding his head in his hands. When he hears our footsteps his head snaps upwards as his hand reaches for the gun he usually keeps on his hip. "What the...?"

"Here." David gives the gun back to Matthias. "You okay?"

"Yeah. Thanks to her, I'm alive." Matthias straps the gun back in his holster.

"What happened?" I ask, trying to force the image of the soldiers out of my mind. "We heard shots and thought you were dead."

"No, the girl stepped in front of me when the bullets started flying, and I watched as they missed us and hit the floor around our feet instead."

"That was Landon," Joselyn says quietly from the corner.

"Either way, ya saved my life." Matthias grunts as he stands up. "Did you make sure the soldiers were taken care of?"

"Yeah. They were already dead," David answers.

"Good. Let's get everyone back on the bus. We need to get outta here."

"You have to stop beating yourself up," I hear Charlotte say to Joselyn. "You did exactly what you were supposed to do. You saved us all."

"I know. It's just—" she stops to take a shuddering breath.

I keep my eyes closed but my ear turned toward them so I can hear what they're saying.

"Just what?"

"I tried something new. I tried to concentrate my ability directly at the soldiers and—and I could feel them. No. Not feel. Sense. I was aware of what I was doing to them. I was aware that I was destroying their brains." She sniffs.

"We felt your ability too, though. We all passed out. Those soldiers probably just died from crashing the helicopter," Charlotte says, trying to comfort Joselyn.

"No. This was different," Joselyn insists.

"Okay, fine. How about we talk about something else?"

I look over at David to see if he heard what Joselyn said. He has his head pressed against the bus window, staring at the scenery passing by. I lay my hand on his arm. "Did you hear what Joselyn just said?"

"Huh?" He blinks as he focuses his attention on me. "No, I wasn't listening."

"Joselyn just said that she concentrated her Rare ability toward the soldiers and sensed what she was doing to them. I didn't realize we could control our abilities like that."

"I wonder how she would have known to do that." David scratches at his jaw. "Maybe she's onto something."

"But how can I concentrate my ability when they're dreams? I have no control."

"I don't know. Maybe it's a question for when we get to the Haven." David turns to look out the window again.

I close my eyes, trying to relax as we jostle around in the bus seat. Matthias is driving as fast as he safely can, which isn't very fast. He told us to keep an ear out for any more helicopters, but for some reason, I feel like that was going to be the only one.

After about three hours, Matthias pulls over for a bathroom break. He finds a rundown gas station and pulls underneath the canopy to hide the bus as best we can.

"Think the toilets would still work?" I ask David.

David pats my back. "Probably not."

As I step off the bus, a biting wind hits my face, making my nostrils almost freeze shut as I try to take a deep breath of fresh air. I stretch out my sore legs as I look around. The sun is close to setting, leaving the sky a mixture of pink and orange on the horizon. It reflects off the sparkly snow, and I take a moment to soak it in. David joins me, hugging me from behind, and we sway back and forth, silently having a moment.

While we're enjoying the view, other people work on picking a spot behind the building to do our business. Matthias, Frederick, and Henry discuss the best way to fill the bus back up with fuel from the barrels. I'm glad to not be standing directly by the fumes coming from the barrels. I can smell it from here.

We join everyone else, and while we wait for our turn behind the building, I look through the gas station window and see it's been looted, but there's still some food left on the shelves.

"Think it's any good?" I ask David.

"I doubt it, but doesn't hurt to check it out."

We slip through the broken glass of the entrance and walk down the aisles in the growing darkness. I grab a package of little chocolate chip cookies and rip them open. They still smell good, so I pull one out and take a nibble. The texture is like eating sandstone, hard at first and then turns grainy in my mouth. I spit it out and put it back on the shelf.

"Ya guys realize this food is from before the war, right?" Matthias asks from the doorway as he washes his hands with a handful of snow. "After the bombs fell, and people were gathered up to go into the city, all this was abandoned. I wouldn't eat it if I were you."

"Is there anything that could still be good?" David calls out from the drink cases.

"Liquor. But ya probably aren't gonna find any of that by the looks of things," he says, then walks away, shaking his hands off.

We head to the alcohol section and find he's right. The shelves have been cleared.

"Too bad," David comments.

"Why? We can't drink. We're not old enough."

"Rebecca could have used it to sterilize medical equipment and stuff. And who's going to enforce the no drinking law? Matthias?" He gives me a devious smirk.

I push him playfully. "Rebel."

"I have an idea." David heads down another aisle. He picks through the stuff on the floor and finds a couple boxes of bandages. He holds them up in triumph.

We sort through the gas station quickly, seeing what we can find. David discovers a half drunk bottle of whiskey behind the service counter.

"The person who worked here must have had their own personal bottle. It's ours now." David shakes the bottle, making the liquor slosh around inside.

After we take our turn behind the building, we tramp back through the snow to the bus and find everyone's back on.

"Here, Rebecca," David says, handing the bandages and whiskey over.

"Um, thanks?" Rebecca says, holding the half-drunk bottle to eye level.

"I thought you could use it for sterilization," David says slowly.

"Oh, yes. Of course. I thought maybe you were telling me I needed it for self-medication," she says with a half laugh. "God knows I could use some." She glances back at Cindy, or at least Cindy's feet because she's sitting upside down with her feet stuck up in the air. Rebecca rolls her eyes and stashes the bottle in her medical bag.

"Matthias, do you think it's such a good idea to drive in the dark? Our headlights will be easily spotted," Frederick points out.

"I think it's a risk worth takin'." Matthias pulls the doors closed. "All right, everyone sit down. It's time to go."

■■■■■

"Matthias, you need a break," Frederick says.

I've been sleeping on and off for the last few hours. These bus seats do not make for comfortable sleeping conditions, but I've been able to doze out of sheer exhaustion.

"Do ya know how to drive a bus?" Matthias's jaws crack with an enormous yawn.

"No, but if you can do it, how hard can it be?" Frederick chuckles.

Matthias must be tired, because he pulls over and lets Frederick take the wheel.

"Anything I should be looking for that would be worth me waking you up?" Frederick asks.

"Not really. We crossed the river a while ago over the bridge Eli told me about. I thought that was gonna be one of the hardest parts of this whole trip. Figured there'd be guards or somethin', but there wasn't. Now that we're in the DMZ, it should be easy sailin' as far as Coalition guards and soldiers go."

Matthias takes Frederick's spot next to Henry and lays his head back on the seat. It'll do him good to get some rest. He's always trying to do too much. I turn back toward David and lay my head on his shoulder and start dozing off.

I stare out the window at the thick gray clouds hanging heavy in the sky. A feeling of unease settles in my mind out of nowhere.

We've had quite a few twists and turns as we navigated around fallen trees or abandoned cars left to disintegrate in the elements. Now Matthias has found a stretch of flat road, cutting through large swaths of nothingness. There's not a soul in sight, and yet I can't shake a feeling of dread.

"You okay, Liv?" David asks when I squeeze his arm a little tighter.

"No. Not really," I say. "I just feel like something bad is about to happen."

At that moment, I spot a wall of white coming toward us quickly from across a field.

"What's that?" I hear someone ask from a seat in front of us.

"I think it's snow. Matthias, we should pull over," Alexandrine says.

"We're fine. We need to keep going," Matthias answers stubbornly.

The wall of snow hits us, causing a complete whiteout. We can't see anything directly in front of us. An abandoned semi-truck suddenly comes into view, and Matthias swerves sharply to miss it. Everyone screams as the bus tips over, throwing the people on my side of the bus onto the opposite side. My head slams into the metal ceiling as David falls on top of me, crushing the air out of my lungs.

I wake up with a throaty gasp, as though I really can't breathe.

"Liv! You okay?"

I take a moment to catch my breath. "No, I just had a vision. We're going to get slammed by a blizzard, Matthias is going to swerve to miss a truck, and the bus is going to tip over."

David instinctively looks out the window, but it's still dark out. "When's it going to happen? Now?"

"No. It was light out when the storm hit," I say, rubbing at my forehead.

"You should let Matthias know."

"It can wait until he's awake." I sigh, settling back in the seat. I do some deep breathing to try to calm my heart down. The way I feel after having these visions makes me wonder if this ability is a gift or a curse.

20

"A blizzard, huh? Well, I guess we'll just keep goin', and when you see the wall of white, let me know, and we'll stop."

I nod and go back to David.

"I'm not sure the blizzard is going to hit us today. Look at how clear and beautiful the sky is," David says, staring up at the sky.

"I wish there were a way to know the timing of my visions," I mutter.

"Hey, at least you have the gift. Now we know to look for the storm." David wraps his arm around my shoulder.

I sigh and go back to staring out the window. I'm bored out of my mind. David and I are running out of things to talk about. I find myself wanting another pendant puzzle to solve or a book to read. I feel like I'm going to die of boredom staring at this vast white void.

The day is half done, and there are still no signs of clouds anywhere. I'm beginning to think the vision wasn't for today.

We traveled through what felt like endless flat nothingness. With the snow on the ground, it's hard to know where the old fields end and the road begins, and if not for random abandoned cars, it would be easy to lose track of where we are.

"Once we find some woods, we need to hunt," Matthias says.

"Would they be safe to eat? Isn't everything radioactive around here?" Tim asks.

"We don't have a lot of options. It's been a long time since the nukes dropped. It'll be fine," Matthias answers.

"What do you think, Denis?" Tim whispers from two seats ahead of me. I've tried to not eavesdrop on people, but sometimes I can't help it; their conversations catch my attention.

"I think we're going to see a lot of animals with defects, but that doesn't necessarily mean they'll be inedible."

"Good," Tim says. "I wonder why these fields haven't turned into forests yet."

"That sort of thing takes time. It's also possible that the nukes fell around this area, making the land unstable for reforestation."

I turn back to David and see he's drawing a heart around our initials in the condensation on the window. I add an arrow to the heart, and as I'm leaning over him, he whispers, "I love you," in my ear.

"I love you too," I whisper back. I let out a happy sigh, realizing the depression clouding my mind has finally released me. For now, anyway. I actually feel pretty good.

We continue driving until late afternoon without any breaks, and I'm getting restless. I want off the bus. Since we don't have much to drink, we haven't had the need to stop, and the kids have been growing rowdy, making a lot of the adults cranky. I feel bad for the children. They're full of energy with no way to expend it.

We finally come up to a little abandoned town, and I'm so grateful to have something to look at other than flat fields. The houses aren't anything special, but they're better than nothing. The town's water tower still stands, but unfortunately, the letters have faded away and are unreadable.

"Think we could stop for the night? Give us a break from the bus for a while?" Rebecca asks.

I hear quite a few people voice their agreement.

"Fine. I'm gettin' tired of drivin' anyway." Matthias pulls the bus into the driveway of a quaint two-story house.

As soon as we're parked, everyone stands up, desperate to get off the bus. The children start a game of tag as soon as their feet hit the ground. Their laughter fills the air, and it makes me wonder how long it's been since this town has had the sound of humans in it. I drop my bag in the snow and stretch, watching the children run, as the adults go in the house to check things out. Sonya toddles by, and I pretend to start chasing her, making her squeal with delight. The other kids take notice and ask me to chase them too. I take off after Noah, careful not to allow my competitiveness and Rare abilities to ruin their fun. After a while, Cass, Charlotte, Joselyn, and even David are running around, getting into the spirit of things.

The last of the day's sunlight fades away, and we hear Alexandrine call from the house, "Time to come inside, kids."

The children let out a groan, unhappy to be cooped back up inside.

I grab my bag and follow David into the house, relieved we will be able to sleep lying down tonight.

One of the adults lit a fire in the house's fireplace, filling the large room with a cozy glow, but that's where the pleasantness of the room ends. The furniture is ghastly: sky blue couches with big orange flowers, yellow square end tables, a purple-and-black zebra-print rug on top of the light green carpet, and thick red curtains framing the window. Whoever lived here must have been trying for a rainbow color scheme, but it looks more like a unicorn visited them after drinking too much and blew chunks all over the room.

Everyone gathers in the living room or the adjoining kitchen, and Matthias suggests we all pile the remainder of our food out on a blanket. David reluctantly adds the last can of soda and bag of chips he got from Angel into the pile.

"This is it?" Matthias strokes his beard.

Alexandrine glances around at everyone. "Looks like it."

"I'm going to have to go hunting sooner than I thought," he grumbles. "All right, share your food with people who might not have any, and I'll go huntin' first thing in the mornin'."

David grabs for his can of soda as Cindy lunges for it. They both stubbornly hold onto the can, waiting for the other person to let go first.

"It's my can of soda, Cindy," David says.

"You heard Matthias. You have to share it." She crinkles her nose and glares.

"He said to share *food*. Technically, this is a drink, not food."

"You guys could split it," I suggest, a little shocked David is fighting so hard for it.

"Ew! I don't want to swap spit with pretty boy."

"Pretty boy?" David looks at me with furrowed eyebrows. "You know what? Fine. Take it." As a big grin spreads across her face, I hear David say under his breath, "I hope you choke on it."

"David! What was that all about?" I ask once Cindy triumphantly waltzes back to Charlotte. We watch as she opens the can and chugs half of it in one go.

"She just rubs me the wrong way. Jokes on her though. I lied about that being my last can." He pulls a Mello Yello out just enough that I can see it. "Wanna share it with me?"

"Let's go to a different room first. I don't want Cindy to know you lied about having another can. We'd never hear the end of it." I grab David's flashlight out of his bag.

David waggles his eyebrows at me. "You okay with swapping spit with me?"

I laugh. "What's wrong with your face?"

"What? That doesn't do it for you? How about this?" He does a half smile, looks at me intensely, and bobbles his head back and forth.

I laugh harder. "Just go," I say, pushing him out of the room.

I follow him down the hallway, peeking into the rooms with the flashlight as we pass by. It turns out the living room wasn't the only hideous room in the house. The bathroom is not only painted pink, with a pink sink and bathtub, but the toilet is adorned with a fluffy pink toilet lid cover and matching floor rug, and the shower curtain is pink lace. We look into the next room and see a bedroom decorated in a country motif with a big wagon wheel hung on the wall above the bed, and what I think is a cowskin rug on the floor. The bed's covered in a busy patchwork quilt made with clashing colors and no visible pattern. There are pictures of barns and livestock hanging on the wall, and little cow figurines on the bedside tables.

"Who the heck lived here?" I ask.

"Should we go upstairs and check out the rest of the house?"

"I don't know if I can handle much more of this." I hear Cindy cackling about something in the living room—probably high on sugar from the soda—and the children fighting over who gets the last peach out of the can and decide I would rather wander around this crazy house in a modicum of silence than be by the chaos in the living room.

I gesture to the stairs. "Lead the way."

We walk up the stairway, our feet hardly making a sound as they sink into the plush gray carpet. We come to the landing and find three doorways up here.

The first bedroom is adorned with pictures of clowns and other circus performers on red-and-white striped walls, a bright yellow bedspread with a cartoon seal balancing a blue ball on its nose, and in the corner is a stuffed animal holder built to look like a cage in a zoo. It has a white wooden frame with bungee cords as the bars. It's still full of stuffed animals, all staring outward, as though waiting for their long-lost owner to return and set them free from their fifty-year imprisonment.

"Maybe we should tell Rebecca and Caroline what's up here so they can surprise the kids with new toys," I suggest.

"Good idea. I bet they would be happy to have something different to play with," David agrees.

We step out of that room and find the next door leads to a remarkably plain half-bath. Everything is white, except for the wood cabinet beneath the sink. It's kind of a shock after seeing such wild decorations in the rest of the house.

The last room looks to have belonged to a teenager. I shine the flashlight slowly around the room. The walls are plastered with posters of people I can only assume were popular before the war. Some of the boys in the pictures are kind of cute, however, if they're still alive, they'd be old enough to be my grandpa. A pang hits me as my thoughts now turn to Saul. I didn't know him well, but I still miss him.

There's a TV on top of a black dresser, directly across from the bed. The bed has a soft purple comforter still disheveled from the last time it was slept in. We walk farther into the spacious room and see a vanity with photos taped to the mirror. There are pictures of teenage girls hugging each other and laughing, lying on towels at a beach, and dressed in pretty gowns standing with boys in suits. At the bottom of the mirror is a picture of a family that I can only assume are the owners of this house, since the girl is the same girl in all the other pictures.

David pulls open a drawer crammed full of stuff. "Check this out."

"Should we really be snooping through someone else's room?" I ask.

"It's not like they live here anymore." He shrugs, pulling a black book with a red flower embossed on the cover out of the drawer and flips through a few pages. "Eh, it's just a diary or something." David drops it back in the drawer.

"Wait. Let me see it." I open the front cover and find the first journal entry was dated a year before the war happened. "This might be interesting to read."

"I thought you didn't want to snoop through people's stuff?" He bumps his elbow into my arm.

I ignore him and grab the pencils and pens sitting in the drawer. I test the pens to see if they still work. They do, so I slip them in my pocket for Cass. There's a couple of notebooks in the drawer too. There are a few pages with math problems and science jargon, but the rest of it is blank. I take those too.

"Anything else you see that we could use?" I ask David.

"You could look through the closet and see if there're any clothes you could wear," David suggests.

"That's a good idea," I say.

I sort through her closet and see she has decent taste, but I don't have a lot of space in my bag, so I have to keep it to a minimum. I pull out a couple of t-shirts and sweaters I like and set them on the bed.

David cracks open the soda, and we sit on the floor, sharing it.

It's been so peaceful up here away from everyone, but our silence is interrupted when a loud humming noise comes from somewhere below us, and a light unexpectedly turns on in the room.

2'1

"What the—" David stands and reaches his hand out to pull me off the floor.

"How are the lights on?" I ask, a little spooked.

As we rush downstairs to see what's going on, we literally run into Frederick, who's standing at the base of the stairs.

"Sorry, Frederick," I say, holding onto his arm as I get my balance back. "What's going on? Why is there electricity?"

"Matthias and Henry found a generator out in the garage. It runs on diesel fuel, so they tinkered with it and got it running," Frederick explains. "I'm surprised it works after sitting for so long, but I'm glad it does." He gives us a big smile under his bushy mustache, pats my arm, and then heads farther down the hall.

David and I continue to the living room.

"I haven't seen electricity in ages." Caroline looks at the lamp and smiles. "I didn't realize how much I missed it until now."

People start to scatter throughout the house, searching the rooms now that they can turn the lights on. Cass is still sitting next to the fire, so I take this opportunity to give her the stuff I found.

"David and I grabbed these for you. There's a few pages in the front with writing on it, but otherwise, it's empty." I hand her one of the notebooks, as well as a few pens and pencils. I decided to keep a notebook and pen for myself in the hope it'll keep me from being bored on the bus.

"No way! Thank you." She gives me a hug.

I head over to my bag and cram all the stuff inside, hoping my zipper doesn't break as I force it closed.

"Well, we still don't have use of the bathroom or anything, but it'll be nice to have some light." Matthias walks into the house, wiping his hands on a rag.

"This is great. Thank you," Caroline says.

"Yeah, thanks," I add.

Everyone one else who's in the room nods or expresses their gratitude. Matthias just nods and gives a half smile as he heads back to the garage.

Looking at Caroline, I remember we were going to tell her about the stuffed animals. "Caroline, there were some t-o-y-s upstairs in a bedroom." I spell it out in case the women don't want the kids to have them. "David and I thought that maybe you'd like to check them out for the kids."

"That's very thoughtful of you. I'm sure they'd love that." She smiles. "C'mon kids. Olivia found a surprise for you upstairs."

The children all jump to their feet in excitement and race up the stairs, with Caroline yelling at them to "wait up."

It's nice and calm now in the living room. David and I take a seat on the couch and find that, even though it's hideous, it's actually quite comfortable.

Our silence is short-lived as Nathaniel and Rebecca come flying into the room.

"Where's Matthias?" Rebecca asks.

"He's in the garage. Why? What's wrong?" David answers.

"We need to go back!" She pulls Nathaniel to the garage.

"Should we follow them to find out what's going on?" I ask David.

David answers by standing. We walk through the kitchen and head to the only door that leads out. The garage isn't heated, and I immediately feel the chill after being warm by the fire.

"Slow down," Matthias grunts. "What are ya tellin' me?"

"There was a TV in one of the rooms. Nathan turned it on and flipped through a few staticky channels until we found one that you could almost see a picture on. There was a guy's voice, broken up a bit, but we could still hear it. He was saying the Haven is a lie—a trap set up to lure people to their deaths. That if you see this broadcast, your lives are in danger and you need to return to a designated city before it's too late," Rebecca says, shaking.

"Sounds like Coalition lies," Matthias growls.

"We have to go back!" Nathan's eyes are wide in fear. "We're going to be killed, and it's all your fault!" Nathan grabs Matthias's shoulders, but that was a bad move.

Matthias blocks Nathan's hands and puts him in an arm bar, slamming him against the wall. "I don't know what's wrong with ya, but we're goin' to the Haven. The Coalition are a bunch of liars, and I will never set foot in one of their cities again."

"But the Haven isn't real!" Rebecca hugs herself.

"Please, Matthias. Take us back. I don't want to die," Nathan pleads with a whimper.

Matthias lets go of his arm and then looks around at David, Henry, and I as though searching for help on what to do.

"You'd be more likely to die going back to the city. They kill people for being traitors, and that's what we are. We can't go back now," Henry argues.

"Maybe Turk would be understanding about the whole thing. The Coalition will take us back. I know it!" Rebecca says in tears. "Please, Matthias. I don't want to die."

Matthias shakes his head as he looks back and forth at Rebecca and Nathan, who are now clinging to each other's hands. They apparently can't be reasoned with while they're like this.

"How about you sleep on it, and we'll talk about it in the morning when the sun's up," I suggest.

Nathan and Rebecca look at each other and nod. Nathan wraps his arm around Rebecca's shoulders and leads her back into the house.

"What was that all about?" Henry asks after they close the door.

"That was weird," I comment.

"If they keep insistin' on goin' back, I'll have no choice but to leave them behind to make their own way. A bullet to their heads would probably be more humane."

"Pop!"

"You can't kill Rebecca. We need her," I say, appalled.

"Let's just hope it doesn't come to that, then." Matthias walks back toward the house.

Henry, David, and I follow.

▪▪▪▪▪

The fire burned out while everyone was sleeping since there wasn't enough wood in the house to keep it lit all night. I wake up to the sounds of sniffling and wonder if it's from the cold or if Rebecca is still crying.

Nathaniel and Rebecca stayed huddled together in the corner of the living room, whispering intently to each other and weeping until it was time to sleep. Rebecca hardly responded when her twins, Joey and Isaac, tried to show her their new-to-them stuffed animals.

I could tell they were hurt when she didn't show as much enthusiasm as they were hoping for.

Caroline saw it too and ushered them back over to where Noah and Emily were putting on a play and then snapped at Rebecca for being distant. It didn't seem to make much difference.

Now I hear Matthias and Henry whispering to each other as they get ready to head out hunting. I feel bad for thinking it, but I'm happy it's them going out into the cold and not me.

"I'm so sorry, Matthias," I hear Rebecca say. "I have no idea what came over me last night."

"I take it you're feelin' better now?"

"Yeah, much. It came out of nowhere. I couldn't shake the feeling we were on our way to our deaths, and it terrified me."

"Well, I'm glad you're back," I hear Matthias say. "We might be stayin' here another day dependin' on how well Henry and I do hunting. Make sure nobody watches the cursed TV while we're gone, eh?"

"Yes, sir," Rebecca says with a nervous chuckle.

Matthias opens the front door, blasting us all with bitterly cold air.

I shiver and pull the blanket up over my head. I'm relieved Rebecca is feeling better, but shouldn't we figure out what caused her to freak out? Whatever it was, I hope it doesn't happen again. Some of the men went out this morning to find burning materials so we could rebuild the fire and melt snow for drinking water. It's good to have water to drink, but my stomach is growling, and I'm tempted to see what canned goods might be in the cupboard. However, getting food poisoning is not worth making my stomach stop growling temporarily, so I stay put.

We all agreed that even though it's nice to have electricity, we should only turn the generator on in the evening, so we can conserve the fuel. It's starting to grow dark, but Matthias still isn't back yet, so we're holding off until they're here to fire it up again.

I hope they were able to find some animals to kill. The kids are all complaining about being hungry, and their whining is getting annoying.

Nathaniel and Rebecca have been putting in extra effort to help people when needed. I think they feel bad for their behavior, even though they can't figure out why they felt that way to begin with. Joey and Isaac are quick to forgive Rebecca when she gushes over the toys they tried to show her last night. She even allows them to choose a second animal to keep, much to Caroline's annoyance, because now all the children want a second one.

"Well, pickin's were slim, but we got enough for supper," Matthias announces as he and Henry come tramping back into the house, holding game bags full of meat.

Frederick sets to cooking the meat over the fire while Henry and Matthias clean up. Tim finds some salt in the cupboard and tests it.

"Still good!" he announces, and everyone cheers. It's the little things that bring happiness nowadays.

The smell of the meat cooking has everyone huddled together in anticipation. Matthias turns the generator back on, and I can't help but feel a sense of home. I know it won't be long before we hit the road, but having electricity has been a creature comfort that everyone seems to be enjoying.

"What kinds of animals were you able to find?" Rebecca asks Matthias as we wait to eat.

Matthias and Henry exchange a look before answering. "A deer, a few squirrels, and a wolf that started following us."

"We're eating a wolf?" Joselyn asks.

"Meat's meat," Matthias answers with a look that dares her to complain.

She takes the hint and doesn't say anything more.

"That's right. Meat's meat, even if it is mutated," Henry adds under his breath.

"Wait, what?" I whisper.

"The deer had some weird growth on the side of its face. After we shot it, we discovered it was a second part of a head. It had teeth and an eyeball."

"Gross!"

"The rest of the deer seemed fine, so we decided it would be okay."

"How about the squirrels and the wolf?" I ask, even though I'm not sure I want to know.

"One of the squirrels had two tails, but otherwise, they were normal."

After knowing what we're eating, I find I don't have much appetite, but this is it for food, so I force it down.

"So, what's the plan? Are we sticking around for another day of hunting, or should we head out tomorrow?" Henry asks Matthias as everyone finishes their supper.

"I think it's best to move on," Mattias answers. "Unless anyone has reason to stay longer?"

Everyone looks around at each other, and we all agree we want to keep going.

"Good. Then, let's get some sleep." Matthias heads back out to the garage to shut off the generator.

22

We've been driving for two days straight. The skies have been crystal clear, without a cloud in sight. It makes the snow sparkle, which is beautiful, but it's painful to look at. Luckily for Matthias, Nathaniel had a pair of sunglasses he could wear, or he wouldn't have been able to drive in the blinding snow.

I started reading the journal I picked up from the house. There's a lot of typical girl stuff about boys and friend drama, but there are a few interesting entries. Like the one I read this morning:

> I don't understand why everyone is freaking out about people being Rare. Isn't it good that we're not all the same? They're always telling you to be yourself.
> Unless you're a Rare, I guess.
> So, I decided to start hiding my abilities from everyone. I know it's going to make playing sports harder, but I don't want to be called out. I'd rather fit in than be able to make every basket I shoot or show off my mind-reading tricks. Those have been getting me into trouble lately anyway. Scott hasn't talked to me in three days because I caught him thinking about Heather and yelled at him. I didn't mean to read his thoughts. It just sorta happened. He told me to stay out of his head and then went home. Maybe I should call him and see if we're still boyfriend/girlfriend. I make such a mess of everything.

She had the ability to read people's minds? I wonder to what extent. Could she do it whenever she wanted to? Or did it come and go like my ability?

I feel a little weird reading about someone's personal life, but isn't that how we learned about things from the past? Besides, I'm too curious not to. I wonder what it would be like to read people's minds. I could see how it would have its advantages, but there would be a lot of disadvantages too. If we can't have our own thoughts be private, then we wouldn't have any freedom. I know I wouldn't want people to hear what I'm thinking at times.

The journal and the notebook have been quite helpful in keeping me from being bored. David and I have been filling my notebook up with endless games of tic-tac-toe and hangman. We're playing our twentieth game of tic-tac-toe, and just as I'm about to beat him again, the bus makes sputtering noises and then stops moving.

The engine shuts off, making Matthias swear loudly.

"What's going on, Pop?" Henry asks.

"We ran out of fuel."

"Can't we just fill it back up?"

"Barrels are empty too."

"Even if we had some fuel, we wouldn't be able to start the engine again until you bled the fuel lines of the air that's now in them," Denis throws in, but nobody's really paying attention.

"Why didn't you tell anyone that we were almost out of fuel?" Alexandrine demands.

"What good would it have done for ya to sit here worryin' about it?" Matthias asks. "We're gonna have to keep goin' on foot. Bundle up, and let's go."

"But my vision of the blizzard happened while we were on the bus. Are you sure you can't get it running again?" I ask, confused.

"No. It musta just been a dream, not a vision," Matthias answers.

I shake my head. "No. It felt just like all my other visions. Something's not right."

"Maybe it's a sign that your visions can't always be trusted. Now, everyone grab your stuff, and let's get going," Matthias commands, ignoring my death glare.

People groan in frustration. This is not going to be fun. I moodily throw on extra socks and another sweater I got from journal girl. Once everyone has on extra layers, we get the kids set up in the sled and continue our way west.

How could my visions be wrong? What's the point of having visions if they can't be trusted? I think about the other visions I had and remember Matthias and Henry tied David and me up after first discovering us instead of being friendly like in my vision. Maybe they only hold part truths, but then, what about the bus? Perhaps the bit of truth is there's going to be a blizzard, or maybe Matthias is going to be stubborn and get us all hurt. It seems at this point, my vision of the future isn't going to help anything, and I will only make the connection after it happens.

How stupid.

After walking for hours, everyone is cold and hungry. We check out houses until we find one with a fireplace. Once settled, Matthias goes out hunting but comes back empty handed. The look of defeat reads loud and clear on his face. He feels like he's failed us all.

We melt as much snow as we can, trying in vain to stop the hunger pangs with water. Everyone sits quietly as we deal with our own discomfort, hoping tomorrow will bring better luck. Of all the things I've been through, I really hope I don't die from starvation.

Thankfully, the morning hunt is successful. Henry and Matthias were able to get two deer. We feast on as much meat as our bellies can hold.

This diet of nothing but meat is going to grow old quick. I'm already missing the meals we had at Eli's camp. I wonder what kind of food the Haven will have. I hope they have tacos.

Matthias bags up the rest of the meat and distributes it among the men to carry. They attach it to the outside of their bags to keep it exposed to the freezing temperatures. Let's hope it doesn't attract predators as we walk.

We walk until night starts to fall, but there aren't any houses in sight. We're moving at such a slow pace, there's no way we're going to find somewhere to stay before it's dark. We make it to the edge of a forest, and Matthias drops his bag.

"We'll build a big fire, and everyone will have to group together to stay warm. I thought there'd be a house nearby, but it looks like I'm wrong. Sorry, everyone."

There are some heavy sighs, but nobody dares complain to Matthias. He's doing the best he can, and we all know it. Instead, everyone uses what's left of their energy to pitch in and gather up wood to build the fire that might be our only lifeline out here. We set up camp by the edge of the woods and cook half of the remaining meat for supper. Matthias walks about a quarter mile away to tie the other half up in a tree for safety.

Sleeping is miserable. From the sounds of all the sniffing and shuffling around, I doubt anyone is getting any sleep. Henry, Matthias, Frederick, and Nathaniel take shifts keeping the fire going through the night, so we at least have a chance to survive. I wake up shivering and see in the light of dawn that Nathaniel is asleep on his post and the fire has burned down to embers. I start blowing into my gloves to bring feeling back into my fingertips, and that's when I hear footsteps approaching. They aren't being made by anyone from our camp. Everyone is here and accounted for. I have just enough time to shake Matthias before the footsteps make it to our camp.

"What in the Sam Hill are you guys doin' out here?" a deep voice calls out, waking everyone else in the camp up.

An old man with a handlebar mustache, a long leather trench coat, and a weathered cowboy hat stands about five yards away, looking at us as though we're crazy.

My breath catches a little when I see he has a rifle resting on his shoulder.

Matthias stands up slowly with his hands out. "We're just passin' through, sir. It got late, and we had to make camp. I'm sorry if we're on your property."

The old man studies Matthias as though trying to decide whether he's telling the truth by staring at him. He then cocks one eyebrow up and asks, "Where're you headed?"

Matthias clears his throat, then lifts his chin up, "Well, sir, we're headed to the Haven."

There is a heavy silence as we all stay still, waiting to find out how he's going to respond.

"So, you're not part of the Coalition claptrap?"

"No, sir. Far from it."

"Good, good. Well, come on. You're all welcome to stay at my ranch for a spell. Let's get your young'uns warmed up, eh?"

Everyone packs their gear away. Matthias sends Frederick to retrieve the meat tied up in the tree as the rest of us follow the man over a hill. In the distance is a two-story house with a large barn and a fenced-in area with about ten cows. Farther behind the house is a beautiful mountain so tall, clouds obscure the top. The whole scene is gorgeous.

"Mind if I ask ya your name?" Matthias's breath comes heavy as we plow through a deep snowdrift.

"Sure can," he responds but says nothing more.

After an awkward pause, Matthias asks, "Okay? What's your name?"

"The name's Jed Chozolt. My wife's Mary Ellen."

"It's nice to meet ya, Mr. Chozolt. My name's Matthias Sloane. That's my son, Henry, and my daughter, Olivia." He points back at us with his thumb.

My heart does a little flutter, hearing the pride in his voice while introducing me.

"Nice meetin' you. And call me Jed. Mr. Chozolt was my father. We'll get you all settled in the house before I ask everyone else their names if you don't mind. It's a bit too nippy out here for an ol' guy such as myself."

"This is quite a hike from your house. What brought ya all the way out here?" Matthias asks.

"I was tracking a grizzly. There was a time grizzlies never came this far south, but things have changed since the war. You're all lucky he didn't visit your camp last night. He's a mean son-of-a-gun."

I start to imagine what it would have been like to have a grizzly bear show up while we were sleeping. I shiver at the thought of waking up to a bear eating me.

As we come closer to the house, it looks to be in fairly good shape and has a feeling of peace about it. A steady column of smoke snakes out of the chimney, filling the air with a comforting smell. A cow moos in the distance as though saying "hello."

Jed leads us to his spacious front porch and asks us to stay put for a moment so he can break the news of guests to his wife. He opens the front door and calls out, "Mary Ellen! We got some company. Be a dear and throw a roast—no, make that two roasts—in the oven, would ya?"

"Two roasts? How many people are we talking about?" Her voice grows louder as she walks toward the front door. She peeks her head out of the door to look at us all. Her hazel eyes grow wide in surprise. "Oh, my word. Where'd you all come from? Come on in, come on in! Make yourselves at home!"

We follow them into their cozy house, making sure to stomp the snow off our boots before walking in.

"I'm afraid we don't have enough seating for you all to relax in the living room, so just find someplace comfortable wherever you can," she says as she heads to the kitchen. "I'll get you all something to drink."

My first impression is that she is the kindest lady I have ever met. Even her appearance exudes a friendly vibe from her floral apron over a denim dress to her long gray hair braided down her back. When she smiles, it deepens her wrinkles, showing off the lifetime of smiles she's worn on her face.

Matthias follows Jed into the kitchen. "Anything we can do to help?"

"Don't you worry yourself, dear. Go be with your people. We'll get everything all fixed up in here, and then you can tell us your story," Mary Ellen responds.

The living room is small, and only half of us can cram ourselves in, sitting on the floor wherever we can. Those who can't fit sit in the dining room. Matthias comes to join us in the living room, and Nathaniel immediately gets up off the couch to offer it to him.

"No, that's all right. Sit by Rebecca. I'll take the floor." Matthias plops down next to Henry.

Everyone is quiet while we wait for Jed and Mary Ellen to come in with the drinks. How are they going to have enough glasses for everyone? I guess they wouldn't have offered if they didn't have enough.

I look around at how clean and quaint the room is, feeling out of place with my poor hygiene and dirty clothes. It's a shame we can't be at our best, since Jed and Mary Ellen are being so kind, but I'm sure they understand.

"Well, I hope you all like lemonade. If not, let me know, and I can get you some water instead," Mary Ellen says as she and Jed bring in pitchers of lemonade and red plastic cups.

"Lemonade will be wonderful. Thank you," Alexandrine says, bringing another smile to Mary Ellen's face.

"I hope ya don't mind me being nosey," Matthias says as Jed and Mary Ellen start handing out filled cups, "where did ya get plastic cups?"

"From town." Jed hands me a half-filled cup.

I take a drink, and the tartness of the lemon is like a jolt to my taste buds, but not in an unpleasant way.

"Town? There's a town around here that still sells stuff?" Matthais looks up abruptly.

"Well, it's quite a ways away, but yes, there're stores and the like." Jed continues handing out cups to the children.

"This town wouldn't happen to be in the Haven, would it?" Matthias's eyes sparkle with hope.

"Why, yes it would," Jed says with a smile.

Everyone starts gasping and speaking at once.

"Are we in the Haven right now?" Henry asks.

"No. We're still in the DMZ, and strictly speaking, we're not supposed to be here, but there's a certain amount of rule-breaking you can do when your grandson's the president," Jed says with pride.

"You're the president's grandparents?" Henry asks with awe.

"And our son was the president before him." Mary Ellen beams. "Of course, Alfred knew we didn't like city living, so he allowed us to keep our farm. We just gotta keep it hush-hush. And now it's Icky who's in charge, keeping our secret."

"Icky?" Rebecca asks in amusement.

"His name's Icarus, but we've been callin' him Icky since he was a young lad. Though, if you meet him, I wouldn't call him Icky if I were you. He hates it." Jed guffaws. His laughter is infectious, and everyone laughs with him. "But enough about us. What's your story?"

Mary Ellen takes the now-empty pitcher to the kitchen.

Matthias gives him a quick summary of our journey, giving him just enough to understand our motive for coming to the Haven as well as some of the hardships we've endured. We wait patiently while he tells it.

I finish my lemonade about the time the bus has broken down.

"That's quite the adventure. So, some of you are Rare?" Jed looks around at all our faces.

"Yes, sir. That's not a problem, is it?" Matthias asks lightly, but his face hardens as he waits to see if we're going to have trouble.

"Not a problem at all. Jed's a Rare. He can tell if people are lying to him just by looking at them, and Icky's got Rare abilities too. We couldn't be prouder!" Mary Ellen gushes as she comes back into the room with another pitcher of lemonade.

"What's his ability?" I ask.

"He's able to help other Rares harness their abilities. He can draw their abilities forward and know exactly how to make them stronger. He's helped so many people out over the years. It's part of what makes him such a great leader," she responds as she hands out the last of the cups. "Here, I got a picture of him over on the mantel."

She walks around everyone carefully and pulls a framed picture off the mantel. She uses her apron to wipe off the dust before handing it to Matthias.

He takes a look and nods before handing it off to Henry. When it's my turn, I hold it so David can look at it with me. You can only see his head and part of his shoulders in the picture. His gray eyes look steadily at the camera as though he's having a staring contest and winning. He has a silvery scar on his left cheekbone, strawberry blond hair, and a red-and-brown goatee.

"He's very handsome," I say to Mary Ellen as I hand it to Tim.

"Yes. He's the spittin' image of his father when he was that age." Mary Ellen sighs. "Now that Alfred's gone, Icky is all we have left. We don't see him that often, but he makes sure he comes to visit us on the holidays."

"Does he live in the town that you mentioned?" Matthias asks.

"'Fraid not. He lives in the capital, of course," Jed answers.

"How far away is that?" Matthias inquires.

"Oh, about a day's train ride from town."

Matthias sits up a little straighter, eyes filled with hope. "Hear that, guys? We could easily be in the capital within a week's time."

"When should we get going?" Alexandrine asks.

"Now, hold on. It's not going to be an easy trek, because the town I spoke of is over the mountain."

I watch Matthias's shoulders slump at the news.

"Traveling by foot is going to take a toll on you. Our old pickup truck has trouble getting over some of the steeper roads. I can only imagine what it's going to be like walking up there, breathing in that thin air. Why don't you give the wife and me a day to get some rations ready, huh?"

"All right. Thank ya for your generosity." Matthias looks around at us with raised eyebrows.

We take the hint, and everyone voices their gratitude as well.

Matthias settles in next to Henry, and we spend the rest of the day cleaning up and getting rest before the next part of our journey. If only Jed could give us a ride over the mountain in his truck, but there's too many of us. At least there's an end in sight. I'm excited to get started and get it over with.

In the morning, we pack our bags with bread, muffins, canned goods, and dried fruit Mary Ellen and Jed give us.

"Remember what I said. Stick to the roads I told you about, and keep an eye out for the wildlife. You're in their territory, and they won't be afraid to let you know that."

"Thank you, Jed, Mary Ellen. We appreciate your hospitality." Matthias shakes their hands.

"Before you go, we also want you to have this." Jed hands Matthias a roll of money. "That should be enough for your train tickets."

"We can't accept this." Matthias thrusts the roll toward Jed.

"You wouldn't dare insult an old man, now would you?" Jed crosses his arms. "It's a gift. If you don't take it, you're going to have to walk all the way to the capital, and that'll take you weeks."

Matthias awkwardly shoves the money into his bag. "What can we ever do to repay ya?"

"Say 'hi' to Icky for us," Mary Ellen says. "And tell him to come visit us as soon as he gets a chance."

"Will do," Matthias says.

We all say our goodbyes and give hugs or handshakes before heading out the door into the mild winter morning. The sky is full of gray clouds, keeping the temperature a touch warmer than normal. I lean down and scoop up some snow to see how it packs. This would be the perfect snow for a snowman, but we don't have time for that, so I squish the snow into a ball and throw it as hard as I can into the field. I almost lose sight of it before it falls to the ground. If only my gym teacher could see me now.

After about a half hour of walking on the snow-covered road, my shirt and head are soaked with sweat. It doesn't help that Mary Ellen filled my stomach past full, practically force-feeding me an enormous breakfast I almost threw up. It was delicious, but I'm not sure that was the best choice before hiking all day long.

By around noon, we make it to the base of the mountain.

"This is where it gets interestin'." Matthias signals for us to stop for a drink break.

"How far up do we want to go before making camp?" Alexandrine asks.

"Like usual. We go until the sun gets close to setting. Frederick? You still have the deer meat, right?"

"Yup. I grabbed it before we left." Frederick holds up the bag of meat.

"Good. We'll cook that up for supper, then burn the game bags so we don't attract animals," Matthias says. "Let's go, everyone."

436

We move a lot slower with the incline of the mountain road. As the sun begins its descent, we keep our eyes open for a good camping spot. We find a clearing, but it's at a slant, making it tough for everyone to find a place to sleep comfortably.

I contemplate asking if Charlotte could sing a couple of notes and knock us all out, but I know Alexandrine would not be happy about us using her daughter as a sleeping aid.

David is put on one of the night watches, much to my displeasure. Without his body heat, I can't seem to stay warm and can't sleep the entire two hours he's keeping watch. I should have gotten up and helped him instead of trying to sleep while shivering uncontrollably.

The next day's walk is even slower. We hit a few hills that were so steep, our feet kept sliding in the snow, making a few of us slip down the hill a little way before we caught traction again.

"Well, guys, the sun's goin' down, and this is the only place that I've seen that's big enough for stoppin'. Problem is, there're no trees here," Matthias says, looking around. "Without a fire, we're in for a cold night."

"Should we use flashlights and keep walking until we find somewhere better?" Henry asks.

"The kids are getting tired. We gotta stop," Caroline says.

"Matthias!" Alexandrine calls from the clearing. "You need to see this."

Matthias walks over to where Alexandrine is staring down at the snow. He crouches to get a better look. "Those are bear tracks. And from the looks of the scat over there,"—he points about ten feet away—"it looks like it's been here recently."

"What should we do?"

Matthias strokes his beard, thinking. "Ya still have your night vision goggles?"

"Yeah, somewhere in my bag."

"Okay. Whoever has watch duty will keep the goggles by them, and if ya hear something strange, use them. We don't have extra batteries though, so make sure you're only usin' them if ya need to."

We settle in, keeping as close together as we can for warmth. With our survival at stake, this is no time to be shy. I'm so close to Cass, her hair tickles my nose, and I jerk away to rub at it. In the process, I bump my head into David's forehead, drawing out a frustrated groan. After shifting around a bit more, I finally settle into a comfortable position, David's warm breath on my neck.

As I'm about to nod off, the hairs on the back of my neck stand-up, and it isn't from David breathing on them. There's a strange huffing noise I can't quite place, and it's getting louder. When I sit up to see where it's coming from, Nathaniel calls out, "Bear!"

Bang!

Nathaniel fires a shot into the air, shocking everyone awake. I hear the children scream, but their screams are drowned out by a menacing roar that fills us all with terror.

I look through the darkness and see a giant mass standing on hind legs.

"Run!" Matthias grabs his weapons bag, searching for another weapon to kill the bear with.

Nathan shoots at it but misses.

As I go to run with the rest of the group, I grab David's hand, but he pulls it out of my grip.

"What are you doing?" Every muscle in my body tenses as my flight response kicks in. I turn to watch the women and children flee, wishing I were with them, but I can't leave without David. I'm completely rooted in place, unable to decide what to do.

I can only stand here as I watch David rush over to Matthias and pull a gun out of his bag. The breeze blows the scent of wet dog mixed with putrid meat at me, upsetting my already nervous stomach.

Matthias shoots the bear, but it doesn't die. It just seems to make it angry. The bear roars again, followed by a pained yell.

"Nathaniel!" I hear Rebecca scream.

Nathaniel is hunched over, holding his face while the bear towers over him, snarling.

Matthias shoots a couple more times as David aims his gun and fires. The bear lets out a little whine and drops straight to the ground.

After a moment of silence, Matthias and David cautiously walk over to where the bear is lying, holding their guns out in case they need to shoot it again. Matthias kicks its paw, and the bear doesn't move. He pulls a flashlight out and shines it at the bear's head.

"Nice shot!" Matthias slaps David on the back. "I could hardly see with it being so dark, and ya shot it right between the eyes."

David smiles as they put the safeties on their guns back on.

My fear eases up, and I walk to where David stands looking at his kill. Once again, I feel bad for an animal having to die for doing what's natural. As Jed said, we're in its territory. We're the intruders. But if David hadn't killed it, it would have killed Nathaniel. It's sad, but it was necessary.

"Coast's clear!" Matthias yells in the direction everyone ran.

"Hold still, Nathan. I need to clean this out, or it could get infected," Rebecca says.

I cringe when I turn and see Nathaniel's face. He has three deep gashes on his right cheek, starting just below his eye.

"How bad does it look?" he asks.

"It looks like a bear clawed your face." Rebecca gingerly wipes at his wound with gauze soaked in whiskey. "You're going to have some scars, but I think it'll look good on you."

Matthias points to his eye patch. "You're lucky he didn't get ya just a little bit higher, or ya would've looked like me."

"Anything but that," Nathan jokes.

Everyone returns to the clearing and congratulates David. He brushes it off as nothing, but I catch a proud smile as he returns the gun to Matthias. Once Rebecca finishes with Nathan, we all try to sleep again, but my mind is racing from what happened, and I don't fall asleep until right before Matthias wakes us up.

It's going to be a long day. Losing a night of sleep often leads to my depression flaring up on me, and since I just got out of a depressed funk, I really don't want to fall right back into one. I've got to keep going, though, even if my mood slips. Existence can be painful sometimes, but I need to always keep moving forward.

2 | 5

We've been walking for days now. Thankfully, no more bears have shown up. Matthias is confident we aren't far away from town, and I hope he's right. We finished off the last of the food Jed and Mary Ellen gave us, and now we're back to eating squirrels and whatever else we can find.

Matthias takes us off road, where we trudge through a forest thick with leafless undergrowth that still manages to trip us up. The adults pulling the kids on sleds keep grunting in frustration and swearing under their breath as they try their hardest to find clear areas to walk.

"Guys? Do you hear that?" Charlotte asks.

I was lost in thought, but now that she mentions it, I do hear something familiar.

"Cars!" Caroline says.

Everyone moves a little bit faster, excitement fueling their steps. We step out of the trees and onto a plowed road. A row of houses in pristine condition line the other side.

Matthias leads us across the road to the sidewalk, and I squeeze David's hand out of nervousness and excitement.

"Are we there? Is this the Haven, Mama?" Noah asks Caroline.

"It looks like it, baby," Caroline answers with a catch in her voice.

Everyone erupts into cheers, jumping for joy and hugging one another. Matthias claps Henry on the back but then hushes us all.

"Everyone calm down. We still have a ways to go," he says, a hint of a smile still lingering. He looks up and down the road, looking for clues to where the train station might be and finally picks a direction to start walking.

Nobody questions his judgment, and we all follow, elated to finally be close to our destination.

After walking for only five minutes, I can't help but notice cars slowing down and the drivers staring at us as they drive by. I suppose we are an odd sight, but I really wish they would stop it.

As Matthias turns right to head down another street, two quick siren sounds come from behind us. My heart skips a beat when I see a police car like the one back at Eli's city. It pulls over next to the sidewalk, and a man steps out dressed in a uniform.

Matthias holds his arms out for us to stand back while he steps forward to talk.

"Good afternoon," Matthias says.

The policeman nods and stops in front of his car. "Quite the crew you got there. Where are you guys headed?"

"The train station. We're on our way to the capital."

"What's in the capitol that so many of you want to visit?" He's friendly enough, but I can tell he's suspicious.

"We need to talk to President Chozolt." Matthias stiffens.

"May I ask about what?" The policeman asks, hooking his thumbs in his utility belt, which puts me on edge when I realize his hand is closer to his firearm.

"We escaped the Coalition and would like to live in peace, sir," Matthias says.

"Is that right? How'd you all get here?" the policeman asks.

"We had a bus, but it ran out of fuel, so we had to walk the rest of the way. It's been a long journey. Could you point us in the direction of the train station?"

The policeman stands still, looking us all over, giving no indication he's willing to help. I can feel the tension rising as we wait to see what he's going to do. It would be our luck to make it this far and then be thrown in jail for breaking some sort of law we couldn't have known about.

Just when I feel like I'm about to yell in frustration, the policeman finally answers, "Sure, can," and I blow out the breath.

"You'll want to continue down this road for four blocks," he says, pointing down the road Matthias was about to turn on, "then take a left. You'll go down two more blocks and take a right. A couple more blocks, and you'll see it."

"Thank you, sir. Much appreciated."

"Good luck." The police officer grabs the brim of his hat and nods.

Matthias heads the direction the policeman gave, and we all follow, mumbling about how lucky we are. After a while, the houses change over to businesses, and the traffic picks up, making me more and more self-conscious. I don't like that our group sticks out like a sore thumb, especially Nathan, with his bandaged face. I want to just get to the train and stop being out in the open.

The discomfort of being stared at ebbs away momentarily when the smell of bread and cake wafts down the sidewalk from the bakery up ahead, making my mouth water at the tantalizing scents.

As we pass by the window, I gawk at the three-tiered cake on display that's covered in white frosting with big pink flowers cascading down the side. I'd give anything to have even a bite of that cake. It's been so long since I've had desserts. I sigh and keep walking.

Matthias leads us straight to the train station, never turning the wrong direction even once. If it were left up to me, I would have ended up leading us all over the place, getting distracted by the store fronts and the different smells coming from restaurants lining the streets.

We walk through the doors into the train station, and I gape at the immensity of this place. The curved ceiling stretches at least three stories above us and is lined with big windows letting in a lot of natural light.

As we walk farther into the building, we see kiosks selling a wide variety of candy, chips, drinks, and newspapers. For one involuntary second, I imagine myself swiping a candy bar because I'm hungry and to see if I could get away with it, but I'm immediately sickened by the thought. I could never live with myself if I did.

The crowds of people bustling past us either don't notice us at all as they go about their business or openly stare at our appearance. I catch one person going out of their way to make a wide berth, side eyeing us as they walk by.

"Everyone take a seat while Henry and I go buy the tickets." Matthias points to a wall lined with long wooden benches.

"Anyone need to use the bathroom?" Caroline asks the children, but now that she mentioned it, almost everyone seems to need to.

As I wait for my turn, I spot Cindy eating a Snickers bar. "Where'd you get that from?" I ask, knowing exactly what she's done.

"From over there." She points at the stand. "I got a five-finger discount."

"You're terrible." I cross my arms and lean back against the wall.

"Thanks! Do you want some?" She holds the half-eaten candy bar toward me. "Or if you want your own, I could go grab one for you."

"No, I don't want any of your criminal candy," I say, even though my stomach growls at the thought of taking a bite.

"Suit yourself." She stuffs the other half of the candy bar into her mouth and chews it obnoxiously.

I wonder why Joselyn is letting Cindy stick around so much. It seems like Joselyn's hardly there anymore. I glance at Cindy and watch as she picks at her teeth with her dirty fingernail. I know I turned a corner with Cindy and decided to be more friendly with her, but she is so disgusting sometimes. I miss Joselyn.

Before too long, Matthias and Henry are back with the stack of tickets.

"Train leaves in about an hour. Jed gave us enough money to buy sleeper coaches, so this trip should be a breeze."

"Do you have any money left over for some food?" Frederick asks.

"Some. I was gonna save it in case we need it in the capital," Matthias starts to say, "but I'm hungry too. Let's find something to eat."

We settle on a pizza place since it's more cost efficient to buy whole pizzas to share. The look of wonder on the kids' faces as they take their very first bite of pizza is entertaining. Noah wolfs his down and is already asking for seconds before any of the adults finish their first one.

With bellies full of greasy pizza and sugary soda, we finally board our train. My stomach cramps a bit from the unhealthy food it's no longer used to, but it tasted so good going down, I'll gladly deal with a little discomfort.

David and I take a sleeper cabin with two blue cushioned bench seats and two bunk beds suspended over the benches. The beds really aren't anything special, but since we've been sleeping on the ground in the snow, it seems like the softest, most comfortable bed I've been on.

The train ride passes by in a blink of an eye. Of course, it helped that I slept half the time. I think it was the best sleep I've had in months.

There was one moment where I thought we were going to get kicked off the train. Cindy and Charlotte had decided to play truth-or-dare, and Cindy went streaking down the hallway, screeching at the top of her lungs. Matthias had to talk to the conductor and explain that she's not right in the head. She was then locked into her car until we arrived at the train station. Serves her right.

We file off the train and gather on the platform.

"What now?" Alexandrine asks Matthias.

"Now I ask where Chozolt's office is located, and we go there. What happens after that all depends on how we are received."

We stay put as Matthias walks off to find someone who can give him directions.

"Don't even think about it, Cindy!" I say as I watch her trying to sneak off toward the stand of food.

She huffs. "Who made you the snack police?"

"You're going to get caught one of these times and make us all look bad."

"I'm hungry." She crosses her arms. "It's not like they'll miss it."

"We're all hungry. Suck it up. We'll probably get some food once we make it to President Chozolt's office."

She rolls her eyes but stays put.

"Out of curiosity..." I start to say but then stop when I realize she'll probably get offended.

"What?"

"How come you're around so much? What's happened to Joselyn? Is she okay?"

"She's tired," Cindy says.

I catch what looks like a hint of guilt in her eyes, but Matthias is on his way back over, so I let it go.

"I got the directions written down. Let's move out," Matthias says.

We pick up our bags and follow Matthias on the last part of our journey.

The building the president works in is nothing special, and I find myself wondering whether Matthias got the wrong location. A plain red brick building about four stories tall is hardly becoming of a president. I guess I was expecting a little more glamour, considering what Turk has set up for himself. But then again, Turk seems to milk his position for everything he can. Who really needs a mansion the size of a castle to live in by yourself?

Once we get up to the front doors, guards block us from entering, but after mentioning we escaped the Coalition to come here, we are escorted inside. They make us pile all our bags in a room and then have us walk through a metal detector.

"Sir, may I ask why you are bringing a gun to the president's office?" one of the guards asks after Matthias walks through the detector and it goes off.

"We've been carryin' our guns for so long, I forgot to remove it." Matthias reluctantly hands over his weapons. He had a knife strapped to his belt too. "We're gonna get them back, right?"

"I'll wait for the president's order," the guard replies.

It takes what feels like forever to get everyone through the metal detectors. We are reassured our stuff will be kept safe, but I don't like having it taken away. It's all we have.

"So much for freedom," Matthias mutters to Henry.

We go up the stairs to the fourth floor and are asked to wait in a big conference room. There are plenty of plastic chairs, but Matthias chooses to pace around the room.

After waiting only ten minutes, the door swings open, and the president comes in. A momentary look of shock crosses his face, but he holds his composure and pulls a chair to the front of the room to face us all. "I wasn't expecting there to be so many people," he says. "I'm President Chozolt. I was told you wanted to speak with me."

He's aged a lot since the picture we saw at Jed and Mary Ellen's. His strawberry blond hair and brown goatee are flecked with gray. Deep lines form around his gray eyes when he gives a courteous smile. He holds himself like someone in charge, and I immediately wonder if he and Matthias are going to get along.

"My name's Matthias. It's an honor to meet ya, Mr. President."

"Likewise, Matthias. So, what can I do for you?" Chozolt says.

"We've traveled all the way here in hopes that we could escape the oppression of the Coalition and live in freedom."

"You all left the Coalition?" he asks skeptically. "How?"

As Matthias gives the brief rundown, it strikes me how much we've been through. I can't believe we're finally in the Haven.

Chozolt leans forward. "That's quite the tale. I believe you're the first group to leave the Coalition and make it here. Why do you think that is?"

"Because some of us are Rare, sir," Matthias answers.

"Ah-ha! Now we're getting somewhere. How many of you are Rare?" He asks with a gleam in his eye.

David, Joselyn, Charlotte, and I all raise our hands.

"Let me be the first to say, 'welcome, and we're glad you're here.'" Chozolt grins. "We have a military compound not far from here, where you can stay for as long as you need."

"You're not just sending those four to the compound to live, right? We're a group, and we stick together," Rebecca says.

"Of course not. We have enough space for you all. Just let me make a few phone calls, and we'll get set up for you to stay in. I'll drop in from time to time to check in with you all and to maybe have some one-on-one time with my fellow Rares. My gift allows me to help other Rares."

"We heard, and we're excited to see what ya can do," Matthias says.

President Chozolt raises an eyebrow at him. "How do you know about my Rare gift?"

"Your grandparents told us. Lovely people by the way. Your grandmother, Mary Ellen, says, 'hi' and would like ya to drop by sometime soon."

"What are the odds that you met my grandparents on your journey?" Chozolt shakes his head. "It would seem as though fate wanted our paths to cross."

"I don't know about fate, but your grandparents are the reason we're here. We can never repay them for the help they gave."

"You can repay them by accepting my offer to stay on the compound," Chozolt says with a wide smile, but there's an eagerness behind his eyes that gives me pause.

"That's a very generous offer. Will we be able to get our weapons back? Your guards took them," Matthias mentions.

"Of course, of course. I do apologize for the protocols. We had a Coalition spy try to kill me once, so security has to be tight. Feel free to grab your stuff, and we'll get a bus ready to take you to the base."

"Thank you," I hear multiple people say enthusiastically.

"I won't be able to accompany you since I'm engaged to be elsewhere, but I would like to set up a celebration feast sometime. I'd like to hear more about your journey and to get to know what you four can do." A hungry look passes his eyes momentarily.

"We'd love that, sir," Matthias says.

Unease settles into the back of my mind, but I pass it off as fatigue and join in the celebration as we are taken to our journey's end.

The military base is unassuming but comfortable. The barracks are plenty big enough for our group to stay in. There's still no privacy, but until we can figure out a more permanent living situation, it'll do. Especially since we finally have the creature comforts we've been missing: electricity, bathrooms, showers, and washing machines.

I can't wait to get all my bedding and clothes washed. I've never been so excited to do laundry in my life. What has become of me? Most teenagers my age are excited about sports or going to parties, and I'm excited about doing laundry? I'm such a loser.

Everyone seems to be in high spirits as we pick out our bunk spaces and begin to unpack. Giggles can be heard as the children chase each other around the room, and I look around to see that even Matthias looks a little more relaxed than normal. Once suppertime rolls around, one of Chozolt's soldiers calls us to follow him to the mess hall. They serve us grilled pork chops, mashed potatoes, and corn, but the best part is the ice cream sundaes they hand out for dessert. I watch the children's faces light up as they take their first bite of ice cream. I can definitely get used to this!

Once we get back to the barracks, the women get to work putting the kids to bed. The rest of us take turns using the bathroom.

"Is there any need to keep watch tonight, Matthias?" I overhear Frederick ask as he's standing next to the doors.

"No. I think it's safe for us all to sleep here. We'll let Chozolt's men do the guarding."

Once again, I'm a little shocked at how much trust Matthias has, but we are theoretically in the safest place we've ever been. It's time we finally get to relax.

Days pass as we wait for Chozolt to invite us to the dinner he promised. Everyone seems to fall into a comfortable routine, which mostly involves relaxing and walking around the military base. We've all caught up on our laundry, and everyone is in better moods now that we smell clean and have three square meals a day. Chozolt's soldiers seem nice enough, but none of them ever take the time to talk with us. They won't tell us where Chozolt is, just that he's out of town.

As days become weeks, things start to get a little hairy. People are getting bored and worry that Chozolt forgot about us. There's even some talk of people thinking about leaving the base and finding a place to live on their own. Matthias shot that down immediately, telling them to be patient as we wait for Chozolt to have time in his busy schedule, reminding them he might have a plan for us.

David and I don't mind this time of peace. We sneak away to be alone as often as we can, but Cass sometimes tags along when Tim is too busy to hang out with her. She can't stand being in the same room as Cindy without me there, and I don't blame her. David and I do a lot less kissing when she's by us, but we make a game

446

out of how often we can distract her and sneak kisses when she isn't looking. I'm sure she's caught on by now, but she's a good sport about it.

After about a month since our initial meeting with Chozolt has passed, we get the news he's back and wants to have dinner with us. The barracks are abuzz with chatter as we get ourselves ready to meet with him.

He has his people fix us a big meal: steak, fried potatoes, roasted vegetables, and freshly made rolls. He goes out of his way to make sure David, Joselyn, Charlotte, and I are seated at the head of the table and served first.

"I'm so sorry about the delay. The life of a president, you know," he says with a chuckle, even though we don't know. "I was truly impressed by your story." Chozolt takes a bite of steak. "From what I understand, civilians who live in the Coalition territory don't know we're here, let alone escape to come join us."

"There are rumors of a Haven that float around here and there, but everything I've ever heard is that it was just a city. It wasn't until we found a USB stick with government information my father had gathered that we discovered the Haven was a third of the country, not just a city. I knew right then and there that we needed to do whatever we could to come over here," Matthias says.

"Government information on a USB stick? What other information was on it?" Chozolt asks with a raised eyebrow.

"There were a lot of encrypted files we were unable to read," I say.

Chozolt leans back, wiping his mouth with his napkin. "You know, I have a guy that works in the NSA. He's the best of the best, and I bet he'd be able to open those files. If you don't mind, of course."

"What's the NSA?" I ask.

"The National Security Agency," Chozolt answers patiently.

I just nod, even though I still don't know what that means.

"We don't mind havin' your guy look into it. We've been curious to know what my dad was hidin'," Matthias answers.

Once again, I'm surprised Matthias has been so open and telling him everything. I know he's been hoping for the Haven for a long time, but it seems a little out of character.

"Good. The NSA headquarters are not from here. I'll let them know we're coming."

"Sounds great," Matthias says. "Thank you again for your hospitality."

After everyone finishes with their dinner, we are served dessert. A happy sigh escapes my lips when I smell the delectable scent of chocolate cake.

"So, my fellow Rares, I'm immensely curious to know what your names are and what abilities you have." Chozolt eyes the four of us like we're precious jewels or something.

It makes me feel uncomfortable, but the attention is right up Cindy's alley. She sits up straighter and twirls her hair.

"Let's start with you, young man." He points at David.

"My name's David. I can't really pinpoint what my abilities are exactly. The best I can describe it is that it's like I have a guardian angel." David blushes slightly. "He shows up before I'm about to get sick or hurt. He saved my life by shoving me right before the explosion happened. Had I still been standing, I would have been decapitated."

"Interesting." Chozolt taps his lips with his finger. "That's the first time I've heard of that kind of ability. I look forward to working with you."

I look up from my cake and see he's looking at me now. I set my fork down and take a drink of water to clear my throat. "My name's Olivia. I guess I can dream the future. I haven't done it much, though."

"Ah! A future reader. There's been a few Rares before you that've had that gift. Sadly, they are no longer around." He frowns. "What if I told you that I could train you to see the future while you're awake?"

"That would be amazing, sir, but my visions aren't always reliable." I remember the blizzard vision.

"Not yet, but we'll work on it." He winks.

Cindy doesn't wait for him to look at her. She's been squirming in her chair as though she can't wait to show off. "My name's Cindy, Joselyn, Landon, and Jack. We have many powers." She wiggles her fingers in the air, trying to be mysterious. Instead, she comes off as creepy with a psychotic smile plastered on her face.

"I don't understand." Chozolt furrows his eyebrows, looking around for someone to explain.

"She has multiple personalities." Alexandrine reaches around Charlotte to poke Cindy's shoulder as a warning to behave.

Cindy shifts away, rubbing her arm with a scowl toward Alexandrine.

"Her real name's Joselyn, but this is one of her personalities, Cindy," I step in to explain.

"People! I can speak for myself." She plasters the smile back on her face as she turns toward Chozolt. "Yes. My name's Cindy. I'm able to protect Joselyn from bad things, like mental trauma and stuff. She's a bit of a coward." Cindy rolls her eyes.

"Okay," Chozolt says slowly.

I can tell he doesn't like Cindy, but he's trying to be inclusive.

"You said you had more than one power?"

"Oh, yeah! Jossy can hurt people. She squeezes their brains or something and makes them pass out from the pain. I bet if she really tried, she could kill them," Cindy says, wickedly, "but she never wants to try it. I would if it were my power, but I wasn't so lucky. Then there's Jack, who can talk to dead people, and Landon, who can deflect bullets, but those two don't come out to play that often."

"This is incredible. Are you telling me you have four personalities, and each one has a different Rare ability?" Chozolt asks.

"Yuppers!" Cindy says with glee.

"So, Jack can talk to dead people, huh?" Chozolt says quietly. "I think I'd like to talk to him sometime." I glance up at Chozolt and see sadness in his eyes as he takes a drink of water.

"We're *all* looking forward to working with you, Icky."

Matthias huffs and rubs his face with his hands. "Sorry about her, sir. Your grandparents told us not to call you that."

"I haven't heard that nickname in a while," Chozolt says with a hint of a smile. "It brings back good memories."

"So, I can keep calling you Icky?" Cindy asks.

"No."

Cindy rolls her eyes again as she takes a big bite of cake.

"How about you, little lady?" Chozolt moves his attention to Charlotte. "You've been quiet this whole time. What's your ability?"

Charlotte stares at her plate. "I can make people sleep when I sing."

"That's a remarkable gift," Chozolt says kindly. "So, do you mean your singing lulls people to sleep?"

"No. More like they drop like flies as soon as a note comes out of her mouth," Cindy answers around a mouthful of cake.

"Really?" he says, intrigued. "How fascinating! Your gift might be a little more challenging to work with, but we'll figure something out. Well, I have to say, I'm quite pleased you all have come to join us. It might be a little too soon to say this, but I think your gifts are exactly what I've been looking for, and I look forward to working with you." He makes a point to look down the table at everyone, but his eyes linger a little longer on the four of us. "Regrettably, I have to cut our time short, but please, feel free to help yourselves to whatever you want. Treat this as your home until we can find you a more suitable living situation."

"Thank you, Mr. President." Matthias stands up to shake Chozolt's hand.

We all watch as he exits the building.

"So, what do you think?" Alexandrine asks Matthias.

"I think he seems like a nice guy," Matthias answers.

"What did he mean, 'Your gifts are what I've been looking for'?" I ask. "I feel like he's got a plan he's not willing to tell us."

"Of course not. He's the president. He's not gonna divulge his secrets to a bunch of strangers who just wandered in here," Matthias says condescendingly.

I cross my arms. "I didn't come all the way here to be manipulated again."

"I think we should stop guessin' what Chozolt's objectives are and just go to bed. We'll get to talk to him again, and we can ask about it later." Matthias yawns, ending the conversation.

I fall asleep almost immediately and sleep the whole night. Unfortunately, the kids wake up early with lots of energy, and their giggles echo through the barracks, waking everyone up for the day.

"Are ya guys ready for trainin' today?" Matthias asks when we get back to the barracks after breakfast.

"Why? Did Chozolt say that's what we're supposed to do?" I ask.

"I have no clue what Chozolt wants us to do. *I* think it's time to start our combat and weapons training back up."

"We've gone this long without it, and now we're someplace safe. Why do we need it anymore?" I ask, feeling stubborn.

"Ya should always be prepared to defend yourself, Olivia." Matthias points his finger at me.

I pout. "I just thought we were finally someplace where we could relax and be safe."

"Liv, it's still a good idea to train. We should be keeping our Rare abilities sharp, not wasting them," David argues.

I huff and stare at the ground. I hate how persuasive David can be. "Fine. You're right. We got these gifts. We shouldn't waste them. When do we start?"

Matthias relaxes a bit. "Meet me outside in an hour. I wanna see if they have any targets for us to practice our shootin'."

I grab my stuff and storm off to the washing machine.

David follows me. "What's the matter, Liv?"

"I was just looking forward to having some peace."

"If you don't want to train today, I'm sure Matthias isn't going to drag you out there to join in," David says, but I can tell he doesn't believe what he's saying.

I cross my arms, and we stare at each other for a moment, but my resolve waivers when he wiggles his eyebrows at me. "No. I'll train." I slam the washing machine lid closed. "But I'm not going easy on anyone."

"Thanks for the heads up." David smacks my butt playfully.

I turn around and punch at his shoulder, but he dodges out of the way, which makes me grumpier.

Everyone from our camp meets outside on the lawn in front of the barracks. The temperatures are milder here, so I only have to wear a sweatshirt instead of a heavy jacket. I'm not sure how much farther south we are than Eli's camp, but I'm enjoying this weather better.

Matthias pairs us all off, putting David and me together. He starts everyone on simple maneuvers at first, but David and I blow through them like it's nothing. He eventually lets David and I spar on our own.

I feel like I'm doing quite well, keeping up with him, but I grow suspicious when I make an obvious wrong move, and he doesn't take the opportunity to move in and take me down. "Are you taking it easy on me?" Sweat drips down my nose.

"No..." he says, hesitantly.

"You are!" I say, annoyed. "Don't! You're supposed to be pushing yourself to get better too. Let's see what you've got."

"Fine," David says.

David and I square off, and I make the first move, punching at his solar plexus. He blocks it, steps in, and does a hip toss before I can even process that I didn't land my punch. He's fast! I'm going to have to give everything I've got to keep up.

I'm concentrating so hard, I don't notice everyone has stopped what they're doing to watch David and I spar. We're moving fast enough that everything around us is a blur. I no longer think about what I'm doing, I'm just reacting.

David does another hip toss and is now on top of me on the ground. I'm about to swing my legs up to put him in a leg lock when I hear someone clapping. We both look to see who's applauding and find President Chozolt smiling like a loon next to Matthias.

"You two are amazing!" Chozolt says.

"Ya think that's something, ya should see David shoot," Matthias comments.

David helps me up off the ground, both of us panting as we try to catch our breath.

"Show me," Chozolt says.

Matthias retrieves the targets and sets them up in the shooting range.

"That's about a hundred yards away. You sure about this?" Chozolt asks.

"Watch."

David blows a nervous breath out and wipes the sweat from his brow. He takes his stance, holds still for a moment aiming at the target, and fires off six shots consecutively.

Chozolt rubs his hands together in excitement. "Let's go have a look."

As we walk to the target, I kind of hope he missed so Chozolt's hungry look goes away, but I know David's shooting ability. He would have to try to miss.

"My goodness, man!" Chozolt pulls a quarter out of his pants pocket and holds it up to the bullseye where the bullet holes are. The holes are grouped close enough to be covered by the quarter. "This is the best shooting I've ever seen, and I have some good men."

David tries to keep a straight face, but his cheeks redden a touch.

Matthias slaps David on the back. "Did we tell you how he killed a grizzly bear about ten yards away in the dark? Shot it right between the eyes."

"In all my years of working with Rares, I have never met a marksman as good as you," Chozolt says, astounded.

"Thank you, sir," David says.

My stomach sinks as I look at the glee on the president's face. I have a weird feeling like he's going to try to recruit David into his army or something as soon as he turns eighteen. I hope I'm wrong, because I think David would agree to it if it meant fighting for freedom.

"How about your daughter, Matthias? Is she a sharpshooter too?"

"No!" Matthias laughs heartily, offending me, even though he's right. "Although, she did kill a Coalition soldier to save David, but no, her weapon of choice is a sword."

"A sword, huh?" Chozolt taps on his lips with his finger. "You can't bring a sword to a gunfight, I'm afraid."

"I have no interest in being in a gunfight, *sir*," I say with more attitude than intended.

Matthias shoots me a warning look, but Chozolt seems to not have heard me.

"I think I would like to start some one-on-ones this afternoon after I'm done with some business in the office. I'd like to get a feel for each Rare ability," Chozolt says. "This is just a preliminary meeting, merely a chance for me to get to know you and your ability, so I have a better understanding of what I have to work with."

"What do you mean 'what you have to work with?'" I ask, but Matthias makes a point to talk over me.

"Sounds like a plan, but I'm not sure Alexandrine will let ya be alone with Charlotte," Matthias says.

"The little sleep singer?" Chozolt asks. "Her mother is welcome to be there, but she needs to be prepared to be affected by her daughter's ability should I ask her to demonstrate."

"Fair enough." Matthias nods.

"Is it possible for us to come together?" I ask, holding David's hand.

"It works best for me to be alone with someone. Less distractions so I can focus myself on drawing out the ability. You'll understand once we start training."

"We look forward to working with you, sir," David answers.

"Me too. See you all this afternoon then." Chozolt turns to leave.

After he's gone, I whisper to David a thought that just came to mind, "What if he draws our abilities out, like takes them from us? What if he collects people's powers or something, and that's why he wants to be alone with us?"

"If he was able to steal people's abilities, I think we would have heard about it since being in the Haven," David says.

I cross my arms. "Or he's just waiting for the right abilities. He seems a little too excited about ours."

David just shakes his head.

"Or what if he has some special task force of Rares he wants us to join, and then he starts a war, and we have to fight?"

"Liv, I think you should just drop it. I don't get any bad vibes from this guy.

And so what if he does ask us to fight for liberating Rares? I think we might have a better chance with this guy than we could've ever had."

"Fine, pick up your gun, and go kill people," I spit out. "I won't be joining."

"Taking down the bad guys in order to save the repressed Rares is wrong to you?" A look of disgust crosses his face. "You know what? You're being selfish, only thinking about yourself and how you feel." David gives me a pained look and storms away.

I start to chase after him but stop. I don't know what to say. Quite frankly, I don't even know how to feel. He's got a point, but I still can't seem to be okay with intentionally going to war to kill people. We're getting ahead of ourselves, though. Chozolt never said anything about war, and now I'm in a bad mood at even the thought of it.

When I get back to the barracks, David isn't there. I flop down on my bed and pull the covers up over my face. I wanted to be happy here. I thought I would be. Maybe I'm the weird one. Maybe I need to change my views on things to match everyone else, and then I can be happy. But that doesn't feel right either. I let out a frustrated sigh, and I close my eyes.

Everything is in flames. It seems like the whole world is burning to the ground. Black smoke pours out of the windows and billows to the sky. It blocks out the sun, leaving only the flames to cast any light.

Screams can be heard in between the sounds of explosions and gunfire. Everywhere I look is as gruesome as the next. Dead bodies litter the sidewalks, staining the pavement red. Blackened holes where bombs exploded dot the streets, still smoking from their recent explosion.

David stands in front of me, dressed in a military uniform. His presence shocks me, and it's like everything switches to slow motion, sounds dulling as though I have ear plugs in. He's screaming my name and waving a hand at me, telling me to get out of here. He looks terrified yet determined as he turns back around, regripping his gun to continue charging into battle. I look at my hands, and I'm disappointed to see I don't have a weapon to go help David with.

I set out to follow him anyway, needing to be by his side to help in any way I can, when a bomb falls from the sky directly in front of him. The explosion blows me backward, landing me on the edge of the sidewalk, breaking my ribs. I lie there in a daze, trying to make sense of what happened. My hearing is gone, and blood trickles down my face from shrapnel wounds, but I hardly notice the physical agony, when I finally realize what happened. I scream David's name at the top of my lungs, pain exploding from my freshly broken ribcage. The torment is too much for my brain to process, and I black out.

I wake up screaming, the sheets wrapped tightly around my sweat-soaked body. I thrash around as I try to free myself, the horror of my vision still playing in my mind.

"Olivia! Liv! Calm down!" I hear Cass yelling.

I topple out of bed, onto the floor, and lie there, wailing. Cass is sitting next to me, rubbing my arm, asking me what's wrong, but I can't find the words to describe the horror. The feeling of fear and loss from my vision continues to tear at my mind like a monster trapped inside my skull fighting to get out.

I feel her stand and then call for David. Doesn't she know David is dead? I can't make sense of what's real and what's not as the bright flash of the bomb exploding right in front of him is seared in my mind's eye. If only I could find the courage to open my eyelids to see that I'm safe. My heart pounds too fast, and my face grows tingly as I struggle to catch my breath between sobs. I have never felt this much sorrow in my entire existence.

"Liv. Liv! Hey, come on. Open your eyes," David says.

My breath catches in my chest at the sound of his voice. David. My David. He's still alive! I open my eyes and stare up into his concerned face.

"What's going on, Liv? Are you okay?" He helps me up off the ground.

As soon as I'm sitting on the bed, I wrap my arms around him and squeeze tightly, sobbing into his neck.

He shushes me and rubs my back until I finally calm down.

"I just had the worst vision I've ever had," I say, sniffing. "We were in the middle of a warzone. Everything was on fire. Dead bodies were everywhere. And then a bomb dropped right in front of you, and you died."

"It was probably just a dream, Liv." He strokes my hair. "We were just talking about war. That put it in your mind, and you had a dream about it."

"No, David. It was real. I know it." I grip his shirt sleeves. "The pain, the terror, the sadness, it was all too real to be just a dream."

"Okay, okay. Shhh." David pulls my hands off his sleeves and wraps me tightly in a hug.

"I'm so scared, David," I say with a shaky voice.

"What's all the fuss?" Matthias marches toward us with Cass trailing behind.

"Liv just had an apocalyptic vision about us going to war," David explains.

"Ya just can't help yourself, can ya?" Matthias shakes his head.

"What?" I ask.

"I can't help but feel like ya like to be miserable all the time. Everything is always negative with ya. Snap out of it."

Cass's jaw drops, and she looks at me with apologetic eyes. She must have fetched him to come help me. Not act like a jerk.

"You don't even know what I saw!" I growl.

"I don't have to. All of your so-called visions are nothing but doomsday material. Ya ever try to be happy? Just once? Maybe it would change what you see in your visions."

"This is not helping," David throws in. "Even if it was just a dream and not a vision, it was a disturbing one, and she doesn't need you being cruel about it."

He crosses his arms over his chest. "Fill me in, then. What was it this time?"

I describe it to him, and then sob as a fresh wave of sorrow washes over me from the vision of David dying.

"Maybe ya need to work with Chozolt to see if he can change the visions to be less violent and more useful. I want ya to be happy. Not tormented. Ya were wrong about the blizzard, and I think you're wrong about this. The idea of us marchin' through the streets with bombs explodin' everywhere is not what I intend on happenin'. My hope is when we go to war, they won't know we're comin'."

"When? Not if?" I ask.

"Yes. When. I think war is inevitable. If it's not us, then it'll be the next generation. The oppression of the Rare needs to end, and I think we have what it takes to do it," Matthias answers, patting my shoulder. "Now, I want ya to give Chozolt your full attention when he starts to train ya. See what ya can do with your Rare ability, and then we can decide how to move forward."

I can feel his eye on me, waiting for me to respond. I glance at his face and nod, which seems to appease him. He gives me another pat on the shoulder and walks out of the barracks.

"I am so, so sorry, Olivia!" Cass gushes once he's gone. "You were upset, and I didn't know what to do, so I got Matthias, thinking he might be able to help. I didn't realize he was going to be mean about it."

"It's okay." I sniff. "Thank you for trying."

"Hey. Let's go get something to eat," David offers.

I'm still full from breakfast, but I want to get out of here, so I agree to it.

On our way to the dining hall, we see Denis and Tim standing by the shooting target. I wonder what they're up to now.

When we get to the kitchen, we're told once again to help ourselves. David has me sit at the counter while he fixes us some sandwiches. I stare at him as he moves around, desperately trying to convince myself it was just a dream and not a vision. I couldn't bear for it to come true.

"Here you go, m'lady." David hands me a perfectly prepared turkey sandwich.

"Thank you, good sir," I say, playing along.

"You know," David says around a mouthful of food, "Matthias is right about your visions. That they seem to be only about bad things. I think it would be great if Chozolt could help you control that."

"Maybe it's just my broken brain being unable to focus on anything happy. I had hoped that getting here to the Haven would make everything magically better, but I'm still a mess."

"You're a beautiful mess." David winks.

I give him an exaggerated eye roll and then smile. "Do you think the vitamins altered my brain? Could I have been happy had I never taken them?"

David takes a bite of his sandwich and sighs. "Unfortunately, we'll never know. It's probably best to not think too hard about it."

We finish our sandwiches and take a walk around the compound. Everyone we pass by gives us a salute or nod. It makes me feel like some kind of celebrity. I'm not sure how to feel about it. I mostly just feel awkward.

Once we get back, we see Chozolt standing outside the barracks doors. "Ah! There you are, my boy. Are you ready to start your training?"

456

"Yeah, sure." David squeezes my hand before letting go.

"Don't go too far, Olivia. You'll be next," he assures me with a smile.

As I watch Chozolt lead David away, I can't help but shiver at the thought of his words being a threat instead of a promise.

30

I pace around the barracks as I wait for David to come back. Tim and Denis return, and I decide to check in on how they're doing. Anything to take my mind off what's happening with David.

"How's it going?" I ask as Denis removes Tim's prosthetic.

"Splendidly." Denis tinkers with the arm. "I was shown where the tools and building materials are, and they told me I could have access to them whenever I wanted. Tim's arm is going to be better than we had hoped."

"That's awesome!" I smile at Tim, but he doesn't return it. "Or...not. What's wrong?"

"I just can't get the hang of shooting with it. I missed the target completely. Not even one hole in the paper."

"Like I already said, you just need practice," Denis says, patiently.

"The kickback of the gun hurts my stump too. That's what Denis is trying to figure out now."

"I'd like to give you advice, but I'm a terrible shot. Maybe David could give you pointers sometime," I offer.

"He won't have time for me. Chozolt seems to have plans for you Rares. I wonder if he's ever going to find something for us regular people to do."

"Give it time. What, do you want him to train you for fighting or something?" I ask.

"Yeah. I want to help in any way that I can," Tim says earnestly.

"Not me. I'm more of a behind the scenes kind of a guy. Let the people who know what they're doing do the fighting. I'd rather stay behind and build the weapons." Denis doesn't look up from the arm.

"But we're finally somewhere safe. Why can't we just live in peace?" I ask, exasperated.

"I'm only talking about if something should ever come up. Of course, we should strive for peace. But if it ever comes to fighting to achieve that peace, then I would rather work behind the scenes," Denis says.

"Maybe I could stay behind and work with you," I say.

"That would be a waste." Denis pushes his glasses up his nose so he can look at me. "You've been given these gifts, and you want to squander them?"

"But I don't want to kill anyone."

"You'd have to be barbaric to *want* to kill someone. It's the goal you stay focused on and fight for."

At that moment, David comes staggering back into the barracks. He makes it over to our bunk, climbs up to his bed, and lies down.

"You okay?" I ask.

"Yeah. I'll be fine. I just need to rest," he answers and then closes his eyes.

"What was it like?" I ask, but David doesn't respond. His breathing becomes heavy and steady.

"Olivia. I'd like to work with you next." Chozolt stands between a couple of guards.

I look at David sleeping and brush the hair out of his eyes. I desperately wish he could come with me. I'm scared.

Chozolt leads me to a small room in a building behind the barracks, dismissing his guards. There are no windows, just a lamp sitting on one of the round end tables. Two cushioned chairs face each other with a soft blue rug between them. It's warm in here and smells of lilac, immediately transporting my mind back to my apartment. Nostalgia and a sense of home cloud my thoughts momentarily, but I remind myself what I left behind, and those feelings go away as fast as they came.

"All right, Olivia. Please take a seat." He holds his hand out to the chair opposite of the one he sat in.

"Why was David so tired?" I flop down in the chair and bounce a few times before coming to a rest.

"My methods can be mentally exhausting. If there was some way I could fix that, I would, but it is the nature of my ability. I promise I won't do you any harm. Besides, today is just a preliminary meeting. I want to get inside the RABI in your mind, get a feel for what your abilities are, and how to work with them."

"RABI? I'm not Jewish," I say, confused.

Chozolt chuckles a bit. "No, not that kind of rabbi. Some scientists who are studying Rare abilities named the part of the brain where our Rare ability comes from 'RABI,' which is short for: Rare Ability Brain Intermediary. It's the spot in your brain where your Rare ability connects with normal brain functions and speaks between the two, making them work together. The more you use it, the faster and stronger the connection will be."

I nod as though I know what he's talking about, but I'm kind of lost. Hopefully, it will make sense once we start working.

"Are you ready to begin?"

"Quick question. This isn't some ruse to try to steal our Rare abilities, is it?" I ask.

"Not at all," Chozolt says. "Even if I could do that, I don't think I'd want to. One Rare ability is enough for me, thank you. I can only imagine what it's like inside your friend's head. That's got to be hard to deal with."

"Enough to drive someone crazy." I let out a quick laugh. I fold my hands in my lap, nervously fidgeting with my fingers.

"Now, I'd like you to relax and rest your head back on the chair."

I do as he wants, remembering what Matthias asked of me.

"Before I begin, I want you to take three deep breaths in through your nose and let them out slowly. I'm going to reach out toward your mind, and you will feel my

459

presence. It might be a little disconcerting, but I want you to stay relaxed. The more you fight me, the harder it will be for me to help you."

I nod and then start taking the three deep breaths, wondering how I'll know when he begins. After I blow the last breath out, I feel a small pressure inside my skull at the front of my brain. I stiffen, my muscles drawing tight as panic starts to set in. I open my eyes and see Chozolt sitting forward in his chair, eyes closed tight, his eyebrows creased in concentration.

"I need you to relax, Olivia," Chozolt says calmly. "I can't help you if you block me. Matthias told me about the nature of your visions. I think I can help. Just stay calm, and I'll try to make this quick."

I take more deep breaths and feel him push his way inside my skull again. I grab hold of the armrests on the chair, bracing myself. He begins to prod through my brain in search of my Rare ability. It feels like a worm slithering inside my skull as he moves to the center of my brain and stops. Several small tendrils creep outward from the central pressure in every direction. They make my brain itch, and it takes everything within me not to scream. Sweat trickles down my temple as I focus on keeping control of myself.

The small tendrils slither around back and forth, like a dog sniffing around for a morsel of food. One tendril works its way to the back of my head and then stops. Everything returns to the central pressure, then moves to the back of my skull.

"There we are," Chozolt whispers.

The pressure pulses around for a few seconds and then finally makes its way back to the front of my brain and disappears.

I slump in my chair once it's gone. I understand why David crawled right in bed. I feel exhausted, like I've been awake for two days straight, but I force my eyes open to look at Chozolt.

"Here, have a drink." He hands me a bottle of water.

"Thanks." I take a sip. "Do you feel tired after probing people's minds?"

"A little tired, but it's different when you're the one doing the exploring."

"So, what did you find?" I lean my head against the chair.

"Your ability has been suppressed for so long, I think it's going to take some doing to unbury it, but I saw some great potential. If we work hard enough, I think we could get it to a point where you could see things while awake. And I'm not making any promises here, but there's a chance we could even get you to control how far in the future you see, but that's going to take time."

"Does it get any easier? Or will it always feel like a worm's crawling inside of my brain?"

"I've never heard anyone describe it that way," he says with amusement. "Now that I've located your RABI, I won't need to search your mind like I just did, so it should be easier."

"Good. Are we done? I need to go take a nap." My eyes droop closed.

"Yes, that was all I was going to do today. I think I'll work with Cindy next, although I'm a little intimidated by her." Chozolt leads me back to the barracks.

"As you should be. Try to stay on her good side. She tried to kill me, but we're on okay terms now." I shuffle my way to the door.

"Thanks for the warning." Chozolt offers a nervous smile. "Rest up, and maybe we'll begin training tomorrow if you're up to it."

I nod, or at least think I do. My head feels so heavy with fatigue, I can't even remember getting here. I push my way into the barracks, find my bed, and fall asleep before I'm even lying down all the way.

31

"Liv. Wake up," David says as he shakes my shoulder.

I snap awake with a sharp breath. "What's the matter?" I rub my eyes.

"Nothing. We've been sleeping most of the day, and we should probably have some supper."

I look at the window and see it's getting dark.

Cass clears her throat, grabbing my attention. She's stretched out on her bunk, working in her notebook. "You guys were out cold. You didn't even wake up when Cindy came crashing back in here in a sour mood." She sets her notebook aside.

"Uh-oh. What was she in a sour mood about?" I look down the line of bunks to try to spot her.

"I overheard her telling Charlotte that Chozolt said he can't help her. That her brain is too much of a mess and that it's too dangerous for him to be in there," Cass whispers.

"That doesn't really surprise me," David chimes in.

"No, but it's still sort of sad," Cass says. "Of all the people who need help, Joselyn is the most deserving."

"Especially with Joselyn's powerful ability," I say. "Maybe I'll have a talk with Chozolt and see if there's something he can do for her."

After a hearty meal of beef stew, corn bread, and peach cobbler, David and I walk around the compound in the twilight to stretch our legs. We spot Chozolt talking to a soldier outside of the building he took us in to do our training. He stops speaking when he sees us walking toward him.

"Ah, my fellow Rares. Feeling better after your nap?" he asks jovially.

"Mr. President," I say ignoring his question, "how come you're giving up on Cindy?"

His face hardens a bit. "I wouldn't say I'm 'giving up' on her. That girl's head is like a tangled-up cord of Christmas lights. I was only in her mind for a few seconds, and I was already getting lost. I pulled back out before it was too late and I got stuck in there for good."

"So, there's nothing you can do for her?" I ask.

Chozolt shakes his head. "It would take weeks, maybe even *months* for me to pick apart the knotted mess that's in her brain and find where her Rare ability lies. I just don't think I have time for that."

"Maybe if you can catch her when it's Joselyn in charge and not Cindy..." I say, but he's shaking his head so vigorously, I stop talking.

"I just don't think I'm equipped to help her."

"What if she were asleep when you worked on her? Charlotte could do her thing and put Cindy to sleep first," David suggests.

462

Chozolt considers, tapping at his lip. "I'll have to think about it."

"Fair enough." David grabs my hand and pulls me back toward the barracks before I say anything more.

"He seemed kind of freaked out about being inside of Cindy's head," I comment once we're standing outside of the barracks.

"Wouldn't you be? I know I would. She freaks me out just being in the same room as her," David says with a nervous chuckle.

"Try sharing a room with her in the nuthouse." I laugh at first but then grow serious as the memories of my city life come back up to the surface. "Things were really terrible before we left, weren't they?"

David tucks my hair behind my ear, looking at me thoughtfully. "I know you aren't going to want to hear this, but I think our pasts are a good reason to want to free the Rare still trapped inside that hell. We were lucky to escape, but there are a lot of people still in there being tormented. We should do whatever we can to save them."

I look up into his golden eyes as his words sink in. "You're right. They don't deserve to be treated that way."

As he gives me a hug, I think about what my words implicate. Perhaps I am willing to join the fight. David was right, I've been naive. Life is not always about being comfortable with every decision. Sometimes I'm going to have to make hard choices and do things I don't want to do. From now on, I'm going to train without raising a fuss. It's the least I can do to help those who need it.

At breakfast the next morning, Chozolt informs us he'll take a group of four to visit the NSA headquarters. We'll get a low-level clearance in order to get in, but we will have to wait in a conference room to meet with his guy who can help us with the USB stick. Matthias, David, Denis, and I are the ones going on this "field trip" today. Everyone else stays behind to continue combat training with Alexandrine and Henry, as ordered by Matthias.

One of Chozolt's soldiers drives us there in an armored SUV. The half-hour ride seems so quick after spending days riding on the uncomfortable bus. We come to a bustling city filled with gleaming skyscrapers, long lines of cars at every stop light, and groups of pedestrians waiting to use the crosswalks. The city I grew up in was busy but never this busy.

Chozolt's soldier pulls up to a sleek black building and finds a parking spot.

"We're here." Chozolt opens his door.

Nobody responds as we stare up at the nine-story building in front of us. It seems to be made entirely of windows, but they are all shaded black. This was more like the building I was expecting Chozolt to be in when we got to the Haven, mysterious and important-looking.

We follow Chozolt into the building and go through another metal detector. We are then led to a room the President called a "SCIF." He explained civilians are not allowed to go into most parts of the building because it's a top-secret facility, but there were unoccupied SCIFs for when information is provided by someone who doesn't work there. We get all sorts of side eyes as we follow Chozolt, and I definitely feel like I shouldn't be here, but I'm looking forward to finding out what's on the USB stick.

We walk into a room that is taken up with a long table, with about twelve chairs surrounding it; only one of them is occupied. "Morning, Elliot. I brought along some people who want to talk to you."

A young guy gives a two fingered wave. My first impression is he breaks all the stereotypes given to computer guys. The movies and TV shows I've seen usually make them seem geeky with pocket protectors and thick glasses repaired with tape, but this guy exudes coolness. He wears a sky-blue button-down shirt with the sleeves rolled up exposing a tattoo of a compass on his forearm, khaki cargo pants, and black boots. His dark brown hair is shaved on the sides but long enough on the top to run his hand through to slick it back. He pulls some glasses out of his pocket, and when he slips them on, they accentuate his features, making him look more attractive.

"Is he old enough to work here?" Matthias whispers to Chozolt.

"He's young, but he's the best at what he does. I know he'll be able to help you guys out."

I pull the USB out of my pocket and hand it to Elliot.

"What is it you'd like me to do with it?" Elliot asks with a smooth voice.

"We'd like to know what's in the encrypted files on this USB stick," Matthias says.

"Easy. Give me a few minutes, and I'll get those for you," Elliot says with confidence.

We all stand around awkwardly as we watch Elliot click his mouse around on his monitor.

"So, how long have you been working for the NSA?" David asks Elliot, attempting small talk.

"About two years now," he answers, not looking up from his computer.

David nods in response, even though Elliot can't see him. "What'd you do before this?"

"Before this, I was just a punk kid who broke into the NSA database for fun. They were going to have me arrested but decided they could use my skills and hired me instead," he says with a sly half grin.

Matthias gives a disapproving head shake behind Elliot's back.

"There we are." Elliot clicks open the files and scans through them. "These look like some pretty juicy secrets. Where'd you get this?"

"My father worked for the Coalition for about a year before he had a stroke. He must have taken some notes while he was there." Matthias peeks at the computer screen over Elliot's shoulder.

"So, what's in the encrypted files?" I ask, dying to know.

"I'm not sure I'm supposed to tell you. These are government secrets." Elliot picks up a pen and clicks it as he looks at Chozolt for direction.

"Secrets my father collected and kept hidden. They belong to us," Matthias says sternly.

Chozolt takes a moment to consider them both and pats Elliot on the shoulder. "Go ahead. These people have been through enough. They deserve to know whatever is on that USB stick."

Matthias gives a quick nod as his way of saying thank you.

"Okay, this one," Elliot clicks the top one open, "looks to be a scientific paper on the chemical composition of the fog. There are some notes at the bottom here that says, 'It's used to keep the people of the city susceptible to the way of the Coalition; a form of mild drug to induce fear when needed, thereby making the influencer more powerful; this combined with the vitamins was ultimately the Rares' undoing.' Heavy stuff."

"Keep going. What's the next one about?" Matthias strokes his beard.

"Looks like the vitamins not only worked with the fog but also with the rain," Elliot says, reading the contents of the file. "Says here, 'The main ingredient is a bio-engineered synthetic compound. When taken regularly, they deactivate the Rare ability, leaving Rares weaker than normal people, allowing the fog to cause anxiety, depression, as well as other major health issues.' Looks like they even recorded instances of extreme side effects: multiple victims had their skin 'melted' in the rain. But they didn't stop. It says further research was canceled, and they just put into place the half measures of 'sounding an alarm and locking everyone inside until the rain stopped.'"

"Just regular rain does that?" Chozolt eyebrow cocks.

"If I had to guess," Denis chimes in, "I'd say that the rain got to be like some kind of acid rain as the fog's chemicals became part of the rain cycle over time. The concentration of chemicals inside the rain mixed together with the chemicals in the fog, combined with whatever was in the vitamins must have become too much."

"That's as good a guess as any." Elliot nods.

"How come nobody outside the Coalition knows about this? And how can people *inside* the Coalition be okay with it? Something's gotta be missing," David says.

"Well, I think this next file might be an answer to one of those questions," Elliot says. "It says here that the four towers on the outskirts of the cities scramble radio waves, making it so nothing can get in or out. The Coalition decides what you can or cannot see and hear."

"Doesn't surprise me," Matthias grumbles.

"But guards use radios inside the city." I remember the guard who almost found me when I was trying to leave the city.

"They're more than likely using short range radios that work inside the perimeter of the towers," Elliot answers. "The towers wouldn't have any effect on them."

"Cell phones? People in our school had cell phones," David says.

"From what I know of the situation, people aren't traveling back and forth from city to city all that often, so anyone you want to call is going to be inside the perimeter. Cell towers could work for the city itself. Landlines would work for outside calls."

Everyone nods as we think about it for a bit.

"What about ham radios?"

"What about them?" Elliot responds.

"Some guy in the city told me to tune into a ham radio station, and when I did, I heard a broadcast coming from the Haven."

"Was it a continuous stream?"

"No, it tuned in for about ten seconds before it cut out again," Denis says.

"It could be that the suppression towers aren't geared toward ham radio frequencies and some slip through the cracks on occasion." Elliot taps the end of his pen on the table as he thinks. "But without a full technical break down of how the towers are functioning, we can't know for sure."

"Is there anything else on the USB?" Matthias interrupts our line of conversation.

"There's one more file." Elliot clicks on it. "It looks to be a personal journal. I'll let you read it." He gets out of his chair so Matthias can have a seat.

"I'm curious about the part in the vitamin file that said fear was making the 'influencer more powerful.' Do you have any idea what that might be?" David asks.

"I have a hunch, but I don't have the proof to back it up." Elliot grabs an orange soda off the table. "We can never seem to get close enough for proof. We think there might be a Rare working with Turk, but we don't know his exact powers. Anytime we tried to send a spy in to extract information, our guy never came back."

"Are they caught and thrown in jail or something?" I ask.

"Nah." Elliot takes a swig of soda. "They end up dead. Our inside help retrieved the camera we placed on one of our agents and returned it to us. We watched as Agent Phillips stepped into a room where some dude was sitting with his back turned. Our guy had his gun drawn, pointed at the back of the dude's head. He stood there for a while, so I'm guessing there was some talking going on, but we didn't have a microphone hooked up. Anyway, we watched as Agent Phillips took the gun away from the guy's head and turned it on himself."

The memory of my vision with the old guy bubbles up, and I'm about to ask him if the guy he saw in the video was in a wheelchair, but Matthias explodes. He knocks the chair he was sitting in over as he slams his fist on the table. Everyone in the room is staring at him in shock.

466

"What? What did you find?" I ask.

"The last entry my dad wrote was about a drug Turk was working on that could induce a stroke. They musta injected my dad with it once they caught him stealing information."

"Hold on. How do you know they caught him stealing info?" I ask calmly.

"He said so in the entry. His laptop had been tampered with." Matthias lifts his head and yells up to the ceiling in anger. "Turk is going to pay for this. I want him dead."

The venom in his words hangs in the air, and nobody dares to move, let alone talk for a moment.

"Then we're on the same page." Chozolt slaps Matthias's shoulder.

32

Chozolt leads Matthias out of the room to talk. Elliot picks the chair up off the floor and takes a seat, blowing a breath out. He clicks around on his computer before removing the USB stick and handing it back to me.

There's an awkward pause as we look around at each other uneasily.

"Chozolt isn't planning on going to war with the Coalition, is he?" I ask, breaking the silence.

Elliot swivels back and forth in his chair before leaning forward and speaking in hushed tones, "Strictly speaking, I'm not supposed to tell you lowly civilians anything, but since I'm not one to follow rules, I'll tell you that he visited a psychic, who told him a weapon was coming that would be the Coalition's undoing. He's been waiting for whatever it is to fall into his lap."

"A physical weapon? Or a Rare he's going to use as a weapon?" I ask, voice tightening.

"He goes to a psychic?" Denis asks with a raised eyebrow.

"He doesn't know what kind of weapon, so he keeps delaying until something obvious presents itself." Elliot turns to Denis. "And yeah, he's been seeing a psychic since his old man died. I think he's hoping to make contact with his spirit."

"That must be why he said he wanted to talk to Jack," I say to David.

"Who's Jack?" Elliot takes another drink of soda.

It's making me thirsty for one, but they haven't offered us anything, and I feel too awkward to ask.

"A girl from our camp has a personality with a Rare ability to talk to the dead."

"What?" Elliot scratches his jaw.

David explains Cindy to him.

"Hold up, hold up, hold up." Elliot waves his hands in front of him. "You for real? Four different personalities living inside a little girl, and each one has its own Rare ability. You're not yankin' my chain, are you?"

"Unfortunately not," I say.

"She sounds like she might be what the president's been looking for. I knew this day would come eventually," Elliot says quietly to himself.

"You don't sound very happy about it," David comments.

"I'm not, but it's not my place to question the president. If he thinks we could win and finally end the Coalition, more power to him," Elliot says.

"But I don't think Joselyn's the weapon," I argue. "Chozolt refuses to work with her because her brain's too much of a mess."

"From what you described, I can see why he might be apprehensive," Elliot comments.

"Do you know a lot about Rare abilities?" Denis asks.

"I should. I am one," Elliot says with a smug look.

"Really? What's your ability?" I ask a little too eagerly. I clear my throat and throw in, "If you don't mind me asking."

He chuckles a bit. "I have a photographic memory."

"I've heard of other people having that," David says.

"Photographic memory is a misconception. Most of the time, they just have really good memories, or they have an eidetic memory," Denis comments.

"What's an eidetic memory?" I ask, annoyed Denis continually uses words he knows we wouldn't understand.

"It's where an afterimage will linger in someone's mind's eye for a few minutes before fading away. They don't retain the information forever," Denis answers.

"Except for me," Elliot brags. "I'm a special edition."

"So, you remember *everything*?" David asks.

"I do." Elliot crosses his arms over his chest.

"That's got to be hard to keep track of stuff. I can't even imagine how crowded it's gotta be in your brain," I comment, overwhelmed at the thought.

"Yeah, well, that's what the president helped me with. We did brain exercises where I envisioned myself filing stuff away into folders, and then I can bring it up when I need it."

"So, you treat your brain like a computer?" Denis asks.

Elliot nods. "Basically."

"Does it get any easier with Chozolt inside your head? When he did his search for my ability, it felt like a worm crawling through my brain. I hated it." I shiver at the memory.

"Yeah. It's weird at first, but you get used to it. Just make sure you let him know if he's pushing it too hard. He can sometimes get caught up in the moment," Elliot says coolly. "So, you're all Rare too?"

"I'm not," Denis says.

"He's just smart," I say. "David and I are Rare."

"So, what're your abilities?" Elliot leans back in his chair and puts his feet up on the table. He opens the side pocket on his cargo pants and pulls out a small bag of Cheetos to snack on.

"I haven't really figured out what my abilities are yet. Someone shows up to protect me when I'm about to get sick or injured. I don't really understand it."

"Interesting." Elliot sucks the cheese powder off his fingertips. "How about you, blondie? What can you do?"

"I can dream the future. It's not always reliable, though, but Chozolt says he's going to work on it with me and that maybe he'll be able to help me see the future while awake," I say, trying to impress him.

Elliot drops his feet off his table and sits up straight, his eyes lighting up. "Now that's an ability we could work with."

"What do you mean?" My heart flutters a bit.

"I mean, if I'm reading the inflection in your voice when you asked about war, you aren't interested in it any more than I am, correct?"

"Nope. Not at all, actually." I glance at David.

He gives me a stony look.

Elliot glances around the room and then whispers to me, "I might have an idea of a way we could take the Coalition down without any fighting, but I need to do some research first. Here's my number. Let me know if you've made any progress with seeing the future while awake." He hands me a ripped piece of paper with his phone number on it.

I slip the paper into my pocket as Matthias and Chozolt walk back into the room.

"You guys ready to go?" Chozolt asks.

I look at Elliot, and he winks at me before I turn to follow David out of the room. I wonder if anyone notices the glow of hope blossoming inside of me. I don't know what his idea is, but any plan that doesn't include war has to be good. Now it's time to get started on my training.

33

Matthias seems to be in a better mood when we pile into the SUV. Less cranky, anyway. I'd love to ask what they discussed while they were out of the room for so long, but I doubt he'd tell me.

"Who's hungry?" Chozolt asks from the front seat.

"Me," David and I both reply.

"Seeing as it's Tuesday, how about we stop at a little Mexican joint before returning?"

"What does Tuesday have to do with Mexicans?" Denis asks.

Chozolt turns to give Denis an incredulous look. "You've never heard of Taco Tuesday before?"

"Did you just say 'tacos'? And they have a whole day dedicated to them?" I ask, my giddiness bursting at the seams as Chozolt nods.

"I'm not sure I'm in the mood for tacos," Denis says dismissively.

"Shut up!" I snap at Denis, then point toward the windshield. "Let's go!"

Matthias looks at me with a hint of a smile as David puts his hand on my shoulder and tells me to settle down. How can these people not understand how earth-shatteringly awesome this is? An entire day dedicated to tacos? Maybe I can get Chozolt's cooks to make tacos every Tuesday; then Henry can finally try one. I tried to save him one when we were in Eli's city, but it didn't survive in my bag back to camp. It ended up making a huge mess too. I should have eaten it like I had wanted to in the first place.

Within five minutes, we're standing outside the restaurant, my stomach growling with anticipation. Chozolt told us to order whatever we want because lunch is on him, so I order the endless taco deal. I eat until my stomach is past full, almost to the point of being sick. I probably shouldn't have, but tacos are my weakness.

When we get back to the compound, there's a line of our people outside practicing knife attack maneuvers. I know they're going to want David and I to join, but I'm not feeling well at the moment and want to sleep it off.

"Ugh, I shouldn't have eaten so many." I flop down on my bed.

"I warned you after your sixth one that maybe you should stop." David takes my shoes off for me. "I can't believe you ate nine of them."

"I have to make up for lost time," I joke as my stomach starts to cramp.

David covers me up with the bedding and kisses my forehead before heading outside.

I've finally dozed off when Cindy wakes me up by complaining loudly to Charlotte. Except the innocence in her tone tells me it's Joselyn and not Cindy. I lie still and listen to what's bothering her.

"I don't know why he keeps asking me if he can talk to Jack. I'm not in control of when Jack shows up. I'm not in control of any of them. Especially Cindy," she says, frustration dripping off every word.

"Cindy's been hanging out a lot lately. You're okay, right?" Charlotte asks, concerned.

"I can't get the feeling of those helicopter pilots out of my head. It's like their ghosts are haunting my mind, but I know that's silly." She pauses, then says, "It's silly, right?"

"It sounds silly," Charlotte says.

They're quiet a moment, and I'm about to get up when Joselyn says, "I have to tell you something, but you've gotta promise not to tell anyone else."

"Okay, I promise," Charlotte whispers.

"Cindy wrote me a note once telling me that I could use my ability to kill people. Actually, she said that I *should* kill people," she scoffs. "You know Cindy. Anyway, I didn't believe her, but when I had ahold of those pilots' brains, something told me that if I just held on for a few more seconds or squeezed just a little harder, I could definitely have killed them and —this is the part you can't tell anyone—a little part of me wanted to, just to see what it was like." Shame seeps into her voice. "I don't know if it was because Cindy put it in my head, or if I'm becoming evil like her, but I wish my power wasn't one that hurt people. I'm glad Chozolt isn't willing to train me. I feel like the only thing he could train me to do is to be better at hurting people or killing them."

"Well, maybe he could help you control it better, like help control how hard you squeeze or something," Charlotte suggests.

"What, just squeeze enough to give someone a headache instead of making them fall to the floor in agony?" Joselyn asks.

"Yeah. Like, maybe if you can control how to work your ability, you won't need to be so scared and Cindy won't need to show up all the time."

"I thought you two were friends?" Joselyn asks.

"I try, but she can be hard to deal with sometimes. I like you better," Charlotte says.

"I like me better too," Joselyn says with a giggle.

They start talking about what they should do after supper, so I take the opportunity to pretend to wake up, which they don't even notice. I should probably go see what David is up to.

I find him outside with Tim and Denis, giving them shooting lessons.

"Hey, how're you feeling?" David asks as I step up by his side.

"A little better," I say.

"I'm surprised you didn't vomit after all that food. Not sure how you fit so much in that tiny body," Denis says.

"I don't joke around when it comes to tacos," I say with a small laugh. "So, what are you boys up to?"

472

"David is teaching me how to be a better shot with my prosthetic. Soon I'll be armed *and* dangerous." Tim laughs at his own pun.

Denis shakes his head and groans.

"You might not have to do that, though," I say. "Elliot, the guy at the NSA, told us he might have a solution that wouldn't involve war."

"Doesn't hurt to practice," David says, sounding a lot like Matthias.

"I know, I know. Be prepared and all that stuff." I fight not to roll my eyes.

"Speaking of which, it's been a while since you've practiced." David bumps me with his elbow. "Maybe you should give it a try again."

I absentmindedly rub at my thumb where I got pistol bit the first time I shot the gun.

"Yeah, let's see if you've gotten any better at it," Tim says enthusiastically.

Everyone looks at me expectantly, so I huff and grab the gun out of David's hand. Having the gun in my hand brings back the memory of shooting the soldier to save David, and for a moment, I feel like I'm about to lose myself, but I refocus on the present, refusing to be dragged down right now.

I square off and wait for everyone else to get a safe distance away from me. I fire all the rounds, taking aim between each one. I'm not nearly as far away from the target as David was when he was showing off for Chozolt, so I can easily see I didn't hit the bullseye like he did, but it looks like I at least hit the target.

"Let's go have a closer look," David says.

"Not bad!" Tim says as we step up to the target. "You must have kept your eyes open this time."

"Oh, shush." I give him a playful shove.

The bullets hit the target, but they're scattered all over the place.

"I could give you pointers if you'd like," David offers.

"Nah, I'm good," I say.

We change out the target and go back to the shooting spot. David starts giving Tim advice again, but I don't feel like sticking around to listen. It's boring, and I have no interest in guns.

I go for a short walk in hopes of wearing off some of my lunch before suppertime. I pass by people bustling around doing their daily duties. It makes me feel a little guilty we're putting more of a burden on them. Maybe I should offer to help with something, but I don't know what I would help with, so I keep walking.

I stop beside a tree and look up at the fluffy white clouds floating lazily by. I'm still amazed by the beauty of it all. I never got to see the sky clearly in the city. Sure, there were times the fog wasn't as thick as usual and you could see it through the haze, but nothing like this. As I stare at a cloud, trying to decide what it looks like, Matthias steps up next to me and looks toward the sky too.

"What'cha lookin' at?"

"Just admiring the clouds," I say.

"Ah." He pauses a moment and then clears his throat. "I'd like ya to work with Chozolt every day, startin' tomorrow."

"Every day? Why every day?" I ask suspiciously.

"Just something Chozolt and I talked about. If he can get ya to the point of seeing the future while awake, he thinks ya might be an asset for finally going to war."

"What if we found another way to deal with the Coalition that didn't involve war? Elliot said—"

"I really don't care what some kid said, and I'm not interested in *what ifs* and *maybes*. I'm interested in gettin' the job done. And as I see it, killin' the S-O-B that hurt Dad—and the countless other people—is the only concrete way to end this."

"Why do we keep having to have this argument? My views are not the same as yours, and it's unfair for you to demand me to change. Yes, it sucks what happened to Grandpa, but we don't *really* know if it's true. We're just assuming the worst-case scenario because it's the Coalition."

"Doesn't matter if it's true or not. What matters is that Turk and the Coalition need to be destroyed. Can we at least agree on that?"

I can tell he's trying his hardest to keep his tone calm, so I do the same. "Yeah, but I'm not going to stop trying to find a different way. I'll learn from Chozolt, but I'm doing it because I want to, not because Chozolt wants me to."

"You're as stubborn as your mother." He lets out a breathy laugh, which puts me at ease.

"You're not exactly the easiest person to work with either," I say with a smirk.

"Just please keep an open mind if ya find out your way doesn't work. We're all on the same side of this, and I think it's fair to say we all want it to end."

"Deal." I hold out my hand to shake on it.

He shakes my hand but then pulls me forward and wraps me up in the first legitimate hug he's given me. For one brief moment, I truly feel like his daughter, being protected from the world by his strong arms. Now that I've agreed to his terms, I really hope I can find another way.

34

Today is my first real lesson with Chozolt. I'm nervous about what it's going to feel like. I hope it won't be as bad as the first time, because I won't want to do this if it is. I've been through a lot in my life, and I'm not sure I can put myself through more torture.

"Ready?" Chozolt asks me as I rest my head back against the chair.

"Um, sure," I say as bravely as I can.

"If for some reason you want me to stop, Olivia, just let me know." He makes sure I'm looking at him when he says it.

I nod quickly while I focus on keeping my breathing even.

He settles back in his chair. "All right, let's see what we can do."

I close my eyes and breathe in through my nose and slowly out through my mouth. A small pressure builds on the front of my brain, and I immediately tense.

"Remember to relax and breathe, Olivia," Chozolt says calmly.

I take a few breaths, but it doesn't really help, so I think about David being here with me, holding my hand, and that seems to do the trick. Chozolt must be able to sense when I've calmed down, because the pressure moves to the back of my brain in the same worm-squiggling way it did the first time, only this time, it's quicker and more direct.

"All right, Oliva, I'm going to try to activate your Rare ability. If you start to experience something that resembles your visions or you feel like you want to stop, let me know," he says.

It's kind of making me more nervous that he keeps saying it. How bad is this going to be?

I take a shaky breath, uncertain whether I want this to work or not. Most of my visions haven't been very nice up to this point, and I don't want to have another apocalyptic dream right here in front of him.

The pressure in the back of my head pulsates, but not in a painful way. It's more like when you get a shoulder rub and someone hits a sore spot that feels good and hurts all at the same time. A good pain.

He prods a little harder, and the pressure reaches an uncomfortable level. I'm just about ready to ask him to stop when a vision explodes in my mind.

"Are you sure?" Nathan stands inside the empty barracks with Rebecca.

"Uh-huh." Rebecca nods with excitement. "You're going to be a daddy again."

Nathan picks her up and spins her around in a circle as they both laugh. He sets her down, and they kiss passionately. Nathan pulls away and places his hand on Rebecca's stomach, smiling proudly.

I snap back into the present, feeling like I watched something I wasn't supposed to see, a private moment not meant for my eyes.

"I just had a vision," I say breathlessly. "Can we stop for now?"

"Sure." He withdraws from my brain.

I blow out a big breath once he's gone. I feel drained again, just like the first time. My eyelids start to droop, so I sit forward in my chair, forcing myself to stay awake.

"This is the first time you've seen a vision while still awake, correct?" Chozolt takes a drink from his bottle of water. I notice sweat beading on his forehead.

"Yes." I grab my own bottle of water. "I feel guilty about what I saw, though. It was a private matter."

"I don't suppose you'd care to tell me what it was about?" he asks.

I chew on my bottom lip, considering whether I want to share it or not. "Well, it was a conversation between two of my fellow campmates discovering they're going to have a baby."

"That's wonderful news!" He claps his hands together. "This was an incredible first step in your development, and I don't think you should feel guilty about it. Perhaps after a while, you'll be able to focus it on matters that pertain to you, but in the meantime, we'll call it a win."

"Am I going to stop feeling tired like this after our sessions, or am I going to have to prepare myself to need naps every time we work together?" I blink slowly. If I don't get back to my bunk soon, I'm going to fall over and sleep right here in his office.

"You'll always be a little tired afterward. I think it's a coping mechanism people have after having someone else's consciousness inside their brains. I do apologize for that. If it makes you feel any better, I feel tired too."

I give a sleepy nod, my eyelids closing.

"Let's call it a day, and I'll help you back to your bed." He grabs my upper arm and leads me out of the room.

I wake up to David kissing my cheek and whispering, "Wake up, sleepy head."

I look around and find people getting ready for bed.

"What time is it?" I croak.

"Quarter after ten. Chozolt told us to leave you alone, but I couldn't wait any longer. You're so cute when you sleep." He brushes my hair off my forehead. "So, what happened? Did you see anything?"

I check if anyone is in earshot before telling him what I saw.

"Really? She's pregnant?" David whispers, looking toward Rebecca.

"I don't know if she is right now," I answer. "Do you think I should tell her what I saw?"

"I'll leave that up to you," David says. "It's not really something she needs to be warned about, so it's your call."

"Maybe I will later." I lay my head back down.

"Chozolt said he wants to work with me tomorrow morning," David says.

"We're never going to spend time together at this rate," I say. "Every time we work with him, we need to sleep it off for the rest of the day."

"I know. That part of it sucks, but I'm excited to see what he can do for me." David shrugs.

"Did he work with anyone else today, or is he just doing one person a day?"

"He was going to try to work with Charlotte, but he got called into his office. We're just extras in his already busy schedule, so I'm not sure how often we'll actually get to work with him."

"Are you two going to talk all night, or can I get some sleep?" Cass jokingly asks from her bunk.

"She's right. I should probably rest up before my session tomorrow. Are you going to be able to fall asleep again?" David strokes my cheek with his thumb.

"I hope so," I say, and he gives me an apologetic look. "Maybe, next time, wake me up to have supper with you. I'm hungry."

David gives me a kiss goodnight before climbing up into his bunk. Someone starts turning the lights off, and I let out a frustrated groan. I'm not even in my pajamas yet.

I get out of bed to use the bathroom, but they're both occupied. After waiting a couple minutes, I go to find something to eat instead of standing around outside the bathroom doors. I put on my winter gear, grab a flashlight, and head off to the kitchen to see if they locked it for the night or if I might be able to sneak some snacks.

Once outside, I find I don't need the flashlight because the moon is out, lighting up the world around me in a silvery luster. Every breath I exhale turns into a glowing white stream as the moonlight shines on the condensation. It's so quiet out here, it feels like a different world during the night. The only sound is my boots crunching on the frozen ground. I almost wish it were summertime and the night bugs were out making their racket. I feel so alone.

I make it to the mess hall and tug on the door leading to the kitchen. Surprisingly, it's unlocked. I instinctively look around to see if anyone is going to catch me but then remember Chozolt said we can treat this place like our home. I slip through the door and close it gently.

Using my flashlight, I walk carefully over to the fridge. There's a container of leftover chicken to munch on. I rip a chunk of chicken breast off and start to eat it, but it's dry and hard to swallow, so I grab a soda out of the fridge door. As I crack it open, I hear someone outside the entrance door. It feels like I'm being caught, since I didn't bother turning on the light, so I make the quick decision to hide, bringing the food with me. I have just enough time to squat in the corner of the room behind a counter before they come in and turn on the lights.

"What's to eat?" A man with a deep voice asks.

"There might be some chicken left," a soft-spoken male voice answers.

My heart starts hammering in my chest as I hold the chicken container tightly in my hands.

"Nah. How about some chips or something?" the deep voice suggests, and I hear them walk farther away from my hiding spot to grab their snacks from a cupboard.

"Did you see the way the president was practically salivating during the briefing? He thinks he's finally found them, doesn't he?" the young voice asks, crunching on chips loudly.

"It seems that way, but the problem is going to be training them."

"Training them to be his war puppet, you mean?" the young guy asks.

"He is the master of puppets," the deep voice says around a mouthful of food. "Sometimes I feel like a marionette, running his errands for him day-in and day-out. I can only imagine what those Rare felt like. I hope he's finally found the right candidate so we can get this whole thing over with. If he takes too long, we're going to lose Canada's help, not to mention Scotland's."

"Maybe he needs to stop putting Rares through so much testing and training. The human mind can only take so much raping before it breaks," the young voice remarks.

"It's not rape, you sicko."

"Well, that's what Claudia said it felt like," the young guy says defensively.

"From what I heard, Claudia wasn't right in the head to begin with. I don't think it took much to push her over the edge."

"Probably not," the young guy says thoughtfully. "Poor Claudia. Can you imagine hearing people's thoughts day-in and day-out? She said she no longer knew if it was her own thoughts or if she was hearing someone else's. She came here seeking solitude, but Chozolt believed he'd be able to help her control it and then pushed her too hard. I think he was hoping to use her to spy on the Coalition or something."

"Well, at least he's learned from his failed attempts. Now he lets people rest in between, for whatever that's worth."

"He better be careful. Their leader doesn't look like someone he should cross."

"Chozolt'll just have *us* take care of him if it comes to that," deep-voice guy says with a huff. "Wanna head over to the rec room and play some pool? You can break."

"You're on," the young guy says.

I listen to their footsteps head to the front door, and the lights turn off, plunging me into a darkness that matches my mood.

I don't sleep one bit all night. It might be from sleeping all day, or from the soda I drank so late, but mostly it was because of the conversation I overheard. No wonder Chozolt was so insistent on making sure I know I can stop at any time. He doesn't want me to break like the other Rares he's "helped."

When David wakes up, he takes one look at me and immediately knows I didn't have a good night.

"I'm so sorry. I let you sleep in too long last night." He rubs my head.

"No, it isn't that. I have something to tell you."

"Let me get dressed, and you can tell me on the way to breakfast." He grabs a set of clean clothes and heads to the bathroom.

I get up and stretch, trying to get the blood flowing to wake me up a little more. I go to use the ladies' room before heading out into the cold air but stop with my hand on the doorknob when I hear crying inside. I panic a little, wondering if I should console whoever is crying in there or walk away and pretend I didn't hear it. Before I make my decision, the door opens, and a red-faced Rebecca almost runs into me.

"Olivia!" she exclaims, startled.

"Are you okay?" I ask.

"Uh, yeah. I'm fine." She wipes away a stray tear, the reassurance in her voice not quite ringing true.

I wait a few seconds, trying to decide what to do, when suddenly I blurt out, "Congratulations on the baby." I squeeze my eyes shut, immediately regretting having said anything.

"How did you—" she stutters. "I *just* took a test and found out. Were you spying on me?" she whispers.

"No! No, nothing like that. I had a vision while I was working with Chozolt yesterday. You were telling Nathan about it." I'm surprised when I realize the vision came true so soon after having it.

"Did he look happy?" Rebecca's eyes fill with fear as she grabs ahold of my arm. "I'm so scared to tell him. I don't know what he's going to think."

"Yes, he was happy. In fact, he was excited," I say reassuringly.

"Oh, thank God." She lets go of my arm and puts her hands on her forehead. "Thank you, Olivia. I'm glad you told me." She gives me a friendly hug, then walks back to her bunk.

I'm glad I told her, but the thought pops in my head: what if my vision was wrong, like the bus vision? What if Nathan isn't happy and now she'll think I'm a liar? I shouldn't have said anything.

After finishing in the bathroom, I find David by our bunk, waiting in his winter coat. "You ready to go?" he asks.

"Yeah, just let me get my stuff on."

People are starting to wake up now, and I want to get our breakfast before the morning rush. We head outside into the crisp air, the ground sparkling where the sun hits the thick layer of frost.

"So, what was it you wanted to tell me?" David asks.

"I was in the kitchen getting a snack last night when two of Chozolt's soldiers came in. I hid because—"

"You hid?" David interrupts me.

"Uh, well yeah. I felt a little awkward being in there, and I panicked. Anyway, I overheard them talking." I lower my voice. "Chozolt has broken people's minds while trying to 'help' them. The guys didn't say it clearly, but I think people have died."

"Died just from him being in their heads?" David asks.

"I don't know. I'm just repeating what they said. They talked about some girl named Claudia and how she had the ability to hear people's thoughts, but she heard them all the time. She wanted to come to the Haven to find solitude, but Chozolt insisted on helping her control it, and she broke or something."

"You had a lesson with him yesterday. What did it feel like?" David opens the door to the mess hall for me.

I walk in, and the smell of sausage and eggs hits my nose, making my stomach growl. "Well, he insisted on me knowing that I can stop any time I want, and I have a feeling it's because of the people he's pushed too hard."

I grab a tray, plate, and fork before joining the buffet line. We stop talking while dishing up our breakfast, then find a table in the back corner in hopes of having some privacy.

"There was a point where the pressure of him being in my head intensified to an uncomfortable level, and that's when I had my vision. So far, I think his methods work in activating my Rare ability, but at what cost?"

David stabs at his eggs with his fork, then takes a bite, thinking.

"What's on your mind?" I take a bite of sausage.

"I was just thinking that if he brings my ability out, he won't be able to hurt me. Bartholomew won't let him."

"Lucky you." I cover up my jealousy with a wink.

"But that also means that if he decides to try to train Joselyn, Cindy would step forward to protect Joselyn if he goes too far. I guess my suggestion of him working with Joselyn doesn't work."

"The guys also talked about Chozolt being super excited about one of us coming here, that we're what he was looking for. It's probably not me, though. You three have more useful abilities than mine."

"I think your ability has the potential to be useful," David says.

"Thanks." I don't believe him.

I think there are too many factors for mine to be useful, but I've only worked with Chozolt once. I have a hard time imagining myself controlling what I see and when I see it, but I guess that's what the training is all about.

"Gotta go." David wipes his mouth with a napkin.

I look up and see Chozolt walking toward us with a smile. "How are you feeling, Olivia?"

"Okay." A large yawn betrays me. "Tired, because I slept until bedtime last night and then couldn't go back to sleep. Maybe we should be doing the training session at night, right before bedtime."

"We can certainly try it, but I believe it works better if both minds are well-rested to begin with. Does this mean you'd like to hold off until this evening, David?"

David looks at me, but I shrug because it's up to him.

"No, we can do it now," he answers.

A big smile spreads across Chozolt's face as David stands up to follow him.

"See you later, Liv." David takes my empty plate with him as he leaves.

I don't know what to do with myself now that David's gone. I'm debating whether I should take a nap or not when I spot Cass, Tim, and Denis sitting together, and decide I'd rather not be alone.

"Is it all right if I sit with you?" I ask.

"Of course," Cass answers. "I need someone to talk to." She side-eyes Tim and Denis, who are discussing bullet velocities and whether his prosthetic will be enough for long range shots.

"So, what've you been up to?" I ask.

"Mostly combat training. You're lucky that you get to skip out on it. I'm not getting much better, and Alexandrine isn't being nice about it."

"She just wants to be sure you got the techniques down," Tim says, jumping into our conversation. "Practice makes habit, and if you practice the moves wrong, you're more than likely going to hurt yourself more than your opponent."

"Thank you, O Wise One." Cass jabs her fork into a sausage. "I can't help it if I'm not good at this stuff."

"Would you rather train with me?"

"You have your lessons with Chozolt to worry about," Cass says.

"I'm not working with him today. David is. So, what do you say? Should we get started after you're done eating?"

"Alexandrine might not be too happy," she says, then smiles. "All the more reason to do it."

We both laugh. I don't know why I offered to help with her combat training. I suppose it could be because I don't want to think about what might be happening to David. I need a distraction from it, and this is as good of a distraction as any.

36

"There you go!" I say from the ground. "I think you've got it."

Cass helps me up, beaming. "I feel more comfortable working with you. Alexandrine's always judging me, hardly helping me get better."

"That's just her way." I brush the dirt and frost off my clothes. "Maybe she's actually a Rare and her ability is being cranky and making people feel small."

Cass laughs. "So, how did your lesson go?" She gets back into a fighting stance.

"It went fine." I lunge at her with the sheathed knife we're using for practice. "I had a vision during our session and was able to use it to help Rebecca."

She hip tosses me onto the ground and disarms me while saying, "Help Rebecca with what?"

I look up into her brown, curious eyes, and choose to confide in her. I explain what I saw, feeling a little guilty that not only did I see it, but I keep telling people about it.

"So, you were able to help her be less nervous?" She helps me stand back up.

"I think so."

Cass stands still a moment, thinking. "What if you see someone die in one of your visions? Would you tell them about it or leave it a surprise as it should be?"

"I would—" I stop. "I don't really know. I mean, I had a vision of David being blown up and I told him, but that was because I was so upset. What would you do?"

"I think it would be hard, but I wouldn't tell them. I'd worry that they would end up living in fear or being depressed for the rest of their days, and that doesn't seem fair," she answers thoughtfully.

"Well, let's just hope I don't have a vision of someone dying." I stab at her stomach slowly so she can do the maneuver. "Speaking of dying, I overheard some people talking about Chozolt pushing Rares too hard during training and breaking their minds, or possibly even killing them."

Cass stops her countermoves and looks at me, aghast. "And you're going to keep working with him, even though he might kill you?"

"That was in the past. I think he learned his lesson, and now he's being overly cautious, reminding me multiple times that if I need to stop, to just let him know."

"I don't know, Olivia. You better be careful. What happens if you're having a vision and you can't snap out of it to tell him you need him to stop?"

As I think about what she said, movement catches my eye, and I see Chozolt half leading, half dragging David back to the barracks. I take off running immediately, spooked by my conversation with Cass.

"What's wrong with him? Is he okay?" I grab David's other arm and wrap it around my neck to help hold him up. David's barely able to keep his eyes open.

"He's fine," Chozolt says. "He's just tired."

"Did you get his Rare ability to work?" I ask.

"Yes, I think so. I got hit in the face by an invisible force I'm assuming was Bartholomew, as he calls it."

I look closer and see swelling on Chozolt's cheekbone that's turning a nice shade of purple. I have a million questions running through my head. I hope he's got time to answer some.

"Why isn't he able to walk himself?" We haul David through the barracks door and lay him down on my bed.

"After the assault, I extracted myself from his head and left the room to get some ice. He fell asleep while I was gone, and I wasn't able to get him to wake up fully." Chozolt grunts as he stands, stretching his back.

"So, what do you think David's ability actually is?" We step out of the barracks to let David sleep.

"I'd say his ability is closest to something called 'subconscious manifestation.' Bartholomew is David's subconscious coming out to protect him."

"Like how Cindy protects Joselyn?"

"Sort of, but different. From what I know about that girl, Cindy is a personality, or consciousness, that stays inside Joselyn's body and protects her mind. Bartholomew can be a projected entity that protects David's body from harm."

"How come David can see him, but you couldn't?" I ask.

"I don't know if we will ever be able to see him," he answers.

My shoulders slump a little when I hear that. I'd love to finally meet Bartholomew. I'd thank him for saving David's life so many times.

"Can Bartholomew see the future or something? He showed up to shove David out of the way before a building exploded and decapitated him with sheet metal."

"Good question. I haven't worked with him enough to know that answer, though. I suppose it could be possible, seeing as Joselyn has four personalities that each have a different ability. It's going to be hard to know much more about him if he punches me every time I work with David." Chozolt rubs at his bruise.

"Sorry you got punched." I hope he isn't too mad to work with David again.

He waves my apology away. "Oh, it's all right. It's all part of the process."

"Out of curiosity, why do you think Bartholomew punched you?"

"I'd guess it was because David felt uneasy with my presence in his mind, and since there were no other threats in the room, he took it out on me."

"Looks like it was a solid punch for just a subconscious entity," I comment.

"It was." He nods. "So, now that I'm done with David, did you want to give it another try? I have a meeting later this afternoon, but I could probably fit in another session beforehand."

"Why don't you work with Charlotte or Joselyn?"

"I haven't devised a way to work with Charlotte without falling asleep yet. I have some men looking into a soundproofing system that would allow me to get into her mind but protect me from her sound. When I have that, then I think I can safely work with her. And I'm still working up the courage to enter back into

Joselyn's mind. I'll try again someday, just not yet. So, what do you say? Want to give your lessons another shot?"

"Yes, she does." Matthias walks up behind me.

I turn and narrow my eyes at him. "For your information, I was working with Cass on combat training."

"That's Alexandrine's job. Let her take care of it. Go with Chozolt," he says with finality.

"I guess I'm coming with you," I say, annoyed.

I follow him to the room, the smell of lilac overwhelming me. It feels warmer in here than last time too. I want to turn around and leave, but I also want to get better so I can help Elliot. I take a breath and flop into the chair.

"All right, before I go in and draw your ability forward, I want you to do a little meditating first. I was informed about your struggles with depression, and I want to see if we can bring your mental state to a positive place before we begin and see what happens. Perhaps your negative mindset has been a hindrance to your ability shining through."

"We can try," I mumble, still annoyed with Matthias.

We begin with some deep breathing, then move to some mental exercises where Chozolt speaks calmly and takes me on a journey in my mind. He tells me to go to the place that's most relaxing to me, and I picture myself sitting in the clearing David and I found when we first left the city. The happiness from the feeling of the sunshine on my face for the first time draws a sigh out of me. I'm so immersed, I can feel the cool breeze on my face, hear the sounds of the birds singing and the bugs buzzing, and smell the comforting scent of decaying leaves and wildflowers. After what feels like an hour, Chozolt ends the meditation to begin our session.

"I can't believe it actually worked. I feel completely relaxed and unafraid this time," I say dreamily.

"Good! This gives me an idea. I'd like you to try being in your meditative state when I begin. Perhaps with a relaxed mind, unhindered by any thoughts outside of your safe place, I will be able to manipulate things better. Want to give it a try?"

The suggestion makes me a little apprehensive, and it must show on my face.

"Remember, you can let me know if you want me to stop at any time," he says, which reminds me of the conversation I had with Cass.

"What if I'm in my meditation or in the middle of a vision, and my brain has had enough, but I can't let you know that?"

"Trust that your brain will do what needs to be done before it's too late," he replies.

I don't feel like that's a good enough answer, but we'll see what happens. I rest my head back and take a few deep breaths, concentrating on the clearing in the woods. It's a little harder, knowing he's about to begin, but after a few more deep breaths, I'm back in my relaxed state, feeling the warmth of the sun on my skin and hearing the breeze blowing through the trees.

This time I'm only half-aware of him entering my mind. He goes straight to where my RABI is, the wormy feeling hardly noticeable. But when he increases the pressure, drawing the same good pain out, I'm pulled from my safe place in the woods and thrown into a vision.

The city is still foggy as ever. My brain gets a little fuzzy from breathing the fog in, but I have to ignore it and stay on task. David, Elliot, and I are heading down a street, keeping our eyes peeled for guards or soldiers. I have a strong sense of duty and determination on my mind.

This is going to work.

"A guard on patrol one block ahead is going to catch us. Let's duck in here," I say, as I see it play out in my mind.

We slip into an alleyway and hide behind a pile of cardboard boxes. After a short wait, we hear the clomping of the guard's boots on the sidewalk as he passes by.

Once the footsteps recede, we leave our hiding spot and continue.

"This fog is impossible to see through. How much farther, Elliot?" David squints.

"We continue this way for three blocks, turn right and walk for four blocks, then a left, and we should be able to see it," Elliot rattles off from memory.

"You remembered to bring the clip, right?" I ask.

"Oh, shoot!" he replies, making my heart skip a beat. "We gotta walk all the way... Yes, of course I remembered to grab it, woman," he says as though I insulted him. "You think I'd forget?"

I come out of the vision and into awareness with a sharp breath. Sweat drips off my forehead as the pressure inside my brain starts giving me a panic attack. Every bit of the relaxed state I was in beforehand is long gone.

"Stop!" I manage to say through my panting.

Chozolt withdraws immediately, and once he's out of my head, I collapse forward, tucking my head between my knees. He lays his hand on my back and pats me between the shoulder blades. The back of my brain where my Rare ability is continues buzzing slightly.

"Are you okay, Olivia?" he asks, a slight edge to his voice.

I focus on my breathing until the panic passes and the buzzing stops. I sit up and rest back in the chair. Chozolt looks at me with concern, so I give him a thumbs up to let him know I'm okay.

"What was your vision this time?" Chozolt grabs his water and chugs half the bottle.

"I was on a mission inside a Coalition city. I don't know what I was doing there," I lie, unwilling to let him know my plans on working with Elliot. "I had a vision in my vision. I was able to see something happening and take measures to avoid it coming true."

"This is great news," Chozolt says.

I watch him blink slowly as he wipes some sweat off his forehead. He looks exhausted.

"I also think our test with you being in a relaxed state worked. It was a lot easier for me to get into your RABI and draw it out. You slipped into your vision almost immediately."

"How do you know? Are you able to see my thoughts?" I narrow my eyes at him.

"No. Your facial expression and body language told me. You tend to tense up and look distraught when you have a vision," he says.

"After you left my brain, the spot felt like it was buzzing." I point at the back of my head.

"That means we're getting closer," Chozolt says. "Once your ability is fully activated and you're in control of it, you'll always be aware of it."

"I'm always going to feel buzzing in my head?" I'm unhappy with the thought.

"Well, not *always*. It would be like your awareness of your heart. If you concentrate on your heart, you can feel it beating, but most of the time, you ignore it and don't even know it's there. Your ability will be like that. It'll be present, and if you focus on it, you'll feel it, but otherwise you'll tune it out."

"Do you have any idea how many sessions we need to do before I'm in control of it myself?"

"I'd wager only a few more. You're showing great strides. In the meantime, I'd like you to work on meditating every day to find peace within yourself. If you can gain control of your mind, I think it will help you control your ability."

I give a big yawn and nod, hardly hearing what he's saying.

"C'mon. Let's get you back to your bed so you can sleep it off."

37

It takes Cass a few attempts to wake me up for supper. I keep falling back to sleep immediately after she stops shaking me. When I finally sit up and stretch, I forget I'm on the top bunk because David's in my bed and almost fall off, grabbing on at the last second. The adrenaline rush does the job of waking me up the rest of the way.

"Olivia, can you get David to wake up? He won't listen to me," Cass says.

I slip off the bed and kneel next to David. I rub his shoulder, saying his name gently. When that doesn't work, I lean in and kiss his cheek. Still nothing. I start shaking him, calling out his name, getting a little nervous. I finally grab his face and plant a big kiss on his lips.

David smiles groggily. "Mmm, good morning to me."

"Actually, it's suppertime, and you had me scared to death," I say.

David wraps his arms around me and pulls me in for a hug, knowing exactly how to get me to calm down. He gets out of bed, and we get ready to head to the mess hall.

"Um, did you happen to talk to Chozolt? Did he mention anything about my session with him?" David avoids eye contact as he scratches at the back of his head.

"You mean how Bartholomew punched him in the face?" I ask, chuckling.

"Oh, man. I feel so bad." David's cheeks turn a bright shade of red.

"Don't. He's not angry. He said it's all a part of the process," I reassure him.

We walk into the mess hall, and the smell of tacos hits my nose, and I squeal with delight. I look at where they serve the food and see they have a taco-making station set up.

David has to tug on my arm to get me to stop trying to run. "Chozolt must have pulled some strings for you," he says.

"I promise I won't eat as many as I did the other day." I grab a plate.

David laughs. "I would hope not."

I make three tacos, then look around to see if Henry is here. I spot him sitting with Matthias. "So? What do you think?" I gesture to the tacos enthusiastically.

He shrugs. "Meh."

My jaw drops. "Meh? You must not have made yours right. Here try mine." I reluctantly hand over one of my tacos.

He humors me and takes a bite. His blue eyes grow big as he chews it. "You're right. I made mine wrong. This is delicious." He chews loudly.

"What did you put on yours?" I ask, trying to ignore that I'm swapping spit with my brother by biting where he did.

"Meat, cheese, and lettuce. Those were the only things I could identify that I like."

"You've gotta add salsa and sour cream, silly," I say. "And you need to spread it out just right so you get an even amount of each ingredient with every bite."

"Enough about tacos," Matthias says impatiently. "Did anything happen with Chozolt today?"

"He got Bartholomew to show up while working with David. And got punched in the face for it," I say around a mouthful of taco.

Matthias looks at me stoically and says, "I meant with you."

"Oh! I had another vision. A vision of me having a vision, oddly. And then, when he left my mind, my RABI—short for Rare Ability Brain Intermediary—was still buzzing for a little while. He said that was a good thing, that it'll feel like that once I'm able to control my ability myself. But I don't remember feeling a buzz when I had the few visions on my own." I take another bite.

"Maybe that's because you were always freaked out after your visions. You didn't notice," David suggests, and I shrug in response.

"He also taught me some meditation tricks and wants me to work on them to calm my mind."

"Good idea," Matthias comments. "I'm excited to see what comes of all this."

"Why? Because you want me to go to war for him?" I accuse.

"No. Because you're my daughter and I'm proud that you're a Rare. I want to see what you're capable of."

My cheeks flush when I look up from my food and see the earnestness on his face. "Thank you," I mutter.

"But, speaking of war," Matthias continues.

"I knew it!" I pound the table with my fist.

"I was just gonna say," he says defensively, "remember the deal we had about keepin' an open mind. I want ya to be willin' to step up if needed."

"I remember," I say to placate him.

"Good," he says with a nod. "Ready to go, Henry?"

"Maybe after Olivia shows me how to make a proper taco." Henry eyes up the last taco on my plate, but I notice Matthias frown at him.

"I'll show you next time. Here. Just take this one. I'll go make myself some more," I say.

After David and I fill up with supper, we try to take a short walk, but the wind picks up, and I become chilled.

"I miss the shelters at Eli's camp. At least we got a little privacy when Cass and Tim were out," I whisper as we step into the noisy barracks. "It's going to be hard to practice my meditation with this racket."

"Maybe do it in the morning before everyone wakes up? Or maybe it's good practice for you to learn how to meditate in any kind of environment."

"Hey, you two!" Cass calls out from over by Charlotte and Cindy. "Want to play cards with us?"

I look at David and raise my eyebrows in a way to say I wouldn't mind playing.

He grabs my hand and leads me over to the little table they have set up. "What are you playing?" We take a seat.

"Your specialty. War." Cindy giggles behind her hand.

"Funny."

"Do you know how to play?" Charlotte asks David and me.

"Yeah, we've played it together."

Charlotte deals out the cards.

"So, what's it like being the golden ones?" Cindy asks, and Charlotte shoots her a look.

"Golden ones?" David asks.

"So far, you're the only two Icky's worked with," Cindy says.

"He said he'd work with Charlotte as soon as his men come up with a way for him to get into her head without hearing her sing when he activates her ability," I answer and see Charlotte nod in understanding.

"And what about *moi*?" Cindy lays her hand on her chest dramatically.

"To be frank, he's scared of you," David answers.

I nudge him with my elbow slightly to warn him to play it cool with her.

"Well, Frank," she says, drawing a huff out of David, "that's a good thing. He should be scared."

"Do you want him to be scared of you or to work with you?" David asks, confused.

"Both. I want him to work with me, but I don't want him to feel too cocky while doing it. We are a complicated bunch."

"You can say that again," Cass mutters.

"We are a complicated bunch," Cindy says, making Charlotte laugh.

"What's training like?" Charlotte asks after she and Cindy stop giggling.

I explain the worm-like feeling and the pressure of him trying to activate the ability.

David adds the part of feeling exhausted afterward.

"Sounds fun," Cindy says sarcastically.

"It's not meant to be fun," I start to argue but stop when I look up and see her bopping back and forth, singing a song to herself. She loses focus so quickly, it's ridiculous.

We play a couple of rounds in silence.

Cindy pipes up, "Did you guys hear that Rebecca is knocked up?"

"Yeah, but how did you hear about it?" I ask, surprised Rebecca would tell Cindy. She's not comfortable treating Cindy like a daughter, let alone confiding in her.

"I eavesdropped," she says as though it's a perfectly acceptable thing to do. "How did *you* hear about it?" She gives me a look as though I ruined her fun of having a juicy secret.

"I saw it in a vision while working with Chozolt."

"Oh, so we both eavesdropped." She stacks up the pile of cards she just won.

"I wouldn't call my visions eavesdropping since I can't control when it happens or what I see. At least for now."

"Whatever you say, eavesdropper," Cindy whispers.

It takes everything in me to remind myself to be nice to her. She makes it so hard sometimes. Once Cass wins the game of war, David and I decide to duck out. I've had my fill of Cindy for the day.

David invites me up to his bunk to have a talk. I wish we could have some privacy, but with everyone chatting and making noise, they won't be able to hear us anyway.

I pick at a stray thread on his blanket. "When do you think I should contact Elliot?"

"Probably not until you have complete control over your visions."

"Complete control? I can't even imagine being able to do that," I say, overwhelmed.

"You can't now, but look at how far we've come already. Can you believe that only like half a year ago we were living in the city, broken and half-dead? Now, not only are we healthy and strong, but we have these amazing abilities too. And there's a guy who wants to help us develop them."

"Yeah, but I feel like it's only for his personal agenda. Of course, I'm using his lessons to help me be able to fulfill my own personal agenda." I smirk. "Oh, did I tell you that my last vision was about you, Elliot, and me doing something in the city? I think it was our city. I don't know what we were up to, but it seemed like we had planned it out, because Elliot knew exactly where we were going."

David looks at me with wonder in his eyes.

"What? Why are you looking at me like that?"

"I can't believe how lucky I am. I have a beautiful girlfriend that can see the future. What did I ever do to deserve you?"

"Eh. You could do better," I say, making a self-depreciation joke automatically.

"Impossible." David grabs my hand and kisses my knuckles.

We sit holding hands for a moment, listening to the laughter and conversations around us. I feel relaxed up here with David while everyone around us is happy. Maybe I should take David's advice and see if I can meditate in these conditions.

"I'm going to do what you suggested and try to meditate while there's noise around us," I say. "I just wanted to give you the heads up, so you don't think I'm sleeping."

"Go for it." He moves over so I can lie down.

I take some deep breaths, tuning out the sounds. I focus my mind on the clearing in the woods. I'm sitting on a rock, feeling the warmth of the sun on my face, when Sonya screeches and pulls me back out. I shake it off and take a deep breath, trying again. I slowly tune out my surroundings and go back into the woods.

The light dances around me as the breeze blows, sending the trees swaying. A bird lands in a branch above me, chirping out its song.

"Emily!" Noah yells as Emily falls off the top bunk while she tries to grab her stuffed giraffe out of his hands.

She hits the hard floor with a sickening thud. She immediately starts screaming and sits up, holding her wrist while Caroline rushes to her side.

I come back to the present with my heart hammering in my chest. I sit up quickly and watch as Emily and Noah are messing around on the top bunk with their stuffed animals.

"Caroline, catch her!" I point at Emily right as she lunges toward the stuffed animal Noah holds out over the edge of the top bunk.

Caroline turns just in time to reach out and stop Emily from falling all the way off the bed. Once she's checked Emily is okay, she starts scolding them for goofing around up there.

I blow out a big puff of air as my brain continues to buzz from using my ability. Other than the adrenaline rush of seeing Emily get hurt in my vision, that felt good. I could get used to this, to being a help instead of a burden.

"She had her eyes closed for like two minutes, then jolts up, yelling for Caroline to save Emily. It was awesome!" David gushes.

Everyone in the barracks listens as we tell Matthias what happened.

"And you were meditatin' before ya had the vision?"

"Yeah. I think there might be a link somehow, but I've only had it happen twice. I'll need to practice more."

"I agree. I think ya should see Chozolt tomorrow, if he's got time," Matthias pushes.

"He's worked with her a couple of times already. I think it's Charlotte's turn," Alexandrine says.

"That's okay, Mama," Charlotte says quietly, but Alexandrine ignores her.

"Your daughter's skills are a danger to everyone around her. Olivia's got some true potential to be an asset to Chozolt," Matthias growls.

"But hers are unpredictable. Remember the blizzard that was supposedly going to happen but didn't?" Alexandrine accuses, pointing a finger at me.

Listening to them fight over whose child is better makes me angry, and it's causing Charlotte to be on the verge of tears. I want to scream at them to stop, but Cindy beats me to it.

"Knock it off!" she yells, and they both turn to stare at her. "They're not your gifts to be fighting over."

"No, but they're our children. Chozolt believes one of you four could be the weapon the psychic said would help take the Coalition down. And of the four of ya, I think Olivia's got the best chance."

"What about me?" Cindy glares at him defiantly, hands on her hips.

Alexandrine and Matthias look at her and then at each other before breaking out in laughter.

I watch as Cindy's bottom lip quivers while trying to hold her resolve.

"That's enough!" a voice shouts from across the room.

To my surprise, Rebecca comes marching over to Cindy's side, wrapping an arm around her shoulders.

Cindy's pale eyes grow in disbelief.

"This young lady is just as deserving of training as anyone. She's helped you out more than the other Rares have. But unlike you two, I'm going to leave it up to her whether she wants to have anything to do with Chozolt's big plans or not. I suggest you two do the same. Cindy's right. They're their gifts, not ours."

Alexandrine and Matthias's jaws drop in stunned silence.

I'm elated Rebecca is finally stepping up and being the mom Cindy needs.

"You're right, Rebecca. Cindy has helped us out a lot, and she didn't deserve to be laughed at. I'm sorry, Cindy," Matthias says sincerely. "However, we need to stay focused on the greater good. If I didn't push Olivia, she probably wouldn't be gettin' as far as she is. Every day we sit idly by, enjoyin' the hospitality of the Haven, goin' about our silly little lives, is another day the Rares are stuck in the cities, bein' mistreated or dyin'. Or have ya forgotten?" Matthias looks around the room.

Nobody looks him in the eye.

"We were fortunate to be able to leave the Coalition to get away from the tyranny, but other people are stuck as prisoners." He points to what I think is the direction we came. "Chozolt has given us hope that there could be a way to end this—to free the Rares from their lifelong oppression. If that means pushin' my daughter to get her Rare ability to a point that she could save other people's lives, then so be it. I will not allow ya to judge me for that. I will do whatever is in my power to see that the sufferin' of the Rares ends. Who's with me?"

It's quiet for a second before people start to raise their voices in a war cry. I join them too as his speech cuts me deep. David grabs my hand, raising it up in the air while he shouts. The noise is so loud, I wonder if Chozolt's men are going to come storming in to see what's going on. My voice starts to go hoarse as the shouting fades away.

"Good. Now everyone, get some sleep. Tomorrow, we train harder." He grabs ahold of Rebecca and Alexandrine's shoulders, leading them over to a couple of chairs in the corner. He signals for them to take a seat and starts talking with them.

"You have to admit, your dad is great at inspirational speeches," David says.

"That he is," I agree, still reeling over what happened.

"We should probably get some sleep, Liv," David says. "And for the record, if I had to place a bet on who could help make a difference, I'd put my money on you." He leans in and gives me a kiss goodnight.

The next morning, everyone wakes up with renewed vigor. Once breakfast is over, we all crowd around Matthias and Alexandrine outside to begin our lessons. Rebecca offers to watch all the kids so Caroline can have a chance to learn some self-defense. She seems to be a natural at it, or else she has a lot of pent-up aggression she's releasing. Either way, she's kicking butt.

Chozolt shows up sometime midmorning, and Matthias pulls him aside to have a chat with him. I want to stop what I'm doing to pay attention to what they're saying, but Alexandrine has us working with sticks she calls batons. The batons smacking together makes it almost impossible to hear her barking out orders, and she's right next to us. Even with my Rare hearing, I'm not sure I'd be able to hear what they're talking about ten yards away.

After about five minutes, they come over to our group, and Matthias tells us all to take a break.

"Matthias told me about your dedication to train for the liberation of the Rares, and although I'm honored to have your support of our efforts, I can't allow you to fight, since you are just civilians," he says, receiving outraged cries. "I have professional military men and women who have dedicated their lives to serving our country. It's their job to do the fighting."

"With all due respect, sir," Alexandrine says with attitude, "we're the ones who've experienced tyranny firsthand. I can guarantee you we want them destroyed more than your men. If you won't allow us to fight because we're just civilians, then how do we sign up to join the military? I will not sit around when it comes time to make the Coalition pay for what they've done. I want revenge."

A few people raise their voices in agreement with her.

"If you are serious about joining the military, then let's look into that. Everyone else is more than welcome to continue training and learning self-defense. In fact, I encourage it. It's better to be prepared in case the fight is brought to us. As for you four Rare, I will be splitting my time with you equally. It's only fair."

Cindy's face lights up at this news.

"I'd like to start the day off with Olivia," he says, and Cindy scoffs.

"Gee. What a shocker," she says.

"I promise I'll get to everyone, but Matthias informed me of the incident last night, and I want to follow up on that," he says to Cindy.

"Why are you bothering to train them? They can't fight in your war. They're not soldiers; they're just kids," Caroline challenges.

"I promise you they won't be in any battles directly. Their skills will be used in a safe manner," Chozolt answers.

Caroline doesn't seem happy with his answer but keeps her mouth shut.

"Are you ready, Olivia?"

"Sure." I hand David my batons and follow Chozolt.

"So, you were practicing your meditation, and it caused a vision?" We step into the session room. The warmth feels good after being outside training all morning.

"Yes, but it happened so fast, I hardly had time to warn Caroline before Emily fell."

"But you were still able to warn her. That's what's important." His eyes shine.

I take a seat in my chair. "So, what are we going to work on today?"

"The same thing as yesterday. I want you to meditate in your safe place while I bring your ability out. My hope is, by doing it this way, you'll eventually be able to trigger your ability just by thinking about your safe place. No deep meditation required."

"That would be helpful," I say.

"And then the next level will be you having complete control to trigger it whenever you want, but that comes later," he says. "Ready to begin?"

I nod, then close my eyes and lean back in the chair. It doesn't take long for me to picture the clearing in the woods this time. I decide to imagine David with me, and we're lying down on a blanket, looking up at the sun-soaked leaves.

I'm momentarily distracted when Chozolt's presence manifests heading straight for my RABI and pulsates. It's still a strange sensation I don't think I will ever get used to, but at least it doesn't freak me out anymore.

I refocus, inhaling through my nose and exhaling slowly out my mouth. David and I lie on our backs next to each other, threading our fingers together slowly, then sliding them apart gently. The feeling sends a tingle up my arm. A breeze brings the scent of ripe apples our way, making me hungry for one.

I'm pulled out of my meditation by the sound of the door opening.

"Mr. President? You have a phone call." A lady peeks in the door. She has curly brown hair piled up on her head in an intricate hairdo and cat-eye glasses accentuating her winged lashes.

"I'm in the middle of something." Chozolt's eyes stay closed, and he concentrates on keeping his presence inside my head.

"I think you better take this, sir." She bites her bright red lips together.

The vision ends, and my mind is back in the present, no longer meditating, but I'm also not feeling panicked like usual after a vision. I feel oddly calm, which to me, feels like the biggest win yet.

"Stop." I look at Chozolt, whose eyes are closed, sweaty brow furrowed in concentration.

He immediately listens and draws back out again.

The spot in my skull buzzes just like yesterday, but now that I know it's normal, it doesn't bother me.

"Were you able to get a vision?" Chozolt wipes his forehead with a handkerchief.

"Yeah. It was kinda lame, though." My eyes start to close, but I force them back open before I fall asleep. "It was a lady interrupting us to say you have a phone call." As soon as I finish speaking, there's a knock on the door.

"Mr. President? You have a phone call," the same lady from my vision says.

Chozolt looks at me with wonder. "I'm in the middle of something."

"I think you better take this, sir," I say at the same time as she does.

She purses her lips at me.

"Who's the call from?" Chozolt asks me.

"I don't know. The vision didn't last long enough for me to find out." I rest my head back against the chair.

"Don't fall asleep on me in here. I'll be right back." Chozolt follows the lady out, closing the door behind him.

The buzzing in my head is still there, so I decide to try engaging it without Chozolt's help. I'm really tired, though, so I don't know if this is going to work, but it's worth a try. Instead of picturing the woods, I focus all my attention on the buzzing spot. The longer I focus on it, the stronger it seems to become.

Chozolt enters the room solemnly. He slowly closes the door, taking the moment his back is turned to wipe his eyes.

495

"Everything okay?" I ask.

He clears the lump in this throat, "That was my Grandma, calling from a city payphone. Granddad passed away two nights ago in his sleep. I wish I could have seen him one last time."

The vision ends abruptly, and instead of being excited I made a vision happen, I'm left feeling morose. I wipe a tear away as I think about Jed and how kind he was. I wonder how Mary Ellen is going to get along without him. Will she have to sell the farm, or can she take care of things alone?

The door opens, and I quickly wipe my face, trying to hide that I was crying. "I'm so sorry," I blurt out as Chozolt closes the door.

"Sorry about what?" he asks.

"Wasn't that your grandma on the phone?"

"No, it was the Canadian Prime Minister. Why would you think it was my grandma?"

I realize Chozolt isn't wearing the same clothes as he was in the vision, a detail I didn't notice until now. Was this a mistake? Another false vision?

"I tried to access my Rare ability while the spot still buzzed, and I had a vision, but it wasn't right. I saw you coming into the room sad because your grandma called to let you know that your grandpa died a couple days ago."

"It wasn't my grandma, but that doesn't necessarily mean your vision was wrong. It just wasn't a vision of today," he says thoughtfully. "How did he die?"

"In his sleep. That's all I know."

"I guess I better go visit them as soon as possible," he comments. "Anyway, good job on tapping into your Rare ability while it was still active. That was smart. You're progressing a lot faster than most people do. I'm very impressed! Is the spot still buzzing?"

"Only slightly. It's fading away again." My head bobs as I almost doze off.

"We'll call it a day. I'm hoping you'll be able to access it on your own soon. Then we can focus our sessions on your timing and control."

"Sounds great," I murmur.

"These sessions are wearing me out too." His jaw stretches in a giant yawn. "Perhaps I should work with Cindy while I still have some energy left."

"I'm sure that would make her happy. Just be careful," I say, not knowing who I'm more worried about, him or her.

3|9

"He left because of you!" Alexandrine yells.

I look up from my plate of French toast and see she's pointing at Cindy.

"I didn't make anyone leave, although I'd be more than happy for you to leave me alone!" Cindy yells back.

Frederick reaches out and grabs Alexandrine's arm as she's about to lunge at Cindy.

"What's goin' on here?" Matthias asks.

Everyone is quiet in the mess hall as we wait to hear what set Alexandrine off this time.

"I just went to talk with Chozolt about having a session with Charlotte, and I was informed that he left town without telling anyone where he was going or how long he'd be gone. *She* was the last person to work with him. Her messed-up brain must have drove him away!"

"It's not Cindy's fault," I pipe up. "He probably left to go visit with Jed and Mary Ellen. I had a vision that Jed was going to die, and Chozolt said that he should go visit them. He must have decided to go sooner rather than later."

"Great. So now he's making decisions based off your unreliable visions?" She throws her hands up in the air. "Meanwhile, Charlotte gets shunted off to the side as though she doesn't matter, while everyone else gets his attention."

"First of all, when are you going to let that one mistake go? One of my visions didn't come true, so what? Secondly, Charlotte doesn't seem upset that she hasn't met with Chozolt yet, so why are you?"

Charlotte is sitting next to Cindy, hiding her face from everyone. I watch as Cindy whispers something into Charlotte's ear, glaring at Alexandrine.

"I just want fair treatment for my daughter. She deserves just as much attention as anyone else here. Why is it that we keep getting pushed to the back of the line?"

"Because Charlotte can already control when she uses her ability. David and I can't, so that makes her ahead of us. Maybe Chozolt's just trying to catch us up so we're on the same page."

"I don't really care what you and David can or can't do. I care what he can help Charlotte do," Alexandrine snarls. "I didn't come all this way to be ignored!"

I watch Charlotte whisper something in Cindy's ear. Cindy stands up from the table, walking away with her ears covered.

"Don't do it!" I yell as Charlotte takes a deep breath and starts singing.

Alexandrine drops to the floor hard, right before I black out.

■■■■■

"Wake up, Olivia," Charlotte's voice calls out while she shakes my shoulder.

As I come to, I notice something wet and squishy on the side of my face. The smell of maple syrup fills my nose, and I groan when I realize my face is in my French toast. I sit up, searching for a napkin or anything to wipe this mess off.

"I'm so sorry, Olivia. I didn't mean for you to fall in your food. I just had to stop Mama from talking," Charlotte says desperately. "She was embarrassing me!"

"It's all right," I say, even though I'm annoyed. "You really shouldn't mess around with your ability, though. Someone could get hurt."

Charlotte hangs her head and looks down at the floor. "It was Cindy's idea," she mutters.

"You shouldn't listen to Cindy," I say, exasperated. "But I get it. Your mom was out of control. If I had your ability, I would probably use it to get out of tough situations too." I pat her on the shoulder to let her know I'm not mad.

The napkin I'm using on my face keeps ripping as it gets stuck to the syrup, so I give up. I'm going to have to take a shower to get this off.

"Out of curiosity, when you sing, do you feel a buzzing sensation in your mind from where your ability is located?" I ask as I shake David's shoulder to try to wake him up.

"I always feel it. Even when I was in the mental hospital, I felt it, but I just thought I was crazy."

"How did you find out you could put people to sleep by singing? Did you know you could do that when you were in the hospital? Is that why you warned me about the 'magic within'?" I ask as a million other questions pop up in my mind.

"I have a memory from when I was really young. I was sitting in a room with some scary-looking guys in suits staring at me, telling me to show them my magic. And I was crying because I didn't know what they were talking about. So they had a lady come in and try to calm me down by singing a silly song to me. I liked the song, so I started singing with her, and everyone in the room fell asleep. After that happened, they put me in the hospital and started giving me the vitamins." Her eyes pool with tears. "I would have flashbacks to that day, and any time I brought it up, someone would tell me it was just a dream I had, and they'd give me a shot to settle me back down, even though I wasn't upset or anything."

I shake my head in disgust as I give Charlotte a hug. I can't believe how much effort is put into keeping Rares weak and ignorant about everything.

"It looks like everyone's starting to wake up," she says.

David finally opens his eyes and looks around the room, worry etched on his brow, until he finds me and lets out a sigh.

"I'm going to be in trouble, aren't I?" Charlotte whispers.

"Probably, but I've got your back," I say.

"What happened?" David asks. "And what is that on your face?"

I had forgotten about the maple syrup mess while talking to Charlotte. I touch my face, and my fingers stick to my cheek. My face flushes. I must look ridiculous.

"Where is she?" Alexandrine sits up with her hand on her head.

"I'm here, Mama," Charlotte squeaks, eyes wide with fear.

"I thought I told you to never sing without warning people first. That was very dangerous! I could have a concussion now, young lady!"

"She did it out of self-defense," I say.

"What are you talking about?" Alexandrine pulls herself into a chair. "I wasn't hurting her." Alexandrine looks like she's about to lay into me, but when she looks at Charlotte, the angry lines on her face smooth. "Is it true? Have I been pushing too hard and embarrassing you?"

Charlotte nods.

"But don't you want to work on your skills to get better at them?"

"I do." Charlotte shrugs. "It's just not *that* big of a deal to me."

Alexandrine gives Charlotte a hug, then leads her out of the mess hall. Once they're gone, everyone loosens up and starts talking to each other.

"I don't care what you guys say. My money is on her being the weapon." Nathan holds a napkin up to his bloody nose.

People start discussing which one of us they think could be Chozolt's weapon, and I don't want to hear it, so we leave, even though I'm still hungry.

After showering, David and I sit on his bunk, talking about what just happened. We're interrupted by a loud knock on the door.

"Excuse me, I was told Olivia was in here," a man dressed in a black suit and tie calls out from the doorway.

"That's me," I answer.

"Elliot Stone sent me over to pick you up and bring you to the NSA headquarters. He's got something to show you."

I look at David, and we both hop off his bed with excitement.

[40

"Oh, good. I'm glad you're here," Elliot says as soon as we enter the room. "I've been working on something I wanted to show you."

"You have the power to send a car to come get us whenever you want?" I ask.

"I didn't ask for permission. I told the driver it was orders from the president before he left, and since he's gone, it couldn't be verified," Elliot says with a laugh. "Anyway, I wanted to show you this."

He takes us over to his computer and hits the play button. We watch a short video with Elliot's voice dubbed in, warning the people of the Coalition they're being lied to, as pictures of my grandfather's files flash on the screen, showing the truth.

"What do you think?" He crosses his arms over his chest proudly.

"I think it's a good start," I say, hoping to not offend him.

"Good start?" he asks.

"Well, it's very factual, but...it's kinda boring," I say hesitantly.

"Woman, it's not supposed to be a box office hit. The goal is to wake people up to the truth," Elliot says.

"Exactly. Wake them up, not put them to sleep."

"David, you gonna let her talk to me like that, man?" Elliot asks in jest. "What do you think of it?"

"Well," David says, scratching the side of his head, "I'd have to say I agree with her."

"Psh. You're just taking her side 'cause she's your girlfriend," Elliot says. "All right, all right, all right. I'll go back to the drawing board, see if I can't come up with something with a little more pizzazz."

"What do you plan on doing with this video once it's made? Like, how are you going to get people to see it?" I ask.

"I think I've come up with a way that we can break into a city's tower and take it offline while simultaneously plugging our video into the Coalition's twenty-four-hour news station. If I do it just right, it will display all over the city, on any tv that's turned on, cell phones, computers, and even the audio on the radio stations. We'll get the truth out to the people and let them know what's really going on."

"What do you think is going to happen when people find out?" I ask.

"People will be outraged. There'll be riots and, hopefully, a revolt."

"And you want us to help you with it?" David asks. "How can we help?"

"You two know Baltimore better than anyone else, and you're Rare."

"Baltimore?" I interrupt.

"That's what your city used to be called. They dropped the name after the Coalition took over and then just started calling it "The City." I guess it fit their propaganda better. Anyway, us Rare have to stick together. If blondie here can start seeing the future while she's awake, maybe we can use that for our mission. Make sure we don't get caught."

"Holy crap!" I exclaim. "That must be what my vision of having a vision was all about."

"A vision of having a vision?" Elliot sits and reclines back with his feet on the table.

"I had a vision while working with Chozolt that I was walking in the city with you two. I asked you if you remembered to bring the clip, and I wasn't sure what that meant, but now I think it must be the video clip you're making. Anyway, I had a vision of a guard catching us, so we hid in an alley behind some boxes until they passed by."

"And there you go. We have to do it now. Blondie saw it happen." Elliot's lips curve into a big grin. "How're your lessons going with the president?"

"I'm getting better, but I'm not seeing things on command like in my vision. I don't know how long it's going to take to get to that point," I say.

"We've got time. I have more work to do on my truth delivery video anyway."

"Is the president going to be okay with us doing this?"

"Of course not. But unless you tell him, he isn't going to know until we're already long gone."

"I don't know," David says. "Chozolt has been good to us since we got here, and he's the president of the United States. Should we really be planning on betraying him?"

"It's not really betrayal. We're trying to take down the Coalition without a war. We're helping him but doing it our own way. Besides, he wants to use us as a weapon, which I think is a jerk move," I say.

David shakes his head.

"Look. If we try this and it fails, feel free to join Chozolt's war. But after the vision I had, I hope you'll decide not to," I say, choking up on emotions.

He notices and gives me a hug. "Okay, fine. But how exactly are we getting there?" David asks. "It's a long trip, believe us."

I start thinking about the days spent on the bus and the weeks of walking. I don't want to do that again.

"With the plane our spies use to travel back and forth. I'm going to hijack it for our little excursion," he answers.

"You're going to get us into trouble!" I laugh.

"It's not worth doing if there isn't a little risk involved."

"Do you know how to fly a plane?" David asks.

"Not yet, but I will," he says slyly.

"You remind me of a movie I saw once where they plug something into their heads, upload information, and then are experts within seconds," I say, trying to conceal my awe and jealousy. I'd love to be able to do what he can.

"Yeah, I saw that movie too. I wish it were that quick, but I still have to read or take lessons in order to know things," he says.

"So, as a recap, you want to make a video and hack into the Coalition system to broadcast it and show people the truth. You're also going to learn how to fly a plane to get us there. And Liv is going to work on her training so she can learn how to see the future on command. What part do I play in all this?" David looks back and forth between Elliot and me.

"Moral support." I grab and squeeze his hand. "I'm basically useless without you. You know that."

"Make the president believe that you guys are on his side. Become his pet soldier so you can get intel on what he has planned. We need to get our scheme into action before the president makes his move, which means we need to know everything he's doing."

"You want me to pretend to be a suck-up in order to spy on him?" David asks slowly.

"Essentially," Elliot says. "But in the meantime, I can send someone out to bring you here every day until the president comes back so you can help me work on the video."

David perks up a little. "I wouldn't want you to get into trouble using NSA cars."

"Nah. I wouldn't be sending a government car. I have a friend who owes me a favor. I'm sure he'd be more than happy to do it."

David looks at me, and I give him a thumbs up.

"Okay, I'll help with the video," David says.

"Good. Well, I got some other stuff I have to get done today, but I'll send Darius to come pick you up around eight in the morning. Make sure you're ready to go. He hates waiting," Elliot says.

[4|1

David is awake and ready when a blue Jeep Wrangler pulls up.

"Yo, yo. You David?" A thin guy dressed in a black oversized puffy jacket and baggy jeans steps out of the Jeep. He takes a black stocking cap out of his pocket and pulls it on his close-shaved head. He crosses his arms and leans back against the car. "I'm Darius."

"Are you sure about this?" I give David an apprehensive look.

"I'll be fine. Good luck on your meditation today." David gives me a quick kiss before hopping into Darius's Jeep and leaving.

I head back inside where it's warm and get myself ready for meditating. It's noisy in here, but I think Alexandrine was planning a sword fighting lesson for later this morning, so it should quiet down.

I lie on David's bed to try to stay out of sight as much as I can. I go through my routine of slow breathing and picturing my mental safe place. The noisiness fades away as I bring the forest clearing into focus. I feel the slight buzz begin in my RABI.

"You didn't put it away. You left it right out there for anyone to see," Cindy says.

"That doesn't give you the right to look at it! It was on my bed!" Cass yells.

"Sor-ry," Cindy apologizes insincerely. "If it helps you feel any better, I didn't see very much of it."

"What did you see?" Cass crosses her arms.

Cindy twirls her hair with her finger. "Just some letter you wrote to your mom."

Cass uncrosses her arms, her fists balling up at her sides as she yells loudly in Cindy's face, making the younger girl take a step backward.

I hop off the bed and grab Cass as she's about to throw a punch at Cindy.

My vision ends, and I look over to the bunk next to me. Cass is propped up on her bed, doodling in her notebook. I feel like these visions are getting more mundane as I progress, but at least they aren't apocalyptic.

As always, my heart beats faster after a vision, so I try to calm down before meditating again. Out of the corner of my eye, I see Cass slip off her bed, leaving her notebook open on her pillow.

"Cass, you should put your notebook away," I warn.

"I just have to go to the bathroom. I'll be right back," she says.

"I just had a vision that Cindy looked in your notebook and you got angry with her."

Cass looks around and sees Cindy glancing our way. She stalks back to her bed and shoves her notebook into her bag, mumbling to herself about privacy and personal space.

I smile when I realize my visions have been showing me things that are going to happen within ten to fifteen seconds before they happen. I think I'm getting closer to my ability actually being useful. If only I could trigger it without having to meditate.

I try to access my RABI with my eyes open this time, focusing on the slight buzz left over from the vision I just had, but it's too much outward input right now. I'm not ready for it yet.

By the time everyone heads out to do sword training with Alexandrine, I've had more visions, all of them insignificant, but the fact I can make them occur more frequently is, in and of itself, significant. Even though I have no interest in seeing people having a conversation or changing their socks, I relish that I can see the future. Who would've ever thought I would go from suicidal thoughts to being able to see the future?

My RABI is buzzing so much, it feels like my brain is vibrating in my skull. I think I've had enough practice for one day. Chozolt's going to be happy with my progress once he comes back. Maybe now he can help me figure out how to use it on command.

I decide to participate in Alexandrine's lesson, even though she's still salty after Charlotte's episode. It's as though she doesn't want to punish Charlotte for anything and, instead, takes her frustrations out on everyone else. She asks Frederick to demonstrate the next series of moves with her, and when she cuts the sleeve of his jacket with her sword, she doesn't even apologize. In fact, she blames him for not following her lead well enough.

By the end, everyone is sweaty and sore, not to mention grumpy.

"You need to talk to Alexandrine," I say to Matthias when he returns from his target practice.

"Why?" He busies himself stowing his gun.

"If she keeps punishing everyone when Charlotte does something she's not supposed to, then nobody's going to want to work with her anymore."

"Fine, I'll see what's up," Matthias says. "How's the ability comin' along?"

"I had about six visions this morning, nothing too important, and I still have to meditate first before I can have them." I play down the progress I made so he doesn't start his 'helping with the efforts' speech he gave me last night at dinner.

"That's some good progress, though. Keep it up." He turns and looks around the barracks, searching for someone. "Where's David? I wanted to talk to him about doin' a target practice tomorrow to get a feel for how far he can shoot accurately with different guns."

"Oh, he, um, he's helping Elliot with something. A project," I say, not wanting to lie, but also not wanting to tell him much more than that.

"What kind of project?" Matthias does not take his eye off me, making me squirm a little.

"Uh, something to do with a machine that emits a sound only Rare can hear. Since nobody else at the NSA is Rare, he asked David to come help." I look up at the ceiling as I talk.

"What's the purpose of a machine like that?"

"I don't know. Why don't you ask him?" I retort, then worry he actually will.

"Sorry for being pushy. I just don't like that one of my people is bein' dragged into something without asking me first."

"I didn't think we had to report to you anymore now that we're in the Haven. Chozolt is the president, and we're to follow his orders, right?" I say, trying to strike at him where I know it will hurt.

Matthias clenches his jaw. "I'm still in charge of our group until the war is over and we go our separate ways. And even then, with ya two being an item, and David's parents not bein' here, I'm playin' the role of his guardian."

"He turns eighteen next month."

"Next month is not today. Tell him I want to talk to him as soon as he gets back." Matthias whirls and stalks away.

I've made this into a bigger deal than it needed to be and more than likely gotten David into trouble. Once again, I'm messing everything up.

[42]

I nervously walk around the base until David gets back. I don't want to be in the barracks with Matthias. I'm afraid he's going to ask more questions and I'm going to spill the beans.

I'm nearly frozen when the Jeep rolls up, and David gets out of it, laughing. He waves goodbye to Darius, then walks over to me, picking me up off the ground as he gives me a hug.

"I missed you." He kisses the tip of my nose. "Brr! You're like ice."

"I've been walking around for the last two hours waiting for you."

"Why would you do that? It's cold out here."

"I might've gotten you in trouble with Matthias," I mumble.

"How? What happened?"

"He asked me where you were. I told him you were working with Elliot on something, a machine that only Rares can hear, and when he asked what a machine like that would be used for, I told him to ask you. I'm so sorry! I panicked and didn't know what to say."

"It's all right." He holds me close as we head inside. He's always so quick to forgive me. I honestly don't deserve this man.

"So, how did it go with Elliot?" I ask.

"Great! Once I started throwing ideas out at him, he got excited, and we made some good progress today. How did your meditating go?"

"I had six visions, only one of them was worthwhile. I tried to have a vision with my eyes open, but there was too much input for me to concentrate. Maybe Chozolt will have some tips on how to do it."

"Six visions? That's great! Elliot wants to put our plan into action sometime in the next two weeks. He said we need to do it before the upcoming free trade summit."

"What's that?" I ask.

"I don't know. It sounds like a big meeting with diplomats from around the world. Elliot says the rumors are that a number of countries are going to meet with Chozolt in secret to sign a treaty. This war might be happening soon if we don't do something about it quick," David whispers.

My heart sinks. I don't think two weeks is enough time for me to get my ability where I would want it for this mission.

"What's wrong?" David asks.

"I'm not ready, and I'm not sure I'm going to be ready in two weeks," I fret.

"I thought this is what you wanted—to find a different way to bring down the Coalition?" David's forehead creases.

"I do. I just didn't know it was going to be so soon."

"Once Chozolt gets back, we'll ask to work harder during our sessions with him. He'll think we're putting in more work to help with the war, but he'll actually be helping us with our plan to avoid it. Sound good?"

"Yeah, okay," I agree, even though I'm still wary.

"Good. Now what's for supper? I'm starving."

We get to the mess hall before anyone else does. A supper of meatloaf, mashed potatoes, peas, fresh baked bread, and frosted brownies is already laid out on the serving table. We're almost done when Matthias comes walking in with Henry. He points in our direction and starts heading this way.

"Here we go," I say.

"Hey, David. I was looking for you today."

"Oh, yeah? What about?" David asks, playing along.

"I was hopin' to do some target practice with ya and see what ya can do with different kinds of guns."

"Sure, I can do that. When?"

"How about tomorrow?" Matthias asks with a look as though he's caught him.

"Tomorrow works. Morning or afternoon?"

"Let's make it midmorning."

"Sounds good." David picks up his tray to signal that he's ready to go.

I stuff the last bite of brownie in my mouth and follow. "I thought you were working with Elliot all week?" I ask once we're out of earshot.

"I was going to, but with Matthias being suspicious, I figured it was worth putting Elliot off for a day so we can keep working without trouble."

"How are you going to let Elliot know? If Darius shows up and you shoo him away, he's going to be pissed."

"It's okay. Elliot gave me a cell phone to use." David shows me a phone that flips open. "He says it's basically ancient technology, but it still works."

"Your first cell phone. Sweet," I say.

"I'll just go call him quick and tell him we'll have to wait a day." He walks out of the barracks.

While he's gone, I might as well practice my ability one more time and call it a night. With almost everyone out having supper, it's exceptionally quiet in here. I lie back on my pillow and stare at the bottom of David's bunk, seeing nothing but the white of his mattress. I focus on my RABI, but it's not working. Frustrated, I roll over on my side and give up for now.

"Elliot was disappointed, but I think he'll get over it." David walks back into the barracks. He tucks the cell phone into his bag and has a seat on the edge of my bed, ducking his head down so he can fit.

"You know, Matthias said that he thinks of himself as your guardian since you and I are a couple and your parents aren't here. Maybe that's why he wants to work with you on your target practice so much. He's proud of you."

"That's a nice thought." David laughs. "It's more than likely he's looking to use me as an expert marksman for his war."

"David, I just thought of something," I say as an unsettling thought hits me. "We've gotta make this work. Your parents are still in the city, and if Chozolt wages war, they could get hurt."

"I've already thought of that. That's why I decided to help you and Elliot instead of Chozolt and Matthias. I'm not totally against going to war, if that's what it takes to end this, but it could mean my parents getting hurt in the process. All the more reason for us to hustle and get our abilities working better," David says, rubbing my arm.

I picture David's mother in my mind. She was always happy to see me. Sure, we had a few awkward conversations when she tried to talk me into dating David, but I still liked her. If only she could see us now. I think she'd be thrilled. His dad was kind of aloof, but he worked hard hours and didn't mind that David and I hung out, so long as we kept the door open.

"What?" David asks as I let out a little laugh.

"I was just thinking about your parents and how your dad used to remind us to keep the door open. I always wondered what he thought we were doing that would require the door needing to stay open."

"Probably this." He pulls me in for a kiss.

"Ew! Get a room." Cindy walks past.

"If you don't like it, don't look," David says.

"I don't like your face. Should I wear a blindfold?" she says with a snicker. She looks to Charlotte to see if she's laughing, but even Charlotte is looking at her like she's gone too far.

We all stare at her until her smile fades.

"Ugh. Fine. Sorry," she apologizes quickly and walks away.

David turns back to me, and I look into his golden eyes as he laces his fingers with mine. The feeling of his fingers brings the buzzing in my RABI back, and suddenly, I'm no longer seeing David's face, or anything around me.

"Help! Somebody get help!" David yells, holding pressure on Mattias's abdomen. Blood is soaking through Matthias's coat, staining David's fingers red.

Just that fast, I'm back to looking into David's eyes. The rush of having a vision while awake has me disoriented and breathing heavy.

"Liv, are you okay? It's like you were looking through me in a trance or something," David says.

"I just saw you holding pressure on a wound in Matthias's stomach. You were crying out for help," I say with a shudder.

"When? What happened? Is something about to happen now?" David stands up.

"No." I close my eyes and rub my head. "You two were outside, and it was light out. It might have been during your target practice tomorrow."

"We better warn him," David says, taking my vision seriously.

"Is this just a ruse to get out of doing target practice with me?" Matthias asks bluntly. "I know you're working with Elliot on something. Care to share what this 'project' is that Olivia felt the need to lie to me about?"

"I didn't lie to you." I look at his forehead instead of his eye.

"C'mon. A device that emits a sound only Rares can hear is somehow useful?" Matthias crosses his arms.

"Liv misunderstood what Elliot was talking about. I've been working with him on drones he invented. He thinks they would be great weapons in Chozolt's war," David says.

"Why would he ask you and not Denis?" Matthias asks. "That sort of thing seems right up Denis's alley."

I look to David to see how he's going to talk his way out of this one.

"Probably because I'm Rare and Denis isn't." David shrugs. "He said he feels like us Rare should stick together and rise from the ashes of being burned at the stake. Metaphorically speaking."

Matthias looks at him for a few uncomfortable seconds before conceding. "All right. I know ya to be a man of honor and integrity. I trust that ya wouldn't dare lie to me."

I watch as David keeps his face steady, but his Adam's apple bobs around as he swallows hard.

"Does the army have a bulletproof vest you can borrow for our practice?" David asks.

"I could check with his men, but I really don't see why I should need it. You're responsible with guns."

"Please, just wear one. It's a simple thing that could save your life. If my vision is wrong, then you wore it for nothing. So what?" I say.

"Fine." Matthias turns to David. "Meet me at the shooting range around nine."

David nods, and Matthias walks back to his bunk.

"How did you get to be so good at lying?" I whisper. "Working on drones? Elliot's only working with you because you're Rare?"

"They were half truths," David says. "I may not be working on drones with Elliot, but he told me about some that he helped program for Chozolt. And the Rare part is mostly true. He said he was happy to finally be working with someone like him."

"On a different note, I can't believe I finally had a vision while awake," I say excitedly.

"I know! I'm so proud of you." David grins. "Do you remember how you did it so you can repeat the process to do it again?"

510

"It was actually you that triggered it," I say. "During one of my meditations, I imagined you with me, holding my hand, sliding your fingers between mine, and the sensation brought on a vision. And now, when you just did that same thing in real life, it made a vision happen."

David looks at his fingers with the corner of mouth curled up mischievously.

"So, all I have to do is this," he says, grabbing my hand and sliding his fingers between mine.

I'm about to kiss David when the light hanging from the ceiling close to our bunk gets hit by a volleyball and shatters.

"Boys!" Rebecca screams.

I'm back to looking at David, my heart racing. "What the heck just happened?"

"Your eyes just went unfocused. You had another vision, didn't you?" David asks with a big smile, then leans in for a kiss.

I put my finger up to his lips and say, "We need to catch a ball the twins are about to kick into the light."

David gets to the end of our bunk just in time to catch the ball midair.

I look at their shocked faces as he tosses it back to them.

"So, the real question here is, why does holding your hand trigger visions?" David asks when he comes back to the bed.

I think about it for a moment. When I was meditating, I was most relaxed at David's presence. Same thing here. It's no secret David brings out the best in me, but I can't rely on him for this. I need to be able to do it on my own. I'm not always going to be around him to have him hold my hand.

"Because you relax me, and I'm happy when I'm around you. I feel safe. But I need to find a different outlet, because you can't hold my hand every time I need to have a vision."

"No, but maybe you can summon the feeling it gives you. Or you could hold your own hand," he says with a smirk.

"Yeah, because that would look normal." I roll my eyes.

"It would look like you were praying."

"I'll try it out tomorrow. I'm too tired right now." I lean against David's shoulder.

He rests his cheek on my head and wraps his arms around me. Out of nowhere, the memory of David pointing a gun at me in a vision, ready to shoot at the stranger's command, springs up in my mind, and I fight it off with a shake of my head. I know in my heart of hearts, David would never pull the trigger. At least, not on his own volition.

In the morning, David and Matthias go off to do the target practice after we make sure Matthias is wearing the bulletproof vest. He seems grumpy about it, but at least he has it on.

I wish Chozolt were back. I'd like to talk to him about my progress and see what he has to say about it, but until he gets back, I'm going to keep practicing.

"Cass, want to help me with something?" I ask, getting an idea.

She hops off her bed. "Sure. What do you need?"

"I want you to hold a card up in front of you, and I'm going to try to use my Rare ability to find out what card it is."

"Okay." She retrieves the cards.

I settle onto my bed, and she takes a seat on hers across from me.

"Ready?" Cass pulls a card out of the deck.

I stare at the back of the card as though I'm going to be able to see through it. I take a few deep breaths to cleanse my mind, and focus.

Nothing.

I try to bring up the relaxed state I feel when I meditate, but I can't seem to do it with my eyes open. I take another deep breath to fight off the frustration settling in. I don't want to have to close my eyes or hold David's hand in order for it to work. I didn't need to do those things in my vision of me having a vision, so what am I missing?

I can tell she's growing impatient with me. I give it one last ditch effort and fold my hands together as though I'm praying.

Cass turns the card around, eyes wide. "You're right! Three of clubs. How'd you do that?"

"It's a three of clubs," I say as soon as my vision ends.

Cass turns the card around, eyes wide. "You're right! Three of clubs. How'd you do that?"

"I saw it happen," I say, elated. I hate that I had to hold my own hand to make it work, but if I get results, then I guess it's what I have to do.

"Let's try another one." She holds up a new card.

I stare at Cass while I fold my hands together, hoping to make the vision come faster this time.

"Are you sure you can't see through these things," Cass asks, flipping the card around to show me a six of hearts.

"Six of hearts," I say and follow up with, "and no, I can't see through them."

"How'd you... Never mind," Cass says, laughing. "Wanna do one more?"

"Sure." I get myself ready for the next one.

Cass holds up a card with a smile. I think she's having fun with this. I unfold my hands and then refold them.

"Got it again!" Cass says excitedly, showing me the Jack of spades.

She gets off her bed and reaches out to give me a high five.

"What are you girls doing?" Cindy asks.

"I'm working on my Rare ability. I'm trying to get a vision of what card she's holding up," I say.

"Cards? You have a one in fifty-two chance of guessing it right. Not very impressive," Cindy puts her hand on her hip.

"One in fifty-two are not that great of odds, Cindy," I argue.

"I bet you can't guess what I'm about to do next," Cindy says with an evil look in her eyes.

Without warning, she kicks her leg out, and her slipper comes flying at my face. My reflexes allow me to duck just in time.

I come back out of the vision, angry at Cindy, but see she's not here yet. It seems like my visions are unpredictable in how long they last, and how far in the future I see things. I don't know how to change that.

"Jack of spades," I say.

"Got it again!" Cass says excitedly.

"Wait, watch this," I say as Cass is about to get off her bed for a high five.

"What are you girls doing?" Cindy asks.

"I'm working on my Rare ability. I'm trying to get a vision of what card she's holding up," I say, playing along with my vision.

"Cards? You have a one in fifty-two chance of guessing it right. Not very impressive," Cindy puts her hand on her hip.

"One in fifty-two is not that great of odds, Cindy," I argue, preparing myself for what comes next.

"I bet you can't guess what I'm about to do next," Cindy says with an evil look in her eyes.

Cindy goes to kick her slipper at me, just like in my vision, but I catch it instead of ducking and throw it over her head, across the room. Cindy's mouth drops open, and she turns around with a huff to retrieve her slipper.

"That was awesome," Cass whisper-shouts.

"I don't know why that vision was longer this time, but I'm kind of glad it was. Did you see the look on Cindy's face?" I say, laughing with Cass.

"I think you might have started something now, knowing her. She's probably going to try to surprise attack you."

I sigh. "Probably. I couldn't help myself, though."

"So, what's it like? The whole vision thing? From here, it looks like you clock out. Like, your eyes go unfocused, and you kind of tense up."

"I don't know how to describe it. I'll be looking at you, and then my RABI will start buzzing, and I see you telling me I got the card right, then you show it to me."

"Wait, so in your vision of the future, you've already guessed the card right?" Cass asks slowly.

"Yeah, it's like seeing a vision of my future self, having already seen a vision. It's weird."

"No, it's cool," Cass says with a grin. "We don't have to understand it fully to appreciate it."

My breath catches when the door swings open, and Matthias walks in, followed by David with a very distressed look on his face.

"I'm fine," Matthias says irritably.

"You'd be dead if Liv hadn't had her vision and insisted you wear the vest," David says as Matthias unzips his coat.

"What happened?" I ask.

"The gun exploded from an incomplete discharge. The first bullet I shot didn't come out of the barrel, so when I shot the next round, it made the gun explode. A piece of shrapnel hit the vest." Matthias points at the small piece of metal sticking out.

"We're lucky that was the only piece to hit one of us," David says as I wrap my arms around his waist.

"Looks like ya were right." Matthias takes the vest off. "Your visions saved my life. Which just reinforces that it's a skill Chozolt could really use."

"Maybe if I could control how far into the future I can see and how long the visions last, but they still seem pretty random," I say, trying to downplay it again.

"Any visions that could help with the efforts are worthwhile," Matthias replies.

"Yeah, but having people rely on me for something I can hardly control would be a lot of pressure, and I don't need that kind of responsibility."

Matthias considers me for a moment. "Keep practicin'." He turns and walks away.

"Easy for him to say," I complain. "I'm the one that will have to deal with the guilt of someone dying because I didn't see it in time or saw the wrong part of the future."

"We don't have to worry about that, though," David says. "We're going to solve it before the war even begins."

"I hope you're right," I say. "Want to hear what happened during my practice today?"

David nods, so I tell him all the visions with the cards and what happened with Cindy.

"You probably shouldn't have done that to Cindy," he warns. "Knowing her, she's going to test you now."

"That's what Cass said," I say. "What do you think about the other stuff?"

"I think if you keep at it, we should be able to leave for our mission soon." David kisses my forehead.

"What about your ability? Shouldn't you be working on it?"

"I have been. When I get a moment alone, I try to summon Bartholomew. Unfortunately, it's usually when I'm in the bathroom, since there's hardly any peace around here, but I've gotten him to show up a couple of times."

"That's awesome, David! So, what does he look like? I'd love to be able to meet him," I say.

514

"He looks kind of like me." David shrugs.

"Now I'd really like to meet him," I say with a playful smirk.

David ignores my comment. "Want to practice some more future seeing with me?"

"Maybe we could use Chozolt's room. It'd be quiet in there."

"Great idea." David pulls me off the bed with him. "Let's go."

They let us in the building after we explain our situation and escort us to the room. David works with me on my future seeing with the deck of cards until I'm exhausted. I get every card right, but there are a few times I would see something other than the immediate future. For instance: we're having spaghetti for supper tonight; Sonya is going to trip over a shoe and hit her head on the floor, but she'll be fine; and Rebecca is going to start suffering from morning sickness. That last one was disgusting, and I hope to never see it again.

I'm finally starting to get the hang of triggering my RABI on command. The buzzing never goes away fully, just like Chozolt said. All I have to do is focus on it, and I can sense it. I'm even able to see some visions without having to fold my hands, which is a relief. I hated having to have a crutch in order to use my ability.

"I need a break, David. It's your turn." Sweat trickles down the side of my face.

I watch as David closes his eyes and leans back in his chair. His chest rises and falls as he controls his breathing. Minutes pass by with nothing happening, and I start to wonder if he fell asleep.

I'm getting bored, sitting here doing nothing, when suddenly, David's body jerks, bringing my attention back to him. He opens his eyes, looking at the wall to my right. He nods with a smile, and his eyes slowly glide toward me as though he's watching something move.

My heart starts pounding in my chest when his eyes stop on me.

"Sure." He gives me a wink as something brushes gently against my cheek.

I stiffen, uncertain of what's going on.

David's gaze is no longer on me, but to the right of me again. "She is." He nods once more, and his body jerks again.

"What just happened?" I ask, eyes wide.

"Bartholomew thinks you're beautiful," David says, slightly out of breath.

"I couldn't see him. All I saw was you spasm, watch something invisible move toward me, you talk to no one, and then feel something that wasn't there brush up against my cheek. I have to admit, it kind of freaked me out."

"I'm sorry. He asked if he could touch your face, so I gave him permission. I should have asked you first."

"That's okay," I say, even though I didn't like that experience. I wish I could see him. It'd be less creepy. "It looks like you're getting better control of your ability. You can summon Bartholomew without having to be sick, injured, or nervous. That's good progress."

"It is. I just need to keep practicing so it can be quicker."

I look at the clock on the wall. We've been here for three hours already. "We probably should have told someone where we were going. They're going to start wondering where we are."

We call it a day and head back to the barracks. Nobody even bats an eye that we were missing. I guess when you're a couple, people assume you're off making out or something, and don't bother asking questions.

For the next couple of days, David and I practice our abilities in the evening after he returns from helping Elliot with the video. I'm less creeped out by Bartholomew now. Even though I can't see him, I've been able to talk to him through David. It's strange but amazing all at the same time.

"The video is done." David returned earlier than normal. "And Elliot is a pilot now. He's just waiting for us to tell him when we're ready."

"I don't know how we're going to sneak away. Chozolt got back while you were gone, and he wants to pick up the lessons this afternoon."

"That's actually a good thing," David says. "We can show him how we've progressed, and he can turn his attention to Charlotte and Joselyn because he won't have much left to work on with us."

"Let's hope you're right," I say.

Later that afternoon, Chozolt finds us in the barracks, playing poker.

"Olivia, I'd like to thank you for letting me know about my grandpa. The time I got to spend with him in his final days was priceless." Chozolt looks at me with sad eyes.

"You're welcome. He was a kind man," I say.

Everyone in the barracks gives their condolences with either kind words or a moment of silence.

"Thank you, everyone." He turns to David and me. "Have you found time to work on your abilities?"

David and I explain to him what we've been able to accomplish, and his eyes light up.

"So, you can start working with Charlotte and Joselyn now that Liv and I have it figured out," David says.

"Hold on, I'd like you to come show me what you can do before we give up on your lessons."

David and I exchange a quick glance.

"Do you have time for it now, Olivia?" Chozolt asks.

"Sure." I grab my coat and follow him.

"I'm going to let you do your thing, and while you're having a vision, I'd like to activate your RABI one final time to give you a little boost. If we can get you using your full potential, I believe you could see the future whenever and wherever you want. Nothing could surprise you. From what you told me, you've basically got it, and I'm proud of you for practicing while I was away. You've come so far, and I think you're ready."

516

"Ready for what?" I ask.

"Ready to help me take down the Coalition. I have a summit meeting in two days, and I'm looking forward to telling them about your Rare gift, Olivia. With you on our side, I think we finally have a chance to always be one step ahead of them and finally end this."

I keep my lips pressed together, afraid I'm about to blurt out something I shouldn't.

He thinks I'm his secret weapon.

I guess I should have known by how much time he was spending with me. Now we only have two days before he tries to parade me around as the chosen one. I cringe at the thought.

"All right, Olivia, settle into the chair, and let's see what you can do," Chozolt says.

I let out a breath slowly as I lean back. He holds a card out in front of him, and I turn my focus onto my RABI.

I'm on the floor, writhing as my head feels like it's about to explode. My RABI pulsates violently in my skull, taking over all my other senses, and leaving me unable to think clearly. If it doesn't stop soon, I feel like my brain is going to be destroyed.

"Oh, no! Not again!" I hear Chozolt say as though he's speaking down a long tunnel. "Olivia, please be okay! I didn't mean to push you so hard!"

I force my way out of the vision as soon as I feel Chozolt's presence touch my brain. If I don't say something soon, he's going to kill me.

"Stop! Get out!" I manage to yell.

His presence in my mind dissipates immediately, and he looks at me with concern. "What is it? Are you all right?"

"I just saw what happens when you give me that 'little boost.' It almost kills me." I glare at him.

Chozolt hangs his head and lets out a sigh.

"You knew there was a chance that that would happen, didn't you? Because you've done it before."

Chozolt can't quite meet my eyes. "I thought I could control it this time. Yes. I've pushed it too far with a special Rare before you."

"Claudia." I watch him squirm a little at her name. "I heard your men talking about her."

"Claudia could hear people's thoughts. I had this idea that maybe I could boost her RABI to make it so she didn't have to be right next to someone to hear what they were thinking. That maybe we could get her to the point of reading thoughts just by watching them on a live surveillance feed," Chozolt says with remorse. "But that last lesson was too much for her mind, and she broke. I caused a young girl to be mute, blind, and wheelchair-bound because I got greedy."

"And you were about to do the same thing to me? Without warning?" I say, disgusted.

517

"I wasn't going to push you quite as hard. Besides, I believe you're stronger than she ever was."

"It doesn't matter if you thought I was Superman. You need to warn people of the risks beforehand."

"Please don't think I was trying to hurt you on purpose or anything. I just got excited that you were progressing so quickly. We don't have to continue working on your abilities together if you don't want to. I'll leave your training in your hands, but please keep working at it. We need you if we have any hope of winning this war."

I don't say anything. As soon as I get back to the barracks, I'm letting David know I'm ready to go ahead with our plans.

[4 | 5

Elliot told us to meet him outside a gas station about two miles away from the compound around midnight. David and I spent the rest of the day packing our bags with extra food and clothing when nobody was looking. Getting out of the compound was a little tricky with the entrance guard on duty, but David got the idea of sending Bartholomew into the guardhouse to spill the guard's coffee on his uniform. There was a moment I thought I saw Bartholomew, but it was just a flash of a figure that could have been a shadow from a tree in the moonlight. Bartholomew succeeds, then returns to David. While the guard is busy cleaning himself off, we take the opportunity to sneak out.

Elliot picks us up and takes us straight to the airport. He lies to the airport employees, telling them we are on a covert operation assigned to us by President Chozolt himself. He has documentation forged with the president's signature, which apparently passes the test, but Elliot insists we hurry, in case they call someone and we get caught.

"We've never been on an airplane before." I buckle into the seat, then rub my sweaty palms off on my pants.

"For real?" Elliot asks.

"How would we have? We lived in the city until just recently."

"There's nothing much to it. It's like riding in a car. Here's some gum." He hands us each a stick of mint gum.

"Do I have bad breath?" I breathe into my hand and smell it.

"It's for your ears." He turns back around to the controls.

"You want me to stick it in my ear?"

"Woman! Just chew the dang gum," Elliot says, slightly exasperated. "The pressure change can hurt your ears."

I pop the gum in my mouth, chewing at it nervously.

Elliot starts the engines, and we take off down a long straight road, moving faster and faster until it looks like we're about to run out of pavement. I grip the armrests tightly as the plane starts to lift off the ground. I have the sensation of sinking into my seat as all my organs seem to drop inside my body. I don't like it, and I can tell by the way David is holding onto his seat with his eyes squeezed shut, he doesn't like it either. After a while, the plane levels out, and we can finally relax. I look out the window and see small lights on the ground. I've never been afraid of heights, but the realization of how high we are unsettles me a little.

Since we left so late at night, we're having a hard time staying awake. Elliot tells us to go ahead and sleep so we're fresh once we land. I settle back in my seat and close my eyes. Before I know it, we're already starting to land.

"Where are we?" I ask, groggily.

"About ten miles outside of Chicago, the city where David said your uncle lives," Elliot answers.

"I thought we were going to Baltimore?" David asks.

"The plane's fuel tank isn't big enough to get us all the way there. We need to refuel. Now hold on. I don't know how deep this snow is, so the landing might get a bit sketchy."

I grab ahold of the armrest, but Elliot gets the plane on the ground and to a stop without any issue.

"Where are we going to get fuel out here?" David looks out his window, but it's too dark to see anything.

"We're at an old airport that our government uses for refueling our planes. It's how we sneak our spies around to get intel. I just have to go open those doors, slip the plane into the garage, fill her up with fuel, and then we can start our hike to the city." Elliot unbuckles his seatbelt.

"What? Why are we hiking into the city?" I ask.

"I caught word of some juicy tidbits that I need to check out, just in case our video solution doesn't work."

"We don't have time to waste! We need to get to Baltimore and get our video up and running before Chozolt decides to make his move."

"Cool it, blondie. Any information I can bring back on what kind of weapons the Coalition has will help our side win. It's not going to take that long. I brought a drone that'll help me get in without having to physically enter the city."

"We're new to the whole drone thing. We never really heard of one until Eli's camp was attacked. What are they?" David asks.

"There are a lot of different kinds, all shapes and sizes. Some are some just for fun that civilians use. This one is a spy drone that has a camera and microphone so we can record conversations and videos. Military drones often have guns."

David and I just nod. I'm still unclear about what they do, but I don't have to know about it. That's Elliot's job.

"So, since you have a drone, we're not going into the city? Shouldn't we sneak inside and get the video up and running so people here can see it too?" I ask.

"I didn't bring enough equipment for planting it here. Baltimore is our target because I believe Turk's videos and updates play in all the cities." Elliot shuffles through his gear.

"Do David and I have to come with you? What can we do to help?" I wish we were back inside the plane as a cold wind whips snow into our faces.

"I'll need you two to keep watch while I fly this in." He holds up the drone—it looks like a miniature airplane with four different propellers. "You have the gun on you, right?"

David pats his hip in response.

"All right, it's a bit of a hike ahead of us. Bundle up, and let's go."

We trudge through snow that's deep in some spots and only a dusting in others, all dictated by the blowing wind. I feel a little queasy coming back to the city we fled with Uncle Eli only a short time ago. What happens if we get caught and never get to Baltimore? This feels like an unnecessary stop.

The sun is starting to come up when Elliot breaks the silence to inform us we're almost there.

"So, what happens now?" David asks.

"Now we find a spot to hunker down, and I fly this baby in. We can watch what the drone picks up on this little screen, and once I get what we need, we fly it back here and leave. Easy peasy."

"What if the drone gets spotted or captured?" I follow them down a small hill toward a group of pines.

Once we get below the peak of the hill, the wind stops blowing, and it feels ten degrees warmer. The branches of the pines hang low and give a nice blind to hide behind. Elliot drops his bag into the snow and starts pulling the equipment out. He tosses granola bars to us as we find a way to sit in the snow without getting frozen.

"If we get caught, there's a button I can push to destroy it if necessary." He shows me the red button on his controller, then steps out from our hiding spot to set the drone down in the snow.

David and I scoot close together, trying to stay as warm as possible. I hope this doesn't take long.

Elliot comes back and pulls a small laptop out of the bag, settling himself into the snow with us. He turns the screen on, hits a few buttons, and then uses the controller to get the drone up off the ground. We watch the trees get smaller and smaller on the little screen as the drone takes off into the air.

"Do you know where you need to fly that thing?" I'm mesmerized by the scenery zipping by.

"I have a hunch," he says and leaves it at that.

He takes the drone up high enough that the screen is white with clouds. An occasional break in the clouds reveals the city below, but nothing is distinguishable from so high up.

"We're getting close," Elliot says, but I can't for the life of me figure out how he can tell. As he starts to lower the drone, we see trucks driving to and from a large building with soldiers standing guard outside. Elliot flies the drone over the top of a truck heading toward the building and lands it on the roof.

"What are you doing?" I'm surprised the soldiers didn't catch that.

"This is a weapons base. We need to get inside to see what we're dealing with."

As the truck pulls into the building, Elliot flies the drone up to the rafters and lands it, balancing it so we can see what's going on.

"Let me just turn on the microphone so we can record what's being said too." He fiddles with the controller.

He zooms the camera in on what look like rows of giant tubes of lipstick or pencil tips or something. I can't quite figure out what I'm looking at.

"What are those?" David asks.

"Those, my friends, are nukes. Things just got a lot more complicated." Elliot clicks a button, and we hear voices coming from the laptop.

"How many more loads you got coming in, Major?" a voice asks.

"Three more after this," someone answers.

Elliot moves the camera around until he finds two men standing off to the side, one holding a clipboard and the other with his back turned to our drone. There's something about the way the guy is standing that catches my attention.

The guy with his back turned whistles, then says, "The president said he had a few tricks up his sleeve. I'd say this is more than a few."

That voice sounds familiar, but it's too hard to place it when it's being distorted from the equipment.

He continues, "I really think this is the wrong way to go about things. If my brother made it to the Haven, then I know he's going to have an influence on their president. He's going to talk them into coming in with guns blazing."

I reach out and grip David's arm.

Eli.

Eli has an in with the Coalition president? My face grows hot as anger bubbles up inside of me.

"I think we should wait and let them come to us. Make them look like the bad guys," Eli says.

"Is that right? And why should we listen to you? You got my men killed when they came out to your camp. What was the reason again? Oh yeah. You wanted your brother to leave."

"That jerk—" I start to yell, but David throws his hand up over my mouth, accidentally bumping into Elliot in the process. Just then, the video feed on the laptop starts spinning, ending with a shot of the cement floor.

"What just happened?" I ask, watching a pair of boots come into view.

"Whose playing with the drones?" the major asks.

"That's not one of ours, sir," a soldier answers.

"We need to leave now!" Elliot pushes the red button to destroy the drone. The screen goes black, and Elliot slams the laptop closed. "Let's get out of here before they send out a search team to find where the drone came from!"

David and I follow behind Elliot as he leads us back the way we came. We run for a few miles, but with the freezing temperatures, we lose our stamina and slow to a brisk walk.

I hear a strange noise coming from behind us. "Stop, guys! Do you hear that?"

David and Elliot stand still, but at that moment, the wind picks up and whistles through the trees.

"It's just the wind, Liv," David says.

"No, I swear I heard something weird," I insist.

"Let's just keep going, and you can let us know if you hear the sound again," Elliot says.

We continue for a few minutes when I hear the sound off to the right of us. It's very faint, but it sounds kind of like a fan.

"There it is! It's over there somewhere." I point.

David and Elliot turn their ears the direction I indicated, and Elliot's eyes grow big. "They found us! Quick, hide!" he yells.

David points at something in the distance. "Isn't that the garage that we hid the airplane in?"

"Yes, but we're not going to make it without getting caught. We need you to get down and shoot the drone when it comes into view," Elliot says.

I push my back up against a tree trunk. "How did they find us?"

"My guess is they sent out a whole army of drones in all directions to spot a clue for who got a drone inside their city. If they haven't spotted our footprints yet, they will soon," Elliot says from a nearby tree. "You ready, David?"

David crouches against a tree, holding the gun. "Yeah, I think so."

I lose track of the sound for a moment, but it comes back louder, this time to the left of us. "Is there more than one here?" I ask.

"No idea," Elliot replies. "It's probably safer to assume so."

I curl into a tight ball, holding my knees up to my chest. I want to leave. I want to go back to the Haven and get away from the Coalition as fast as possible. It was a terrible idea to come back here.

The drone grows louder as it gets closer. Gunshots ring out, but it was too many in a row to have been David. I look up and see the drone has a gun attached to the bottom of it.

"Olivia! Run!" Elliot yells. "Get to the airplane now!"

"Where's David?" I scream. I look to where he was crouched and can't find him.

"Go, Liv! I'm right behind you," David yells.

The drone shoots another round of bullets, and one whistles right past my ear. I push myself to run harder than I have ever run before, desperate to get to the safety of the airplane. The snow hardly slows me down this time, and it feels like I'm gliding on top of it. As I make it to the door of the hanger, a loud shot reverberates off the metal walls, and my heart stops for a moment. I turn around in time to see the drone fall out of the sky and drop into the snow.

"Nice shot." Elliot slaps David's back as he runs past him. "Now run!"

The boys make it to me in no time. David helps Elliot open the doors, and then we stand back as Elliot hops in the plane, starts it up, and drives it out. I work with David to close the doors once the plane is out of the way, and then we climb inside. We just make it to our seats when something hits the windshield.

"Another one's shooting at us! Sit down and buckle up. We gotta move!" Elliot yells.

I look at the windshield and see it only left chips in the glass. Will the plane's metal frame be able to stop bullets?

David and I buckle up as Elliot starts speeding down the runway. The plane slides a little on the snow, but Elliot gets it back on track. The drone shoots at us again, putting a couple of small holes in the side of the plane. I grab David's hand, but he squeezes it and lets go.

"Stay here." David heads up toward Elliot, but as David is about to go into the cockpit, the plane starts lifting off the ground. David loses his balance and falls to the floor, his gun sliding down the aisle toward me.

I reach down and grab it before it slides past to the back of the plane. Another round of bullets puncture holes into the side of the plane, shooting right where my head would have been if I hadn't been reaching down to grab David's gun.

David reaches down to me for the gun. I hand it over, and he forces his way up to the window in the cockpit. I stay lying on the floor, the seat holding me in place, so I don't slide to the back of the plane. I don't dare sit up where the drone just almost shot me. I watch as David wedges himself behind Elliot's seat and slides the window open. The icy wind blows back on me, and I gasp.

"Can you see it?" Elliot shouts over the noise of the plane and the rushing wind.

"No," David yells back, and my stomach sinks.

"We need to take this drone down, or it's going to end up shooting our fuel tank or killing one of us," Elliot yells. The plane lurches to the right, and Elliot shouts, "There it is!"

I hold onto the legs of the seat, trying hard to not slide all over. I close my eyes and pray David can hit it.

I barely hear the gunshot over the noise of the wind and the engines. Then another one.

"Got it!" David yells as he slams the window closed.

Elliot levels the plane out, and I let go of the seat, my fingers frozen stiff. David comes back by me and helps me up off the floor. I sit down and buckle up, my heart still racing. David grabs ahold of my hand and squeezes, his own hand shaking slightly. I desperately wish this trip were over.

We ride in silence, lost in our own thoughts. The bullet holes let in freezing air, and by the time we're landing, I'm chilled to the bone. I should have put on extra layers before we left.

"We're about twenty miles outside the city." Elliot unbuckles his seatbelt.

Once Elliot refuels and stashes the plane, we set off on yet another long hike in the snow. We make good time, but it's getting dark, and we're all exhausted. We find an abandoned house to break in to and stay for the night.

The house is unassuming but cozy. We start up a fire in the wood burning stove and have a quick supper.

"So, Elliot. Tell us something interesting you've been able to do with your Rare abilities." David settles onto the couch after we move it closer to the fire.

"I graduated from college when I was only twelve," he starts.

"Twelve?" I ask, astounded. I think back to what I was doing when I was twelve and scoff. I had already made an attempt on my life at that point. What could I have accomplished if I had been born in the Haven? Things could have been so different.

"Yeah, well my ability to remember everything I read allowed me to blow through all my schooling with straight A's. I got into computers when I was about thirteen, and by eighteen, I was hacking into government systems, and that's when I got hired into the NSA."

"Why were you hacking into their systems?" David asks.

"Just for fun," he says nonchalantly.

"You have a skewed sense of fun," David says with a chuckle.

"I just thought of something," Elliot says. "With my ability to memorize things, blondie's ability to see the future, and your ability to send out your—whatever it is— to spy on people, we could make a killing at poker."

"That's cheating," I say as David laughs next to me.

"You really are a goody-two-shoes, aren't you?" Elliot jests.

"Is there something wrong with that?" I ask.

"Nah. Actually, we need more people like you," Elliot answers. "This world is full of crooks and con men. It's refreshing to meet someone with principles."

David leans over and kisses my head as my cheeks blush slightly from the compliment.

After a while, we settle in to get some sleep. I feel a sense of vindication from Elliot's compliment. I'm constantly being told I should be okay with hurting people or doing bad things for the right reasons. It's nice to finally hear I'm good the way I am.

It's nice to not hate myself for once.

[4|7|

"How are we going to get inside the city fence?" It's morning, and we're getting ready to continue our journey.

"I contacted our inside person. They're picking us up at the secret entrance."

"There's a secret entrance?" I ask.

"Sure. How else do you think our spies get in? It's a section of fence on the west side of the city that gets ignored because it's surrounded by water. The land it was sitting on flooded a long time ago. All we have to do is take a boat across the river to the hole that's been cut in the fence, hide the boat, then hitch a ride with our helper."

"Let's go," I say.

As we walk closer to the city, a feeling of finality grows inside me. Either our mission will succeed and we will liberate the Rare without violence, or our mission will fail and Chozolt will have his way through forced peace.

I turn my focus to my surroundings, and déjà vu hits me. This part of the city looks like the part I wandered through when I returned to confront my mom. The snow-covered ruins of war-torn buildings stand as a reminder of what used to be: a great city once a part of the United States and free from the oppressive rule of the Coalition.

The horror people must have felt when bombs were being dropped is overwhelming to think about. I look over at David and see a hardened look on his face. He's feeling the same righteous anger I am. I reach out and hold his hand as we march on through the destruction. I sure hope we end the Coalition soon.

Finally, we make it to a wide river, and Elliot finds the boat hidden under carefully placed sheets of metal siding. I tentatively step into the boat, afraid it is going to tip over. I chuckle a little to myself when I realize this is yet another mode of transportation I am experiencing for the first time. I really lived a sheltered life.

As Elliot rows us closer to the city, the fog starts to thicken, making my hair damp, which leaves me chilled. I try to scoot closer to David for warmth, but my movement rocks the boat and I stop, once again afraid the boat is going to tip over. Now that I've experienced all these different ways of travel, I'd have to say I prefer cars. Warm, safe cars.

"Now I just need to find where they said the hole was," Elliot mumbles as we row along the fence. "Ah, here it is."

He pulls the fence apart, and we all duck as we squeeze the boat through it. He bends the fence back into place as best he can before continuing. My nerves are on edge, being back in the city. That, or it's the fog starting to take effect. Either way, I really don't want to be here, even though our mission is important.

When we finally hit land, we help Elliot pull in the boat and hide it in some scraggly bushes, hoping it's enough to conceal it. A set of headlights cuts through the fog, and I instinctively hit the ground, afraid we got caught.

"It's okay. That's our ride," Elliot says with a little laugh.

I stand and brush off, hiding my face in embarrassment.

"Hey, Elliot," a voice calls out.

I look up, startled. "Mom? What are you doing here?"

"Olivia? What are *you* doing here?"

"She's with me on a mission." Elliot looks back and forth between us in confusion. "Your mom is our inside guy?"

"I told you I was helping Haven spies," Mom says directly to me. "I didn't realize you were going to be with them."

"Yeah, well, you wouldn't know anything I'm doing, would you? Your work is more important than me, remember?" I accuse.

"Do we really have to do this, Olivia?" She pinches the bridge of her nose. "I've worked too hard to get to where I am now to just up and quit. Besides, had I run off with you, I wouldn't be here helping you with whatever it is you're doing."

"She's got a point," Elliot chimes in.

"Stay out of it," I snap at Elliot, then turn back to my mom. "Do you even care to know what we went through to get to the Haven?"

"I think that's a story for another time." She heads back over to the car.

Her disinterest in my life rubs me the wrong way.

"Well, do you care to know what we're doing now? We're on our way to—" I start to say, but she holds her hand up.

"Stop. I don't want to know details. Plausible deniability. I'll help you get in, but that's as far as I go. What you do after that is none of my business. Just let me know if and when you need a ride back out here."

I hold back a frustrated scream as we all climb into the vehicle and she takes off driving toward the city. We ride in silence after I try to make conversation with her a couple of times, and she shushes me because she doesn't want me to let anything slip.

"This is as far as I'm willing to take you. I don't want to be caught driving you around. Good luck with whatever you're doing." She stops the car in front of an empty church.

"Thank you for the ride, Mrs. Sloane," David says politely.

"Goodbye, Mom," I say even though I'm annoyed with her. I don't know how this mission is going to go, so I figure it's better to say goodbye just in case.

"Be careful with whatever you're doing, Olivia." She furrows her eyebrows as she looks at me.

"I'll call if we need a ride. Thanks again," Elliot says.

As soon as we close our doors, she drives off.

"Well, that was a fun ride," Elliot says sarcastically.

I ignore him. "How do we find out which way to go?" I look up at the cross on top of the church barely visible in the thick fog.

"Follow me," Elliot says confidently.

We begin down the labyrinth of side streets and city blocks, keeping our eyes peeled for guards. Luckily, Elliot seems to know exactly where we're going. I can feel my brain getting a little fuzzy now from breathing the fog in.

For some reason, I feel a sense of familiarity as I look around, like I've been here before. This is from my vision. I grab onto the boys and stop them from walking. "A guard on patrol one block ahead is going to catch us. Let's duck in here," I say, seeing it play out in my mind just like before.

We slip into the alleyway and hide behind a pile of cardboard boxes. After a short wait, we hear the clomping of the guard's boots on the sidewalk as he passes by.

Once the footsteps recede, we leave our hiding spot and continue.

Elliot pats my shoulder blade. "Good work, blondie."

"This fog is getting impossible to see through. How much farther, Elliot?" David squints.

"We continue this way for three blocks, turn right and walk for four blocks, then a left, and we should be able to see it," Elliot rattles off from memory.

"You remembered to bring the clip, right?" I ask, even though in my vision he said he did.

"Oh, shoot!" he replies. "We gotta walk all the way... Yes, of course I remembered to grab it, woman," he says as though I insulted him. "You think I'd forget?"

And that's where the vision ends. I'm back to the unknown for now.

"So, tell us the plan again," David says.

"We break into the tower, using the gun you brought if necessary. We find the server room. I do my magic of hacking and whacking: pull the plug on the government mumbo jumbo, and get our video up and running. Once the people see the lies they're being fed, we should have a full-blown riot on our hands. Knock Turk right off his throne."

A tingle of excitement runs down my spine as we get closer to our goal.

"I wonder if Chozolt or Matthias have figured out what we've done yet," David says.

"Hang on. Let me see if I can focus on Chozolt while I tap into my ability and get a vision of what he's doing," I say, feeling newfound confidence in controlling my skill.

"I understand that, Prime Minister, but my greatest war asset has run off with my best NSA worker. I need to retrieve them before we can move forward with this war," Chozolt says.

"*You're relying too heavily on the word of a fortune teller, Chozolt. With the help China granted us, we don't need your Rare child to defeat the Coalition. I say we get our troops rallied up and send our men out as soon as possible.*"

"*And when do you think that would be? How soon will you be able to mobilize?*" Chozolt taps a finger on his chin.

"*Give me two days,*" the Prime Minister says proudly.

"*That soon, huh?*" Chozolt raises his eyebrow.

"*Every day we hesitate is another day of agony for our Rare folk. It's time to end this.*"

Everyone else in the room voices their agreement.

"We'd better hurry," I say out of breath. "They're coming in two days."

"Chozolt has his summit meeting today, and the other leaders are going to push to start making a move in just a couple of days. We need to get this finished today, or we're going to be in the war, whether we like it or not, only this time as collateral damage," I answer.

"Well then, let's quit chatting about it and get going," Elliot says.

We walk so quickly, we're practically running until we finally see the tower up ahead, half hidden in the fog.

Elliot pulls us off to the side of the street and squats behind a tree, unzipping the bag he brought. "Watch this." A devious smile lights his face.

He pulls a machine shaped like a bird out. He sets it on the ground and turns it on with a controller. The bird flies upward, its wings flapping robotically. It doesn't look real to me, but from a distance, it would probably look realistic enough to pass. He propels it toward the tower's entrance and has the bird land on a surveillance camera. With a push of a button, the bird poops all over the front of the camera.

I laugh. "Ew!"

"It's not real poop, of course." Elliot lands it on another camera and does the same thing.

"I would hope not."

He flies the bird back to us and tucks it in his bag. "I invented it myself," Elliot says. "I call it 'the party pooper.' Like it?"

"Clever," David says, laughing.

"We better get going before they come out to clean it off," Elliot says.

We follow him to the front door, where there's a keypad to get inside. I think we're about to be stuck out here when Elliot pushes a series of numbers and unlocks it on the first try.

"I hacked into their database before we left and found the keycodes to the towers," Elliot explains nonchalantly. "Now, act like we belong here, but keep your hand on the gun, David."

We step through the door and see a guard sitting at the desk. He looks up at us, and David and I both freeze when we see his face.

It's the guard we shot to escape the city.

"You!" David yells, drawing his gun and aiming it at the guard's head. He hesitates when recognition lights up in the guard's eyes and he jumps to his feet.

"Wait!" The guard holds his hands up in the air.

"Don't wait! Shoot him!" Elliot shouts.

Panic sweeps over me as David and the guard stare at each other for what feels like an eternity. I want to use my abilities to look ahead to see what happens, but I can't take my eyes off him to be able to concentrate.

"Wait!" he says again. "Before you shoot me, I want to say thank you. You two saved my life."

I look over at David and see his eyebrows crease, but he doesn't lower the weapon.

"We shot you. How is that saving your life?" I look back at him.

"If you hadn't, the doctors wouldn't have found the mass that was growing on my lung. I owe my life to you," the guard says.

"How do we know this isn't a trick?" Elliot asks.

We watch as the guard answers by slowly lowering his hands to unbuckle his utility belt. He drops it on the floor, leaving him unarmed.

"What do you need? I'll help you with whatever it is." He slowly walks around the counter.

David lowers the gun, then tucks it into his holster.

"Can you take us to the server room?" Elliot asks.

"Sure. Follow me." He turns to lead us down the hallway. "My name's Luke, by the way."

"Nice to meet you, Luke," David says.

Luke stops short when someone steps out of a doorway and almost runs into him.

"Who are these people, Luke?" the man with a bushy mustache asks.

"These are my friends, Mr. Miller. They just dropped by for a visit," Luke says cheerfully.

"Where are you taking them?" Mr. Miller studies us with suspicion.

"They had to use the bathroom," Luke whispers behind his hand as though using the bathroom is embarrassing.

"Fine, just don't let them out of your sight. They're not supposed to be back here."

When the man turns around to walk toward the entrance door, Luke flips him the middle finger. "That was my boss. C'mon. It's just down here."

We pass by a couple more doors before he stops and pulls a keyring out of his pocket. He unlocks the door and looks up and down the hallway before opening it to let us in, but then stops with his hand on the doorknob.

"You're not setting off any bombs or anything, right?" Luke asks. "I owe you my life, but I'm not going to let you hurt people."

"No, actually we're trying to save more lives and stop a war from happening," David answers.

Luke lets out a whistle then says, "Is that so? Well, good luck to you then." He finally opens the door to let us through.

"Thanks, Luke." David holds his hand out, which Luke shakes enthusiastically.

"Anytime. Just don't do anything to get me into trouble either, eh?" He grins, closing the door gently behind us once we're in the room.

It's cooler in here than the other parts of the building. There are cabinets with glass doors full of equipment with blinking lights. I have no idea what I'm looking at, but Elliot seems to know exactly what he's doing when he pulls out a mini laptop and plugs it into one of the machines.

David and I watch his fingers fly over the keyboard, typing in some kind of gibberish I can't understand.

"Just about got it." His face scrunches with concentration. "There! Our message should be up and running."

I'm about to congratulate him when he mutters, "Wait. Something isn't right."

His fingers clack on the keyboard some more, and his face falls. "Looks like we're going to have to take out another tower or two to get this message playing across the entire city. The three remaining towers triangulated their signal, keeping our message out of that area."

David's shoulders slump. "How are we going to have time to take out two more towers? We got lucky with this one having Luke here to help us out."

"We'll split up and make it happen, man," Elliot responds calmly. "I brought this little doodad along just in case something like this happened."

He hands David a little black square with a USB port on the end.

"Get yourselves into the server room and plug that baby into one of the servers. I'll be able to talk to it from my laptop and take them both out. Once you finish, meet me at the church Janice dropped us off at."

I take a deep breath and blow it out slowly. I don't like the idea of going separate ways, but if we're going to make this happen before Chozolt's war, then we have to do this now.

David goes to open the server room door, and it's locked.

"Maybe it's protocol to keep it locked," David says with uncertainty.

"Try knocking," Elliot suggests.

Just as David raises his fist to knock, we hear shouting in the hallway coming toward the server room.

"You idiot! You can't let civilians in there," Mr. Miller yells.

"They said they're here to stop a war. Now, let them out!"

"If there was a war about to happen, we would know about it. I'm not unlocking that door until the soldiers arrive," the boss says.

There's a moment of silence and then a loud bang against the door we're standing by. We back away as we hear swear words being shouted as the two men start to fight. My heart leaps into my throat when a gunshot blasts from right outside the door. I look over at Elliot and see him searching the walls.

"Is there another way out of here?" I squeak.

"Unfortunately not."

"What about through the ceiling?" David looks up at the panels.

"We're in the center of the tower, on the first floor. Where would we go? Besides, the ceiling isn't strong enough to hold our weight," Elliot answers.

"We can't let the soldiers get us!" I say.

David puts his arm around me. Just then, the doorknob rattles. He immediately drops his arm and pulls the gun out of his pocket, ready to fight our way out of here. Elliot hides behind a server and pulls a screwdriver out of his bag, brandishing it like a knife. I find myself wishing I had a sword, but I didn't come prepared, so I duck down in the corner and pray I don't get shot.

The door opens, and Luke steps in the room. "You guys okay?" he whispers.

"Yeah." David drops the gun down to his side, but he doesn't put it away. "What's going on out there?"

"Mr. Miller called you guys in. Soldiers are on their way. I had to shoot him in order for you to escape, so you better not have been lying to me," Luke says, holding his sleeve against his bloody lip.

We step out of the server room and into the hallway, where Mr. Miller's body now lies lifeless.

"I promise I'm not lying." David puts the gun away. "Keep tuned into the president's channel. Everything will be explained soon."

Luke gives a quick nod. "All right. You better get going. I have some explaining to do to my coworkers, and the soldiers will be here any minute."

At that moment, I notice pounding on the door down the hallway. I look back at Luke, and he jiggles his keychain.

"Thank you, Luke." David holds out his hand for another handshake.

"Just repaying the debt I owed. Good luck to you." He gives David's hand a quick shake and then turns to head toward where his coworkers are locked in.

"I never thought I'd be happy to have shot someone," David whispers, and I let out a nervous laugh.

Elliot, David, and I run out of the building and down the street. As we are about to turn a corner, I look back at the tower in time to see a black truck pull up to the entrance, and soldiers spill out of the vehicle.

"We don't have a lot of time," I say, worried. "We've got to get out of here."

"How do we find the next tower?" David asks Elliot.

Elliot pulls a piece of paper out of his bag and quickly writes down the directions. He hands it to us, and with a salute, he says, "See ya on the flip side."

"Be careful," I call out as he starts jogging down the sidewalk. Let's hope David and I don't screw this up.

"I recognize some of these road names. They're not far from my house. Do you think it'd be okay to go swing by and peek in at my parents? I want to know they're okay," David says.

"I don't know, David. We don't have a lot of time, and we might be seen," I say carefully, not wanting to hurt his feelings. I know how much he misses his mom.

"But it's starting to get dark, and with the fog, it's getting hard for even us to see clearly," David argues with puppy dog eyes.

I look at him, and my resolve melts. "Fine. We'll take a quick look."

David gives me a kiss, and we set off, following the roads Elliot wrote down. We duck in and out of alleyways whenever cars drive by so we don't get caught. The sunlight is fading fast, leaving me worried about how much time we're wasting. We finally come to his road, and flashbacks of all the times I've walked this street hit me. I almost feel nostalgic, but that would imply happy times. My life before leaving the city was rarely happy.

It hits me how far I've truly come. Spiraling into the abyss used to be a daily occurrence, but now it's days, maybe weeks, between my bouts of darkness. And with the love I now feel for David, I can almost say I've found a modicum of happiness, something that seemed impossible before I left. I grab David's hand and rest my face against his shoulder as we walk on.

His house is up ahead. It's dark inside, except for a light in the kitchen. I wonder what his mom made for supper. Something delicious, no doubt.

In the cover of darkness, we creep up to the window and peer inside. His parents are sitting at the table across from each other, eating frozen pizza. They aren't talking, or even looking at each other; just staring at their plate as they eat. David continues to peer in the window at them, and a look of longing crosses his face.

I can't imagine how hard it must be to be this close to your family but not be able to talk to them.

His parents finally finish their meal, and David pulls me down, crouching under the window so they don't see us.

"Ready to go?" I ask gently.

David nods, and we start to crawl away when a black car pulls up to the curb.

"Run!" I yell, but we're too late.

"Freeze!" A voice yells as two soldiers get out of the car, shining flashlights in our faces and pointing guns at us. They're too far away for us to disarm them, so we stand slowly with our hands in the air.

The front door of the house opens behind us, and David's dad calls out, "What's the meaning of this?"

David turns around, and his mom cries out, "David? David!"

"Stay right there, ma'am!" a soldier yells at her as she steps out of the door.

"This is a mistake. David is our son. Let them go!" Mr. Beckett yells.

The two soldiers move away from their car toward us, and David's parents race out to stand in front of us.

"I'm so sorry, David. Turk made us set up surveillance cameras that would alert his men if you were to come home. I never should have agreed to it!" Mrs. Beckett says quickly as the soldiers march right up to them.

I watch in horror as one of them punches David's dad in the stomach, making him double over in pain, while the other one shoves David's mother, and she falls to the ground.

David lets out an angry yell and springs into action. He grabs the soldier who punched his dad and puts him in a headlock. For a moment, I'm afraid he's about to break the guy's neck, but instead, he's squeezing tightly, and the soldier's eyes start fluttering closed as he gets close to passing out.

I finally snap out of my shock and am about to take the other soldier out, but I hesitated too long. He's got a gun pointed toward me, and when I take a small step toward him, he shoots.

"Liv!" David screams.

My hand instinctively goes to where he shot me, but instead of a bullet hole, I feel a needle sticking out of my neck. I pull it out, but whatever was in the needle does its job, and I black out.

■■■■■

I wake up with a groggy moan. There's something in my mouth, and it's making my tongue so dry, I can't swallow. I go to take it out, but my hands won't move. They're tied behind the back of the chair. I take some deep breaths to keep my cool. Now is not the time to freak out.

Someone moans behind me, and a small weight lifts off my chest when I realize it's David. He's alive.

"Mr. Archer, they're waking up," a voice says from behind me, followed by a phone receiver being dropped back into place.

I try to turn to look at who spoke, but they're too far behind me to see. The room is dimly lit, and I can see the blue glow of a computer screen off to my left. There's nothing else of significance to see, just a white wall and a tiled floor. I have no idea where we are.

Crap! Elliot is expecting us to plug his device into a tower server, and now we're stuck here. He gave us detailed directions of what to do, and we still managed to screw everything up. How long have we been knocked out? Is Chozolt on his way to begin his war? What's about to happen to us?

There's only one way to find out. I close my eyes again and focus on my RABI. The buzz I usually feel is dull, almost nonexistent. Whatever drug they used is affecting my Rare ability. It feels like my RABI went to sleep and is just starting to wake up too.

I hear the door open and something rolling across the floor.

"Untie them, and then leave. They aren't going to hurt me," a deep, shaky voice says from behind me.

That voice sounds familiar, but I can't quite place it. I search my memory as the soldier unties my hands and pulls the gag out of my mouth. I reach up to rub my cheeks where it was digging in.

"Hands down, Olivia," the voice says.

My hand immediately drops to my side.

"Now, stand and face each other."

I stand involuntarily, trying to fight the urge to turn and face David, but there's nothing I can do. It's like my body is on autopilot, listening to the man's commands instead of my own thoughts.

"Who are you?" I croak, my throat too dry to get the words out right.

"My name's Benjamin Archer," he responds. "Now forget I told you."

"What? That your name is Benjamin Archer?" I repeat, confused.

"I said forget," Benjamin says, then lets out a frustrated sigh. "Never mind. It won't matter soon."

I finally recall where I've heard that voice before. My vision. Tears spring to my eyes as I remember what's about to happen.

"Now stare into each other's eyes, and don't move," he commands.

I stare at David, everything else going slightly blurry around the edges. He looks more angry than scared, which is what I'm feeling right now. I'm desperate to find out if he's truly about to kill me, so I focus on my RABI again. The buzz returns, but the old man's voice breaks my concentration before I can try to see the future.

"David, you're going to kill Olivia for what she's done," he says.

David's eyes are unfocused, as though he's looking through me.

I try to move against this invisible force holding me in place, but I can't.

The man rolls around me in a wheelchair and stops in front of David. He holds a gun out to David with a frail, quivering hand.

David looks at the gun quizzically.

"Take it, and point it at her," the man says.

"No," David says.

The invisible force holding us in place disappears, and we take a step toward each other before Benjamin notices.

"I said face each other, and don't move," the old man yells.

I notice his milky eyes look fearful just before turning angry, but I see it for only a split second, because I have involuntarily turned to face David again.

My heart is hammering in my chest as my brain screams at my legs to move, but they are firmly rooted in place. The realization of what's going on finally sinks in. I don't know how I never realized it before. This man is a powerful Rare with the ability of mind control. This must be how the Coalition is controlling people. With him!

"Now, take the gun, David," Benjamin commands, "and point it at her."

David reaches out and takes the gun. He waits for the man to roll back out of the way and then points the gun at my chest.

"Why are you doing this to us?" I whimper.

"Because I can. And Turk asked me to do it, so here we are," he says.

"So, you're Turk's puppet?" David asks bravely.

"I am nobody's puppet, boy! Other way around. *I* run the show. Turk is *my* puppet. They're *all* my puppets," he says with a cackle that turns into a cough.

"Then why aren't you president?" David asks.

"I don't like the limelight. I like to control things behind the scenes. Now, both of you stop yapping, and let's get on with this," the man says.

I try to scream, to cry out to David, but I can't seem to form the words. They're lodged in my throat. All I can do is plead with my eyes. For one brief moment, there's a flicker of recognition in David's eye as he holds the gun toward me. He looks scared, but then his body jerks a little, and he winks at me.

How can he be flirting at a time like this?

"Say goodbye, and shoot her," he says with sick pleasure in his voice.

David's eyes glaze over once more, "Goodbye, Liv," he says.

This is it. I'm about to die.

How did I see this coming yet do nothing to change it from happening?

I stare into David's unfocused eyes, wondering if he can even see me right now. Will he see the light leave my eyes as I die? What is the old man going to do to David after he has him kill me? Is he going to make David turn the gun on himself?

I close my eyes as I wait for David to pull the trigger. An odd sense of peace seems to settle in my mind.

BAM!

The gun goes off, but I don't feel any pain. I thought getting shot in the chest would hurt a lot more than this. My body releases from the invisible force again, and I stagger from the change. I look down at David's hand and see the gun's missing. He's holding his fingers out at me like a gun. What is happening? Was I dreaming all of this?

I turn my attention to the old man and find there's someone else in the room with their back turned to me, holding the gun. He's standing over the old man's lifeless body, now slumped in his wheelchair, a bullet hole in his temple leaking blood onto the floor.

The person holding the gun turns around, and I gasp.

It's David!

Only this David is more grizzled, with a stubble beard grown in, scars running up and down his chiseled arms, and a wild look in his eyes.

"Bartholomew?" I whisper.

"M'lady," he says with a bob of his head. He steps over to David, hands him the gun, and then their bodies meld together, leaving just David.

"What just happened?" I ask, shaking.

David grabs ahold of me and hugs me tightly. "I thought I was going to shoot you. I was trying to fight it as hard as I could, but I couldn't make my body listen to me. So, in that one brief moment, the one where I winked at you, I realized I might not be in control of my body, but I was in control of my mind, so I sent Bartholomew out before it was too late."

"You saved my life, David. I could kiss you a million times over, but we need to get out of here," I say desperately.

David grabs my hand, and we race over to the door. It's locked from the outside. David kicks at the door, but it doesn't open.

"Stand back." David points the gun at the doorknob. He pulls the trigger, but the gun only clicks. "It's empty. They only loaded one bullet in it." David tosses the gun to the side.

"Is there some other way out of here?" I look around at the ceiling and walls.

The doorknob rattles as someone unlocks it from the other side. David pushes me behind him, preparing for a fight. The door swings open, and my mom rushes into the room, sweat dripping down her face.

"Mom? What are you doing here?" I run over to give her a hug.

"David's mom called me as soon as you two were taken, and I came as fast as I could. Are you all right?" She holds me at arm's length as she checks me over for any injuries.

"Yeah, thanks to Bartholomew and David." A little smile slides across my face.

She looks past me and sees the old man's body. "We need to get you out of here now. Turk's going to be here any minute." She tugs on my arm.

"Who did we just kill? He said he was the puppet master, and Turk was his puppet that he was controlling behind scenes." I dart after my mom down the deserted hallway.

"I don't know who he is. Turk has kept his identity a secret." She turns the corner and drops to her knee to shoot a guard coming toward us. She stands back up and keeps running.

I look at the guard as we run past, and my stomach gets queasy.

"But you knew about him? Did you know what he could do?" David asks.

"No. I only saw him one time. The guy was sleeping, and Turk was quick to dismiss me, angry I was in that room, and that memory always stuck with me as odd." She stops at a door to unlock it.

"The guy was controlling people with his Rare ability," I say as we take off down another hallway.

"That explains a lot actually," she says.

As we come to the entrance, almost free of this place, a few men step up outside the glass door. The man in the lead lifts his head up to look at us through the window, his face red with anger.

It's President Turk.

50

He yells at his bodyguards to stay put outside as he yanks the door open and storms in, bearing down on my mom. "Jan? I just got a call from my men! Did you have something to do with this?"

"To do with what?" Mom raises her brows, feigning innocence.

"Don't play dumb with me! I'm sick of your lies." Spit flies from Turk's mouth. His hair that's usually slicked back is falling in his face, making him look crazed. "I never should have trusted you!"

"There are a lot of things you never should have done," Mom says disgustedly.

Turk snarls, taking a threatening step toward her.

"If you're referring to killing Benjamin Archer, it wasn't her," David says defiantly. "It was me."

"You?" His face turns a darker shade of red. "You've destroyed me!"

I stand with my muscles tensed, ready for him to attack David, but he stays put, his chest heaving. Turk finally breaks the silence, "Well, since you killed someone important to me, how about I return the favor." Hatred hangs on every word. He pulls a gun out of his suit jacket and instead of pointing the gun at David, he points it at me.

Time slows. Turk's hand shakes from rage. Although his words and body movements are full of anger, his eyes show nothing but unbridled fear. This is worse than if he was just angry. Now he's unstable.

Before David or I make a move to take him out, my mom jumps in front of me as Turk's gun goes off.

I scream as her body jerks from the bullet hitting her.

She raises her gun and shoots Turk before she crumples to the floor. He falls backward, his head cracking against the hard floor.

"Mom!" I drop down beside her as Turk's bodyguards come charging into the building. Before I can worry about whether I need to fight them off, David takes them out, knocking them unconscious. He grabs their guns and disassembles them before checking on Turk. For the first time in my life, I want someone to be dead. Maybe I'm being hypocritical, but he shot my mom. He deserves it.

"Do you believe me now that I love you?" she asks weakly.

I press my hand onto her wound, trying to stop the blood flow. "Shh. Mom, you're going to be okay. Everything's going to be okay." I start crying as I watch the puddle of blood grow with each beat of her heart.

"Turk's dead," David announces, and my mom lets out a little sigh as she closes her eyes.

"I love you, Mom. Please don't leave me!" I plead as she goes still, her chest no longer moving.

Our attention is pulled away by a guard who comes shuffling down the hallway. David grabs the gun out of Mom's hand and holds it up at the soldier, but instead of the soldier reaching for his own weapon, he holds his hands out in front of him and drops to his knees.

"Please, don't shoot me," he begs. "I don't know what's going on. It's like I just woke up. I don't know what I'm doing here."

David lowers the gun and tells him to leave. The soldier obeys, standing up and running out the door, never looking back.

I turn my gaze back to my mom and brush the hair off her forehead as hot tears blur my eyes and run down my face, dripping off my chin.

"Liv, c'mon, we gotta get that device plugged into a tower and finish this. We'll come back for her, I promise." David places a comforting hand on my shoulder.

"I can't leave her," I cry.

"I know, but we don't really have a choice. We can't take her with us."

I let out a sob as I look at my mom's beautiful face. We never got along well—she held so many secrets and lied all the time—but she was my mom, and she truly did love me. In the end, she did what she does best. She protected me.

David tugs lightly on my arm, coaxing me to go. I lean over and kiss her between the eyebrows before using both hands to lay her head down onto the floor as gently as possible. David helps me up, and I wipe my eyes and nose with my coat sleeve, trying hard to be okay.

"Do you still have the device Elliot gave you?" David asks.

I reach into my pocket and feel the little plastic square with my fingers. I nod, and David grabs my bloodied hand to lead me outside.

When we step out of the building, there are people milling around in the fog as though they're lost. At first, David and I are wary, trying to avoid them, but after a while, we realize they hardly notice we're even there. They all seemed dazed.

"What's going on with everyone? Why are they all acting like zombies?" I ask.

"I don't know. Maybe it has something to do with Benjamin Archer being dead," he says as we watch someone walk past us, then stop and turn in circles looking around at the buildings. He scratches at his head with a dumbfounded expression. "C'mon, Liv. This way. We're only a few blocks away from the tower."

"How do you know?" I ask, my brain feeling as foggy as the city. I can't believe my mom is dead.

"This is the Capitol building, which means the tower is that way." He wraps his arm around me to try to speed up my walking.

We make it to the tower quicker than I thought, but it could be I wasn't paying attention whatsoever. I picture my mom's face, her eyes closed as though she were sleeping and not lying there dead, imagining her waking up and everything being okay.

But it's not.

She's gone.

We walk up to the tower's front door, keeping an eye out for any guards or soldiers who could stop us, but nobody does. The door has a keypad like the last one.

"What do we do?" I ask.

"I think that's what these numbers are for," David says, pointing at three lines of numbers under the directions Elliot wrote out. He types one in, but the screen flashes 'access denied' while making a buzzing sound. He types in the next one, and it's the same thing. "Third times a charm," he mutters, punching in the last line.

Nothing.

"Now what?" I ask, frustrated to come so far to be thwarted by a door.

"Do you think you could use your ability to see someone in the future punch the numbers in?" David asks.

"I can't. I don't think I'd be able to concentrate, David." I hang my head, looking at the blood on my hands. The remnants of my mom's life force coat my palms in a sticky crimson reminder of her love for me.

David lifts my chin so I can look him in the eyes. "Liv, I know you can do this." He raises his voice a little when I shake my head, "Your mom just gave her life to save yours. You can use this opportunity to save countless other lives. I know you're hurting, but people are counting on you. Please, put aside the pain and sadness until later, and let's finish what we set out to do. Heck, I'll even cry with you if you want. But later, okay?"

My first reaction is to get mad at him. How can he be asking me to ignore that my mom just died? Doesn't he know my heart has been ripped out of my chest? But the more I think about it, the more I realize he's right. This will be the only way we can finish what we started. We need to get inside that building. I can allow myself to wallow in misery later.

I pull out my gloves from my jacket pocket and slip them on before grabbing David's hand. I take a few breaths, filling my lungs up until I can't possibly fill them anymore. I blow it out slowly, focusing on my RABI.

Keycode. Keycode. I repeat in my head as the buzzing intensifies.

David and I are hiding in a bush as a guard comes running up the sidewalk toward the front door.

"Quick, send Bartholomew out to see what the code is!" I whisper.

David squeezes his eyes shut, and Bartholomew materializes in front of us.

"Go see what numbers the guard types into the keypad. Hurry!" David instructs.

I watch as Bartholomew creeps up behind the guard, but suddenly, he winks out of sight. I can't see him anymore.

"Where'd he go? I ask.

"He's looking over the guard's shoulder right now. Can't you see him?"

"I could at first, but now he's gone," I say as the guard pulls the door open, never turning to look at Bartholomew even once. As the front door closes, Bartholomew reappears right in front of us, causing me to jump a little.

"What'd you see?" David asks.

Bartholomew rattles off six digits while David writes them down on Elliot's sheet of directions.

"Thank you, Bartholomew," I say awkwardly when his eyes land on me. My heart flutters in my chest as heat radiates from my face. I feel a little guilty being attracted to him, but he's David, or at least a part of David, so it's okay, right?

Bartholomew grabs my hand and brushes my knuckles with his lips, never taking his eyes off me.

"Would you knock it off! We don't have time for this," David scolds, standing up and melding back together with him.

I come back to the present with a sigh. My heart is beating fast, and I wonder if this time it's partly because of Bartholomew flirting with me.

"Seven, nine, five, five, three, one," I rattle off.

David goes to type it in, but we hear rapid footsteps coming our way, so I grab David and pull him into the bushes.

"This happened in my vision. Then you sent Bartholomew to go spy on what the numbers were," I whisper as we wait for the guard to go inside.

"Bartholomew didn't try anything with you, did he?" David narrows his eyes at me.

"Why? Would you be jealous if he did?" I ask.

"Maybe a little." David scratches at the back of his head. "He talks about you every time I bring him out."

"He's a part of you. You're getting jealous of yourself," I say, momentarily amused.

"I know it's silly." David's smile doesn't reach his eyes. "Just remember this when you're having a bad day and questioning whether I love you. Not only do I love you, but even my subconscious loves you too."

"C'mon, let's get this over with."

David puts in the code, and we pull the door open.

"Stop! You're not supposed to be in here...I think," a young guard says uncertainly from the desk. He has his gun out, but his hands are shaking as he points it toward us.

David and I raise our hands up in the air slowly. I feel more concerned about a nervous guard pointing a gun at me than I would from a confident one.

"We were told to come here," David says.

The guard narrows his eyes at David as though he's trying to decide whether David is lying or not.

"President Turk sent us over to work on one of your servers. He said he's got a new message from the Coalition he'd like to broadcast."

"See, it's right here in my pocket." I pull the device out of my pocket to show him. "He gave this to us to bring here. Can you help us get to the server room?"

543

"I just saw President Turk this afternoon. If you saw him, then what was he wearing?" the guard challenges.

I close my eyes and picture Turk's lifeless body lying on the ground after my mom shot him. A flood of emotions crashes over me as I picture the scene, but I manage to focus on what Turk was wearing, trying hard to not think about my mom.

"A dark blue suit, white dress shirt, black tie, and a red pocket square," I say, then blanch when I realize the pocket square was white, but it turned red from his blood soaking into it after he was shot. "No, wait, the pocket square was white," I mutter.

"Good enough for me," the guard says, putting his gun away. "I honestly don't know what's going on. I know that I'm a guard, hence the getup, but I'm not really sure what I'm guarding or what my orders are."

"Everything is about to become clear," David promises.

We follow him to the server room, my fingers crossed that this is going to work. David takes the USB from me and sticks it into one of the servers. I look around the room, expecting something to happen, but nothing does.

"Now we wait for Elliot to do his magic," David says.

"Let's get out of here. We need to take care of my—" I choke up as I'm about to say "mom."

David holds me as we leave the room.

"All done in there?" the guard asks from the desk.

"Yes. Pay attention to the president's channel. Everything will be explained soon," David says.

David and I walk hand in hand as we head back to the Capitol building to move my mom's body somewhere safe until we can call an ambulance. As we get closer, we hear cries of outrage through the fog.

"We're being lied to!" a woman's voice cries out from the left.

"We're not being kept safe! We're being kept prisoners!" a man shouts, followed by a few people in the vicinity voicing their rage.

Glass shattering puts me on edge. If people are going to start breaking things, I want to go somewhere safe.

"Elliot must have gotten through." David pulls me faster as the Capitol building comes into view.

Once inside, we look at the TV mounted on the wall. Elliot's video is playing on the screen, divulging all the secrets of the Coalition's lies. We stand in silence as we watch the truth broadcasted on a loop. I hope Elliot was able to get the truth spread to everyone.

I grab ahold of David's hand and whisper, "It was you all along, you know. You were the secret weapon Chozolt was looking for."

He looks in my eyes intently and says, "It wasn't just me. We're a team. I would be nowhere without you by my side."

544

I give him a hug in response, choked up from the emotions of the day.

"I think we won." He motions for me to look out the window at the people marching down the street. "Let's get out of here and find somewhere safe to be."

We carry my mom's body to a nearby church and use their phone to call an ambulance. As we wait for them to come get her, we sit on the floor next to the entrance door and listen to the chaos erupting outside, my heart heavy with everything that has happened. The sounds of shattering glass and yelling sets me on edge, and now a strange flickering light is emanating from the window.

David peeks out the window. "They're burning down buildings now." David shakes his head.

"Do you think we'll be safe here?" I have a hard time feeling the fear I should probably be right now.

"Yeah. I'll keep watch. You just rest now." He kisses the top of my head.

The weight of the day pulls me under, and I lie down on the floor, releasing the sorrow that has built up. I weep, uncaring that David is here to hear it. He rests his hand on my back as he keeps watch. I hear him sniffle a few times too. He's true to his word that he would cry with me, and a small piece of me truly appreciates that.

After a while, the tears no longer flow, but the hurt is still like a knife piercing my heart. We won the war, but a battle was lost today. The last vestiges of my depression come into full swing, and I feel like I'm drowning.

I grab David's hand as one last attempt to keep myself from sinking below the surface.

His grip makes the promise ring dig into my other fingers, and it's like a reminder there is more than just this pain ahead of me. David and I have a future if I just hold on. Someday we can be happy. It may feel like the day that never comes, but time marches on. It's up to me to make the choice to march on with it.

EPILOGUE

Elliot was able to get word to Chozolt about what we had done before they started moving troops in for a war. Instead, Chozolt had to send military into the cities to keep the peace. More riots broke out all over the Coalition as soon as people heard the truth of what's been going on, of how they have been kept prisoners and how they were being drugged with a mild fear-inducing drug through the fog. Everyone started turning on the soldiers and guards, blaming them for being a part of it, not knowing that they, too, were being manipulated.

It was discovered Turk had been playing recordings of Benjamin Archer's voice commands in every city, keeping them all under his control the whole time. It was quite a mess trying to get word out to every single person in the Coalition, but Elliot worked tirelessly until he did.

Chozolt was appointed interim president until order could be restored and an election could be held. It's uncertain how long that's going to take, but everyone seems to be happy with him in charge.

The whole world is in shock at the news of what was happening in the Coalition. Nobody seems to remember much about Benjamin Archer. In fact, hardly anyone knows he existed. He used his rare ability to hide himself on top of everything else he was doing.

They got one recording of a UN meeting where the microphone had fritzed out on the camera, and you can see Benjamin sitting in the back of the room, but nobody was paying any attention to him, as though he were invisible. Elliot zoomed in on his face and read his lips saying at the beginning of the meeting, "You can't see me. Forget that I was ever here." Without the microphone working on the video, anyone watching it was still able to see him because his ability didn't work without sound. This video was a big oversight on someone's part.

When Chozolt's men searched Turk's mansion, they found a secret room hidden behind a bookcase that turned out to be Benjamin's bedroom. There was an old journal hidden between the mattresses, dated before the big war. People were horrified by what was written in it.

Benjamin was the sole cause of the war.

His journal gave a detailed description of how he was going to execute his plan, and of all the pieces he needed to get into place before he could run the show hidden in the shadows.

He worked as a security guard at the UN building while Rares were still revered as special and useful. One day, he made his move and cornered the US president, poisoning his mind against Rares. The next day, after the president returned from the UN summit meeting, he declared all Rares were dangerous and needed to be locked up. It sparked a civil war. Benjamin manipulated the other government leaders to aid in the war, fighting against the Rare and those sympathetic to their plight. Finally, the people now referred to as the Haven retreated to the West. The DMZ was put into place, and Benjamin organized the Coalition, always making sure he was never seen. He had been the behind-the-scenes guy ever since, making the Coalition presidents run things how he wanted.

Chozolt shook his head. "The world wasn't against the Rares at all. This whole thing was all because of one guy—one powerful Rare who wanted to rule the world. Or at least a part of it."

"He was starting to lose his touch, though," Elliot said. "I found some of his medical records in the database. It was under an anagram, but I figured out it was him. Archer was getting dementia and struggling to keep everything under control. I think that's why Turk was desperately trying to screen Rares for a specific ability. He was looking for a replacement. He knew his reign was about to end with Archer, and he needed to find another mind controller to keep it going."

"The level of deception is astounding," Chozolt said. "This is going to take months, if not years, to get everything cleaned up."

"You have the whole world on your side now. Just ask, and people will come to help," Elliot reminded him.

And that's exactly what happened. Less than three months have passed, and countless countries have come to Chozolt's aid. Cities are being rebuilt at an amazing rate. The DMZ is being tested to find habitable sections, using the radioactive parts as a landfill for all the leftover debris from the cities. The fog generators were found and destroyed, leaving the air in the cities clean and clear.

We've been told the United States will never be what it once was before the war, but nobody cares. Anything is better than being under the oppression of Benjamin Archer, a man who will go into every history book as the biggest criminal of our time. He wanted to remain anonymous, and instead, he became infamous.

As for me, Matthias and Henry came as soon as they could when they heard about Mom. We decided to bury her ourselves, not wanting to wait for things to settle down first. I would have loved to bury her in the clearing in the woods I picture so often, but I'm not sure I would ever find it again. We found the graveyard her grandparents were buried in and put her next to them. I think she would have liked that.

The loss of my mom was too much for me, and I came dangerously close to giving up on life again. I didn't eat for days, no matter how many times David and Cass tried to persuade me. Tacos didn't even hold an appeal to me. I stopped using my Rare abilities and caved in on myself.

David finally convinced me to see someone, so I've been going to a psychiatrist for the last couple of months. We've made a lot of progress, but I truly believe my depression is a part of me that's never going to go away. I have more good days than bad now, but there's still a piece of darkness lodged in my psyche that comes to the surface from time to time. Lucky for me, David is always there to comfort me when it happens. The light to my darkness. I still haven't found the desire to use my Rare ability. I'm sure it will come back to me, but for now, I'm happy to just live in the present.

Cindy won't let me live it down that we left without her. She thinks Joselyn could have finished our task in half the time if we had brought her along. I think she's just angry we're getting all the attention for saving the day. If there's one thing Cindy likes, it's attention.

David's parents moved here to be with us. They didn't want to spend one more second without David. His mom was over-the-moon happy when she found out David and I are a couple. She keeps talking about us getting married. David tried to get her to stop, but he finally gave up after the twentieth time and nods when she talks about it.

Matthias's group of people have started to go out on their own, no longer needing him to be their leader. They keep in touch, of course, but everyone needed to start a fresh life.

Alexandrine surprised everyone when she offered to take care of Cindy. Rebecca seemed to have mixed reactions to it. She seemed slightly relieved, but also uncertain of whether she should be the one to care for Cindy. I think she finally realized it was the best decision for everyone involved. Charlotte was bursting at the seams that she now has a sister.

Denis took Cass and Tim in with him to be their guardian. Tim was delighted because Denis has been like an older brother to him this whole time anyway. It was the perfect fit.

Tonight, David and I are going out to dinner with his parents and Matthias to celebrate our engagement. He chose to do it the old-fashioned way by asking Matthias for my hand in marriage first. He was nervous Matthias was going to say no because I'm only seventeen, but Matthias not only told him yes, but that he would like to get ordained so he could be the one to marry us.

His proposal was simple yet magical. David drove me out to a forest and found a clearing—a lot like the one I picture when meditating—and set up a picnic lunch for us. It was a little chilly with it only being early spring, but the sun was warm, and it felt good to be in the woods again. When he got down on one knee, my heart leaped into my throat. I was already saying 'yes' before he even finished asking the question.

I have a lot of doubts rolling around in my head, but my love for David isn't one of them. I can't promise him a happily-ever-after kind of life, and he knows that, but I can promise him one of love.

A love so powerful and precious, you could almost say it's Rare.

SUICIDE PREVENTION

If you are feeling suicidal or an urge to harm yourself,
please, find someone to talk to.

You are not alone.

If you can't talk to a family member or a friend, reach out to
the National Suicide Prevention Lifeline:

9-8-8
or
www.suicidepreventionlifeline.org

You have a purpose.
Don't ever give up.

ACKNOWLEDGMENTS

First and foremost, to God be the glory!

I would like to thank my husband, Sage, for the support you've given me through the good times and the bad. It has been a long road, but I'm grateful to have Jeeped it with you.

Thank you to my best friend, Lydia, for reading my manuscript and giving me tips along the way. You are the best!

Thank you to my parents for everything you do for me. I love you.

Thank you to the lovely ladies at Authors 4 Authors Publishing Cooperative for giving me a chance. You have been so great to work with. I am truly blessed.

ABOUT THE AUTHOR

Diane lives in central Wisconsin with her husband and three boys. When not reading or writing, she likes to go hiking as often as she can. Her favorite trail—so far—is the Ice Age Trail with Skunk Foster Lake being her favorite section of it.

Diane's fascination with superheroes sparked the idea for her first novel, *Supernova*, taking some inspiration from X-Men.

Diane can also be found serving as an Awana leader at her local church. She has been serving there for ten years.

Follow her online:

www.dianeanthony.info
Twitter: @DianeMAnthony
Facebook: @DianeMAnthony

Also by Diane Anthony
SUPERNOVA

When librarian Madeline Hayes wakes up in the front yard with no memory of why she's there, her simple life in a small town becomes more complicated than she ever imagined. Strange things start happening: her father heals an injury with a touch, her elderly neighbor seems to become younger, and everyone starts getting this strange blue light in their eyes—and in their veins.

And then people start dying.

Can Madeline unravel this mystery and stop the strange transformations before it's too late?

books2read.com/supernova

Authors 4 Authors Publishing

A publishing company for authors, run by authors, blending the best of traditional and independent publishing

We specialize in speculative fiction: science fiction, fantasy, paranormal, and romance. Get lost in another world!

Check out our collection at https://books2read.com/rl/a4a or visit Authors4AuthorsPublishing.com/books

For updates, scan the QR code or visit our website to join our semi-monthly newsletter!

Want more YA Science-Fiction? We recommend:

Hard as Stone
by Beatrice B. Morgan

Seventeen-year-old Raven Thane wants an adventure...and she's going to get one. Just not the way that she expected. Bored and disinterested with a routine life in her remote underground community, she fails to notice a thief during her turn at guard duty. Zander, a charming sharpshooter, tasks her with helping him retrieve the mysterious stolen item. Can Raven fix her mistake and prove herself more than a simple country girl? Or will she create even more chaos?

books2read.com/hardstone